Return of the Plumed Serpent

Graham Hancock is the author of the worldwide non-fiction bestseller *Fingerprints of the Gods*, and of the fantasy adventure novels *Entangled* and *War God: Nights of the Witch*. His books have been translated into twenty-seven languages and have sold more than nine million copies worldwide. His public lectures and broadcasts, including two major TV series for Channel 4, coupled with his strong presence on the internet, have put his ideas before audiences of tens of millions and further established his reputation as an unconventional thinker willing to explore extraordinary ideas in fresh and unusual ways.

GRAHAM HANCOCK

War God

Return of the Plumed Serpent

CORONET

First published in Great Britain in 2014 by Coronet
An imprint of Hodder & Stoughton
An Hachette UK company

First published in paperback in 2015

1

A CIP catalogue record for this title is available from the British Library

ISBN 978 1 444 78836 5
Ebook ISBN 978 1 444 78838 9

Printed and bound by Clays Ltd, St Ives plc

Hodder & Stoughton policy is to use papers that are natural, renewable and
recyclable products and made from wood grown in sustainable forests. The
logging and manufacturing processes are expected to conform to the
environmental regulations of the country of origin.

Hodder & Stoughton Ltd
Carmelite House
50 Victoria Embankment
London EC4Y 0DZ

www.hodder.co.uk

For Santha

Graham Hancock on Facebook:
www.facebook.com/Author.GrahamHancock

Graham Hancock on Twitter:
@Graham__Hancock

Graham's website: www.grahamhancock.com

Part I

20 April 1519–12 May 1519

Chapter One

'That lurcher's growing into a fine, warlike animal,' said Telmo Vendabal.

'He is, sir,' Pepillo conceded.

'Strong, by the look of him. What you been feeding him on?'

'Goat's milk, sir, when I first got him, and now galley scraps.'

'What you calling him?'

Pepillo shifted uncomfortably from foot to foot. 'Melchior, sir,' he mumbled.

'Melchior? After that blackamoor friend of yours who went and got hisself killed?'

'Yes, sir.' Pepillo bit his lip and added. 'He was brave, sir.'

'Aye, brave enough, I suppose. But black as the devil's own buttocks.'

A brutal, heavy-set hunchback, Vendabal was the expedition's chief dog handler. A calculating glint sparked in his small eyes. 'Think this Melchior's brave too?'

Pepillo felt a bead of sweat roll down his brow. It wasn't because of the sun. 'I'm sure I don't know, sir. I'm rearing him as a pet.'

'Pet eh? Pet my arse! No room for pets on a fighting expedition.' With a sour twist of his mouth, Vendabal dropped to his knees beside the lurcher, a wolfhound-greyhound cross, grasped the pup by the lower jaw, lifted his upper lips and examined his new white teeth. Melchior whined anxiously, attempted to back away and rolled his intelligent amber eyes towards Pepillo in mute appeal as he discovered he was held fast.

'Don't fret, boy,' Pepillo said. 'Stay!'

Melchior was obviously uncomfortable, but Pepillo was training him to be obedient and he remained still while Vendabal prodded at his

3

mouth and rubbed the filthy thumb of his left hand along the dog's gums. When the hunchback's right hand snaked out towards the pup's hind-quarters, however, and attempted to grasp his testicles, Melchior's nervous whine turned to a menacing growl and his teeth flashed in a sudden bite. Uttering a stream of foul oaths, Vendabal snatched his hand away and dealt Melchior a heavy blow about the head, sending the lurcher yelping and tumbling across the deck, then followed him at a run and aimed a ferocious kick at his ribs, eliciting another agonised yelp.

Reacting instinctively, Pepillo leapt forward as the dog handler stood poised to deliver a second mighty kick; he tangled his legs and brought him crashing down.

Very rapidly, a crowd of twenty or more crew and soldiers, jeering and yelling, had gathered between the masts to observe the action while others scurried into the rigging for a better view. Flushed and panting, Vendabal struggled to his feet, hauled Pepillo up by his lapels until their faces almost touched and blasted him with a gale of stinking breath. 'You little shit,' he bellowed, 'your lurcher's mine. Next battle we fight, he'll be first out against the enemy.'

'No, sir, please,' Pepillo begged. 'Melchior's not a war dog. He wouldn't even be alive if you'd had your way. After his dam died in the fighting at Potonchan, you had your men kill all the rest of the litter. You said pups were too much trouble to feed by hand. Don Bernal Díaz told me that, sir. It was he who rescued Melchior.'

'Díaz, eh? So where's he now when you need him?'

'On Don Pedro de Alvarado's ship, sir, as you know very well, but he'll vouch for me when we reach land. Melchior was his gift to me and you can't take him away!' Pepillo was feeling stubborn now, anger rising in him, though his feet were off the ground and he was helpless in the hunchback's iron grip.

'Vouch for you?' Vendabal's voice rose almost to a scream. 'Vouch for you? I'll show you vouch for you!' And with that he shifted his stance, still holding Pepillo by the lapels with his left hand while slap-ping him once, twice, three times across the face with his right. As the fourth blow landed, Pepillo heard a snarl through the ringing in his ears and saw a streak of brindled fur as Melchior launched himself at Vendabal and sank his teeth into the hunchback's thick, heavily

4

tattooed forearm. At once the grip on Pepillo's lapels loosened; Pepillo dropped to the deck with a heavy thud and could only watch, dazed, as Vendabal shook Melchior loose, threw the puppy down and loomed over him with murder in his eyes.

'*Desist!*'

The voice was thunder. It cut through the excited cries of the spectators, stopping Vendabal in his tracks. '*Desist, I say!*' All eyes turned to the navigation deck, where Hernán Cortés, captain-general of the expedition, had emerged from his stateroom. Since the slaughter of the Chontal Maya at Potonchan, his rages had become legendary, and it was obvious to Pepillo, who knew him better than most, that his master was in a dark mood. It was never good to awaken him from his customary afternoon siesta, but to awaken him rudely was to risk the worst of his wrath.

Wearing only a length of colourful native cloth wrapped around his waist, Cortés strode barefoot to the railing at the edge of the navigation deck overlooking the main deck and glared down at Vendabal and Pepillo. 'What's the meaning of this?' he asked.

'Bastard cur bit me,' complained Vendabal, pointing at Melchior, who stood with hackles raised and bared teeth as though daring him to do his worst.

Suddenly and surprisingly, Cortés smiled. 'And I suppose that soft flesh of yours has never felt a dog's teeth before, Don Telmo? No doubt those scars you carry were left by the talons of jealous lovers.'

Vendabal looked confused. 'Of course I've been bit before,' he said truculently. 'A hundred times! But no dog that bites me gets away without a beating. They have to know who's master.'

'You've already beaten Melchior,' Pepillo objected. He had picked himself up and now crouched beside his pet. 'He's learned his lesson. Look, he's trembling.'

It was true, Melchior was trembling, but not with fear, Pepillo thought. A low snarl rumbled in the lurcher's throat and he seemed ready to leap at Vendabal again.

'Be damned he's learned his lesson,' Vendabal roared. 'That dog needs a whipping. Then he goes in the pack with the others to be trained for war.'

'No,' Pepillo yelled. 'He's mine! You can't have him.'

Cortés watched from the navigation deck, his features registering a strange, cruel amusement. 'The dog stays with my page,' he said finally. 'For now.' He turned his back and began to stroll towards the open door of his stateroom, then added over his shoulder. 'But whip him, Vendabal. By all means, whip him.'

Chapter Two

Guatemoc leapt high into the air, all grace and style, and Man-Eater's blade whistled by harmlessly beneath the soles of his feet. Then, in the same smooth movement, the handsome Mexica prince brought his own weapon down on the crown of his opponent's head, halting the blow less than a finger's breadth from its target. 'You're dead, Man-Eater,' Guatemoc drawled. 'Your skull is cleft in twain. I do believe that's your brains, scant though they are, lying in the dust before us.'

Man-Eater was a bad loser. This was the fourth time he'd been spectacularly bested in less than an hour of sparring, and now he growled furiously and attacked again, his blade a blur of rapid movement, too fast for the eye to follow. Yet somehow Guatemoc evaded him, his lean, scarred, heavily muscled body weaving from side to side, ducking and swaying as he retreated before the furious onslaught until suddenly – Tozi could not see it coming – he swivelled, let his opponent slide by, and chopped the edge of his blade into the back of Man-Eater's thick neck, reducing the force of the blow but yet allowing it to strike home with a loud slap that laid out his friend, face down and inert in the dust.

Invisible, insubstantial as air, able to pass unseen wherever and whenever she wished, Tozi was the silent and unknown observer of the bout. Indeed, she had observed Guatemoc many times since Moctezuma's plot to poison him, when she'd used sorcery to save him and to bring him healing for the terrible wounds he'd received in battle against the Tlascalans. It was, she had to admit, most inconvenient that she had fallen in love with this noble prince, nephew of that noxious creature Moctezuma, who for the entire fifteen-year span of

Tozi's life had been enthroned as the Great Speaker of the malevolent empire of the Mexica. But having accepted the truth of her feelings, Tozi supposed she was better able to deal with them.

Above all else, a dalliance of any kind was out of the question.

Guatemoc was of the blood royal, while Tozi was a witch and the daughter of a witch. Besides, he was her enemy and the nephew of her enemy. She must use her magic and her wiles to turn him against his uncle and the war god Huitzilopochtli, 'Hummingbird', whom his uncle served – either that, or she must bring Guatemoc to the same ruin she planned for Moctezuma.

Quetzalcoatl, the Plumed Serpent, god of peace, ancient antagonist of Hummingbird, was coming, coming as prophesied in this year One-Reed, to overthrow a cruel king and abolish the war god's vile cult of human sacrifice forever. Tozi felt a momentary qualm – for her own magical powers, most particularly her ability to render herself invisible, had been enhanced by none other than Hummingbird himself when she had stood before his altar of sacrifice. Her friend Malinal, who had stood there with her that night two months before, and who had been freed with her following Hummingbird's intervention, had seen a terrible danger in this. For if Hummingbird had freed them from sacrifice at the hand of his puppet Moctezuma, then it must mean the war god had a plan for them and, since Hummingbird was a being of pure evil, then it followed that only evil could come of it.

Tozi had dismissed all such concerns when she'd sent Malinal on her way to the coast to seek out Quetzalcoatl. Certainly there was a plan – a great plan – but it was not of Hummingbird's making. And certainly she and Malinal had their parts to play. Tozi remembered the words of reassurance she'd spoken to her friend: 'Moctezuma too is playing his part, and even the wicked and deluded god he serves must play his part.'

'I don't know,' Malinal had replied. 'I don't understand any of this.'

'You don't need to understand it, beautiful Malinal. This is the year One-Reed and you just have to play your part . . . Don't you see, it's not an accident that you are of the Chontal Maya and that those who came to herald the return of Quetzalcoatl first appeared in the land of your people, and in Potonchan, the very town where you were born? None

8

of this is an accident, Malinal. That's why you must go back to Potonchan now, without delay. That's why you must start your journey at once.'

And so she had sent Malinal off on a perilous journey to her homeland, and to her family who had sold her into slavery with the Mexica – sent her off to seek out the returning god of peace. Tozi's magic was strong now, stronger than it had ever been, but still she had no idea what had happened to her friend in the sixty days or more that had passed since then. She could only guess, could only hope, that she was well and that her mission to find Quetzalcoatl, and lead him back to the city of Tenochtitlan to overthrow Moctezuma, had been crowned with success.

Meanwhile Tozi's own business was here with Guatemoc.

To win him over to the cause of the Plumed Serpent would be a great victory, yet Tozi could barely trust herself to approach him. Indeed, since the last time she had shown herself to him in her disguise as Temaz, goddess of medicines and healing, the very thought of him was enough to make her dizzy – for then the prince had swept her up in his arms and kissed her full on the mouth, and she had tasted his tongue and he had tasted hers. Even now, observing him unseen from the sanctuary of her invisibility, the memory made her breathless.

Dressed only in a simple loincloth of plain white cotton, Guatemoc had been sparring with his friend Tecuani – nicknamed 'Man-Eater' – in the spacious courtyard of his townhouse in the royal quarter of Tenochtitlan. Both men were armed with *macuahuitls* – swords of hardwood stripped of their razor-sharp obsidian teeth for today's purpose – and both their bodies were sheened with sweat. Presently, however, Guatemoc was on his feet while Man-Eater lay face down on the ground, a livid red welt standing out on the back of his neck where the prince had struck him.

'Come on,' said Guatemoc, dropping to his knees beside Tecuani, 'I didn't hit you that hard.'

Silence.

Guatemoc sighed. 'I know you can hear me, Man-Eater. I know you're just playing dead.'

Silence.

Now Guatemoc was seriously concerned, shaking his friend by the shoulders, getting no response.

'Wake up, Man-Eater! What's this?'

Still getting no answer, Guatemoc leaned closer, and that was when Man-Eater, a powerful, heavy-set noble of thirty years of age, a Jaguar Knight but with the shorn head and sidelock that also marked him out as a member of the formidable Cuahchic class of warriors, exploded into action. He threw himself on top of the prince and wrestled him onto his back on the ground. 'Surrender, Guatemoc,' he yelled. 'Your time has come.'

'Hardly, dear chap,' Guatemoc laughed. 'Since I've spilled your brains and cut off your head, I don't think you're in any shape to accept my surrender.'

'Well, we'll call it a draw then,' Man-Eater said after a moment's thought. 'You've got to admit I had you fooled.'

'A draw it is,' replied Guatemoc with another easy laugh, and they both stood, slapping each other on the shoulders for all the world like two schoolboys reconciled after a playground fight.

Still hidden by the shield of her invisibility, Tozi watched. The knife wounds Guatemoc had received to his belly, throat and forearm two months before were now almost completely healed . . .

Thanks to her magic!

His life force was back.

Thanks to her magic!

And, by dint of much exercise and determination, his strength had returned.

Soon, therefore, it would be time, Tozi decided, to reveal herself to him again, disguised as the goddess Temaz – the only form in which he knew her – and perhaps even to share once again the bliss, the hot roiling warmth, the endless promise of a kiss . . .

But no! Not that! Though she felt a sweet heat in her loins, she would permit him no contact with her. She would not repeat the same mistake she had made before.

There would be no contact, only spoken words.

Perhaps even tonight, after Man-Eater was gone, after the servants had retired to their beds, she would find Guatemoc alone and win him to her cause.

Chapter Three

Tenochtitlan, Wednesday 21 April 1519, evening

Moctezuma sat at his dinner, choosing a morsel here, a morsel there from the three hundred dishes laid out before him, but taking no pleasure from them. The images that crowded in upon his mind were of the Tzitzimime, the star demons of darkness, those monstrous spiders that attack the sun at the end of a world age, diving headfirst upon him from heaven.

An almost inaudible scurry of slippered feet across the polished mahogany floor of the dining hall, along with a faint perturbation of the air, announced the arrival at his side of his lugubrious steward Teudile, the seventh most important lord of the Mexica empire. Tall, gaunt and hollow-cheeked, his temples and brow shaved, his long grey hair gathered in a topknot at the back of his head, and his cherished personal dignity enlarged by the star-spangled robes of office that he alone was permitted to wear in the presence of the Great Speaker, Teudile held sole responsibility for all matters concerning the running of the royal household. At dinner it was his particular honour and privilege to describe the dishes to the Speaker and hand him whichever took his fancy, but tonight and for many previous nights Moctezuma had dispensed with this service, caring nothing for the delights of the menu and preferring to eat and brood alone.

'Sire, with humble apologies—'

'Go away, Teudile! You disturb me at your peril.'

Out of the corner of his eye, Moctezuma saw the steward wringing his long thin hands.

'Forgive me, sire, but I fear your wrath if I fail to bring this matter to your attention . . .' More wringing of hands. 'It is better you yourself should decide.'

Moctezuma's fury was building. It was not for nothing that his name meant 'Angry Lord'. But he also felt apprehension, indeed a sense of impending catastrophe. 'Very well,' he said quietly – for he almost never raised his voice. 'Tell me of this matter.'

Teudile's fear was palpable now. 'Sire,' he said, 'at the door, is a *pochtecatl* called Cuetzpalli. I would have sent him away with a severe beating, but he carries your seal, and he claims you told him to discover certain information for you. He says he is in possession of that information now, and he is certain you will want to hear it.'

The blood drained from Moctezuma's face. He had summoned this Cuetzpalli to a private meeting at the palace last year, soon after the first inconclusive sightings of white-skinned beings, resembling men but possessing supernatural powers, who had emerged from the eastern ocean in boats that moved by themselves without paddles. Moctezuma had reason to fear such tidings. There was much to suggest that the beings had come to prepare the way for the return of Quetzalcoatl, the god of peace who, it was prophesied, would drive him from the throne of the Mexica empire, end the rites of human sacrifice over which he presided, and overturn the existing order of the world.

The young merchant Cuetzpalli, a member of one of the powerful *pochteca* guilds, travelled and traded amongst the Chontal Maya of the Yucatán, in whose lands the beings had passed a brief sojourn. He was therefore ideally placed to keep watch for any further sign of them. 'If they are sighted again,' he had told Cuetzpalli before sending him on his way to the Yucatán, 'then gather intelligence and bring it to me swiftly. You may approach me with it at any hour of the day or night. No information is of greater importance to the safety of our realm.'

'You were right to disturb me,' Moctezuma sighed, putting Teudile out of his misery. 'I will see the *pochtecatl* in the House of Serpents. But before you bring him there, summon Namacuix and tell him I will require two captives, both males – youths – for sacrifice.'

Because the best-known manifestation of Quetzalcoatl was in the form of a plumed serpent, it seemed to Moctezuma it would be appropriate to be amongst the creatures of Quetzalcoatl if, as he very much feared, he was now to receive tidings of that god's return.

The House of Serpents was part of the royal zoo, and there, in the pits and ponds surrounding the main viewing floor, could be found serpents of all sizes and colours, from the dullest rattlesnakes to the brightest coral and parrot snakes. The collection included bushmasters, nauyaca vipers, eyelash vipers, dwarf pythons, ribbon snakes, black rat snakes, milk snakes, garter snakes, boa constrictors and many other species, including a variety of aquatic snakes. The great walled court-yard built to display these monsters was in part open to the stars and additionally illuminated tonight by flickering torches, bringing to life richly painted murals of serpents arranging themselves in geometric patterns. Ichtaka the zookeeper and his young assistant were still busily lighting the torches when Moctezuma entered. They at once fell on their faces, as was proper in the presence of the Great Speaker, but he waved them to their feet, ordering them to complete their task and leave.

Namacuix, the lean zealot with burning eyes, recently appointed to the role of High Priest following the mysterious disappearance of his treacherous predecessor Ahuizotl, arrived soon afterwards. He was accompanied by four black-robed assistants carrying a portable wooden execution platform, which they set down in the middle of the viewing chamber. With them, guarded by six soldiers, came two captive Tlascalan youths, dressed in paper loincloths, their bodies already covered in chalk. Although they were drugged and compliant, their eyes brimmed with fear and horror. Finally Teudile entered with a servant carrying two stools – a high one for Moctezuma to sit on and a much lower one for the *pochtecatl*.

'Shall I bring in the merchant, lord?' Teudile asked.

In one of the pits, a sinuous boa constrictor was in the process of swallowing a very large agouti. Watching gloomily, Moctezuma was struck by the symbolism. The serpent must represent Quetzalcoatl while the agouti, now bulging in the serpent's gullet, must be himself.

'Yes,' he said. 'Bring him in.'

It was most unusual for any man, let alone a travel-stained and weary *pochtecatl*, to be seated in the presence of the Great Speaker, but Cuetzpalli's mission justified the honour. When the merchant had completed his obeisances, Moctezuma gestured to the stool and got straight to the point: 'Have the white-skinned beings returned?' he asked.

'They have, my lord,' Cuetzpalli replied. 'They came, as they did before, from across the eastern ocean, in boats of enormous size that move by themselves without paddles.'

Moctezuma nodded slowly. *In this way*, he thought, *as the ancient prophecies foretold, my doom approaches.* He made a sign to Namacuix and, very quickly, with no ceremony, the two Tlascalan youths were bent backwards over the killing platform, their breasts hacked open and their hearts torn out. When the work was done, the High Priest dipped his fingers into their welling chest cavities, crossed over to Moctezuma and Cuetzpalli, and sprinkled them liberally with blood.

There followed a brief interval as the bodies were removed; the parts not fit for human consumption would be fed immediately to the jaguars and other carnivorous beasts kept in the zoo. The assistant priests and soldiers then filed out. Finally, only Namacuix and Teudile were left standing, one on either side of their ruler. 'Very well,' Moctezuma said to the *pochtecatl*. 'You may proceed.'

'You are gracious, sire,' the merchant replied. 'But before I begin it is my duty to inform you that the events I am about to speak of took place twenty-seven days ago.'

Moctezuma frowned. 'Twenty-seven days?'

'Yes, great lord, for the lands of the Chontal Maya are very far from here. I travelled fast, by forced march, sleeping little and eating while on the move. I left my caravan far behind, retaining only my Cuahchic bodyguards to secure my safety. Even so, we were twenty-seven days on the road.'

Though Moctezuma endeavoured to keep his face calm and free of emotion, his heart was thudding. If the white-skinned beings had been seen in the lands of the Chontal Maya twenty-seven days ago, then who was to say where they might be today? If they were truly gods, as he suspected, it seemed likely they would travel much faster than mortal men, in which case might they not even now be approaching Tenochtitlan?

That prospect, terrifying in itself, grew even more horrible and

14

immediate for Moctezuma as the *pochtecatl* told his story, supporting it with many detailed paintings done by his own artist during a great battle – a battle that had taken place twenty-seven days previously, in which the Chontal Maya had sought, and failed, to drive the white-skinned beings back into the ocean.

Moctezuma knew the Maya to be ferocious fighters; indeed their ferocity was one reason why the Mexica had never tried to force them to become tribute-paying subjects of the empire. They were also numerous as flies in the summer and thus able to put large armies in the field, which made conquering them a costly prospect that his generals had always advised against.

Yet the white-skinned beings, whose own numbers, Cuetzpalli reported, did not exceed a paltry five hundred, had, in a single day, destroyed and put to rout an army of forty thousand Chontal Maya! Of particular significance was the fact that they had done so with the use of Xiuhcoatl – fire-serpents. The war god Huitzilopochtli, 'Hummingbird', had appeared to Moctezuma in visions to warn him that those who sought his doom would be armed in exactly this way.

The Mayan chiefs, Cuetzpalli continued, had foolishly persuaded themselves that the beings were not gods and that their Xiuhcoatl were merely manmade weapons of some ingenious sort. Having seen them in action, however, the *pochtecatl* had no doubt that supernatural powers were involved. 'Their fire-serpents roared,' he said, 'and their noise resounded like thunder so loud as to steal a man's strength and shut off his ears.' Moreover, the beings possessed not just one but at least three different types of these miraculous weapons! The smallest killed one or two men at a single blow, those of medium size easily killed fifty, and the largest ones killed hundreds. 'The discharge of a large Xiuhcoatl is terrifying, lord,' Cuetzpalli said, his voice filled with wonder. 'A thing like a ball of metal shoots out from its entrails, showering fire and blazing sparks; it travels a great distance through the air and when it hits the ground it bounces and rolls, killing all in its path, breaking men apart and dissolving them as though they never existed. The smoke that comes out with it has a fetid odour, like rotten mud. It can be smelled from afar and it wounds the head and penetrates even to the brain.'

Moctezuma had an overwhelming sense of a great danger that had been closing in on him for several years, now slowly and menacingly fulfilling its dreadful promise.

First there had been the signs and omens, unexplained visitations, incoherent and unclear but no less terrifying for that, stretching back a decade or more. Then two years ago a strange bird had been brought to his palace. The bird had a mirror in its crest, and in that mirror Moctezuma had seen white-skinned, golden-haired creatures dressed in metal armour, some resembling humans, and some part-human, part-deer that ran very swiftly. Next, less than a year ago, reports had reached him from the Chontal Maya that beings exactly like those he had seen in the mirror had appeared in the Yucatán. Later, Hummingbird had given him further tidings of them, telling him that they were masters of unknown metals and that wild beasts fought for them in battle, 'Some carrying them faster than the wind, others with monstrous teeth and jaws that tear men apart.' Now, witness to a battle that had taken place just twenty-seven days ago, Cuetzpalli had brought paint-ings of these same wild-beasts – 'deer that bore them on their backs and were tall as roof terraces', and other monsters the size of jaguars that he had seen only from a distance but that ran across the battlefield in great numbers, seizing and devouring the Mayan soldiers. Both types of beast moved with terrifying, unnatural speed, flying over the ground and leaping through the air; and both, like the white-skinned beings themselves, wore armour made of a mysterious metal that gleamed like silver but was so strong that none of the Mayan weapons could penetrate it. 'Their trappings and arms are all made of this metal,' Cuetzpalli said. 'They dress in it and wear it on their heads. Their swords are metal, their bows are metal, their shields are metal, their spears are metal.'

The artist had painted awe-inspiring images of the white-skinned beings with their strange beasts, and their terrifying metal war array. As Moctezuma studied the paintings and heard Cuetzpalli's account, the suspicion that these beings must be gods, which he had all along entertained, began to solidify and take definite shape in his mind. Although Cuetzpalli had not had the opportunity to approach them closely, witnessing the battle from a hilltop, he had questioned a Maya chief who had negotiated with them for some days before the fighting began. This chief, Muluc by name, had described the beings as 'very white. They have chalky faces; they have yellow hair, though the hair of some is black. Their beards are long and yellow, and their moustaches are yellow.'

The description accorded perfectly with all ancient testimony concerning the bearded, white-skinned god Quetzalcoatl whose return, it had long ago been prophesied, would take place *this very year* – the year One-Reed. Indeed Quetzalcoatl's full name was Ce-Acatl Quetzalcoatl meaning 'One-Reed Quetzalcoatl'. Moreover, there was a venerable tradition that 'years with the sign of the Flint come from the north, those with the House from the west, those with the Rabbit from the south, and those with the Reed from the east.' It was therefore a matter laden with meaning that these white-skinned gods, whose description answered so closely to that of Quetzalcoatl, had entered the Yucatán *from the east*, across the eastern ocean. Also, the place where they had arrived and given such a fearsome demonstration of their supernatural powers was Potonchan – the exact spot from which Quetzalcoatl was said to have made his exit long years before, and to which he had promised he would return to begin the overthrow of the devotees of Hummingbird, the war god who had driven him out. *Quetzalcoatl has appeared!* Moctezuma thought. *He has come back! He will come here, to Tenochtitlan, to the place of his throne and his canopy, for that is what he promised when he departed.*

'In the year One-Reed,' the prophecy said, 'a king will be struck down and made a slave.'

Certain now that he himself must be that doomed king, Moctezuma found it increasingly difficult to disguise the awful, mind-numbing, gut-wrenching fear that was overtaking him like some deadly curse, shrivelling his heart and loosening the sinews of his knees.

That same fear, inspired by the earlier omens, had led him to initiate a holocaust of two thousand female victims on the pyramid sixty days before. The great sacrifice had produced its desired effect. Hummingbird had appeared to him and promised to fight at his side, and in return Moctezuma had sworn to the war god that an even larger harvest would follow – a harvest consisting entirely of virgin girls. He'd felt confident he would be able to keep his word because Coaxoch, his greatest general, had then been in the field commanding an entire army with a full complement of four regiments, each eight thousand men strong, dedicated to the sole purpose of seizing huge numbers of additional victims. But what Moctezuma had not known that night, what he could not even possibly have imagined, was that Coaxoch's army of thirty-two thousand fighting men would be annihilated the very next morning by a superior Tlascalan force – demolished so completely by the Tlascalan battle-king Shikotenka that barely three thousand demoralised survivors had limped back to Tenochtitlan. Nor could Moctezuma have predicted the puzzling escalation in fighting that erupted soon afterwards, much closer to home, with the rebel forces led by Ishtlil, the treacherous prince of Texcoco. This flare-up had so preoccupied the five remaining Mexica armies that there had been scant progress in the further search for sacrificial victims.

Deep in his roiling guts, Moctezuma knew he need look no further to explain why, despite all his efforts and his desperate need for reassurance and advice, Hummingbird had not reappeared or even sent him a single unambiguous sign. It was obvious the war god would remain remote until he received the large basket of virgins promised to him. Henceforward, Moctezuma resolved, he would once again devote four full regiments of his best men exclusively to that sacred task.

When Cuetzpalli's report was complete, Moctezuma spoke gently to him. 'You have suffered fatigue,' he said, 'and you are exhausted from your long journey, so you may go now and rest and when I have need of you I will call you again. But know this. What you have said to me tonight and what you have shown me has been in secret. It is only within you. His glance took in Teudile and Namacuix and he made his voice stern: 'No one shall speak anything of this. No one shall let it escape his lips. If any here present lets any of it out, they will die. Their wives will be killed by hanging them with ropes. Their children will be dashed to pieces against the walls of their houses and their houses will be torn down and rooted out of their foundations.'

As he stood to leave, Moctezuma's eyes fell on the boa constrictor in the pit. He noted with interest that the agouti had proved too large to swallow and the serpent's gullet had burst explosively open.

Both creatures now lay dead.

Chapter Four

Wednesday 21 April 1519, night

Guatemoc sat alone on the roof garden of his townhouse in the royal quarter of Tenochtitlan, gazing up at the starry sky. In the midnight depths of the darkness, the glittering Mamalhuaztli, the seven bright stars of the Fire-Sticks constellation, were setting and would soon enter their period of invisibility when they would be seen no more until the late summer.

Strange, Guatemoc thought, how the stars came and went – now seen, now not seen. They were as inscrutable and mysterious as Temaz, the goddess of healing and medicines, to whom he owed his astonishing recovery from the terrible wounds inflicted on him two months previously by Shikotenka, battle-king of Tlascala, and also from the deadly *cotelachi* poison he'd been given while he lay convalescing in the royal hospital. His uncle Moctezuma had, of course, denied any direct involvement in the plot, had ordered the royal physician Mecatl to be flayed alive for administering the poison, and had presented the doctor's skin to his nephew as a token. Even so, Guatemoc and his father Cuitláhuac, whose loyalty to Moctezuma had hitherto been unshakable, both knew perfectly well that the Great Speaker had been behind the whole scheme.

Ah Temaz, Temaz . . . Guatemoc couldn't believe how lovesick he had become! He was sitting out here actually sighing under the night sky! He was missing her, longing for her sweet touch, remembering the uncanny healing warmth that had poured from her fingers into his wounds, bringing him back to life. More than fifty days had passed since their first encounter in the royal hospital, when she had come to him to expose Moctezuma's plot. Then, after he'd been taken to the safety of his father's estate at Chapultepec, she'd materialised thrice more to give him further healing and to speak to him of impossible things – of the return of Quetzalcoatl, the Plumed Serpent, the god of peace, who, she said, would overthrow Moctezuma. Even now, so many days later, though he had not seen her again since that last extraordinary night, her words still echoed in his ears: 'You must not, Guatemoc, *you must not* place yourself in opposition to Quetzalcoatl. A war is coming and you must be on the right side. You must be on the side of peace.'

'Peace?' Guatemoc had been genuinely puzzled. 'I am a warrior, my lady. I can never be on the side of peace . . .' Besides, 'What sort of god of peace would resort to war in the first place? Surely if he wishes to rid the world of Moctezuma, he will find a way to do that by peaceful means?'

'Moctezuma is evil,' Temaz had insisted, 'and sometimes evil over-whelms good, and when it does it can't just be wished away peacefully. It has to be fought and it has to be stopped, and that's what Quetzalcoatl is returning to do.'

'So Quetzalcoatl, then, is a god of war, just like our own war god Hummingbird?'

'No . . . Yes!'

'Which is it to be, my lady? Is this Quetzalcoatl of yours a god of peace? Or is he a god of war? He can't be both!'

'Then he is a god of war! But his fight is against Hummingbird himself, the wicked ruler and authority of the unseen world, who contaminates and pollutes everything he touches with evil and dark-ness, whose puppet Moctezuma is, just as the physician Mecatl was Moctezuma's puppet in the plot to poison you . . . So the question you must ask yourself, Guatemoc, is this – will you, too, be Hummingbird's puppet in the great conflict that is to come, or will you fight on the side of the good and the light?'

'Lady Temaz,' Guatemoc had replied, 'if you are asking me to fight against Moctezuma, then I will tell you now I am ready to do so! He is a weakling and a fool and, besides, he sought to murder me! But if you are asking me to fight against Hummingbird, my lady . . . well, that is quite another matter and by no means so easily undertaken.'

'The time will come, Prince, when you will have to choose,' Temaz had said. 'I can only hope you choose wisely.' He remembered how she'd pressed her fingers one more time against the wounds that scarred his naked belly, sending more healing warmth into his body. 'I will see you again,' she'd said, straightening, relinquishing the contact.

And then . . .

Well, then he'd kissed her, a passionate kiss, deep and filled with hunger – his hunger, her hunger – which could only be satiated in one way, which *should* have been satiated in that way, except that at that precise moment the Lady Temaz had turned to smoke in Guatemoc's arms and disappeared, leaving him embracing empty air.

What just happened? he remembered thinking. *Who is she? A goddess, as she claims? Or something else?*

He'd touched his lips again, glowing, alive, tingling with sensation. But when he brought his fingers away he saw they were smeared with red.

He'd frowned. What was this? Blood? He'd tasted his lips with his tongue. No! Not blood! Something else. Something familiar.

He'd found an obsidian mirror and examined himself. This red stuff, whatever it might be, was not confined to his lips but smeared all round his mouth. He'd tasted it again and suddenly he had it. Tincture of cochineal! Rare and exotic, yes, but quite definitely a woman's lip paint.

Why would a goddess need lip paint?

He'd pondered that question back then, and pondered it still, but had not yet come to any definite conclusion. It remained possible that he had been healed by a goddess. But his intuition suggested another, even more extraordinary, possibility: that the goddess Temaz had all along been a human woman in disguise. A witch, perhaps, with some strange power to render herself invisible and visible at will?

Guatemoc sighed again. The thought that he might have been duped would ordinarily have plunged him into a rage but, in this case, strangely, it did not. The single, unassailable truth was that this Temaz, whoever she was – whether goddess or woman, phantom or witch – had brought him the miracle of healing and saved his life.

He ran the tip of his tongue around his lips. Even now, after so much time had passed, he often imagined he could taste her sweetness and feel the hot, wet warmth of her tongue roiling against his.

And, on occasion – was it also his imagination, or something more? – he was overtaken by a strong intuition that she was present, invisible, watching silently over him. He felt the hairs rise on the back of his neck. Was now one of those times?

'Temaz,' he said softly. 'Sweet goddess. Show yourself to me.'

There! What was that? A disturbance of the air? A hint of form emerging out of shadow? Was tonight the night the goddess would return to him? Guatemoc sat forward eagerly, his eyes probing the darkness. 'Are you there?' he asked, surprised by the tremor in his voice. He stood, walked hesitantly to the place where he thought he had seen her, reaching out with his arms. 'I have longed for you,' he said – but then immediately felt foolish because there came no reply and the night air was still again, the shadows just shadows and empty of substance.

Enough! He was behaving like a callow youth.

It was time to put this nonsense behind him. Tomorrow, he resolved, he would begin to involve himself in affairs of state again. Moctezuma would resist, but Moctezuma's days were numbered. If Quetzalcoatl was indeed about to return, then a true warrior must step forward to confront him.

As to women . . . well, women were as plentiful as the fish in the sea. Guatemoc had held himself aloof from them long enough because of his foolish loyalty to Temaz.

Might as well be loyal to a dream!

He was ready to move on.

Chapter Five

Thursday 22 April 1519

The great lord called Cortés, wearing the gleaming metal jacket that these Spaniards called a cuirass, was seated under an awning on the same grand and ingenious folding chair that Malinal had seen him use for his diplomatic encounter with the defeated chiefs of the Chontal Maya. But time had passed since then, and the man in front of Cortés today, seated cross-legged on a mat on the ground and thus obliged to look up at him from a position of inferiority, was no Maya. Instead this was a plain and stocky middle-ranking noble of the Mexica, Pichatzin by name, whom Moctezuma had appointed as provincial governor of the coastal town of Cuetlaxtlan. In her five years as a sex slave of the Mexica, Malinal had attended a number of dinner parties in Tenochtitlan at which Pichatzin had been present before he was sent to rule this far-flung outpost of the empire. But, since his rank amongst the *pipiltzin* – the noble social class – was too low for her ever to have been given to him as a lover, it was not certain he would remember her. For the same reason, she knew none of the five other relatively low-ranking nobles accompanying him as an entourage, who were presently obliged, for want of space, to stand outside the awning in the full glare of the afternoon sun. In addition, Pichatzin had brought along an artist who was also squatting in the sun and working industriously on a series of paintings.

Cortés's own entourage consisted of red-bearded Puertocarrero, who Malinal knew all too well, and the lords Alvarado, Escalante, Ordaz and Montejo, whose names she had memorised. Though standing, they had all found a place under the shade of the awning. The boy Pepillo, who was never far from Cortés's side, except when

24

tending to his injured pet dog, sat on the ground clutching a pen and a sheaf of papers, ready as always to keep a record of his master's doings. In addition the interpreter Aguilar was present; however, since he spoke only Castilian and Maya, while Pichatzin and his entourage, like most Mexica, spoke only Nahuatl, he presently had very little to do. It was obvious from the repeated use of sign language and frustrated smiles that the two groups did not understand each other at all well.

Spying on the meeting over the steam rising from the cooking pots, and between the bustling figures of the other serving girls in the makeshift kitchen of the Spanish camp, Malinal saw the chance she had been denied until now to prove her worth to Cortés. In her first extraordinary glimpse of the white men on horseback twenty-eight days before, it had been the eye of Cortés himself that she had caught as he rode past her, clothed from head to foot in shining metal armour, to join the great battle outside Potonchan. The very next day she had been presented to him as a peace offering by her stepfather Muluc, the ruler of Potonchan, who had of course survived the fighting in which so many thousands of the Chontal Maya had died. Along with her had come heaped jaguar skins, bales of costly cloths, a chest full of precious jade objects, some gems, some small items of gold and silver, and nineteen other women – all of them, like Malinal herself, offered as slaves to be used for any purpose the Spaniards saw fit. 'You said you returned to us to meet the white men,' Muluc had reminded her, 'so now you're going to get your wish – and good riddance to you. I hope you're as much trouble to them as you've been to me.' Her mother Raxca had wept but had raised no objection as her repulsive husband got Malinal out of the way permanently and placated a powerful enemy at the same time – thus, he gloated, 'killing two birds with one arrow.'

Malinal had found it hard to conceal her joy. After she and her friend Tozi had narrowly escaped sacrifice at the hands of Moctezuma himself, she had walked all the way from Tenochtitlan to find these white 'gods', only to be diverted from her quest by Muluc – yet fate had now conspired to make him the very instrument that would put her into their hands! For a moment everything had seemed to be moving smoothly towards its foreordained conclusion but, soon after she had been marched from the regional capital Cintla back to Potonchan, and delivered to the Spaniards, Malinal's sense of being swept up in some divine scheme was again rudely shattered. The special connection she had felt with the Spanish leader as she'd watched him ride into battle, the way he had turned his bearded white face towards her, the way his eyes had seemed to fix on her and root her to the spot, had filled her with hope and a strange yearning. Yet, when she had been brought before him in Potonchan, he had accepted her from Muluc as a gift of less importance than the jade, gold and jewels (which themselves had seemed to please him very little), paid her no special attention, rejected her attempt to speak to him through Aguilar and finally *given* her to his friend Puertocarrero.

Thereafter she had seen little of Cortés during the twenty-three further days the Spaniards had remained in the lands of the Chontal Maya. He had spent much of his time away from Potonchan, often in the company of his cruel but handsome second in command Pedro de Alvarado. She soon learned from servants who Muluc had sent to work for them in the palace that the Spaniards were ransacking all the towns of the region for gold – which seemed to obsess them as much as it obsessed the Mexica, though it was of little interest to the Maya. It was even said that Muluc and the paramount chief Ah Kinchil had been tortured to persuade them to surrender stores of gold the white men believed they had hidden – but of course they had none to give. She neither knew nor cared if these reports were true; the two chiefs had conspired to ruin her life and, in her opinion, deserved whatever bad things came to them.

When not hunting for gold, Cortés's other favourite activity – to which he showed great dedication – was destroying the idols of the gods kept in the temples and preaching to the people of Cintla and Potonchan about his own strange and incomprehensible religion. Since everyone was terrified of him, he won many converts.

On the occasions when he was not preoccupied with these activities, Malinal several times asked Aguilar's assistance to approach Cortés and speak to him. From the very first day, however, the Spanish interpreter had been unhelpful. She'd made him understand she was fluent not only in Maya but also in Nahuatl, the language of the Mexica, yet for some reason she couldn't grasp, he was obviously determined not to let her talk to Cortés.

Then she'd found out why.

One evening Cortés had made an announcement to the assembled army, which Aguilar had been required to translate for the benefit of all twenty of the female slaves who would be accompanying them; he'd said that the Spaniards had concluded their business with the Chontal Maya and would soon be moving on to the lands of the Mexica. They would go first by ship to the coastal town of Cuetlaxtlan – everyone must be ready to embark in just three days' time – and from there they would strike inland to Tenochtitlan, the Mexica capital. This they would seize by force, take its emperor Moctezuma 'dead or alive', and help themselves to the vast hoard of gold his empire was reputed to have amassed.

Reputed? Malinal had thought, even as her heart soared. *Reputed!* If she'd been allowed to talk to Cortés she could have told him weeks before that it was not just a matter of 'reputed'. The Mexica were the richest people in the entire world, Tenochtitlan overflowed with gold and Moctezuma's treasuries were stuffed to bursting point with it.

Clearly Aguilar had acted so strangely because he knew Malinal was fluent in Nahuatl – which he spoke not a word of – and could see she was already learning Castilian. The foolish man must have feared, since it was inevitable the Spaniards' lust for gold would sooner or later lead them to the Mexica, that she would then usurp his privileged place at Cortés's side. While not actually lying to his master about the fabulous wealth of Tenochtitlan, the interpreter had therefore done all he could to divert and delay this important intelligence and to prevent Cortés from discovering how indispensable Malinal might prove to the Spanish cause.

Perhaps Aguilar had even hoped the slaves would be left behind when the Spaniards continued their journey! But there was no way Puertocarrero or any of the other officers who'd been given women were going to do without their all-purpose cooks, cleaners and bed companions, and Cortés had made a point of confirming they would accompany the army in its advance on Tenochtitlan.

So once again, Malinal realised, she had been reunited with her fate. Very soon Cortés would meet the lords of the Mexica and find he was unable to talk to them. When he did, no matter how Aguilar might try to block her, she had resolved she would be there to take her rightful place in history.

Three days later, as Cortés had promised, they left Potonchan. Then had followed a sea voyage in the great boat, named the *Santa Luisa*, owned by Puertocarrero. This vessel was so much larger and grander than any Malinal had ever seen or dreamed of, that she had at first been overawed, even a little terrified, by its mountainous size and by the cunning way its wings of cloth caught the wind and drove it forward across the foaming waves.

Moreover, the *Santa Luisa* was only one of eleven such boats under the command of Cortés, with his own *Santa Maria* being the largest and most magnificent of them. All these 'ships', as the Spaniards called them, had sailed together along the coast of the Yucatán after departing from Potonchan and again, since they were on different vessels, there had been no opportunity for Malinal to speak with Cortés. What soon became clear to her, however, was that they were travelling faster than a man could walk and that they kept this speed up, hour after hour, day after day, and night after night, soon leaving the lands of the Maya behind and moving ever closer to territories settled and governed by the Mexica.

Finally, on the morning of the fourth day at sea, Cortés ordered the fleet to drop anchor off the coast a few miles north of Cuetlaxtlan and immediately began to disembark the larger part of his army. Within hours camp had been pitched high up on the sand dunes, Pichatzin and his entourage had arrived to find out what was going on, only to be frustrated by a seemingly insuperable language barrier, and Malinal, slaving over the cooking pots, had seen her opportunity to catch Cortés's eye again, as she had on the day of the great battle outside Potonchan.

Then, as he'd thundered by on horseback, she might still have been persuaded that he and his fellow Spaniards were gods, but she knew better now. Indeed the smell of Puertocarrero's farts alone had been enough to convince her that she was dealing with men, like any other men – with all the weaknesses, follies and stupidities of the male sex.

To be sure, they looked very different from the Maya or the Mexica, and their language – which Malinal had already begun to master – was quite unlike any other she had ever heard. Admittedly, also, their customs and behaviour were strange. Although most of them never washed, with the result that their bodies were filthy and stinking, they were unusually disciplined and determined, and their weapons, their tame animals and their ships were extraordinary. Nevertheless, when all was said and done, they were men, and nothing more than men, and as such, no matter how fearsome and alien they might seem, they could be understood and manipulated.

Malinal checked her cooking pots one more time. The stew was ready. She ladled two generous helpings into the bowls she would offer to Cortés and Pichatzin, told the other girls to serve out the rest, and made her way across the sand to her destiny.

'Surely there must be some common ground between the Mexica and the Maya?' Cortés asked Aguilar. 'Something you can use to communicate with these savages?'

'No, Hernán,' Aguilar replied. 'Their languages are not like French and Italian, with many shared words. They are utterly different. I can't make myself understood at all.'

'Well we have a problem then,' said Cortés. 'If we can't speak to the Mexica, we can't negotiate with them or impress them with our arguments, or learn their minds. It will make them harder to defeat.'

'Nonsense!' said Alvarado, who was standing with Puertocarrero beside Cortés. 'The language of the sword is plain. We need only speak to them in that and they'll understand us well enough!'

Cortés laughed wearily. 'I wish it were so simple, Pedro, but in my experience the tongue is a mightier weapon than the blade.'

As he spoke, Cortés saw the tall and very beautiful Mayan woman he had given to Puertocarrero approaching them across the sand; she was holding two steaming bowls of the afternoon meal he had ordered the kitchen to prepare. He had first seen this striking creature on the day of the great battle outside Potonchan, standing with a group of other observers atop one of the low hills that overlooked the plains, and he'd recognised her the following morning when the barbarian Muluc had brought her as a tribute. She had made an impassioned appeal to speak to him then, but Aguilar had persuaded him – against his own instincts – to ignore her. Now, noting again the elegance of her stride and the seductive curves of her body, Cortés reflected that he should have claimed her for himself. But rebellion was brewing amongst the Velazquistas – as he called the faction of conquistadors still loyal to his rival Diego de Velázquez, the governor of Cuba, who he'd betrayed by sailing from Santiago without permission two months before. His own friends outnumbered them, but they had to be kept sweet, and this decorative sex slave had been an easy way to satisfy Puertocarrero, who loved women at least as much as he loved gold.

She stooped under the awning, ignored the lustful stare she received from her master and brought the first bowl straight to Cortés, her eyes fixed on him. There was intelligence in those eyes and something else – some urgency, some attempt at connection, some message she seemed to wish to communicate. 'Gods!' Montejo muttered to Puertocarrero, 'you're a lucky man to take that one to your bed.'

'Her tongue struggles mightily with my blade each night,' agreed Puertocarrero. There was a general outburst of lewd sniggers from the Spaniards, but Cortés refrained from joining in. He sensed that the woman somehow knew she was being mocked. She turned to Pichatzin, stooping to offer him the second bowl. Then, as the Mexica reached out his hands to take it from her, she spoke some words to him in what sounded like his own language. His eyes widened, his thin lips narrowed, a beat of silence followed and then he replied. There was, Cortés thought, anger in his tone. The woman addressed him again. Her voice was husky, deep and rich, but at the same time soothing and gentle. Pichatzin relaxed and in a moment there was a smile on his face. He spoke further to the woman and she answered with a musical chime of laughter.

Cortés turned to Puertocarrero. 'It seems your woman is quite the diplomat,' he observed. 'What's her name?'

Puertocarrero shrugged. 'Malinal . . . or something such.'

'And this Malinal,' Cortés addressed Aguilar, 'she is Maya? She speaks the Maya tongue?'

'She is Maya,' Aguilar replied. There was something evasive in his tone. 'She came to us with the other Maya slave women. You'll recall she made a scene when they brought her. Since then she's many times asked to speak to you – some nonsense about you being a god – but I didn't think you'd wish to be bothered with the babble of a serf.'

'That was a mistake,' Cortés snapped, putting steel into his voice. 'Make no such decisions for me in the future!'

Aguilar's shoulders slumped: 'Yes, Don Hernán. My apologies.'

'It seems she speaks the language of these Mexica,' Cortés observed. 'Find out, therefore, if she truly does, whether she is fluent and where she learnt it.' Leaning forward in his chair, with the Mexica officials also looking on eagerly, he watched and listened as Aguilar and Malinal held an animated conversation that lasted for several minutes.

'Spit it out, man!' Cortés said to Aguilar the moment they fell silent. He couldn't hold down the impatience and rising excitement he felt.

'She is of the Chontal Maya,' said Aguilar. 'But she claims to have complete mastery of the Mexica language, which she says is called Nahuatl. She claims to have lived in the Mexica capital city – this Tenochtitlan of which many have spoken – for five years and learnt it there.' Aguilar lowered his eyes and added: 'She also says she knows much about the Mexica that will be of value to you—'

'Things I might have learned weeks ago if you'd done your job properly . . .'

'Yes, Don Hernán. I can only apologise . . .'

Cortés nodded. 'Very well, but let's learn from this. In future you will tell me everything she says.' He bounded from his chair, walked into the sunlight and paced restlessly. 'The two of you will work together,' he said to Aguilar. 'When the Mexica speak, Malinal will translate their words into Maya and you will put them into Castilian for me, missing nothing out. When I speak you will translate my words into Maya and Malinal will put them into Nahuatl. Tell her! Tell her now this is the plan. Tell her if she accepts she'll do no more menial kitchen work. She'll be elevated to a place of honour amongst us.'

'By all means she accepts!' growled Puertocarrero. 'I'll give her a good slapping if she doesn't.'

'Fie, Alonso! That won't be necessary. This is clearly an intelligent woman of some breeding. Any fool can see that! I would prefer she worked happily with us of her own free will.'

As Aguilar and Malinal talked, Cortés observed them closely, and he was happy to see a broad smile break out on her face and hear her laughter. Damn, but there was something about this girl that touched his heart! 'What does she say?' he asked.

'She says, yes, of course,' Aguilar replied. 'She will be honoured to serve in any way that pleases you.'

Once introductions had been properly made by Malinal, Cortés had a much better idea about who he was dealing with. Pichatzin was the servant of that powerful king or emperor whom the Chontal Maya had spoken about with such reverence, whose title was the 'Great Speaker' and whose name was Moctezuma. It seemed this Moctezuma ruled vast territories and huge numbers of people from his splendid capital city Tenochtitlan, which stood on an island in a lake somewhat less than two hundred miles inland from the place where the Spanish were presently camped. There was no doubt in Cortés's mind that this must be the same golden city Saint Peter had promised him in his dreams as his reward for punishing the Chontal Maya at Potonchan. As to Pichatzin, he had been appointed a year ago on Moctezuma's orders to be the governor of the good-sized town called Cuetlaxtlan, lying a few miles further south down the coast and identified as such by Juan de Escalante in an earlier reconnaissance. Now Cortés learned Cuetlaxtlan had been conquered and settled more than seventy years earlier by Moctezuma's race – the fabled Mexica, about whose great wealth in gold and treasure he had already heard so much. However, the majority of the inhabitants of this region were a subject people called the Totonacs, who were ruled by the Mexica and paid tribute to them.

Through Malinal, Pichatzin then asked Cortés what the Spanish wanted here, why they had come across the ocean in their ships and what their plans were.

'We have come,' Cortés lied, 'because the fame of your emperor the great Moctezuma has reached us even across the ocean. I desire to see him and trade with him, and to this end in a very short while I propose to march with my men into the interior of your country and make my way to Tenochtitlan.'

Pichatzin replied that this would be unwise without the permission of Moctezuma, who commanded a standing army of more than two hundred thousand men. 'Allow me to send a message to my emperor,' he said. In the politest possible language, but nonetheless with a clear undertone of threat, he advised Cortés to keep the Spanish in their camp until they had received an answer.

'If Tenochtitlan is two hundred miles away,' Cortés objected, 'this going to and fro of messages will surely take a long time.'

'Not so long,' said Malinal. Speaking directly through Aguilar, without reference to Pichatzin, she explained that the Mexica had excellent roads on which the journey could be made in six days – or sometimes less at a fast march. However, messages travelled very much faster than that. There were relay posts on the roads, separated by intervals of just five miles. A messenger would leave at once running at top speed. When he became tired he would stop and hand the message on to another runner, who would do the same at the next relay post – and so on. In this way Pichatzin's message would be carried very quickly to Moctezuma, reaching him in less than twenty-four hours.

'So we can expect a reply in two days and two nights?' Cortés asked.

Malinal put the question to Pichatzin.

'Yes,' he replied. 'In two days and two nights you will have the Great Speaker's answer.'

'If we wait,' said Cortés, 'my men will need food, water, better shelter than we have now. Can you provide us with these things?'

'The Great Speaker is generous to his guests,' Pichatzin replied. 'I will see to it you have everything you need.'

Pichatzin proved true to his word. Within hours of his departure, hundreds of bearers arrived bringing huge quantities of fresh food and drink and the promise that at dawn the next day a gang of labourers would be sent to build temporary dwellings for the Spaniards. Meanwhile, though far from comfortable, and plagued by swarms of tiny biting insects, the camp occupied a good defensible position on the dunes. Francisco de Mesa, the grizzled and enormously competent chief of artillery, had already set up cannon around its perimeter to protect against any surprise attack.

All in all, Cortés decided, things could be very much worse.

With night already well advanced, he dismissed his captains and, despite some grumbles from Puertocarrero, summoned Aguilar and Malinal to his tent for a private meeting. If he was to take on the military might of the Mexica empire, then the brute force with which he had won his battles against the Chontal Maya would not be enough. Above all else, he needed to know Moctezuma's weaknesses if he was to defeat him – and, in this, some intuition told him, Malinal had been heaven-sent to help.

It had been a long day for Pepillo, an exciting day that seemed lifted from the pages of *Amadis de Gaula*, that great romance of adventure and chivalry, of brave knights and monsters and of savage, exotic kingdoms, that Cortés kept in his travelling library and had allowed Pepillo to read. The Mexica ambassador and his entourage, so colourful, so barbaric in their bright feather cloaks and headdresses, with their lip-plugs of turquoise, with thin rods of gold and jade passed through their ear lobes and noses, with their strange weapons of wood, flint and obsidian, and their mellow, fluid language like a river running over stones and a breeze sighing through trees, had seemed unutterably alien, more alien even than the Maya, as though they were creatures not of this earth but of another realm entirely. How wonderful, then, that the slave woman Malinal not only spoke Maya but also spoke Nahuatl, the language of the Mexica, and therefore could work alongside Aguilar to make communication possible between Cortés and the dangerous savages whose lands he very soon intended to enter.

'You may go, lad,' Cortés had told Pepillo as he'd ushered Aguilar and Malinal into his tent to talk long into the night, and Pepillo, though curious, had been pleased enough to be set at liberty. Poor Melchior was still suffering from the whipping Vendabal had given him at sea, the stripes of his wounds open and raw. Indeed, since that day on board ship, Pepillo had feared for Melchior's life. So he ran helter-skelter through the darkness to the shelter behind the kitchens where he kept the pup, crouched down beside him and loosened the chain that held him fast. 'Come on, boy,' he said, 'let's get you exercised.'

Melchior rose stiffly and a little unsteadily and nuzzled Pepillo's hand. He was well fed on scraps here by the kitchen, and gaining weight, but his injuries pained him. Before taking him out onto the dunes to stretch his legs, Pepillo removed yesterday's blood-caked bandages, cleaned the dog's wounds, gently smoothed in the salve made from pig fat infused with herbs that Dr La Peña had given him, and finally applied new dressings.

It was a fine, cloudless night, the bright stars glittering, the moon – past full – flooding the sky with its pale light, and a soft breeze blowing in from the ocean carrying the sound of gentle waves lapping against the beach.

Pepillo left Melchior off the leash and the two of them walked side by side, the lurcher occasionally stopping to sniff the sand or cock his leg and piss against a clump of sturdy grass. Before Vendabal had whipped him, the dog had been an irrepressible ball of energy, enthusiasm and curiosity, but now there was something cautious, something tentative, about his manner. Not fear exactly – Pepillo did not think that Melchior felt fear the way he himself felt fear – but a new understanding of the random cruelty and wickedness of the world.

After a little time they came to the edge of the dunes overlooking the moonlit ocean – the ocean that stretched away from here in an unbroken expanse encompassing the islands of Cuba and Hispaniola until it reached the shores of far-off Africa and Spain.

Africa, whence his best friend Melchior had been brought as a slave, only to die in the New Lands in that last great battle against the Maya.

And Spain, where Pepillo himself had been born, but which he could hardly remember now, only knowing, in a distant sort of way, that he had been orphaned there, and taken in by the Dominicans and brought across the ocean to start the new life that finally had brought him to this time and this place.

He rested his hand on Melchior's floppy ears and scratched his brindled head – his new Melchior who could never replace the great friend he had lost, but who yet had become his only true companion in this strange and terrible world.

The lurcher's ears suddenly shot up and a low whine vibrated in his throat. Off in the distance, in the heart of the camp, could distinctly be heard the snarls and growls of two dogs fighting. They would be two of Vendabal's war dogs, set against one another in a pit for the men to lay wagers on. Very rarely the hounds in such contests would be allowed to battle it out to the death, and Cortés tolerated this, claiming to be persuaded by Vendabal's argument that it toughened the animals up, but more often they were whipped apart before too much damage was done. They were, after all, valuable and irreplaceable weapons, and not to be lightly squandered.

Pepillo sighed. Since the voyage from Potonchan he'd felt Vendabal's evil eye increasingly focused on Melchior. The fact that Cortés had refused to give the dog over to become a member of the pack had merely served to heighten this unwelcome attention.

But what would the next move in the game be?

Pepillo shuddered and sighed again, and Melchior, sharing his misery, nuzzled up against him.

Chapter Six

Friday 23 April 1519, night

After Cuetzpalli's departure from the House of Serpents, Moctezuma gave firm instructions to Teudile that if there was any further word concerning the whereabouts of the white-skinned beings, it was to be reported to him immediately. 'Tell me even if I am sleeping,' he insisted.

That night passed without sleep, day followed, and then a second restless night and another day. The Great Speaker felt himself falling ever deeper into despair. He wandered the halls of his palace in torment, sighing, filled with weakness, talking to himself, saying: 'What will happen to us? Who will outlive it? Ah, in other times I was contented, but now I have death in my heart! My heart burns and suffers as if it were washed in chilli water. Where can I go?'

Food was offered to him but he could not eat it. The time for his afternoon rest came, but when he closed his eyes he was haunted by visions of white, bearded faces and weapons of gleaming metal, and fearsome beasts, and again he could not sleep. Lost in the deepest gloom and sorrow, he picked at his dinner, leaving it largely untouched. Even the most delicate dishes, in which he had once taken such delight, failed to awaken his senses. Tobacco tubes were brought to him but, as he inhaled the smoke, he imagined he smelled the sulphurous fumes of fire-serpents and vomit rose in his throat.

Finally he retired to his chamber where he was greeted by four naked girls from his harem. They were young and beautiful, they quivered in their fear of him, their *tepilli* parts became moist when he touched them, yet they failed to arouse even the slightest reaction from his limp and useless *tepulli*. Sad and dejected, he sent them away, determined to face the night alone.

At last he slept, but it seemed only a moment had passed before he awoke again to find Teudile standing over him holding a lantern. An expression of deep anxiety lurked in the cadaverous hollows of the steward's face. 'Lord,' he said in a shaking voice, 'forgive me for disturbing your rest, but in this I obey your command. Relay messengers running for a night and day have brought a report from your servant Pichatzin, governor of your city of Cuetlaxtlan in the conquered territories of your subject people the Totonacs. It seems the boats of the gods appeared there yesterday and the white-skinned beings have descended from them and made their camp upon the land. Pichatzin met and talked with them. They wish to see you, sire, and for that purpose they have stated their intention to march to Tenochtitlan . . .'

With a horrible groan, Moctezuma sat bolt upright in his bed. He was filled with such terror that he felt certain he must die of fear, and only with the greatest difficulty was he able to compose himself. 'Meet me in the audience chamber,' he told Teudile. 'We will study Pichatzin's message together and I will decide what must be done.'

Cloaked in the spell of invisibility, Tozi had been following Moctezuma around his palace for hours. The ability to magnify others' fears had been added to her witch's repertoire on the night of the holocaust at the great pyramid, when all her other powers had also been mysteriously enhanced, and she'd sent fear to Moctezuma often enough in the sixty days since then to wear the murdering bully down and deeply undermine his resolve.

There were risks.

Her friend and ally Huicton, who walked the streets of Tenochtitlan in the guise of a blind beggar (but who in reality was neither blind nor a beggar but a spy for Moctezuma's enemy Ishtlil, leader of the rebel faction in the vassal state of Texcoco), had warned her that powerful magicians protected the palace and posed real dangers to her when she entered its halls. 'If you encounter such a one in your invisible form,' Huicton had said, 'you might be snuffed out like the flickering flame of a lamp, or else imprisoned in some sorcerous realm from which you can never escape.'

'Their strength cannot match mine,' Tozi had replied, not boasting but simply expressing the quiet confidence she felt in her own magical skills.

Huicton had looked at her with disapproval: 'Never be too sure of yourself. In this world of the strong and the weak, there is always someone stronger than ourselves.'

And perhaps what the wise old spy said was true, but Tozi judged the risk worth taking to fill Moctezuma's nights with chilling dreams and his days with nameless dreads, gradually eating away at his self-confidence and plaguing him with uncertainty. Her purpose was to render him weak, timid and ineffective, so he would be unable to put up a fight when the time came – as it soon must – for the return of Quetzalcoatl, the god of peace, who would usher in a new age free of human sacrifices, free of torture, free of slavery, free of pain, free of suffering.

Now, on her first visit to the palace for five days, she listened with growing excitement to the news that Teudile brought Moctezuma in his bedchamber – news deemed important enough to wake him from his tormented sleep. Her senses quickened as she heard the steward speak of the 'boats of the gods' and of the 'white-skinned beings'. And, as she witnessed Moctezuma's reaction, all the while feeding him more fear, she knew in her heart the time had come.

A little later, after Moctezuma had dressed, the two men met again in the audience chamber, where they made reference to other intelligence Tozi had been unaware of until now, most notably that a great battle had been fought outside the Mayan town of Potonchan – the home town of her friend Malinal! – less than thirty days previously. Since the white-skinned beings had been armed with Xiuhcoatl, fire-serpents, the characteristic weapons of the gods, and had been served – as the gods were – by wild creatures they had tamed, it was therefore obvious to Tozi that they could be none other than Quetzalcoatl himself and his divine companions. No wonder they had been victorious! Having defeated the Maya, they had then moved on in their great boats to Cuetlaxtlan where Pichatzin had met them.

Like many official Mexica documents, the codex containing Pichatzin's report was illustrated with detailed paintings, which Moctezuma and Teudile now pored over intently. Unknown to them, protected by the magic spell of invisibility, Tozi studied the paintings too.

The first showed the leader of the *tueles* – gods – as Tozi was certain they were. He had the appearance of a man, very handsome, white skinned, with a full beard and bright eyes of uneven sizes, and he wore a jacket of shining metal. 'This must be the god Quetzalcoatl himself,' Moctezuma exclaimed. 'He has come to seize his kingdom from my hands.' Tozi could only agree. Enthralled, she gazed at the painting and had no doubts. It depicted Quetzalcoatl returned to earth to usher in a new age of peace and harmony, when humans would no longer be offered as sacrifices to the gods, but only fruits and flowers.

Then Teudile turned the page and another figure appeared – a woman whose thick black hair had once been much longer, and whose beauty shone out like the sun. It was all Tozi could do not to gasp with the joy of recognition, for again there could be no doubt. The artist was skilled and this woman standing beside the human manifestation of Quetzalcoatl was none other than Malinal herself . . .

Moctezuma's jaw dropped open. 'I know her,' he said. He seemed dazed, shocked, unable to take his eyes off the painting. 'Her face haunts my dreams . . .'

Because I have made you dream of her, thought Tozi. *Because I have made you see her again and again as she lay before you on the sacrificial stone. Because I have made you remember how you were forced to release her. Because she is the one chosen by the gods to destroy you . . .*

Teudile was reading the pictographs. 'She is a woman of our land,' he told Moctezuma, who still stared fixedly at the image as though confronted by a ghost. 'Her name is Malinal and she is of the Chontal Maya, but it so happens she speaks our Nahuatl tongue. It was through her, Pichatzin tells us, that he was able to talk to the white-skinned ones who have amongst their number one who speaks the language of the Maya.'

'I know her,' Moctezuma repeated. 'And you also, Teudile! You know her too!'

'Forgive me, lord, but I do not think so.'

Moctezuma frowned: 'You speak true,' he said. 'I had sent you on a mission to Azcapotzalco that day. Had you been present, matters might have turned out differently. It was last year, Teudile, the year Thirteen-Rabbit, and this Malinal was summoned to serve as my interpreter when I received the message of the Chontal Maya concerning the first appearance in their land of a number of the white-skinned beings. Once she had performed her task, since the matter was sensitive, I naturally ordered her strangled, but Ahuizotl cheated me. After I had left the room, he took her to join his kept women in Tlatelolco. You know the story now, I think?'

'Yes, lord. I regret I was not there to prevent his treachery and wickedness.'

'It is not your fault, Teudile. It seems this Malinal is favoured by heaven. Four months after Ahuizotl flouted my order for her execution – I suppose he had had his fill of her – he placed her beneath my knife on the stone of sacrifice, but Hummingbird himself intervened and commanded her release. I obeyed and now she appears again as the tongue of the god Quetzalcoatl who has come to fulfil the prophecy and reclaim his kingdom. I feel the hand of doom upon me, Teudile, and here is what I want you to do. You must go to Cuetlaxtlan. Go at once! Do not delay a single moment. Do reverence to our lord the god Quetzalcoatl. Take him rich presents. Say to him: "Your deputy Moctezuma has sent me to you. Here are the presents with which he welcomes you home to Mexico."'

The steward seemed aghast. 'My lord,' he said. 'Will you allow me to offer some words of caution?'

To Tozi's surprise, Moctezuma agreed: 'You have always advised me well, Teudile,' he said in a small voice. 'You may speak freely.'

'Sire, we do not know for certain these white-skinned strangers are gods. You would be wise to learn more about them before welcoming them into our lands.

'Did we not hear enough from Cuetzpalli two nights ago? They have fire-serpents! They defeat armies of tens of thousands. Wild beasts obey their commands! A woman of our land is twice saved from death to become their voice. Of course they are gods!'

'It *seems* they are gods, sire. It is *very likely* they are gods. But it is not yet certain. Let me go to them as you have commanded. I will study them closely – their food, their clothing, their manner of behaviour, their weapons, their wild beasts, and I will bring you back a full report. Then you can decide . . .'

Moctezuma fell silent for a long while. 'Very well,' he said at last, slowly nodding his head. 'You are right.' He leaned over the codex again and turned the page back to show the white-skinned bearded countenance of the leader of the *tueles*. 'Present yourself to him, Teudile, and discover with absolute certainty if he really is the one our ancestors called Quetzalcoatl. Our histories say he was driven out of this land, but left word that he or his sons would return to reign over this country and to recover the gold, silver and jewels they had left hidden in the mountains. According to the legends, they are to acquire all the wealth we now possess. You must order the governor of Cuetlaxtlan to provide him with all kinds of food, cooked birds and game. Let him also be given all types of bread that are baked, together with fruit and gourds of chocolate. Give these things to him so that he and his companions may eat of them. Notice very carefully if he eats or not. If he eats and drinks what you give him, he is surely Quetzalcoatl, as this will show that he is familiar with the foods of this land, that he ate them once and that he has come back to savour them again. Then tell him to allow me to die. Tell him that, after my death, he will be welcome to come here and take possession of his kingdom. We know that he left it to be guarded by my ancestors and I have always considered that my domain was only lent to me. But let him allow me to end my days here. Then he can return to enjoy what is his.'

Another long pause followed, during which the steward also remained silent, watching his master expectantly. Finally Moctezuma added: 'Do not go with anxiety, or fear death at his hands, since I swear I will honour your children and give them my wealth and make them members of my council. If by chance he is desirous of eating human flesh, Teudile, and would like to eat you, allow yourself to be eaten. In such an event I assure you that I will look after your wife, relations and children—'

Teudile blinked. 'I must allow myself to be eaten, sire?'

'Yes, Teudile. That is my wish.'

How entirely typical of Moctezuma, Tozi thought. *The coward doesn't*

42

hesitate to put others forward to die for him, but he trembles and weeps like a terrified child every time he imagines any threat to himself!

The steward remained calm. 'Your will, sire. I am ready to offer myself . . . But if I am eaten, I will be unable to bring you back any report. May I propose, therefore, that I take captives with me to the coast and sacrifice them there in the presence of the white-skinned beings and offer their flesh and blood instead?'

The Great Speaker brightened. 'Ah yes, of course. Very well, Teudile. Let it be as you suggest.'

'Now, as to the matter of presents, lord. Even if the leader of these strangers is a god, we cannot be certain he is Quetzalcoatl. Perchance he is the lord Tezcatlipoca taken human form, or perchance he is Tlaloc? In addition to many other rich gifts, let me therefore take the finery of each of these gods from the royal treasure house and we shall see which he prefers.'

'A good plan, Teudile. You advise me wisely.'

'And one more suggestion, sire. Allow me to take with me some of our great magicians to put the strangers to the test . . .'

Moctezuma brightened further: 'You advise me well, Teudile. With the help of our sorcerers, we will learn what sort of beings the strangers truly are.' Tozi was watching the Great Speaker closely and saw that a look of cunning had entered his small, darting eyes. 'Perhaps after all they are just men,' he mused, with a new note of hope in his voice. 'Just white-skinned, bearded men . . . Therefore take Tlilpo, take Cuappi, take Aztatzin, take Hecateu. Let them try their wizardry upon the strangers to see if they can work some charm against them – perchance to put them to sleep or terrify them with visions, or direct a harmful wind against them, or send serpents, scorpions, spiders and centipedes to bite them, or cause them to break out in sores, or injure them in some other way so they might take sick, or die, or else turn back whence they came. While you must pretend to the strangers that you have come amongst them only to serve them, let our sorcerers do everything in their power to kill them!'

'It will be done as you order, lord,' said Teudile. 'I will begin preparations at once, but it will take a little time to gather the wizards and

43

the captives and the finery of the gods and to make everything ready for the road.'

'You will work through the night, Teudile, and you will depart our city no later than noon . . . It is not so very far to Cuetlaxtlan. How long do you suppose the journey will take you?'

'If we make the greatest possible haste, lord, I believe it can be done in five days and five nights.'

'Our runners traverse the same route in a single day and a night, Teudile! I understand, of course, that you cannot run, that your embassy must transport much baggage . . . Nonetheless, I expect you to reach Cuetlaxtlan in four days and nights, or I will have your skin.'

'Yes, lord.'

'When you arrive, spend a further day and night with the strangers and discover if they are gods or men, then return here and bring me your report . . .'

'All will be done as you command, lord.'

The steward was already backing out of the audience chamber, bowing with each step, the hems of his star-spangled robe brushing the floor, when Moctezuma stopped him with a movement of his finger. 'One more thing, Teudile,' he said. 'If word of the strangers' victory at Potonchan, or of their presence now at Cuetlaxtlan, or of your mission to learn the truth about them reaches anyone here in our city, even the highest nobles of the land, then I will bury you under my halls, your wife and your children, your parents and all your kin will be killed, and your house will be razed to the ground.'

'Your will, my lord,' said Teudile, his face ashen.

Silent and invisible, Tozi followed him from the audience chamber and made haste to the place where her friend Huicton awaited her.

What Moctezuma wished kept secret, it was their duty to reveal.

Chapter Seven

If Shikotenka, battle-king of Tlascala, had not seen it with his own eyes, he would not have believed it. A small army of white-skinned, bearded men had set up camp on the dunes three miles north of the Mexica coastal town of Cuetlaxtlan – the very town he had come here to reconnoitre and that he hoped soon to destroy.

'What in the name of the gods are they?' muttered sharp-eyed Chipahua, who was sprawled next to him under cover of the long dune grass. He was staring at the distant strangers with slack-jawed amazement, revealing jagged gaps in his front teeth where he'd been hit in the face by a Mexica war club two months before.

'The gods themselves?' wondered Ilhuicamina, whose own face bore the marks of a much earlier encounter with the enemy – in his case a wide, puckered scar where a *macuahuitl* had struck him, the ugliest part of the injury concealed by a prosthetic nose made of small jade tiles.

'Then what are those?' asked Acolmiztli, at forty-two, lean and sinister, he was the oldest man in the squad, but as formidable a warrior as Tlascala had ever produced. He was pointing at a herd of extraordinary beasts, tall as houses, that had just now emerged from behind a dune. In their lower parts these beasts somewhat resembled deer, though they were much larger than any deer Shikotenka had ever hunted. But out of the midst of their backs sprouted the upper bodies of white-skinned bearded men! How was that to be explained? Men seated on deer, perhaps? Or some sort of completely unknown hybrid entities? Anything seemed possible on this day of miracles and wonders.

Another oddity was that the men who stood on two legs on the ground, some busily performing various tasks, others just sauntering around, were decked out in shining, flashing silver that caught and reflected the rays of the sun! So, too, were those formidable man-beasts which now broke into a run, charged up the side of a towering dune and disappeared over its summit in the direction of the beach.

'They're wearing some sort of metal armour,' observed Tree. The big man had a belligerent scowl on his broad, stolid face, and now rose to a crouch, shaking his massive head, his long, tangled hair falling about his powerful shoulders. 'I say we go grab one or two of them, find out what sort of creatures they are, see if they can fight.'

'Don't be so eager,' Shikotenka hissed, pulling his friend down again. 'I want to watch them for a day or two, get the measure of them, see how the Mexica are treating them . . .'

'They're licking their arses,' said Chipahua dryly. 'Just look over there!' He gestured to the space between two dunes where wooden huts were being erected by teams of Totonac labourers and carpenters under the watchful eye of armed Mexica overseers. The sounds of hammers and saws could be heard faintly on the morning air, and there was a general atmosphere of industrious activity. Many of the white-skinned bearded men – if indeed they were human at all – stood around watching, seemingly on good terms with the Mexica supervisors. Soon afterwards, a long file of Totonac bearers appeared, carrying food baskets on their heads, which they delivered up as though they were sacred offerings.

'They're housing them,' said Chipahua, 'they're feeding them, they've put their Totonac vassals at their disposal . . . In short, they're treating them like royalty.'

'Or like gods,' suggested Ilhuicamina.

Shikotenka thought long and hard. The month before, wily old Huicton, spy and emissary for the Texcocan rebel leader Ishtlil, had come to him in Tlascala and offered him an alliance against the Mexica. Shikotenka had turned the offer down, arguing that he had just destroyed an entire Mexica army of more than thirty thousand men, and that Moctezuma was unlikely to trouble him again for a very long while. But Huicton had disagreed: 'I much regret to inform you that your victory will not be an end to the matter. There is another factor at work, one you may not even be aware of, but I have reason to believe that because of it you and your people will face more – not fewer – attacks from the Mexica in the months ahead. The same will unfortunately be true for Ishtlil's people and for many others. So, despite your commendably proud and independent stance, the truth is that there has never been a time when an alliance would be more expedient or more worthwhile for Tlascala than it is today . . .'

Huicton had then gone on – and at great length! – to tell an incredible story. It seemed Moctezuma was convinced that the white-skinned, bearded god Quetzalcoatl, the fabled 'Plumed Serpent', was about to return from across the sea to overthrow him, and to abolish the sacrificial cult that honoured the Mexica war god Hummingbird. It was not just that this was the year One-Reed, in which it had long ago been prophesied that Quetzalcoatl *would* return; far more ominous had been – a few months earlier – the appearance amongst the Chontal Maya of the Yucatán of a small band of white-skinned, bearded strangers, who possessed the weapons and the attributes of Quetzalcoatl's legendary demigods. The Maya had driven them off at great cost to themselves, but it seemed Moctezuma was convinced they would return in force, led by Quetzalcoatl himself. The Great Speaker's whole focus now, therefore, was to gather victims – for some reason exclusively pure, undefiled virgin females – who were to be offered up in a spectacular festival of human sacrifice to feed and flatter Hummingbird, thus persuading the war god to fight alongside the Mexica to defeat Quetzalcoatl.

Although he could not understand the special interest in virgin female victims, Shikotenka was forced to admit that Huicton's story was not entirely without merit. He, too, had heard rumours of white-skinned bearded strangers being sighted in great ships off the coasts of Mexico, but he refused to believe there was any such god as Quetzalcoatl, or that he would ever return.

'With respect, Lord Shikotenka,' Huicton had argued, 'what *you* believe or don't believe isn't really the issue here. All that matters is what Moctezuma believes. He is mad, of course, you already know that – so please allow me to assure you that he does indeed most certainly believe, and fear in the depths of his black, demented heart, that the return of Quetzalcoatl is imminent. He will let nothing stand in his way; he will sacrifice thousands of virgins, tens of thousands if he can find them – Tlascalans, Totonacs, rebel Texcocans, and any others he can lay his hands on – to prevent that happening. It is for this reason, I urge you, before more lamentable harm and suffering is caused, to accept the alliance that my lord Ishtlil offers you and to join forces with him to bring Moctezuma to his knees.'

'Tell Lord Ishtlil,' Shikotenka had replied, 'that I am grateful for his offer and that I regard him as the enemy of my enemy and therefore as my friend. Nonetheless, we Tlascalans have always walked our own path, and we do not resort to alliances and intrigues. Let us continue, therefore, to fight Moctezuma in our own separate ways – Ishtlil's Texcocans in their way, we Tlascalans in ours – obliging the madman to divide his forces and do battle on two fronts. If the gods are with us, he will fall.'

It had been a proud statement of Tlascalan independence, but Shikotenka had already had cause to reflect deeply on it over the past month. Huicton's warning had proved uncannily accurate. True, Shikotenka had destroyed one Mexica army consisting of four full regiments, but five other armies of the same size, twenty regiments in all – a total of one hundred and sixty thousand men – remained in the field, and it seemed that at least one of these armies had been tasked exclusively with the capture of virgin females for sacrifice, just as Huicton had predicted.

He'd been right about the raids on Tlascala too. Far from ceasing, they had intensified. Indeed, it was in an attempt to create a distraction that would draw Moctezuma's forces away from the Tlascalan highlands that Shikotenka had conceived his plan to attack and destroy the coastal city of Cuetlaxtlan. This outpost of the Mexica empire, so important for the prosperous trade with the Yucatán, had been seized from the Totonacs some seventy years before; the Totonacs themselves were now vassals of the Mexica. Shikotenka had reasoned that if he could take the prize of Cuetlaxtlan, and slaughter its Mexica settlers, then the Totonacs might be persuaded to rise against their overlords.

That was why he was here now, with his four most trusted lieutenants, on this mission of reconnaissance to lay plans for a full-scale attack. But instead he found himself confronted by a war camp of white-skinned, bearded strangers, dressed in metal armour, allied with strange beasts, and waited on hand and foot by the Mexica's Totonac vassals – clearly acting on the orders of the Mexica – as the gods themselves might expect!

So, yes, Huicton had been right to predict that Shikotenka's great victory of the past month would not see the end of the Mexica's quest for sacrificial victims, but – eerily – it now seemed that he had also been right about the return of Quetzalcoatl, or at any rate of beings who had the look of Quetzalcoatl.

But here was the very odd thing! Quetzalcoatl was supposed to be the enemy of Moctezuma, and the enemy of the vile god Hummingbird whom Moctezuma served. So if these strangers had anything to do with Quetzalcoatl, then why were the Mexica feeding them and sheltering them, and why would gods camp out on these pestilential, windblown, fly-infested dunes?

The whole situation was a riddle wrapped inside a puzzle enclosed within a conundrum.

'I want to catch one,' said Tree stubbornly. 'I want to catch one and kill one tonight.'

Shikotenka thought about it.

Maybe Tree was right. When you were confronted by something you didn't understand, the best thing was to get as close as possible to it.

That way, the truth would come out.

Chapter Eight

◆

Monday 26 April 1519, night

Pepillo pointed at himself. 'I am a boy,' he said. He pointed again –
'boy'. He pointed to Malinal: 'You are a woman.' He spread his hands
and looked at her expectantly.

Now it was Malinal's turn. She pointed to herself: '*Ne cihuatzintli.*'
She pointed to Pepillo: '*Titelpochontli.*' Then she softened her tone and
added: '*Noquichpiltzin*', which meant not just 'you are a boy' but rather,
as a mother might say to her child, 'my beloved boy'. He was sweet,
innocent and lonely, and she felt pity for him, understanding, as she'd
discovered yesterday, that he'd lost his closest companion in the fighting
at Potonchan, a friend named Melchior after whom he had named his
pet dog.

Pepillo pointed upwards now and said: 'Sky.'

Malinal looked up, wondering – did he mean sky? She made an
expansive gesture towards the heavens with her hands, raised her
eyebrows in query, and said: '*Ilhuicac?*' Or did he perhaps mean a
specific star? She selected one of the brightest, pointed to it, sighting
along her arm and said, '*Citlalin.*'

Pepillo nodded, getting the distinction immediately, pointed at the
same bright star and said 'star', then copied her expansive hand movement and repeated the word 'sky'.

It was a cloudless night, and the two of them sat alone in the
lantern-lit area in front of the kitchen, after the evening meal had been
served and all the men had dispersed. Malinal no longer worked in
the kitchen, but Cortés had ordered the boy to teach her Castilian –
she in return was to teach him Nahuatl – and Pepillo had chosen this
place for their classes because he kept his beloved Melchior nearby.

The caudillo – the title meant military leader, as Malinal had quickly learned – was plainly a man who understood the power of language, and she was happy he had made his young page her instructor, rather than that envious snake Aguilar, with whom she was forced to work day to day.

Delegations of Mexica officials constantly scurried back and forth between the Spanish camp and the town of Cuetlaxtlan. Their job was to carry the incessant demands made by Cortés for more food, more fresh water, more bearers, more labourers, more carpenters, more women to serve as bedslaves – more of everything! – to the wretched and overburdened governor Pichatzin, and to return with Pichatzin's responses. These were usually affirmative, but always with qualifications, quibbles, excuses and prevarications. So it was a tedious, time-consuming task. First she must listen to Aguilar as he put the caudillo's words into Mayan, next she must translate those words into Nahuatl for the benefit of the Mexica officials, and finally she must put the words of the officials into Mayan so that Aguilar could convey them in Castilian to Cortés.

Moreover, there was the complicating factor of Aguilar's jealousy. His resentment at the privileged position Cortés had given Malinal was driving him – she was beginning to realise – to make deliberate interpreting errors that resulted in confusion and misunderstandings, which he then steadfastly blamed on her. Since the caudillo continued to favour her greatly, she liked to think he saw through Aguilar's wiles, but still it was disturbing and meant she had to be constantly on her guard. How much easier everything would be if Aguilar could be got out of the way!

Fortunately Malinal had a gift for languages and had always been a fast learner. Indeed, her survival and success during her years amongst the Mexica had depended at least as much on those skills as upon her sexual prowess. She was finding Castilian easy to grasp, though tonight was only her second formal lesson. Of course, she'd already taken every opportunity to learn what she could since she'd been handed over with the other women after the battle at Potonchan, always carefully listening and watching and picking up vocabulary and snatches of conversation. And now, with her new role as interpreter, every minute of every day offered her fresh opportunities as she wrestled with Aguilar's subterfuge and paid close attention to the words he and Cortés spoke to one another. It was amazing how constant jeopardy and uncertainty focused the mind, but Malinal had high hopes that her work with Pepillo would bring her on even faster in this new language, and she was pleased with the progress they'd made since their first lesson the evening before.

What helped was Pepillo's sweet nature as did the fact that he was plainly as eager to learn Nahuatl from her as she was to learn Castilian from him. So they both entered into the process with enthusiasm, as though it were a kind of game, fun rather than a chore, and there was even some laughter between them.

But this laughter was tempered with the deep sadness Malinal sensed within Pepillo. Like her friend Tozi, who was about the same age, not more than fifteen years under the sun, it seemed that he had already seen too much of the cruelties of the world and grown old before his time. And, like Tozi, he had a good heart and a generous spirit. Unlike Tozi, however, this boy had no magical powers, no burning purpose, no thirst for revenge. He was just kind and decent and good – and damaged. More important almost than his role in her life as a language teacher was the other lesson he had already taught her, which was that these Spaniards, for all their formidable powers, were exactly like any other people – vulnerable, in need of love, and even capable, in their own way, of giving it.

'Puertocarrero,' Pepillo said suddenly.

Malinal looked up. She couldn't bear the rough, barbarous, stinking creature, to whom Cortés had given her as a bed slave.

Pepillo then said something else, a short string of unfamiliar words, the meaning of which Malinal could not grasp. She gazed at him blankly.

'Puertocarrero,' he repeated, at the same time making the face of someone who has smelled a bad thing and she suddenly understood. Pepillo was trying to tell her that he knew she didn't like Puertocarrero. He said the words again: 'You don't like him, do you?'

'No,' she answered, in halting Castilian. 'Don't like. Don't like Puertocarrero.'

* * *

Much later, after Malinal had retired with a grimace to Puertocarrero's hut, Pepillo untied Melchior and headed out past the guards and into the dunes. He was happy to see how the young lurcher was rapidly overcoming the effects of the whipping Vendabal had administered six days before, shrugging off the stiffness of the wounds, rebuilding his strength and day by day recovering more of his exuberant spirit.

Pepillo often wished that he could be a dog, living in the now, reacting immediately to everything and quickly forgetting pains and woes, but unfortunately it was not so easy for him. The worst of it was he could not forget – indeed, he swore, he would *never* forget – the original Melchior, his best and only friend. Nor could he cast from memory how the two of them had followed that evil, murderous friar Gaspar Muñoz into the forest on the island of Cozumel, or what had happened after – their capture, their near murder and their rescue at the last moment by Bernal Díaz, Francisco Mibiercas and Alonso de la Serna. Pepillo shivered as other images streamed unbidden into his mind – the hatchet in his hands as he'd hacked at Muñoz's skull, his own part in the disposal of the friar's body and, a month later, the desperate fight on the summit of the great pyramid of Potonchan, the long-haired Mayan warrior who'd straddled Melchior, viciously stabbing him with a flint blade, Melchior's death a few hours later, his burial, and finally Bernal Díaz's kindly gift of the lurcher pup – the new Melchior, now off somewhere excitedly exploring the dunes.

Pepillo came to his usual spot overlooking the ocean. He sat down to watch the light of the stars and the waning moon reflecting from the waters, to listen to the soft sound of the waves lapping against the beach below, and feel the cooling southern breeze in his hair. Melchior ranged further and further every night, but sooner or later he always came back, appearing like a ghost out of the darkness, and Pepillo was content to wait here and think his thoughts and dwell in his memories.

They had made a long detour to the north of the camp and now approached it by way of the beach, moving silent as ghosts in the darkness. Shikotenka had chosen this route because a fair breeze was blowing from the south that would carry their scent away from the strange beasts resembling deer that some of the white-skins rode. The notion that the creatures might be hybrids had already been laid to rest when several of the white-skins had been seen to dismount from their backs, but extreme caution was still in order until the nature of the strangers and their animals was better understood.

Shikotenka led the climb up the side of the dunes from the beach. Like him, all his crew were skilled night fighters; the darkness held no terrors for them. They'd fought so many engagements together that they didn't need to plan, didn't need to speak – every movement, every action, was second nature to them, so perfectly coordinated that they were more like a single creature, united in single-minded intent, than five separate men.

Near the summit of the dune, sensing something, Shikotenka suddenly stopped, reaching back his hand to touch Acolmiztli right behind him, bringing the whole group to a soundless halt.

There was someone there, not ten paces above them.

One of the white-skins sitting alone looking out over the ocean.

Shikotenka held a finger to his lips. *Silence! Silence!* He signed to Acolmiztli – *go that way, circle round* – and to Ilhuicamina – *go that way, the other side, circle round*. To Chipahua and Tree he signalled simply: *Follow me*.

There was no hesitation. Acolmiztli and Ilhuicamina vanished left and right into the darkness. Shikotenka counted *one . . . two . . . three . . . four . . . five . . .* and then charged the last few paces up the dune, smashed into the unsuspecting white-skin who sat at the top, bowled him onto his back, and left it to Tree to clamp a huge hand over his mouth to stop him from crying out. It was all done in seconds leaving nothing for Chipahua, Acolmiztli and Ilhuicamina to do but keep watch.

Silence . . . just silence. In his head, Shikotenka counted slowly to a hundred. No other white-skins appeared, but out of long practice no one said a word in the interval. Still holding his hand clamped over the struggling captive's mouth, Tree was the first to speak. 'Definitely not gods then!' he whispered. 'Let's take this bastard off a mile or two and see if he can fight.'

Chapter Nine

Before their departure from Tenochtitlan, Tozi and Huicton had sought out every one of their ragged band of beggars, malcontents, thieves, lookouts and spies, and crisscrossed the city to whisper in the ears of certain more respectable members of Mexica society – people Huicton had cultivated who also covertly supported the insurrection. They had informed them all of the spectacular victory of the white-skinned bearded strangers over the Chontal Maya at Potonchan and of the strangers' arrival at Cuetlaxtlan, and had charged them to spread the rumour that Quetzalcoatl had returned to overthrow Moctezuma and usher in a new age. Only then had they set off on the journey of two nights and the greater part of three days that had brought them to the camp of Huicton's patron Ishtlil, leader of the rebel faction in the Mexica vassal state of Texcoco. Reaching the camp, they had been obliged to negotiate an obstacle course of officials and bodyguards, before finally being ushered into Ishtlil's command tent, a towering structure of white maguey fibre stretched over a framework of great poles, furnished with mats, stools and map-strewn tables, and lit within by guttering torches.

The previous year, following the death of King Neza of Texcoco, Moctezuma had intervened in the succession and placed Neza's compliant and sycophantic younger son Cacama on the Texcocan throne rather than the independent and free-thinking elder son Ishtlil. Used to getting his own way in all things, Moctezuma had assumed that Ishtlil would simply accept this arrangement, but instead he had seized control of Texcoco's mountain provinces and declared a rebellion, leaving only the lakeside city of Texcoco itself, and its valley provinces, in Cacama's hands.

Huicton had previously worked as a spy for wily old Neza, who'd had a mind of his own; after Neza's death, seeing the weakness of Cacama, Huicton had given his allegiance to Ishtlil. Since then Ishtlil had waged a bloody war against the forces of Cacama and Moctezuma, and had made increasing use of Huicton, not only as his spymaster in Tenochtitlan, but also as his ambassador in secret negotiations with the Tlascalans and others who suffered under Mexica tyranny. Now, with Tozi seated on a mat by his side, Huicton first praised her as the best of his spies, and the only one able to infiltrate Moctezuma's household, then slowly and carefully outlined to his master the intelligence she'd gathered about the strangers with the aspect of *tueles* – gods.

Ishtlil was a big man, with broad, swarthy uncouth features, beetling eyebrows, a large, misshapen nose broken in some battle years before, and a mane of thick, black, greasy hair tied back in a pigtail. Aged about forty, he had the looks and the huge calloused hands of a peasant farmer, but his voice and haughty manner were those of an aristocrat and his shrewd, deep-set eyes seemed to miss nothing. He turned those eyes on Tozi now: 'This is interesting information, girl, but what makes you so sure these white strangers are *tueles*?'

Huicton was proud to see that Tozi didn't flinch under the Texcocan's scrutiny. 'Pichatzin's messenger,' she replied, 'brought Moctezuma a written report of his meeting with these "strangers".' *My goodness, thought Huicton, is the girl risking a note of sarcasm?* 'The paintings were done by Pichatzin's own artist,' Tozi said, 'who was present to record his meeting with the "strangers".' *That note of sarcasm again.* 'I was able to observe the paintings over Moctezuma's shoulder,' she continued, thrusting out her lower lip, a sign of stubbornness that Huicton had come to know all too well, 'and I have no doubt that the "strangers" depicted by the artist are *tueles*. Their leader has the appearance of a man but he is white-skinned and bearded, as the lord Quetzalcoatl is described in all our legends. He wears a jacket of shining metal. He and his companions are armed with fire-serpents and other weapons of the gods.'

'And Moctezuma?' prompted Ishtlil. 'How did he react to this news?'

'With fear, Lord Ishtlil. When he looked upon the painting of the leader, he acknowledged the truth. "This must be the god Quetzalcoatl himself," he said. "He has come to seize his kingdom from my hands.'"

Suddenly Ishtlil bounded to his feet, crossed to Tozi in a single stride and towered over her. 'If you're telling me the truth,' he said, 'then Quetzalcoatl's cause and mine are one and the same and I should seek to unite my forces with his. But how do I know you're telling the truth? How do I know you're not just inventing all this simply to impress me? Or perhaps even to mislead me? Perhaps you're working for Moctezuma? How do I know? Ha? How do I know?'

'My Tozi always tells the truth,' Huicton said, 'and no one hates Moctezuma more than she does. She's not inventing anything.'

'If I'm to make policy based on her word, I need to be sure,' Ishtlil growled. 'But how can I be sure this slip of a girl spied on Moctezuma as she claims?' His eyes bored into Tozi: 'Ha, child? How can I know? You tell a far-fetched story. Do you really expect me to believe you were able to get so close to the Great Speaker that you could study the paintings over his shoulder and he didn't even notice your presence?'

Huicton shifted uncomfortably: 'I have explained to you before, lord, that this girl has special powers.'

'Ha! Special powers! Anyone can claim special powers. I'll need proof.'

Huicton looked at Tozi and raised a quizzical eyebrow. 'Would you be willing to show Lord Ishtlil what you're capable of, my dear?'

'What do you mean?' Tozi whispered.

'Make yourself invisible. Then he'll believe you.'

'I'm not some circus tumbler putting on a show,' Tozi hissed. 'I'm a witch.'

'A witch?' Ishtlil exclaimed, his voice rising. 'The girl is a witch?'

'She has special powers,' Huicton repeated. The encounter was moving in a dangerous direction. Ishtlil was a good man – in his way, a far better man than his brother Cacama – but he was deeply superstitious and shared the common prejudice against witches that had led Tozi to the fattening pen in Tenochtitlan and almost to sacrifice at the hands of Moctezuma. Indeed, suspected witches were as frequently offered for sacrifice by the Texcocans as they were by the Mexica.

'Don't heed the foolish child,' Huicton said. 'She imagines herself a witch but the truth is she has been given a gift from the gods, a gift meant to help us in our war against Moctezuma.'

Ishtlil was pacing up and down inside his command tent now, the flat planes of his big face shadowed into hollows in the flickering torchlight. 'Then show me this gift!' he stormed. 'Show it to me! I would decide for myself whether she is indeed a foolish child, in which case I'd be a fool to trust her, or whether she's a witch, or a liar, or a gift from the gods as you claim.'

Huicton nudged Tozi. 'Now would be a good time for you to vanish, Tozi.'

'Suppose I don't want to.'

'Then you may get us both in a great deal of trouble.'

Tozi shrugged and began to chant softly – under her breath at first, but rising in pitch and tone until her voice became almost a snarl, furious and wild. A look of mild surprise came over Ishtlil's coarse features, then of fear, and finally – to Huicton's astonishment – of terror. He had known the Texcocan since he was a boy and never once had he seen him afraid. Now, with a gasp, Ishtlil slumped to his knees, his eyes wide and rolling.

'Tozi!' Huicton snapped, 'what in the name of all the gods are you doing?'

'Showing the lord Ishtlil what I'm capable of, as you asked.'

'I asked you to make yourself invisible.'

'But I'm capable of more than that,' Tozi smiled, and it was the smile of skull, the smile of a death's head. 'Ishtlil made you afraid with his threats. He tried to make me afraid . . . So I'm feeding him fear.'

'He made no threats . . .'

'Yes he did. He said he wanted to decide if I was a witch. You were afraid of what would happen if he decided I was—'

Ishtlil was clutching at his throat now, making horrible gasping and gurgling sounds.

'Stop!' Huicton demanded. 'Stop right now, Tozi. Any more of this and his guards will be in here and we'll be slaughtered.'

'Not me,' said Tozi. There was a glint of malice in her eyes. 'They won't catch me. I can make myself invisible, remember?'

Huicton looked at her long and hard, his little protégée, the girl he'd rescued from the mob all those years before. What had become of her? He hardly recognised her now. 'Let Ishtlil go, Tozi! Free him now before it's too late. I command you.'

'You *command* me?'

'I request you. I beg you! Let him go.'

'Very well then,' said Tozi, 'I will.' She whispered a string of words in some strange tongue that Huicton had never heard before, closed her hands into fists and opened them again, extending her fingers towards Ishtlil, and suddenly the Texcocan rebel leader was released. He slumped forward, his face resting on the richly embroidered carpet that covered the floor of his command tent, spittle dribbling from his slack lips, his chest heaving as though he had run some great race, his breath coming in ragged gasps. Finally, still on his knees, he raised his upper body again and stared fixedly at Tozi. 'You . . .' he said. 'You . . .'

Huicton knew what was coming next.

With just the faintest shimmer of the air, Tozi vanished.

Chapter Ten

Monday 26 April 1519, night

Pedro de Alvarado had walked out into the dunes, a few bowshots away from the camp, for a clandestine meeting with two of the ring-leaders of the Velazquistas, the nickname that he and Cortés had given to the large and powerful faction amongst the conquistadors who remained loyal to Diego de Velázquez, the governor of Cuba.

'Surely you can see, Don Pedro, that your so-called caudillo has taken leave of his senses?'

The speaker was lantern-jawed Juan Escudero, a man who had long hated and envied Cortés, and whom Cortés loathed and despised in equal measure. Some years before, Alvarado recalled, Escudero had taken immense pleasure in arresting Cortés and throwing him into jail on Velázquez's orders. The charge of treason – which carried an automatic death penalty – had been trumped up by Velázquez because Cortés had got the governor's favourite niece, Catalina, pregnant, and had refused to marry her.

After eight months rotting in prison, with the thought of being hanged, drawn and quartered to focus his mind, Cortés had finally agreed to marry the hell-bitch and recognise the child as his own. In return he had been readmitted to the governor's inner circle and in due course given command of the expedition to the New Lands. But before the fleet left Cuba, Velázquez had grown suspicious of Cortés – rightly fearing he intended to declare the expedition his own once the New Lands were reached – and had once again given orders for his arrest.

Alvarado himself had brought the news of the governor's plan and, on the stormy night of 18 February 1519, only a few hours ahead of the arrest warrant, Cortés had persuaded the other captains of the fleet to sail, winning the support of even the most ardent Velazquistas with phoney intelligence about a rival expedition being mounted from Jamaica to seize control of the New Lands. 'If we don't beat them to it,' Cortés had argued, 'there'll be no prize left for us to win.' Greed had persuaded most of the captains to agree with him, so that in the end Escudero was the only Velazquista who still felt the matter should be referred to the governor. Again Alvarado had come to the rescue, goading Escudero to draw his sword, and giving Cortés the excuse he needed to throw his old enemy into the brig that night. By the time Escudero was released the next day, the fleet had sailed far beyond Velázquez's reach.

But Escudero's resentment had remained a problem ever since. From the moment the expedition reached the New Lands, he'd worked tirelessly against the caudillo's interests, lobbying and inflaming the other Velázquez loyalists and urging them to imprison Cortés and return to Cuba. Such incitements to mutiny – and it was plain they were nothing less than that – won ever more support as the weeks passed and it became clear there was no rival fleet. Then there had been the gigantic battle with the Maya at Potonchan. True, only four Spaniards died in the fighting itself, but close to a dozen had subsequently expired from infected wounds, and more than eighty, some in great pain, were still suffering from the injuries they'd received. Despite all Cortés's efforts, the mood of the expedition was turning sour.

Standing with Escudero and Alvarado – out of the breeze and out of sight of the camp in a hollow of the dunes – was Juan Velázquez de León, Diego de Velázquez's own cousin, a bull of a man with a bushy black beard, an aggressive chin and angry green eyes that glinted in the moonlight. Bound as he was by blood to the governor of Cuba, he was a natural Velazquista; still his greed was such that he might easily have been bought off if there had been gold to be had. In its absence, however – the Chontal Maya of Potonchan had turned out to possess almost none – Velázquez de León was siding more and more openly with Escudero, and had several times joined him in calling for the expedition to return to Cuba.

'We fought that damned battle against the Maya,' he complained to Alvarado, 'and what did we get in return? Gold? No. Jewels? No. Honour? No. Trade advantage? No. Now we're here, camped on these noisome dunes, and still we see no gold – nor any prospect of it. The plain truth is we've campaigned for more than two months, expended treasure, expended lives, incurred the governor's disfavour and all for—'

'All for nothing,' Escudero completed the sentence. His jaw shut like a trap and then opened again as he added, 'Or rather: all to satisfy Cortés's pride. I say enough is enough. Join us, Pedro – I know we've had our differences, but I've always recognised your qualities, and with you on our side no one will dare stand in our way.'

Despite the well-known fact that he and Cortés were friends, Escudero and the other Velazquistas never relented in their attempts to win Alvarado to their cause. He understood very well why! First and foremost, they'd witnessed Cortés publicly rebuke and shame him on the island of Cozumel, the expedition's first port of call; secondly, because Alvarado's love of gold was legendary, they naturally assumed that the lack of it would make him as restless as it was making them.

On both points they were at least partly correct. Alvarado was still smarting from the dressing down that Cortés had given him on Cozumel – even forcing him to return the few miserable trophies he'd managed to extract from the filthy Indians there. And Potonchan, where Cortés had raised such high expectations, had proved to be a huge disappointment. Fifteen thousand pesos' worth of gold was all the Chontal Maya had delivered in the aftermath of the battle, and the next month spent ransacking the region had produced little more.

So, yes, of course Alvarado was dissatisfied!

This did not mean, however, that he was about to betray his friend. He still had confidence in Cortés and believed that he would, sooner or later, deliver on his promises of riches beyond their wildest dreams. Indeed Cortés had confided in Alvarado that this was precisely what he expected of the Mexica, overlords of the town of Cuetlaxtlan, outside which they were now camped. It seemed his new interpreter, the woman Malinal, had lived amongst the Mexica for five years and according to her they were rich as Croesus. So, it was just a matter of patience.

Meanwhile Alvarado saw no harm, and much to his advantage, in playing the Velazquistas along. Should Cortés continue to fail, he could easily switch sides. And if Cortés succeeded, then intelligence on the plans of the mutineers would surely have a value.

'Who's with us and who's against us?' Alvarado asked Escudero, as though he had already joined the mutiny.

'A hundred good men for sure,' the ringleader replied confidently, 'and a hundred more tending our way.'

Two hundred! Alvarado thought. If this was true it was bad news indeed for Cortés. But he kept his face expressionless. 'Pah!' he said. 'I'm not interested in the riffraff, only the captains and the officers – men of my own class. How many of them?'

Escudero and Velázquez de León eyed one another shiftily, looked back at Alvarado, but said nothing.

'Francisco de Montejo?' Alvarado guessed. 'I know he's always been loyal to the governor, despite taking a hefty loan from Cortés . . .' He paused, turned towards Velázquez de León: 'I seem to remember that you, too, are in Hernán's debt, Juan? What was it again? Two thousand gold pesos or thereabouts to refit that worm-eaten caravel of yours . . .'

'That's irrelevant,' spluttered Velázquez de León. 'I am steadfast in my opposition to Cortés and steadfast in support of my cousin the governor.'

'Oh yes, yes of course,' Alvarado replied. 'Steadfast. I don't doubt it for a moment. You are steadfast; Escudero here is steadfast. If I am right, Diego de Ordaz is steadfast too . . . '

'His Excellency assigned him to the expedition specifically to keep watch on Cortés,' said Escudero pompously. 'He won't hesitate to declare for us when the time is right.'

'And Cristóbal de Olid, I presume?'

'We may count on him absolutely,' blustered Velázquez de León. 'Olid was the governor's major-domo. His loyalty to our cause is not in doubt.'

'And who else?' asked Alvarado. 'Who else can we count on?'

Another shifty glance.

'Well come on, gentlemen!' Alvarado urged. 'If I'm to throw my lot in with you, the very least I need to know is who my associates will be.'

That look again. Finally Escudero spoke: 'The question, Pedro, is whether *you* are with us or not. If you are with us, then we'll make you privy to our plans and give you the names of all our senior people, but while there's doubt—'

'While there's doubt,' Velázquez de León cut in, 'we've already told you too much.'

'It seems, gentlemen,' said Alvarado, 'that we have reached an impasse. You want me to commit to your cause absolutely, without full knowledge of those I will be committing myself to. But I, for my part, require that knowledge before I am willing to com—'

'Damn you, Alvarado!' exclaimed Escudero, 'I've had enough of your procrastination.'

'I do not procrastinate! If I'm to turn against my lifelong friend, and risk being hanged as a mutineer, I want to know I'll be doing it for men I can respect and rely upon. Olid, Ordaz, Montejo, the two of you – there's nothing new here. Any fool can guess whose side every one of you is on. But you must trust me with new names if you want me to trust you.'

Without explanation, Escudero took Velázquez de León by the arm and walked off a few paces with him. *Ridiculous*, Alvarado thought. *Like children!* He looked on in disbelief as the two men engaged in a heated, whispered conversation. When they returned, Escudero said: 'We'll think on your request, Don Pedro. Meanwhile we must have your vow of silence. Our meeting tonight—'

'What meeting?' asked Alvarado.

Velázquez de León uttered an awkward, braying laugh. 'Exactly!' he said. 'It never happened.'

And with that the two plotters turned away and walked briskly back towards camp, leaving Alvarado alone under the stars.

Fools, he thought. *They still don't realise I'm playing them.* And then he thought: *But I can't spin this out much longer.*

In a way it was a miracle, and a tribute to his own superior negotiating skills and capacity for dissemblance that he'd managed to keep the plotters on the hook as long as he had. But unless something changed, and changed radically, they were going to see through him very soon.

Unless, after all, he did join them.

He began to whistle cheerfully, loosened his fine Toledo rapier in its scabbard and set off down the dunes towards the beach. He was wide awake, his mind full of plans and schemes. Before retiring to his bed, he decided, he'd walk for half an hour, enjoy that southern breeze that was blowing and get the sour stink of Velázquez de León and Escudero out of his nostrils.

Chapter Eleven

Still struggling for breath, Ishtlil staggered to his feet, his fingers fluttering at his throat, his face flushed. 'A demon!' he gasped. 'Your girl is a demon. No human can do what she did to me. No human can disappear like that.'

'She is human, lord,' Huicton said. Tozi was touched by the worried look on her mentor's wizened face. 'She's just a girl like any other. A sweet girl. A good girl with a kind heart, but blessed by the gods with special powers to aid our cause.'

Shielded from their eyes by the spell of invisibility, Tozi had not left the tent, had not, in fact, moved at all, and she did not move now as Ishtlil lurched towards her, his arms sweeping the air in front of him. When she made herself invisible her connection to the stuff of the world became different, more complicated, than when she was in physical form. Her clothes and the contents of her pockets always faded with her, and she had learned she could spread the field of magic to other things, and the people around her, if she concentrated her will. She could pick up objects and use them if she chose to do so, but she was also able to make herself as insubstantial as thought, and flow in this form even through solid matter, or allow solid things to flow through her. In every case, she had discovered, the keys to control were focus and intention, so she focused now, as Ishtlil's huge, groping hands passed through her body, giving him no clue that she was even there. The Texcocan rebel leader then careered around the tent, rather comically Tozi thought, his arms spread wide, groping and feeling but finding nothing. 'Has she gone?' Ishtlil eventually asked. 'Or is she still here?'

'Well, that's the thing with my Tozi,' Huicton said mildly. 'When she's invisible you never know where she is—'

'Which is why she makes such a good spy,' Ishtlil mused. He was beginning to calm down now. Tozi read his mind and found no anger there towards herself, none of the suspicion about witchcraft he'd begun to radiate earlier, just surprise, some lingering fear and . . . and . . . What was this? Something like greed? Something like cunning? What Ishtlil's reaction most reminded her of, she realised, was the opportunistic pleasure of a street trader who has just made a winning deal. He was calculating how he might use her, and in immediate confirmation of this he turned to face Huicton and said: 'How about we get this Tozi of yours to kill Moctezuma? She could enter his bedchamber undetected, slit his throat and be gone with no one any the wiser.'

'With respect, lord,' Huicton replied, 'we've already thought of that and decided against it.'

'Against it?' Ishtlil sounded aghast. 'Why?'

'Consider this, Lord Ishtlil. Moctezuma is the weakest and most incompetent Speaker the Mexica have produced in a hundred years. If Tozi were to kill him as you suggest, then anyone else they might put on the throne – Cuitláhuac, perhaps even Guatemoc – would do a better job than him. If we're truly to end Mexica power, then it may be that the best way to do so is to let Moctezuma live and exploit his deficiencies and his failings, his superstitions and his fears . . . Indeed, lord, that is what we are already doing, and very successfully. Tozi has the power – I think she showed you this just now? – to magnify a man's fears—'

'Ha! She showed me all right!' Ishtlil looked around the tent again. 'Girl!' he said. 'Are you there? Are you spying on us?'

Tozi said nothing, preferring to keep Ishtlil guessing.

'If you won't slit Moctezuma's throat,' the Texcocan rebel leader now said, still addressing empty air, 'how about slitting Cacama's throat? How about that, girl? Would you do that for me?'

I'm not an assassin, Tozi thought. But then she remembered how she'd killed the corrupt high priest Ahuizotl by the lakeside on the night she and Malinal had escaped sacrifice and she thought: *Why not?*

Huicton spoke again. 'Kill Cacama, lord,' he told Ishtlil, 'and risk a more effective leader being placed on the throne of Texcoco to confront you. Cacama and Moctezuma are both great fools and they both serve our cause better alive than dead.'

Ishtlil glowered, then grinned. 'Ha! I suppose you're right,' he said finally. 'Clever Huicton! What would I do without you?'

The two men's talk soon turned to strategy. It seemed Ishtlil needed no more convincing of the value of the intelligence Tozi had brought. Some new force had entered the land, perhaps indeed the god Quetzalcoatl and his divine companions. Huicton was therefore to make his way to the coast where these *tueles* had set up camp, attempt to speak to their leader and offer him Ishtlil's support in overthrowing the tyranny of the Mexica. 'Go by way of Tlascala,' Ishtlil added. 'Try again to forge an alliance with Shikotenka. With the prospect of a god on our side, perhaps he'll reconsider our offer . . .'

Tozi's heart was thudding with joy. The coast! The coast! She would travel with Huicton, she would be reunited with her dear friend Malinal and she would see the face of the god Quetzalcoatl himself. She was suddenly so excited she could not keep still, and rushed out of the tent to run unseen through the night where the hosts of men at Ishtlil's command sat around their campfires taking their evening meal. A great army was building to overthrow evil and usher in a new age, so of course that stubborn Shikotenka would want to be part of it! Once she and Huicton convinced him of the truth about Quetzalcoatl, any other outcome was unthinkable.

Chapter Twelve

This was what terror felt like. He had known it before when he had nearly been washed overboard during the great storm that scattered the fleet on the night they'd set sail from Cuba. And he'd known it again when he lay hogtied on the forest floor on the island of Cozumel while Father Muñoz strode back and forth, ranting and mad. But tonight, terror had reached a new peak for Pepillo, when his moments of quiet reflection overlooking the ocean had been suddenly cut short by a muscular Indian who'd thrown him onto his back while another had clamped his mouth shut, stifling his cries of alarm, and his nostrils were filled with the musky, alien smell of his attackers and they had dragged him off through the dunes and down onto the smooth, hard sand of the beach, lifting him bodily when he lost his footing, spiriting him away, he knew not where or why, at tremendous speed.

He guessed there might be four of them, or five; in the rush and the confusion he could not be sure. They spoke little amongst themselves, but when they did he thought he recognised snatches of their words. Their language was the same Nahuatl that Malinal had begun to teach him, or something very like it, yet these rough men seemed wilder, more savage by far than the semi-civilised and officious Mexica whom Pepillo had grown used to seeing around the camp, and he feared he was about to be murdered. 'Let me go,' he tried to say. 'What have I done to you?' His words were Spanish, and of course they would not understand, but even if by some miracle his abductors spoke the King's own Castilian, that massive, uncompromising hand clamped across his mouth prevented him from uttering anything more than stifled grunts and sobs.

His feet slipped from under him and he was lifted bodily again, his head almost wrenched from his shoulders, when there came a snarl, menacing and low, and his pup Melchior launched himself out of the darkness, a missile of fur and teeth and fury, and seized that clamping, stifling hand and tore it loose in an instant, extracting a bellow of pure horror from its owner and allowing Pepillo to shout at the top of his voice: '*Help! For God's sake, help!*' In the same instant, Melchior let go the hand and dropped back to the beach, sinking his teeth into one of the attacker's ankles. There came another shriek and suddenly Pepillo was free, stumbling over his own knees, then rising and running and shouting again and again: '*Help! For God's sake, help!*' The breeze was still blowing, carrying his cries away from the camp, which now lay hundreds of paces to the south, so there was little chance he would be heard, but it was his only hope.

As Alvarado strolled down from the dunes towards the beach, he felt the hairs on the back of his neck stir – something was amiss here – and his hand fell to the hilt of his rapier. He had long since learned to trust his instincts, but at first he wasn't sure what it was that troubled him except perhaps a sense of motion, of agitation – and that not very far away. Then he heard a dog snarl and a yell of surprise followed by a boy's voice, high-pitched and terrified, shouting '*Help! For God's sake, help!*'

Alvarado drew his steel and broke into a run. In seconds he had reached level sand. Directly ahead of him, not fifty paces distant and dimly lit by the crescent moon, he made out a scrum of figures – Indians, by the look of them, naked but for breechclouts and feathers. Closing he saw a small figure break free, heard again that high-pitched plea for help and now recognised the boy Pepillo, Cortés's own page, running and stumbling away, still calling for aid and seemingly unaware that his wish had been granted. The boy was followed by two of his attackers, while the other three seemed fully preoccupied with the furious dog, no more than a pup, that was amongst them, snarling and snapping its teeth, and clearly doing some harm.

Alvarado changed direction, put on a burst of speed, and came up with the boy just as one of the filthy savages, streaking after him, reached to grab him. 'Not so fast, my lovely,' Alvarado said, striking down on a dusky arm with the edge of the rapier and feeling the satisfying resistance of human flesh. 'Pick on someone your own size, why don't you?' The second heathen came at him with a hideous yell, wielding one of those crude wooden paddles edged with blades of obsidian that the Indians used as swords. Alvarado parried, but the rapier lodged with a *clunk* deep in the wood of the other man's weapon; for a moment he could not pull it free, and suddenly he was surrounded by a press of stinking Indians thrusting at him with their primitive stone knives. Just as well, he'd buckled on his cuirass this evening! He felt the blades break and turn on his armour, ducked to avoid a huge club that came whistling at his head, drew his own dagger of Toledo steel, plunged it into a leg here, a torso there, and was rewarded with cries of pain and a sudden drawing back of the men around him. In the same instant, with a twist and a jerk, he pulled his rapier free and dropped into the guard position fencers call the plough, holding the slim blade out before him, hilt down close to his centre of gravity, point up, turning through three hundred and sixty degrees to see where the next threat was coming from.

He glanced at Pepillo. The boy was still with him, still alive. 'You're doing good, lad,' he said, 'but I want you to run now. Run back to camp. Yell at the top of your voice all the way. Get us help. I'll keep these bastards busy.'

'No, sir. With respect, sir. I don't see my dog.'

'Bugger your dog, lad. Dog'll look after himself. Get running, unless you want us both to end up in the cooking pot.'

'Very well, sir. As you say, sir . . .'

But it was already too late. Their attackers had formed a rough circle around them and there was no way the boy was going to make it through. Alvarado laid a gloved hand on his shoulder. 'Change of plan,' he said. 'Stay close. Watch my back. It's hard to credit but it looks like these Indians know how to fight.' He raised his voice. 'Come on, you godless barbarians. Have at me if you dare.'

Shikotenka was beginning to wonder whether the white-skinned, bearded, golden-haired man confronting them might after all be some kind of *tuele*. With odds of five to one, the five being without a doubt the flower of Tlascalan warriors, their opponent should be lying, bleeding his last, in the sand by now. Instead he was standing there taunting them, apparently uninjured and protecting the boy they'd snatched. The boy was human, no doubt about that, but this man, if he was a man, seemed possessed of supernatural powers. Shikotenka had aimed a thrust straight at his heart – a good thrust, a true thrust – and yet his war knife had been turned by the stranger's metal armour.

Surely some witchcraft must be at work here, some sorcery – for while the white-skin was as yet untouched, Chipahua had taken a deep wound to the muscle of his right forearm, forcing him to switch his *macuahuitl* to his left hand, Tree had been stabbed through the thigh, and Ilhuicamina between the ribs.

And what was that monstrous *animal* that had come at them and then disappeared? Shikotenka looked down at his own ankle, bleeding copiously where its fangs had slashed him. Was it some species of wolf that the white-skins had enchanted to their service? And where was it now? He hoped it had not gone to fetch others of its kind.

He looked around at his crew, closing in for the kill. All were still in the fight and none were complaining, but they were losing blood and time. Only Acolmiztli remained completely uninjured. 'I can take him,' he hissed. 'Give me my chance, Shikotenka. Great honour in it for me when I bring this one down.'

'Shit on honour,' growled Tree. 'I say we all just rush him, club him into the ground . . . '

But Alcolmiztli wasn't listening. Raising his *macuahuitl* in a two-handed grip, he uttered a shrill battle cry and darted forward.

With a roar, Tree followed him.

Signalling Chipahua and Ilhuicamina to stay back – their injuries made them liabilities in a fight with an opponent as skilled as this – Shikotenka circled silently out into the darkness, aiming to get behind the white-skin.

Deep in a claustrophobic dream in which a fiend hunted her through narrow corridors and passageways, Malinal heard the sound of whining and scratching at the door of the wooden hut she shared with

Puertocarrero. She was immediately wide awake, her mind working fast, sensing trouble. She leapt out from the bed, ran naked to the door and opened it to find Pepillo's dog Melchior standing there shivering, covered in blood. The moment it saw her it turned and ran off a few paces, then turned back, looked at her and barked.

Malinal had no doubt what this meant. Pepillo must be in some terrible danger. 'Puertocarrero!' she yelled, 'wake up!' She realised she'd spoken the words in Castilian, even as she dashed back to the bed, pulled off the sheets and gave the hairy slumbering figure a shove. No reaction! She was already pulling on a tunic and slipping into her moccasins; moments later, with a final shriek at Puertocarrero, she ran out into the night, heading for Cortés's nearby pavilion. Melchior followed at her heels.

The guards were asleep in the portico and Malinal barged past them without a second thought. 'Caudillo,' she shouted, 'be awake. Trouble. Danger.' At once Cortés sat up in the bed, the dim light of the candles revealing a chubby Totonac girl by his side. Malinal felt an instant stab of jealousy – that should be her place! – but ignored it. 'Caudillo! Caudillo! Come quick. Pepillo! Great danger!' Melchior scurried around her feet, barking, and Cortés at once jumped up, his *tepulli* half-engorged, swinging from side to side, his *ahuacatl* large and heavy. Hastily he donned a pair of breeches, boots, and strapped on his sword. He asked no questions, just charged outside, slapping the guards about the head. Within seconds there were a dozen men around him, all armed, some holding blazing firebrands, and they streamed down across the dunes towards the beach after Melchior, Cortés calling over his shoulder: 'Vendabal! Follow with the dogs!'

As the two Indians charged towards him, one small and wiry, the other massive and heavily muscled with a tangle of wild hair, time seemed to slow, as it often did in battle, and Alvarado had a moment to wish he'd brought his heavy falchion with him this night rather than the slim and elegant rapier now gripped in his right hand. The rapier was a fine weapon to be sure, the work of the great swordsmith Andrés Nuñez of Toledo, but it was not well suited to a fight with savages. The way it had become trapped in the first scuffle for example. Not good! Not good at all! He'd have to make damn sure that didn't happen again or they might yet get the better of him. If he'd had the falchion it would have broken that wooden sword in half, leaving him free to carve its owner into mincemeat, but – well – he didn't have the falchion, so he'd just have to make the best of a bad job.

The first man swung at him, another of those infernal wooden swords, but since the blow was aimed at his chest where his cuirass protected him, he allowed it through, feeling the obsidian blades shatter harmlessly. He spun sideways and let the Indian's own momentum carry him past, dodged left to avoid a whistling blow from the other attacker's huge club, shoved Pepillo roughly out of the way, fell into a stance, his right knee flexed, his left leg and left arm extended almost straight behind him, and executed a rapid powerful lunge, the long blade of the rapier thrust out ahead, its needle point seeking, questing for flesh to pierce, for vital organs to puncture.

But the wiry little Indian with the sword was fast – damned good, in fact! – and swivelled to avoid the strike, backhanding a second useless blow into Alvarado's cuirass even as the other came in yelling, whirling that monstrous club. They thought they had him now – Alvarado could see it in the triumphant glint of their eyes – but he was an accomplished athlete; he threw himself into a backflip, a technique that had saved his life more than once in battle, landed poised on the balls of his feet and went at once into the counterattack, slashing the razor edge of the dagger in his left hand across the face of the Indian with the club, tearing loose a great flap of skin, then leaping high into the air and – *Yes! Yes!* – perfectly skewering the other man. The point of the rapier slid in just below the savage's Adam's apple and emerged from his lower back, doing terrible damage along the way. Alvarado had already whipped the blade out before his feet hit the ground and, as the giant Indian with the club came at him again, he struck him through the belly, not centre mass as he would have preferred, but somewhat to one side, a blow that would not be immediately fatal but that would surely slow him down.

The smaller of the two attackers had already collapsed to his knees, making the choking, gurgling sounds of a man drowning in his own blood, and Alvarado was about to deliver the *coup de grâce* to the giant when he was shocked to discover his sword arm seized in a powerful grip and the rapier snatched from his grasp. Where the hell was the boy Pepillo, who should have warned him of this, he thought furiously, even as he switched his dagger to his right hand and swung to face his new assailant.

Creeping up on the boy was easy. He didn't make a sound when Shikotenka smashed his fist into the side of his head, laid him out flat, and rushed forward to grab the golden-haired warrior's sword arm just in time to stop him killing Tree. With the advantage of surprise, Shikotenka wrestled the strange metal weapon from his hand but, not being practised in its use, he cast it down and faced the white-skin knife to knife. Out of the corner of his eye he saw Tree advancing, bleeding mightily from face, thigh and side, while Ilhuicamina and Chipahua also edged closer. 'Stay back!' Shikotenka commanded. 'He's mine.'

Everything about the white-skin's stance, the calm, steady glare of his pale eyes, the relaxed way he moved, light on his feet, poised, deadly, told Shikotenka that he confronted a practised knife-fighter, a slayer just like himself. This was not going to be easy, and what made it even more difficult was the silver armour that sheathed the other man's torso. Pointless to attempt another thrust for the heart. Shikotenka knew that if he were to kill this enemy, he would have to strike home to his unprotected legs, or throat or head, while he himself would remain vulnerable to a body blow throughout the contest.

They were still circling – each looking for an opening in the other's defence, knives lashing out, probing, neither yet committing to a full attack – when Shikotenka saw something that made his blood run cold: a line of men holding blazing torches aloft, running full tilt towards them along the beach from the direction of the camp. Behind them, further back, was a shadowy mass of other figures, and from their midst arose the horrible baying of the white-skins' wolves.

Shikotenka made an immediate decision. Although it was dishonourable, Alcolmiztli's corpse would have to be left behind. He did not know how fast the war animals of the white-skins could run, but Tlascalans – even injured! – were the fastest runners in the world, and the wind would carry their scent away from the beasts, not towards them.

He issued the order, broke off the fight, nodded to his opponent and said: 'This isn't over, white-skin. We'll meet again.' Then he turned and ran. Glancing back he saw the man's golden hair gleaming in the moonlight and heard him call out in his foreign tongue. The words themselves meant nothing to him, but their tone of mockery was unmistakable and the skin of Shikotenka's face grew hot with shame.

Chapter Thirteen

Wednesday 28 April 1519

Following the attempted abduction of Pepillo, which Alvarado – and the dog Melchior – had spectacularly foiled, many of the Spaniards wanted to attack the town of Cuetlaxtlan that very night, kill its governor Pichatzin and wipe out the large Mexica garrison there. Just as well for Pichatzin, then, Malinal thought, that Alvarado had slain one of the abductors whose breechclout, hairstyle and tattoos left no doubt, as she herself was able to affirm, that he was a Tlascalan warrior, a sworn enemy of the Mexica. It was unthinkable, therefore, that the Mexica were in any way responsible for his actions and, in the end, after Malinal had explained this to Cortés through Aguilar, reason prevailed. Not that she cared much one way or another whether the Spaniards fell upon the local Mexica, but ultimately it was Tenochtitlan and Moctezuma she was after, not a provincial town and its poor harassed governor.

The hunt for the rest of the little Tlascalan war band was soon called off. Somehow they'd escaped into the darkness, even evading Vendabal's bloodhounds, and must now be well on their way back to their mountain stronghold. Why they'd launched the assault in the first place was not clear, but Malinal suspected it must be to do with the close cooperation that seemed to have been struck up between the Spaniards and the Mexica. The two thousand Totonac labourers, whipped into line by Mexica overseers, busily at work constructing the temporary town of wooden dwellings on the dunes, the teams of bearers bringing food and other supplies out from Cuetlaxtlan, the women sent as bedslaves, even the frequent visits Pichatzin himself made to the camp – all would have been regarded as highly significant.

77

The Tlascalans might have heard the rumours, rife throughout the area, of the return of Quetzalcoatl, but nothing they could have seen would have persuaded them that the Spaniards were here to overthrow Mexica tyranny. On the contrary, witnessing all the activity, only one conclusion would have been possible – that the strangers were not gods but powerful men and that the Mexica were in the process of forging a strong alliance with them that must surely, sooner or later, be turned against Tlascala.

Yet still, even with her own eyes wide open to the truth, Malinal could not quite shake off the astonishing ways that Cortés, with his striking pale skin and handsome bearded face, seemed such a plausible fulfilment of the prophecy of the return of Quetzalcoatl. Nor was it simply a matter of appearances, or the fact that he and his companions had arrived in great boats that moved by themselves without paddles in the year One-Reed – or any of the other eerie resemblances. Whether it was pure coincidence, or resulted from the workings of some supernatural design, Cortés also shared what was probably the most important and the most distinctive of Quetzalcoatl's legendary characteristics. Malinal had hardly begun to understand the Christian faith the caudillo professed, his reverence for the tortured god-man depicted nailed to a cross, and the frequent sermons, translated by Aguilar, that he directed at her. One thing was completely clear, however, and this was his abhorrence of human sacrifice as practised by the Maya, the Totonacs and most particularly by the Mexica, under whom, as she had informed him, it had been elevated to the status of a national obsession, with tens of thousands going under the knife each year.

Now, two days after the attempted abduction of Pepillo, Malinal sat with Cortés in his newly built wooden pavilion, roofed with fine cloth, provided by Pichatzin. The caudillo was listening with rapt horror, making occasional remarks such as 'disgusting', 'vile', and 'an abomination', as Malinal told him of her own close escape from the killing stone in Tenochtitlan on that terrible night, months before, when the hearts of more than two thousand women had been plucked from their breasts. The air within the pavilion was redolent of split pine, refreshed by the soft morning breeze that blew in off the ocean and ruffled the canopy over their heads, but as Malinal relived those hours of horror and dread, she smelled again the awful reek from the tide of blood that had washed down the steps of the pyramid, and imagined she could hear the beat of the snakeskin drum and the screech of the conch. Speaking slowly, allowing Aguilar time to grasp her meaning fully in Maya and put it into Castilian, listening closely as he did so in order to add to her growing vocabulary in this strangely soft, lilting language spoken by the Spanish, she explained how she had been imprisoned in the fattening pen with her friend Tozi, how they had mounted the steps with all the other women and how at the last moment they had been freed by the intervention of Huitzilopochtli – 'Hummingbird' – the very god to whom the sacrifices were dedicated.

Her grasp of the Castilian tongue was already sufficient for her to realise that Aguilar was disparaging her even as he translated her words to Cortés, suggesting indeed that she was making the whole story up. Anger gripped her and she exclaimed in Castilian: 'No! Not make up. Truth! All truth!'

A flicker of a smile crossed Cortés's face and he said something to Aguilar about her being a 'clever woman – very clever.' But she couldn't follow the rest. Then he put a question directly to her, waiting to see if she could understand it, which she could not. Finally Aguilar translated: 'Explain why this devil Hummingbird whom the Mexica worship should wish to set you free?'

She shrugged: 'I don't know. Who can comprehend the ways of gods or devils?' An idea occurred to her which she thought might prove persuasive to Cortés, so she looked him straight in the eye and said: 'I think perhaps it is because your god, the god of the Christians, is more powerful than Hummingbird. I think he made Moctezuma release us so we could help you to defeat him.'

Cortés allowed that this was indeed possible, since Malinal had already helped him a great deal with the descriptions she had provided over the past days about the vast wealth of the Mexica and their treasure houses filled with gold, silver and jewels – which made him all the more determined to visit them – coupled with her accounts of their vile and diabolical religion, with its addiction to human sacrifice, which was an abomination and which it was his duty as a Christian to suppress. In addition he had learned much from her about the size, weapons and disposition of the Mexica armies, which had made him aware that he must proceed cautiously and in strength. In all this, he said, he could indeed see the hand of god and of divine providence at work.

At this point Aguilar, who Malinal already disliked because his jealousy had unnecessarily kept her apart from Cortés for so long, objected in Castilian, and then again in Mayan for her benefit, that pure coincidence seemed a better explanation than any god-directed process for her presence in Potonchan at the time of the Spaniards' arrival. He also wanted to know why she considered her supposed 'friend' to be relevant, since she wasn't even here.

A lengthy argument followed between the two Spaniards, during which the caudillo spoke in the special rolling, lilting tone that Malinal had noticed he liked to use for sermons. When he seemed to be finished she said in Castilian, 'I speak now?' and Cortés, with another smile that she very much liked, waved her on. Reverting to Mayan she turned to Aguilar: 'This is important,' she said. 'Please try to translate what I say very carefully and very exactly into Castilian because your idea about coincidence is wrong and I will tell you why and the caudillo needs to know this.'

Aguilar looked at her with much the same dislike that she felt for him. He had status because he was, or had been, Cortés's chief interpreter; he feared, now they had moved out of the lands of the Maya and into territories ruled by the Mexica, about whose language and culture he was ignorant, that he would no longer have a role. Well, he was right! She'd always had a good ear for languages and she already understood much more Castilian than he realised.

For the moment, however, she still needed him, so she told him what she had to say in Mayan and listened very intently to his translation into Castilian, not only to improve her vocabulary but also to be sure the caudillo was not being misled.

'There is something,' she said, 'that neither you, Aguilar, nor you my lord Cortés, know yet, and this concerns a god whom the Mexica fear and respect almost as much as the demon Hummingbird. I will tell you about this god – who is called Quetzalcoatl, the Plumed

Serpent – not only because what I have to say about him proves that it was not coincidence that brought me here, but also because if you Spaniards arm yourselves with this knowledge, it will help you to lay low the great armies of the Mexica and destroy their powerful cities and take their wealth and make it yours and end forever their cruel and evil reign in these lands.'

She then recounted the whole story of Quetzalcoatl, and his human manifestation, so similar to that of the Spaniards, as a bearded, pale-skinned man who detested human sacrifice. She told of the ancient prophecy that the god and his companions would return in this very year, in great ships that would come from the east, moving by them-selves without paddles. Lastly she spoke of the promise that Quetzalcoatl was said to have made – to overthrow the wicked and bloodstained cult of Hummingbird and replace it with a religion of peace and love such as the Christian faith as Cortés had repeatedly described it to her.

When Aguilar had put all this into Castilian, the caudillo leaned forward in his chair, rubbing the point of his beard with his left hand, and the two Spaniards again talked animatedly for several minutes. Cortés then had Aguilar explain to Malinal in Mayan that it was possible, in his opinion, that a 'saint' – a holy man – called Thomas had visited these lands one thousand five hundred years before to preach the Christian faith and that it was his memory, and a promise that he had no doubt made to return, that was preserved in the story of Quetzalcoatl. He then invited Malinal to continue. She said that whether Quetzalcoatl was this Saint Thomas or not, the prophecy of his return was believed by all the Mexica, and especially by the Great Speaker, who was utterly terrified of what it would mean for him. She described how she had been called to the palace in Tenochtitlan the year before to serve as a translator when a message had been brought to Moctezuma from the Chontal Maya concerning the first visit to these lands of white-skinned, bearded strangers. They had been fewer in number than Cortés and his men; nonetheless, they had defeated a Mayan army ten thousand strong.

Cortés slapped his thigh with his hand as this was translated for him, and said something in Castilian about a captain called Hernández de Cordoba.

After that, Malinal continued, Moctezuma had been seized by a terrible foreboding that those strangers, who had arrived near the end of the year called Thirteen-Rabbit in the Mexica calendar, had come to announce the return of Quetzalcoatl, which was therefore to be expected this year – which happened to be the year One-Reed as the prophecy had long ago foretold. Driven mad with fear that he was about to lose his throne, Moctezuma had initiated a new cycle of sacrifices, intended to strengthen Hummingbird with human hearts and blood and win the war god's support to drive Quetzalcoatl and his companions back into the sea. Malinal repeated that she and her friend Tozi would have been amongst those sacrificed for this cause, but for the mysterious intervention of Hummingbird himself – surely compelled by the one and only true god of the Christians. After they had been released from the killing stone, she told Cortés, she and Tozi had pledged to do everything in their power to bring about the overthrow of Moctezuma and the end of human sacrifice. To this end Tozi had remained in Tenochtitlan to work what harm she could against the Great Speaker, while Malinal had made the long journey overland to Potonchan, her hometown, to welcome Quetzalcoatl, should he appear there, and help him to win back his kingdom.

'I do not believe you are Quetzalcoatl,' she now said to Cortés, 'and I do not believe you are a god, but it is very strange that you look the way you do and that you have come from the east in the year One-Reed. I think you can now see that Aguilar was wrong to imagine it was coincidence that brought me to Potonchan at exactly the time you arrived there.'

When he had heard all this, a strange light came into Cortés's eye. The rolling, lilting tone was back in his voice and – as he often did – he required Aguilar to translate into Mayan a verse from the sacred texts of his religion. This one stated: 'Thou art the God that doest wonders; thou hast declared thy strength among the nations.'

'What does it mean?' Malinal asked.

'It means,' explained Aguilar, 'that God works in mysterious ways to perform his wonders. The caudillo is of the opinion, which I do not share, that the lord of all created things has chosen to work through

82

you and through this prophecy about Quetzalcoatl to strengthen our hand here and put us on the path to victory.'

Cortés spoke again, his eyes seeming to burn into Malinal.

'The caudillo asks,' Aguilar translated, 'how you think he might best take advantage of the prophecy. Should he perhaps pretend to be this Quetzalcoatl? He says he finds such an idea repugnant and contrary to his Christian faith.'

'There is no need to pretend anything,' Malinal replied. She returned Cortés's gaze as she spoke. 'It will not serve your interests to make a claim that will later be proved false. I advise you always to tell the truth about who you are, as you have told it to me. So when you are asked, say you are just a man, a Spaniard, from a land across the seas and you serve a great emperor who rules that land and many other lands. But know while you say these things that the Mexica believe their gods to be tricksters, very deceitful and dishonest, great lovers of masks and disguises, who like to pretend to be other than what they are. Regardless of what you say, their own imaginations will convince many of them, especially that fool and coward Moctezuma, that you really are a god. You have ships, guns, steel, horses, war dogs – and these things will seem like wonders to them. So say you are a man, but act like a god, that is my advice to you.'

'You see,' Cortés said triumphantly to Aguilar, 'I told you she was clever!'

They had been aware for some minutes of a clamour of shouts in the camp, but now it suddenly increased in intensity. As Cortés sprang from his chair to investigate, Alvarado appeared at the door. 'We've got visitors,' he said with a grin. 'There's a whole delegation of Mexica notables in robes and feathers down by the main gate. What shall we do with them?'

Malinal understood and turned to Aguilar. 'They must wait,' she said in Mayan. 'Tell the caudillo! Let me see who they are first, then I will advise.'

With Malinal at his right hand, Aguilar at his left, and his senior captains behind him, many decked out in full armour, Cortés sat overlooking the beach on the highest point of the dunes, under a much larger and grander awning than the one he had used a few days before to meet Pichatzin. The fine white cloth out of which this new awning was woven had been supplied by the obliging governor of Cuetlaxtlan, along with many other useful gifts that he had delivered to the Spanish camp since that meeting, and was supported on a framework of sturdy pine posts erected at great speed especially for this occasion by a gang of Totonac labourers. The two hundred fittest and strongest soldiers in Cortés's army were arrayed round about, bristling with swords, spears and battle-axes and carrying their shields, crossbows and muskets.

Other preparations, every one of them orchestrated on Malinal's advice, were under way all around the camp. She predicted that the Mexica delegates would already have heard from Pichatzin about the horses, would ask to see them, and could easily be frightened by them. To this end a mare in heat had been tethered close to the awning for the past hour and only just now led away. After the meeting had started, the plan was to bring up Alvarado's randy stallion Bucephalus and tether it in the same place; the mare's scent, lingering on the ground, could be relied upon to make it boisterous. Meanwhile the rest of the cavalry were being prepared to stage a grand demonstration down on the firm sand of the beach, Telmo Vendabal's assistants were armouring fifty of the most ferocious dogs, and Francisco de Mesa's Taino slaves were hauling all three of the lombards to positions close to the awning, where they would be loaded with seventy-pound cannon-balls and very large charges of gunpowder.

Cortés nodded towards the crowd of Mexica delegates. 'Shall we let them come up?' he asked Malinal. It had been her idea, but a good one he thought, to keep them waiting, clustered in the sun in a hollow of the dunes close to the camp's latrines, where swarms of pestilent flies and biting insects were always encountered.

She narrowed her eyes. 'Yes,' she said through Aguilar, 'let them come.'

She had already pointed out the tall thin figure of a man of mature years, dressed like some wizard of old in a conical cap and a long black robe embroidered with silver stars. He was the leader of the delegation. She recognised him from court occasions in Tenochtitlan,

84

she said, but she had never met him personally. His name was Teudile and he was Moctezuma's own steward, the seventh most important official in the land after the Great Speaker himself.

Pichatzin walked by Teudile's side, and a group of five other Mexica nobles wearing colourful carmine robes clustered round them. 'They're not important,' Malinal said. 'Not even Pichatzin. Only Teudile matters.'

The delegation included five artists equipped with their sheaves of paper, paints and brushes, several dozen bearers carrying an assortment of baskets and boxes, and an honour-guard of twenty fearsome-looking soldiers from the class called the Cuahchic. These, Malinal explained, were the most formidable and skilled of all Mexica warriors. Except for a scalp lock tied with a red ribbon above their left ears, they were shaved bald, with their heads completely covered in glistening paint, red on the left side and blue on the right. Dressed only in loincloths and sandals, they showed off superb, heavily muscled physiques, and were armed with the long, two-handed wooden swords, edged with blades of obsidian, that the Spaniards had already confronted amongst the Maya.

In addition there were four men in lusciously colourful shimmering cloaks woven out of feathers. Three of them were elderly with lined faces and long grey hair, while the fourth was young and wore his hair in a curious crest across the middle of his otherwise shaved head. All had exceptionally long, twisted, dirty fingernails, and all clutched rattles that they shook from time to time as they walked. They muttered rhythmic phrases in lowered voices and looked around from under glowering brows with suspicious, hostile glances. These curious creatures, Malinal said, were Moctezuma's court sorcerers, and had been sent to cast evil spells and generally work harm on the Spaniards. She seemed to believe they might really be able to do this, but Cortés told her firmly that the idea was laughable: 'We are protected,' he said, 'by the Lord God himself.'

The final element of the delegation now winding its way up the slope towards them was equally strange. There were two male captives amongst them, heads bowed, hands bound behind their backs. One was a boy, perhaps fourteen or fifteen years old, about Pepillo's age. He was scrawny and hollow-chested, with coarse black straight hair cut in a fringe over his acne-covered forehead. He sobbed continually as he walked, tears running down his cheeks and snot dripping from his nose. The other, who spoke sharply to him from time to time, as though admonishing him, was older, broad shouldered and powerfully built, with long braided hair and coppery-red skin marked by many scars – some old, some still livid and fresh – on his chest and arms. His face was heavily tattooed with blue zigzags and curlicues, and his earlobes and lower lip were stretched and greatly extended by large bone plugs. Both captives had been daubed with some sort of white paint, were barefoot and wore flimsy loincloths that seemed to be made of paper. Leading them by ropes looped around their necks were five fierce-looking men with wild, matted hair wearing filthy black robes.

'Who are they?' Cortés asked.

'Priests of the war god Hummingbird,' replied Malinal.

'And their prisoners?'

'Totonacs. They've prepared them for sacrifice. Looks as if they intend to offer them to you.'

'By God,' Cortés exclaimed. 'Nobody will be sacrificed here.'

Teudile was a sallow, hollow-cheeked bag of bones whose sunken eyes glittered with a curious mixture of intelligence, malice and fear as he sat cross-legged on a mat on the ground in front of Cortés, flanked by Pichatzin and the other Mexica officials. He spoke, giving his name, and held forth a gold ring in which was set an engraved gemstone. This, it seemed, was the seal of Moctezuma himself. Malinal translated Teudile's words into Mayan while Aguilar put them into Castilian: 'Pray that the god will hear us. Your lieutenant Moctezuma, who has in his charge Tenochtitlan, the city of Mexico, sends us to give homage to you . . .'

'So he's already addressing me as a god?' Cortés asked.

'He's assuming you are Quetzalcoatl,' Malinal replied through Aguilar. 'That's the safest course of action for him at the moment, but remember what I told you. Don't make such a claim yourself. Say you're a man but overawe him – fuel his superstitions, keep him guessing.'

86

'Tell him we accept his homage and ask him if there is any particular thing he wants with us,' Cortés said.

'I wish to know from this god,' Teudile replied, 'why he has come here, where he is going and what he seeks?'

'Tell him I have come to greet his master Moctezuma and that I intend to go to the city of Tenochtitlan to salute him.'

'The lord Moctezuma will be much pleased to hear this,' Teudile replied. 'However, he asks that you delay your journey and leave him in peace until the time of his death. After that you will be welcome to journey to Tenochtitlan, where you will recover your kingdom just as you left it long ago. Meanwhile he wishes you joy after your long journey. He has sent you foods and fruits of this your homeland, so that you may be restored.'

Teudile then waved forward several of the bearers, who unslung large, wood-framed baskets from their backs and set them down on the carpets that had been rolled out over the sand under the awning. The baskets were filled with cloth-wrapped packages, from which the rich scent of cooked meats arose; as the packages were carefully opened, a sumptuous feast was revealed.

Looking on, with Alvarado and the other captains peering over his shoulders, Cortés had two thoughts uppermost in his mind. First: was this food poisoned? Second: although the local breads, eggs, vegetables, guavas, avocados and prickly pears were obviously harmless, might there not be human flesh amongst the many different cooked meats – none obviously recognisable – being offered here? The rich sauces could disguise a multitude of sins.

'Ask him to describe the meat dishes,' Cortés told Malinal.

With some pride and apparent relish, taking time to explain how they had been cooked and the sauces that accompanied them, Teudile pointed out dishes of quail, turkey, duck and other fowl, several types of fish, and also wild peccary, deer, monkeys, hares and dogs.

'They have dogs here?' asked Cortés with surprise, and some concern, because the Maya – to the advantage of the Spaniards – had been terrified by the war hounds and had not seemed to understand what sort of creatures they were. Malinal explained this was because the dogs of the conquistadors were much larger and very different in appearance from the animals the Mexica called *itzcuintli*, also known to the Maya, which were small, hairless, did not bark and were bred almost exclusively for the kitchen, though some were kept as pets. Nonetheless she had taken the opportunity to study the Spanish dogs over the past weeks and confirmed they did indeed belong to the same tribe as the *itzcuintli*. 'Their meat is good,' she said. 'Try it. You will enjoy.'

Cortés nodded. He had no objection to eating dogs. 'Ask if there is any human flesh or blood amongst these dishes,' he said. 'Question him closely. Make sure I get a truthful answer.'

But no sooner was the question put than Teudile was on his feet with a worried expression on his face. 'I regret not *tuele*,' he replied – Cortés now recognised the Mexica word for 'god' – 'but we are ready to serve.' While speaking he had produced a small flint knife from some pocket of his robes with which he now slit the lobe of his own left ear.

'What in God's name is the man doing?' Cortés exclaimed.

'He thinks you're angry that they didn't provide human blood,' said Malinal, 'so he's offering you some of his own.'

One of the black-robed priests bounded forward, clutching a small silver cup that he held under Teudile's ear, collecting the stream of blood flowing from it. He then approached Cortés and attempted to press the brimming cup to his lips, but Cortés dashed it angrily aside, and dealt the priest several blows about the buttocks with the flat of his sword, making the man jump and screech in pain. Driven out from under the awning into the sun, the priest took shelter behind the escort of Cuahchic warriors, who were lined up in two ranks of ten, frowning and grimacing mightily at the Spaniards.

An idea occurred to Cortés and he turned ferociously on Teudile. 'Tell him this,' he said to Malinal through Aguilar. 'Tell him I don't like and *will not permit* blood sacrifices.' He pointed to the two Totonac captives who were standing surrounded by the other four priests near the edge of the awning. 'Tell him to release those men. That is my wish. That is my order. Tell him it must be done now.'

'But Lord,' objected Teudile, 'your lieutenant Moctezuma commanded they be sacrificed for you and that we prepare their flesh for you while it is fresh and offer it to you to eat.'

'What you are proposing is *abominable* to me!' Cortés yelled. 'Do you hear? *Abominable*. Release those men at once.' He strode over to Alvarado who was watching with amusement. 'Time to bring up Bucephalus,' he said with a wink. 'You'll send for him?'

Moments later, while Malinal was still embroiled in what appeared to be a heated argument with Teudile, there came a great neighing and whinnying as Alvarado's groom walked Bucephalus up the slope and tethered the huge creature close to the awning where the mare had earlier stood. The stallion, which was fully barded in its gleaming steel armour, at once began to paw the ground and snort menacingly, and twice reared up, lashing the air with its hooves, causing consternation amongst the Mexica. The formidable Cuahchics, who stood closest to it, drew back in horror while Teudile gazed at it from under the awning, his face grey and his eyes bulging. Only the artists, to their credit, did not break off from sketching and painting even when, in the midst of all this, Telmo Vendabal appeared with five of his largest wolfhounds, also decked out in armour. When they scented the Mexica delegates, they began to snarl and bark and strain on their leashes towards them.

'As you can see,' said Cortés to Teudile, 'our war animals are angry with you because of your sacrifices. Will you obey me and release your two captives now?'

'It is not what my lord the Great Speaker wishes,' said Teudile stubbornly.

'But it is what I wish,' said Cortés, 'and has not my lieutenant Moctezuma ordered you to please me?'

Teudile barked a command to the priests, the bonds of the captives were cut and they at once ran off through the camp.

'Good,' said Cortés. 'Now we're making progress.'

'Will you eat the other dishes they have prepared for you?' Malinal asked.

'Do you think we should?'

'Yes. I advise it. It's probably some sort of test. If you are Quetzalcoatl returning, they'll expect you to relish the food of your homeland.'

'Very well, we will eat,' said Cortés. 'But I suspect poison. Tell them if we eat that they must eat also from the same dishes.'

89

Malinal smiled. 'The food will not be poisoned,' she said.

'Still, they must eat with us.'

After a pause while they waited for Teudile and Pichatzin to sample all the dishes first, Cortés persuaded his captains to join in the meal; soon a positive atmosphere had been restored with some small talk exchanged between the two sides. The food proved to be excellent and the final course, gourds filled with the dark drink called *chocolatl*, elicited particular praise from the Spaniards.

'The ambassador apologises,' Malinal told Cortés as the dishes were cleared away. 'He says he doubted the ancient traditions of Quetzalcoatl and his hatred of human sacrifice, but now he knows that every word was true.'

While she spoke, Teudile had signalled bearers forward, who set down three large baskets in front of Cortés. 'These are presents for you,' Malinal explained after Teudile had spoken. 'They've been sent by Moctezuma himself. He wishes you to choose the one that most pleases you and to give the others to the gods who are here with you.'

The baskets were piled high with folded cloths and featherwork. On top of one was a cone-shaped helmet of gold, to which Cortés felt his eyes strongly drawn. On top of the second was an elaborate head-dress adorned with green feathers. On top of the third was a mask in the form of a serpent's head, a woven pectoral with a small gold disk in the centre and earrings with curved gold pendants.

'Choose the basket with the serpent mask,' Malinal advised through Aguilar.

'I prefer the helmet,' Cortés said. 'There's more gold in it.'

'The impact will be greater if you choose the basket with the serpent mask. It's the one that contains the finery of Quetzalcoatl.'

Cortés chose accordingly and Teudile, seeming suitably impressed, insisted on dressing him up in the regalia from the basket. Cortés went along with this, examining the items as they were hung around his body. There was disappointingly little gold.

'Is this all he has for me?' Cortés asked, taking off the serpent mask and setting it down. 'Is this your gift of welcome? Is this how the great Moctezuma greets his visitors?'

Teudile gave orders to his minions and a great many more baskets of presents were laid out on the carpets under the awning. 'Now we're getting somewehere,' said Alvarado excitedly as he opened the baskets one by one. 'Gods! There's a king's ransom here!' He delightedly picked up a heavy gold plate and hung a gold pectoral around his neck. Meanwhile Puertocarrero had helped himself to a pair of golden cups in the shape of eagles with outstretched wings and was studying them greedily. Cortés noticed how Juan Escudero, the most fanatical of the Velazquistas, weighed everything in his hands, no doubt calculating the value of this hoard so that he could report it to his master Diego de Velázquez as soon as he got back to Cuba. Here were gold necklaces worth thousands of pesos, gold earrings – even golden sandals. Here were heaps of precious stones. Here were beautiful figures of birds and beasts and strange mythical creatures, all fashioned in gold and silver, some with emeralds for eyes. There were also piles of woven cloth, and curious, richly coloured items of featherwork, some shaped like shields, some in the form of capes and hats. But these last were largely ignored; it was around the items of gold that the Spaniards clustered most eagerly.

Teudile was watching, his hooded eyes glittering. 'I see you *tueles* like gold very much,' he said.

'We have need of it,' Cortés said bluntly. Remembering his conversation with the savage Mayan chief Muluc by the riverside in Potonchan, he added with a straight face, 'Many of us suffer from a disease of the heart that can only be cured by gold . . . Say, how are the reserves of this metal in your country? Do you have mines? Or do you bring your gold here from faraway places to be worked?'

'Our land is rich in gold,' Teudile answered proudly. 'We find it in our rivers. We find it beneath the ground.'

Fool! Cortés thought. *If I were in your shoes I wouldn't have shared that information.*

But the ambassador's attention was already elsewhere. His eyes had settled on Bernal Díaz, the leg wound he'd received at Potonchan healed now, who was wearing as he often did a battered, somewhat rusty, half-gilt *morion* helmet. 'Might I see that?' Teudile asked.

'Surely yes,' said Cortés. He waved Díaz over. 'Mind if His Excellency here takes a look at your helmet, Bernal? It seems to have taken his fancy.'

'He's welcome to,' said Díaz, a grin lighting up his big honest face as he passed the *morion* over. 'Be happy to exchange it for some of that gold of his.'

Teudile, Pichatzin and the other Mexica delegates examined the helmet, turned it over in their hands, held it up to the light and peered inside its peaked dome. Finally Teudile said: 'It greatly resembles a helmet that was left to us by our ancestors; we keep it now in the temple of our war god Hummingbird. May I take this one with me when I return to Tenochtitlan? I'm sure my Lord Moctezuma will wish to see it.'

'Any objection, Bernal?' Cortés asked.

That farmboy grin again. 'Tell him to bring it back full of gold,' Díaz replied.

Good idea, thought Cortés. *It can settle once and for all whether they really have mines or whether that is just a boast.* 'You know, Teudile,' he said, 'I'm curious whether the gold of your country is the same as the gold we find in our own rivers and mines. Like you I serve a great lord who rules many lands, so can I suggest after you have shown the helmet to your emperor that you bring it back to me filled with grains of gold as a present for my emperor?'

'It will be done,' said Teudile suspiciously. 'But if you are a god, how is it that you serve a great lord?'

'I am no god,' Cortés answered gravely. 'I am a man, just like you.'

'My Lord Moctezuma says you are Quetzalcoatl, come to reclaim your kingdom—'

'I myself claim no such thing! My name is Don Hernándo Cortés. I serve a great emperor across the seas who rules my country, which is called Spain. Both my emperor and I worship the one true God who resides in Heaven and rules over the earth, whose son is Jesus Christ, and beside whom there are no other gods.'

Teudile was looking deeply confused. 'Then tell me, man or god or whatever you are, why have you come here to our land? What do you want with us?'

Cortés said that he was here because his religion, called Christianity, was the only true faith on earth, and that it was his duty as a Christian to bring news of it to other peoples around the world. In particular he was required to teach those who lived in ignorance of Christ to abandon their false gods, such as this Hummingbird whom the Mexica worshipped, who in reality was not a god but a demon, sent to mislead mankind and damn the souls of those who followed him to burn in hell for eternity.

Teudile's face clouded while Malinal put all this into Nahuatl for him. He then asked again why Cortés had chosen to come to the lands of the Mexica rather than to other lands. This, Cortés lied, was on account of the emperor he served, Don Carlos, the greatest lord on earth, who had many great princes as his vassals and servants. 'Even on the other side of the ocean, rumours of your land and of your emperor have reached my lord, and because of these he sent me here to meet the great Moctezuma, and establish friendship with him, and bring the Christian faith to him, and tell him many things that will delight him when he knows and understands them.' To this end, Cortés added, it was his intention to travel to the place where Moctezuma was and to meet with him at the earliest possible moment.

'You have only just arrived,' spluttered Teudile, looking shocked. 'You admit to being a man and not a god, yet already you wish to speak with our emperor?'

'That is my wish and my intention,' Cortés said.

'Such a meeting was not to be arranged, even if you were a god,' Teudile countered. 'Our Great Speaker is no less a monarch than this Don Carlos of yours, being likewise a mighty lord served by lesser lords. Nonetheless, I will go to him to discover what his pleasure may be in this matter and return to you with his answer. In the meantime,' he indicated the gifts that the Spaniards were still eagerly examining, 'I ask you to enjoy these presents, which have been bestowed on you in Moctezuma's name.'

Cortés rubbed his hands together. 'Ambassador Teudile,' he said, 'I am glad we understand each other so well. And in return for the gifts you have given us, we also have gifts for you. He turned to a box that had been placed earlier at the side of his chair, pulled out some Spanish beads of coloured, twisted glass and ceremoniously handed these over.

'Kindly send these to your towns and summon their inhabitants to trade with us, for we have many more of these beautiful beads, which we would like to exchange for gold.' Teudile, whose expression was unreadable, gave thanks and passed the beads to a retainer.

Cortés then signalled to two of his soldiers to bring over some more glass beads, necklaces and bracelets, some pearls, a silk coat, looking glasses, scissors, straps, sashes, shirts, handkerchiefs, an inlaid folding armchair, similar to his own, and a crimson cap, to which was attached a small gold medal stamped with a figure of Saint George on horseback killing a dragon. These, he said, were presents for the great Moctezuma himself, and he would like it if Moctezuma would sit in the armchair and wear the crimson cap when he himself came to visit him. He added: 'In the temples where you keep the idols that you believe to be your gods, I wish you to set up the cross of Christ and an image of Our Lady with her precious son in her arms. If you do that, you will prosper.'

Teudile appeared aghast. 'Such a thing is impossible,' he said flatly.

'Nevertheless, kindly convey my wishes to your lord Moctezuma. I am sure he will agree, and when he does I will arrange to have these sacred objects sent to him or bring them to him myself.' A sudden change of subject: 'Now tell me please, Ambassador Teudile, about the great Moctezuma. What sort of man is he? Is he a young man, or mature, or in his old age? Is he an old man now, with white hair? And if old, is he still able or is he aged and infirm? Kindly describe his appearance for me so that I already have a picture of him in my mind when I meet him face to face, which most assuredly I will.'

As Malinal put the question into Nahuatl, Cortés noticed that all the Mexica delegates were paying close attention and that the four sorcerers made strange signs with their hands and muttered ferociously under their breath.

'Our Great Speaker is a mature man in the prime of life,' Teudile eventually replied, 'not stout, but lean with a fine, straight figure. He is vigorous and powerful in battle and has led our forces to many victories over our enemies . . .' A pause: 'We have heard that you *tueles*, or Spaniards, or whatever you call yourselves, are also powerful warriors.

We are informed that you defeated a great army of the Chontal Maya at Potonchan. Is this true?'

'It is true,' Cortés allowed.

Teudile was eyeing Bucephalus, quieter now, still tethered outside the pavilion. 'We heard,' he said – and Cortés did not think he had ever seen a man more obviously fishing for military intelligence – 'that your war animals played a decisive role in your victory.' As Malinal had predicted, the steward then requested a demonstration of the prowess of the horses and dogs.

'Of course,' Cortés said. 'Nothing would give me greater pleasure. Allow my men a few moments to prepare.' He turned to Puertocarrero, Ordaz, Olid, Escalante, Morla, Montejo, Davila and the others he'd selected to ride today and said quietly, 'You know what to do.' The horses stood tethered just out of sight at the foot of the next dune and, as the cavaliers hurried away to mount up, Cortés cast a long glance at Malinal, trying to let her know by the warmth in his eyes how grateful he was for her cleverness in second-guessing the needs and wishes of Moctezuma and formulating this plan to impress and overawe his ambassador. He had always believed that to know one's enemy was more than half the battle of defeating him, so Malinal was rendering a service of inestimable value by showing the Spaniards how to look beneath the daunting appearance of the Mexica to see and understand the primitive fears, superstitions and ignorance that governed everything they did and thought. Yes, Cortés and his conquistadors had now entered the heartland of Moctezuma's power; yes, this savage emperor would be able to throw overwhelming numbers against them – hundreds of thousands! – when war broke out, as it surely would; and yes, his warriors would possess huge advantages arising from their knowledge of the terrain and their access to virtually limitless supplies and reinforcements. Nonetheless, Cortés was confident that working with Malinal to undermine and demoralise Moctezuma in the arena of the mind before he ever met the emperor's forces on the battlefield would ultimately give him victory.

Undoubtedly this woman had charisma, and it was, he thought, something more than simply the enchantment of a great and noble beauty. There was depth to her, and a mystery, that touched his heart and put fire into his soul. As she returned his glance, and he sensed again that special private communion that had somehow grown up between them, he felt a burst of annoyance that she was still obliged to return to Puertocarrero's bed each night after her work of interpreting was done. To be sure the man was his friend, and a useful and important ally, but what had he been thinking of when he had so carelessly handed this treasure over to him?

Alvarado was standing by. At Cortés's signal, he strode out from under the awning with a wide grin, untethered Bucephalus and bounded into the saddle. The massive stallion reared, gave a spirited whinny and wheeled round twice, its front hooves lashing the air again, sending up a spectacular spray of sand, before Alvarado urged it into a rushing, plunging gallop down the dunes. In his gleaming cuirass, with his blond hair flying in the wind, he did indeed have the aspect of some god, Cortés thought; as he looked at the astonished faces of the Mexica delegates, he saw a numinous fear written there as they whispered urgently to one another.

'What are they saying?' he asked Malinal through Aguilar.

'They are calling him Tonatiuh,' she explained. 'It means the sun. They imagine he's the sun in human form. It's a great compliment.'

Alvarado had disappeared from sight, but moments later he reappeared, holding a long lance. The rest of the cavalry, all similarly armed, trotted behind him. They made a splendid sight, their armour sending off dazzling reflections as they descended the soft sand of the dunes, and the hundreds of little bells that Malinal had suggested should be attached to the horses' barding chimed and jingled melodiously as they made their way onto the wide expanse of the beach. There they arrayed themselves into a long line, spurred immediately into a gallop, and with yells of 'Santiago and at them!', levelled their lances and charged off at tremendous speed.

'Would you like to look closer, Ambassador Teudile?' asked Cortés. 'Perhaps we may all walk out a little into the sun to observe the display better?' Malinal translated the proposition and the Mexica delegates, including their wizards, priests, artists and the twenty Cuahchics, all followed Cortés to the edge of the dune, where the lombards had been set up on their carriages and aimed inland towards a copse of pines, half a mile distant, that had taken root in the sandy soil. All three of the heavy cannon were primed and ready to fire, their gun crews, under Mesa's command, standing by with lighted tapers.

'Your war animals are very fast,' observed Teudile as he watched the receding line of horsemen.

'As fast as the wind,' said Cortés.

Teudile's eye was suddenly caught by the fleet of great carracks and caravels moored out in the bay; though visible from beneath the awning, it was as though the ships had only now attracted his attention. He and the other delegates stood staring at them, speaking amongst themselves in hushed tones. 'What do they say?' Cortés asked Malinal.

'They wonder if your ships are your temples,' she answered, and again her eyes seemed to communicate something private and personal to Cortés. 'They are interested in the sails because Quetzalcoatl is a god of the wind.'

A mile away on the beach, the cavalry split elegantly into two files, a standard battleground manoeuvre, curved out left and right in great semicircles, reformed into a single line and came charging back.

Tearing their gaze away from the ships, the Mexica officials watched open mouthed as the horsemen galloped full tilt towards them, their hooves drumming on the packed, wet sand, their bells jingling, lances and armour flashing in the sun. Cortés waited until the troop had passed beneath the viewpoint and gave the signal to Mesa; at the same moment he, Malinal, Aguilar and all the other Spaniards nearby raised their hands unobtrusively and covered their ears. The Indians were so absorbed in the display of the cavalry, and the ships looming out in the bay beyond, that they noticed nothing until all three of the lombards discharged at once with a tremendous, earthshaking concussion and recoil, fire billowing from their barrels, great clouds of noxious smoke rising up and the whistle of the three seventy-pound balls flying through the air.

Cortés found the effect on the Mexica comical, and it was only with great difficulty that he was able to stop himself laughing out loud as every one of them, even the painted Cuahchics, threw themselves down with great shrieks and howls of fear, rolling and moaning in the sand. Nor was their ordeal over. Even as Teudile tried to get to his feet and recapture some of his shattered dignity, Cortés gave another signal and his entire corps of fifty musketeers marched forward, levelled their weapons at wooden targets that had been set up thirty paces distant and fired over the heads of the Indians, provoking more groans and screams of terror. With a despairing cry, Teudile threw himself once more onto the sand.

Again, Cortés noticed, it was only the artists who maintained any kind of self-possession, quickly returning to their paints and parchments to sketch accurate images of the cannon, the muskets and the galloping cavalry.

Over the next two hours, with looks of awe and sighs of wonderment, the Indians were shown the splintered and shattered targets, inspected the shredded and flattened pines in the copse where the cannonballs had struck, and were allowed to see the lombards fired again and a further demonstration of sharpshooting by the musketeers. The fifty dogs that Vendabal and his assistants had armoured were then brought out in a pack and paraded before them, and half a dozen of the largest animals, fed to satiety to reduce the risk of a serious accident, were let loose amongst the delegates and bounded threateningly around them, sniffing and snarling at their feet. A mastiff knocked one of the priests to the ground, planted its forepaws on his chest and dripped gouts of saliva on his face through bared fangs before an assistant drove it away from him with a whip. A greyhound cocked its leg and urinated on the hem of the young magician's ornate feathered cloak.

The last marvel, to which Teudile, Pichatzin, one of the carmine-cloaked officials, two of the artists, two of the priests and all four of the magicians were treated, was a visit by longboat to the *Santa Maria*, bobbing at anchor in the bay. Malinal advised strongly against allowing any of the sorcerers on board, but Cortés convinced her that he, his men and his ships – and she too – were invulnerable to their spells. 'Let them do their worst,' he laughed. 'It will avail them nothing.'

The Mexica were struck dumb with amazement, their eyes wide and their jaws gaping as they were shown around the great carrack, taken above and below decks, and even into the stateroom. Then, since a good breeze was blowing, Cortés ordered the crew to put the ship under full sail, provoking gasps and exclamations of childlike amazement from the visitors who picked their way gingerly from side to side, looking down over the railings at the foaming waves as they raced around the bay. Not long afterwards, however, they all became seasick – an affliction that Malinal, who'd proved to be a good sailor, had ceased to suffer from after her first day at sea – and lay about miserably on deck, groaning and clutching their bellies until the short excursion was over and the *Santa Maria* was again at anchor. Cortés then brought out two large jugs of a potent red wine he kept under lock and key in his stateroom. 'Tell them this is medicine that will help them,' he said to Malinal with a wink. She poured cups for each of the delegates, from which they drank hesitantly at first, then enthusiastically, and were soon much restored.

'Since we have eaten your food,' Cortés told Teudile, 'I desire now that you eat some of ours, even though it is very different.' He offered them biscuits, bacon and beef jerky, washed down with so many more draughts of strong red wine that they all quickly became drunk – which rendered them merry and sentimental. Pichatzin led them in a rendition of several Mexica love songs for the benefit of the Spaniards, and the eldest sorcerer went so far as to kiss Cortés's hands, telling him that he had never in his life enjoyed such a fine drink. Even Teudile admitted that his heart was 'gladdened' by the medicine.

As darkness fell, fatigue overcame the delegates, their eyelids drooping closed. Cortés offered to have them ferried back to shore but Teudile, who had stretched himself out full length on the deck, refused. 'We will sleep here,' he said drunkenly.

Moments later, he was snoring.

Cortés grinned at Malinal. 'You've done very well today,' he said. 'I'm grateful to you.'

'It was nothing,' she replied in Castilian, understanding and answering without help from Aguilar.

'You've done well too, Jerónimo,' Cortés said, clapping Aguilar on the shoulder. 'A good day's work. But I believe the lady and I can manage these fellows until the morning.' He nodded towards the sleeping Indians. 'Take the longboat back to shore; send it out for us again at daybreak.'

'I am not required here?' The ugly emotion of envy was plainly written on Aguilar's face.

'Tonight? No.'

'And Puertocarrero? Will he not need his woman?'

'You trespass, Jerónimo, on matters that do not concern you. Return to shore. I'll see you in the morning.'

Chapter Fourteen

Covered in the dust of the road, footsore and offended, Tozi reached Tenochtitlan on the afternoon of the third day after her departure from Ishtlil's camp. She was offended – or more accurately, she thought, deeply *hurt* – because Huicton had not permitted her to accompany him on his journey to Tlascala for further negotiations with Shikotenka, and from there to the coast to deliver Ishtlil's message to Quetzalcoatl. 'This is diplomacy,' the old man had insisted bluntly, 'and your presence will not be helpful. Where I need you now is back in Tenochtitlan, invisible, spying on Moctezuma, keeping us up to date with his schemes and manoeuvres, not at my side in full view in the courts of powerful men.'

'But I can help you,' Tozi had protested. 'I can work magic. I can make them see things our way. I made Ishtlil see things our way, didn't I?'

'You don't seem to realise how close to disaster we came with Ishtlil,' Huicton had replied gravely. 'Your rash behaviour put us both in great danger. I'm not prepared to take the same risk with Shikotenka, much less with this foreigner camped at Cuetlaxtlan who you continue to insist must be Quetzalcoatl.'

Tozi stamped her foot. 'He *is* Quetzalcoatl! I am called to his service.'

'Perhaps he is,' Huicton reflected, 'and perhaps you are. But perhaps not. Either way, I won't have you there.'

'You can't stop me,' Tozi sulked. 'I'll make myself invisible. You won't see me until I choose to show myself.' Even as she uttered the words she realised how childish she suddenly felt and sounded.

Huicton sighed. It was the weary sigh of an old, old man. 'My dear,' he said, 'I trust you to do what you are good at – and you *are* a very good spy – but you must also trust me to do what I am good at. I've been a diplomat and a negotiator for half my long life. This next meeting with Shikotenka is one I must hold alone, and our first encounter with Quetzalcoatl, if that is who he really is . . . well, I must hold that alone also. I will not keep you apart from him for long, I promise, but now is not the time for you to meet him. Besides, I mean what I say, Tozi, your place is in Tenochtitlan. Observe Moctezuma. Continue to undermine his confidence and his judgement, work on the destruction of his mind. This is where your skills are needed.'

But now, as she entered the Mexica capital from the north along the Azcapotzalco causeway, now as she made her way through the bustling market square of Tlatelolco in the late-afternoon sunlight, now as she approached the sacred precinct overshadowed by the great pyramid, now as the gates of the royal palace itself lay before her, Tozi found that Moctezuma was not the first focus of her thoughts.

A woman! What was this? How dare he?

To Tozi's horror, when she stole invisibly into Guatemoc's bedchamber later that night he was not alone.

Instead, in that room lit by flickering torches, she found him naked with a girl named Icnoy, a girl with a slim waist and big breasts and round buttocks, who she recognised as a member of Moctezuma's own harem. But in the Great Speaker's lavish bed, thanks in large part to her own efforts, Tozi had never once seen the effect that a ripe and willing female body could have upon a man; Moctezuma's little *tepulli* was always limp and thin, like some foul worm, no matter how Icnoy or the other women of the harem sought to persuade it.

Not so with Guatemoc. His *tepulli* was long and thick and wrapped around with pulsing veins, and at this very moment he was thrusting it vigorously in and out of Icnoy, who was on all fours in front of him like some animal, the lips of her *tepilli* swollen and glistening as he entered her deeply, withdrew until almost his whole *tepulli* became visible, then plunged in again whilst she wiggled and circled her bottom, all the while uttering little grunts, gasps and yips of pleasure. Now his hands moved forward to fondle and squeeze her breasts, now he gripped and spread her plump cheeks, now he reached back to squeeze her feet, now he caressed her sleek black hair which hung down damp with sweat around her face.

Altogether it was a disgusting, intimate, unsettling scene, and yet . . . and yet . . . Tozi could not tear herself away, and felt her own *tepilli* parts grow hot and moist between her legs as she watched, spellbound, for what seemed like hours. Finally, when the two of them were done, they lay exhausted, legs and arms intertwined, sighing and stroking one another, and then – worse in a way than all the rest of it – Guatemoc rolled on top of Icnoy and pressed his open mouth against hers, and they kissed, and kissed, and kissed, their tongues working, slurping and sucking at each other, saliva dripping.

Horrible! Tozi thought. Truly horrible! She couldn't believe it. Guatemoc was hers! In her own mind she had already sworn herself to him, and yet here he was, surrendering himself so completely to another.

At last the kiss stopped and the pair, still entangled, seemed to fall asleep. Icnoy snored gently. Guatemoc rolled onto his back, his breathing heavy and regular. Silent, invisible, insubstantial as air, Tozi watched. She had intended to show herself to the prince tonight, reveal herself, and there had been so much she had wanted to say. Instead she had witnessed this shocking, deeply disturbing scene.

Nor was it over! Soon enough, the couple stirred again, Guatemoc's hand slipped between Icnoy's thighs, and she moaned and writhed and coiled herself around him.

Unable to bear it a moment longer, Tozi fled from the room and out into the night.

Chapter Fifteen

◆

Friday 30 April 1519

Before dawn, Icnoy arose and dressed, fretting she would be caught.

'Don't worry,' Guatemoc reassured her as he stretched and yawned on the bed. 'Moctezuma's got . . . what? Fifty concubines? A hundred?'

'He has more, great lord,' the girl replied. 'Close to two hundred.'

'Well, there you go then! Out of two hundred girls, you don't think he's going to miss one, do you?' He slipped his hand under the hem of her tunic and caressed her smooth inner thigh. 'Although mind you,' he added, 'you are a little bit special, I have to admit.'

Icnoy giggled shyly. 'The great lord flatters me.'

'It's no more than you deserve,' said Guatemoc. He'd passed her in a corridor of the royal palace yesterday. She'd caught his eye, so he'd followed her into one of the secluded gardens where they were hidden from view amongst the fruit trees, propositioned her – if you don't try your luck in this world you never win anything – and, to his amazement, she'd agreed to slip out that night and visit him in his town house.

And what a night it had been! She'd told him Moctezuma, never a sexual adept, had been entirely impotent for several months – which perhaps explained her willingness to take the incredible risk of cuckolding the monarch; she had fallen into Guatemoc's bed with truly delightful enthusiasm and excitement. What they'd done was dangerous for both of them, but Guatemoc wasn't worried. On the contrary, he rather thought he'd try his hand with a few more of the Great Speaker's women; poor, needy creatures such as he now knew them to be, it would be uncharitable not to offer them the same consolation he'd given to Icnoy.

Not bothering to dress, he escorted her to the servants' entrance, which opened discreetly onto an unfrequented alley, gave her a passionate kiss and a playful slap on the bottom, and watched her as she slipped away into the darkness pulling a shawl over her head. In the east, where the sun would soon rise, a blush of the softest pink touched the sky. The morning air was cool and fresh. Guatemoc took a deep breath, then another. By all the gods of the thirteenth heaven, he was glad to be alive!

Too energised to return to bed, he performed his ablutions, called on his butler for breakfast, and strolled out into the courtyard to work up an appetite with an hour of vigorous exercise.

Around mid-morning, Guatemoc's closest friends Man-Eater, Starving Coyote, Fuzzy Face, Big Dart and Mud Head paid him a call. High-born scions of five of the noblest, wealthiest, and most powerful families of Tenochtitlan, Eagle and Jaguar warriors every one, they were the captains of his own elite fighting squad. It was they who had carried Guatemoc off to safety after Shikotenka had left him for dead on the night of the great battle with the Tlascalans. But for these five and their decisive action, Guatemoc, helpless at death's door, would certainly have perished when the Mexica field army, more than thirty thousand strong and under the direct command of general Coaxoch, had first been divided into two parts by a clever ruse of Shikotenka's, and then slaughtered so efficiently that hardly three thousand shattered and demoralised men had made it back to Tenochtitlan alive.

But it was a reverse, not a disaster. The Mexica nation was populous, its resources immense, and though one army had been destroyed, five more of equal size were still intact, ready to mete out revenge and gather victims for sacrifice. With four regiments per army, and eight thousand men per regiment, this meant a combined total muster remaining of one hundred and sixty thousand regular soldiers – and that before the hundred thousand auxiliaries available from vassal states were counted, or the fifty thousand Otomi and Chichemec merce-naries Moctezuma had also recently hired. All in all, the vast Mexica war machine was unmatched by any other nation, and was big enough to smash Tlascala to pulp; big enough to crush Ishtlil like a bug; big enough, despite recent reverses, to impose and maintain Mexica hegemony throughout the One World for a thousand years.

If – and this was the point – *if* there was the will.

'We require, indeed we demand, in fact we insist,' said Man-Eater to Guatemoc, 'that you be appointed commander in chief of the five armies.'

It was what Guatemoc wanted, it was what he had begun to manoeuvre for, and his friends and their powerful families played a crucial role in his strategy. But there were obstacles in the way that would first have to be cleared. Most notably, no one could be appointed commander in chief unless he was first a member of The Thirty, the Supreme Council that advised Moctezuma on all matters of State. The problem here was not Guatemoc's blood; as the Great Speaker's own nephew, that could hardly be questioned. Nor was it his age – for younger men of exceptional quality had served amongst The Thirty during previous reigns. No, the heart of the matter was that every place on the council was already filled by nobles in good health, and a vacancy would be needed if Guatemoc were to join.

'There's the problem of The Thirty,' he said casually.

'We've thought about that,' replied Nezahualcoyotl, whose name 'Starving Coyote' was entirely appropriate, since he was small, fast and lean-flanked, with shrewd brown eyes and somewhat prominent ears.

'And what conclusion have you come to?' Guatemoc asked.

'I have received a vision,' said Starving Coyote with a straight face. 'The spirit of prophecy has come upon me and revealed to me that by tomorrow The Thirty will become The Twenty-Nine. Councillor Tototl is to meet with a tragic accident tonight.'

'I see,' said Guatemoc. He smiled. 'You feel there can be no doubt over this prophecy?'

'None at all. Which means, of course, in these troubled times, that a new councillor will have to be appointed immediately. Our fathers are with us on this. They will raise the matter with Moctezuma when the council meets tomorrow and you must ask your father to do the same.'

Guatemoc's father was Cuitláhuac, younger brother of Moctezuma and now the second most powerful lord of the Mexica following

106

Coaxoch's humiliating death at Shikotenka's hands. Cuitláhuac was a stickler for procedure; three months ago there would have been no chance of him supporting a bid by his firebrand son to be appointed a member of The Thirty and commander in chief of all the nation's armies. Following Moctezuma's cowardly attempt to have Guatemoc poisoned, however, things had changed. 'Under the circumstances,' Guatemoc agreed, 'he might lend his weight to this.'

'Nothing could be more urgent,' said Cuatalatl, whose nickname 'Mud Head' had been with him since childhood, its origins long forgotten. 'Moctezuma is losing his grip. We all know it.' So strong he could lift a dozen men on his arms and shoulders, Mud Head was deeply insecure. Now he looked around at the others for reassurance, as though he feared he'd gone too far, said too much.

Ixtomi – 'Fuzzy Face' – grinned through the straggly beard that he'd been unsuccessfully attempting to grow since he was a teenager. 'Losing his grip?' he echoed. 'I'd say he lost it long ago. He's not fit to rule this nation. If we face a crisis as the rumours suggest, then we have to take matters into our own hands.'

'We *need* you in The Thirty, Guatemoc, and we need you at the head of our armies.' It was Huciimuh's – 'Big Dart's' – turn to speak. He was handsome, somewhat long-nosed with unusually round eyes, high cheekbones and a firm chin, but he got his nickname from the fabulous size of his *tepulli* which, it was often jokingly suggested, could be used as a weapon in battle and would soon have all the enemy on the run. 'I believe the rumours,' he added, 'and I think we're about to face a great test. I feel it in my bones. We must put ourselves in a position where we can sweep Moctezuma aside when the need arises. If we fail to do so, the day will come when all will be lost.'

The rumours concerned Guatemoc greatly – far more than he had allowed his companions to realise. They concerned him because they seemed in every way to bear out the warnings of the return of Quetzalcoatl that the elusive goddess Temaz – if she was indeed a goddess! – had given him. He did not know, yet, exactly what to make of this. He only knew that for days Tenochtitlan had seethed with alarms concerning the white-skinned bearded strangers – perhaps gods – who had destroyed an enormous Mayan army at

Potonchan and had since appeared at Cuetlaxtlan, within the borders of the empire. Rumours of gloom and destruction had spread everywhere, dangerously undermining public morale. Although civic laws forbade gatherings of more than twenty people in any one place, assemblies of scores, even hundreds, were seen every day on every street corner, where the gossip was of imminent destruction. As Temaz had uncannily foreseen, many said that Quetzalcoatl had returned to overthrow Moctezuma and all who stood by him, to end human sacrifice, to tear down the temples of Hummingbird and Tezcatlipoca, and to punish the Mexica for their wickedness and cruelty. Terror, astonishment and dejection filled the air and the people were everywhere in distress, some exchanging tearful greetings, some seeking to encourage others. Here was a father smoothing his little son's hair, comforting him against what they all believed was about to come to pass. Here was a mother, weeping, bidding farewell to her children as though she feared she would never see them again. It was said that the white men were few, that they were many, that their bodies were made of shining metal, that they possessed fire-serpents, that wild beasts obeyed their commands, and that they had been seen riding on great deer, tall as houses, and flying on the backs of eagles. Now they were a day's march from Tenochtitlan, now they were at the gates, now they were already within the city, cloaked with invisibility but about to materialise and strike the populace down at a single blow.

It had so far proved impossible to discover the source of the rumours that seemed to proliferate simultaneously, in endlessly new variants, in every quarter of the capital and, moreover, were not confined to Tenochtitlan, but were equally prevalent across the lake in Texcoco and Tacuba. Such was the turmoil, such the unrest, that yesterday the Great Speaker finally conceded what he had attempted to keep secret before – namely that he had already opened negotiations with the strangers, who he indeed believed to be gods; that his steward Teudile had met with them and that he must even now be making haste along the road back to Tenochtitlan.

It was eerie, Guatemoc thought, uncanny really, how the one who called herself Temaz had foreseen all this. He called to mind her words again: 'The time will come, Prince, when you will have to choose. I can only hope you choose wisely.'

There was no doubt in Guatemoc, no hesitation at all. If Quetzalcoatl was really coming, then the only choice for him was to confront the interloper, fight him tooth and nail. Clearly this was not what the Lady Temaz wanted, but he could not concern himself with the whims of a fickle and elusive goddess when the fate of the nation hung in the balance.

Chapter Sixteen

By age-old custom, the meetings of the Supreme Council were held in the assembly room of the House of the Eagle Knights, an imposing rectangular structure of dressed ashlars that dominated the south side of the great plaza adjacent to the pyramid of Hummingbird. Moctezuma sat upright on a stone plinth at the centre of the room, arrayed in his purple robes of state with golden sandals on his feet. The walls around him were painted with richly coloured scenes of ritual warfare, and jutting out from their base were low stone benches decorated with panels in bas-relief, showing intertwined serpents above processions of warriors holding blood-letting instruments and giving homage to Mictlantechutli, the god of death. On these benches sat the councillors, numbering only twenty-eight today since Teudile was still on his way back from the coast, and since Tototl, one of Moctezuma's staunchest supporters, had fallen to his death from his roof garden the night before. Moctezuma was quite certain poor Tototl had been murdered, and his suspicions grew all the darker as he listened first to one councillor then another proposing that Guatemoc – that swollen-headed upstart! – should be appointed to fill the vacant place.

Amongst Guatemoc's principal sponsors, Moctezuma noted, were Chancellor Maxtla, Chief Judge Yayau, Apanec, the Keeper of the House of Darkness, Zolton, the Keeper of the House of Arrows, Tzoncu, the Keeper of the Chalk and, last but by no means least, Cuitláhuac, the royal younger brother, who he'd recently appointed to the role of Serpent Woman, the second office in the land, following Coaxoch's unfortunate demise in battle. It was surely no accident that Cuitláhuac was Guatemoc's father, while the other five were the fathers of Guatemoc's closest associates. Moreover, they'd somehow managed to get the support of Aztaxoch, the Chief of the Refugees from the South. Totoqui, the poet-king of Tacuba, was also with them. Even that snivelling, ungrateful worm Cacama, Lord of Texcoco, who Moctezuma had recently elevated over Ishtlil, the rightful heir, was now enthusiastically praising Guatemoc's qualities. Many others, like a mindless flock of little birds, were swinging the same way.

A discordant note was struck by Chimalli, titular head of the Pochteca guilds, who proposed Xipil, one of Tenochtitlan's richest merchants, as his candidate. When he had finished speaking, Cuitláhuac again took the floor. 'With respect, revered Chimalli,' he said, 'your own presence on our noble council, in itself unthinkable even a generation ago, is more than adequate recognition of the importance of the merchant class. No doubt the day will come when even street traders and stallholders will claim a right to sit amongst The Thirty, but now is not that day. We do not face an auction or a property deal. We face war with a powerful enemy. My son Guatemoc is the pre-eminent warrior of the land and a hero whose miraculous survival of horrific battle injuries leaves no doubt he is beloved of our gods.' Cuitláhuac turned to face Moctezuma: 'The decision is of yours alone, sire,' he said, but I urge you to reflect deeply and appoint Guatemoc not only to your council, but also as commander in chief of our armies. No man could be better suited to the task or to the responsibility.'

As a sigh of approval echoed around the room, Moctezuma kept his face grave and expressionless, aware – as others were not – of the subtle undertone in Cuitláhuac's words and in his manner. A few months ago, his younger brother would never have dared to speak out in this way, but then, crucially, had come the failed poisoning plot, instigated by Moctezuma himself in the hope of doing away with Guatemoc once and for all while he lay gravely wounded and already close to death in the royal hospital. Unfortunately – and, rumour had it, through supernatural intervention – Guatemoc had discovered the plot, Cuitláhuac had intervened and the poisoner Mecatl had been caught red handed. Of course Mecatl had claimed he was acting under Moctezuma's orders and had failed to recant while being flayed alive.

111

Moctezuma, for his part, had absolutely denied any involvement, but it was obvious that Cuitláhuac suspected the truth.

It was this, more than anything else, that distorted today's discussions. If Moctezuma had not in fact tried to have Guatemoc poisoned, he would have found it much easier to exclude him from the council. As it was, however, any attempt on his part to keep the upstart at bay was bound to be seen by Cuitláhuac as further evidence that he had after all been behind the plot. Besides, there might be a virtue to be made of necessity here. 'Keep your friends close,' in the words of the famed strategist Tlacaelel, who had formalised the rituals of human sacrifice a century before, 'but keep your enemies closer.'

'Very well,' Moctezuma announced abruptly, noting with satisfaction how the chattering, whispering voices that had filled the assembly room at once fell silent and twenty-eight pairs of eyes swivelled in his direction.

He paused for effect. Twenty-eight heads tilted and twenty-eight pairs of ears quivered with anticipation.

'I have decided,' Moctezuma continued, 'that the loyal and worthy Guatemoc, hero of our nation, is appointed a member of The Thirty with immediate effect.'

A further collective sigh of approbation.

'He is young, true, but he is skilled in war and we will value his counsel.'

'I am grateful to the revered Speaker,' Cuitláhuac said, 'but as to the other matter raised—'

'What other matter would that be?'

Cuitláhuac's posture slumped. Clearly, and this was as it should be, he had not yet forgotten his habit of deference to his older brother. Nonetheless, Moctezuma noted with displeasure, he was determined to speak.

'It is the matter of our armed forces,' Cuitláhuac continued. 'We cannot leave them long without a commander in chief.'

'And you wish me to consider Guatemoc for this role also?' Moctezuma's tone conveyed deep disapproval, even disgust.

'I do, sire, if it pleases you.'

'I do not know yet whether it pleases me or not. Let us first see how your son – my royal nephew – performs in his new position as councillor. If he does well, who knows, we may even decide to appoint him to the high office you seek for him. But if he fails, then that will be another matter.'

Some minutes later, after a number of routine points of order had been dealt with, Moctezuma adjourned the meeting. Though they coloured everything that had been said, he had pointedly refused to discuss the rumours of the return of Quetzalcoatl. In a very few days, his loyal steward Teudile would arrive from the coast with his own first-hand impressions of the god.

Until then, the only appropriate course for the royal dignity was to remain silent.

Chapter Seventeen

During Huicton's previous visit to Tlascala, he had been permitted to call upon Shikotenka in his home, and even to meet his clever and beautiful wife Xilonen, but there was no such informality about today's encounter, which took place on the floor of the Senate with almost every high notable of the fiercely independent mountain republic attending.

'Ambassador Huicton,' said Shikotenka, 'I am told you are here to persuade us to join forces not only with your master Ishtlil, but also to throw in our lot with the white-skinned strangers who presently infest the dunes outside the Mexica vassal city of Cuetlaxtlan.'

Infest the dunes?

Shikotenka's tone was that of a man describing an outbreak of head lice, not the miraculous arrival of strange and powerful gods. And whereas at their last meeting it had been his roguish charm that had shone through, today what Huicton noticed more were the flat, impassive planes of his face, the determined set of his wide, sensual mouth, and the calculating cruelty of his eyes. In his home the young Tlascalan battle-king had worn only a colourful length of cloth wrapped around his waist that covered his legs to just below his knees, not hiding the combat scars that crisscrossed his shins, abdomen, chest and arms, and Huicton remembered thinking – *this is a man who stands and fights; this is a man who does not run away.* Now the same steadfast solidity and warrior pride that he had sensed in Shikotenka was even more apparent, and it was clear that for some reason he had taken an intense dislike to the white men on the coast.

'You speak,' said Huicton, following an instinct, 'as though you have direct experience of these strangers.'

'I do,' said Shikotenka, his voice filled with malice, 'and you are a fool to imagine they will aid Ishtlil against the Mexica. Quite the opposite is true. They are hand in glove with the Mexica. I saw the evidence of this myself, for I was there at Cuetlaxtlan just days ago and observed a close alliance in the making. The Mexica have given these white-skins every hospitality, lavished sustenance upon them, built shelters for them to make them comfortable, and are showering them with honour and respect. The white-skins return the favour! Their arrival, in my view, is a deadly threat to all of us, for they are doughty warriors and with their support the Mexica may prove impossible to defeat. We should drive them back into the sea now, before it is too late, not seek to ally ourselves with them.'

'Doughty warriors, you say? May I take it then, Shikotenka, that you have had direct experience of their battle skills also?'

An expression that Huicton could not read momentarily crossed the Tlascalan's face and then was gone. 'I fought one of them,' he said.

'And . . . ?'

'I have never met his like in combat. We were five but he killed Acolmiztli – you know who I speak of?'

'The great captain Acolmiztli? Yes of course.'

'He's dead now, slaughtered by the white-skin, and three more of my men lie in the infirmary recovering from their injuries.'

'But how? How is this possible?' Knowing the martial qualities of the Tlascalans, Huicton was genuinely stunned that five of them could have been vanquished by a single foe.

'The white-skin was unafraid of us. He wore metal armour that turned our knives. His weapons were of metal too, of a kind never seen before in the One World. I came face to face with him, dagger to dagger, but other white-skins appeared with a pack of their war wolves and we had no choice but to flee the field—'

'War wolves?'

'They have animals, somewhat like wolves, that they have trained for war.' Shikotenka lifted the hem of the full-length tunic he wore today, showing bloody lacerations at his ankle. 'Their wolves pursued us but we outran them.'

That expression was back on the battle-king's face, and this time

Huicton knew it for what it was – anguish at the loss of his comrade in arms, shame at having been forced to turn his back on an enemy, and a cold-blooded thirst for revenge.

'What of the notion that they are gods?' Huicton asked. 'I have it on good authority that Moctezuma believes their leader to be Quetzalcoatl returned.'

'As ever, Moctezuma is a fool. What we face here is not the return of the Plumed Serpent but the arrival on the shores of the One World of a new and terrible kind of men.'

'Nonetheless, Moctezuma believes they are Quetzalcoatl and his divine companions and that they have come to overthrow him. He has sent a mission to them.'

'We saw no mission from Tenochtitlan while we were there. Only Pichatzin and his lackeys from Cuetlaxtlan, licking the white-skins' arses.'

'Moctezuma's delegation was led by his steward Teudile. Perchance it reached the white-skins after your own, er . . . departure.'

'After we had *fled* you mean? Perchance. But what of it?'

'I am of the opinion, lord, that there is something in this situation that we enemies of Moctezuma may exploit. True you have seen these white-skins enjoying Mexica hospitality, but we do not know yet what their real motives are—'

'That is my view also,' interjected a quiet, somewhat unsteady voice. Huicton looked up to see that the speaker was Shikotenka the Elder, civil king of Tlascala and father of Shikotenka the battle-king. Neither the aged, wizened father nor the vigorous and virile son held their positions through blood, but had been elected on merit by the Senate and could be removed from power by the same body at any time.

'Just because you've taken a thrashing from a white-skin warrior,' Shikotenka the Elder addressed his son, 'just because your pride is hurt . . .'

'Just because I mourn the loss of a dear friend . . .'

'Even so, it does not mean we should rush to judgement. You were, if I understand correctly, in the process of carrying off one of these strangers – a mere boy, you conceded in your report to the Senate – when the man who bested you intervened?'

'It is so,' Shikotenka admitted.

'Well then, this man, whoever he was, can hardly be blamed for putting up a fight to protect one of his own people. That he did so tells us nothing whatsoever about the plans of the white-skins. I agree with Ambassador Huicton. We should find out more about them before we commit ourselves to opposing them.'

'I second that view,' said Maxixcatzin, a venerable chief of some sixty years of age, still very strong and active, who served as deputy to both Shikotenkas. 'If an alliance with the white-skins can make the Mexica impossible to defeat, then we should do everything possible to displace the Mexica and secure such an alliance for ourselves.'

'Pah!' Shikotenka was actually shaking with rage and looked furiously from his father to Maxixcatzin and then to Huicton. 'I am tired of the counsel of old men! I have faced these white-skins, which none of you has done, and I tell you that they are not our friends. Perhaps you are right. Perhaps their seeming alliance with the Mexica is only a ruse. Perhaps in time they will eat Moctezuma up; it would not surprise me. In fact, I believe they will eat us all up! Our only hope is to confront them while they are newly arrived, while they have still not gained a proper foothold in these lands, and to destroy them utterly.'

The deliberations of the Senate went on all morning and the upshot was that Shikotenka the Younger was forbidden to mount an attack on the mysterious strangers he called the 'white-skins'. Only if they marched in force against Tlascala itself was such a move to be contemplated. Meanwhile no state of war with them was deemed to exist. They were to be watched, and watched closely, in an effort to learn what it was they really wanted, but that was all.

As he made his way out of the Senate, Huicton was approached by Shikotenka the Elder and Maxixcatzin. 'We will be pleased,' the aged civil king said, 'to hear the result of your mission to the white-skins.'

'It will be my honour, and it is my master's wish, that I should share it with you,' Huicton replied. 'I'll make a point of passing through Tlascala on my way back to Ishtlil.'

'My son opposes all alliances,' mused Shikotenka the Elder. 'Whether with the white-skins, or with Ishtlil and his rebels, he's loath to compromise our independence.'

'That is understandable,' said Huicton, ever the diplomat.

'Even so, these are times of miracles and wonders,' Shikotenka the Elder said. 'We cannot stop the river of history when it flows in spate.'

'Better to flow with it than be swept away and destroyed,' Maxixcatzin added.

'Indeed so,' Huicton agreed. 'Indeed so.'

Later that day, as he began the long trek down from the mountains to the coast, he thought long and hard on that brief conversation. The only possible interpretation was that Shikotenka the Elder and Maxixcatzin were after all in favour of an alliance with the white-skins, if one could be made. Despite its elected kings, Tlascala was a democratic place, and if they could get enough votes in the Senate they could strike a peace, even if Shikotenka the Younger opposed it.

But what if the battle-king was right? What if these white men's presence spelled the doom not just of Moctezuma, as Tozi fondly imagined, but of Texcoco and Tlascala and indeed of all the myriad peoples and all the vibrant cultures of the One World?

Despite the heat of the afternoon sun, Huicton shivered as the chill of a great responsibility settled like snow upon his aching shoulders.

Chapter Eighteen

Tuesday 4 May 1519

Watching Moctezuma's reactions as the four leading sorcerers of the court delivered their report to him, the word that came into Guatemoc's mind was *coward*. But he kept silent. Even his father Cuitláhuac, who stood second only to the Great Speaker, would not yet dare to voice such an insult. Still, there was no doubt. Now that he had been put severely to the test, Moctezuma was proving himself to be not only a treacherous deceiver and poisoner, but also a weakling and a fool.

The four sorcerers, none of whom Guatemoc had the least respect for, were squatting in a semicircle on mats on the floor of the House of the Eagle Knights, at the feet of Moctezuma, who sat on his plinth, gasping with fear and actually weeping as they recounted their dismal failure to drive the strangers away with magic. Guatemoc suppressed a yawn as ancient Cuappi tried to excuse his own utter uselessness by claiming the strangers were not human beings but gods who were so powerful that all sorcery was ineffectual against them. 'We are not their equals,' he bleated. 'We are as nothing compared with them.' Young Hecateu, with his ridiculous crested hairstyle, then claimed that the strangers were constantly on guard and this was why it had been impossible to send poisonous animals against them or cast a deep sleep upon them. Tlilpo said he had conjured up many fearsome visions but the strangers had paid no attention to them. Aztatzin supported Cuappi's view that the strangers were indeed gods, adding, 'Their flesh was so tough that even our magical needles couldn't penetrate it, their entrails were dark and their hearts were impossible to locate. Try as we might, we couldn't harm them at all.'

'Your words have vanquished me – ' Moctezuma shed more womanly tears – 'and thrown me into confusion. Must these gods then come to Tenochtitlan? Does the future hold no hope for me?'

The magicians sat silently, their long faces filled with fear.

'Speak!' Moctezuma said. 'I command you to speak.'

Tlilpo looked at the others and seemed to share a silent communication with them. They all nodded their heads and he uttered a series of dry coughs. 'We must tell you the truth, great lord,' he said finally. 'The future has already been determined and decreed in heaven, and Moctezuma will behold and suffer a great mystery which must come to pass in his land. If our king wishes to know more about it, he will learn soon enough, for it comes swiftly. This is what we predict, since he demands that we speak, and since it must surely take place, he can only wait for it.'

'Nonsense!' Guatemoc couldn't stop himself from crying out. 'The ramblings of imbeciles and cowards!' He stood and glared at Moctezuma. 'Your sorcerers offer you a counsel of despair, sire. I implore you not to heed it. Under no circumstances should we wait here passively for doom to descend upon us. We must march out, today, and fight these white men – for they are surely men, not gods, and even if they are gods we must still fight them.'

Guatemoc could feel his father's hand tugging at his robe, pulling him back to his seat, and heard low, fearful whispers from other councillors. To stand in this way in the presence of the Great Speaker was an unprecedented breach of etiquette. 'Sit!' Cuitláhuac hissed. 'Sit and apologise!'

Guatemoc remained standing and addressed Moctezuma again. 'Forgive me, lord,' he said, 'but I believe it is my responsibility to speak my mind. These strangers must not be permitted to do to us what they are said to have done to the Chontal Maya at Potonchan. We must crush them now while they still linger on the coast. We must under no circumstances allow them to come to Tenochtitlan.'

Moctezuma blinked twice and wiped the tears from his cheeks with the sleeve of his robe. 'Nephew,' he said, 'you are newly appointed to our council, you have not yet learnt our ways, and your mind is still much troubled by your recent injuries. I will therefore overlook your discourtesy on this occasion,' his voice rose abruptly, 'but you will be seated *now*. Should I require your advice again I will ask for it.'

As Guatemoc subsided onto the bench, seething with indignation, Moctezuma turned to Teudile. 'Good steward,' he said, 'before we hear your report, we would like to know why it is that the whole city is informed of the strangers' victory at Potonchan, their arrival at Cuetlaxtlan and your mission to them there. Did I not caution you to keep these matters secret until we had the opportunity to consider them fully?'

'Yes, lord, you did so caution me.' Teudile had already suffered a severe public rebuke by the mere fact that the Great Speaker had asked the sorcerers to report first. His voice was now shaky and so small as to be almost inaudible. 'I assure you that I told no one.'

'Then how do you explain the rumours? The gossip? The panic.'

'Sire, I fear a spy must be at work in the palace.'

'A spy? How can that be? We two were alone when we studied the message from the governor of Cuetlaxtlan.'

'It was not me, sire,' Teudile blubbered. 'I told no one the reason for our mission, not even the magicians, not even the priests. I kept everything to myself until we reached the coast.'

'Hmm,' pondered Moctezuma. 'Do you suppose the leak came about through our relay messengers?'

'Perhaps, sire,' said Teudile. 'Or perhaps the merchant named Cuetzpalli.'

'He knew about Potonchan only,' objected Moctezuma, 'and nothing about Cuetlaxtlan.'

'It is a mystery, sire, but I swear, on my life, I was not responsible.'

'On your life,' mused Moctezuma. 'Yes, exactly. I will think on the matter. Meanwhile give us your report, gentle steward.'

Unlike the sorcerers, who had spoken only of their own magical dealings, Teudile's report was lengthy and detailed, and was brought to life by dozens of sketches and paintings produced by his artists. Featuring prominently amongst these, standing by the side of the leader of the strangers, was the figure of a beautiful Mayan woman. It seemed she was fluent in Nahuatl and worked with another of the strangers – who somehow spoke the Mayan tongue – to interpret the leader's words. If there were mysteries everywhere, one of them certainly surrounded this woman who, it emerged, had been held for sacrifice some months before in the fattening pens of Tenochtitlan. She had come beneath Moctezuma's knife on the night of the great holocaust – the same night Guatemoc lay bleeding from the wounds Shikotenka had inflicted on him – and, astonishingly, the Great Speaker had released her. It seemed many of the Supreme Council, including Guatemoc's own father Cuitláhuac, were aware of this shameful breach of sacrificial tradition, which had otherwise been hushed up. But the fact that the woman now served as an interpreter for the strangers was obviously highly significant.

Moctezuma took it as further proof of their divine status and there was, admittedly, much other evidence that seemed to point in this direction. Of particular note, amongst the paintings, were images of the great boats the strangers had arrived in, including one the delegates had been allowed to board, which Teudile described as 'a thing more divine than human, a work of genius.'

Guatemoc found he had to agree. The immense and powerful structure the artists had depicted was unlike any boat known to the Mexica, seeming a thousand times bigger even than the great royal canoe that Moctezuma had commissioned to carry him on his voyages across Lake Texcoco. Moreover this craft, in which the strangers had reached Mexico, was not moved by paddles but by huge sheets of cloth that caught the wind and apparently caused it to rush forward at terrifying speeds.

Despite himself, Guatemoc could not help but be reminded of the legends of Quetzalcoatl, which told of how he would return to claim his kingdom in a boat that moved by itself without paddles.

Was this that legendary boat?

Moctezuma thought so, and was already giving way to fresh tears as he looked through the paintings in which he seemed to find certain proof – if the words of the magicians were not enough! – that a great and terrible doom awaited him.

The appearance of the strangers – their white skin, their luxuriant beards, and some with hair as yellow as the sun – added further to his anguish. Priests were summoned to open the temple archives and bring ancient books containing images of Quetzalcoatl and his demi-gods, and these were found to match very closely with the paintings of the strangers that the artists had produced. Moreover, it seemed the leader of the strangers, while cunningly denying that he was a god and stating his name as Don Hernándo Cortés, had behaved exactly as Quetzalcoatl would have been expected to behave over the matter of sacrifices. He had become furiously angry when human blood and hearts were offered to him, had beaten one of the sacrificing priests black and blue and had insisted the victims be freed. Equally telling, when offered the finery of the gods Tezcatlipoca, Tlaloc and Quetzalcoatl, he had unhesitatingly chosen the latter, and when offered a banquet of the fruits and meats of the land he had eaten everything that was put before him, thus showing himself to be familiar with the food of Mexico, as was to be expected if he was indeed Quetzalcoatl returning to claim his kingdom.

For Guatemoc, the paintings of the strangers' weapons and armour, and the descriptions given of them by Teudile, were impressive and intriguing, but for Moctezuma they were obviously terrifying. It was clear the Great Speaker already had some knowledge of these things from an earlier informant, the merchant Cuetzpalli?, whose testimony he had not shared with the Supreme Council. But it seemed they had been viewed only from afar. Now Teudile and the artists provided close, detailed observations of the strangers' deadly fire-serpents, the horrific crashing noise they made, the clouds of smoke that emanated from them and their terrible destructive power. Then too there were the long knives and the armour of the strangers, crafted from some unknown metal, which made them deadly and invulnerable in battle.

Moctezuma had also heard before of the wild animals that the strangers commanded, already the subject of so many fearful rumours doing the rounds in the city. Teudile had not at any point seen them mount up on the backs of eagles, but he was most impressed by the huge deer they rode, faster than an avalanche in the mountains, and by the ferocious beasts that did their bidding, which he took to be some hitherto unknown species of dog. 'These dogs are enormous,' he said. 'They have flat ears and are spotted like ocelots. They have great dragging jowls and fangs like daggers and blazing eyes of burning yellow that flash fire and shoot off sparks. Their bellies are gaunt, their flanks long and lean with the ribs showing. They are tireless and very powerful. They bound here and there, panting, their tongues dripping venom.'

Guatemoc was almost more fascinated by the expression on Moctezuma's face as he heard this report than he was by the report itself. It was as though the heart of the Great Speaker had fainted, as if it had withered, as if the strangers would not even need to confront him in battle because his own fears had already utterly defeated him.

And worse was to follow, because Teudile next told of how the leader of the strangers had taken a special interest in the Great Speaker himself, frequently expressing his intention to visit him and meet him face to face, asking many probing questions about him and wanting to know details of his age, his physical strength and his exact appearance. At this Moctezuma covered his head with his hands and said: 'I cannot fight these gods; my only choice is to flee. I know a certain cave out by Chapultepec; I will hide myself there.'

Guatemoc was about to risk his own life a second time by objecting to these craven words when, to his amazement, Namacuix, who had recently replaced Ahuizotl as the High Priest, spoke up: 'What is this, O mighty lord,' he said to Moctezuma in a tone of outrage. 'What folly is this in a person of such courage as you? If you run, if you hide, then what will our enemies the Tlascalans say? What will Huexotzinco, Cholula, Tliluhquitepec, Michoacan and Metztitlan say? Think of the contempt they will have for Tenochtitlan, this city that is at the heart of the entire world. Truly it will be a great shame for your city and for all those who remain behind you when the news of your flight becomes known. If you were to die, and they had seen you dead and buried, it would be a natural thing. But how can one explain flight? What will we say, what will we answer, to those who ask about our king? Will we have to say that you have abandoned us? This cannot be, lord! You must strengthen yourself! You must stay on your throne!'

A terrible hush had fallen on the councillors gathered in the assembly room, all of them no doubt waiting, Guatemoc thought, for Moctezuma to order the High Priest's summary execution. Instead the Great Speaker, with a mournful look, merely sighed and said: 'You are right, Namacuix. Thank you for reminding me of my duty. I will master my heart and await my doom here in this city, for my fate has been ordained and Quetzalcoatl has returned to vent his ire against me. But know this! All of us will die at the hands of these gods, and those who survive will be made their slaves and vassals. They are to reign now, for it is fated that I am to be the one to be cast from the throne of my ancestors and leave it in ruins.'

Again, to the profound embarrassment of all present, Moctezuma began weeping.

Guatemoc looked round at the other councillors. Here were his sponsors – Apanec, Zolton, Tzoncu, Maxtla, Yayau – the fathers of his friends. Here was Aztaxoch, the Chief of the Refugees from the South, Here was Cacama, lord of Texcoco, Moctezuma's picked man elevated over Ishtlil, the rightful heir. Here was Totoqui, the poet-king of Tacuba. Here was Guatemoc's own father Cuitláhuac, here Namacuix, here Teudile – and all the others sitting stunned and mute as they observed the catastrophic disintegration of their Great Speaker, the man they had feared above all others, the man they had all sworn to follow and to obey unto death.

It was Teudile who broke the silence. 'It may not be as bad as it seems, sire,' he sought to reassure Moctezuma. 'There is yet hope! I have met these gods, if they are gods, and men if they are men, and they showed great warmth and friendship towards me and towards you, Your Majesty. They embraced our delegation, they ate our food and shared theirs with us, and they insisted that they mean us no harm. In my opinion, lord, you should do everything in your power to gratify them in order not to anger or displease them in any way.'

'Did they indicate,' asked Moctezuma with a sniff, 'how they might be gratified?'

'Yes, lord,' answered Teudile. 'There are two matters that seem to be of paramount importance to them. The first is their great desire to journey here, to Tenochtitlan. Claiming to be men, as they do, they say they serve a powerful emperor who dwells across the eastern ocean, where he rules a rich land called Spain. They say it was he who sent them here for the express purpose of meeting with you and establishing diplomatic relations between his land and ours.'

'That seems harmless enough,' offered Cacama, the smooth and pampered ruler of Texcoco. 'Perhaps they are indeed men, as they say they are, in which case I think we should agree with this request.'

Moctezuma sat brooding on his plinth. 'I don't like the idea of them coming here,' he said finally. 'I don't like it at all.'

'Nonetheless, sire,' persisted Cacama, 'my advice is that if you do not admit the embassy of a great lord such as this King of Spain appears to be, it is a low thing, since princes have the duty to hear the ambassadors of others. If they come dishonestly, you have in your court – ' and at this he looked pointedly at Guatemoc – 'brave captains who can defend us.'

'And if they are in fact gods?' asked Cuitláhuac, who had kept silent until now.

Moctezuma looked up: 'Speak, brother,' he said.

'Suppose they deceive us with this talk of being men, as gods are known to do? Suppose the leader of these strangers really is Quetzalcoatl come to overthrow you?'

Moctezuma nodded: 'Suppose it is so . . . What then, brother?'

'My advice,' said Cuitláhuac, 'is not to allow into your house someone who will put you out of it.'

Moctezuma nodded again and turned his eyes back to Teudile. 'You said, gentle steward, that there is a second matter of great importance to the strangers by which we might gratify them.'

'There is, lord . . .' Teudile reached down to the floor beside his bench and brought up a battered metal helmet. 'The second matter is gold. The strangers say they have great need of it. They say, indeed, that they suffer an ailment of the heart that can only be cured by it.'

From the moment that the strangers' love of gold was mentioned, and their impudent ploy in claiming they needed it for their health, Guatemoc ceased to have any doubt about their identity. As he'd suspected from the outset, these were not gods but audacious men, bandits, risk-takers armed with powerful unknown weapons, but men nevertheless. Serving as their interpreter, the Mayan woman Malinal would of course have informed them about Quetzalcoatl, who their leader Cortés resembled simply by chance, enabling him to act the part. Yet it was notable he had never in fact claimed to be Quetzalcoatl, leaving that conclusion to the gullible and superstitious minds of the Mexica themselves.

Clever, Guatemoc thought. *Very clever!*

Then there was the business of the strangers' helmet. Moctezuma had called for the sacred helm kept in the temple of Hummingbird to be brought forth, and almost lost his senses when he saw similarities between the two objects. Guatemoc was less convinced by the likeness; what interested him more was Cortés's opportunism in asking for the helmet to be returned filled with grains of gold from the mines, supposedly as a present for his far-off emperor. Were that request to be granted, Guatemoc reasoned, then this daredevil pirate would gain valuable and dangerous knowledge. It would confirm that the land of the Mexica was rich in gold and therefore well worth attacking!

So, as the meeting of the Supreme Council went on from afternoon into evening, with many different points of view and many competing arguments expressed, Guatemoc found himself increasingly opposed to the emerging consensus. This was that excuses should be made to refuse the strangers' wish to come to Tenochtitlan – that the road was too long, that it abounded in thieves, that it was beset by the enemies of the Mexica, that there were dangerous cliffs to scale and rivers to cross, that the passes were too high and frozen all year round . . . and so on and so forth. At the same time, the strangers' other wish – that the helmet should be returned filled with grains of gold – was to be granted. And not only that. Moctezuma, who was gaining courage from the idiotic notion that these predators could simply be bought off, was in favour of giving them other gold presents – and in huge quantities. He had in mind the spectacular calendar disk of solid gold, as tall as a man and a span thick, that he had commissioned the year before. To this he would add, since the strangers had also expressed a desire for presents made of silver, a second disk of similar size cast from the highest grade of silver and representing the full moon. There would in addition be ten basket-loads of beautiful gold figures – of animals, birds, gods and goddesses – and ten basket-loads of costly gold jewels, including necklaces, pectorals and arm rings, ankle rings, and many other fine things. Warming even further to the idea, the Great Speaker now insisted that this vast treasure should be prepared with the greatest haste and a caravan made ready to set off for the strangers' camp near Cuetlaxtlan the next day.

'Sire,' said Guatemoc. 'May I be permitted to speak?'

Moctezuma glared at him: 'Speak, nephew, but be brief. My mind is made up.'

'Sire, I beg your forbearance but I believe we are about to make a terrible mistake. The reasons it has been suggested we give to the strangers to persuade them they cannot make the journey to Tenochtitlan are foolish and obviously untrue. They know already from Teudile's visit to them that our own emissaries can make the journey in less than six days, and this will be proved to them again when the caravan reaches them so soon. If we can travel the roads in so short a time, and suffer no harm, then the strangers will realise that they can do so also. They will rightly take our excuses as signs of our vulnerability and fear. At the same time, the golden treasure you propose sending them will not satisfy but whet their appetites, convincing them if we can be so generous that we must have much more in reserve – and I have no doubt they will want that too. In short, we will show them our weakness while at the same time igniting their greed and inducing them to attack us. Nothing could be more dangerous, sire. I urge you to consider another plan.'

'Which would be what, exactly?' Moctezuma asked.

'Give them death, not gold. Allow me to assemble ten of our most seasoned regiments, eighty thousand fierce warriors, and lead them at once on a forced march to the coast. While the strangers wait unsuspecting for the rich presents they believe they have bullied us into giving them, we will approach their camp by stealth and fall on them without mercy. Permit me to do this, lord, and I promise you not a man of them will be left alive to carry news of their fate back to their native land.'

Chapter Nineteen

Thursday 6 May 1519

'I couldn't help noticing you keep a diary, Senor Díaz,' Pepillo said, 'and how often you make entries in it.'

'I've noticed you do the same, lad.'

'I keep mine for the caudillo so events can be fresh before him when he comes to write his memoirs. And you, sir – do you plan some such thing? By the end of this campaign I warrant you'll have an incredible story to tell. I'm sure there's many who would want to read it.'

'What? A story by an illiterate idiot like me?' Bernal Díaz always felt enormously uncomfortable when other soldiers made jokes about his constant scribbling. Along with his good friend Gonzalo de Sandoval, he'd been promoted to the rank of ensign by Cortés before they'd sailed from Cuba. But, unlike Sandoval, who was of noble stock, though fallen on hard times, Díaz had never become used to officer status, and always felt himself to be one of the men, indeed one of the lowliest amongst them. As such it was somehow unfitting – almost unseemly – to reveal that he could not only read but also write fluently.

Díaz was doing his rounds of the camp perimeter, accompanied this early evening by Pepillo and the dog Melchior, which he himself had given to the boy after the battle against the Maya at Potonchan. The dog, though still very young, had proved its worth ten days before when it had played its part in saving Pepillo from abduction, and probably murder, at the hands of a group of Indians. Since then security had been strengthened and a fence of thorn bushes now ringed the camp, incorporating the cannon emplacements that artillery chief Francisco de Mesa had set up when the Spanish first arrived. Previously the main gate on the south side of the camp, through which flowed the constant stream of supplies from Cuetlaxtlan, had been more symbolic than functional, but now it was one of only four openings in the fence – the others lying to the north, east and west. All were kept under permanent guard.

'With respect, sir, you're neither illiterate nor an idiot,' Pepillo responded. 'You're a brave soldier with a gift for words who was in the thick of it at Potonchan and will likely be in the thick of it again.' A grin: 'Turn your memoirs into a romance and you might sell thousands of copies, as did García Rodríguez de Montalvo with *Amadis de Gaula*. You could make yourself a rich man.'

'Ha!' Díaz laughed. 'That'll be the day. Money's never stuck to me, unfortunately.'

'Still, sir, if you'll permit me to say so, you shouldn't dismiss the idea. This adventure we find ourselves launched upon is in many ways more strange and fabulous than anything in Amadis. The people of this land – so savage and yet so fine. Their practice of human sacrifice, their beautiful and wondrous clothes of feathers, their pyramids, sir, their way of battle. Someone has to write all this down, or in later times it will never be believed.'

'But if I write it as a romance, Pepillo, it will never be believed anyway.'

'Well, that's true, sir, no doubt, but still I and many others would like to read it.'

Díaz chuckled. Since the strange events on Cozumel soon after the fleet had first reached the new lands, he'd felt a special responsibility for this boy who seemed always to be getting himself into scrapes and difficulties. The death of Pepillo's close friend Melchior at Potonchan had all but destroyed the lad, which was why Díaz had gifted him the lurcher pup Melchior, which now bounded around happily at their feet.

Pepillo threw a stick and the lurcher went after it, barking madly, tearing through the long grass of the dunes.

'Your dog's doing well,' said Díaz, 'despite that whipping Telmo Vendabal gave him and the fight he got into with those Indians.'

'Oh yes,' said Pepillo proudly. 'He's quite a hero . . .' A worried look crossed his face and the energy went out of his voice, 'But I'm afraid, sir, very much afraid, that Don Telmo will take him away from me and put him with the other hounds to be trained for war.'

'Surely the caudillo wouldn't allow that,' exclaimed Díaz. 'His own page's pet dog!'

'But that's just it, sir. Since the fight with the Indians, my master keeps saying that Melchior's no pet – that his rightful place is with the pack. He says we need all the fighting dogs we can get, sir.'

'He's jesting with you, lad.'

'I don't think so. Vendabal's always whispering in my master's ear, trying to convince him I should give Melchior up.' A sudden frown: 'I'll never give him up, sir! If they try to take him from me, I'll run away!'

'Run, lad? Where would you run to in these unknown lands?'

'I don't know, sir, but run I would! I won't see Melchior put to war.'

What the boy was too plucky to mention, yet must be connected to his obviously serious resolve to flee the camp if things got too bad, was the way he was repeatedly harassed and bullied by a gang of Vendabal's assistants. Three of them in particular, youths of about Pepillo's own age but much harder and nastier characters, seemed to regard it as their duty to their own master to make the page's life a misery. Díaz had witnessed several of their acts of spiteful cruelty and bullying, but had refrained from intervening until now, for fear it would simply make things worse. After all, no young lad, growing into manhood, would wish to be accused of being a snitch or of hiding behind others. On the other hand, Díaz thought, he'd never forgive himself if Pepillo did go through with his foolhardy escape plan.

'I'll try to convince Vendabal to lay off,' he now said. 'I'll talk to the caudillo if I have to. I'm sure this can easily be resolved.'

Even as Díaz spoke, however, the thought occurred to him that there might be no easy solution. Vendabal was enormously stubborn; he had leverage because his dog pack gave the conquistadors a unique edge over the enemy. Cortés was a practical man, not at all sentimental in leadership matters, and most likely wouldn't want to invite trouble to keep a mere page happy. As to the bullying – well, Cortés would probably approve of it rather than disapprove, on the grounds that it would toughen Pepillo up.

By now they had walked almost the full circuit of the perimeter fence and were nearing the main gate when an altercation broke out. An elderly Indian, stooped and grizzled, was speaking urgently to Allonso Gellega, a known brawler and troublemaker who happened to be on duty.

'Look, bugger off will you!' shouted Gallega. He had big hands and thick forearms covered in a dense mat of black hair, and he now made an aggressive shooing gesture.

The Indian continued to address him in a peculiarly resonant, droning, nasal voice. Very curiously one of the words he was saying over and over again sounded like 'Malinal', the name of the beautiful Mayan woman who was now serving Cortés as his interpreter.

'I don't understand your heathen gibberish,' Gallega yelled, spraying spittle in the Indian's face, 'but if you don't clear off *now* you're going to feel the toe of my boot in your arse.'

'Did I just hear him say Malinal's name?' Díaz asked Pepillo.

'I think so sir, yes. I heard it too.'

Just then the little Indian, showing remarkable agility for one so ancient, dodged round Gallega and darted through the gate. Gallega bellowed and gave chase, drawing a dagger, but the old man was swift and kept ahead of him.

'Come on,' said Díaz to Pepillo, 'let's find out what's happening here,' and with a few loping strides he blocked the elder's path, grasped his shoulder and dragged him to a halt. Up close he was amazed to discover that the Indian's eyes were clouded with cataracts. Not only old, then, but blind!

As Gallega came pounding up, already out of breath and brandishing his dagger, Díaz raised a warning hand. 'No need for violence! This old man is blind. Can't you see that, you idiot!' He turned to Pepillo: 'You speak some of the local lingo, don't you?' he asked.

'A few words, sir. Malinal's been teaching me.'

'A few words should be enough. Let's find out what this is all about.'

Chapter Twenty

Thursday 6 May 1519

'You are more beautiful by far than Tozi described you,' the old man called Huicton said. 'I was anticipating wonders, but in every respect you excel my expectations.'

It had taken Malinal some time to get used to the idea that this ancient could see at all through his clouded eyes, but somehow he could – and clearly!

What was harder to accept was the claim that he knew her friend, and furthermore had known her for many years.

'Tozi never spoke to me about you,' Malinal said suspiciously. 'Not a word.'

'Ah yes, perhaps . . . but how long were you and she together?'

'A day only, in the fattening pen at the foot of the great pyramid of Tenochtitlan where we awaited death together. At the end it was as though we had known each other all our lives.'

'As no doubt in every meaningful sense you had, since you both believed that was your last day on earth. Even so, you would not learn all there was to know about each other in such a short time. Certain pieces of information would inevitably have been missed.'

Malinal allowed that this must be so; still she was doubtful, and it took more than an hour of close questioning to allay her fears. At the end of it she left Huicton in front of the kitchens enjoying a bowl of soup and went to Cortés in his pavilion. Aguilar was there waiting to play his part.

'I believe the old man is genuine,' Malinal said. 'He has knowledge of my friend that only someone close to her could possess.' She listened attentively as Aguilar translated and was reasonably sure he had represented her correctly. 'I think you should see this Huicton,' she continued, now speaking directly to Cortés in Castilian. She switched back into Mayan: 'He claims to have information, and an offer, that will be of value to you.'

When Aguilar had interpreted her words, Cortés nodded. 'Very well,' he said. 'Bring him in. I'll hear what he has to say.'

Malinal went to fetch Huicton, who was finishing up the last of the soup, smacking his lips with satisfaction, and led him to the pavilion where Cortés greeted him graciously, introduced himself, embraced him in the Spanish fashion, and indicated a stool on which he should sit down.

'Thank you, my lord,' said the old man. 'I have been on the road for many days and my bones ache.' In affirmation of this there came a mighty creaking and cracking of his joints as he lowered himself onto the stool.

Huicton was trying very hard not to seem impressed, but even with years of experience of bluff and counter-bluff it was difficult to keep the astonishment he felt from showing on his face. These 'white-skins', as Shikotenka had called them, were indeed a new and terrible kind of men, and certainly not gods. Yet it was their very humanness, exemplified by the reek of their latrines, by the ripe, unwashed stink of their bodies, and by the lice that crawled in their beards, that made them so remarkable. Their discipline and coordination, their exotic metal armour and weapons, their huge and monstrous war animals, one of which had grazed Huicton's leg with its fangs as he was first brought into the heart of the camp while another, tall as a house, had nearly trampled him down – all these things radiated an alien and remorseless power, the like of which he had never known before, but which was yet plainly the product of human ingenuity and skill, not of supernatural forces.

At least this one called Cortés, the leader, he whom Tozi in her childlike purity had assumed to be Quetzalcoatl, did not smell as bad as some of the others. Apparently he washed and there were no lice seething in his beard. Moreover, it was obvious the woman Malinal was infatuated with him. How, Huicton wondered, would Tozi react to that?

134

'You are an ambassador?' Cortés asked. The meaning of his words reached Huicton through the other white-skin – the little, pungent, hairy one who spoke the Mayan tongue – and thence through Malinal. 'Ambassador for whom? Whom do you represent? Why are you here?'

'I am the ambassador of Ishtlil, rightful ruler of the kingdom of Texcoco,' Huicton replied. 'And I am here to bring you his salutations and his offer of friendship.'

'And why would I seek the friendship of this Ishtlil?' Cortés asked carefully.

'Because the great power in this land is Moctezuma, emperor of the Mexica,' Huicton replied immediately. 'If you wish to remain here and prosper, then it is certain that sooner or later you will either have to become his vassal or you will have to fight him. If it turns out that you must fight him, then I believe you will need allies. I am here to smooth that path for you.'

When his answer had been translated into the language of the white-skins, Cortés sat forward and studied him with an expression of keen interest. Huicton was fascinated by the other man's eyes: the left was large, round and grey, while the right was smaller, oval and black. These surface features, however, did not disguise the deeper message of character to be read there – a message of cunning, of resolve, and of a cold, ferocious concentration that would have been formidable in any leader, but was somehow doubly impressive when encountered in one so foreign as this.

'May I take it, then,' Cortés said finally, 'that your master Ishtlil is at war with Moctezuma?'

'He is, lord.'

'But how can that be? I am led to believe by Moctezuma's own envoys, who have visited me here, that all his enemies lie crushed at his feet.'

'With respect, lord, the Mexica are notorious deceivers and Moctezuma's envoys are the most practised amongst them.'

Cortés laughed. 'But you yourself, of course, tell only the truth?'

'I tell the truth when it serves my master's interests to do so, lord, as it does now.'

Another laugh: 'Well and good then. So tell me about your master and his enmity towards Moctezuma.'

Speaking through the two interpreters, Huicton gave an account of the Texcocan rebellion. He did not exaggerate or fabricate anything, being convinced that the truth would indeed serve him best here. When he had finished, Cortés and the other white-skin, whose name it seemed was Aguilar, talked animatedly to one another for a few moments. 'What are they saying?' Huicton asked Malinal quietly.

'I do not follow everything in their language yet,' she replied, 'but if I understand correctly, my master makes the observation that in all lands the concerns of rulers are very much the same. I think he says that for a younger son to be placed on the throne ahead of his elder brother would lead to trouble in Spain, just as it has in the case of Texcoco. In other words, he believes your story.'

'Which is right and proper, since my story is true.'

Cortés then asked questions about the size and disposition of Mexica and rebel forces, which Huicton answered with the same honesty as before. The numbers of those supporting Ishtlil were growing every day, but he could not yet put more than twenty thousand men into the field. Despite a recent catastrophic defeat at the hands of the Tlascalans, on the other hand, Moctezuma still had one hundred and sixty thousand regular soldiers at his command, divided into five separate armies, each thirty-two thousand men strong. In addition a hundred thousand auxiliaries from vassal peoples such as the Tacubans, the Cholulans, the Mixtecs and the Totonacs stood ready for immediate call-up at a snap of his fingers, and in the past year he had also hired fifty thousand unruly Otomi and Chichemec mercenaries.

Cortés raised his eyebrows. 'Impressive numbers,' he said, although he did not look very impressed. 'But you mentioned a defeat inflicted on Moctezuma by a people called the Tlascalans. I have heard something of these Tlascalans already – for a small band of them came here some days ago and attempted to kidnap my own servant, a mere boy. Pray tell me more about them and their famous victory over Moctezuma's huge armies.'

Cortés listened with careful attention as Huicton told him the story of the independent mountain kingdom of Tlascala, its fierce resistance against Mexica tyranny and the incredible coup orchestrated less than three months before by the battle-king Shikotenka, in which almost an entire Mexica army of thirty-two thousand men had been annihilated.

This time Cortés did look impressed. 'So the Tlascalans themselves must command large forces?'

'They do, lord. I believe the number stands close to a hundred thousand men.'

Cortés whistled. 'Useful!' he said. He rubbed his hands together, the unconscious gesture of a man coveting some great hoard of treasure. 'So, if I should contemplate an alliance with your master Ishtlil, and with these formidable Tlascalans, how would you advise me to set about it?'

Ah, Huicton thought. *Now we're getting to the point.* He looked Cortés straight in the eye. 'May I ask you a question, great lord?'

'You may ask me anything you like, but whether I'll answer it is another matter.'

Huicton swallowed. He felt strangely nervous, as though he confronted a puma in its den. 'My question is this, lord. Do you intend to fight Moctezuma? Or will you allow him to make you his vassal?'

A look of anger crossed Cortés's face and he seemed about to speak, but Huicton held up his hand. 'Hear me out, great lord, I pray. Before coming down to the coast to find you, I had an audience with Shikotenka, battle-king of the Tlascalans. He was here himself spying on you just a few days ago – indeed it was he who attempted to kidnap your servant. He did so because he is convinced you are in the process of allying yourself with Moctezuma – and you should know that all Moctezuma's allies become his vassals in the end. The Great Speaker of the Mexica brooks no equals.'

'By God!' Cortés barked, 'I'll not be Moctezuma's vassal, nor will he be my equal. I'm here to conquer him, nothing less.'

The moment he'd said it, part of him wondered if he'd gone too far, but then he thought – *caution be damned* – and allowed Aguilar to give the words to Malinal, who in turn put them into Nahuatl for Huicton's benefit. Cortés trusted her judgement that the old man was genuine, but even if it turned out that he was a spy for Moctezuma, what would really be lost by telling the truth? His strategy was to keep the Mexica leader guessing as to his motives, so it could do no harm to show friendship to his envoys like Teudile while offering a completely different face to his spy. If on the other hand Huicton did work for Ishtlil, as he claimed, and had connections with the warlike Tlascalans as well, then the sooner he opened negotiations with these enemies of his enemy, the better.

'It is a matter of great joy to me,' Huicton said, 'that you have entered our land to rid us of the tyrant Moctezuma. Undoubtedly this noble lady who serves as your tongue' – a gesture in Malinal's direction – 'has already told you that your presence here, in this very year, bears out an ancient prophecy of the return of the god-king Quetzalcoatl?'

'Yes, she has told me of it, but I am just a man . . .'

'Even so, the coincidence is quite remarkable, and will work to your advantage when you begin your march on the Mexica capital of Tenochtitlan.' A pause: 'When, by the way, do you intend to do that?'

'Soon enough,' said Cortés gruffly.

'You will find that Tlascala lies along your route,' Huicton continued. 'You may avoid it, of course, by following the highway that runs through the territories of several Mexica vassal states. I imagine that this is exactly what the Mexica will seek to persuade you to do. But I suggest you ignore their advice and pay a call upon Shikotenka instead. If you can convince him you seek the downfall of Moctezuma, you will have won a powerful ally.'

'You speak of Tlascala, whose ambassador you are not, but what of this Ishtlil whose ambassador you are? When does Ishtlil's offer of friendship come in useful to me?'

'Only after you've settled things with Shikotenka. You must make him your friend. The mountain provinces of Texcoco that Ishtlil controls lie next to Tlascala and, proceeding from there, through my master's lands and supported by the warriors he will provide you with, you can continue your march on Tenochtitlan.'

'So, in other words, I've no choice. If I'm to benefit from Ishtlil's alliance, I must go through Tlascala. That's the burden of what you're here to tell me.'

'More or less, my lord. More or less.'

'Very well,' said Cortés. 'I'll consider what you've said. Feel free to visit me again at any time and, meanwhile, please carry these gifts that I send to Shikotenka of Tlascala and to your own master Ishtlil.' Cortés paused while he went to the chest he kept at the rear of his pavilion and pulled out two handfuls of twisted-glass beads. He placed the beads in separate velvet bags, which he handed over to Huicton. 'For the lord Shikotenka,' he said, 'and the lord Ishtlil, as tokens of my friendship. Please tell them we have been happy to receive their embassy, for we share a common enemy in Moctezuma and we must work together to bring the tyrant to his knees. Say I promise them my help, and the help of my men, and of all the weapons at my disposal, in this great and worthy endeavour.'

Before dawn the next morning, Huicton met with Malinal. She asked him to remember her to her friend Tozi, and agreed to send him messages from time to time through his network of spies. With that accomplished, he slipped away from the camp of the white-skins. He knew now they called themselves Spaniards and, having seen Cortés, he was confident their presence in the One World would end badly for Moctezuma.

Shikotenka was a fool to imagine anything else. Though by no means Quetzalcoatl and his demigods, these powerful strangers were the instruments sent from heaven to destroy the evil rule of the Mexica, just as the ancient prophecy had foretold.

Before reporting back to Ishtlil, Huicton resolved to see Shikotenka again to attempt to convince him of this.

If he failed to do so, he had no doubt that Cortés would be more persuasive.

Chapter Twenty-One

A morning of tedious haggling had been concluded with Pichatzin, the governor of Cuetlaxtlan, who for the past three days had not sent food to the Spanish camp in anything like the quantities promised by Teudile before his departure for Tenochtitlan on 29 April. There was no serious problem as yet, but the shortfall was annoying and had caused some unrest. Speaking as usual through Aguilar and Malinal, Cortés had threatened Pichatzin, who had just taken his leave, and extracted a commitment from him to deliver an increased supply tomorrow.

Perhaps because of the strange food, or perhaps because of the unhealthy conditions of the camp itself – heat, dust, clouds of insects, overflowing latrines – many of the Spaniards were suffering from stomach ailments. Aguilar had been hit particularly badly and now, with a groan that required no explanation, he made for the door of the pavilion clutching his belly. 'A good distance away if you please, Jerónimo,' Cortés called to the unfortunate interpreter as he stumbled outside.

Aguilar closed the door behind him and, in the same instant, Cortés rose from his chair, stepped over to Malinal, swept her up in his arms and pressed his lips and tongue against hers in a forceful kiss. She closed her eyes and relaxed into this stolen moment, wrapping her arms round his neck as he held her close, enjoying his strength, feeling his *tepulli* harden against her, taking pleasure in the immediate response of her own loins.

It was strange, she reflected as the kiss lengthened and his hands explored her body. Her mission had been to find a god and bring him to Tenochtitlan to inflict her hatred upon Moctezuma. But instead of Quetzalcoatl she had found Hernán Cortés and become his secret lover! After the night they had spent together in the stateroom of the *Santa Maria*, while the Mexica envoys snored on deck, she had felt like a giddy girl again, in the throes of her first crush. And the fact they had to keep their passion secret – in particular from Hernán's close friend and ally Puertocarrero – somehow made everything so much more intense. Yes, Malinal was constantly by Cortés's side, interpreting for him, anticipating his wishes, acting in his interests, even when he did not know it, in his dealings with Pichatzin and his deputies. But Aguilar was almost always present, and if not him then one or other, or many, of the captains, until finally, when each day's work was done, she would retire with Puertocarrero to his wooden cabin, plead 'women's problems' to defer his incessant and increasingly violent sexual demands, and fall asleep by his side to dream of Cortés.

Since that surprising night of ecstasy in the caudillo's stateroom, there had only been one other opportunity to make love, and that had been no more than a bungled and uncomfortable fumble behind a dune. Otherwise their intimacy had been limited to glances and whispers and now and then a snatched kiss like this one – so where it was all leading Malinal had no clear idea. Perhaps it would come to nothing. Cortés had few enough real allies amongst the captains, and could hardly afford to alienate Puertocarrero over an affair of the heart – if it even amounted to so much. More likely it was merely an affair of the loins, and he would have her a few more times and discard her, with Puertocarrero none the wiser. Malinal knew enough of men to be prepared for anything, but meanwhile she was making good use of her special access to the Spanish leader. Her true purpose, in which she remained unwavering, was to destroy Moctezuma, and Cortés certainly had the means and the will to do that.

He also had the senses and reactions of a jaguar, heard the footsteps scurrying across the sand before she did, and broke away from her as a knock came at the door. Smiling with his strange, odd-sized eyes, he signalled to her to sit down, returned to his own chair and said 'enter'.

It was Pepillo, Malinal's friend and language teacher, flushed and breathless from running. 'It's Teudile, sir,' he told Cortés. 'He's back!'

'Peaceful or hostile would you say, Pepillo?'

'Hard to know, sir. But he's brought a whole caravan of bearers with boxes and baskets.'

It was a moment of triumph, Cortés thought, but also a moment of danger. Since Teudile's departure twelve days before, as conditions in the camp had deteriorated and more and more of the men grew sick, the Velázquez faction, led by Juan Escudero and Juan Velázquez de Léon, had become increasingly vocal in its demands for a return to Cuba. It was true that thirty-four conquistadors had already died in the camp, most succumbing to wounds received at Potonchan, but it was the treasure Teudile had brought on 28 April that had given the Velazquistas their most persuasive argument. 'We should take our profits and get out while we're ahead,' Escudero had demanded, and it seemed that a good number of the men – perhaps as many as a hundred – agreed with him. So, now Teudile was back with an army of bearers and what looked to be an even greater treasure, it was obvious the Velazquistas would seize the opportunity to press all the more strongly for the expedition to sail home and make an accommodation with Diego de Velázquez, the powerful governor of Cuba.

Cortés had no intention of allowing his hated rival to be handed the prize in this way. He was here to conquer a land and write his name on the pages of history; no matter how great the inducements, he would not settle for anything less.

As before, he had summoned the Mexica delegates to meet him and his captains under the great cloth awning set up on the dunes overlooking the sea. As before, carpets had been rolled out onto the sand on which Moctezuma's gifts could be displayed. As before, Malinal sat at Cortés's right and Aguilar, hunched and grey faced, sat at his left.

At the head of the new delegation, Teudile now touched the ground and put his hands to his mouth – the traditional 'earth-eating' gesture used both by the Mexica and the Maya when they wished to honour a person of great importance. Pichatzin, who had been on his way out of the camp after his earlier meeting with Cortés – but had clearly been obliged by Teudile to return – did the same, and both of them together then perfumed Cortés and his captains with the smoke of some fragrant incense they had brought in earthenware braziers. Pointedly refusing to take part in these ceremonies was a third notable member of the delegation – a much younger man with long black hair, high cheekbones and an aquiline nose, who stood haughty and aloof behind Teudile, glaring at the Spaniards with burning, hostile eyes. He was tall and powerfully built, his upper body clothed in a splendid tunic made of jaguar skins, and the scars of recent battle injuries stood out livid on his throat and right forearm.

'Do you know this man?' Cortés whispered to Malinal.

'Don't know,' she replied. 'But recognise. He is Prince Guatemoc, nephew to Moctezuma and a famous warrior in Tenochtitlan.'

'What can you tell me about him?' Cortés asked. They weren't even bothering to put their simpler exchanges through Aguilar now, so proficient had Malinal become in Castilian.

'People say he is honest. Brave. Takes risks. Sometimes foolish. Likes to fight.'

'Sounds like a troublemaker. Think he'll make trouble for us?'

'Not sure. Probably.'

Teudile began the formal part of the proceedings by producing Bernal Díaz's battered old helmet, now filled to the brim with grains of gold, and addressing Cortés. 'You said,' the steward recalled, 'that you and your countrymen suffer from a certain disease of the heart that can only be cured by gold, and you asked to see the gold from our mines. The great Moctezuma sends you this gold as a gift. Will it cure your strange ailment, do you think?'

Alvarado, Velázquez de Léon, Escudero, Puertocarrero, Montejo and the other captains all pressed forward, passing the helmet from hand to hand and sifting its glittering contents through their fingers. While they were thus preoccupied, Cortés looked around for Bernal Díaz and saw him standing behind the others, exchanging some joke with his friend Gonzalo de Sandoval. Cortés had promoted the two of them to the rank of ensign just before sailing from Cuba and had never regretted the decision. Though from very different backgrounds – Sandoval was an aristocrat whose family had lost its fortune, Díaz was a commoner – they got on well together, commanded the respect of the men who served under them and had both fought with tremendous bravery at Potonchan. 'Hey Bernal,' Cortés called out. 'Come here! See your helmet is returned filled with gold as we asked.'

The young ensign pushed through the throng, took the helmet and stared into it. 'With so much gold a man could retire,' he said wistfully, 'and never work again.'

'Nonsense!' said Alvarado. He had produced an empty canvas money sack from somewhere and now decanted the gold grains from the helmet into it and weighed the bag in his fist. 'Five thousand pesos at the most,' he declared. 'Hardly enough for a man to retire on.'

'That would depend on a man's needs,' said Díaz stiffly as he set the emptied helmet back on his head.

Cortés reached out, gently prised the sack from Alvarado's grasp and laid it on the carpet before his chair. Five thousand pesos was a goodly sum but the real value of these grains lay in the absolute proof they provided that rich mines did exist in this land – intelligence worth ten thousand times as much as the meltdown value of the gold itself.

'Thank you, Ambassador Teudile,' Cortés said. 'I will see to it that this generous present reaches my emperor in Spain. Now, what else do you have for us?'

Cortés called in Pepillo to keep an account and compile an inventory of the presents.

Item: Two golden necklaces with jewellery, one of which has eight strings of two hundred and thirty-two red jewels and one hundred and sixty-three green jewels. And hanging from the border of this necklace there are twenty-seven small gold bells; and among them there are four figurines made of large gemstones mounted in gold.

Item: Four pairs of screens, two pairs of fine gold leaf with adornments of yellow deerskin and the other two pairs of fine silver leaf with adornments in white deerskin. From each of these hang sixteen small gold bells.

Item: A large paten of gold weighing sixty pesos de oro.

Item: A fan of coloured featherwork with thirty-seven small rods covered with gold.

Item: Sixty-eight small pieces of gold, each of which is as large as a half-cuarto.

Item: Twenty little golden towers.

Item: A bracelet of jewellery.

Item: A large head in gold that seems of an alligator.

Item: A helmet of blue jewellery with twenty small gold bells, which hang all around, with two strips over each bell.

Item: Another helmet of blue jewellery with twenty-five small gold bells and two gold beads above each bell hanging round the outside of it.

Item: A reed container with two large pieces of gold to be worn on the head, with the shape of a seashell.

Item: A sceptre of red jewellery, which resembles a serpent with its head, teeth and eyes that seem to be mother of pearl.

Item: A large buckler of featherwork. In the centre of this buckler is a gold plate with a design such as the Indians make, with four other half-plates of gold round the edge which together form a cross.

Item: Sixty-two marks of silver.

Item: Six bucklers; each one has a gold sheet which covers the whole buckler.

Item: A half-mitre of gold.

Item: Twenty golden birds of fine and realistic workmanship.

Item: Two rods, twenty inches long, all modelled in fine gold.

Item: Thirty loads of cotton cloth of various patterns, decorated with feathers of many colours.

And thus the list went on and on, covering page after page in Pepillo's small, neat hand, with items of immense value mixed in with items that were merely beautiful. As the hot afternoon wore on into evening, and seemingly limitless varieties and combinations of these rich gifts were laid out before him, Cortés felt increasingly stunned and amazed, as though he had become immersed within some fantastic dream or vision. Unlike many of his captains, however, he made sure he kept a straight face and did nothing to reveal his delight and lust for the great wealth that was simply being handed over here without even a fight to obtain it.

Finally, with full night now descended upon the camp and a hundred flickering torches lighting up the lurid scene under the awning, Teudile unveiled his *pièces de résistance* – two gigantic disks, each a hand-span thick and big as cartwheels. One was of solid gold, and worth two hundred thousand pesos, Alvarado thought; the other was of silver. Both were intricately engraved with figures from the Mexica calendar, which Teudile insisted on explaining. In the centre of the silver wheel, he said, was the image of Toncacihuatl, the moon, in the form of a woman's face, symbolising the female realm – the waters of lakes and oceans, the night and darkness, and all the compliant, passive, yielding principles of life. By contrast the male face at the centre of the gold wheel was Tonatiuh, the sun – active, masculine, luminous, celestial, his features wrinkled with age and his tongue, sharp and pointed, jutting out hungrily.

'Tonatiuh?' said Alvarado. 'That's what you people call *me!*'

'Because of your golden hair,' said Teudile.

'But my features are youthful and handsome,' protested Alvarado, running his fingers over the grotesque image, 'not like this! Why do you show him so old and so ugly?'

'We Mexica believe the sun of our own epoch is the fifth to have shone down on mankind and that there have been four previous suns, or ages of the earth, each one ended by a terrible cataclysm that destroyed the greater part of humanity. We believe that our Fifth Sun is already very old and very cruel, and that he is only kept alive, is only able to continue shining down on us, if we offer him constant nourishment and rejuvenation.'

Cortés knelt to examine the figure. 'The tongue,' he said, 'is strange. It's almost like a dagger.'

'It is the obsidian knife of sacrifice,' Teudile answered with a gruesome smile. 'The rejuvenation that we offer daily to the sun, and to our war god Hummingbird, is in the form of human blood and hearts.'

Cortés felt anger grip him like a fist. 'You Mexica know how to make beautiful and wonderful things,' he said, 'but your practice of human sacrifice is an abomination and the foul creatures you worship are not gods but demons. You must set them aside, you must set aside sacrifice and your other evil rites, you must destroy your accursed idols and you must turn to the worship of the one true God, the creator of Heaven and Earth, whose son is Jesus Christ and whose ways my sovereign, Don Carlos of Spain, has sent me here to teach you. It is for this purpose I must now travel with my army to your city of Tenochtitlan, there to meet your sovereign Moctezuma and correct him on the many errors he commits and attempt to save his soul.'

As Aguilar put the words into Maya for Malinal, Cortés saw her turn towards him, her large dark eyes glowing. 'Are you sure you want to say this, lord?' she asked him in Castilian.

'Yes!' he snapped. 'By all means I am sure.'

Her next point required clarification by Aguilar: 'Perhaps it would be wise not to tell these Mexica your plans, lord? Don't say what you mean to do. Rather do as you wish with them when you are ready, giving them no warning or mercy.'

But Cortés was still angry and shrugged off her advice. 'Put what I said into their heathen tongue, Malinal, and exactly as I said it. These savages must learn the truth.'

'Your will, lord,' Malinal replied. As she switched into flowing Nahuatl, Cortés watched the faces of the Mexica delegation. Pichatzin looked afraid, Teudile, he thought, looked shifty and dishonest, but on Guatemoc's face he saw pure anger, pure hatred.

'Whore!' snarled Guatemoc as soon as Malinal had finished translating Cortés's admonitions. 'Why do you serve these bandits? Why be their tongue? You are a woman of our land. I command you to leave them now.'

Did Guatemoc *know?* Malinal wondered. Had he learned how Moctezuma released her at the climax of that terrible night on the great pyramid? Did he call her a whore because he'd found out her story, her life as a sex slave, the men she'd served in Tenochtitlan – including his own father – before she was sent for sacrifice? The very presence of this prince, though he himself had never been amongst her lovers, filled Malinal with feelings of horror and terror – feelings she refused to reveal, refused to betray on her face, refused to give way to. Instead she laughed and looked him straight in the eye, showing him more disrespect in that single, simple act than he would ever in his life have received from any of the subservient women of the Mexica.

'You cannot command me, Guatemoc,' she said. 'I am free of you, free of the bullying and cruelty of your race, free to do as I choose – and I choose to help these white-skinned *tueles*.'

'*Tueles*. Ha! So you think they are gods then?'

'You will find out for yourself what they are and what they are not.'

Malinal realised she was trembling, so unnatural did it seem to her to address a prince of the blood in this way, and yet she had to admit it gave her exquisite pleasure to do so. Ignoring Guatemoc completely, she turned towards Teudile. 'What do you say to the lord Cortés?' she asked.

Teudile's mask of patrician disdain had not slipped. 'Our revered Speaker has charged me with a message for your master,' he said, 'and it is this. He is to accept these gifts he has been given with the same grace as Moctezuma has shown in sending them, and he may divide them as he wishes amongst the *tueles* and men who accompany him. Our revered Speaker furthermore says he hopes one day to see the face of the great emperor, Don Carlos of Spain, of whom the lord Cortés speaks, but under no circumstances will he meet with the lord Cortés. Our revered Speaker is ill and cannot descend to the sea, and it will be extremely difficult and laborious for Cortés to come to him, not only on account of the many high mountains that lie between, but also because of the great and sterile deserts he would have to traverse, where he would necessarily suffer from hunger, thirst and similar hardships. Besides, much of the country through which he would have to pass is in the hands of Moctezuma's enemies, who are cruel and evil people and who will kill him as soon as they learn he is travelling as Moctezuma's friend. The lord Cortés is therefore to take these presents and return across the sea whence he came.'

Malinal needed Aguilar's help to put Teudile's speech into Castilian, and as the message was conveyed she saw Cortés's face cloud over. When he had understood everything, he said: 'Tell Teudile, and that bad-mannered young upstart beside him, that I will be coming to Tenochtitlan with my army whether their revered Speaker likes it or not. I have journeyed from distant lands, crossed thousands of miles of oceans and fought battles with savage foes solely to see and exchange words with Moctezuma in person. My great king and lord Don Carlos will not give me a good reception should I return to him without

148

achieving that goal, so tell these Mexica dogs that nothing will stop me – not mountains, not deserts, not men – and that wherever their Speaker may be, I intend to go and find him.'

From that point the negotiations became extremely heated, and Malinal watched with growing interest as harsh words were exchanged not only between Cortés and Teudile but also between Teudile and Guatemoc. Technically the steward outranked the young prince, but it was clear that Guatemoc was not only higher born but also the stronger personality, and ultimately his will prevailed.

After Cortés had insisted for the fourth or fifth time, and in increasingly bullying language, that nothing would stop him marching on Tenochtitlan and that in fact he felt the Mexica were simply making excuses to delay his progress, Guatemoc flew into a wild rage and shouted at him: 'You've got everything you came for – gold, jewels, more wealth than thieves like you have ever dreamed of. You'd have had none of this, believe me, if Moctezuma had followed my advice. So consider yourselves lucky, get back in your boats and return to your country now, or I warn you, Cortés, you will perish in my land and all your little army with you.'

Cortés smiled: 'The Chontal Maya made exactly the same threat to me at Potonchan, and look what happened to them.'

Guatemoc's face was tense with fury. 'We are not the Chontal Maya,' he said. 'You make a great mistake if you imagine we are.'

Another mocking smile from Cortés. 'I don't see much difference. You're all heathens and savages worshipping false gods, and none of you has a clue about how to win a real fight. If I choose to march on Tenochtitlan tomorrow, you'll not be able to stop me.'

Guatemoc drew himself up to his full height. 'My soldiers are as numberless as the sands of the sea,' he boasted, 'and undefeated in battle. March on Tenochtitlan and I will teach you the Mexica way of war.'

'That is a lesson I await eagerly,' said Cortés, 'and, when we have thrashed you, be sure I will pay Moctezuma a visit in his palace.'

After she had translated this, Malinal could not resist adding a few words of her own. 'When a man has to lie,' she said quietly to Guatemoc, 'I take it as a sign of weakness.'

'Silence, whore,' the prince sneered. 'You have no voice of your own here.'

'But I have ears,' she said, 'and I know, as the lord Cortés also knows, that your warriors *have* faced defeat. Do you think the loss of an entire Mexica army in battle against the Tlascalans is a matter that can be kept secret? So the only sense in which your soldiers are numberless is that they now indeed number less than they did before, great Prince, while your enemies multiply.'

Malinal looked slowly round at the grim Spanish captains beside Cortés, their armour shining in the torchlight, and at Cortés himself, his eyes hooded and pitiless, his hand resting on the hilt of his sword. 'Are you so certain,' she said to Teudile, 'that Prince Guatemoc is right to add these *tueles* to the roll of your enemies? You have not seen *their* way of war as I have. You cannot yet imagine the deeds they are capable of.'

Teudile stepped close to Malinal and peered into her eyes, but he did not answer her question. 'We know your story,' he said in a tone filled with menace. 'And the lord Moctezuma remembers you.' Then, without another word, leaving all the golden gifts behind, he led his delegation away down through the dunes and out of the camp.

Chapter Twenty-Two

Small hours of the morning, Wednesday 12 May 1519

Moctezuma felt joy, an emotion he had almost forgotten. His heart beat like a drum threatening to burst forth from his chest. Excitement welled in his throat. He'd made no sacrifice, he'd eaten only a small dose of mushrooms, yet here was the god Hummingbird, looming over him, gleaming like the risen sun in the darkness of the night. 'Lord,' he said. 'You have returned to me.'

'I never left you,' said Hummingbird. 'I've been watching your progress . . . with approval.'

'Thank you, lord. So you approve, then, that I resisted Guatemoc's demand for ten regiments to attack the white-skinned *tueles* in their camp?'

'I approve, my son! I approve mightily! Now is not the right time to fall in force upon the white-skins. Disaster would have been the result if you had allowed Guatemoc to proceed with his foolish and importunate plan. You made the right choice and I applaud you for it.'

Moctezuma's feelings of pleasure were so intense that for the first time in several months he felt his *tepulli* flush with blood and grow erect. 'Instead of making war on the white-skins,' he told the god, 'I thought it wise to assign additional regiments to the sacred duty of hunting out virgin girls to offer you in sacrifice. I had originally set four regiments to this holy work, but in the days since the last meeting of my council I have increased the size of the task force to ten regiments – eighty thousand skilled men; the same number Guatemoc demanded – and I am confident now that the enterprise will proceed to your satisfaction. My regiments have been sent out far and wide, like the fingers of two great hands stretched across the empire. Runners reach me daily with reports. We have already begun to extract additional tributes from our subject peoples, we have begun to raid enemy cities, and the fattening pens of Tenochtitlan are being prepared to accept a ripe harvest of virgin girls.'

The Great Speaker, lord and master of the Mexica nation, lay spreadeagled on the floor of his darkened chamber. Standing over him, the god licked his lips: 'I have seen your preparations,' he said, 'and I delight in them.'

Moctezuma's *tepulli* swelled further. 'My aim,' he said, 'is to gather an immense basket of virgins in your name. The target is ten thousand. If it is acceptable to you, lord, I will sacrifice them on your altar in the four days that culminate with the annual celebration of your birth.'

Hummingbird's tongue darted out again. 'How very thoughtful of you, and how very appropriate. Ten thousand virgins will make a splendid birthday gift!' He stooped, placed his huge hand on Moctezuma's head and gently caressed his hair. 'I shall await the offering with . . . anticipation,' he said. 'Meanwhile, allow me to offer you a little something in return.'

'A gift, lord? You have a gift for me?'

Moctezuma was both excited and flattered at the prospect and found the sensation of the god's hand caressing his hair deeply arousing. 'I have something to show you,' Hummingbird now said. A jolt of energy radiated suddenly from his fingers and at once, by magic, a vision was conjured forth. Without even being aware of the transition, Moctezuma discovered he was no longer in his palace, no longer in Tenochtitlan, no longer immersed in darkness, but flying like a bird in bright sunlight over his beautiful vassal city of Cholula and above its remotely ancient pyramid dedicated to Quetzalcoatl. From that aerial vantage point he looked down on the vast walled enclosure that surrounded the antique shrine of the once and future king – the only one of its kind still permitted to function with an active priesthood throughout the domains of the Mexica.

'This is the place, O great Moctezuma,' said Hummingbird, 'and this is the time of the unmaking of prophecy. When the leader of the white-skins comes to Cholula and enters the shrine of the Plumed Serpent, he will lose his power.'

Moctezuma's heart stirred with a sudden flutter of panic. 'But I have every hope, lord,' he hastened to reply, 'that the white-skins will not penerate so far into my territory as Cholula! I have sent them a huge treasure of gold, in exchange for which I expect them to return across the sea whence they came.'

'They will not do so, my son,' said Hummingbird flatly. 'The treasure you have sent them has only whetted their appetite for more. On that matter Guatemoc was right, and in the months ahead they will swarm over your lands and march upon you, arrayed for war.'

Moctezuma groaned, terror rising in his throat like vomit.

'But have no fear,' Hummingbird continued, 'because at Cholula you will stop them and destroy them utterly. Observe now and I will show you.'

Moctezuma obeyed, gazing down in vision on the city of Cholula and on the pyramid and shrine dedicated to Quetzalcoatl that lay at its heart and – behold! – he saw a great battle between Mexica soldiers and the white-skins raging within the precincts of that immense enclosure. As the fighting reached its climax, he saw companies of his brave jaguar and eagle knights laying low the white-skins and taking them prisoner, trussing some in hammocks so they could not move, holding others like slaves at the end of long poles with collars fastened tight round their necks and leading them off towards Tenochtitlan for sacrifice.

The spectacle was so uplifting and reassuring to behold that it took Moctezuma's breath away. 'Will it be so, lord?' he asked.

'It can be so,' Hummingbird replied, 'if you make it so, but before this high objective can be accomplished, there is something I require of you first.'

'Anything, lord. Anything . . .'

'The sorcerers of your court, Cuappi, Hecateu, Aztatzin and Tlilpo, are all empty vessels. They have no skill. They have no power. They are mere performers of mummery and ritual.'

'Yes, great lord.' Moctezuma hung his head. 'Even I, who am merciful, have seen this. They failed in all their attempts to work magic against the white-skins. They are nothing—'

'They are worse than nothing. They are frauds. They are imposters! I want them burnt.'

'Burnt, lord?'

'Yes, you heard me. Burnt alive. Roasted in a fire-pit. You will arrange this immediately.'

Moctezuma felt his fear rising again. 'Who then will be my sorcerers, lord?'

A new image swam unbidden into his mind. It was an image of a man dressed only in a loincloth whose powerful body from his bare feet to his shaved head was covered in such a dense web of swirling, interwoven tattoos that he seemed to be almost entirely black, black as night, black as a jaguar in the depths of the jungle. Excepting his eyes – terrible, terrifying eyes – which shone and blazed like firebrands amidst a pall of smoke, and from which darted forth the complex interconnected patterns, the sacred geometry, the mathematical lightning bolts of high magic.

'This man,' said Hummingbird, 'will be your sorcerer, the only sorcerer you will ever need. His name is Acopol and he is one of the pure ones of the Chichemec tribe, out of the northern deserts. He is a *nagual*, a shape shifter who has served me well for many a long year and now I, even I, have called him out of the ocean of sand to serve you. You must not keep him at your court, however. Instead appoint him to the role of high priest in Cholula. Do that, my son, and he will prepare the way for your great victory there.'

Moctezuma had misgivings. How could he feel secure in his own court with no sorcerer to protect him from magical attacks? But Hummingbird read his mind and reassured him. 'Acopol is powerful. He will cast warding spells around your palace, and around my temple where you come to commune with me, and even from Cholula he will keep you safe.'

'In that case, lord,' said Moctezuma, 'I am ready. I will do as you require.'

'Of course you will, my son. Of course you will.'

The vision widened, beginning to show more of the background in which the tattooed figure stood. He perched, Moctezuma suddenly realised, on the summit platform of the immense and unspeakably ancient pyramid of the Sun at Teotihuacan, 'the place where men became gods', which lay some thirty-five miles north of the Mexica capital.

'Despatch an honour guard to bring Apocol here to Tenochtitlan,' Hummingbird continued. 'Let him oversee the burning of your sorcerers; let him put his warding spells in place to protect your palace against intrusion, and then send him to Cholula to prepare the final doom of the white men.'

'Your word is my command,' said Moctezuma as the vision slowly faded from view.

Part II

12 May 1519–16 August 1519

Chapter Twenty-Three

Awakened by Melchior's wet nose nuzzling his face, Pepillo shifted position on the hard ground beneath his blanket and gazed sleepily into the cold ashes of last night's kitchen fire. He was overtaken by an uneasy premonition that something was wrong.

Melchior whined and nuzzled him again.

'What is it, boy?' Pepillo asked, still drowsy. 'What's the matter?'

The dog replied with a muffled bark and this time Pepillo sat up, wide awake, his spine tingling. He looked around. On the ridge of the dunes he saw sentries at their post, the barrel of the small falconet they manned silhouetted against the rising sun. The soldiers' postures were alert, their gaze was directed to the south, and the tone of surprise in their voices was clear on the morning air.

South lay Cuetlaxtlan, from whence any Mexica forces that were to be thrown against the Spanish camp could be expected to make their approach. And the threat of an attack, after yesterday's menacing encounter with Moctezuma's ambassadors, seemed very real. Pepillo bounded to his feet and ran up the side of the dune, scattering sand, with Melchior loping at his side. 'What's happening?' he asked, as he burst in amongst the sentries.

'See for yourself, lad,' said Miguel de La Mafla, a young musketeer promoted to the rank of officer cadet after the fighting at Potonchan. He pointed to the rough bivouacs that had been pitched a few hundred paces to the south of the camp's perimeter to house the thousands of Totonac labourers and serving women who the Mexica had put at the disposal of the Spaniards. The bivouacs were deserted and empty now, not a soul moved amongst them, and it was obvious the workers had fled. 'They stole away in the night,' La Mafla said. 'Didn't make a sound, the buggers.'

'What does it mean?' asked Pepillo.

'It means we have to shift for ourselves,' complained La Mafla with a rueful smile. 'Pity. I was getting used to being waited on hand and foot.'

'And to tupping a different woman every night,' added another of the sentries with a ribald laugh.

Pepillo blushed. 'But what does it really *mean*? Will we be attacked?'

'Ask your master the caudillo,' said La Mafla, patting the brass barrel of the falconet. 'But if they come, we're ready.'

No attack materialised, but neither did the additional supplies of food and drinking water that Pichatzin, the governor of Cuetlaxtlan, had promised the day before. As evening fell, Cortés was therefore not surprised to be confronted in his pavilion by a delegation of Velazquistas led, as usual, by Juan Escudero. Escudero's by now steadfast companion Velázquez de Léon was with him, and they were supported, predictably, by Cristóbal de Olid. Less predictable (not because his Velazquista sympathies were unknown to Cortés, but because he was usually not forward in revealing them) was the grizzled, authoritative presence of Diego de Ordaz, and an even more unexpected member of the group was Alonso de Grado, hitherto a staunch and vocal supporter of the expedition. Francisco de Montejo was also there, wearing a hangdog expression. Last but not least the Velazquistas had even brought along a man of God, a one-eyed priest with lank black hair and a bad smell about him named Pedro de Cuellar, another of the many distant relatives of the governor of Cuba who had sailed with the expedition.

Quite a formidable troop, Cortés thought as he called for Pepillo to light the torches that stood in brackets around the walls of the pavilion, to bring wine, and to be ready to take notes. Arranging himself comfortably in his folding campaign chair, Cortés then made small talk regarding the weather, the insects and the probable causes of the bloody flux that still afflicted a quarter of the expeditionaries. He finally turned to Escudero. 'So Don Juan, I gather you have some concerns,' he said as the wine was poured. Pepillo was settled cross-legged on the floor, quill in hand, a fresh sheaf of milled paper resting ready on his knees.

'Concerns?' Escudero spluttered with a spastic jerk of his wine glass. 'Concerns! Have you not observed that we have been deserted by our native labourers? Have you not observed that no food has been brought to us? Does it not occur to you that the treasure handed to us yesterday may be about to be snatched back from us tomorrow?'

Cortés treated his old enemy to an unblinking stare, saying nothing, but reflecting inwardly on how much he loathed this former mayor of the town of Baracoa, whose pronounced underbite gave him the look of the grouper, caught fresh from the sea, that the cooks had served up for luncheon. It was not so much that Escudero had been the one to arrest and lock him up in Baracoa's filthy jail on Velázquez's orders over the matter of Catalina, but that the man's strutting and sneers at the time were as unforgivable as the trumped-up charges of treason the governor had used to force Cortés to marry his insipid niece.

'Well?' stormed Escudero as the silence drew out. 'Do you have nothing to say?'

Cortés smiled. 'The labourers have done their work for us, Don Juan. The camp is complete and we can manage well enough without them. As to food, the bounteous ocean is near at hand – ' a gesture through the open flaps of the pavilion to where the fleet floated at anchor in the bay – 'and our sailors know how to fish. I myself enjoyed an excellent grouper at luncheon and shall dine on lobster tonight.'

'You get the choice of the catch!' complained de Léon, a man of prodigious appetites.

'Yet you have not been deprived,' replied Cortés, raising a quizzical eyebrow at de Léon's huge belly. He looked around at the others: 'You are all still eating well, I think?'

'It's not ourselves we're concerned about,' said Ordaz gruffly, his strong, stubborn miller's face set in a look of deep disapproval. 'It's the common soldiery who'll grow hungry if the supplies from Cuetlaxtlan aren't resumed.'

When Cortés had led the decisive cavalry charge at Potonchan, he had given Ordaz command of the infantry. The old swordsman had performed the task well, but now seemed to feel it entitled him to the role of spokesman for the needs of the ranks.

'Fie, Don Diego,' said Cortés in a tone of gentle reproval. 'They need not go hungry. We are Spaniards after all! We can fend very well for ourselves – hunt, fish and take what we want from the indigenes whenever we wish. None of us will go hungry, I promise you that—'

'All this is beside the point,' cut in Escudero.

'But, with respect, Don Juan, it was you who raised this point.'

Escudero's eyes bulged. 'As I have every right to do.' He thrust out his lower jaw even further than usual. 'However, what we're really here to discuss is the gold.'

'Ah, yes, of course, the gold.'

'We received enough yesterday from those stinking savages to make every one of us rich – not just the officers, but the men as well. We must not squander or risk this great treasure, Don Hernán. We have no allies here, no reserves to fall back on. We must sail at once for Cuba, and for safety, and make account to His Excellency the governor.'

'I agree that we must not squander or risk the treasure,' said Cortés, 'but to cut for Cuba now when there is still so much to be gained seems the ultimate folly. I should not like to think, Don Juan, that you have grown shy?'

'Shy? You dare call me shy?'

'Your great desire for safety raises the question—'

Escudero lunged to his feet, upsetting his stool, his knuckles white around the hilt of his sword. 'You will withdraw that remark,' he said, a bubble of spit popping at the corner of his mouth, 'or you will give me satisfaction . . .'

Cortés stood also. 'My dear Don Juan,' he said, 'I shall be delighted to give you satisfaction.'

The trouble with being an officer, even a relatively junior one, was the infernal need to make decisions, and after being called to the sentry post at the camp's northern gateway, Bernal Díaz found himself confronted by yet another judgement call – in this case whether to disturb the caudillo during his meeting with a group of the expedition's senior captains, or to leave the matter until the morning.

A knot of about twenty Indians – most outlandish Indians – had gathered outside the gate in the darkness. They had a wild look, with muscular tattooed bodies and great holes in their lower lips and in their ears, in which they had inserted large disks, some of bone, some of stone spotted with blue, some of gold. They were unarmed and their manner seemed friendly enough, but what on earth did they want, and what was it they were saying in their foreign, incomprehensible jabber?

Díaz despatched a sentry to bring the woman Malinal and her counterpart Jerónimo de Aguilar, who collectively provided the expedition's interpreting services, but when the sentry returned he was accompanied by Malinal alone. It seemed that Aguilar was laid up with the bloody flux and claimed to be too unwell to come.

As ever when he found himself in close proximity to the beautiful raven-haired native, Díaz's heart pounded and his tongue froze. What was he to say to her? What could he possibly say to her? He knew that she was learning Castilian – the boy Pepillo was teaching her and Díaz himself had sometimes heard her speak in halting Castilian to the caudillo – but he feared he would not be able to make himself understood.

He bowed awkwardly. 'My lady,' he began. It was not the right term of address for a native; Puertocarrero, who owned her, simply called her 'woman' or 'hey, you', but there was something ladylike, even aristocratic, about her. 'Thank you for coming. Please tell me, do you understand my language?'

Malinal's huge almond eyes twinkled in the torchlight. 'Yes. Understand. And you? You understand me, Don Bernal?'

Good God! This was better than he could have hoped. She even – wonder of wonders – knew his name.

'I understand you very well,' he said. For a moment he was lost for words and just stood there staring at her.

That twinkle in her eyes again. 'Can help you?' she asked.

'Yes! Oh yes! Very much.' He jerked a big, dirty thumb towards the gang of Indians outside the gate. 'I need to know what they want. Will you ask them?'

'They Totonacs. I don't speak they language. Maybe one speak Nahuatl? Wait . . . I ask.'

She stepped forward, slim, graceful, wrapped in a tight-fitting smock that left little of her figure to the imagination, passed between the guards on either side of the open gateway and addressed the Indians in a firm, clear voice.

One of them, a tall, muscular savage in his prime with the look of a warrior, immediately replied, and the pair were soon engaged in urgent conversation.

As was her habit, Tozi waited until after nightfall to enter Moctezuma's palace. Although her invisibility protected her even in broad daylight, she always felt safer, more sure of herself, in the hours of darkness. Tonight, though, she sensed something different, something ominous, something *terrible* in the air. And as she floated weightless and invulnerable through the vast echoing corridors, as she passed oblivious guards with their useless obsidian-tipped spears, she experienced . . . what was this?

Something new?

Something unfamiliar.

Something strange.

Was it . . . could it be . . . fear?

No! Surely not. For she was Tozi, she reminded herself – Tozi the witch! – and she was never afraid. She had no reason, since Hummingbird had so mysteriously multiplied her powers, ever to be afraid!

Even so, what was this? She didn't like the feeling at all.

She had been aware for some moments of a commotion ahead in the further of the two great inner courtyards of the palace: a blaze of torches, an eerie glow and the hubbub of a thousand voices. Tozi had intended to haunt Moctezuma tonight, but first she must discover the cause of this unusual activity. Some celebration? Some ceremony? If so, then most likely Moctezuma would preside and she might have the opportunity to disturb the balance of his mind in public. Her own intimations of fear would be as nothing beside the fear she would feed him.

'The Great Speaker will not be pleased,' said Teudile, his sepulchral voice emanating from behind the curtains of the gilded and feather-strewn palanquin in which his bearers carried him aloft.

Disdaining such a womanish transport, Guatemoc loped easily alongside and now, in the darkness, bared his teeth in a wolfish grin. The steward's remark must rank, he thought, as the understatement of the year. Far from being merely displeased, Moctezuma would be furious, livid and likely murderous when he discovered what the prince had done and – worse! – what he intended to do next. Not only had he antagonised and threatened the white-skins during their meeting on the dunes, something Moctezuma had expressly forbidden; not only had he ordered the withdrawal of the Totonac labourers who had previously served the white-skins' camp; but Guatemoc had also spirited five hundred elite Cuahchic warriors out of Tenochtitlan, his personal squad, and they awaited him at the next way station less than a mile ahead. His plan, as he had just informed Teudile, was to make a forced overnight march back to Cuetlaxtlan with his fiercely loyal Cuahchics, and begin at once to test the white-skins' strength.

'I'd rather I had the eighty thousand men I asked for,' Guatemoc now added. 'My uncle was a fool not to grant my request. With such a force I could have overwhelmed the foreigners, regardless of their weapons and war animals. But I'll warrant I can cause them enough trouble with my picked five hundred to stir up a hornet's nest, and I fully intend to draw Cuetlaxtlan's garrison into the fight as well. Then Moctezuma will be obliged to send reinforcements or stand revealed for the fool and eunuch that he is.'

'It is you who are the fool, young prince,' said Teudile gloomily, 'and I fear I, too, will pay the price for your folly. The Great Speaker will not forgive my failure to stop you.'

Guatemoc laughed. 'Stop me? Absurd! How could you stop me?'

'I cannot, of course. Yours are the arms, yours is the might, yours is the royal blood. But the lord Moctezuma will see none of this. He will have me flayed alive.'

'Not if I return to Tenochtitlan with a conspicuous victory—'

'Even if you do,' said Teudile, 'I shall have been parted from my skin by then.'

'I hope not, old man! Still, I must do what I believe is right to save our nation from these interlopers.'

The way station loomed ahead and figures emerged from the

darkness. 'Hey, Mud Head,' Guatemoc roared, recognising his friends leading the Cuahchic contingent. 'Big Dart, Man-Eater, Fuzzy Face, Starving Coyote, well met! Are you ready for a fight?'

'No, no – gentlemen please! – *No!*' The small, wiry Francisco de Montejo had jumped to his feet and stood between Cortés and Escudero, a hand extended towards each of them as though he intended to hold them apart physically. 'You must not duel, gentlemen,' he said. His voice was trembling. 'We must not fight amongst ourselves while we are in hostile territory. As a friend to you both, I cannot allow it. It simply will not do.'

A long-faced, olive-skinned man with something of the Moor about him, wearing a neatly trimmed spade beard that showed some grey amongst the black, and with close-cropped salt-and-pepper hair, Montejo seemed older than his thirty-four years. He'd been nicknamed El Mozo – 'The Novice' – in his early twenties, when he had, indeed, still been a fresh-faced and optimistic young fellow, but the last five years of heavy drinking, womanising, gambling and crushing debt had aged him terribly, eating up the small fortune settled upon him by his aristocratic Salamanca family and threatening his honour. His financial needs had put him in the pocket of the governor of Cuba, who'd appointed him to the expedition to spy on Cortés and nip in the bud any act of mutiny, as he'd admitted during a drinking bout with Cortés himself. In the weeks before their unauthorised departure from Cuba on 18 February, Cortés had therefore carefully cultivated Montejo, enjoying a few raucous nights out with him, sharing some rough whores and some very fine wines, and settling a gambling debt of two thousand pesos for him, in an attempt to undermine his loyalty to Velázquez. As it happened the same sum, with the same purpose, had gone to Velázquez de Léon, the governor's cousin, and it was therefore no accident that neither had opposed the precipitous escape from Cuba. But Cortés prided himself on understanding human nature, and expected that these two fundamentally weak men would continue to play both ends against the middle, now appearing to side with him, now with Escudero, until they were more certain how things would turn out.

'In God's name you must not fight,' said the one-eyed priest De Cuellar at this point. Velázquez de Léon rumbled his agreement with the peacemakers, and the enormously strong Cristóbal de Olid, short, squat and gnome-like, with a wild black beard and twinkling blue eyes, bounded to Escudero's side and restrained him as he attempted to draw his sword.

So far Alonso de Grado, the surprise new convert to the Velazquista cause, had said not a word, but now he strode into the centre of the floor to join Montejo. He addressed Escudero. 'Don Juan,' he reasoned, 'there is no need for you to seek satisfaction. The caudillo did not mean to impugn your courage, I am sure.'

'He said I was shy,' sulked Escudero, 'and I am not shy, as I will prove to him with my blade.' He struggled fruitlessly against Olid's iron grip. 'Release me, Don Cristóbal! It is my right to defend my honour.'

'Your honour is not at issue here,' De Grado insisted. He was a tubular, stooping, bulbous-nosed man, whose fair skin and thinning blond hair, combed over his crown in a vain attempt to hide a bald patch, gave him more the look of a tax collector or an office clerk than a bold conquistador. 'The caudillo did not say you were shy,' he now told Escudero. 'His exact words were that he should not like to *think* you shy, and that, you must agree, is a very different matter.'

Cortés had been watching the whole scene unfold with wry amusement. All the Velazquistas knew that he was a far better and more experienced swordsman than Escudero and that barring some mischance there was only one plausible outcome to a duel. Part of him was eager to get on with it, run the pride-addled fool through and end their feud then and there, but another part of him – the stealthy, more calculating side of his character – preferred to wait and find a legal pretext to hang Escudero. It should not be too difficult; indeed an idea was already beginning to form in his mind as to the manoeuvres needed to bring it about when there came the sound of footsteps and raised voices and Bernal Díaz poked his head through the door of the pavilion.

The young ensign pointedly ignored the Velazquistas. 'Caudillo,' he said. 'My apologies for disturbing you, send me away if I am wrong, but there's an urgent development I think you should know about . . .'

Tozi lurked invisibly amongst the nobles, warriors and royal attendants crowded into the courtyard, trying to make sense of what was happening there. Open to the sky, it was an immense rectangular space perhaps a hundred paces in length and eighty wide, and encompassed by a paved and covered walkway bordered on its inner side by a colonnade. The courtyard itself was floored with polished flagstones, but at its centre these had been removed and a pit dug in the earth beneath them – a pit five paces square filled with blazing logs that sent up billows of pungent smoke to the heavens. On the north side of the pit, set back from it some fifteen paces, an imposing throne, presently unoccupied, had been positioned with benches arrayed next to it, on which sat some thirty of the leading notables of the land. Opposite them, on the south side of the pit, but much closer to the fire, four male captives dressed in the paper loincloths of sacrifice, their hands tied behind their backs, their bodies smeared with chalk, their shaved heads decorated with raven feathers attached with a glue of molten rubber, stood in line. A row of guards behind them were armed with long, obsidian-bladed spears. Held back by more guards, the crowd nevertheless pressed in impatiently, faces lurid in the flickering flames and alight with bloodlust. Never let it be said that the Mexica were not eager to witness death!

Who were these captives to merit such a public display? Tozi drifted closer, much closer, but it was not until she was right beside them on the south side of the pit that she recognised their twisted, tortured faces. These were none other than the royal sorcerers Tlilpo, Cuappi, Aztatzin, and Hecateu, who until recently had been accorded high status, even though their spells had failed utterly to keep her out of the palace or detect her presence when she was there. It seemed that Moctezuma had at last discovered how useless they were and decided to rid himself of them.

She felt a thrill of excitement. Had he learned about her? Or was it some other failure on their part that merited this spectacular execution?

Even as the thought crossed her mind there came a disturbance at the east side of the courtyard; a procession entered with a splendid palanquin borne aloft by royal bodyguards. With hatred in her heart, Tozi watched the members of the crowd, young and old, aristocrat and commoner, cringe back as one and throw themselves to the ground as the Great Speaker passed, as the palanquin was brought forward, and as Moctezuma, dressed in robes of the finest purple, was helped down and took his place on the waiting throne, finally lifting his hand to wave the spectators again to their feet.

There was such pomp, such pride, such a sense of entitlement about him! Casually Tozi sent a dart of fear his way and watched with satisfaction as he jerked upright, his eyes casting about, now left, now right.

Oh my, she thought, *oh my! This is going to be such fun!*

But she wouldn't rush, she decided.

Better to draw out the humiliation, better to let the evening unfold to its climax, before she showed the monster the real meaning of terror.

When Moctezuma had regained his composure, he leaned to whisper in the ear of the high priest Namacuix who stood by his side. Namacuix in turn barked an order and attendants rushed to surround the fire, raking the burning logs, subduing the last of the flames until the pit was filled only with fiercely glowing red embers. On another command, the guards levelled their spears and pushed the four captives forward until they stood squirming and begging for mercy at the very edge of the pit, so close that their paper clothing shrivelled, blackened and burned away entirely, leaving them naked and weeping with pain.

An expectant hush fell. The guards stood poised ready. The captives teetered on the edge of the pit and then, quite suddenly, Tozi felt a chill enter her heart. Moctezuma raised his hand again and the crowd on the west side of the courtyard parted as though divided by a knife.

Through the lane that opened up in the midst of the throng someone – some *thing* – was approaching.

Some terrible, unspeakable thing.

* * *

'Well, speak up, man,' Cortés said to Díaz. 'What's this urgent development?'

'Indians, Caudillo. Twenty Totonac Indians. I've taken the liberty of having Malinal talk to them, sir – one of them speaks her lingo – and it seems they want to help us fight Moctezuma.'

'Twenty,' scoffed Escudero. 'Fat lot of good twenty will do us.' His hand was back on the hilt of his sword, Olid having released his hold on him the moment Díaz had entered.

'No, you misunderstand me, Don Juan,' Díaz said. 'These twenty are just a delegation, but they claim they have tens of thousands of warriors ready to fight at our side if we'll take Moctezuma on.'

It was plain from the look on the young ensign's face that he'd not failed to sense the explosive antagonism between Cortés and Escudero, and he stood by uncertainly, waiting for an answer.

'Well, well,' Cortés said, to put him out of his misery. 'Interesting, eh . . .' He rubbed his hands together and gave Escudero a hard stare. 'Don Juan, what say you and I settle our differences later, and meanwhile let's hear these Indians out. What they tell us may have bearing on your plans to return to Cuba.'

'Not a chance,' Escudero sneered.

'Still, we should hear them,' Ordaz said firmly.

'I agree,' said De Grado. 'An excellent idea.'

'No harm in it that I can see,' said Montejo, after which Olid, Velázquez de Léon and the priest also quickly fell into line, leaving Escudero no choice but to concede also.

Cortés turned to Díaz. 'Very well, Bernal, you can bring in their spokesman – but leave the other nineteen outside, eh!' He laughed: 'You say Malinal is with you to interpret?'

'Yes, Caudillo.'

'What about Aguilar?'

'Indisposed, sir.'

Pepillo recognised the Totonac spokesman the moment he entered the pavilion, and it was immediately clear the caudillo did also. 'Isn't he one of the pair the Mexica wanted to offer us for human sacrifice?' he asked Malinal.

When she didn't immediately understand his question, Pepillo was able to clarify for her in a mixture of Castilian and his own halting Nahuatl.

'Ah, I see, I see,' she said, getting the gist quickly as she always did. She turned to Cortés. 'Yes, lord, same. He owe you life he say. He want pay debt.'

'Has he told you his name?'

'His name Meco.'

Cortés stepped forward to greet the tall, broad-shouldered, heavily tattooed Indian, while Pepillo gazed at the numerous scars on the man's body – some old, some fresh – and at his long, braided hair and the bone plugs in his lips and ears, which together gave him a wild, savage demeanour. His eyes, however, were intelligent and forthright, and Pepillo noticed that he didn't look away, or even blink, under scrutiny.

'You are welcome here,' Cortés said finally, holding out his hand.

Malinal put the words into Nahuatl and the Indian seized Cortés's hand in his own, shaking it up and down vigorously.

When the formalities were over, the negotiation began – and it was, Pepillo recognised as he made notes, a negotiation from the very beginning. The Totonacs obviously thought they had something to offer and equally obviously believed the Spaniards had something to give in return.

'Do you belong to the same Totonac tribe as the labourers who were sent to us from Cuetlaxtlan?' Cortés asked, 'the labourers who have now fled?'

Meco replied that he did belong to the same tribe.

'But your dress and appearance are very different. You look like a free man. They seemed like slaves.'

With some difficulties in interpretation, which Pepillo was again able to help untangle, Meco explained that his people were from the great city of Cempoala, the Totonac capital, two days' march to the north, and that unlike their kin on this part of the coast, they had preserved a degree of independence from the Mexica. Even so, they were vassals, and as the tortuous conversation continued, with many stops and starts for clarification, their intent gradually emerged.

Along with everyone else in the region, they had heard of the spectacular defeat of the Maya at Potonchan, which had greatly impressed them. Moreover, said Meco, placing his hand over his heart, he could never forget the events of two weeks before when the Spaniards had stood up to the feared Mexica and Cortés had forced Teudile to release him and his son – for that was who the other intended victim had been. They had fled to Cempoala and reported the matter to their paramount chief, a man called Tlacoch, who had conceived the hope that Cortés might liberate the Totonacs from their hated overlords and sent Meco back to watch for an opportunity to approach him. He had been unable to do so while the labourers and their Mexica overseers were present, but now they were gone and Teudile's delegation had been sent 'running off home to Tenochtitlan', as Meco put it, he had seized his opportunity. The burden of his message was this: would Cortés consider a visit to Cempoala to meet with Tlacoch for discussions that might prove to be of mutual advantage?

Cortés replied with flattery and friendly words and told Meco that the answer was yes; there were some matters he needed to attend to first, but very soon he would come to meet the great chief. 'By the way,' he asked casually, 'can Cempoala be reached by boat?'

No, Meco replied, that would not be possible, since the Totonac capital stood somewhat inland.

'Is there another city on the coast that is close?'

Meco replied that there was. Its name was Huitztlan, and it lay within a sheltered bay a few hours' march north of Cempoala.

When Cortés had satisfied himself as to all this, he ushered Meco from the pavilion, beckoning to Malinal to accompany them. Muffled words were exchanged outside. When Cortés returned, Malinal was no longer with him.

'Well, gentlemen,' he said, beaming at the Velazquistas. 'What did you make of our visitor?'

'Filthy savage,' said Escudero, scratching a livid mosquito bite on his brow.

'Filthy he may be, but what he came to say changes things, does it not?'

'It changes nothing.'

'Really?' said Cortés, sounding amazed. 'I feel quite differently. The noble Meco revealed dissensions amongst the Indians. I believe we can exploit such dissensions to set them one against the other, and go on to win the great prize of Tenochtitlan and the mountains of gold we know the Mexica possess. To be sure they have given us a king's ransom in treasure already, but think how much more we stand to gain if only we persevere – all the more so now we have a real prospect of winning allies who can provide us with auxiliaries, reserves, supplies – even a sheltered port, for God's sake; everything we need to mount a sustained campaign.'

'Savages with bones through their noses,' scoffed Escudero.

'But savages who hate the Mexica and will fight for us if we give them encouragement,' Cortés continued reasonably. 'Come, Don Juan, don't be so quick to dismiss this sign that God has given us of his blessings for our enterprise.'

'I'm with the caudillo,' announced De Grado. He laid a hand on Escudero's shoulder: 'I was all for your plan to return to Cuba,' he explained. 'It seemed wise. But this proffered alliance with the Totonacs changes the calculation. With respect, Don Juan, I wish to see how it develops before I agree to sail.'

'There's nothing to lose,' added Montejo, 'and everything to gain. I say we go to Cempoala.'

'We should go to Cempoala,' agreed Olid. 'Two days' march! What's that when there's so much at stake?'

Continuing to take notes, Pepillo wondered at the inconstancy of the Velazquistas, so easily swayed first one way then the other. It was a stroke of luck for Cortés – luck was often on his side! – that the Totonacs had turned up when they did; even so, most of these men, with the single exception of Escudero, were like clay in his hands, easily bent to his will. Indeed even Escudero could be manipulated, Pepillo saw, as Cortés now skilfully turned the conversation back to the matter of the ringleader's honour the moment it was clear the majority opinion amongst the Velazquistas had swung firmly against an immediate return to Cuba.

'Juan,' he said magnanimously, 'let us bury our differences. Francisco was right earlier when he said I did not mean to impugn your honour.

We should not fight – a fight in which one of us must certainly die – over such a petty misunderstanding of words . . .'

'You will apologise to me then.'

'Certainly I apologise for expressing myself clumsily. I have no doubt of your courage. I have never doubted it. Indeed, I hope to rely on it in the months ahead as we pit ourselves against the might of the Mexica.'

'But it is not yet settled that we shall do so,' objected Escudero. He looked around at his companions. 'I accept that we should discover the value of an alliance with the Totonacs, but if it proves to be worthless, as I suspect, then I trust you will all agree on an immediate return to Cuba. Even you, Cortés – will you agree to that?'

'It is my responsibility as captain-general to act in the best interests of all the expeditionaries,' Cortés said smoothly. 'And I make no secret of my view that our best interests will be served, with or without the Totonacs, by marching on Tenochtitlan and taking everything the Mexica have and making it our own. But I tell you what, Juan, let us put this to the test. We will learn more of this Totonac offer and then at some suitable time we will call for a vote of the whole army on whether to stay here in Mexico and take it by conquest or whether we return to Cuba as you wish. Will you abide by such a vote? What do you say?'

'I say yes, of course.' Escudero was visibly discomfited with the eyes of all his allies upon him. 'We will take a vote and we will abide by it.'

He could, Pepillo realised, hardly say otherwise. But what game, exactly, was Cortés playing here?

Sometimes his master's mind was as impenetrable to him as a thick fog.

At first what Tozi saw padding through the crowd was a huge jungle beast with burning yellow eyes, a black jaguar, massive and relentless, as tall as a fully grown man at the shoulder. As the creature drew closer to the pit, however, a transformation overcame it, shadows seemed to surround it, its form shimmered and faded, and finally – some sorcery was at work! – it resolved itself into the appearance of a lean and muscular Chichemec nomad. He was dressed only in a loincloth, but his entire body from his bare feet to his shaved head was covered in swirling black tattoos.

Tozi felt a prickle of fear – fear again! – but also of fascination. Who was this man? Only an immensely powerful sorcerer, a *nagual* of the highest order, could shift his shape so effortlessly.

Silent, invisible, undetected, fixed in her place on the other side of the sacrificial fire, Tozi watched as the bizarre tattooed figure advanced towards the royal throne on which the Great Speaker sat stock still, as though hypnotised. She saw that the *nagual* approached and did not prostrate himself – did not even bow his head. Who was he that Moctezuma should accord him such a high and unprecedented public honour? How could it be that he was allowed to come so near? Now he leaned forward. Now his face brushed the face of the Great Speaker. Now he whispered something in the royal ear.

Without consciously having willed it, Tozi realised she was no longer in the place where she had stood a moment ago, but was moving slowly, inexorably forward, as though drawn by some magnetism. She skirted the west side of the sacrificial pit and by slow increments came closer, and closer still, to the twined figures of the *nagual* and the ruler seemingly locked in some intimate exchange. Now she was ten paces from them and the nobles on their benches surrounding them, now five paces, now just an arm's length, and then suddenly, shockingly, the *nagual* whirled around and looked straight at her, *as though he could see her*, his yellow eyes reflecting the red glow of the embers in the pit, burning like molten gold.

There was recognition and intelligence, ferocity and cunning also, and a malign hunger in those unblinking eyes. Yet it was less them that fixated her attention than the writhing, intricate tattoos covering the broad, flat, cruel face in which they were set – tattoos that twisted and intertwined, as though filled with a life of their own, revealing, in their dots and swirls and tendrils, a thousand transient, half-recognised shapes and forms.

Tozi gasped and staggered back, feeling the scorching heat of the pit behind her and in the same instant the *nagual* raised his face to the dark skies above and laughed – HA, HA, HA, HA, HA, HA, HA, HA, HA, HA, HA; a horrible, reverberating, mocking bray that seemed to go on for ever, while beneath its noise, not speaking aloud but somehow conveyed by thought, a hissing reptilian voice breached her sanctuary of invisibility and penetrated her skull and said: '*Of course I see you, girl. You cannot hide from me.*'

Vaguely aware that Moctezuma had given an order and that the four captives had been tumbled howling and thrashing into the pit where they would be held in place by the spears of the guards and roasted alive, Tozi turned and fled.

It was late, and the Velazquistas were long gone, when Cortés had Pepillo bring Juan de Escalante to the pavilion. Escalante had saved Cortés's life on the first day of fighting at Potonchan, when a sudden ambush had threatened everything, and was the most trusted of his captains and friends – more trusted even than Alvarado, who had too much self-interest ever to be entirely reliable. Escalante was also a discreet, confidential man, who'd been dead set from the beginning against the Velazquistas, who was not given to boasting and loose talk like Alvarardo, and was therefore in every way ideal for the task that Cortés now had in mind for him.

'Juan,' he said, 'welcome. My apologies for disturbing your rest at this late hour.'

'It's nothing,' said the other man. 'I wasn't sleeping anyway.'

'May I offer you a little wine? I have a very fine Galician red from my private reserve.'

'That would be nice, Hernán.' A smile. 'I'm guessing you want something from me.'

'Yes . . . well, as it happens I do, but let us drink first. Pepillo! See to it.'

Escalante was long-limbed and lean, almost gaunt, with prominent cheekbones, a wolfish, heavily bearded face and startlingly blue eyes. He was somewhat vain of his appearance and his straight black hair hung down to his shoulders in order to conceal the sword wound from the Italian wars that had left a deep scar along the side of his skull and deprived him of the top two-thirds of his right ear.

'To the success of our expedition,' Cortés said, raising his glass, 'and to the glory of His Majesty Don Carlos.'

'And to the confusion of our enemy Diego de Velázquez,' Escalante added. 'May he grow boils on his backside and may all the schemes of his sycophants and supporters come to naught.'

'I'll drink to that!' Cortés laughed. They drained their glasses at a draught and he poured again. 'Indeed, a strategy to confuse and confound Velázquez further is very much on my mind at the moment, since I've spent the evening dealing with Escudero and his gang; it's why I've called you here.'

Cortés proceeded to tell his friend about the meeting with the Velazquistas and about the distraction from their endless complaints that the surprise arrival of the Totonac embassy had brought. 'But I fear this respite will be brief,' he concluded, 'and since I have offered a vote on whether to return to Cuba or not—'

'A hostage to fortune if ever there was one!' Escalante interrupted.

'Since I have offered a vote,' Cortés continued, 'I intend to do everything in my power to make certain it goes our way. It occurs to me that one factor weighing against us is the extreme discomfort of our present quarters here on these unwholesome dunes.' He slapped at a mosquito to make his point; indeed both men were surrounded by clouds of the biting insects that infested the camp, making everyone's life a misery.

'Bloodsucking little bastards,' agreed Escalante with feeling. 'Just when the mosquitoes are done with us at dawn, the sandflies take over for the rest of the day. There'll be a big boost in morale if we can find another site.'

Cortés nodded. 'We're also too close to Cuetlaxtlan, with its large Mexica garrison. We could thrash them, I've no doubt of it, but I'd prefer to do so at a time of my own choosing. I don't want to tempt them to some folly by staying in this godforsaken shit-hole a moment longer than we need to.'

'So you want me to go and recce some other sites?' said Escalante, divining Cortés's purpose.

'Yes, Juan, absolutely. Find us a site, and not just for another camp. I believe we must put down permanent roots in this land, establish a colony—'

'A colony! Now there's an idea that will drive the Velazquistas mad!'

Establishing a colony had been explicitly ruled out by Velázquez when the mandate for the expedition had been granted, but then so had just about everything else that Cortés had in mind.

'Escudero will oppose it tooth and nail,' he conceded. 'He'll stir up trouble. He'll claim it as yet another sign of my perfidy, but I think I know a way to outmanoeuvre him – so yes, Juan, please find us a site where we can build a town. The sooner the better. Go north. That's where our newfound Totonac allies say they're strongest. Their chief city is called Cempoala. It's two days' march from here and somewhat inland, but I learned from them of another city they control on the coast – what was its name, Pepillo?'

Pepillo consulted his notes. 'Huitztlan, sir.'

'Very good, yes, Huitztlan, a few hours' march north of Cempoala. That's where I'd like you to head for, Juan. I've reason to believe it will provide a safe anchorage for our fleet and a good place to plant our first colony in these new lands.'

'How will I know it when I see it?'

Cortés could not resist a broad grin of self-satisfaction. 'I have a guide for you,' he said, 'none other than the Totonac emissary Meco himself. I told Malinal to ask him to return the day after tomorrow. Will you be ready to sail by then, do you think?'

'My *Santa Theresa*'s full of leaks like the rest of the fleet, but nothing the pumps can't handle, so I'm happy to sail. But how am I to communicate with this . . . what's his name – Meco?'

'Malinal must stay with me,' Cortés said. 'I need her here in case further negotiations are called for with the Mexica, but my page speaks a few words of the Nahuatl language – eh, don't you, Pepillo?'

'Yes, sir, a few.'

'More than a few I'd say. You were very helpful tonight. And it seems Meco speaks Nahuatl too . . .'

'He does, sir.'

'So there you are, Juan. Pepillo will accompany you to serve as your interpreter and I wish you sweet sailing and a swift return.'

'Sir,' said Pepillo hesitantly.

Cortés frowned. 'Yes?'

'I would like to take my dog with me, sir, that is if you and Don Juan do not object.'

'Your dog?' frowned Cortés. 'What use is a dog on a ship, lad? Leave him here I say. It's high time he was put in with the rest of the pack anyway.'

'But, sir—'

'I'll tolerate no buts from you, boy. The dog stays. You go.'

Chapter Twenty-Four

Friday 14 May 1519 to Sunday 16 May 1519

'We'll have that cur of yours for the pack,' Miguel Hemes yelled. 'The caudillo won't protect you much longer.' A filthy, ragged, lice-infested, pimply urchin of fifteen, one of Telmo Vendabal's assistant dog handlers, Hemes had been following Pepillo around the camp on his errands all morning, taunting and tormenting him. Now, suddenly and ominously, he was reinforced by two of the others, fat Francisco Julian, also fifteen, puffing and perspiring as he appeared over the top of a dune, and Andrés Santisteban, Vendabal's senior apprentice, nigh on seventeen years old, whose sparse black beard did nothing to hide the mass of smallpox scars on his face, but whose constant smile success-fully disguised – for those who did not know him well – a vindictive and malicious nature.

Of the three, Pepillo feared Santisteban the most because of the consistent bullying he meted out: the kicks, the sly shoves and kidney punches when no one was watching; the choke holds and the dirty tricks designed, whenever possible, to put Pepillo in a bad light with the caudillo. It had all got so much worse in the past three weeks; Melchior's courage and fighting spirit during the kidnap attempt by the Tlascalans had only served to inflame Vendabal's desire to possess the young lurcher and it seemed that Cortés was persuaded by the hunchback's arguments. His refusal to let Pepillo take Melchior on the voyage north in Escalante's carrack, his insistence that it was time for the dog to join the pack and the fact that the promised intervention by Bernal Díaz had also failed to materialise were bad signs. Although Melchior had not yet, in fact, been wrested away from him, Pepillo had decided to take matters into his own hands.

'Leave me alone,' he yelled as he hurried through the dunes towards the beach. He broke into a run but Santisteban soon caught up with him, grasping him firmly by the shoulder. 'Not so fast,' the older boy said. 'We want to speak with you.'

Pepillo struggled to free himself but Santisteban was much stronger than him; he kicked Pepillo's legs out from under him, forcing him to his knees on the sand. 'Give up your dog,' he said. 'Bring him to Don Telmo tonight, make a gift of him, and we'll leave you alone. Otherwise—'

'Otherwise what?' Pepillo spat. 'You'll beat me up again?'

Santisteban punched Pepillo square on the nose, a hard blow that drew blood. 'Yes,' he said. 'We'll beat you up again.'

'Beat me up all you like,' Pepillo was defiant. 'I don't care.' He used his sleeve to wipe blood and snot from his face. 'I'll never give you Melchior.'

'Then we'll kill your precious Melchior. Don Telmo's orders. If he can't have him for the pack, he doesn't see why you should have him as a pet.'

'We'll poison him, see?' It was Hemes speaking now, his voice going high and low, still not fully broken. 'We got wolfsbane to put in his meat.'

'But it'll be dog's bane for him,' tittered Francisco Julian. 'Unless you do what we say.'

'You wouldn't dare,' Pepillo protested. 'It would be a waste of a good dog. I'll tell the caudillo you did it. You'll be punished.'

'He'll never believe you if you tell him,' said Santisteban, reaching down to punch Pepillo again, this time low in his belly, knocking all the wind out of him and leaving him sprawled, gasping on the sand. 'No one will believe you. It'll just be one of those accidents that can happen to a dog.'

After the three boys had gone, Pepillo picked himself up, dusted off his clothes, wiped his face again and made a beeline for the beach. Wolfsbane was deadly. A few drops on a piece of meat would be enough. Melchior, growing larger and heavier by the day, had a huge appetite; he would gobble down any scraps he was offered so fast he wouldn't even notice the foul taste of the poison.

But at least that wouldn't be happening tonight. A stiff wind was blowing from the southwest, a good wind for sailing and, as he'd arranged earlier, Malinal was waiting for him by the longboat with his bounding, happy dog. 'You be in big trouble with caudillo about this,' she said as she passed the leash to him. 'He no like disobey.'

'I know, but I have to disobey him. I just have to. Thank you for understanding.'

'Sweet boy,' said Malinal. She kissed his brow and dabbed, with a look of concern, at the blood drying under his nose. 'Sail well. Come back safe.'

The Totonac warrior Meco had taken his place in the longboat and the crew were at the oars ready to row them out to Don Juan de Escalante's carrack *Santa Theresa*, which was bobbing at anchor in the bay. 'Come on, Melchior!' Pepillo yelled. The dog barked excitedly and the two of them charged through the surf and leapt aboard.

Guatemoc watched the small boat move out through the surf towards the fleet of vastly larger vessels in the bay and noted two things with interest. First one of the war animals, undoubtedly some monstrous species of dog if its behaviour was anything to judge by, was being carried in the boat. Second, a Totonac warrior was also a passenger. What were the implications of this, Guatemoc wondered. He'd ordered all the local labourers away from the camp, and they'd done as they were told, but this man had the look of a Cempoalan, and the Cempoalan Totonacs were a bloody-minded lot.

Guatemoc narrowed his eyes as the small boat bumped against one of the giant ones and its passengers climbed to the deck above by means of a rope ladder; the dog was last to follow, hauled up in a basket. Moments later came the sound of shouts carried distantly across the water, and men could be seen scurrying to and fro in a frenzy of activity. As though by magic, huge wings of cloth, which billowed as they caught the breeze blowing off the shore, sprouted from the three tall poles soaring high above the mountainous vessel, and suddenly it was on the move, slow at first but soon gaining speed, cutting through the waves like a knife, sending up a spray of foam to either side and leaving a lasting trace of its path in the bay behind it.

Guatemoc watched spellbound – he had to admit that he was impressed – until the giant craft rounded the headland and disappeared northwards in the direction of Cempoala.

The forced march back to the coast had been as fast as any Guatemoc had ever achieved, with Cuetlaxtlan reached soon after dawn. Leaving his five hundred Cuahchics to catch their breath and enjoy Pichatzin's reluctant hospitality, he'd then hurried forward with Mud Head, Big Dart, Man-Eater, Fuzzy Face and Starving Coyote to observe the interlopers at close quarters. There was nowhere to hide five hundred Cuahchics out here – their presence would have amounted to an open declaration of war – but he and his friends were light enough on their feet to conceal themselves amongst the dunes, avoiding the regular patrols of white-skins mounted on strange deer sent out to scout the terrain between the camp and Cuetlaxtlan. After observing the pattern and regularity of the patrols, following a few of them at a distance, Guatemoc satisfied himself that they almost never consisted of groups larger than just three mounted men – more usually two – and that they typically ranged a few miles southwards, coming within sight of the outskirts of Cuetlaxtlan before turning back. He resolved that tomorrow, or at the latest the day after, he would deploy a hundred of his Cuahchics to ambush one of these patrols close to Cuetlaxtlan, snatch the men and the beasts they rode, and then kill them in such a way that a response from the main force would be inevitable.

'What do you reckon?' he asked his friends after he'd shared the idea with them. 'Can it be done?'

They all agreed that it could. Admittedly the battle skills of the foreigners and their deer were unknown, other than the rumours – surely exaggerated – of their prowess against the Maya at Potonchan; but it seemed inconceivable that one of the smaller two-man patrols could outfight a hundred Cuahchics.

'By the gods, we'll be no better than women if we can't pull this off,' exclaimed Mud Head.

'Indeed I will personally volunteer to bend over and let them fuck me up the arse if we fail,' said Starving Coyote with a straight face.

* * *

The raiding party was three hundred men strong, all of them Chichemec mercenaries recently hired by Moctezuma to reinforce his armies. They were bandits, not trained warriors, but they were seasoned snatchers of victims for human sacrifice, and they were used to getting their way in the defenceless villages they targeted.

Villages like Teolo where Shikotenka had finally caught up with them. It was their last call before fleeing back over the Mexica border with their shameful haul of a thousand captives, all of them women and girls.

Teolo, a poor hamlet of a few hundred wattle-and-daub huts encircling a muddy central plaza, lay at the bottom of a valley, surrounded by densely forested slopes providing excellent cover for the fast-moving Tlascalan force of two hundred picked men that Shikotenka led. Tree and Ilhuicamina were still recovering from their wounds, and Acolmiztli was dead at the hands of the accursed white-skins, so the only one of his original captains to accompany him on this rescue mission was Chipahua, his right forearm still bound in bandages but healing fast.

'We're outnumbered,' Shikotenka observed to his friend.

'Not that we've ever been bothered by that,' Chipahua replied, clenching and unclenching the fist of his right hand twice before reaching back over his shoulder to draw his obsidian-edged *macuahuitl* broadsword from its leather scabbard.

After slaying the handful of guards posted around the edge of the forest by the overconfident Chichemecs, Shikotenka had sent contingents of men to encircle the village so that when he gave the signal to go in they could do so from all sides at once. Under normal circumstances, given the disparity of numbers, he would have preferred to launch a couple of *atlatl* volleys into the mass of the enemy milling in the plaza, but that was unfortunately out of the question today, since their captives were there with them, bound and huddled in a pathetic mass, while the last of the villagers were rounded up. The mercenaries, many already drunk on looted pulque, were well ahead with the butchery of men, boys and mature women, while the younger women and girls, screaming in terror and outrage, were being herded into place with the other prisoners who, again, were all females.

'No rapes,' Chipahua observed.

'As has been the case elsewhere,' Shikotenka mused. He'd been inclined to discount the reports he'd heard about this new and strange behaviour, but now he was seeing it for himself. Mass rapes were a hallmark of the Chichemecs, something they regarded as a perk of the service they gave the Mexica. With such an abundance of female prisoners at their disposal, there must be some very good reason why they were acting so delicately.

The mercenary leader was easily identified, strutting about in the middle of the plaza, striking off the heads of a row of kneeling men with savage blows of his *macuahuitl* and bellowing with pride whenever he managed it at a single stroke. He seemed to be taking real pleasure in the task.

'Let's try to grab that one alive,' Shikotenka said to Chipahua. 'I've got some questions for him.'

Chipahua grinned, a gruesome sight since many of his front teeth were broken. 'So,' he said, 'are you going to give the signal?'

Shikotenka nodded. Everyone should be in place now and, even if they weren't, he wasn't prepared to witness this slaughter a moment longer. He raised the war conch to his lips and blew a single long, furious blast.

'I've come for the cur,' said Vendabal. The hunchback's manner was more than usually surly and disrespectful.

'Go and get him then,' Cortés replied. 'He's tied up by the kitchen.'

'No he's not . . .'

'It is normal to call your leader by an honorific, Vendabal. "Sir" will do nicely, "Captain-general" if you prefer or, perhaps, "Caudillo". I will even accept "Don Hernán" at a push. But you may not address me as though I am a common soldier.'

'Sorry . . . Caudillo.' Vendabal made a vain attempt to straighten, and his horrible features creased into a sycophantic leer. 'But I've been hunting for that dog since I got your message, sir, and he ain't in the camp.'

'What do you mean he's not in the camp? Of course he is. Where else can he be?'

'Perhaps you should ask the boy, sir?'

'Pepillo? I've sent him on a reconnaissance mission with Don Juan de Escalante. Won't be back for a few days . . .'

'Well, there's your answer, Captain-general. He must've taken the mutt with him.'

'Nonsense, man. I gave strict orders that the dog was to stay behind.' Overtaken by a sudden intuition, Cortés wheeled on Malinal who was seated on a stool just inside the door of the pavilion. 'Do you know anything about this?' he asked.

'Pepillo take Melchior,' she said. There was something defiant in her tone and she looked Cortés straight in the eye.

'What?' he exploded.

'Pepillo take Melchior. Why not? Dog his friend.'

'I see,' said Cortés. The red tide of a great rage was building inside him, but he would not show it with Vendabal present. 'Go!' he told the dog handler. 'I'll see you get the animal the moment my page returns.'

Against superior numbers, the right tactics were maximum surprise and maximum ferocity. But it made things so much easier, Shikotenka reflected as he led the attack, when you commanded the best shock troops in the world.

In seconds he'd passed the last of the huts with Chipahua right beside him and fifty elite Tlascalans formed up behind them in a thundering, unstoppable wedge. Roaring war cries, they hit the surprised, already panicking Chichemec rabble at a full charge. Shikotenka swung his *macuahuitl* low and lopped the left leg off a big, red-painted mercenary, who tried to bar his way, took a knife wound on his upper left arm, swung high and decapitated the man who'd given it to him, smashed his heavy hardwood shield into the face of a third attacker scattering teeth in all directions before trampling him underfoot for one of the men behind to skewer. The phalanx was a killing machine, maintaining perfect order, each Tlascalan warrior using his shield to defend the warrior next to him, each specialised unit within the whole – spearmen, axemen, swordsmen, daggermen – working in perfect coordination with the others. Gaps opened up in the Chichemec defence by the *macuahuitls* and hatchets were exploited by the daggermen, who finished off the maimed and the injured at close quarters while the spearmen jabbed overhead, impaling men two or three ranks in front of them whose bodies fouled the feet of those trying to flee.

Meanwhile, other Tlascalan units closed in all around the circle to cut off every route of escape, forcing the terrified, jabbering mercenaries who sought shelter in the forest to turn back into the melee, where some even cut down their own comrades in their mad desperate rush to escape murder. A handful of Chichemecs, rather than fight the Tlascalans, were running amok amongst the captive women and girls, cutting throats, splitting heads, seeking to do whatever harm they could before they died, but Shikotenka's corps of twenty archers, darting around the edge of the fight looking for targets, put arrows into every one and the captives, with howls of fury, rose up and finished them off, tearing them limb from limb.

Shikotenka and Chipahua spotted the Chichemec leader at the same moment and began to work their way towards him through the heaving, bloody scrum. He was a big man with his head shaved, but for a crest of thick hair running from his brow to the nape of his neck. He'd lost his *macuahuitl* but had armed himself with a huge war axe, and as Shikotenka and Chipahua converged on him, he felled a Tlascalan with a killing blow to the temple, then hacked his weapon so hard between the ribs of another that it became lodged there. Chipahua darted forward and grabbed his arms as he tried to tug the weapon free; Shikotenka dropped to the ground and used his dagger to cut the Chichemec's hamstrings, crippling him in an instant. The man fell to the ground screaming and gushing blood as Chipahua prised his fingers away from the axe haft and trampled his face to silence him.

A few moments later the short, intense battle was over, the few surviving Chichemecs were rounded up, and Shikotenka dragged their unconscious leader to the edge of the plaza where he propped him against the wall of a hut.

'What shall we do with the others?' asked Chipahua, glancing in the direction of the remaining twenty or thirty dejected mercenaries now held captive.

'Use knives,' snarled Shikotenka. 'Gut them like peccaries.'

As the executions began, the Chichemec leader's eyes flickered open and filled with hate. 'Welcome back,' said Shikotenka, looming over him. 'I've got a few questions to ask you before you die.'

The Chichemec proved to be surprisingly hard-bitten, and night had fallen – after hours of patient torture – before he told Shikotenka the news that he already half expected to hear; news that had been conveyed to him by Huicton months before.

'The Great Speaker wishes to honour Hummingbird.'

'That's obvious, you stupid bastard!' Shikotenka turned the point of his knife, which was buried between the metacarpals of the Chichemec's hand. 'But why do you take only female victims?'

A groan. 'Because that's what Hummingbird wants.'

Shikotenka turned to Chipahua. 'Makes no sense,' he remarked. 'Hummingbird's a god of war. Why would he want female sacrifices?'

'Should be warriors,' grunted Chipahua. 'Fine warriors with big *tepullis* for the war god.'

The Chichemec laughed suddenly, his face twisted into a foul grimace and he coughed up a spray of blood. 'Hummingbird wants women,' he croaked. 'Women and girls, the younger the better.' A horrible leer: 'He wants them innocent. He wants them pure.'

Shikotenka leaned forward and stared into the mercenary's eyes. 'Is that why you don't rape them,' he asked?

'Pain of death if we rape them,' the Chichemec coughed. 'Moctezuma wants only virgins for Hummingbird.'

It was all beginning to make a twisted kind of sense, Shikotenka realised. There had been a few escapees from the raids over the past weeks, and more than one had reported that female prisoners were physically inspected to discover if they were intact; those found not to be virgins were killed. This would explain why the capture squads were focusing ever more intently on targeting female children rather than grown women during their raids.

Innocence, Shikotenka reflected . . . *purity*. These were the key words and thoughts; this was the new information he'd extracted during the interrogation.

Hummingbird didn't want virgins for their virginity.

What he wanted was their innocence!

Somehow the murder of innocents empowered both the war god and that vile creature Moctezuma who served as his regent on earth.

Judging there was nothing else to be learned from the Chichemec, Shikotenka opened the man's throat with a swift cut from ear to ear. He stood and looked around at his warriors. Only five had been killed in the fight against the mercenaries and no more than a dozen injured. It was a good result.

'Do we stay here, or head home?' Chipahua asked.

'We head home,' said Shikotenka, glancing at the wound on his left bicep, an ugly rip still dripping blood.

'You need to bind that,' observed Chipahua.

'No time,' said Shikotenka. If we march through the night we should reach Tlascala by noon tomorrow. I need to talk to my father and Maxixcatzin. We've got plans to make.'

Long after dark, with most of the crew who weren't on watch already snoring in their hammocks, Pepillo brought Melchior to a quiet corner on the main deck of the *Santa Theresa* to continue his education. The young lurcher was extremely clever and attentive and already knew how to sit, stand, stay, come hither and walk to heel on command. Tonight's lessons were 'leave it', 'take it', and 'bring it', and for these Pepillo was using a bone to which Melchior was very much attached. He dropped the bone to the deck, hauled Melchior back by means of his leash when he darted forward and ordered him to 'leave it'. He repeated this exercise a second and a third time. By the fourth try, Melchior had got the idea, and when Pepillo said, 'Leave it!' the dog waited, panting, eyeing the bone but not going for it. 'Good boy,' Pepillo said, slipping him one of the scraps he'd collected earlier from the galley and further rewarding him with elaborate praise and hugs. 'Very good boy!' He took off the leash, dropped the bone again with the command 'Leave it!' and Melchior remained still, ignoring temptation, looking up adoringly at his master and wagging his tail. Pepillo gave him another scrap of meat and rewarded him with further hugs and praise.

'So that's how it's done,' came a gruff voice, very close.

Pepillo looked round to see that Juan de Escalante had approached so silently that even Melchior, intent on his tricks, hadn't noticed.

'I'd always wondered,' the captain continued, 'how dogs were trained. Where did you learn this thoroughly useful skill?'

'I was raised by the Dominicans, sir, in their monastery in Santiago. We kept two dogs there to catch rats. Brother Rodriguez trained them and I helped, sir.'

'Ah . . . Brother Rodriguez, the librarian? I met him once. Seemed like a nice old duffer. Not like that bastard Muñoz who disappeared when we were on Cozumel. Quite a mystery, eh?'

Pepillo bit his tongue – Muñoz's disappearance was no mystery to him – and stayed silent.

'You worked for Muñoz, didn't you?'

'I was to be his page,' Pepillo admitted, 'but the caudillo required my services.'

'And you're happy serving the caudillo?'

'Oh yes, sir. It's a privilege. I'm learning a lot.'

'Including the local lingo! I saw you jabbering away with that Totonac today.'

It was true, Pepillo had been trying to talk with Meco most of the afternoon while the *Santa Theresa* sailed steadily north along the coast of Mexico. The two of them had managed to communicate reasonably well with a mixture of sign language and Pepillo's limited but growing Nahuatl vocabulary.

'I hope I will be able to interpret for you properly, sir, when we get where we're going. I'll try my best.'

There was a kindly twinkle in Escalante's blue eyes and his lean, weather-beaten face creased into a smile. 'I'm sure you will, lad,' he said. 'I'm sure you will.'

Pepillo had not had occasion to get to know the captain well in the months since the expedition had sailed from Cuba, but what little he had seen of him – a dashing warrior on the battlefield, a skilled sailor who treated his crew with respect – made him instinctively like and respect the man.

'You named him after your friend,' Escalante now said, looking down at the dog.

'I did, sir.'

'He was a good lad. He fought well atop the pyramid at Potonchan. I was sorry he died.'

'I too, sir.'

'I'm told you fought bravely yourself,' Escalante added.

'It was nothing,' Pepillo said, feeling suddenly embarrassed. 'I froze up with fear for a while, then I stuck my spear in an Indian. That was about it.'

'It takes a brave man to admit to fear,' Escalante said softly. 'It was your first action?'

Pepillo gulped and nodded. He didn't suppose the killing of Muñoz, which had anyway been done by Díaz and his friends Mibiercas and La Serna, really counted. 'Yes, sir, my first action.'

'So I take it you've never been taught how to wield a sword?'

'Never in my life, sir.'

'Would you like to learn?'

Pepillo's heart leapt. Reading *Amadis de Gaula* had fired him with a very private and secret ambition to become, one day, a swordsman and a hero of renown. But that ambition could never be achieved if he didn't even know how to use a sword.

'I'd love to learn, sir,' he blurted excitedly. 'I can't think of anything else I'd rather do more.'

'Good! Then you shall have your wish. Meet me here tomorrow morning an hour after dawn and I'll give you your first lesson.'

'Thank you, sir. You're very kind. I'll be here, sir.'

'It's nothing,' grinned Escalante. 'Oh, and stop calling me "Sir", will you! Don Juan will do very well.'

Coldly furious and silent, Cortés had dismissed Malinal right after Vendabal's departure from the pavilion and sought no further communication with her that day. She was now in Puertocarrero's quarters, struggling to avoid the foul-smelling Spaniard's latest attempt to penetrate her, when a messenger came rapping at the door and she leapt up to answer.

'The caudillo requires your presence,' the boy said with a cheeky look at Malinal's half-clad form, 'quick as you like.'

'It's late,' complained Puertocarrero from the makeshift bed of blankets strewn on the floor. 'Can't it wait till morning?'

'The caudillo says now, sir.'

'Then we'll both come,' said Puertocarrero, standing, his small pink *tepulli* fully erect in its nest of furious red hair.

'The caudillo's orders are for me to bring the interpreter only,' said the boy, suppressing a giggle that brought Malinal dangerously close to a laugh herself. 'He was quite definite about that, sir.'

Puertocarrero's erection was wilting fast. Seemingly aware of it for the first time, he snatched up a sheet to cover himself. 'Oh very well, go then,' he snapped at Malinal. 'But be quick about it. You've a woman's duties to perform here.'

When Malinal entered the pavilion she found Cortés in a better mood than when she had left him, naked but for a length of cloth around his waist, a smile on his face and a glass of wine in his hand. 'Here, drink this,' he said pouring another and passing it to her.

She accepted, cautiously. The drink the Spaniards called wine was tasty but made her head spin; she had taken some on board the caudillo's ship the first night he'd seduced her and it had made her feel foolish and wanton. No doubt he hoped it would elicit the same feelings in her now. She took a sip. 'You want see me?' she said. 'Got some interpret to do?'

'No, my dear. No work tonight, only play.' He moved in on her fast, enclosed her in a fierce embrace and kissed her. She tasted the wine on his tongue and broke free, almost dropping her glass. 'You sex me now and Puertocarrero find out,' she said, taking another, longer sip and looking Cortés knowingly in the eye.

'Damn Puertocarrero.'

'Damn him very good but if he smell you on me he beat me sure. Maybe kill.'

'Do you think I'd allow that?' Cortés asked. He took her glass from her hand and set it down with his own on his writing table before forcing himself on her again. This time she returned his embrace, caressing his hair and responding with enthusiasm to his kiss. She felt his hand lift the hem of her robe and part her thighs, felt her loins melt in automatic response, then jerked back—

'No, Hernán! Not now! Not good!'

'Yes, now! Yes good!' He stroked the moist lips of her *tepilli*, opening her and slipping a finger inside her, finding the hard knot of the neck of her womb as he shoved her back to lie across his desk, sweeping maps and papers to the floor. There came a crash as the wine glasses followed. 'No, Hernán!' she beat feebly at his face. 'Puertocarrero maybe follow, maybe hear us.'

He ignored her, lifted her robe over her head and cast it aside, leaving her naked; kissed her breasts, softly biting her nipples, moved down to her belly, kissed and sucked her *tepilli*, his tongue hot and eager, then moved up her body again, entered her with his *tepulli* – so much bigger, so much nicer than Puertocarrero's poor thing! – and began to thrust rhythmically.

'Wait!' she cried wriggling away from him, pushing her hand against the matt of dark hair covering his chest.

'Wait be damned!' He grasped her by the hips and pulled her down onto him, but once more she fought away. 'Pepillo,' she said, 'his dog, what you do?'

Sudden fury, combined with disbelief, raged in the caudillo's eyes as it had this morning. 'You're talking to me about Pepillo *now*? You're talking about that bloody dog *now*?'

'Pepillo my friend. He good boy. Don't want you hurt him. Want you be kind.' Malinal could cry at will, a skill she'd learnt in Tenochtitlan, and wept now, tears gushing hot down her cheeks.

Cortés's anger passed as swiftly as it had appeared. 'Come come, my love,' he crooned, 'don't cry.' His *tepulli* found her *tepilli* again, the rhythmic, pleasant thrusting resumed. 'I won't hurt the boy, I promise.'

'You let him keep dog?'

'Dear god, woman!'

Malinal clenched her buttocks, made a circling motion with her hips that no man she'd ever known could resist. 'Let him keep dog,' she urged again. 'Master, please, do this for me.'

Another swirl of her hips and Cortés groaned, his thrusting becoming stronger. She tried to pull away from him again but he stopped her with a gentle touch of his hand. 'All right,' he said, 'you win. I'll let Pepillo keep his damned dog and I won't punish him. You have my word on it.'

'Ahhh, yes . . . yes . . .' Malinal closed her eyes, relaxed, arched her back luxuriously, sighed deeply and at last committed herself body and soul to this unexpected act of love with her master. It wasn't difficult because she did love him after all, but there'd been no harm in transacting a little business along the way. Men were easier to manipulate when they were aroused.

She stayed with Cortés through the night, made love thrice more, and returned to her quarters at dawn reeking of sex. Strangely Puertocarrero was not there, and it crossed her mind, as she fetched a bucket to wash, that he might have been out all night too, lurking by the pavilion, spying on her, listening to the unmistakable sounds of coupling.

If so, it was hard to say what the outcome would be. Malinal yawned and stretched and found she was too tired, and too happy, to care.

As morning came the *Santa Theresa* scudded northwards, her sails billowing in a fine following wind, her keel slicing through the water and sending up a powerful bow wave.

Excited at the prospect of a lesson in swordsmanship, Pepillo had slept only fitfully, and dawn found him already at the spot where Escalante had told him to wait. He caught glimpses of the captain moving around the ship, in conversation with the boatswain, even climbing a mast and peering northwards, but more than an hour passed before he disappeared into his stateroom and then reappeared with not one but two scabbarded broadswords tucked under his arm.

He passed the smaller of the weapons to Pepillo. 'I was going to give this to my son,' he said, 'when he reached your age.'

Pepillo noticed the past tense and an undertone of sadness in the captain's voice and felt awkward. 'You have a son, sir?'

A rueful smile from the captain. 'Call me Don Juan as I told you last night. All these "sirs" make me uncomfortable. And to answer your question, I had a wife and son both, but they were carried away last year by the smallpox.'

'I'm so sorry. I don't know what to say.'

'Nothing to say, lad. Let's get to it, eh? Draw your sword.'

The hilt of Pepillo's weapon was wrapped in criss-crossed leather and copper wire. He closed his fingers around it and drew . . . and drew . . . and drew. The blade, bright, double-edged, with a deep wide groove running from the guard almost to the tip was somehow much longer than he had expected.

'It's heavy,' he said.

'Has to be heavy to do its job. That's why the first thing you'll need if you want to be a swordsman is strength.'

Pepillo felt anxious and bit his lower lip. 'I'm not strong, Don Juan.'

Escalante leaned forward, inspected him from head to foot, pinched his biceps between a calloused thumb and forefinger and said: 'Tut tut . . . Too much time in Brother Rodriguez's library, eh; not enough time out in the fields?'

'I suppose so, sir . . . I mean Don Juan. And since we left Cuba, my work has mostly been done sitting down.'

'Well, don't worry. You're not on the battlefield yet. There's plenty of time for you to make yourself strong. From now on, if you're serious about this, I expect you to do every bit of manual labour you can volunteer for, as well as physical exercises for an hour or two a day. I'll teach you some basic routines that'll build muscle, and you need to exercise for flexibility as well . . . How do you like the feel of the sword?'

Pepillo looked in awe at the beautiful, deadly thing in his hands, admiring the reflections of ocean and cloud in the polished steel of its blade. He tested its edge – sharp! – and made a few experimental slices, revelling in the swishing sound the weapon made as it passed through the air. He was entranced. 'I love it,' he said.

'Well, you'll have to love it and leave it for now. Put it back in its scabbard and give it here.'

'Why?' Pepillo asked, crestfallen.

'Because swordsmanship's all about footwork, balance and speed, and until you grasp at least the basic principles, there's little point in playing with the blade.'

Pepillo returned the weapon and Don Juan placed it on the deck with his own. 'Take a stance,' he said.

'A stance?'

'Yes, stand as strong and as firm as you can. I'm going to try to push you over. You try to stop me.'

Pepillo stood with his feet parallel and slightly apart.

'Ready?' asked Don Juan.

'Yes, ready.'

Suddenly the captain's hand shot out, fingers closed into a fist. The blow felt like being kicked by a horse and Pepillo went tumbling head over heels. Some members of the crew who were passing by sniggered. As Pepillo picked himself up, Don Juan asked: 'What did you learn from that?'

'I placed my feet wrongly?'

It was a wild guess, but the captain nodded his approval. 'You're weak with your feet close together and parallel like that . . . Here.' He reached down and guided Pepillo's leg. 'Slide your left foot forward . . . Good. Now slide your right foot back a little and turn the toes out to the side. Good! Yes. You've got it. That's a strong stance.' He placed his hand against Pepillo's chest and shoved, making him stagger back a step but not fall. 'See how you're able to resist me?'

'I . . . I think so.'

'But there's still something not quite right. Your centre was turned to the side then, and it needs to be turned to the front.'

'My centre?'

'Yes. Imagine a point about the width of two fingers beneath your belly button. That's your centre. When you took the stance your centre was turned to the right, in the direction of your right foot. It should have been aligned forward in the direction of your left foot. To fight with swords, Pepillo, is to dance with life and death. You are more likely to live, less likely to die, if you take care that your centre always faces your opponent as you dance and that every move you make originates from your centre. See this?' He pulled back the long hair that hung down almost to his shoulders. 'I got it in the Italian wars because I forgot my centre in the heat of battle.'

The old wound that Don Juan showed was an ugly one. Usually hidden by his hair, the top two thirds of his right ear was missing and a deep, puckered groove – long since healed into a pink mass of scar tissue – ran along the side of his skull.

'The blow reached me when I was off balance, hit me fast as a bolt of lightning. I lost my senses, fell like a poleaxed ox, and my attacker followed through with this.' The captain pulled up his shirt and revealed a second jagged scar crossing his belly. 'I was rescued by a good comrade. He killed the man just before he delivered the *coup de grâce*, dragged me out of there – though the fight raged all around us – and got me to a surgeon in time. He saved my life but I wouldn't have needed saving if I'd just watched my centre. Do you understand what I'm saying?'

Pepillo nodded his head vigorously. 'Strong stance,' he said, 'good balance, centre always facing the enemy.'

'And that way you stay alive.' The captain smiled. 'Had enough?'

'No, Don Juan.' Indeed Pepillo had never felt more invigorated or wide awake.

'Good! Then it's time to teach you the basic steps. No point in a nice strong stance if you don't know how to move.'

Moments after Malinal had slipped out of the pavilion, Cortés fell into an exhausted, satiated sleep, amongst the rugs they'd used on the floor when the hard surface of the desk had lost its charms. He slept and, as was often the case, he dreamed.

Dreamed of the golden city of Tenochtitlan that lured him on.

Dreamed of conquest and of honour.

Dreamed of Saint Peter, his patron, his guide, who held the keys to heaven and whose intercession, after so many sins, was his one sure route to salvation.

This time the setting was the place – he had travelled there in dreams more than once before – that Cortés took to be heaven itself, filled with beautiful, ethereal figures, male and female angels, he thought, all dressed in white, going placidly about their business. There was a great wall of mother-of-pearl around heaven, entered through high gates, but they always swung open to admit him when he arrived and he was wafted now, on the wings of a warm, soft wind, into the throne room, vaster than any cathedral, all made of scintillating amethyst and radiant sapphire, and thence forward until he stood in the mighty presence of Saint Peter himself.

Dressed in a simple hemp tunic, its sleeves rolled up revealing forearms knotted with muscle and huge hands made more for gripping a sword then bestowing blessings, the holy saint was a tall, robust man, as massive as Hercules, powerful in the chest and thighs, rugged featured, clean-shaven with thick fair hair, in which the blond of vigour was shot through with the grey of wisdom. He seemed in the prime of life, perhaps forty years of age; a nimbus of brilliant light shone from his body, particularly dazzling around his head, and there was an animal magnetism, a dangerous allure, a raw, overwhelming charisma and the unmistakable demeanour about him of a soldier used to command.

But it was his eyes, above all else, that demanded, required, indeed *compelled* attention, and that drew Cortés in towards him, helpless as a lamb to slaughter – eyes pitiless and remote, hard as diamonds, black as coals, yet paradoxically brilliant as the sun.

'Welcome, Captain-general,' said the saint. 'Your army is the army of God, and heaven blesses your venture.' He reached forward and placed his heavy hand on Cortés's head, seeming to press him down with the weight of the world.

'Thank you, Father,' Cortés replied, his voice choked with emotion.

'But you must not tarry long at the coast,' Saint Peter continued. 'Your enemy Moctezuma has summoned the help of the devil. Make haste to Tenochtitlan, my son, or you will face defeat.'

'My plans are already in motion, Father.'

'Good! Excellent! Yet hear me, my son. You must go by way of a city called Cholula, a vassal city to the Mexica. I am preparing a great victory for you there.'

'Cholula . . . Yes, Father. I will remember. I will be sure to place it on our route of march. But—'

'Yes?'

'There is something I must settle first. A problem. A difficulty . . .'

'Tell me, my son.'

'Certain of my captains conspire against me. I must flush out their plot and destroy them utterly before we begin our march. If I fail to do so, I run the risk of mutiny at some vital moment.'

'I know of this plot,' said the saint. 'I have already inspired you with the strategy to defeat it.'

Cortés looked up at him, surprised.

'Do you really think all your ideas are your own, my son?' Saint Peter laughed, a great rumbling bellow that began low in his gut and worked its way up through his chest to burst forth from his throat. No sooner had it died away, however, than there was a sudden change of subject: 'The native woman I arranged to have the Maya give you. You like her?'

'She's proving to be a gifted interpreter, Father.'

A sly smile. 'And gifted in other ways as well?'

Cortés hung his head, knowing nothing could be hidden. 'She is my lover, Father.'

'A tasty morsel, eh?'

It seemed a strange choice of phrase for a saint. 'Yes, Father,' Cortés replied.

That huge hand clapped down on his head again. 'Do not worry. Every good soldier deserves his bed slave and I am glad to provide her for you. Yet take care! She is a cunning serpent. You must treat her firmly. You must not let her lead you astray.'

'Astray, Father?'

'As she led you astray tonight . . .' The saint's fingers tightened in Cortés's hair, taking a powerful grip. His voice suddenly boomed: '*Teach her a lesson, my son!*'

'A lesson, Father, how?'

'Show her you are a man by denying her demands. Punish your page severely when he returns from his voyage. Take his dog from him and throw it in with the pack.'

'Your wish is my command, Father,' Cortés said as his dream dissolved into mist and he awoke in his pavilion, hot and covered with sweat.

He stood, staggered to the door, poked his head out and looked up. The sun was high, past midday, and waiting outside, chatting amiably with the guards, was Puertocarrero.

Huicton had been in Tlascala for three days waiting for Shikotenka to return from a renewed campaign against the Mexica. Now he was in conference with his father, Shikotenka the Elder, and with

199

Maxixcatzin, who served as deputy to both leaders, when the battle-king strode in to the audience chamber, his tunic covered in blood, and a fresh knife wound, as yet unbound, livid on his left bicep.

'Did we prevail?' asked Shikotenka the Elder in his dry, somewhat tremulous, ancient voice.

'We prevailed, father.' The younger Shikotenka seemed to see Huicton for the first time. 'You!' he said. 'Strange to find you here, now! You've been very much on my mind.'

Huicton studied the younger man. 'That's a nasty injury you've taken,' he said. 'Will you let me attend to it? I have some knowledge of medicines.'

'It's nothing. Just a flesh wound.'

'Nonetheless, it should be salved and bound. Flesh wounds can fester. I have an ointment in my quarters that's just the thing. Can I send for it?'

Shikotenka looked distracted. 'If you wish,' he said – immediately Maxixcatzin signalled to an attendant and sent him off to collect the salve – 'and since you're here, let's review again the offer you renewed a few days ago, of an alliance with your master Ishtlil.'

'An offer you turned down then, as you did once before.'

'I'm open to reconsidering it now, so long as it's not tied to any foolish plan to befriend the white men at Cuetlaxtlan.'

Huicton chose his words with care: 'For the moment the two matters can remain separate.'

'Then let's talk,' said Shikotenka, drawing up a stool.

'You've been tupping my woman,' Puertocarrero got straight to the point once they were sitting face to face within the pavilion. 'Don't deny it, Hernán. I followed her here last night, I saw her leave at dawn and I heard the pair of you hard at it.'

Cortés raised his eyebrows and spread his hands. 'What can I say, Alonso? You have caught me in the act . . .'

'You could start by saying you're sorry.'

'Look, let's have a glass of wine, shall we?' suggested Cortés. 'My head's pounding. A drop of the poison that caused it might cure it, as the saying goes.'

Puertocarrero's beady eyes brightened and his bushy red beard twitched. He was a man who liked a drink. 'A bit early, isn't it?'

'Oh to hell with that!' Cortés skirted the broken glasses still lying on the floor, found two more on a shelf, reached for the wine jug and poured. 'Here's to Malinal,' he said, 'a fine woman.'

'A whore!' said Puertocarrero, emptying his glass at a single swallow and holding it out for more. 'A damned scheming, conniving, libidinous whore. I've a mind to beat her to death.'

'Do that and I'll hang you for a traitor,' said Cortés. 'She's a vital asset to the expedition. Without her interpreting skills, we'd be lost in this land.'

'Traitor! It's you who's the traitor. You've betrayed our friendship by cuckolding me. I'll be the laughing stock of the whole camp.'

'The whole camp doesn't need to know, Alonso. I'll see to it the guards say nothing. This is just a matter between you and me.' Cortés was struck by a sudden intuition. 'Come on,' he added, 'admit it; you don't even like her.'

Puertocarrero had finished his second glass of Galician red and now helped himself to a third. 'Can't stand the stuck-up, whining bitch,' he agreed. 'Useless in bed – don't know what you see in her frankly – a shrew and a nag, thinks too highly of herself.' He looked defiantly at Cortés. 'She's been nothing but trouble since you gave her to me.'

'And what I gave is mine to take back,' Cortés reminded him, draining his own glass. 'I am your captain-general after all.' He pointed at the jug. 'More?'

'Don't mind if I do,' said Puertocarrero.

As Cortés poured again for both of them, his mind was working fast. This might prove much easier than he'd feared. With enough enemies already amongst the Velazquistas, he didn't want to alienate his old and hitherto reliable friend if he could possibly avoid it, and he now thought he saw the way out. He must nurse Puertocarrero's pride, persuade him to view what had happened with Malinal not as a personal slight but as a kind of *droit du seigneur* of the captain-general, and he must make sure the whole matter was kept discreet. He fully intended to continue – indeed increase! – his liaisons with

Malinal, but she would have to go on living with Puertocarrero if the proprieties were to be observed, and of course the word 'cuckold' must never cross anyone's lips.

But how? How was that to be achieved in the long term? Granted Puertocarrero really didn't seem to like her, but the man was by no means a complete fool, and surely he would expect, and must get, some great reward in return for his complicity in the affair. A picture of the huge treasure that the Mexica ambassadors had brought took shape in Cortés's mind and he thought: gold . . .

Gold would do it, as it always did.

He was considering which pieces would be sufficient to buy Puertocarrero off once and for all, and to keep his loyalty, when a new idea presented itself to him in a flash, a fully formed idea, immaculate and perfect, with which he could kill two, nay three; nay a whole flock of birds with one stone.

'The mountain provinces of Texcoco under your master's control share a common border with Tlascala, across which our troops – and yours – can move back and forth with ease,' said Shikotenka. 'As a first step in our new alliance, how about we guarantee your men refuge and reinforcements when they're under hot pursuit by Mexica forces? And how about you do the same for us?'

As the discussion continued, Huicton washed and dressed Shikotenka's wound. The battle-king seemed to have a great oppression hanging over him, and Huicton learned with careful probing that it was to do with the new Mexica practice of seizing virgin females for sacrifice. Shikotenka's loathing for this abomination, Huicton discovered, was what had sparked his change of mind on an allegiance with Ishtlil, and by the time the meeting was drawing to a close, they'd agreed not only on mutual Tlascalan and Texcocan support against Mexica hot pursuit, but also, in the longer term, on the need to create a unified army of both peoples – something that had been inconceivable to the independent-minded Tlascalans even a month before.

Only when all this had been talked through and settled did Huicton bring up the matter of the white-skinned strangers again. 'I have visited their camp,' he said. 'I have met their leader.'

Shikotenka's face darkened. 'And . . .'

'He told me frankly he's here to conquer Moctezuma.'

The battle-king frowned. 'How did you communicate with him?'

'He has a woman as his tongue, Lord Shikotenka, a Mayan woman called Malinal who was a slave in Tenochtitlan for many years. She is as fluent in our Nahuatl language as she is in her native Maya, and there is a man, one of the white-skins, who also speaks Maya. When words are to be interpreted from Nahuatl she puts them into Maya and this man in turn puts them into the language of the white-skins. When the white-skins wish to put words into Nahuatl they first speak to the man who puts them into Maya for Malinal, and she in turn renders them into our language. Between them they are able to provide effective interpretation.'

Shikotenka fell silent for a moment. 'Gods do not need interpreters,' he said eventually, 'let alone an arrangement as complicated as the one you describe.'

'Quite so! Whatever they are, these white men are not gods.'

'What are they, then, do you think?'

'Men like us, Lord Shikotenka. But peculiarly powerful and dangerous men . . .'

'On that we are agreed!'

'Yet I believe they are heaven-sent to aid us in our fight against Moctezuma.'

'On that we are *not* agreed.'

Huicton reached into a satchel lying at his feet and pulled out the small bag containing the handful of shining, brightly coloured beads of a most curious design that he had brought for Shikotenka from the coast. 'The leader of the white men is called Cortés,' he said. 'For what it's worth, I believe he does mean to destroy Moctezuma as he told me.' He poured the beads into his hand and passed them to Shikotenka, who took them and looked at them with puzzlement. 'Cortés asked me to deliver these to you,' Huicton continued, 'and gave me a message for you.'

'Then discharge yourself of your message, Ambassador.'

'I am to say, Lord Shikotenka, that you and Cortés share a common enemy in Moctezuma and that the lord Cortés will be pleased to work together with you to bring the tyrant to his knees. I am to say that the lord Cortés promises you his help and the help of his men and of all the great weapons at his disposal to achieve this worthy end.'

Shikotenka poured the beads thoughtfully from hand to hand. They tinkled like little bells and caught the light, sparkling in a way that seemed to fascinate him. Then abruptly he dashed them down onto the hard flagstones at his feet, where they shattered into a thousand pieces. On impulse Huicton bent to gather them up, but the shards were as sharp as obsidian razors and he jumped back, cursing, with blood dripping from the many small wounds opened in his fingers.

Shikotenka looked on gravely. 'The white men's promises are as pretty as their beads,' he said. 'I fear they will break just as easily and make us all bleed before the year is out.'

By late afternoon Puertocarrero was very drunk, and singing sentimental songs. Cortés, who was not so drunk, chose this moment to strike. 'I have a plan, Alonso,' he said. 'One that will solve all our problems at a stroke and make you a very wealthy man into the bargain.'

Although Puertocarrero was from a respected aristocratic family, he was the second son and they'd settled no fortune on him. He looked up sharply, his eyes glittering at the prospect of riches. 'Tell me more,' he said.

'Should it not wait until the morrow?' Cortés asked. 'When you're sober?'

'Bugger the morrow, Hernán. Tell me now.'

Cortés leaned closer. 'How would you like to go home?' he asked.

'To Cuba? Not very much. I'd rather stay here and get rich with you. You'll have to find me another woman, though, to replace that fucking whore.'

'I'm not speaking of Cuba, Alonso. I'm speaking of Spain. How would you like to go home to Spain and take with you all the treasure the Mexica have given us?'

'The treasure?' Puertocarrero asked. Cortés had his attention now and the man was sobering up fast.

'Yes, the treasure. All of it.'

'All of it! I don't understand, Hernán. What are you talking about?'

'It's very simple really. Our expedition is illegal. It has always been illegal since we sailed contrary to the wishes of Diego de Velázquez . . .'

'That prick!'

'Indeed. But unfortunately that prick is the governor of Cuba, and his powers in this region are godlike. He can, and will, have every one of us hanged if he gets the chance.'

Puertocarrero rolled his eyes. 'So we make sure he doesn't get the chance.'

'Of course,' said Cortés. 'Nonetheless, Velázquez's arrest warrants will cast a shadow over us for the rest of our lives unless we can find a way to neutralise him completely.'

'And you've thought of a way?' Puertocarrero held out his empty glass for more wine.

As he poured, Cortés asked quite casually, 'Who has more power than the governor?'

'The king?' Puertocarrero hazarded after a moment lost in frowning thought.

'The king! Exactly! If we can win the king to our cause, then Velázquez will be lost.'

The light of comprehension was beginning to dawn on Puertocarrero's face. 'You're going to bribe the king to intervene against Velázquez by making him a gift of the treasure we've already won!'

'That's right, my friend, and with your family connections you're just the man to take it to him. You may keep a tenth portion for yourself – ' at this Puertocarrero's eyes widened – 'but I expect you'll return here. Once we're rid of Velázquez, we'll be free to do as we wish in these New Lands and to take what we want. We'll be richer than kings!'

Tozi had left Tenochtitlan immediately after fleeing the palace. She'd been so shocked and afraid – yes, afraid! – that she'd run the full two-mile length of the Tacuba causeway. Cloaked in invisibility, she'd passed unnoticed, but the undeniable fact was she'd been seen by Moctezuma's new Chichemec sorcerer.

'Of course I can see you, girl. You cannot hide from me.'

The words echoed in her head even now, almost three full days later, where she'd gone to ground in the lakeside city of Tacuba. Huicton kept a safe house there, owned by Yolya, a burly middle-aged woman with a sweet, gentle nature. Tozi had stayed with Yolya before when Huicton had first sent her to 'charm' Guatemoc, then lying convalescing in his father's mansion in nearby Chapultepec, and it had seemed the obvious place of refuge in her present pass.

Moctezuma's sorcerer was a man of power, a *nagual*, a shape shifter, and Tozi was convinced he would find her and kill her if she came within range of his senses again. No more venturing into the palace on her nightly missions! Indeed, she was not sure she was completely safe here in Tacuba, even in this unobtrusive single-roomed shack, halfway along a narrow, rubbish-strewn alley and surrounded on either side by other identical dwellings.

'I might be putting you in danger, Yolya,' she said to her host. But the older woman, who made her living as a laundress, and who was even now at work in her yard folding baskets full of sheets and blouses in the late afternoon sunshine, merely laughed. 'Nonsense, Tozi. No one will think to look for you here. We're safe enough . . .'

'Maybe I should go,' Tozi continued, as though Yolya hadn't spoken. 'The god Quetzalcoatl is at the coast – that's where Huicton's gone. That's where my friend Malinal is. I should join them.'

'Hush, child. Huicton will return soon. Wait here until he does and then decide your next move.'

Tozi sighed. All her pride, all her strength, all her courage had evaporated, revealed to her as no more than a foolish girl's bravado. For the first time since Huicton had rescued her from the mob that had killed her mother eight years before, she didn't know what to do.

It was the late afternoon of Saturday 15 May, and after a smooth and uneventful voyage with a fair wind from the south, the *Santa Theresa* hove in sight of a fair-sized native town, perched on a headland overlooking a crescent-shaped bay, sheltered by high cliffs. The Totonac warrior Meco hurried to Pepillo's side, pointed excitedly, and said 'Huitztlan.'

Pepillo ran at once to Captain Escalante: 'It's the town we've been looking for, sir, Meco confirms it.'

Escalante smiled. 'That's good news, boy, for it seems to offer a sheltered anchorage just as the caudillo hoped. Now let's find out if the natives are friendly.'

The *Santa Theresa* dropped anchor close to the town, from whence hundreds of Indians poured. They came leaping down the steep steps cut into the cliff and spread out twenty-deep on the little pebble beach skirting the bay. There were men – for the most part unarmed – and colourfully dressed women and children, all laughing and crying out excitedly. But when the longboat was launched and Meco was recognised, their excitement grew wilder and they burst out into a cacophony of shouts, whoops and ululations. He called back to them – some words that Pepillo couldn't understand.

'Ask him what's going on,' said Escalante. He was seated at the front of the longboat, armed with sword and dagger and wearing his steel cuirass. Five other swordsmen, five pikemen and two musketeers were also in the landing party – 'just in case of trouble,' Escalante had said.

Meco was grinning from ear to ear and Pepillo found it hard to get sense out of him as the longboat approached the shore, but eventually understood that the Totonac had sent word ahead after his meeting with Cortés on 12 May, that they were expected, and that all was well. They were to be the honoured guests of the chief of the town and a banquet awaited them.

'He says there's nothing to fear,' Pepillo reported. 'We're their honoured guests. They've prepared a feast for us.'

'I hope they don't mean to feast *on* us,' Escalante laughed. 'I don't intend to be any savage's dinner!'

The cannibalism so much relished by the natives of Mexico was something all the Spaniards held in mortal disgust, and nervous glances were exchanged by the soldiers as the boat ran ashore. The crowd rushed in upon them, a jabbering cacophony of voices and outreached hands. The pikemen raised their weapons, the musketeers levelled their arquebuses, and Indians would certainly have been killed but for Escalante, who called out: 'Hold fire, belay those pikes, I'll hang the first man who strikes a blow,' and strode into the midst of the throng with the greatest confidence.

At once he was lifted shoulder high by a group of smiling, laughing youths, who placed a garland of bright flowers around his neck and carried him towards the steps. 'Come on, you laggards,' he yelled, looking back at his men still clustered around the boat. 'What are you waiting for?'

Guatemoc had waited all day with a hundred of his Cuahchics to ambush a white-skin patrol, but although pairs of scouts mounted on their odd-looking deer had approached several times, they had never come close enough to be snatched. The deer were too fast to be chased far on foot and Guatemoc didn't want to risk revealing his position until he was sure he could spring the trap he'd prepared.

'Complete waste of time,' he said to Mud Head in disgust. 'Yesterday, when we weren't ready, they came within a bowshot of the town three times; today, when we are, they keep their distance.'

'Perhaps they suspect we're here?' ventured Big Dart.

But the others disagreed. 'Patience!' said Starving Coyote. 'They'll be back tomorrow. We'll have better luck then.'

Night was falling and lanterns were being lit on the outskirts of Cuetlaxtlan. Reluctantly Guatemoc gave the order to return to the town.

The remainder of his force, four hundred men, had spent the day in the walled compound provided for them by Pichatzin, the governor of Cuetlaxtlan. The compound, which contained dormitories, an extensive kitchen and an eating hall, had been built to house visiting Mexica nobles and their entourages, and was luxuriously appointed with its own staff of cooks, servants and cleaners.

Pichatzin was waiting when Guatemoc returned. The governor seemed anxious, nervous, somehow out of sorts, sweating profusely and asking many questions about the white-skins, and about Guatemoc's strategy for the morrow, as the two of them sat down to enjoy an excellent dinner.

'I fear,' said Pichatzin, 'if you bring captives into my town, that the white-skins will attack us in full force.'

'That's precisely what I want them to do,' said Guatemoc, 'and if you fear their attack, I suggest you leave.'

When the engagement that he sought to provoke with the

white-skins came, Guatemoc had already resolved to commandeer Cuetlaxtlan's garrison, a full regiment of eight thousand fighting troops whose normal purpose was to suppress dissent amongst the rebellious Totonac factions in the countryside to the north around Cempoala. It still might not be enough to deal with an army that had routed forty thousand Maya at Potonchan, but at least it would force Moctezuma to send reinforcements. This seemed as good a moment as any to share the plan with the governor.

'You may take a personal escort,' Guatemoc continued. 'Fifty of your men should be sufficient to bring you to Tenochtitlan in safety; but I'll require you to leave the rest of your garrison with me.'

'My garrison,' spluttered Pichatzin. 'You want my garrison for this fight you're picking with the white-skins?'

'Of course I do.'

'On whose authority?'

'On my own authority. I am – or have you forgotten? – a prince of the blood.'

Pichatzin's eyes bulged. His position in the Mexica aristocracy was too low for him to even contemplate refusing the orders of a member of the royal family. At the same time, he knew from Teudile that Moctezuma did not want war with the white-skins.

'It is not wise, Prince,' he said carefully. 'We must seek approval from Tenochtitlan before engaging—'

Guatemoc cut him off. 'There simply isn't time,' he said. 'I would have taken command of your troops today if things had gone as I intended, and I put you on notice now that I'll need them tomorrow; not for the ambush – my specialists will look after that – but for what comes after.'

He beckoned a serving girl with a particularly delicious rump and ordered more pulque before turning back to Pichatzin. 'Go to Tenochtitlan, Governor; you have my blessing. Take fifty men with you by all means, travel fast, and tell Moctezuma what's happening here. I'll be pleased to have his support. It's a matter of vital importance that we stop the white-skins now, at the coast, before they consolidate their strength and march inland. The very survival of our nation is at stake.'

*   *   *

The chieftain of the Totonac town of Huitztlan was named Yaretzi, a small, wiry middle-aged man with a receding hairline and a pointed nose whose jerky head movements and watchful beady eyes reminded Pepillo strongly of a farmyard hen. The Spaniards had been brought directly to his palace – a sprawling, flat-roofed, two-storey stucco structure that overlooked the bay – and ushered into an inner court-yard, open to the starry sky, where a sumptuous banquet was laid out on tables. There they were joined by the Council of Elders – twenty grave tribesmen dressed in ceremonial robes – and the heaped plates were inspected.

'Tell them we don't eat human flesh,' said Escalante, sniffing a colla-tion of strange meats.

Pepillo communicated the thought to Meco, who laughed uproari-ously and said he already knew this since, after all, the white men had saved him from being offered up as a dish to them. 'Don't worry; only peccary.' He pointed to other plates: 'There turkey, there sea fish, there monkey – very nice! – there parrot, there dog.' He looked down at Melchior who stood impatiently salivating at Pepillo's side. 'Not like your intelligent dog, though. Dogs we eat very small, very stupid. Anyway, no human meat here, I promise.'

Pepillo was realising that the more he heard of Nahuatl, and the more he was forced to rely on quick understanding, as he had been in his conversations with Meco these past two days, the better he got at it. Very few of the other Totonacs spoke the Mexica tongue, however; even Yaretzi had only a smattering, so the whole evening would depend on what he and Meco were able to convey to both sides.

The strong local drink called pulque was served and Escalante sent down to the ship for wine, which the Totonacs tried and at once declared their love for. Some heavy drinking followed, with much slurping and smacking of lips and, as the evening wore on, a great, mellow feeling of camaraderie descended over the whole group. A particular rallying point was mutual distaste for the Mexica. Escalante was forthright in expressing his loathing for these 'bullyboys', and informed the Totonacs that the Spaniards were here for one purpose only, which was to conquer Moctezuma and free all those who suffered under his unjust rule. The Totonacs for their part complained bitterly of the onerous annual demands for tribute in goods, crops and services that the Mexica levied on them, especially the 'human tribute' of sacrificial victims, which was growing increasingly impossible for them to bear. It seemed there had been some marked change in this aspect of the Mexica overlordship of the Totonacs in recent months – something about children – but Pepillo was not able to understand exactly what was being said to him.

'Never mind,' said Escalante, brushing aside the need for details. 'The gist is clear enough. Tell them we're the men to get Moctezuma off their backs but we'll expect some help from them in return.'

Pepillo conveyed the message to Yaretzi who replied: 'Anything within my power. The great lord Tlacoch has told me to put myself at your service, and this I do willingly . . .'

'Tlacoch?' said Escalante. 'Who the hell's he?'

'The paramount chief of the Totonacs,' Pepillo remembered. 'Has his seat in the city of Cempoala, a few hours' march south of here – the caudillo mentioned him to you, Don Juan.'

'I can't be expected to remember every one of these damned names . . .'

'Tla-coch,' Pepillo repeated, emphasising both syllables. 'He's the one who sent Meco to us to seek out an alliance in the first place. It seems Yaretzi answers to him.'

'Well and good, whatever he's called,' said Escalante, draining his fourth mug of pulque with a grin and switching to wine. 'By God I like these fellows, Pepillo, and it seems they like us, so now's the time to put our proposal to them. Tell them, if your language runs to it, that we want the right to build a town of our own here on these cliffs next to theirs. Tell them we delight in their company so much that we want to be their neighbours. As their neighbours we will become their friends, their brothers and their family, and as their family we will join in the great enterprise of ridding them of Moctezuma.'

It was a difficult interpreting challenge, and Pepillo and Meco went back and forward on it for some time, often resorting to sign language, before it could be conveyed, but Yaretzi's response was immediate and enthusiastic. 'We are very happy that you will build your town here,' he said. Our labourers, our craftsmen, our materials – all will be put at your disposal. We are honoured,' he concluded, 'that the gods wish to live amongst us.'

'Tell him we're not gods,' said Escalante.

Pepillo tried but Yaretzi would have none of it. 'Of course you are gods,' he insisted. 'Everyone knows this.'

Escalante stood up a little unsteadily from the table, walked round to where Yaretzi was sitting, lifted the chieftain to his feet and wrapped him in a strong Spanish embrace. 'We are not gods,' he said, 'we are men like you. We are your brothers, and as brothers we embrace you.'

Yaretzi, who was also very drunk, returned the embrace. 'Still you must be gods,' he said. 'For only gods could hope to destroy Moctezuma.'

On the morning of Sunday 16 May, after breakfasting with his friend and fellow ensign Bernal Díaz, and attending the short service in the makeshift chapel on the dunes, Gonzalo de Sandoval donned his cuirass, strapped on his sword and walked to the stables. Alonso Puertocarrero would ride out with him on this first patrol of the day; he was already mounted on his silver-grey mare Ciri and impatient to be off.

Sandoval took his lance from his groom and climbed into the saddle of the chestnut mare, Llesenia. He was far too poor to own a horse, but the caudillo had put this one at his disposal at Potonchan, and allowed him to keep her ever since. Rather than place his lance in the scabbard attached to his saddle, as Puertocarrero had done, he kept it in his hand; some intuition told him he might need it. 'A fine morning for a gallop, Alonso,' he said, trying to sound cheerful.

'A fine morning indeed, Gonzalo. What say we go as far as Cuetlaxtlan? Give those Mexica a bit of a scare. I could do with a spot of action.'

Puertocarrero was a braggart and a blowhard, and had not done well at Potonchan where others, including Sandoval and Díaz, had been commended by the caudillo for conspicuous bravery. Perhaps this explained why the red-bearded aristocrat so often seemed to feel the need to prove himself.

'I'd prefer to avoid action if at all possible,' Sandoval replied. 'Our mission is to scout, not start a fight.'

'Oh bah!' said Puertocarrero. He spurred Ciri and set off at a gallop. Sandoval followed in his dust trail.

Guatemoc had prepared his ambush with the greatest possible care.

To approach Cuetlaxtlan, the white-skinned deer riders would need to wind their way through a range of low dunes. There were four possible paths and on either side of each of these, dug into the sand so they were as near to invisible as possible, he had distributed the hundred Cuahchics he'd selected for the task – his most skilled, most violent warriors. Twenty were with him, while the other three groups, each also twenty men strong, were led by Fuzzy Face, Big Dart and Man-Eater. Reserves of ten under Starving Coyote and another ten under Mud Head were held back, out of sight, in houses at the very edge of town, able to join the fight in a matter of moments wherever they were needed most.

And a fight it seemed there would be! A short while before, two long trails of dust had appeared in the north, and now, beneath them, coming on at fantastic speed, could be seen two riders, their upper bodies shining silver in the sun.

These were not gods, Guatemoc reminded himself; he refused to believe such superstitious nonsense. Yet how fast they moved! How extraordinary they seemed! How they loomed and threatened as they approached! How the hooves of their deer thundered and shook the earth! Already the lead rider had chosen his path; it would not take him past Guatemoc's position, but between the dunes commanded by Big Dart. The second rider was a hundred paces behind on the same trajectory, yelling something in his strange language, his words torn away by the wind. As the first rider passed from view into the reach of Big Dart's ambush, Guatemoc barked an order and his twenty surged from their hides and rushed to join the fray.

Sandoval was furious at Puertocarrero's rashness and stupidity. What had got into the man, to approach so close to Cuetlaxtlan with its huge garrison – and at such an impetuous pace? Still, there was nothing for it but to follow and try to rein him in. Shouting, 'Stop, you bloody fool' at the top of his voice, he spurred Llesenia, aiming her at the gap between two dunes that Puertocarrero had already entered, when everywhere he saw painted Indians dressed in loincloths, armed with spears and obsidian-edged broadswords, erupting from the sands. Twenty of them were straight ahead, swarming around Puertocarrero and – ye gods! – one of them shoved a spear between Ciri's legs, making her stumble, sending her idiot rider flying out of the saddle and crashing to the ground on his face before he'd even had time to draw his lance from its scabbard. Riderless now, Ciri quickly recovered her footing and bolted free, evading other groups of attackers, yelling war cries and beating their swords against their shields, who converged from dunes to the left and right. With no time to think, only to act, Sandoval bellowed 'Santiago and at 'em', dropped the tip of his lance to take an Indian full in the chest, jerked the weapon free in a spray of blood, raised it high, stabbed down to kill another, bowled three more men over with the force of his charge, smashed his iron-clad stirrup into a warrior's screaming face and wheeled Llesenia in a tight arc, her hooves lashing the air, before driving back a pair of Indians who already had their hands on the seemingly unconscious Puertocarrero and were trying to drag him off.

Now Sandoval himself was surrounded, and the little valley between the dunes was rapidly filling with scores of screaming, heavily armed warriors. Steadying Llesenia, he bent low, grabbed Puertocarrero by his wiry red hair and, with a mighty effort, hauled his limp, unconscious weight up into the saddle in front of him – at the cost of his lance, which was torn from his grasp by a glowering savage. Releasing the reins, gripping Puertocarrero round the midriff, clinging onto Llesenia by his knees alone, Sandoval drew his broadsword, cleaved the skull of the damned Indian who'd taken his lance and urged the prancing chestnut mare onward into the scrum. Hemmed in by contorted, painted faces that streamed with sweat, their eyes flashing white, their filed teeth bared, it was a scene from his worst nightmare. Some projectile bounced harmlessly off the backplate of his cuirass, an arrow grazed his thigh and, as a thicket of strong brown hands reached to unseat him, his sword scythed down, taking an arm off at the elbow here, severing a man's fingers there, hacking so hard through the neck of a third that his head, smeared with yellow and red paint, took flight, ending up bouncing and rolling a dozen paces away.

Poor Llesenia, though trained for battle, was spooked by the blood and the din, the ululating howls of the Indians, the clash of weapons and the unaccustomed weight of two men on her back. She reared madly, nearly throwing off Sandoval and his still unconscious charge, and he only brought her back under control with the greatest difficulty. He buried the point of his sword in the eye of a warrior who leapt up to wrestle Puertocarrero from him, cut deep into a naked shoulder, tore open a throat – and suddenly the crowd ahead was just two ranks deep. Had he been alone on her back, he had little doubt that spirited Llesenia could have jumped them, but Puertocarrero's weight made such a feat impossible. Sandoval spurred the mare forward, yelling his battle cry, *'Santiago and at 'em . . . Santiago and at 'em'*, clinging to the hope that he might somehow break through, even though it would be in the direction of the town and not back towards the camp.

There was an imminent danger the white-skins and their animals would escape, Guatemoc realised. The deer whose legs had been fouled by Big Dart's spear had already galloped off over the dunes, placing itself out of reach in a heartbeat, while its fallen rider had been rescued by his companion, a formidable warrior who'd worked terrible slaughter on the Cuahchics and seemed as unstoppable as a whirlwind.

But Guatemoc had already signalled to Mud Head and Starving Coyote to bring up the reserves and, as the white-skin broke through the last men encircling him, driving his animal out of the pass between the dunes in the direction of Cuetlaxtlan, he was suddenly confronted by twenty fresh warriors blocking his path. Guatemoc threw down his *macuahuitl* – he wanted a living prisoner, not a corpse – sprinted forward, leapt up onto the back of the deer, wrapped his arms around the white-skin's neck and succeeded in unbalancing him and wrestling him to the ground. There Big Dart and Fuzzy Face also fell upon him, pinning him down despite his struggles. In the same instant of intense action, the second white-skin, who'd seemed stunned and helpless, abruptly woke up, took control of the deer and – quite astonishing this! – goaded it into a run, jumped it over the reserves barring his way and fled without looking back, first towards the town but soon veering onto the smooth, compacted sand of the beach, where the animal's stride lengthened to such a pace that it left all pursuit far behind as it thundered northwards.

Sandoval couldn't believe Puertocarrero's cowardice – or, rather, knowing the man, he *could* believe it, but was stunned to have been its victim. He had plunged into the thick of battle for him, fought for his life, come close to pulling off a successful rescue, yet when the tables were suddenly turned, when Sandoval had been pulled from his horse, Puertocarrero had simply run, making no effort to help, *not even looking back*, and had left him in the hands of the Indians who would undoubtedly sacrifice him to their vile gods and make a cannibal feast of his carcass.

Sandoval had been beaten savagely about the head until his ears bled, his arms had been tied behind his back, and a strangling noose had been fastened round his neck. It was fixed to the end of a long pole, which was held by the cruel savage who now shoved him, stumbling and choking, towards the outskirts of Cuetlaxtlan, taking great pleasure in pulling him back abruptly if he hurried too far ahead and pushing him forward if he lagged.

Sandoval recognised his tormenter.

Though dressed then in splendid robes, and this morning wearing only a loincloth that revealed the scars of recent knife wounds disfiguring his muscular belly, he was without a doubt the same tall and powerful Mexica prince with long black hair, high cheekbones and a prideful sneer, who had come to the Spanish camp five days before as a member of the delegation from Moctezuma – the delegation that had brought so much treasure and left with so many threats. The prince's name, Sandoval remembered, was Guatemoc. Through Malinal he'd had the temerity, the huge *cojones*, to order Cortés to leave, warning him that he and all his men would be wiped out if they did not. 'My soldiers are as numberless as the sands of the sea,' Guatemoc had boasted, 'and undefeated in battle. March on Tenochtitlan and I will teach you the Mexica way of war.'

Cortés had said something about awaiting that lesson eagerly, but now it looked very much as though Guatemoc was about to pre-empt the caudillo's plans and nip the Spanish advance in the bud – for out of Cuetlaxtlan, marching rapidly to meet them, surged thousands of Mexica warriors fully armed for battle.

Chapter Twenty-Five

Sunday 16 May 1519

There came an urgent drumming of hooves, yells from the guards, a sliding skid, a furious neigh and a scatter of sand as a horse at full gallop was brought to a near-catastrophic halt and Puertocarrero burst into the pavilion, his face as white as his hair was red. 'An ambush, Caudillo,' he screamed. 'There were hundreds of them. They overwhelmed us. They've captured Sandoval . . .'

Cortés, who had been drafting a long letter to the king and regretting the absence of Pepillo to take dictation, leapt up from his desk. 'Who ambushed you?' he asked. 'Where? When? How was Sandoval captured?' But as Puertocarrero told the story, the words vomiting forth in a confused, urgent, unpunctuated mass, Cortés held up his hand. 'Slow down, man,' he said. 'Catch your breath . . . Here, drink this.' He poured wine and, as the aristocrat slurped greedily from the glass, sent a guard to bring Pedro de Alvarado and Bernal Díaz to the pavilion and issued orders for a general muster. The entire army was to form up and be ready to march within the hour.

By the time Alvarado and Díaz arrived, Cortés was beginning to notice certain oddities and lacunae in Puertocarrero's story. He seemed most intent on painting his own actions in a good light, while blaming Sandoval for rashly putting them both in harm's way by insisting the morning patrol pass much closer to Cuetlaxtlan than was safe. Now came an accusation of cowardice: 'I do not wish to impugn young Sandoval's name, Hernán, but the truth is he deserted me at the moment of greatest danger. I was surrounded! I had to fight my way out alone. I killed many! By the grace of God I escaped.'

'Caudillo, I object!' said Bernal Díaz. 'I object most strenuously.

Gonzalo would never leave another man in the lurch – and besides, he is not here to speak for himself.'

Cortés gave Puertocarrero a hard glance. 'If Sandoval deserted you and fled,' he asked, 'how is it that you were the one to return safely to camp?'

'And how, pray tell,' said Alvarado, 'did you manage to do so on Sandoval's horse? I saw you leave the stables earlier. You were riding your Ciri and Gonzalo was mounted on Llesenia, yet it is now Llesenia I see tethered outside, while of Ciri there is no sign. It is passing strange, is it not?'

'We were both unhorsed,' blustered Puertocarrero, a blob of spit flying from his mouth. 'In his haste to flee, Sandoval mounted Ciri and made off but was brought down. I fought my way through a mass of Indians to Llesenia and escaped by the skin of my teeth.'

'So then it was you who left Gonzalo behind, not the other way round,' said Díaz, his jaw thrust forward pugnaciously.

'No, not at all. He abandoned me—'

'I don't like the stench of this,' said Alvarado. 'Sandoval's not the man to run from a fight.' He stepped closer to Puertocarrero and loomed over him. 'Let me see your sword,' he demanded. 'If you struck blows against the Indians as you claim, then it will be marked, it will be bloodied . . .'

A look of mingled horror and fury now appeared in Puertocarrero's eyes. 'Are you calling me a liar?' he shouted.

With a grunt of impatience, Bernal Díaz grasped the hilt of Puertocarrero's sword and drew the weapon. All could see that the blade was clean and unmarked.

'Yes, I'm calling you a liar,' said Alvarado coldly. 'And now I call you a coward as well.'

'I fought with my lance,' Puertocarrero protested.

'So where is it?' asked Alvarado. 'Show it to us.'

'It . . . it was wrested from my grasp.'

'Ha!' Alvarado exclaimed, showing his disgust. 'You have an answer for everything.'

Cortés's mind was working fast. He did not want his plans for Puertocarrero ruined by the charge of cowardice now raised against him. On the other hand, might there not be ways he could use it to his advantage to press and further dominate and control the aristocrat? He would have to give the matter careful thought. 'Gentleman,' he said, 'please! We'll settle this later. Our priority now must be the rescue of Gonzalo and the punishment of the Indians who took him.'

'What if he's already been sacrificed?' asked Díaz.

'If he has, then we will sack Cuetlaxtlan, annihilate its garrison and kill every man, woman and child there—'

'Annihilate its garrison?' said Puertocarrero aghast. 'There are eight thousand of them.'

'We faced forty thousand at Potonchan,' Cortés reminded him, restraining himself from striking the red-haired fool across the face. That the man was a coward he had no doubt, but he could still be a useful coward. Important, therefore, that he was not shamed into demanding satisfaction from Alvarado, who would certainly slaughter him if it came to a duel.

Fortunately at that moment the tension was broken by the arrival of García Brabo, a lean grey-haired sergeant from Cortés's home province of Extramadura, with the announcement that the army was formed up and ready to march. Brabo, an efficient, ruthless killer who Cortés had relied on for many years to do his dirty work, had a hooked nose and a permanently sour expression. The smell of sweat and garlic hung about him like a threat. 'Where do we march to, sir?' he asked.

'To Cuetlaxtlan. Leave a squad of fifty, two of the falconets, all three of the lombards and their crews, and twenty dogs to defend the camp. Everyone else goes with us.' Cortés turned to Díaz: 'Bernal, I'll be scouting ahead with the cavalry, so find Malinal and bring her along with the infantry. Keep her by you. I'll need her for any parley.'

'Do you want Aguilar as well?' Díaz asked.

'He's still in the infirmary shitting his guts out. Doesn't matter, though. Malinal's Castilian is getting better. I reckon she can handle this on her own.'

As Cortés led the way out of the pavilion, one of the stable boys approached, leading Puertocarrero's horse Ciri. 'She came back by herself, Caudillo,' the boy reported. 'I thought you'd want to know.'

Unmissable in its scabbard attached to Ciri's saddle was Puertocarrero's lance.

Sandoval couldn't understand what was going on.

He'd assumed the army of thousands that had surged out from Cuetlaxtlan had come to join Guatemoc to march at once on the Spanish camp. But that was not at all what had happened.

Instead, as the two groups converged on the outskirts of the town, the warriors Guatemoc had used for the ambush moved into a defensive formation around him, bristling with weapons, and angry words began to be exchanged between the prince and another man whom Sandoval recognised as Pichatzin, the governor of Cuetlaxtlan. Pichatzin was holding a glittering object in his right hand – was it a ring? – which he insistently thrust towards the prince and which the prince equally insistently ignored.

The argument went on for a great while, with much posturing and brandishing of weapons by both sides. Several times Guatemoc seemed to speak over the governor's head, addressing the ranks behind him directly, but the men stood stony faced and made no response. Pichatzin shouted back at the prince and again offered him the object he was holding. Finally Guatemoc strode forward, took the object from Pichatzin – Sandoval could see now that it was definitely a ring, a gold band set with a gemstone – studied it and then threw it down in the sand at his feet. This provoked a groan of evident horror from the ranks and a gasp of fury from the governor. He barked a command and suddenly two hundred archers stepped to the fore, raised their bows and trained their arrows on Guatemoc's much smaller force.

The prince turned and walked back towards his men, the muscles of his face working, twisting his handsome features into an expression of black fury.

Guatemoc was so angry that for a moment he considered ordering his Cuahchics to attack Pichatzin, who'd brought out four thousand men, half the garrison, to arrest him. But with such odds there could only be one result – even the governor's contingent of archers outnum- bered his tiny force by two to one and would riddle them with arrows before they could strike a blow. True, there were still the four hundred Cuahchics he'd left in the town, but they weren't sufficient to sway the balance, regardless of their ferocity, and, besides, they would not come. Pichatzin had undoubtedly told the truth when he said he'd had the rest of the garrison surround them in the walled guest compound and that they were prisoners there.

Guatemoc beckoned Mud Head, Starving Coyote, Big Dart, Fuzzy Face and Man-Eater. 'Friends,' he said, 'we're done for. I don't want to see any of you or any of our brave Cuahchics killed needlessly, so I'm going to surrender.'

'Surrender!' spat Mud Head. 'Never.'

'Let's fight the fuckers,' said Big Dart.

'At least we'll die with honour,' said Man-Eater.

Guatemoc forced a smile, calmed his breathing. 'No,' he said. 'I won't allow it. Surrender is our only course. Pichatzin has the Great Speaker's signet ring, his mandate of authority, and clear orders for us to stand down. You won't be arrested, boys! I have the governor's word on it. Our Cuahchics will be free to return to Tenochtitlan and rejoin their regiments. It seems it's only my skin that Moctezuma wants.'

'But how did this happen?' Starving Coyote demanded. 'How did Moctezuma get intelligence of what we planned here? How did he get his orders to Pichatzin so fast?'

'I'll warrant that toad Teudile was behind it,' snarled Man-Eater.

'You're right,' said Guatemoc. 'It was Teudile. I should have realised the risk when he started moaning about how he'd be punished for not stopping me. He used relay runners to send a message ahead to Tenochtitlan while he was still on the road. He revealed our plans, and Moctezuma had runners carry his order to stop us straight back to Pichatzin with his signet ring to confirm it.'

'That bastard,' said Mud Head. 'But it would be suicide to give yourself up, Guatemoc! If you let them take you back to Tenochtitlan, it's certain you'll be killed.'

'And I suspect in a very horrible way,' Guatemoc said wryly. 'No one defies the will of the Great Speaker as I have done over this matter of the white-skins and lives to tell the tale. But truly I have no choice.

We're outnumbered and we've been outmanoeuvred and I have to accept that.'

Fuzzy Face looked at the prisoner, the Spaniard, who was watching their conversation intently. 'What happens to him?' he asked.

'Pichatzin's going to free him,' said Guatemoc. 'More's the pity. He's a fine warrior and a brave one. He would have made a noble sacrifice.'

The expedition had eighteen heavy horses, but only seventeen were going into battle today. Puertocarrero kept Sandoval's mare Llesenia, since Ciri's legs had been badly bruised in the earlier skirmish and she would need attention before she would be fit again. Cortés had not commented on the implications of the scabbarded lance still mounted on Ciri's saddle – Alvarado's sneer was more eloquent than any words – and had insisted that Puertocarrero ride with the rest.

They were two miles ahead of the infantry, and Cuetlaxtlan was already in sight, when they saw a small band of Mexica warriors, not more than twenty, approaching them. At once Cortés spurred his dark chestnut stallion Molinero into the charge, the rest of the corps spreading out in a line on either side of him yelling, 'Santiago and at 'em,' the ancient war cry of Spain that had echoed for centuries across the bloody battlefields of the Reconquista. Now it was not reconquest, Cortés thought grimly, but conquest that was at issue, and it would not be the Moors of the old world who would fall under Spanish lances today but the Indians of the new.

That was when he recognised Sandoval placed at the front of the savages, waving and shouting.

With great reluctance, Cortés reined Molinero in and called to the other cavaliers: 'Hold . . . hold!' As they all slowed to a canter, he beckoned Alvarado to his side and the two of them rode forward at a trot. 'Do you reckon it's a trap, Pedro?' he asked conversationally.

'If it is,' said Alvarado, 'it's a mighty strange one. Those Indians are unarmed.'

Cortés squinted. 'True enough. Wonders to behold.'

A few more seconds brought them within hailing distance of Sandoval.

'Ho, Gonzalo!' called Cortés. 'It's good to see you. Are you well?'

'Never been better,' said Sandoval. 'Come and meet my friends – whatever you do, don't kill them.'

'Why not?' shouted Alvarado.

'It would be churlish,' Sandoval replied, 'since they just saved my life.'

The unarmed Mexica warriors were led by Pichatzin, the governor of Cuetlaxtlan. Sandoval was mystified to have been released when he'd fully expected to be sacrificed, and could only report the bare facts. He and Puertocarrero had been ambushed by Prince Guatemoc leading a force of about one hundred men. Puertocarrero had escaped; Sandoval had been taken – Cortés noted with approval that the young ensign made no criticism of Puertocarrero's behaviour. There had then followed a confrontation between Guatemoc and Pichatzin, who had arrived in the nick of time at the head of a much larger force. The outcome was that Guatemoc had appeared to surrender to the governor, and had been bound and led away, amidst much outcry from his men, while Sandoval had been freed and brought immediately towards the Spanish camp by Pichatzin and this small escort.

Despite the gesture, Alvarado was in favour of pressing on to Cuetlaxtlan and destroying the town and its garrison but, with Sandoval back safely, Cortés was in no hurry. 'There's some strange business afoot here, Pedro,' he mused. 'I'll need a better understanding of what's happened before I decide a course of action.'

He beckoned Puertocarrero, told him to ride back to the infantry column, find Malinal, who would be with Díaz, and return with her posthaste. While they waited he took Alvarado aside.

'This business of Puertocarrero's cowardice,' Cortés said. 'Don't shame him to the point where he has to challenge you—'

Alvarado snorted. 'If he challenges me, he'll die . . .'

'Exactly, and I don't want him dead. I've got a job for him to do. It doesn't look like Sandoval is going to pursue the matter, and I'd prefer it if you didn't either.'

'I can't abide cowardice,' said Alvarado.

224

'Who can? But Puertocarrero won't be with us much longer, I promise you.'

Alvarado raised a quizzical eyebrow.

'I plan to send him back to Spain with all our treasure as a gift for the king,' Cortés explained.

'What? Are you mad, Hernán?'

'No! I'm a gambler. And I know you like a throw of the dice yourself, Pedro.'

Alvarado's eyes lit up, as they always did at the prospect of a bet. 'What's the wager?' he asked. 'What are the stakes? What do we stand to win?'

Cortés looked about and gestured towards the distant ranges of blue mountains that could be seen rising far inland.

'Mountains?' said Alvarado in disbelief. 'We're to win mountains?'

Cortés laughed. 'No, you idiot! I want what lies beyond those mountains. I want Tenochtitlan, the Mexica capital, and all its fabled gold and jewels. The treasure we've been given is a pittance by comparison with what awaits us there, but I'm gambling it will be more than enough to buy the king's favour and get Velázquez off our backs forever.'

'They say a bird in the hand is worth two in the bush . . .'

'Come, come, Pedro! That's never been your philosophy.'

'All right,' agreed Alvarado slowly. 'Tell me more about this plan of yours.'

When Puertocarrero returned, Malinal was perched in the saddle in front of him, riding astride like a warrior, even though she'd never been on horseback before. She was grinning mischievously, and obviously exhilarated by the gallop. *Gods*, Cortés thought. What a beauty she was. Brave too. And clever! His true ally and comrade-in-arms in this great struggle to take the New Lands from their present owners. He rather regretted that he would have to disappoint her over the matter of Pepillo and his damned dog, but Saint Peter had spoken and was not to be denied.

Within minutes of her arrival, Malinal had begun to make sense of the morning's events.

In conversation with Pichatzin she first learned, and then informed Cortés in her halting but workable Castilian, that Guatemoc had been acting against Moctezuma's orders when he had set his ambush and seized Sandoval. This, Pichatzin said, was quite the opposite of what the Great Speaker wanted, which was for peace, harmony, tranquillity and love to govern relations between his people and the *tueles* – as it seemed he continued to believe the Spaniards to be. The order to withdraw the Totonac workers and serving women had come from Guatemoc without sanction from Moctezuma, but neither Pichatzin, nor even Teudile, could defy a prince of the blood. Learning of Guatemoc's plans to cause further trouble for the *tueles*, however, wily Teudile had sent runners forward to Tenochtitlan with a message for Moctezuma, telling him all; Moctezuma had received the message and sent runners back, reaching Pichatzin just in time for him to mobilise the garrison of Cuetlaxtlan and prevent Guatemoc from committing further crimes. Now, as a token of good faith, it was Pichatzin's honour to return the *tuele* Guatemoc had captured unharmed to the lord Cortés.

'Too little, too late!' fumed Alvarado, who was listening closely. 'I say kill the lot of them, then march on their filthy town and burn it to the ground.'

Malinal looked up at Cortés. 'Don Pedro idea maybe not good,' she suggested.

'Damned impertinence!' Alvarado muttered.

'Why's it not a good idea, Malinal?' Cortés asked.

'Attack Cuetlaxtlan now, Moctezuma know your mind. Know you attack Tenochtitlan next. Spare Cuetlaxtlan and he not sure. He hope maybe you spare Tenochtitlan also.'

'Ye gods!' Cortés exclaimed. 'It seems the woman has a grasp of tactics!'

'Bugger tactics.' Alvarado made a sour face. 'Attack first, ask questions later – that's my motto.'

'We'll attack them soon enough,' Cortés said, 'and in their heartland, where the blow will be mortal. Until then I'd prefer to keep them guessing about our intentions.'

As they spoke, the infantry, more than four hundred strong, arrived at the meeting place on the dunes. Cortés gave orders for them to stand at ease. He could see plain terror in Pichatzin's eyes at the sight not only of the Spanish soldiers in their battle panoply, with their muskets and their cannon, pikes, swords and shining armour, but also of the eighty baying and snarling war dogs that Vendabal and his handlers had brought – the dogs likewise armoured in plate and mail; many wearing collars inset with metal spikes.

It was a good moment to win some concessions. 'Tell Pichatzin he did the right thing giving us Sandoval back,' Cortés said to Malinal. 'But tell him Alvarado here is very angry and wants me to burn Cuetlaxtlan and slaughter everyone in it. Tell him my other captains feel the same way. I don't think I'll be able to restrain them.'

Pichatzin broke out in a sweat and began to tremble. His voice was urgent, tremulous and high as he replied.

'He say he hoped you happiness for get Sandoval back. Wants peace with you, he say. No war.'

Cortés deliberately made his face stern and his voice harsh: 'I'll need more than fine words and the return of a prisoner who shouldn't have been taken in the first place.'

'He say what you want?' Malinal translated when Pichatzin replied.

'Gold!' said Alvarado. 'That'll be a good start.'

Pichatzin agreed at once. Tomorrow all the gold in Cuetlaxtlan would be delivered to the Spanish camp. There was not a great deal, but he hoped it would prove sufficient to compensate the *tueles* for their inconvenience.

'We'll want our labourers and serving women back as well,' Cortés added. 'And our food supplies restored.'

Again Pichatzin agreed.

'And that upstart Guatemoc. Tell Pichatzin to hand him over to me for punishment.'

Pichatzin replied with a single word and Malinal translated: 'Impossible.'

'No! I don't accept that. Tell him to give me Guatemoc.'

A longer reply from Pichatzin this time. 'He say Moctezuma want punish Guatemoc,' was Malinal's translation. 'Guatemoc not for you. On way to Tenochtitlan now. Many guards.'

'Insolent little shit!' exploded Alvarado with a murderous glare at Pichatzin. 'Give me the word, Hernán, and I'll take the cavalry after Guatemoc, drag him back here in chains.'

Cortés frowned. 'What do you advise?' he asked Malinal. 'Shall I accept what Pichatzin says, or shall I send a troop of horse after Guatemoc? I'd like to see the man hanged.'

'What you gain if you take and kill Guatemoc now, Caudillo?'

'Considerable satisfaction,' said Cortés.

'Lose more!' Malinal exclaimed. 'Kill Guatemoc here, he dead; let Guatemoc go Tenochtitlan he trouble Moctezuma very much before Moctezuma kill him. Guatemoc have friends, supporters. Good to divide Mexica peoples, no?'

'It's Guatemoc who should be divided!' Alvarado said. 'Hang him, draw him and quarter him. Make him suffer for what he did.'

'I sure Moctezuma will make suffer,' Malinal observed. 'Wait. I ask.' She turned aside, put a question in Nahuatl to Pichatzin, listened to his answer. 'Punishment for Guatemoc,' she continued in Castilian, 'is . . . how you say?' She pinched the skin on the back of her hand, pulled it up.

'Skin?' Cortés suggested.

'Yes skin! Pichatzin say Moctezuma skin Guatemoc, like animal.'

'After he's dead, of course?'

'No, Caudillo! Skin alive. Make suffer very much.'

Cortés thought about it. 'That'll do nicely,' he said.

Chapter Twenty-Six

Don Juan de Escalante was a great man, Pepillo decided. A really nice man! This must be what it was like to have a father – to be treated kindly, with honour and respect, to be advised well on the ways of the world and, above all else, to be taught how to fight with a sword!

Their business with the Totonacs successfully concluded on the night of Saturday 15 May, Escalante kept the *Santa Theresa* anchored in the bay on Sunday the 16th while he explored the headland, looking for and eventually finding a suitable site on which to build the Spanish town. It was a mile away from Huitztlan, surrounded by well-watered fields, close enough to take advantage of all the help, labour and supplies that had been willingly offered, but not so close as to encourage too much familiarity, and with excellent access to the sea.

On the morning of Monday 17 May, after saying elaborate farewells to Yaretzi and all the elders, and to Meco (who was to go on foot to the Spanish camp by way of Cempoala, where he would report everything that had been agreed to the Totonac paramount chief Tlacoch), Escalante gave the order to raise anchor and the *Santa Theresa* sailed.

On the voyage, Pepillo learned much more about the art of the sword, mastering the basic step, the passing step, the switch step, the step pivot and other elements of footwork to such a degree that the captain said he was now ready to continue his practice with a weapon in hand; he brought out the beautiful blade he'd shown Pepillo so tantalisingly a few days before. Escalante took up his own sword so that they could spar, and they then spent some hours practising the four primary guard positions, known as the plough guard, the roof guard, the ox's guard and the fool's guard.

'Why the fool's guard?' Pepillo asked of the strange posture in which the hands were held below the waist and the tip of the sword was allowed to drop down, almost touching the ground. 'Does it mean only a fool would use it?'

Escalante laughed. 'Far from it! The idea is to make your opponent *think* you're a fool, when in fact you're not. Along with strength, balance, footwork and speed, deception is one of the pillars of swordsmanship.'

There was, for Pepillo, an almost fairytale quality to the return voyage, as though he were in a place and time entirely different from and unconnected to the rigours, challenges and ordeals of the daily life he'd grown used to in Mexico. But soon enough reality was restored, and with it an abiding sense of gloom and hopelessness, when the Spanish camp on the dunes came into view on the afternoon of Tuesday 18 May.

'You're looking glum, lad,' said Escalante, joining him by the rail on the navigation deck.

'I defied the caudillo,' Pepillo admitted. 'He ordered me to leave Melchior behind and I brought him.'

'Well, that doesn't sound too serious. I've been happy to have your dog on board.'

'It is serious, Don Juan. The caudillo believes Melchior should be cast in with the dog pack and trained for war.'

'And you don't agree?'

'Never! If the caudillo doesn't relent, I'll take Melchior and run.'

Escalante's reaction to this idea – that Pepillo must not even consider it – was much the same as Díaz's had been a few weeks before, and like Díaz he promised to intervene with Cortés if necessary.

'I'm grateful,' Pepillo said, 'don't think I'm not. Don Bernal Díaz also said he'd help me, but I don't even know if he's spoken to the caudillo yet. If he has, it's made no difference.'

'I'm not Don Bernal,' said Escalante. 'The caudillo and I go back a long way. I like to think I have some influence with him.'

Three days later, on 21 May, as Pepillo sat miserably staring through the bars of the filthy pen where Melchior now lived, it was clear that

230

neither Don Juan, Don Bernal or Malinal, who'd also tried to help, had any influence whatsoever with Cortés. Pepillo and Melchior had gone ashore in the longboat with Escalante on the 18th, but after they'd beached and were making the boat fast, Telmo Vendabal and his triumphant, sneering assistants came sauntering down the dunes from the camp.

'We're taking your dog,' said Vendabal. 'Hand me his leash, there's a good lad, and don't make trouble.'

Pepillo had turned to run but Andrés Santisteban had blocked and held him and Vendabal had prised the leash from his hands.

Escalante gave them a dangerous look. 'The boy's under my protection,' he said. 'Let him go. Let his dog go. I'll be talking to the caudillo about this.'

'It's the caudillo's orders, sir,' said Vendabal. Although his tone was obsequious, his manner was supremely confident and, moments later, when Cortés himself appeared, Pepillo understood why.

'Welcome back, Juan.' Cortés strode down the beach to embrace the captain, not sparing so much as a glance for Pepillo. 'A successful mission?'

'Very successful,' Escalante replied. 'I've much to tell you . . . But I'd like to see this little misunderstanding resolved first. Don Telmo seems to feel he has a right to take Pepillo's pet dog.'

'There's no misunderstanding,' Cortés said with a hint of impatience. 'Don Telmo's acting on my orders.'

'But Hernán—'

Cortés held up his hand to silence Escalante. 'Not now, Juan. This is a trivial matter when we have the future of the expedition to discuss. Come away to my pavilion—'

'It's not a trivial matter for me,' Pepillo dared to object, but Cortés turned on him with a face of thunder. 'Boy,' he said, 'you are asking for a beating. The dog goes with Vendabal. Now! You will follow Don Juan and me to my pavilion and when our meeting is done I'll have dictation for you to take.'

Thereafter, any attempt by Pepillo to raise the subject of Melchior with Cortés had led to a cuff about the ear, and now, three days later, he was beginning to accept that he would never get the pup back.

But there were consolations. Most important of all, Melchior was not dead yet, for it seemed that even in the dog world – perhaps more so than in the human world – there was such a thing as a code of honour. Whenever he could, Pepillo stole away to the kennels to see how his pet was doing. Twice he'd witnessed Melchior being attacked by a full-grown jet-black mastiff whose name, he learned, was Jairo – an animal no taller than Melchior (for Melchior had grown very tall despite being so young), but much more massive through the chest and withers, scarred from old battles and rippling with muscle.

On the first attack, which came suddenly, with stunning ferocity and seemingly without provocation, Melchior had tried to fight back and had been badly mauled, the flesh of his shoulder torn open and his throat seized in a death grip. But then, whimpering, he had fallen still and Jairo had released him, cocked his leg and pissed on him, then stalked off, seemingly satisfied.

On the second occasion Melchior had made the mistake of going for a scrap of meat lying on the earth floor of the kennel close to Jairo. No other dog had claimed the morsel, and the big dog seemed uninterested in it, but as Melchior edged closer, Jairo bounded to his feet, snarling horribly, his yellow fangs bared. This time Melchior knew what to do. Rather than resist, he crouched and grovelled, lowered his back to make himself appear smaller, tucked his tail between his legs, flattened his ears and dribbled urine. The mastiff stood over him, hackles raised, a rumbling, deep growl vibrating in his throat, and Melchior responded by rolling on his back, exposing his belly and throat to Jairo's teeth – complete, abject surrender. Jairo sniffed him, his growl subsiding, his hackles falling back, picked up the scrap and swallowed it, then walked away, again seemingly satisfied.

Was there a lesson to be learned here, Pepillo wondered? Although they'd got what they wanted, Santisteban, Hemes and Julian continued to torment him. Should he, then, grovel to them, just as Melchior had grovelled to Jairo? Would that persuade them to leave him alone? Somehow Pepillo doubted it. Dogs were more honourable than humans. And besides, he would not grovel. He simply would not! Instead, he was determined, he would learn to fight and make himself strong – and soon, he promised himself, he would pay them out.

Two days before, on the 19th, Don Juan, regretful at being unable to help reunite him with Melchior, had suggested they resume the sword practice that had begun on board the *Santa Theresa*. Pepillo had accepted with alacrity. The captain had also shown him a system of exercises he must pursue to strengthen his legs and arms, his belly and his shoulders, and he had begun to perform them religiously. There was, likewise, much manual work to be done around the camp, from the digging of latrines to the construction of ramparts, to the running out of the lombards – those great guns, so effective at Potonchan, that could throw a seventy-pound cannonball a distance of two miles. Although Pepillo had hitherto been excused such duties, he now volunteered for them whenever his responsibilities as Cortés's page and secretary allowed.

Plucking up her courage, Tozi entered the gates of the sacred precinct of Tenochtitlan nine days after she had fled Moctezuma's palace. She had doubted her powers, but this was the proof they had not deserted her, for she was able to pass in front of the guards without them seeing her, just as she had done on many occasions before, then cross the grand plaza and skirt the eastern side of Hummingbird's immense pyramid, where a priestly ceremony was in full flow – all, again, without her presence being detected. She shivered and mastered the fear that rose like vomit in her throat as the vestibule of the palace loomed ahead, patrolled by a dozen royal spearmen. All she had to do was pass them unnoticed, as she had the others, and the palace would lie open to her: its halls, its meeting rooms, Moctezuma's chambers of state and Moctezuma himself would be as vulnerable to her as they had ever been before the arrival of the *nagual*. To make sure that she truly was invisible, Tozi drifted to within an arm's length of the two nearest spearmen, turned her back on them, bent forward and lifted her skirt, showing them her bare arse, but they did not blink at the insult, did not react; absolutely, undeniably, did not see her. She braced herself and moved closer.

Though Huicton was still absent, word from his network of spies had reached the safe house in Tacuba that the Great Speaker's new *nagual*, the tattooed one from the north, had left Tenochtitlan the very next morning after the public burning of the sorcerers Tlilpo, Cuappi, Aztatzin, and Hecateu. The *nagual*'s name, the spies had discovered, was Acopol, and his destination was the city of Cholula, sacred to the god of peace Quetzalcoatl. What his purpose was there and when, if ever, he would return, were unknown, but the fact was he had gone and the responsibility to resume her work for Quetzalcoatl preyed so insistently on Tozi's mind that she resolved to return to the palace, resume her campaign of terror against Moctezuma, and discover what she could about Acopol's mission.

She was within the vestibule when the first knives pricked her, the first razors sliced her, the first talons tore her, the first arrows of horror entered her brain. She gasped, aloud – she could not help herself – and the guards turned as one towards the place where she stood. They spun round and yet they could not see her . . . Relief flooded through her as she realised her magical protection was still intact but then . . . wait! Wait! What was that sound? *Pitter, patter, pitter, patter*, like rain on a roof. She looked down and saw drops of fresh blood – her blood! – falling to the marble-tiled floor. She gasped again. Three guards thrust at her with spears but the weapons passed harmlessly through her invisible form; yet in the same instant she felt other unseen spears drive into her and she screamed in agony, turned and ran, leaving a trail of blood to mark her path, a trail that the guards followed.

Not until she was streaking back along the flank of the great pyramid did Tozi realise that none of the blood was coming from her body, arms or legs where she had felt so many wounds inflicted. All of it was coming from her nose! Clapping a hand around her nostrils she stemmed the flow, cut off the telltale trail, abruptly changed direction and struck out across the plaza for the towering enclosure wall. She hurtled towards it at a speed that was only possible in her invisible form, reached it, penetrated it, and was out the other side with no more resistance than passing through a light shower of rain.

Tozi fled on, only stopping to catch her breath and still her pounding heart when she reached a shadowy alcove in a narrow street. Emerging into visibility, she held her sleeve across her nose until the bleeding stopped. She examined herself carefully. Though the agonies she'd suffered had felt like murder, she could find not a single wound. Not one! What then were those stabs and cuts she'd felt; those rips, those piercings? The pain had been beyond imagining; she did not think she could ever bear it again. But what had caused it? What had attacked her? Slipping back into invisibility again, she made her way across the causeway to Tacuba, reaching the safe house after nightfall. Yolya awaited her, tutting and clucking at her dishevelled state. 'Wherever have you been, my dear?' the washerwoman asked. 'You've had a nosebleed . . . Look, your ears have bled as well.'

There had been a time when Tozi had suffered terrible bleeding from her nose and ears whenever she had tried to maintain invisibility for longer than a few seconds. The bleeds had stopped months ago on the night she and Malinal had been marched up the great pyramid of Tenochtitlan to face sacrifice at Moctezuma's hands and Hummingbird had intervened to save them. On that same night, for mysterious reasons that had never been explained, the war god had also enhanced and multiplied Tozi's powers, her bleeds had stopped, and she had become able to maintain invisibility indefinitely, suffering no harm.

Did tonight's bleed – following the strange sorcerous attack she'd suffered – mean her powers were waning again? The source of the attack, of course, could only be Acopol, even though he was not physically present in the palace. The thought that he had ways to reach her from afar, and to destroy her strength, filled her with desolate apprehension, and she realised how much she had come to love her powers.

'But I want to kill him, great lord. I must kill him. I missed my opportunity before. This is my chance—'

'Restrain yourself, my son. It does not serve our purposes for Guatemoc to die now . . .'

'I want his skin. I want to drape it wet and warm over my own naked body and dance in your honour wearing it, lord . . .'

'A noble thought, and entirely understandable. It pleases me greatly. Yet unfortunately I cannot allow it. I have another death planned for Guatemoc, another destiny for him to fulfil, and until then I command and require you to keep him alive.'

In the darkest hour of the night, lying in the skull room of Hummingbird's temple, surrounding by the grinning, dripping heads of recent sacrificial victims skewered ear to ear on the racks, Moctezuma had entered into deep communion with his god after consuming ten large *teonanácatl* mushrooms. He was only distantly aware of the hard floor beneath his back and of the flickering lanterns around him because he was out of his body, soaring through the heavens on an enchanted shield, with Hummingbird radiant beside him in his form as a tall, powerfully built man dressed only in a simple loincloth. Yet Hummingbird emanated force and authority; he was massive through the chest and thighs, with the fair skin and golden hair of the gods, but with eyes black as obsidian, and with exceptionally large, strong hands – strangler's hands, warrior's hands, knotted with bulging veins.

'I am yours to command, lord,' said Moctezuma, accepting the inevitable. 'Tell me what I must do with Guatemoc and it will be done.' Even in trance, the idea filled him with an impotent, rebellious, petulant fury and he added: 'Surely you do not expect me to allow him to return to my council, though?'

'No, my son,' chuckled Hummingbird. 'That would be too merciful.'

'Imprisonment, then,' said Moctezuma hopefully. 'I have a certain pit where I keep those whom I wish to be neither alive nor dead.'

'No, that will not do. It serves my purposes better for Guatemoc to be free but not free. Perhaps you might think of banishing him to Cuitláhuac's estate at Chapultepec? Place him under house arrest?'

Cuitláhuac, Guatemoc's father, was Moctezuma's brother, the second most powerful man in the land. There had been tension between them ever since Moctezuma had tried to have Guatemoc poisoned a few months before.

'You're right,' said Hummingbird, divining his thoughts. 'Cuitláhuac's support for you has waned. He is becoming a danger to you. Be merciful to his son in this way and you will win him back.'

As they flew through the night, Moctezuma found the thought of not killing Guatemoc but keeping him under house arrest increasingly appealing. Very soon it seemed to him that it had been his own idea all along.

'You are so very clever, my son,' Hummingbird said as he brought the shield swooping down out of the night sky, over a vast plaza surrounded by a high perimeter wall, lit by a thousand torches and dominated by an immense pyramid. It was immediately recognisable as the sanctuary of Quetzalcoatl in the heart of the sacred city of Cholula.

'I have brought you here,' Hummingbird whispered in Moctezuma's ear, 'to witness the work of our favourite, Acopol. The burnt offering of his predecessors that you made to me in your palace was most satisfactory, my son. Most satisfactory. The smoke of their flesh delighted my nostrils . . .'

'It is my honour to have pleased you, great lord.'

'And afterwards you did well to send him at once to Cholula as I had ordered.'

'It was hard for me, lord, though your word is my command and I hastened to obey. Before his departure for Cholula, Acopol told me of a magical intruder, a witch who watched me from the shadows. He said he had driven her away, but I fear she has returned. This very afternoon I received a report that my guards became aware of an invisible presence. They attacked it with spears. They saw blood fall from empty air to the ground . . .'

'You are right that the witch returned, my son, but you have nothing to fear. Acopol has placed warding spells of great power around your palace, and within the sanctuary of this, my temple. Those are spells that no witch can overcome. They will protect you, as they protected you today, for the whole of Acopol's sojourn in Cholula.'

'And that sojourn, lord – will it be long?'

Hummingbird's laughter was thunder that rose from his belly and burst forth from his throat. 'Long enough for him to work the doom of the white-skins, my son! Long enough to weave the web of blood and sorcery that will destroy them. See now what he has done here in my name – here in Cholula, in the very sanctuary of my ancient enemy Quetzalcoatl, whose likeness the white-skins have stolen.'

On the eastern horizon, the first pink flush of dawn had now touched the sky and Hummingbird brought the flying shield close, very close, to the summit of the pyramid and to the great temple that stood there – the temple of Quetzalcoatl with its two distinctive wings, like the wings of a dragon, joined in the centre by a great hollow tower of stone, itself in the shape of a pyramid. Moctezuma had visited the temple two years before, the only active and functioning shrine to the god of peace that he permitted in his realm, but now he saw with approval that there were new additions, both placed at the east side of the temple complex, set back from the top of the stairway. The first was a bulky hemisphere of green jasper, an execution stone across which sacrificial victims would be stretched to offer up their hearts. Such a thing had never been seen before in Cholula, since Quetzalcoatl had forbidden human sacrifice. And the second modification to the age-old customs of the sacred city, even more pleasing to Moctezuma's eye, was that a giant idol of Hummingbird himself, an idol glinting with gold and gemstones, its gaping maw barbed with fangs and tusks, had been set up beside the execution stone.

But best of all was the sight of twenty weeping, fresh-faced boys, Tlascalans by the look of them, none more than ten years of age, nearing the top of the eastern stairway. Dressed in the paper clothes of sacrifice, their bodies streaked with chalk, they were kept in order by laughing, jeering guards, who prodded them with the obsidian blades of their spears, drawing blood at every step.

'Look!' Hummingbird hissed, directing Moctezuma's attention to the eastern doorway of the temple, out of which Acopol now appeared naked, but for the swirling mystery of his tattoos. Behind the *nagual* came four priests in black robes – priests of Hummingbird! – the killing team, who would hold the victims down over the stone.

'They are your priests, lord!' Moctezuma observed.

When he had sent Acopol to Cholula he had given him full authority to implement whatever changes he desired in the sanctuary of Quetzalcoatl, and orders had been carried to Tlaqui and Tlalchi, the joint rulers of the sacred city, that they should obey the sorcerer and not impede him in any way. Still, he had worked fast to get all this done – the altar, the idol, driving out the priests of Quetzalcoatl and replacing them with the war god's men – in just a few days.

'Yes,' purred Hummingbird. 'I am well pleased.'

As the limb of the sun broke the horizon, the killing began, and Moctezuma could not help but admire Acopol's technique. Rather than first splitting the breastbone, then cutting away the ligaments and arteries and finally removing the heart, he had somehow combined all three operations into a single, graceful, scooping flow of the obsidian knife that culminated with the dripping organ, still pulsing, still pumping blood, raised high above his head and offered to the sun – Hummingbird's symbol in the heavens. And oh, joy: in his visionary ecstasy, Moctezuma saw great rays of light and life rising like steam from those sacrificed hearts, vibrating waves and arcs and spirals, in colours brighter and stranger than any he had ever known, colours ethereal and mystical, colours that seemed to belong to another order of existence entirely, transcendental and unearthly, filled with a preternatural vigour that the war god drew into himself, gorging and feasting until the last of the victims lay dead.

'Ahhh,' said Hummingbird, 'you see? That's what I call a sacrifice.' He licked his lips: 'But I relish even more the basket of ten thousand virgin females you have promised me for my birthday . . . I trust that your preparations continue to go well.'

'The preparations go well, lord.'

Unfortunately this was not entirely accurate. Moctezuma had received word only the day before that more than a thousand young girls from Tlascala, whose arrival in Tenochtitlan he had hotly anticipated, would not, after all, be swelling the as yet inadequate harvest in the fattening pens. A band of Chichemec mercenaries had gathered the girls in during a month in the field, only to be intercepted by that demon Shikotenka just before crossing the border. All the captives had been freed and almost the entire mercenary squad efficiently slaughtered; only one of them – just one out of three hundred! – had escaped to tell the tale.

'You lie,' said the war god. His voice in the dawn was a soft, menacing susurration.

'I do not lie, great lord. There has been a setback but I have redoubled our efforts. The ten thousand will be gathered in for your birthday feast as I promised. All the resources of my empire are deployed to achieve this noble end.'

'Do not fail me, my son. Nothing will go well for you if you fail me. But keep your promise and I will give you the world.'

Abruptly Hummingbird was gone, the magic shield dissolved and Cholula vanished. With a start and a stifled scream, Moctezuma awoke on the floor of the skull room of the temple of Hummingbird, atop the great pyramid of Tenochtitlan.

Glaring down at him was the severed head of the Chichemec mercenary who had brought the news of Shikotenka's ambush.

In the last ten days of May 1519, as they worked together on the long, immensely complex and legalistic letter that Cortés was drafting to King Carlos of Spain, Pepillo found himself observing his master carefully. For the first months of the expedition he had admired him, indeed all but worshipped him, but he had always, also, been aware of a devious, calculating, manipulative side to Cortés's nature, and it was this, now, that came increasingly to the fore.

The immediate focus of the caudillo's formidable intelligence and will, Pepillo saw, was less on his long-term strategy to crush and utterly destroy Moctezuma, than on a much more pressing need to crush and utterly destroy the faction led by Juan Escudero and loyal to Diego de Velázquez, the governor of Cuba. In some way that Pepillo could not at first fully understand, the mission he had gone on to Huitztlan with Escalante, and the agreement with the Totonacs that the Spaniards could build a town of their own there, was the key to this. But gradually the picture began to clear as Pepillo watched how Cortés worked tirelessly to cultivate allies at all levels of the soldiery. To be sure some, perhaps quite a large number, broadly supported the Velazquistas' call – which Escudero had made publicly several times – for a quick return to Cuba with the treasure they had already won. But the majority were still either undecided or frankly against such a solution, not wishing to turn their backs on the even greater wealth that Cortés had persuaded them they might win in Tenochtitlan.

In the minds of those who were willing to continue, Cortés carefully planted the suggestion, which he had so far shared only with his closest confidants, that the best way forward might be to establish a permanent colony here in Mexico, which would be a legal entity in its own right, able to provide for the needs of its members. An ideal site at which to establish such a colony had, as it happened, already been found in the explorations along the coast recently conducted by Don Juan de Escalante – a location with a safe harbour, set amidst productive, well-watered farmlands that had been offered as a permanent gift to Spain by friendly and tractable Totonac Indians, who would prove strong allies if war with Moctezuma were to come. Cortés lamented he had no authority from Velázquez to found such a colony, but, 'We should never forget,' he hinted, 'that the interests of Spain and of our sovereign Don Carlos are paramount.' He then made sure that word of these discussions leaked out to the Velazquistas who, predictably, were outraged, accusing him of going far beyond the governor's plans for the expedition, which had been strictly for trade and exploration, calling once again for an immediate return to Cuba, and announcing their own intention to depart.

Making a great show of injured dignity, Cortés convened a meeting of all the soldiery on Monday 31 May. There he spoke gravely and with convincing humility saying he had no desire to exceed his instructions – indeed, he had never had such a desire – and that if the majority wished to leave then he would not stand in their way. He even went so far as to issue a proclamation ordering the troops to make ready to embark and sail for Cuba.

But he'd prepared his ground well; the order caused a sensation as his allies stirred the men to fury, generating a storm of resentment within the camp at the selfish folly of the Velázquez loyalists. The idea of staying and establishing a colony, which had come from Cortés in the first place, now took root among the soldiers as though it was their own invention. 'We came here,' Pepillo overheard one of the men say, 'expecting to form a settlement and we'll not be frustrated just because there's no warrant from the governor to make one. There are interests, higher than those of Velázquez, which demand it.' The words could have been Cortés's own! Another likewise argued that Mexico wasn't Velázquez's personal property and that his partisans had no right to act as though it was. 'These territories were discovered for the king; we have to plant a colony to watch over the king's interests.'

Cortés was now in a position to claim that the idea of a colony was not his but had arisen from the patriotic zeal of the majority of the conquistadors in their desire to expand the overseas possessions of Spain and to serve the best interests of King Carlos V – fundamental virtues that he could hardly be against. He was obliged, he said, to assist so worthy a process; to this end, during a second long and emotional public meeting, he appointed his ally Puertocarrero, who Pepillo noticed had become peculiarly compliant and agreeable after the skirmish outside Cuetlaxtlan two weeks before, together with Francisco Montejo, formerly one of the ringleaders of the Velazquistas, as joint chief magistrates of the new colony. The *alguacil*, *regidores*, treasurer and other councillors – all personal friends of Cortés – were then sworn in. Finally the colony, which as yet existed only as a concept, was given a name – Villa Rica de la Veracruz – with the stated intention that it should be founded at the earliest possible opportunity at the location near the Totonac town of Huitztlan previously scouted by Escalante. With all this done, and entered into the minutes by Pepillo, Cortés dramatically resigned the commission as captain-general of the expedition, conferred on him by Diego de Velázquez, which indeed, he said, had necessarily expired, since the authority of the governor of Cuba was now 'superseded by the magistracy of Villa Rica de la Veracruz'.

Cortés then returned to his pavilion beckoning for Pepillo to follow him. 'What happens now, master?' Pepillo asked.

'I get my way lad,' the caudillo replied. 'Stick with me and you'll see how these things are done.'

Sure enough, within the hour the newly appointed councillors called Cortés back to the meeting ground and told him there was no one else as experienced and as well qualified as himself to govern the community, both in peace and in war. They asked him specifically to lead them in the continuing invasion and conquest of Mexico and to be their captain-general, chief, and *justicia mayor*, 'to whom we will have recourse in arduous and difficult situations and in the differences that might arise amongst us'. They told Cortés: 'This is our charge to you, and, if necessary, our command, because we hold it as certain that God and the king will be well served if you accept this authority.'

Pepillo recalled the old saying, 'Press me harder but I'm very willing' – for after some show of modesty and reluctance Cortés did, of course, accept the commission, but not before he had secured extraordinary terms for himself, including one fifth of all the treasure that would be won during the conquest.

This last concession, an amount equivalent to the share – known as 'the king's fifth' – that all expeditions were required to allocate to the king himself, outraged the Velazquistas again. They had been taken by surprise by the defection of Montejo and by the speed of the coup that had, at a stroke, stripped the governor of Cuba of all authority in Mexico, and vested supreme civil and military power in Cortés. Now, however, the governor's kinsman Velázquez de Léon, his former major domo Diego de Ordaz, and Juan Escudero, whose hatred of Cortés grew visibly more intense as each day passed, made the mistake of attempting to start a full-scale rebellion.

Cortés clapped the three of them in irons, and locked them in the brig on his flagship. There, after letting them cool off for a few days, he visited them on 6 June, the day before the entire army would decamp towards Huitztlan, and released them again after buying their compliance with gold. 'Every kingdom divided against itself is brought to desolation,' he explained to Pepillo, citing the Book of Matthew, 'and every city or house divided against itself shall not stand.'

It all sounded very convincing, very conciliatory. But in his heart Pepillo didn't believe the caudillo really wanted to reconcile with the Velazquistas at all. The cunning way he had provoked them into a rash and hasty act of insubordination, and the way he now forgave them, were surely just moves in some subtle game of wits and strategy he was playing. Even the bribe of gold offered to them seemed insincere, since Cortés fobbed them off with just a fraction of the modest treasures he'd received from Pichatzin to compensate for Guatemoc's attack on Sandoval and Puertocarrero. The lion's share, he told Pepillo, he'd already used to detach Montejo from the Velazquistas and buy his loyalty in the manoeuvres to found the colony.

Chapter Twenty-Seven

Twenty-six days had passed since Tozi's precipitous flight from Moctezuma's palace, and fourteen since her single disastrous attempt to re-enter it. Other than that she had remained with Yolya in the safe house in Tacuba, helping with the laundry work, sleeping a great deal, eating little, her confidence shattered. She had almost given up hope that Huicton would ever return when one morning she heard the familiar shuffle of his feet and the tapping of a stick outside in the lane. The green gate opened and he hobbled into the yard, bent over, dressed in rags, a filthy sack dangling from his shoulder, utterly convincing in his role as a blind beggar.

Tozi ran to him, embraced him wildly, tears pouring down her face. 'I've failed,' she said. 'I can't do my work any more. Moctezuma has a new sorcerer, a great *nagual* from the north, one of the tattooed ones. I fear him, Huicton. He could see me even when I made myself invisible. Such power he has! He's no longer in Tenochtitlan, yet his magic still protects Moctezuma—'

'My dear . . . wait. Slow down . . .'

But Tozi was in no mood to be interrupted: 'I know Huicton! I tried. Truly I tried to enter the palace but spirit knives and spirit razors attacked me until my head burst and my brains bled.'

'That is not good, Tozi.'

'I know,' she sobbed. 'I fear I'm losing my powers. I'm nothing without my powers.'

Huicton guided her to a bench in the yard and they sat together under the lines of drying laundry for a long while until her weeping subsided. Finally the old spy spoke, the vibrant nasal hum that characterised his voice peculiarly resonant this morning: 'This sorcerer who you say is no longer in Tenochtitlan . . . has he gone to Cholula?'

At this Tozi looked up sharply. 'Yes,' she said. 'He has.'

'And is his name perchance Acopol?'

'Yes! It is. How do you know this?'

'I have come here directly from Cholula, my child. After I left the Spanish camp near Cuetlaxtlan—'

'The Spanish?'

'They are the white-skinned ones you believe to be the companions of Quetzalcoatl. They call themselves Spaniards.'

Tozi felt her pulse quicken. Here was the end of all her woes. Here was the fulfilment of all her hopes. 'And did you meet – O tell me it is true, Huicton! – did you meet Quetzalcoatl? Did you meet the god himself?'

'I met the leader of the Spaniards,' Huicton replied carefully. 'He is a man called Cortés, Hernán Cortés, and – I cannot deceive you, Tozi, for I love you dearly – he is no god.'

As fast as Tozi's hopes had risen, so now they threatened to come crashing down. 'You lie, Huicton!' she protested. 'He *is* a god. I know he is a god. He will destroy Moctezuma! He will destroy Moctezuma's bastard sorcerer! He will destroy them all.'

'Well there, my dear, you may very well be right – for I believe that Cortés will indeed destroy Moctezuma and all his henchmen, and I am willing to believe that Cortés has been sent to us from heaven, even perhaps that he may be the manifestation of Quetzalcoatl in human form. Nonetheless, you must accept, Tozi, that he *is* a human being, with all the faults and frailties of a human being. Your friend Malinal knows this better than any other since she has become his lover.'

'If she is his lover,' said Tozi fiercely, 'then she is the lover of a god.' She took Huicton's hands. 'Tell me of Malinal! Is she well? Is she working to bring Quetzalcoatl here?'

'She is well and she is undoubtedly working to bring Cortés here. She has not faltered for a single moment in the mission you and she agreed, and she's promised to send me messages through my spies to keep us informed.'

'I knew it,' said Tozi. 'I knew she wouldn't let me down . . .' A pause: 'She is beautiful, is she not?'

'She is possibly the most beautiful woman it has ever been my privilege to know.'

Tozi's mind was flooded with memories of the brief, intense time she and Malinal had spent together in the fattening pens of Tenochtitlan, and of the way they had cheated sacrifice at the hands of Moctezuma, thanks to the inexplicable intervention of Hummingbird – that wicked god whose servant Acopol undoubtedly was. All of this, everything that was happening, must be tied together in some deep, secret, hidden way, and the fact that Acopol was now in Cholula only added to the mystery. Why would the murderous sorcerer go to the last sanctuary of the living worship of Quetzalcoatl in Mexico, if not to work murder and magic there?

'You said you came here from Cholula,' Tozi reminded Huicton.

'Yes. I have travelled far, child. I have been with the Spaniards at the coast, I have been with Shikotenka in the mountains of Tlascala and I have been with my master Ishtlil. It was Ishtlil who sent me onwards to Cholula to gather intelligence of certain happenings there . . .'

'Happenings that involve the sorcerer Acopol?'

'Yes, my child. I watched him for many days.'

'And did you discover what he's doing in Quetzalcoatl's city?'

'If you can still call it that! Acopol has imposed his will on it, in Moctezuma's name, and made vassals of its rulers Tlaqui and Tlalchi. They are weak men, foolish men. They've even allowed him to build an altar to Hummingbird on Quetzalcoatl's pyramid!'

'To Hummingbird?' Tozi was stunned.

'I know. It's unbelievable. But the old high priest was set aside, taken away – no one knows what's happened to him – and Acopol was put in his place. He sacrifices twenty young boys to Hummingbird every morning, Tozi. He kills them at dawn just as the sun rises.'

'Why?' she asked. Her head was spinning. Never in this age of the earth had humans been sacrificed at Cholula. Because of its ancient sanctity, it was the last place in Mexico where Moctezuma had allowed the cult and worship of Quetzalcoatl to persist. 'Why would they turn the world upside down?'

'I believe it is all to do with the Spaniards,' said Huicton, 'who – I repeat – are not gods but mortal men of flesh and blood who can be killed. I heard rumours in Cholula that a trap is to be prepared for them there.'

'A trap? How? Even if they are mortal men, and I know they are not, they're still miles from Cholula.'

'This is what I wasn't able to discover. It's a closely guarded secret. All I know is that Moctezuma has raised this sorcerer Acopol very high.' Huicton tapped his nose. 'I don't like the smell of it. I had been thinking, my little spy, that perhaps you could go there and find out more, but now that I have heard your story, I cannot ask you.'

Tozi thought about it. She could not spy on Acopol. He would find her out in a moment.

On the other hand, if his purpose in Cholula was to prevent the return of Quetzalcoatl, then surely it was her duty to try?

Preparations for the move north to Huitztlan were set in motion immediately after the public meeting of 31 May, and on 7 June the fleet, under the command of Juan de Escalante, embarked for the new site, with orders to break the ground there and begin construction and fortification of the colony of Villa Rica de la Veracruz as a permanent base for future operations. With the fleet went half the army, while Cortés, guided by Meco, led the rest of his force overland on an indirect route by way of Cempoala, the Totonac regional capital, where meetings of the greatest importance were to be held with Tlacoch, the paramount chief.

Although still unhappy to be separated from Melchior, Pepillo had accepted his lot. There were times, now, when his pet, growing rapidly stronger and more savage in the company of the other dogs, did not even seem to know him. Melchior had developed a special friendship with Jairo, the black mastiff who had previously attacked him, and the two of them were now inseparable. If other dogs threatened the lurcher pup, Jairo would come ferociously to his aid. Melchior was cunning to seek protection in this way, Pepillo realised, and he watched with pride as his pet loped forward with the rest of the pack; he was already bigger than many of the full-grown dogs and soon he would be able to fight his own battles.

Meanwhile it was a joy, it was a delight, to be leaving the miserable and boring dunes on which the Spanish camp had been pitched since April, to cross the barren coastal plains and to advance into landscapes that became greener, richer and more interesting with every mile, offering glimpses in the distance of a towering, snow-capped volcano. Finding himself unable to resist the mood of excitement amongst the soldiers, Pepillo began to join in with their marching songs.

They crossed a river by making rafts and requisitioning some native canoes left lying on the banks, and thereafter found themselves on rolling plains, richly carpeted with tropical vegetation, overgrown with graceful palms and teeming with wild creatures. There were species they recognised, including large herds of deer – Alvarado gave chase on Bucephalus and wounded a buck with his lance, but it escaped into a palm forest and could not be caught. Other animals, however, were completely unfamiliar, and the skies were filled with strange, brightly coloured birds whose raucous cries rang out from morning to night. It seemed that all the towns and villages on their route had been deserted by their inhabitants – no doubt out of fear of the Spaniards – and in several they found temples with blood-spattered shrines and mutilated human corpses bearing witness to recent human sacrifices. The contrast between these horrors and the terrestrial paradise through which they passed could not have been more stark.

On 10 June, in the morning, they came in sight of Cempoala, its stuccoed walls gleaming like silver in the sun, and advanced on it with cavalry, cannon, muskets and crossbows ready. Twenty dignitaries hastened to intercept them, bringing cakes of finely scented rose petals, which they presented to the horsemen, greeting them with every sign of friendliness and telling them, through Malinal, that lodgings had already been prepared for them. The paramount chief, Meco explained, was too fat and heavy to come out and receive them personally, but eagerly awaited their arrival.

Pleased by such a warm reception, Cortés reached down to Pepillo, who was walking at his stirrup, and lifted him up into Molinero's saddle as they rode through Cempoala. The city was so green with trees and bushes that it looked like a garden, and proved to be far larger and more beautiful than any other they had so far seen in Mexico, with a population of perhaps thirty thousand living in well-built stone houses thatched with palm leaves. Crowds of men, women and children thronged the streets, smiling and welcoming the conquistadors with wreaths of flowers – one of which was hung around Molinero's neck, while Cortés was given a chaplet of roses to decorate his helmet.

Seated beneath a huge sunshade, Tlacoch was waiting to greet them as they entered the courtyard of the spacious lodgings he'd put at their disposal near his palace. Though tall, the paramount chief was indeed truly and enormously fat, a veritable mountain of wobbling flesh. He was so fat, in fact, that he could not walk unaided for more than a few paces. Inevitably the Spaniards began to call him 'the fat cacique' – 'cacique' being the word for chief they had adopted from the Taino Indians of Hispaniola and Cuba.

Cortés kept the men on their guard during the night, but there were no signs of hostility and the following morning, 11 June, he held a long meeting with the fat cacique, which Pepillo attended and kept note of. Meco and Malinal interpreted, with assistance and clarification where necessary from Jerónimo de Aguilar, who had at last recovered from his stomach ailment.

As usual the caudillo began by announcing himself to be the subject of a great monarch, dwelling beyond the waters, who had sent him to abolish the false religions and the vile practice of human sacrifice that prevailed in Mexico, to overthrow the foul demons mistakenly worshipped as gods by the Indians and to convert them to the true religion of Christianity.

To this Tlacoch replied that he was very happy with his own deities, who sent sunshine and rain, and that he too was the vassal of a powerful monarch, Moctezuma, whose capital city Tenochtitlan stood in the midst of a great lake far off in the mountains where, being surrounded by water, and approachable only along narrow, well-defended causeways, it was effectively impregnable. He then went on to paint a terrifying picture of Moctezuma and to reveal his hatred of him and of the burdensome tribute the Mexica extracted from him which, as well as gold, jewels and crops, included large numbers of young men and women, the flower of the nation, carried off each year for sacrifice on the altar of the Mexica war god Hummingbird.

The problem was getting worse, Tlacoch complained, as the years went by. Moctezuma had, for example, recently demanded an onerous new levy of sacrificial victims – a thousand virgin girls to be delivered to the fattening pens in Tenochtitlan in good time to celebrate the supposed birthday of Hummingbird at the beginning of the month the Mexica called *Panquetzaliztli*, a date corresponding with 20 November. When Cortés learned of this, his eyes lit up with fury; he said he had been sent here by his own monarch precisely to stop such abuses. He invited the Totonacs to join forces with him to overthrow the oppressor before this wicked holocaust of virgins could occur.

The fat cacique's response was ambiguous. On the one hand it was clear he wanted to take up Cortés's invitation – indeed this was why he had asked him to come to Cempoala in the first place – and he hinted he might be able to provide the Spanish with as many as a hundred thousand warriors to support their conquest of Mexico. But, on the other hand, he was obviously deeply afraid of 'the great Moctezuma', as he always referred to him, opining that if he betrayed him, vast Mexica armies would 'pour down from the mountains, rush over the plains like a whirlwind and sweep off the whole Totonac nation to slavery and sacrifice'.

Cortés endeavoured to stiffen Tlacoch's backbone with reminders of what his soldiers had done to the Chontal Maya at Potonchan, declaring that a single Spaniard was equal to a thousand Mexica, and gradually extracting more information from him, much of which Malinal endorsed as true. The fat cacique spoke at some length of Ishtlil, the rightful monarch of the kingdom of Texcoco, who had been ousted by Moctezuma and replaced by his more compliant brother Cacama. 'As well as ourselves,' said Tlacoch, 'Ishtlil can prove an important ally for you.'

'We have already received representations from him,' Cortés was able to reply. 'His envoy approached us and offered us his master's friendship. I understand, though, that my army must pass through the lands of a people called the Tlascalans if we are to join up with Ishtlil's forces.'

'That is correct,' said Tlacoch, who was clearly taken aback that Cortés knew so much and was already in discussions with other leaders.

'I'm told these Tlascalans are great fighters,' Cortés added.

The fat cacique confirmed that this was indeed the case. The Tlascalans, he said, lived in a state of permanent warfare with the Mexica and might perhaps be recruited as allies. There was also a tribe named the Huexotzincos, smaller and less powerful than the Tlascalans, but likewise vehemently opposed to Mexica overlordship. In short, if Cortés were to make an alliance not only with the Totonacs but also with the Tlascalans, the Huexotzincos and Ishtlil, then there might be a real chance of defeating Moctezuma.

After translating this last point, Malinal interrupted the discussion and, relying very little on Aguilar, told Cortés in Spanish that the situation was not nearly so simple as Tlacoch was painting it. First, he was talking nonsense about the Totonacs; there was no way they could support Cortés with an army of a hundred thousand, or even a tenth of that number, and they were not renowned for their bravery on the field of battle. Second, the Huexotzincos and the Tlascalans hated each other at least as much as they both hated the Mexica, and had never before been known to cooperate. Thirdly, while it was true that the Tlascalans would make excellent allies, they were a ferocious, unpredictable and independent-minded people, and there was no guarantee they would join the Spaniards; on the contrary, they were just as likely to fight them.

'Even so,' Cortés replied, 'if I can unite all these peoples in an alliance, what say you? Will we win?'

'If you can do it,' said Malinal, 'then certainly you will win.'

That was the moment, Pepillo realised much later, when Cortés's strategy for overthrowing Moctezuma began to take proper shape in his mind. He smiled, a broad smile, showing his teeth, and just for that instant he looked less like a man and more like a wolf.

Guatemoc was here! It seemed he'd committed some act of insubordination against the Great Speaker – something to do with the *tueles*. Could it be, Tozi hoped, that he'd listened to her after all? Could he have made an overture of peace to Quetzalcoatl? Huicton had been unable to glean any definite intelligence on the true nature of the prince's crime, but whatever it was, his punishment was to be held under house arrest on his father Cuitláhuac's estate at Chapultepec, just a few miles from Tacuba. Months before, when he'd been recovering from his battle wounds and from the poison Moctezuma's physician had given him, Tozi had visited Guatemoc there in her disguise as the goddess Temaz and helped him to heal. Now she longed to pay an invisible call on him again, to appear to him again as Temaz, and to discover what had happened between him and the *tueles*, but Huicton would not allow it. 'In truth, I can't stop you, girl,' the old spy said. 'If you want to go I'm sure you will go. But if you are truly to face Acopol as you say you must, then you first have to renew and strengthen your powers; I fear the prince will prove a distraction.'

Huicton's idea was that Tozi must go on a vision quest. She must travel, alone, into the northern deserts, through the lands of the Chichemec nomads whence Acopol himself had come. She must go at once.

'And why must I go, Huicton?'

'Because our cause needs you, dear girl, but you cannot help us when you are as damaged and afraid as you are now. You must journey to the place of your ancestors, to the lost land of Aztlán, you must find the Seven Caves of Chicomoztoc, and there you must seek a vision from the masters of wisdom.'

Aztlán was the home of the gods, though nobody knew where it was any more, and nobody had been there for hundreds and hundreds of years. The Seven Caves of Chicomoztoc were believed to lie within the borders of Aztlán and were the mystic place of origin of the Mexica, the Tlascalans and all other Nahuatl-speaking peoples. The masters of wisdom were workers of the highest magic, said to have concealed themselves from common sight in the caves long ages ago. So much, every Mexica knew, but what Tozi knew in addition, or at any rate had believed since her childhood, was that she came from Aztlán – not in some distant, remote, centuries-old, ancestral sense, but in the sense of actually having been born there and having migrated from there to Tenochtitlan in her infancy. Her mother had told her this – her mother who had passed on the gift of withcraft to her but who had only just begun to teach her the path when she was killed by a mob, leaving Tozi an orphan. Tozi had been reared by Huicton, who had found her in the hole she had hidden in after her mother's murder; he had nurtured her skills and made her one of his spies. Now he stood over her in the yard of the Tacuba safe house and told her it was time for her to go.

'Don't delay,' he urged. 'Don't think about it, even for a moment. Go! Find your vision, discover your power and return to me. Then and only then will we see what can be done about Acopol.'

So Tozi gathered up her few belongings, bundled them into a deerskin backpack and left without a backward glance. 'Head north,' Huicton called after her. 'Go first by way of ancient Teotihuacan. There is a ruined pyramid there, said to have been built in the long ago by Quetzalcoatl himself, and from its flank protrudes the effigy of the plumed serpent. Seek guidance from the god you revere and then continue on your journey north . . . always north. Your feet will know the way.'

Tozi's feet did know the way. Before Teotihuacan they took her directly to Chapultepec, where she slipped into invisibility – she did not fear the failure of her powers with ordinary mortals, only in the presence of adepts such as Acopol – and entered Cuitláhuac's estate.

Huicton be damned!

If she was going to trudge hundreds of miles north into the Chichemec wilderness on some crazy quest for a mythical land, Tozi was absolutely determined that she would see Guatemoc first.

An hour later, Tozi lurked invisibly in the audience chamber of Cuitláhuac's mansion, watching Guatemoc and his father locked in an intense, furious, but *whispered* argument. Their voices were lowered, she understood, because a small army of paid informers and secret policemen had been sent by Moctezuma to infiltrate the Chapultepec estate. Indeed she had passed several suspicious-looking characters as she had sought Guatemoc out, two of them loitering by the door to the audience chamber with their ears obviously pricked. She had thought of exposing their presence by some trick, and would perhaps have done so, had she not been so angry at Guatemoc because, once again, as when she had seen him performing unspeakable intimacies with another woman, he'd shattered her romantic image of him – in this case her foolish dream that he might have been persuaded to embrace the cause of Quetzalcoatl. She now knew that quite the opposite was true. The reason the prince had been placed here under house arrest – 'you might so easily have been executed instead', his father complained – was not that he had sought to make common cause with the *tueles* to bring Moctezuma down, as she had fantasised, but rather because he had tried to attack them, and had even taken one of them prisoner with the intention of sacrificing him, contrary to the wishes of the Great Speaker. Weirdly it seemed to be Moctezuma who was making peace overtures towards Quetzalcoatl, sucking up to him in every possible way and trying to curry favour, while the prince fought and opposed the return of the god.

The one thread of hope for Guatemoc, however, was that his hatred for Moctezuma plainly remained undimmed. 'Father, we must act,' he now whispered. 'We must overthrow that monstrous fool before it's too late.'

'Overthrow the Great Speaker?' replied Cuitláhuac, as though Guatemoc had suggested they turn the earth upside down. 'But that would be treason. Such a thing has never been done in the whole history of our nation.'

'It's a short history, father, hardly two hundred years, and there is a first time for everything. I say the time has come – indeed is long overdue. If we do not act, my uncle will surrender to the white-skins and make slaves of us all.'

'I won't be part of any plot against him,' Cuitláhuac insisted.

'Even though he plotted to poison me?'

'Even so.'

'Even though in his every action he betrays the high office of Speaker?'

'Even so! You are proposing a rebellion, Guatemoc, and that is unthinkable. It will always be unthinkable.'

Tozi wanted desperately to intervene, to shoot out from invisibility like a thunderbolt and put both these stupid, stubborn men right! Cuitláhuac needed to understand that a revolt against his wicked brother Moctezuma was absolutely, immediately, imperatively necessary. But it was even more important for Guatemoc to understand that the

254

tueles, who he so dismissively called the 'white-skins', were not the enemy; rather they were his natural allies, since they had come across the eastern ocean to abolish the foul rule of Moctezuma and restore justice to the world.

'I will not – I cannot – sanction rebellion,' Cuitláhuac now whispered. 'There must be some other way. I'll speak to your uncle again in the council and try to get him to see reason.'

'It won't do any good, father,' Guatemoc sighed, 'you know it won't! The man is far beyond reason.'

'Nonetheless I have to try. Anything else is—'

'Unthinkable?'

'Yes. Unthinkable! Moctezuma has his faults but he is our ruler, sanctioned by the gods, loved by the people. We must never forget that.'

Tozi drifted closer to Guatemoc. She knew she must not speak to him in the presence of his father. She was tempted to wait until he was alone and then reveal herself, but she had brought none of the finery of the goddess Temaz that she'd used for disguise in their previous encounters, and she was under no illusions about how the prince would react to her real appearance as a street urchin and a witch!

She hated him, yet loved him, despised him, yet admired him, and above all, as had been the case since their first encounter in the royal hospital months before, when she'd gone to cut his throat and ended up saving his life, she felt powerfully drawn to him as though some deep and ancient connection bound them.

She was close enough to touch him now. Invisible, he could not see her, could not feel her, so what was the harm? She rested her hand on his arm. Closer . . . Closer still. Now she sensed that faint, strange resistance that was always there when she moved through a solid object. And then – she could not help herself – she merged with him, just for an instant occupying the same space filled by his strong, masculine body. She was within him, part of him, feeling the firm, steady beat of his heart, the vigour of his blood as it pulsed through its channels, the great reservoirs of warmth and courage that fed his vitality. She was within him and then she emerged beyond him, ending

255

their fleeting union, and in that instant he turned, turned suddenly and looked at her – really *looked* at her – and she fled.

It must have been an illusion, Guatemoc decided much later as he worked out in the exercise yard, sparring not with Man-Eater or Mud Head as he would have preferred – for it was a strictly enforced condition of his house arrest that his closest friends must not visit him – but with two of Cuitláhuac's bondsmen, trained warriors both, though not in the same league as any of his five comrades in arms. It must have been an illusion and yet . . . and yet . . . he had felt the most unsettling sensation within his body, something intimate, almost orgasmic. And then as the sensation abruptly ceased, he had turned and seen the diaphanous, translucent form of a woman there in the audience chamber between himself and his father – a young woman, strangely familiar, with the look of the goddess Temaz but yet also different, more fierce, with something wild and flighty about her, like a feral animal caught in a trap.

Guatemoc rolled his shoulders and deliberately dismissed the vision from his mind. He struck a blow – a very good one, he had to admit! – that brought one of the bondsmen to his knees with a gasp of pain, then on the backswing he struck again and laid the second burly soldier flat. Throwing down his *macuahuitl* – stripped of its obsidian blades for sparring purposes and thus toothless as a crone – he said, 'Thank you, dear fellows, that will be enough for today', and stalked off to the private apartments he now occupied in the south wing of his father's mansion.

He needed to be alone. He needed to think. Why his mad uncle had let him live was a mystery to him, for he had fully expected to die. Indeed the night before he was to be killed, specialised priests had come to prepare his body for ritual slaughter by the ordeal of flaying. He had broken one priest's jaw and pulled the arm of another out of its socket before they subdued him and began the process of softening his skin with unguents and hot towels to ensure it could be removed without tearing so Moctezuma could pull it over his own body like a glove.

But then, soon after dawn, the Great Farter himself had come to

256

his cell, dismissed the priests and ordered Guatemoc's release into the custody of Cuitláhuac. Moctezuma had seemed flustered, excited, anxious, with a strange fixed smile and staring eyes. He had acted, almost, as though he and Guatemoc were friends!

What was the reason for this sudden change of heart? What had happened to Moctezuma during that night? Guatemoc realised that he might never know, that his uncle was so crazed that his mental processes were beyond rational enquiry – which was precisely why he could no longer be trusted to rule the nation. Since Cuitláhuac was a weakling, Guatemoc resolved, it fell to him and him alone to plot the death of Moctezuma and to prepare a proper strategy for dealing with the threat of the white-skins. If they all fought like the man in the dunes had fought, they were going to prove to be very formidable enemies indeed.

After her eerie union with Guatemoc, an experience that had left her aching with an unaccountable sense of loss, as though there were now some void within her that could never be filled, Tozi walked steadily and determinedly north from Chapultepec through the spectacular beauty of the One World. She passed beneath the twin aqueducts that carried fresh water into Tenochtitlan from the springs on Chapultepec hill by means of a pair of gleaming ceramic pipes, each with a bore as wide as a man's torso. Assembled from hundreds of short interlinked sections, the pipes were carried on marching lines of stilts and scaffolding that followed the curving decline of the hillside for two miles down to the edge of Lake Texcoco, and then soared out for a further two miles over the lake itself, finally entering the island metropolis in the district of Tlatelolco. The whole amazing construction was needed to keep Tenochtitlan alive because the lake waters were brackish and practically undrinkable, and there were few functional wells within the city. For this reason the aqueducts were guarded and patrolled along the full length of their overland transit by squads of warriors, from a permanent garrison of twelve thousand who were camped at the point where the springs emerged from the earth. Tozi saw no need to hide in invisibility as she passed the heavily armed patrols. Their vigilance was reserved for warriors like themselves – Tlascalans perhaps, or rebel Texcocans. Skinny, dirty, dressed in rags, she posed no apparent threat and was already effectively invisible to them.

She continued her journey north, leaving Chapultepec with its military hustle and bustle behind as the day wore on. The colours of the One World were lush fern green and rich loam for the fertile fields of the farmers that she passed on her left, deepest cerulean blue flecked with the snow-white of the wavelets that lapped the lake to her right; above her was the azure sky, in which slow-moving clouds floated like feathers, and the molten gold of the sun. Long, welcoming shadows were cast by stands of trees; the drab clothes of peasants contrasted with the bright stalls of market traders, standing amidst the red and yellow painted adobe buildings of the town of Tepuca on the north side of the lake, which she reached very late in the afternoon.

Tozi had no goods to barter with her – Huicton had insisted on that – so she begged shelter for the night from a widow in Tepuca, a stranger who took her in kindly and would accept no service in exchange for her food and lodging.

The following morning, early, Tozi was on her way again, heading north, constantly, unerringly north through the valley of the One World. Something plucked at her heart and she turned back for a last view of distant Tenochtitlan shimmering in the midst of the great lake – an impossible mirage of towering pyramids, palaces and mansions, separated by the perfect geometry of intersecting avenues and canals. The whole eye-achingly beautiful vista, which yet concealed so much ugliness, so much cruelty, so much woe, was encompassed, surrounded, defined, by distant ranges of jagged snow-capped mountains that soared to west and east, their descending slopes richly carpeted in the blue-green of forests that had already been remotely ancient when the Mexica, then a poverty-stricken but ferocious nomadic tribe, had first arrived in these lands.

And something else, even older, had been here to greet those first Mexica scouts as well. On the afternoon of her second day on the road, after begging a few cobs of maize for sustenance, Tozi's quest brought her, as Huicton had told her it must, to the long-abandoned city of Teotihuacan, 'the place where men became gods', with its three ruined pyramids that had been built, the Mexica believed, at the very beginning of this present age of the earth. She advanced along the broad, straight, two-mile-long avenue called the Way of the Dead, mixing in with a group of hymn-singing pilgrims from Tenochtitlan as they visited first the small, ruined step-pyramid believed to have been the work of Quetzalcoatl because of the sculptured head of a plumed serpent that jutted from its steep side, thence onward to the gigantic pyramid of the Sun, which rose in five tiers towards the heavens, and finally, at the northern end of the avenue, to the slightly smaller pyramid of the Moon.

Like everything else the Mexica touched, Teotihuacan had become a focus of monstrous perversion in recent years. Age-old lore concerning this sacred ground held that the previous age of the earth, the Fourth Sun, was brought to a close by a cataclysmic flood, after which primeval darkness fell. The gods chose Teotihuacan as their gathering place to decide who was to sacrifice himself so as to become the new Fifth Sun and bring light again to the world: 'Even though it was night, even though it was not day, even though there was no light, they gathered, the gods convened, there at Teotihuacan.'

Two of them, the legends said, competed for the honour to throw themselves into the sacred fire from which the Fifth Sun would be kindled – the handsome and worldy Tecciztecatl, arrogant and greedy for glory, and humble, self-effacing Nanahuatzin, ailing and covered with pustules. At the last moment Tecciztecatl baulked before the fierce heat of the flames. Nanahuatzin, however, closed his eyes, rushed forward and leapt into the fire where he began 'to crackle and burn like one roasting'. As a result of his self-immolation, the Fifth Sun finally arose, ushering in the present epoch – 'it took sight from the eyes, it shone and threw out rays splendidly, and its rays spilt everywhere'.

In this tale, which was not their own but had been passed on to them by the peoples they had encountered and conquered when they migrated into the valley two centuries before, the Mexica found cause to carry out mass human sacrifices by burning at Teotihuacan on two occasions each year, once at the winter solstice, *Atemoztli*, when the sun rose furthest to the south of east, and again at the summer solstice, *Tecuilhuitl*, rapidly approaching, when the sun rose furthest to the north of east. These holocausts, at which Moctezuma danced publicly and distributed gifts to the onlookers, were supposedly conducted to nourish the Fifth Sun with the suffering of the victims as they crackled and roasted on the sacred flames, thus preventing the untimely end of the age.

But once all the pious nonsense was set aside, what it was really all about, Tozi knew, was the sick pleasure and delight the Mexica took in finding ever more inventive and spectacular ways to degrade, humiliate, and terrorise others. And in the process of their wicked rituals, the true significance of 'the place where men became gods' was all but forgotten. She recalled the ancient and time-honoured words her mother had taught her about the meaning of Teotihuacan:

> Thus they said, 'When we die, truly we die not, because we will
> live, we will rise, we will continue living, we will awaken . . .'
> Thus the dead one was directed, when he died: 'Awaken, already
> the sky is rosy . . .' Thus the old ones said that he who has died
> has become a god; they said: 'He has been made a god there.'

And here lay the truth – the sacred ground of Teotihuacan was for renewal and rebirth, not for hopeless destruction and death of the kind the Mexica liked to celebrate. Transformation of the soul was intended here, not brutal murder of the body. After the party of pilgrims had left and evening was falling fast, remembering Huicton's suggestion that she should seek guidance from Quetzalcoatl, Tozi walked back alone to the ruined pyramid he was said to have built and settled down cross-legged beneath his effigy of the plumed serpent.

She had failed him by submitting to terror when Acopol had set his eyes on her in Moctezuma's palace, and proved he could see her even when she was invisible to others. Her ability to fade was her power, and Acopol had brushed it aside as though it were nothing, stealing her confidence, stealing her courage. Perhaps this was why Huicton had sent her away – not so much to find the lost land of Aztlán and seek a vision from the masters of wisdom in the Seven Caves of Chicomoztoc, as to find her courage again.

She gazed up into the stern features and the snarling teeth and jaws of the plumed serpent, the once and future king who had returned, after so long an absence, to claim the lands and the heritage that were rightfully his. Where was he now, she wondered, the warrior Huicton called Cortés, Quetzalcoatl taken human form, and his army of demigods? Something in her bones told her they were already marching inland from the coast, these 'Spaniards' who had come to work the doom of Moctezuma, and that great events lay close at hand.

'I will find my courage,' she said aloud. 'I will be ready to fight by your side.'

'In that case,' replied a voice, 'bide here nine days longer. I have work for you to do when Moctezuma comes to celebrate the festival of *Tecuilhuitl*.'

Tozi leapt up, looking in every direction, but there was not a sound, not a footstep. Night was falling, all the other visitors had gone, and she was alone amidst the ancient ruins.

'You have work for me to do?'

'Yes, little one.' The voice was deep and resonant and it reverberated in the settling darkness. It seemed to emerge, Tozi now thought, from between the bared teeth of the sculpted head of the plumed serpent. It could only be the god Quetzalcoatl himself, speaking to her from his effigy of stone!

'I long to serve you, lord,' Tozi said. 'Only tell me what I must do.'

'Listen, then, bold one, brave one, here are my commands for you . . .'

On Saturday 12 June, friendly relations and possible military cooperation with the fat cacique having been set on a proper footing, Cortés led his men out of Cempoala and down to Huitztlan at the coast – a march of less than six hours – to find that the fleet carrying Escalante and the other half of the army was already anchored in the bay and that the ground had been broken for the foundations of Villa Rica de la Veracruz. Totonac dignitaries had been sent ahead to prepare lodgings for the Spaniards to use in Huitztlan while the new town was being built, others under the direction of Meco accompanied Cortés to smooth the way, and in addition Tlacoch provided four hundred porters – called *tamanes*, Pepillo learned – to transport all the baggage the conquistadors had previously been obliged to carry themselves.

Arriving on the late afternoon of 12 June, Cortés convened a meeting that same evening in Huitztlan's main square with Yaretzi, the town's chief, and the Council of Elders; Meco and Malinal, supported to some extent by Aguilar, served as interpreters. The meeting was also attended by the fat cacique in his capacity as paramount chief. He'd had himself carried down from Cempoala on a litter and treated Yaretzi and the elders as his subordinates, often speaking over them, his voice booming out across the square.

Once again the atmosphere was friendly, with most of the towns-people crowding round to look on, and the talk soon turned to Moctezuma and what was to be done about him. Tlacoch's complaints at the heavy toll of sacrificial victims demanded by the Mexica were echoed by the other dignitaries present, who added that this ghastly tribute was extracted every year from every one of the thirty principal towns and villages where the Totonacs lived. The new levy of virgins to be killed for Hummingbird's birthday was particularly resented, and in addition Moctezuma's tax gatherers were hated as bullies who felt free to rape and even permanently abduct any man's wife or daughter if she was beautiful, leaving husbands and fathers humiliated and bereft.

By a strange coincidence, at the exact moment these depredations were being discussed, a tangible ripple of fear went through the crowd in the square, a commotion broke out and people fled in all directions. Two Indians rushed to Tlacoch and Yaretzi and whispered in their ears. Both men at once lost colour and began to tremble and sweat in a manner that would have been comical if they hadn't been so obviously terrified. An almost hysterical conversation broke out amongst the elders, many of whom were now on their feet. Meco spoke urgently to Malinal and Malinal turned to Cortés: 'A delegation of Mexica tax collectors just arrived,' she explained.

Cortés seemed delighted at the news. 'Good! Now we'll see how serious these Totonacs really are about their rebellion.'

Moments later, five haughty, cocksure men entered the square where Cortés and his captains still sat with the fat cacique and Yaretzi. The new arrivals, preceded by a host of servants with fly whisks to keep mosquitoes and other night insects away, had the appearance and bearing of overlords used to subservience. Their black hair seemed to shine, they wore richly embroidered cloaks and loincloths, and each held a crooked staff in one hand and roses in the other, which they raised disdainfully to their nostrils as though not wishing to smell the local air. They passed the Spaniards rudely, refusing even to acknowledge their presence, and made their way to a stately house. They were immediately followed by Yaretzi and, once he had been hoisted into his litter, by Tlacoch.

A little later the two caciques returned, crestfallen, and told Cortés through Meco and Malinal that the *calpixque*, 'stewards of tribute', as the tax collectors were known, were offended and outraged at the entertainment and hospitality the Totonacs had dared to extend to the Spaniards without prior permission from Moctezuma. In addition to the cruel tribute of a hundred virgin girls they had come to collect, part-payment of the quota of a thousand the Totonacs were required to provide, they were therefore now demanding an extra levy of twenty young men to be handed over to them within the hour and prepared for sacrifice to Hummingbird that very night.

Pepillo remembered why he had once loved and admired Cortés when the caudillo realised the caciques fully intended to obey the order. In the strongest possible terms he required them not only to refuse it but to arrest the tax collectors instead and confine them in a room next to his quarters, where his own Spanish soldiers would keep them under guard.

Yaretzi and Tlacoch were horrified by the idea and fell into a panic. Manhandle Moctezuma's officials? They didn't dare! But Cortés quietly and firmly insisted. He reminded them that his lord, King Carlos, had sent him to this land to chastise evil-doers and prevent sacrifice and robbery, and that now was the time, under his protection, to throw off the Mexica yoke forever. Finally he persuaded them. The order was given and the *calpixque* were arrested and secured, humiliatingly, with long poles and collars. One who resisted was soundly beaten into submission with clubs. Cortés then told the fat cacique to send messengers at once to all other Totonac towns and villages that were subject to him informing their chiefs what had been done here and ordering them to treat any tax collectors sent to them in the same way, with a full guarantee that the Spanish would protect them.

Meanwhile the townsfolk had gathered again in the square and there was much talk of these astonishing events; the view emerged, as Malinal explained with some amusement to Pepillo, that the Spaniards must indeed be *tueles* – either gods or demons – because no ordinary humans would have dared defy Mexica power so blatantly. As for Yaretzi and Tlacoch, they quickly recovered their courage, and were now pressing for the *calpixque* to be sacrificed forthwith – thus ensuring that none of them escaped to carry the tale back to Tenochtitlan. Cortés naturally refused: they must not be sacrificed, no one must be sacrificed, but there was nothing to fear since he had taken charge of the prisoners.

It being after midnight, everyone retired to bed, but Cortés was far from done and had his men bring two of the five Mexica prisoners quietly to his quarters. When they stood before him, he put on a manner of complete innocence and asked them through Malinal on whose orders they had been taken prisoner. They replied, rightly enough, that Tlacoch and Yaretzi had imprisoned them and that the Spaniards must have encouraged them to do this foolish thing, which would bring the wrath of Moctezuma down on their heads. Cortés, for his part, insisted he knew nothing of the matter, professed to be very sorry about the way they'd been treated and added that he'd arranged to free them, without the knowledge of his Totonac hosts, because he'd heard many good things about Moctezuma and was troubled to think of the officers of so great a monarch being treated in such a shabby way. Announcing he would provide them with a means to escape Huitztlan, he told them to return at once to Moctezuma, explain that he had released them to save them from harm at the hands of the treacherous Totonacs, and inform him the Spaniards were his good friends and were at his service. Furthermore he would do all in his power to ensure their three companions were not harmed and would endeavour to have them released as well. He then had six of his men take the grateful tax collectors down to the bay under cover of darkness, put them in a longboat and row them a few miles up the coast to a place where they were safe from the Totonacs and could make their way back to Tenochtitlan.

The next morning, 13 June, there was consternation in the town when the escape was discovered. Even though they had been under Spanish guard, Cortés and Malinal somehow managed to convince the caciques that the Totonacs were to blame for the loss of the prisoners. Cortés pretended to be angry, ordered a chain to be brought with which he bound the three remaining tax collectors, and had them transported to the *Santa Maria* for 'safekeeping'. Once on board, however, he released them, treated them in a friendly and hospitable way and told them he would soon return them to Moctezuma – a promise he fulfilled that night when they, too, with the Totonacs none the wiser, were ferried up the coast and set free.

All in all, Pepillo had to admit, it was a masterstroke. Having effectively risen in rebellion against Moctezuma by imprisoning his tax collectors, two of whom had then immediately escaped to tell all, the vacillating Totonac chiefs were now too deeply committed to change course or ever hope to be forgiven. They therefore had no choice but to throw their lot in completely with Cortés, accept his protection and make a determined effort to win their freedom from Mexica overlordship. At the same time, by freeing the tax collectors, Cortés could hope he had sent quite a different signal to Moctezuma, a signal of friendship and complicity that would, at the very least, confuse him!

Tozi was a practised beggar so it was not at all difficult for her to sustain herself during the nine days she waited at Teotihuacan for the midsummer ceremonies to begin. Crowds of pilgrims visited the site and as she sat on the Way of the Dead, sheltering from the sun under the retaining wall on its east side in the morning and on its west side in the afternoon, her little striped maguey-fibre mat spread out beneath her, dirty rags on her back and a sorrowful look on her face, there were many who gave her gifts that she could later barter for food and shelter. Not wishing to strike up any friendship or attract attention, she stayed in different homes in the nearby villages every night: now an outhouse, now a stoop, now a corner of the floor in a crowded one-roomed adobe hut, now a lean-to, now a roof terrace shared with a poor family making the trip of a lifetime. At no point did she invoke her powers of invisibility because it was unnecessary to do so. As she'd learnt long ago, it was often possible to be invisible without using magic at all – just common sense. Don't stand out, don't offend anyone, don't get yourself noticed; these were the important rules to follow. As the days went by and the numbers of visitors to Teotihuacan grew rapidly, with many camping out in vast transitory settlements near the ruins, it grew easier and easier for her to blend in – literally to vanish amidst the crowds.

On the eighth day, a thousand crack troops from Moctezuma's personal regiment marched in and bivouacked in front of the pyramid of the Moon, setting up guard posts at intervals all along the Way of the Dead. They were there to prepare for the Great Speaker's arrival on the morrow and to guarantee his security. Meanwhile, a team of skilled craftsmen set to work erecting a splendid royal pavilion on the plaza by the pyramid of the Sun, while between the pavilion and the pyramid itself the blackened fire-pits, sealed for the last year by stout planks, were opened and packed with logs and kindling in preparation for the holocaust.

Next to appear were the sacrificial victims, two hundred of the finest male prisoners from the fattening pens of Tenochtitlan. They were escorted by a further thousand troops, who kept them under strict guard while the decoration of their bodies with paints and feathers began. Because the victims were all warriors taken in battle, some Texcocan, some Tlascalan, there was no wailing and crying amongst them; rather they remained steadfast throughout the whole degrading procedure.

Finally, after nightfall, troupes of clowns, tumblers and dancers took up their places under torchlight. They began to perform at once for the benefit of the huge throngs of pilgrims and sightseers who had already gathered to ensure the best vantage points from which to witness the sacrifices the following midday. Tambourines, drums, conches and trumpets threw up a harsh, jangling cacophony, mingled with thousands of excited voices, which from time to time broke into a roar of approbation at some incredible acrobatic feat. Food sellers with baskets of their wares slung around their necks offered snacks of fried and honeyed grasshoppers, maguey worms, ants, grubs, popcorn, beans, squash cakes, algae cakes, and more specialised and expensive delicacies of human flesh. As well as the ever-popular pulque, a wide range of alcoholic drinks were on sale, made from fermented maize, honey, pineapple, cactus fruit and a variety of other plants.

Tozi was there in the midst of the press, silently witnessing it all, slipping through the crowds unnoticed. She had her orders from the god himself, she'd made her plans, and when Moctezuma came the next morning, she knew exactly what to do.

Chapter Twenty-Eight

Moctezuma was nervous, tormented by dark imaginings and filled with apprehension. Ever since he'd brought that marvellous sorcerer Acopol to his palace, he had felt strong, free and confident. The sense of being constantly watched had ceased, the nameless fears that had formerly haunted him had evaporated, his vigour had returned and his *tepulli* had begun to stand up again, enabling him to service his wives and concubines. Even more important, his bowels had stopped betraying him with strange rumblings, gurglings, cramps, flatulence and sudden, wrenching urgencies that he could not control.

And all this was so, even though Acopol was long gone on his mission to Cholula and was therefore not physically present to provide protection. Hummingbird had spoken of 'warding spells of great power' that the sorcerer had placed around the palace, and within the sanctuary of the god's own temple, and there could be no doubt, now, that these spells worked!

But what would happen when Moctezuma travelled beyond the warded zones that Hummingbird had named? Would Acopol's magic still keep him safe then? It was this question that had once again sent his stomach into uproar, requiring frequent comfort stops as he journeyed north on the night before the summer solstice to ancient Teotihuacan, where he was to officiate at the ceremonies of *Tecuilhuitl*. He bitterly resented the inconvenience and the danger of the journey, since *Tecuilhuitl* was not even – by any stretch of the imagination – his favourite festival. Quite honestly it was amongst his least favourite! He was expected to mingle with vast, stinking crowds of paupers and peasants from all over the empire, even to the extent of allowing himself to be touched by them – something that was forbidden on pain of death at any other time. He was expected to hand out gifts. Worst of all, he was expected to dance for them like some circus performer. Were not the weight of tradition so solidly behind it, he would have abandoned *Tecuilhuitl* years before. But Moctezuma prided himself on being a great student and respecter of tradition, and it was for this reason, despite his fears, that he had resolved to favour the festival with the royal presence as he had done each year since his coronation.

Held aloft in his palanquin by bearers who knew how important it was that he be carried smoothly without any jolts, missed steps or rocking motion, Moctezuma brooded also on the other dark cloud looming on his horizon as he approached sacred Teotihuacan on this morning of *Tecuilhuitl*. That dark cloud, admittedly still distant yet growing closer, was the prospect of the *tueles* and their manoeuvres along the coast. Spies followed their every movement, reports reached him daily, and he found himself mightily confused by their recent behaviour.

First, there was the matter of Guatemoc's attack on them. Now, though not dead as he deserved, the troublesome prince was confined to Cuitláhuac's estate at Chapultepec, where he would be unable to cause any further chaos or disruption. Perhaps it would have been better, Moctezuma reflected, if he had skinned Guatemoc alive as he'd originally intended. On the other hand it was a good policy – particularly with one's own brother's son – to show a little mercy.

Besides, the damage had been minimal in the end. Moctezuma's orders for his nephew's arrest had reached Pichatzin in time, and the governor of Cuetlaxtlan had carried them out swiftly and released the captured *tuele*. Better still, this gesture by Moctezuma seemed to be paying off. Eight days ago the leader of the *tueles* had responded with a gesture of his own by releasing a group of *calpixque* tax collectors who had been seized in Cempoala and were about to be executed by the rebellious Totonacs. Whether the *tueles'* leader was in fact Quetzalcoatl, or perhaps an avatar of Quetzalcoatl in human form, or just a man called Cortés as he cunningly claimed, remained unclear, as did his precise intentions. Yet the fact that he had freed the *calpixque*, and returned them to Tenochtitlan with messages of friend-ship, was undoubtedly a most auspicious sign.

Less auspicious, indeed downright worrying – and this was the source of Moctezuma's confusion – were other aspects of the *tueles'* behaviour. They had been in a position to intervene over the *calpixque* because they had abandoned their camp on the dunes near Cuetlaxtlan and marched inland to Cempoala, and there, the spies reported, they had negotiated an alliance with that fat slug Tlacoch, paramount chief of the Totonacs – an alliance against Moctezuma himself! Moreover, they had then moved on to Huitztlan on the coast where, with the help of the Totonacs, they had begun to build a permanent town of their own.

All this was unprecedented and alarming and called for immediate action. Yesterday, therefore, before leaving for Teotihuacan, Moctezuma had despatched an embassy to the *tueles* led by two of his younger cousins, Zuma and Izel by name, mere youths who were in awe of him and thus completely reliable. Their orders were to proceed to Huitztlan by forced march with a caravan of rich gifts for the *tueles*, ostensibly to thank them for their intervention in the matter of the tax collectors. They were to inform the leader of the *tueles* that his request for a meeting on the coast with Moctezuma could still not be granted since the Great Speaker was in ill health, and anyway too busy to leave Tenochtitlan; however, they were to add that the other request, namely that the *tueles* might come up to Tenochtitlan themselves and meet the Great Speaker there, was now viewed favourably, and that they would be provided with a *laissez passer* and even guides to facili-tate their journey.

The invitation, of course, was a trap. Should the *tueles* accept it, the guides would bring them by way of Cholula and there, as Hummingbird had promised, and as Acopol was already working his sorcery to ensure, they would be destroyed.

With all that already set in motion, there was really nothing more to be done until Zuma and Izel returned with their report – nothing more to be done, that is, except burn two hundred victims for *Tecuilhuitl* and attempt, so far as possible, to enjoy the festival.

So thinking, Moctezuma tugged softly at the curtain of his

palanquin, opening a gap of no more than a finger-width, and peeped out. As he had thought from the growing din, his bearers had already brought him into the sacred precincts of Teotihuacan and were now advancing north along the Way of the Dead. The pyramid of the Sun towered ahead to his right, with the solar disk itself climbing the sky behind it. Midday, when he could begin to light the sacrificial fires, was little more than two hours away, but first – onerous duty – he was required to hand out gifts to the poor and dance – dance! – for them.

The ornate palanquin halted outside the pavilion set up to shade the royal party from the sun and Moctezuma was helped down. Teudile and Cuitláhuac had come out to greet him. After they had made their expressions of deference he took their arms and walked within.

Tozi chose this moment to fade into invisibility. None of the people around her saw her disappear because all eyes were fixed on the ground in fear at the presence of the Great Speaker. Besides, no one had noticed her anyway – she was too small, too ordinary, too insignificant to stand out in such an immense crowd.

The masses were kept a hundred paces back from the pavilion by an unbroken cordon of guards which Tozi, now as elusive and intangible as air, effortlessly slipped through. Momentary anxiety gripped her. Would the magical defence that Acopol had placed around Moctezuma, which had hurt her so badly and nearly exposed her the last time she tried to enter the palace, be in place here? She drifted into the recesses of the pavilion itself, coming closer and still closer to the Great Speaker, who reclined on a throne drinking red pitaya juice chilled with ice from the high sierras.

No sorcerous attack came. No stabs of pain. No aura of supernatural danger.

Tozi was so close now she could have seized the goblet from Moctezuma's slim brown fingers and dashed it to the ground, but she had other, graver plans for him and chose to bide her time.

As each moment passed, she became more convinced that he was unprotected and at her mercy. Her confidence grew.

*   *   *

His confidence grew. He was relieved that no magical attack had been attempted on his person. Acopol's warding spells were clearly so powerful that they protected him even here. Moctezuma yawned, licked his lips and handed the empty goblet to a retainer. The time was approaching when, as age-old tradition demanded, he must mingle with the public. Normally it was forbidden for any mere mortal to have contact with him, who was so close to the gods, but today, *Tecuilhuitl*, that taboo was lifted for the single hour before noon. Teudile stood ready with the basket of cacao beans and silver trinkets that the Great Speaker would distribute as gifts; after that was done, he must perform the ritualised slow-stepping dance of the star-demons in a special costume of green quetzal and red parrot feathers before the sacrifices could begin.

Dismissing the little shadow of apprehension that lingered at the back of his mind, despite his attempts to reassure himself, Moctezuma stepped out into the sunlight and walked with dignified steps, Cuitláhuac at his right, Teudile at his left clutching the basket, across the boundary of cleared space that separated him from the masses. A hundred soldiers specially selected for their intimidating size had already surged forward into the crowd, opening a lane through which Moctezuma could pass and yes – ghastly thought! – the paupers would be permitted to reach between the guards to touch the Great Speaker's garments, his hands, and even his gold-slippered feet. He shivered in disgust and progressed into the armed gauntlet. As he did so, complete silence fell. This was partly a matter of custom – silence had always been required at this moment – but it was partly, also, because the people pressing in all around were utterly, unspeakably terrified.

As well they might be, Moctezuma thought. *As well they might be*. After all, a veritable god walked amongst them, who could order the death of any or all of them with a single, simple word, who could require them to cut their own throats right here, right now, who could command that their children's brains be dashed out, or wrest their wives or their husbands from them at his whim, without any recourse on their part.

Uggh . . . His flesh crept at the stinking smell that invaded his nostrils as thickets of filthy hands stretched out towards him, past the guards, grubby fingers clutching his robes, caressing his hands and arms. Others snaked out at ground level in order to reach his feet. And all these unwashed limbs and digits that so urgently sought for him belonged to people – his people! – who fervently believed that this fleeting connection would cure their ills, bring them wealth, make them fertile and fulfil whatever other hopes and dreams sustained them in their short, ugly, meaningless lives.

Moctezuma was now twenty, now thirty, paces into the throng. The guards were having some difficulty keeping the crowd back. Better get on with it! He reached into the basket that Teudile carried, scooped up beans and silver jewels and began to pass them out, now to the left, now to the right, revolted at the massed hands that took them from him like so many hungry, grasping mouths.

That was when, suddenly, in the space the soldiers had opened directly in front of him, and so close that it seemed to emanate from a place no more than a pace away, a woman's voice spoke up through the silence, very high and very clear in the ringing tones of a proclamation. '*Behold, Moctezuma,*' the voice trumpeted, '*the last days of your world are upon you and very soon you will be dead, crushed under the foot of the god Quetzalcoatl, but not before you have been punished for your crimes . . .*'

There came a massed gasp of shock and horror and whispers began to spread, passing the astounding words that had been spoken from person to person back into the furthest reaches of the crowd where they had not been heard. For his part Moctezuma stopped in his tracks, his jaw hanging open, stunned, surprised beyond measure by this unexpected and unprecedented voice which now continued: '*Repent, Great Speaker, for the vengeance of the god will be great and mighty upon you; give up your evil ways, make recompense to your people and to all those of other nations who have suffered at your hands.*'

Again there was that susurrating whisper of rumour as the words were repeated and passed on, rippling through the crowd at incredible speed while the guards cast about wildly, their *macuahuitls* drawn, pushing people aside, searching for someone – anyone – to arrest. Several women were grabbed, a man shouted hoarsely and was struck down by a savage blow, and hundreds more soldiers from the security battalion came rushing out, shouting, stamping their feet, striking their *macuahuitls* against their shields in an attempt to quell the swelling riot. Meanwhile, Moctezuma, Cuitláhuac and Teudile had been encircled by a dozen Cuahchics who hacked indiscriminately at the rabble around them. A head rolled, an arm flew through the air spouting blood and, amid the chaos, that voice again, that terrible haunting voice somehow rose above the sea of sound, incredibly close yet with no obvious source: '*Oh foolish and cowardly Moctezuma, you are undone; your wickedness has caught you out and the reckoning has come to you sooner than you imagined. Abandon today's sacrifices! Forswear them or you will pay the price.*'

'Never!' Moctezuma yelled. It was the charge of cowardice that got to him, and he could not restrain himself from responding even as the bodyguards rushed him, Cuitláhuac and Teudile into a tight group, pushing them through the screaming masses and back behind the cordon of troops protecting the pavilion. At the last moment Moctezuma turned and shook his fist impotently at the throng, only to feel a sudden inexplicable stab of pain. He looked down and saw that a gaping wound from which the royal blood gushed forth like a river had opened between his great and his first toe, slicing up from there towards the arch of his foot. 'Witchcraft!' he yelled – for at the moment he was struck, no one had been standing close enough to him to inflict this wound – 'Witchcraft!' He staggered and, as Cuitláhuac rushed to support him, he fell in a dead faint.

Well, thought Tozi, *that was a good start*. She was grimly pleased with herself, especially because she had managed to stab the Great Speaker – not fatally; she did not want to kill him; she had long ago been persuaded by Huicton's arguments about the merits of keeping him alive and using his own folly and weakness of character to undermine Mexica power, rather than getting him out of the way and making room for a stronger man to take the throne. To inflict that rather nasty injury on the royal foot, she had of course been obliged to allow her right arm and her hand holding the flint knife to materialise for an instant from the field of invisibility with which she had surrounded herself, a risky manoeuvre because of the possibility of detection; but she had done it so fast she'd got away with it. Now, with cries of 'witchcraft' going up all round, Cuitláhuac and Teudile leaping here and there like headless toads, armed guards storming back and forth, Moctezuma flat on his back, unconscious and bleeding from an inexplicable stab wound, and the huge crowd on the verge of a full-scale riot, she had every reason to hope that matters might spiral completely out of control.

In the event, however, and within the hour, Mexica discipline and the judicious use of terror contained the crisis. Not a single member of the crowd was allowed to leave. After recovering from his faint, Moctezuma was patched up – weeping like a baby – by the royal physician. And Teudile announced that the *Tecuilhuitl* sacrifices would go ahead.

Tozi had eavesdropped the conversation between Moctezuma and Cuitlahuauc that had preceded the announcement. Predictably the craven Speaker had wanted to return at once to Tenochtitlan and to his palace – the only place now, he was convinced, that he could be safe from magical attack.

'No, sire,' Cuitláhuac had said with surprising firmness. 'You cannot even contemplate such a course of action. Whatever mysterious force has afflicted us today you must not be seen to give way to it; to do so, I believe, and before so many witnesses, would prove fatal for your rule.'

'But I cannot,' Moctezuma had sobbed. 'I simply cannot, dear brother. See – ' he pointed at his foot – 'I am injured. It was a witch who did this to me, the witch Acopol warned me about. If I stay here she will attack again. In my palace, Acopol's warding spells protect me.'

'Nevertheless, my lord, you must strengthen your will. The honour of the throne is at stake. Look . . .' Cuitláhuac signalled through the door of the pavilion at the vast, sullen crowd, still waiting, hemmed in by soldiers. 'Consider what your people must think – must say! – if you leave Teotihuacan now without performing the sacrifices. You will never be able to command them again.'

Finally, after much more of this, Moctezuma was reluctantly persuaded. 'I'm sure the witch has gone, brother,' Teudile said. 'She would not dare strike twice in the same place.'

We'll see about that, thought Tozi.

'There must be no hint of witchcraft being worked against you, great lord,' Teudile added, 'and that word is already being bandied about. While the surgeon stitched and bound your foot, I therefore took the liberty of having a man and a woman seized from the crowd. The man I accused of stabbing you and I found witnesses to swear to it. The woman I accused of throwing her voice and I found witnesses to swear she was indeed the one responsible for those utterances. I suggest a summary trial before the public, a guilty verdict pronounced by yourself and then their immediate execution.'

'You have done well, Teudile,' Moctezuma said. 'We will flay them both alive before we begin with the sacrifices.'

'*We'll see about that too*,' thought Tozi.

It was an hour past noon, the first time in the annals of the Mexica that the sacrificial flames of *Tecuilhuitl* had been kindled late, when Moctezuma, seated on his throne, was carried by sweating slaves to the twin fire-pits between the pavilion and the pyramid of the Sun and cast a burning brand into each of them. Designed to hold a hundred human bodies packed close, each pit was filled with dry logs, which were at once set alight with much cracking, a burst of heat and a great pall of smoke, and soon two giant conflagrations were under way. The two hundred victims sat under guard in twin enclosures nearby. They would not be thrown into the pits until the flames and smoke had died down and a mass of red-hot embers had formed that would roast them slowly, stripping their flesh and melting the fat beneath their skin until they themselves became fuel for their own immolation.

Moctezuma was deeply uneasy and his wounded foot was causing him a great deal of discomfort – indeed, he thought, the worst pain he had ever suffered in his life. His every instinct was to flee Teotihuacan at once, but he accepted that he would lose face if he failed to see the ceremonies through. Only another hour needed to pass, two at the most, for his departure to seem normal enough. So he must simply grit his teeth and endure.

And meanwhile there was another piece of theatre to perform.

He had been carried back a hundred paces from the fire-pits, and now with Teudile and Cuitláhuac positioned in front of him, and representatives of the noblest families of Tenochtitlan all around him, he raised a finger to signal that the accused should be brought into his presence.

The man, in his middle years, was thickset and bald, the woman was young and heavily pregnant and both were gratifyingly terrified.

'I did nothing, great lord!' the man protested as the guards dragged him forward.

'In the name of the gods,' shrieked the woman, 'I caused Your Majesty no harm.'

'Mercy!' sobbed the man.

'Mercy!' wailed the woman. 'I am with child.'

Moctezuma gave them his stony face. There would be no mercy here. At his signal, both were forced to their knees as Teudile read the charges. The man, Ohtli, was an assassin; he had been seen to strike the Great Speaker with a knife, injuring the royal foot. Witnesses were called and gave mumbled confirmation that this was so. The woman, Tlaco, was a witch. She had thrown her voice and uttered treasonous statements; again witnesses confirmed the truth of the charge. With eyes lowered, trembling, choked with fear, the defendants continued to protest their innocence until, at a word from Teudile, they were beaten into silence. All that remained now was for Moctezuma to pronounce the verdict. Leaning on Cuitláhuac, whom he used as a crutch to avoid putting weight on his injured foot, he stood with all the solemnity he could muster and then . . .

And then . . .

A sudden bolt of terror struck him. Fear that was at once hotter than the fiercest fire and colder than ice drilled into his brain like an augur, causing him first to gasp and then to scream uncontrollably in insufferable pain. He raised his hands to his head, clasped his temples, lost his grip on Cuitláhuac, stumbled and fell forward before anyone could catch him. He barely noticed the renewed agony in his foot, for it was as nothing compared with this ripping, grinding horror within his skull, as though his brains were being diced and pulped and pumped out of his ears and nose. For some moments he remained fully conscious,

277

seeing everything, aware that he was writhing, biting his tongue until blood poured from it, tearing with his fingers at the skin of his own face, vomiting bile as Cuitláhuac and Teudile stooped over him and lifted him bodily upright again. Worse still, even as they did so, he knew that all of this was unfolding before the silent, awestruck witness of a vast multitude of his people. He saw their startled, staring faces, their wide eyes. So shaming! So humiliating! But worst of all – unendurable, unbearable – was the terror that afflicted him. Oh, gods, the terror, the dread, the unstoppable galloping panic that seized him by the throat, by the guts, by the bowels, and that now caused him to void himself in a hot wet, explosive, rumbling evacuation that soaked his robes and ran down his legs and splattered onto the ground for all to see. His consciousness began to dim. He heard shouts, hoarse cries, the thud of many footsteps as guards closed around him – too late! – cutting him off from public view. Then blackness, darker than the darkest night, closed over him, and for a very great while he knew no more.

Tozi watched the wreck of Moctezuma that her magic had set in motion with deep satisfaction. Since Hummingbird had reached out to her on the summit of the great pyramid of Tenochtitlan on the night she was to be sacrificed; since he had, for unknown reasons, multiplied her powers, she had known she could send fear to those she chose to punish. But it was not until now, until this very moment, as the Great Speaker slumped before her on the arms of Teudile and Cuitláhuac, that she fully understood how powerful a weapon the war god had placed in her hands.

Regardless of its origins, it was a weapon she intended to use to bring only good to the suffering people of the One World. Sadly there was nothing she could do for the two hundred young men bound and awaiting sacrifice; even if the festivities today were cancelled, as now seemed inevitable, they would be held for use in some later event. But Tozi was determined, at least, to save bald Ohtli and pregnant Tlaco, falsely accused of acts that she herself had committed, from a most painful and terrible death. They still knelt on the ground where they had been forced down awaiting sentence, but there were no guards

around them now and no one was paying them the least bit of attention. Moreover, the soldiers who had been posted at the outer edges
of the crowd to keep order after the earlier riot had been called in
over the past moments to defend the Great Speaker, and so there was
no longer any force to prevent people slipping away. This they were
already doing in their hundreds, rapidly growing into thousands, none
wanting to stay to face the consequences – quite possibly mass execution – of the extraordinary scenes it had been their misfortune to
witness this day.

But there was no time to lose – the situation could change again
at any moment – so Tozi moved rapidly, still invisible, to stand between
Ohtli and Tlaco. 'You must run,' she whispered. 'Run now! Mingle
with the others who are leaving; lose yourselves amongst them and
be gone if you want to live!'

Infuriatingly, neither of them moved. They were still so frightened,
so dazed after their beating, that this voice from nowhere merely
seemed to disorient and panic them further.

Realising she had no other option, Tozi took a deliberate, calculated
risk and re-emerged into visibility between them. Ohtli gasped. Tlaco
groaned and clutched her swollen belly. 'Who are you?' she asked.

'Never mind who I am,' said Tozi. 'Get up, both of you! Get up!
Get out of here!' Since they still stayed where they were, quaking
fearfully, she took their hands and pulled them to their feet. 'You
have to come with me,' she said. Then very firmly but quite slowly,
not wanting to attract the attention of Teudile or Cuitláhuac by
running, she walked with them into the dispersing crowd, walked
and walked, gripping their hands tightly until they were far from the
pavilion, lost amongst hundreds of others fleeing south along the Way
of the Dead.

Only when she judged them to be out of danger did she release
their hands. 'Get as far away from here as you can,' she told them,
'as quickly as you can.' A thought struck her: 'When they arrested
you, how much did you tell them? Do they know where your homes
are?'

'Not me,' said Ohtli. 'There wasn't time. They just took my name.'
'Me too,' said Tlaco.

Tozi grinned: 'Good! Then you can go to your homes. You'll be safe and they'll never find you. I doubt if they'll even look. They'll have too much else to think about for a while.'

'But who *are* you?' Tlaco asked again. Her face sharpened: 'Are you the witch everyone's talking about?'

'I'm nobody,' said Tozi. 'You never saw me and this never happened.'

Then she turned her back on them, faded and was gone.

For some time Huicton had only been able to track Tozi's invisible progress from the spectacular chaos she had caused, but when she made herself visible to lead the man and the woman to safety he followed her, using all his tricks of fieldcraft, only to see her vanish again.

He wasn't behind her but parallel, roughly twenty paces west of her on the broad thoroughfare of the Way of the Dead, and well hidden amidst a hurrying knot of people. He didn't think there was any danger she would spot him since she'd turned back north, against the flow of the crowd, just before she disappeared. Still, it was an eerie feeling to know she might still be nearby somewhere, seeing everyone – perhaps even him! – while remaining completely unseen herself.

What power the child had. What amazing potential!

Huicton only hoped he'd done enough by hiding in the secret chamber behind the effigy of the plumed serpent in the ruined pyramid of Quetzalcoatl nine days before, when he'd spoken to her as the god himself, giving her the commands that she'd carried out today.

But the question remained – would this strategy, and its stunning outcome, free her from the crippling anxiety and self-doubt that her encounter with that fiend Acopol had caused and thus bring her back to herself? Huicton rather thought it would, for Tozi had acted with incredible courage and shown amazing initiative. She had not only utterly wrecked the midsummer ceremonies with their vile sacrifices, but had also forced Moctezuma into a deeply embarrassing public display. The result could only be a serious weakening of Mexica power and prestige throughout the empire.

What would she do next, his little protégée? Huicton rather imagined she would continue the quest he had sent her on, because that was her nature. He would have liked to be able to tell her she didn't need to because she'd already recovered her power. But to do that he'd first have to find her – probably impossible – and then reveal his subterfuge to her.

Something told him she would not take it well if he told her he'd posed as her beloved Quetzalcoatl.

All in all, he decided, it was better to leave things as they were. Tozi could look after herself and she would return to Tenochtitlan in her own good time.

Chapter Twenty-Nine

Friday 25 June 1519 to Friday 9 July 1519

On 25 June, a Friday, four days after midsummer, a Mexica delegation presented itself to Cortés at the new site of Villa Rica de la Veracruz, where construction work, with the willing help of the Totonacs, was already well advanced. The delegates – two youths whom Malinal identified as relatives of the Great Speaker, and four elders – were all highly placed nobles; they arrived with a large retinue of servants bearing rich gifts of gold and cloth. These they gave to the caudillo with thanks from Moctezuma for his actions in freeing the tax collectors. They further stated that Cortés's kindness in that matter had persuaded the Speaker to overlook the great offence he had caused in taking shelter with such wicked people as the Totonacs. The meeting that Cortés had requested remained difficult, since Moctezuma was in ill health, and anyway too busy with wars and other matters to leave Tenochtitlan. On the question of Cortés going up to the Mexica capital, however, there was a marked change of tone. Despite earlier refusals, it seemed this would now be countenanced – and Moctezuma was even offering to provide guides.

'Don't trust him,' Malinal warned in her increasingly workable Castilian. 'This trap! If Great Speaker invite you in his city it means he hope kill you easy there.'

'I wasn't born yesterday,' Cortés answered, all the time smiling at the delegates and showing them a friendly and welcoming face. 'I'd sooner trust the devil than trust these Mexica. We'll pay Moctezuma a visit when we're good and ready, but I plan to win us some more allies first.'

He therefore answered the invitation with diplomatic prevarication.

He was grateful and honoured, and he would send word across the sea to his monarch King Carlos, who would undoubtedly be pleased, but there were matters he needed to attend to here before he could travel – he gestured to the buildings and fortifications of Villa Rica rising up around them. He would come as soon as all this was complete.

The delegates professed themselves satisfied and set off on the journey back to Tenochtitlan with a present of blue and green glass beads for Moctezuma. No sooner had they gone, however, than the fat cacique appeared, bringing Yaretzi in tow. The chiefs reminded Cortés of his instructions that all Totonac towns and villages should rebel against Moctezuma and expel or arrest his tax collectors. These instructions had been followed to the letter throughout the region. Now, however, four thousand Mexica troops, one of many such demi-regiments that had been sent out across the empire to gather victims for sacrifice (and thus most likely acting independently from the delegation that had just left) had taken it upon themselves to punish the Totonacs for their rebellion. The fat cacique called upon Cortés to fulfil his promise of protection.

Pepillo remained in Villa Rica with the small garrison left to defend the new town, while Cortés led almost his full force, around four hundred men, to deal with the threat. However, the Mexica demi-regiment, which had mustered at a hill called Tizpacingo, immediately and cravenly fled the field the moment they saw the Spanish cavalry and guns. The result was that Cortés received another massive boost to his prestige, and at very little cost apart from a few days' inconvenience. Passing through Cempoala on 29 June on his way back to the coast, he seized the moment and required the fat cacique to destroy the idols in the temple that sat on the summit of the pyramid in the city's main square.

Pepillo had the story later from Bernal Díaz, who had been there. It seemed that Tlacoch at first refused and sent warriors to defend the pyramid. Cortés responded by seizing Tlacoch himself and holding him at sword-point, threatening to kill him if he did not order his men out of the way. There was a tense standoff, but the fat cacique eventually lost his nerve and Díaz was among the fifty conquistadors who climbed the pyramid and one by one threw down all the idols.

'Some of them,' he said, 'were in the form of fearsome dragons as big as calves, and others half man and half puma and hideously ugly, but all were smashed to pieces in the fall.' There was much howling and wailing, for the Totonacs believed the smashing of the idols meant the end of the world; when the world did not end, however, they were soon mollified, and accepted Cortés's next demands, which were that their priests should all have their long, filthy hair shorn, that the temple should be whitewashed inside and out, and that a cross and an image of the Virgin should be set up in its inner sanctum where the idols had formerly stood.

The next morning, when all this was done, Father Olmedo, the Mercedarian friar who had served as the expedition's spiritual leader since the disappearance of Father Gaspar Muñoz at Cozumel months before, said mass; following this, the most important caciques of the region, summoned thither by Tlacoch, submitted to baptism. Eight young maidens, all daughters of the chiefs, were also baptised and afterwards presented to the Spaniards to consolidate the alliance. Cortés divided them amongst his captains, giving the most beautiful of them to Puertocarrero, who after that date relinquished all claim to Malinal.

As far as Pepillo was concerned, this was a much more important development than the conversion of the Totonacs. He'd been aware for a long while how unhappy his friend was to be living with Puertocarrero, but when she returned with the army to Villa Rica, walking at Cortés's stirrup, her lovely face glowed with joy. She was baptised that same day, 2 July, and moved her residence permanently to Cortés's headquarters.

This was obviously a sensible arrangement, Pepillo thought, since they worked so closely together anyway.

Two days had passed since Malinal had allowed herself to be 'baptised' into the peculiar Christian religion so admired by her lover and master Cortés. Despite all the sermons she'd been obliged to listen to, she really knew nothing about this faith, and cared less. But if it pleased the caudillo for her to call herself a Christian and pray to the tortured god-man on the cross, and if it made it easier for her to be acknowledged as his woman in bed and out of it, then she was happy to oblige.

They were in bed at the moment, this night of 4 July 1519 in the Christian calendar, and Cortés, mercifully, slept quietly by her side – mercifully because on the preceding two nights he had been troubled by dreams in which he spoke aloud the name of Saint Peter and tossed and turned like a man possessed. They had made love, with passion, with joy, as they always did – he knew some tricks, her caudillo! – and then he had fallen into a deep slumber, leaving her to think in the darkness, lying on her back, her legs slightly apart, feeling his warmth and his hard muscled body next to her.

Was it a miracle – these Christians often spoke of miracles – that Cortés had succeeded in prising her away from Puertocarrero without any apparent ill feeling or consequences? For a long while their liaison had seemed dangerous, a thing to be kept secret, but then Puertocarrero had found them out. Malinal had expected a beating, perhaps worse, but he had returned from a long talk with the caudillo seemingly indifferent to what she had done; thereafter, although they had continued to share a bed until the expedition to rout the Mexica from the hill of Tizpacingo, Puertocarrero had ceased absolutely to seek sex with her. Malinal had no way of knowing what private agreement must have been reached between the two men, or what strange power it was that Cortés held that made Puertocarrero now so obliging, obsequious even, and sometimes evidently fearful, but she was grateful that because of it she could in the future be openly acknowledged – not only as the caudillo's interpreter but also as his mistress. He was already married, of course, but he detested his wife, the 'hell-bitch' Catalina, and it was true, was it not, that a mistress was sometimes higher than a queen?

Malinal thought about this as sleep began to overcome her, and found she rather liked the idea. She had been born a princess, after all. Why should she not become a queen? Who knows, she and her caudillo might even have children together – a boy, she hoped! A prince for their royal family. This notion in turn brought suddenly to mind the image of Coyotl, the little boy who had shared the fattening pen with her and Tozi, and from whom they had been separated the night they had been led out to be sacrificed. It made her sad, filled her heart with guilt, that they had never seen the innocent child again, and that he had gone to his death alone with no one to comfort him. She remembered how the High Priest Ahuizotl, whose head Tozi had later smashed with a rock – another memory – had snatched Coyotl away and how she'd been impotent to keep her promise to care for the sweet little boy and protect him. And she remembered the astonishing events that had led Moctezuma to release her and Tozi, and the ghastly scene afterwards as they had searched for Coyotl amongst both the living and the dead, but had failed to find even his poor, mutilated body.

She shuddered and her thoughts drifted to Pepillo, another innocent child also caught up in the events of this strange and terrible time. Malinal knew she had failed him too. She'd tried hard to persuade the caudillo to let the boy keep his dog and had even extracted a promise from him that he could, but Cortés had reneged on that commitment just a few days later and the dog had been cast in with the pack, exactly as Pepillo had feared. Unlike the death of Coyotl, Malinal consoled herself, this was at least no great tragedy. Pepillo seemed to have come to terms with the loss of his pet, although she'd often seen him watching Melchior amongst the other hounds, as Vendabal put them through their paces, training them for war.

Pepillo, too, had begun to train for war. Almost every day, Malinal went to watch him sparring with the good Captain Escalante, and showing increasing mastery of the sword. In this way, taught to accept loss stoically, taught to bear arms, and growing noticeably taller and heavier as the weeks went by, it seemed to her that the boy was rapidly becoming a man.

And that was surely no bad thing, for Malinal knew that Cortés would soon march on Moctezuma and when he did they would all be tested. There would be no time for finer feelings then, no time for soft hearts and weak limbs, no time for love.

Failure was as likely an outcome of this venture as victory, and if the Spaniards failed, then only death would await them.

On that thought, with a shuddering sigh, Malinal fell asleep.

Since 12 June, the construction of Villa Rica de la Veracruz had proceeded at a tremendous pace. Many of the wooden buildings were already complete, and the town was protected by a high stockade, with guard posts at intervals all around, and a single massive gateway. As Pepillo walked out through the open gates shortly after dawn on Monday 5 July, making for the stretch of headland beyond a stand of trees where he was to meet Escalante for their morning's practice, he happened upon his old tormentor, Andrés Santisteban, flanked as usual by Miguel Hemes and Francisco Julian, holding a dozen dogs on leashes. Amongst them was Melchior. Although at times in the past weeks he'd shown no recognition, he now bounded out of the pack, his tail wagging furiously, barking with joy, tearing his chain from Julian's pudgy hand, streaking in front of Hemes and leaping up at Pepillo. Huge shaggy paws were placed on Pepillo's shoulders as the dog licked his face enthusiastically. The show of affection enraged Santisteban, who strode forward, plucked a whip from his belt, unfurled it with a sharp crack and lashed out once, twice, thrice in quick succession.

With the first strike the tip of the rawhide tore a gash in Pepillo's cheek, while the second and third lashes opened bleeding welts along Melchior's back, causing him to drop back to the ground with a snarl. There was no fourth strike because Pepillo, in an explosion of fury, ran straight at Santisteban and punched him hard in the eye, sending him reeling.

Pepillo was a changed boy since May, the last time Vendabal's assistants had picked on him. It wasn't just that he was eating more and growing taller and heavier as he approached his fifteenth birthday. Regular sword practice with Escalante had improved his balance, speeded up his reflexes, and somewhat habituated him to combat, and he had begun to exercise obsessively, for as many hours as he could snatch for himself, building muscles in his legs, belly, arms and shoulders that simply hadn't been there before. The construction of Villa Rica had given him numerous opportunities to volunteer for hard manual labour when he wasn't tied up with secretarial work for Cortés, and, last but not least, again on Escalante's advice, he ran five or six miles every evening, which had increased his wind and stamina.

All this work, all this effort, all this training, all the momentum of his charge and all his pent-up anger at the frequent persecutions he'd endured, Pepillo therefore put into his attack on Santisteban, which took the older boy completely by surprise. Nor did he stop with the first blow. Something Escalante had impressed on Pepillo repeatedly was the need to follow up any advantage won in combat immediately and without mercy, so he didn't hesitate to step in on Santisteban as he staggered back, punching him in the belly and treading hard on his ankle, tripping him and making him fall. He might have won the fight with a few well-placed kicks ('There's no such thing as a dirty trick in battle,' Escalante had drummed into him; 'anything goes') but Hemes and Julian came to their friend's rescue, grabbing Pepillo's arms and slowing him long enough for Santisteban to stumble to his feet, shaking his head like an enraged bull. 'You're for it now, you little shit,' he yelled, as he lurched forward and headbutted Pepillo, who was still struggling to free himself from the grip of the two other boys.

'My, my, what's this?' came Escalante's deep voice as Santisteban drew back his massive fist for a killer punch. 'Three against one. That hardly seems right.'

Suddenly Pepillo was released. Santisteban stood before him, panting and shaking with rage, a huge bruise swelling beneath his right eye, hatred twisting his pockmarked face. Hemes and Julian had jumped back, as though they'd come too close to a hot fire. Melchior was circling at Pepillo's feet, snarling. The other pack dogs, their leashes dropped, had scattered back into the town. The sentries in the guard posts on either side of the gate were peering down with amusement, and appeared to be placing bets.

'What am I to make of this?' Escalante wondered. He was carrying the two swords he and Pepillo would use in practice. 'Item: one dog, formerly a pet, bleeding from the back, seemingly whipped. Item: one Caudillo's secretary, bleeding about the face.' He stepped closer and examined the wound on Pepillo's cheek. 'Also seemingly whipped . . . Item: one senior apprentice dog handler who will soon have a shining black eye, knocked down, beaten in a fair fight as I saw it, but given succour by Messrs Hemes and Julian, which he used to unchivalrous advantage to head-butt aforesaid caudillo's secretary.'

Escalante paused, rubbed his chin. 'Well, lads,' he said finally, glaring at the three dog handlers, 'what do you have to say for yourselves?'

'It was him as started it,' sniffed Hemes, pointing a finger at Pepillo.

'Tried to take his dog off us,' said Santisteban. 'I had to stop him. I'm responsible for the dogs, see . . .'

'Well I must say you're not doing a very good job,' observed Escalante, 'since a moment ago there were twelve dogs here and now there is only one. The others will be causing havoc in the town, I'd venture.'

As he spoke, as though in confirmation, there came the sound of distant barks and growls, a yelp, angry shouts. Hemes, Julian and Santisteban looked at one another nervously.

'This isn't over,' Santisteban said. He signalled to the others and backed away towards the gates, dragging Melchior by his leash. 'We'll catch up with you when you don't have no noble captain to protect you,' he told Pepillo. There was murder in his eyes. Then, remembering himself, he cast an oily glance at Escalante. 'Begging your pardon, sir, of course. No offence meant to Your Excellency, but this is a score to be settled amongst us lads.'

'I don't get offended by scum like you,' said Escalante. 'But I do know a bit about settling scores, and I'll tolerate no ambushes or gangs, nor harm worked on that dog either. The only right way for this to be done is for you and Pepillo to square up to each other, man to man, at an agreed time and place . . . Do you have the spleen for that, Santisteban?'

'Course I do,' said the dog handler. 'Name the time, name the place, I'll be there.'

'Dawn, a week from today, out on the headland – ' Escalante pointed – 'past the trees there. Are you agreed, Pepillo?'

'Yes, Don Juan, I am.'

'And you, Santisteban. Agreed?'

'Agreed.'

'Oh, one other thing,' said Escalante. It seemed to be an afterthought. 'I propose that this battle be fought with staves. So much more elegant, so much more like the real thing than fisticuffs. Any objection to that, Santisteban?'

The dog handler frowned, looked at his companions, looked back at Escalante.

'Well?' said the captain. 'I'm waiting.'

'Staves it is,' Santisteban finally agreed, but Pepillo could see he didn't like the idea.

'And you, Pepillo? No objection to staves, I take it?'

'None.'

Escalante looked pleased with himself. 'So,' he said, 'that's settled. Staves at dawn, on the headland, a week from today.'

The dog handlers turned and hurried off into the town, where more growls and barks could be heard.

'Are you feeling all right?' Escalante asked Pepillo. 'That whip cut is superficial; bleeding's already stopped. But how about the blow you took to your head? Has it left you groggy?'

'I'm fine, Don Juan.'

'Excellent. In that case let us proceed to the headland and continue with your training. You were lucky and fast today, but Santisteban is much bigger and stronger than you and there's a lot of work to be done if you're to be ready for him. Your great advantage, which we must build on, is that the principles of sword and stave work are much the same. You're already well on your way to mastering those principles and, unless I'm very much mistaken, Santisteban is not.'

Today's lesson focused on what Escalante called 'the binding of swords', when contact between the two blades was maintained for some interval during a fight. After repeated attacks and defences, Pepillo began to understand that he could 'feel' the intention of his opponent through the pressure of his blade and react accordingly. Thus, if his opponent pushed strongly against him, then he must become weak and wind his blade away, seizing the opportunity to break out of the bind and strike. On the other hand, if the push was weak, then the objective was to apply strength to manipulate his opponent's blade with his own into a position where it would be possible to deliver a thrust or a slice.

'And once you break out of the bind,' Escalante added, 'don't be afraid to grapple. The closer you are to your enemy, the more difficult it is for him to cut you. So close with him, throw him and run him through. Here, let me show you,' he said – and suddenly Pepillo found himself tipped onto his back with the point of Escalante's sword against his throat. 'Now, your turn,' the captain grinned. 'Get up. Bind . . . That's right. Step in . . . Grapple! Now try to throw me . . . You know, you're getting better and better at this.'

They repeated the exercise six more times until Pepillo's arms ached. 'Use elbows, knees, the pommel of your sword, whatever comes to hand in the grapple,' Escalante said. 'Anything that gives you the advantage. Never hesitate, keep on pressing your opponent every way you can—'

Abruptly he broke off the bout and turned his gaze out to sea. There, coming into the bay under full sail, and no more expected than if Aphrodite herself had chosen that moment to emerge from the foam, was a beautiful Spanish caravel.

Cortés was knee-deep in the surf, with his arms outstretched in greeting, as the longboat from the caravel *Gran Princesa de los Cielos* ran its prow up onto the sand and his old friend Francisco de Saucedo leapt out.

'Francisco!' Cortés exclaimed, wrapping the small, wiry, fork-bearded captain in a warm *abrazo*. 'Ye gods! It's good to see you! How did you find us?'

'Hernán! So good to see you too! We knew you'd be along this shore somewhere, so we just coasted, coasted, and suddenly here you are!'

Saucedo, in his early forties with short-cropped hair showing more iron grey than it had when Cortés had last seen him in February, glanced up at the headland where the rooftops and stockade of Villa Rica were visible. 'It seems you're setting down permanent roots here.'

'Indeed so! We are a colony now. You gaze upon the mighty towers and spires of the noble town of Villa Rica de la Veracruz.'

'A fine name and a fine plan, but I have news for you, Hernán – most urgent and important news. Shall we get our feet out of the water and go somewhere dry?'

As they climbed the steep path to the headland, joined now by other captains and friends, Saucedo said jokingly: 'You might have waited for me!'

Everyone knew what he meant. The *Gran Princesa de los Cielos* had been undergoing a refit in the Santiago dockyard when Cortés had sailed precipitously with the rest of the fleet on 18 February after discovering that Diego de Velázquez, the governor of Cuba, planned to relieve him of command. There had been no time to inform Saucedo and, besides, his caravel hadn't been seaworthy. But after the repairs were complete, he explained, he'd quietly recruited sixty soldiers, 'hard-bitten types, ready for adventure', purchased four heavy cavalry horses, 'two of them mares, both good breeding stock', and slipped out of Santiago a few days ago without the governor's knowledge. 'That shit Velázquez,' Saucedo said with feeling as he and Cortés walked in the midst of a rapidly growing throng of well-wishers through the gates of Villa Rica. 'He wants your blood, you know.'

'I don't give a damn what the old fart wants,' Cortés replied. 'As the captain-general and justicia mayor of Villa Rica de la Veracruz, I answer only to my fellow colonists now. It's all legal and above board.'

'I wouldn't be so sure of that,' said Saucedo, lowering his voice as they reached the splendid new pavilion in the heart of the town. 'Indeed, the urgent news I bring you concerns your legal position . . .' He looked around at the crowd that followed them and lowered his voice still further. 'Perhaps we should discuss this in private?'

Some instinct for his own advantage made Cortés take Saucedo's arm and steer him away from the pavilion towards the public meeting hall that stood nearby. 'What I may hear, all may hear,' he said in booming tones. He sought his secretary and saw him in the crowd. 'Pepillo, summon the rest of the community. Everyone who's not on guard duty. We have word from Cuba.'

While the colonists assembled, some finding places on the benches that served as pews (the meeting hall doubled as a church on Sundays), others standing around in small groups speculating as to what was about to be announced, Cortés took Pedro Alvarado aside and whispered in his ear: 'If this comes to a showdown with the Velazquistas over the future of the colony, as I suspect it will, don't state a view.'

Alvarado looked puzzled. 'I'm not sure I understand you, Hernán.'

'I'm assuming Escudero and his gang are still courting you?'

Alvarado yawned, showing his perfect white teeth. 'Every day.'

'And you're still leading them on?'

'As best I can, but they're getting rather tired of foreplay. If I don't

292

surrender my virginity to them soon, they're going to throw me out of bed.'

'Say nothing at this meeting to hasten that process! Rather let them think you're ready to consummate the liaison.'

With that, Cortés clapped Alvarado on the shoulder and rejoined Saucedo. 'Shall we begin?' he said.

'If you wish, Hernán, but I still would have preferred to meet with you privately first.'

'Too late for that now, my friend.' Cortés cleared his throat. 'Gentlemen,' he addressed the packed meeting hall, 'I give you Francisco Saucedo, who needs no introduction here. He is fresh from Cuba and he tells me he has urgent news for us.'

Saucedo had always been a man of few words, and now, in characteristic style, he got straight to the point. After the expedition had sailed from Cuba against the governor's wishes on 18 February, Velázquez had acted swiftly to secure his own interests, sending a fast ship to Spain just two days later. The ship carried an embassy to the court of King Carlos, with a petition that Velázquez be granted an exclusive licence to colonise the New Lands, the profits to go to him and his heirs. Rodriguez de Fonseca, the powerful and influential Bishop of Badajoz, a relative of the governor and his closest crony in Spain, had ensured that the petition was delivered directly to the king, and the king had acceded without demur to all that was asked of him. Astonishingly and exceptionally, he had even agreed that if gold was found, only a tenth of its value (rather than the usual fifth) was to be paid to the Crown; the rest would be for Velázquez to keep. The same fast ship then brought the signed, sealed and fully executed licence back to Cuba and delivered it to the triumphant governor.

Cortés had expected that some such manoeuvre would occur. Despite his bravado, he knew that his legal cover as captain-general and justicia mayor of Villa Rica de la Veracruz was most unlikely to be sufficient to protect him from so vengeful an enemy as Velázquez. Indeed, this was precisely why, in parallel with his manoeuvres to establish Villa Rica as an independent authority, he had also developed the plan – as yet discussed only with Alvarado and with Puertocarrero who was to be his messenger – of sending King Carlos all the treasure so far won by the expedition as a bribe for his royal support. What he had not anticipated, however, was that Velázquez would move so fast to pull the rug out from under his feet and would himself petition the king for powers that would allow him to claim control of any colony that Cortés might establish! This was chess-playing at a more advanced level than he had believed the governor capable of, and meant he now had no choice but to bring his own plans forward.

Might as well make a virtue of necessity, Cortés thought. But he would choose his moment, because others were already on their feet venting their fury and, over the next half-hour, a consensus emerged amongst the colonists. The new licence that Velázquez had somehow hoodwinked the king into issuing posed a direct, indeed an existential, threat to their interests, since he would certainly use it to argue that Villa Rica de la Veracruz should be placed under his authority, with all its profits going straight into his pockets.

'All our hard work these past months will have been wasted,' one of the settlers opined.

'The risks we've run, the dangers we've faced, all for nothing,' protested another.

'We can't allow this, Hernán,' said Juan de Escalante gravely. 'We all have too much at stake here at Villa Rica – something must be done.'

Seeing the way the wind was blowing, Montejo and Puertocarrero now rose to add their voices. They were both bought and paid for, with the latter additionally compromised by the cowardice for which Cortés had never allowed him to be called to account, and as he'd expected they divined his wishes correctly.

'Caudillo,' Puertocarrero said, 'we who have appointed you as our leader call upon you to find a solution.'

'Velázquez must be stopped,' squeaked Montejo, with a nervous look at his former Velazquista cronies, who were gathered in a glowering knot around Jean Escudero and the governor's cousin, Velázquez de Léon. 'Action! I demand action!'

'No action is needed,' sneered Escudero. 'We all serve the king, Governor Velázquez is his appointed representative in these parts, and he now has the royal warrant to administer this and all other colonies.

All that's wanted to put things to rights is to send a ship to Cuba at once – I will captain her myself – and formally place Villa Rica under the governor's authority.'

'Here, here,' echoed Velázquez de Léon.

'I'm with you,' added that treacherous swine, Diego de Ordaz, who'd taken Cortés's gold, agreed to stay out of trouble after his participation in the last rebellion, and was now clearly up to his tricks again.

Likewise Alonso de Grado, Cortés's one-time 'friend', who'd first revealed his links to the Velazquistas a few weeks before, once again hoisted his true colours by sidling over to stand beside Escudero and professing: 'Since the king has ruled in favour of Diego de Velázquez, as Don Francisco Saucedo now informs us, then who are we to go against him? No one here wishes to commit treason. I'm sorry, Hernán, but I vote we place ourselves under the governor's command as soon as possible.'

A few other supporters of Velázquez also crawled out of the wood-work now, while more, Cortés suspected, were biding their time before they declared openly for one side or the other, but the mass of the colonists remained outraged, indeed horrified, at any suggestion of giving up their hard-won toehold in the New Lands. It seemed the meeting must soon come to blows.

Judging the moment, Cortés called for silence. 'Gentlemen,' he said, 'gentlemen. Bring yourselves to order. You are not savages. As justicia mayor, my first responsibility is to preserve and safeguard the future of Villa Rica de la Veracruz, and look to the best hope for success and prosperity – dare I say even wealth? – for all of us here gathered. The crux of the matter, as Don Francisco has made very clear, is His Majesty the King who, it appears to me, has been misled and misadvised by that venal self-serving cur Diego de Velázquez . . .'

Roars of anger erupted from Escudero and his followers at this, but Cortés waved them down. 'Gentlemen, silence please! You have had your say, now allow me to have mine – for unless my memory plays tricks with me, I am still your elected chief . . .'

Roars of 'Yes, Don Hernán, speak up, we're with you', and suchlike encouragements, burst forth from the mass of the colonists, and a scuffle broke out between Velázquez de Léon and a huge, dour soldier named Guillen de Laso, who accused the governor's cousin of sodomy. Suppressing a smile, Cortés again called for silence and continued. 'As I was saying, that vile pederast and bestialist Diego de Velázquez has plainly misadvised the king in order to win a wholly spurious and undeserved exclusive licence to colonise these New Lands. I believe it is our responsibility – nay, our duty! – to aquaint His Majesty with the facts, and I am confident, once we have done so, that the licence given to the governor of Cuba will be revoked and our right to rule our own affairs and serve the king in these New Lands will be confirmed.'

More cheers and yells from his supporters, more boos and catcalls from the Velazquistas, *and now*, thought Cortés, *comes the difficult bit*.

'Gentlemen,' he said, 'I have a plan. Are you willing to hear it?'

From the massed drumming of feet, entirely drowning out the protests of the Velazquistas, it was clear that the majority of the colonists were indeed willing to hear Cortés. He waited again for silence and then, in measured tones, outlined the idea he had already shared weeks before with Alvarado and Puertocarrero. What was needed, he said, needed above all else, and needed all the more urgently now since hearing the news that Saucedo had brought, was that the settlers of Villa Rica, under Cortés's leadership, should find a way to win direct royal sanction for their venture. 'If we can only do that,' he said, 'then the threat posed by Velázquez will be lifted forever.'

But how best to achieve this goal? Cortés looked around the crowded meeting room before answering his own question. Since gold was the fastest route to a man's heart, since Don Carlos, too, was a man, and since his court, like every great court in Europe, was always in need of funds, the wise solution, surely, was to sweeten him with gold? Indeed, Cortés suggested, summoning every ounce of his eloquence and persuasive powers, the settlers of Villa Rica must send to the king all the gold, all the treasure, in short everything of any value they had won by barter and wrested as 'gifts' from the Maya, the Totonacs and the Mexica since their arrival in the New Lands in February. This would include even the two spectacular wheels, one of pure gold, one of pure silver, they had received from Moctezuma – presents so rich and so valuable they were bound to win the king over to the settlers' cause.

The initial reaction from even the most loyal and enthusiastic of his supporters was one of stunned silence, while the Velazquistas bellowed and howled with outrage. But once again, when the hubbub had died down, Cortés began to work the crowd, and after another hour had passed it was clear that many were seeing things his way. He used the same arguments here in public that he had used to persuade Alvarado in private in the middle of May, namely that a relatively small sacrifice now – the treasure they'd gathered in just four months at the periphery of the Mexica empire – would secure for them the vast and immeasurable treasure that surely awaited at the heart of that empire in the fabled city of Tenochtitlan. By all means what they had won already was enough to make them all modestly wealthy, but if they would only keep their nerve and follow his advice, he promised – nay, he swore on the holy cross and on the name of Saint Peter his patron – that he would make them all as rich as kings. Indeed, within a year, two at the most, every one of them from the greatest lord to the lowliest soldier could look forward to becoming veritable kings in their own right, for these New Lands were vast and their potential limitless. It would be folly, utter folly, for which their children and grandchildren would never forgive them, if they were to forgo the greatest opportunity of their lives in favour of a man like Velázquez for want of a little courage and expenditure now.

'You want us to give the king *all* our treasure?' stormed Escudero in disbelief. '*All* of it? And you call that a "little expenditure"? Damn your eyes, Cortés, you're a bigger fool than I took you for.'

'Well, let's see who's the fool and who is not,' Cortés replied. 'Heated opinions have been expressed openly and it's plain there are at least two very different views as to what we should do. I propose we take a few days to deliberate on these weighty matters as a community before we come to a final decision. Each side may freely make their case and try to win support, and then we'll take a vote to settle things – shall we say here in this meeting room exactly one week from today at noon?'

It was an eminently reasonable suggestion, and even the staunchest Velazquistas could find no good argument to oppose it.

'A week from today then,' said Cortés as he brought the meeting to a close. He looked directly at Escudero: 'And may the best man win.'

'It's a damned insult,' said Escudero.

'I couldn't agree more,' said Alvarado.

Having been ferried out from the shore by longboat around noon, the two captains were alone on opposite sides of a table in the state-room of Alvarado's carrack *San Sebastian*. It was Friday 9 July and, after four days of tireless lobbying, it had become clear to all that Cortés was going to win his vote by a huge majority – so huge, indeed, that he had taken the liberty of circulating the letter that Escudero was now waving. Already signed by more than three hundred and fifty colonists, with every likelihood that many more would follow, the letter repeated the proposal to give all the treasure to the king, but cleverly shifted the source of the idea away from Cortés and placed it squarely on the shoulders of the colonists themselves, thus ensuring, Alvarado noticed with admiration for his friend's cunning, that none who signed it would later be able to claim they'd been coerced.

'Gentlemen,' the letter read, 'you already know we wish to send His Majesty a present of the gold we have obtained here. Because it is the first we are sending from these lands, it should be much more than the king's usual fifth. It seems to us that all we who serve him should give our shares. We gentlemen and soldiers have signed our names here as wishing to take nothing, but to give our shares voluntarily to His Majesty in the hope that he may bestow favours upon us. He who wishes to keep his share may do so. But let all those who renounce theirs do as we have done and sign here.'

'He's got us in a fork, the devil,' Escudero now continued. 'If we sign the letter it makes us disloyal to Don Diego de Velázquez. If we refuse to sign it, he makes us disloyal to the king . . .'

'Either way we can't win,' Alvarado prompted.

'Exactly. Which is why some of us have decided to take action,' said Escudero. 'Governor Velázquez is the rightful authority here, by the king's own command and licence, and it is the governor, not that madman Cortés, who must decide how the treasure we've won is to be divided . . . I tell you what, Pedro, Cortés is pulling the wool over everyone's eyes. His plan to send the treasure to the king is a trick. I have impeccable intelligence on this . . .'

Ah, gods! thought Alvarado. *Intelligence of any kind from this stuffed codpiece? I somehow doubt it.* But he did his best to summon an expression of keen interest.

'First,' Escudero continued, 'have you observed the urgency with which the *Santa Luisa* is being refitted?'

The *Santa Luisa* was Puertocarrero's carrack, and Alvarado had not only observed but also knew exactly why she was being refitted. Like virtually every vessel in the fleet, his own *San Sebastian* not excluded, the *Santa Luisa* had taken a beating and suffered badly from rot and storm damage over the past few months. She'd sprung a hundred leaks, her hold was rarely less than thigh deep in stinking bilge water (the pumps were always working, even now in the sheltered harbour beneath Villa Rica), and her bottom was fouled with weed and barnacles. There was no possibility of putting her in dry dock, which would have been the ideal solution, but her leaks would nevertheless have to be made sound by the carpenters, and as much of her keel cleaned as possible before she could attempt the journey across the Atlantic to Spain.

'I've noticed,' Alvarado answered. 'I assume it's because she's in more urgent need of repair than our other ships. My own *San Sebastian* could do with some work,' he added innocently, with an airy wave towards the closed stateroom door and the navigation deck beyond it.

'Bah!' exclaimed Escudero. 'There is only one reason for this haste. Cortés has chosen his lapdog Puertocarrero to carry away the treasure and – I assure you of this, my friend – it will not be carried to the king, but to Cortés's own father Martin, who will hold it in safekeeping for him. Our great leader, who is in truth nothing more than a common thief, plans to divide everything we have won between himself and Puertocarrero.'

'The swine!' growled Alvarado. He summoned the required frown of outrage: 'What's Puertocarrero's share for his treachery?'

'Thirty per cent, I'm told, with a third of that going to his crew to buy their silence. After the treasure's delivered, the *Santa Maria* will be scuttled, the men will pull away to safety in the longboats and the story will be put about that our so-called "gift" to the king was lost at sea.'

'Damn!' Alvarado was in fact beginning to feel quite angry now. Escudero spoke with such conviction, and the story was in many ways so plausible that he almost found himself believing it. He wouldn't put such a scheme past Hernán, who was capable of anything. 'So what do you propose?' he asked Escudero. 'You said you'd decided to take action.'

'That I have, but before I tell you more, are you with us, or are you not?'

'I'm with you!' said Alvarado with conviction. 'I've had enough of Hernán and his tricks. He made me return the gold I'd taken from the savages in Cozumel and I had to swallow the insult. He promised us gold after Potonchan and we found none. Now we've finally extracted a king's ransom from the Mexica, I'll be damned if I let Cortés take it for himself.'

'Can I trust you?' Escudero said. 'Some in my group believe you're still a friend to Cortés . . .'

'Friends come and go,' Alvarado replied smoothly, remembering he'd said the same exact words to Diego de Velázquez himself in answer to exactly the same question in February, 'but gold is a constant companion. If you don't trust me, trust gold.'

'How much buys your loyalty?' asked Escudero, all business now.

'Why, thirty per cent, of course.'

'Thirty per cent of what?'

'I must guess you aim to wrest the treasure from Cortés. I'll want thirty per cent of the total if I'm to join you.'

'Thirty per cent of the total?' fumed Escudero. 'That's absurd!'

'If Cortés bought Puertocarrero with so much, I don't see why I should settle for less from you, Don Juan.'

'But Velázquez will have to have his share. And we of the rebellion are many. I can only offer you ten per cent.'

'Ten per cent won't answer, Juan. Twenty at the least, or I'll be speaking to Cortés next.'

After further haggling they settled on fifteen per cent, a bigger cut than the king's under the new licence granted to Velázquez.

Why was Escudero prepared to go so far? Alvarado wondered. To be sure the Velazquistas had told him too much over the past months, shared too many of their secrets with him, made themselves vulnerable to exposure by him. Now that they were about to take some definite action, therefore, he could understand why they wouldn't want to leave him on the loose. Murder must have been an option they'd considered, but he was Pedro de Alvarado, a notoriously hard man to kill, so perhaps they'd decided not to risk an assault that might easily backfire on them? Still, he felt, there was something missing from the picture, some other motive lurking in the sewers of the plot that must surely soon emerge.

'Very well then,' said Alvarado. 'I'm one of you now. Tell me what's to be done.'

'We sail tonight for Cuba,' said Escudero. 'With fair winds and current we can reach Santiago in five days. Three more days for Don Diego de Velázquez to mobilise his forces and take ship, then five days again to return, let us say six. In summary we can be back in two weeks. It will require at least that long for the refit of the *Santa Luisa* to be complete, so we'll be able to take command here and seize the treasure before it's sent to Spain. Your presence amongst us and your good name as a respected man and a former ally of Cortés will help persuade the loyalists of Villa Rica that their beloved caudillo was in error, and with luck we'll be able to settle everything without a fight . . .'

Alvarado had to laugh; even if the sailing and muster times for the governor's troops could be achieved, which was most unlikely in his view, the whole idea was still so patently ridiculous it would look downright suspicious if he just went along with it. 'Without a fight!' he exclaimed. 'You're joking, of course. We'll have the fight of our lives on our hands. Cortés isn't the man to take such a thing lying down, and he's loved by many. Be sure he'll whip up stiff resistance. You'll need a big force if you're to have any hope of defeating him.'

'We've thought of that,' said Escudero with a sly smile. 'It's why I agreed to your extortionate demand for fifteen per cent. Your participation is important, of course; it will send the right signals to the others. But we expect rather more from you than that, dear Pedro—'

'More? What do you have in mind?'

'We need you to kill Cortés before we sail tonight. You're the only one of us who can get close enough to him to do it. He still has allies, of course, they'll try to rally the men, but with their beloved caudillo gone they'll lose their stomach for defying Velázquez, and when we return from Cuba their surrender will be easily negotiated.'

Alvarado thought about it for a long while, saying nothing. Finally he spoke. 'For killing Cortés,' he said, 'fifteen per cent won't answer. I'll need fifty if you want this done.'

Eventually they settled on twenty-five.

When they were ferried back to shore around 4 p.m., Alvarado knew everything about Escudero's plans and exactly who his accomplices were – all the usual suspects, of course, and some surprising additional players. Had he in fact been willing to murder Cortés, there was even a possibility the plot might have succeeded, and perhaps for fifty per cent he would have considered it! But amongst Escudero's many faults was a severe lack of imagination, coupled with a deep-rooted meanness of spirit – hence his refusal to go up even a whisker beyond twenty-five per cent. In so doing he had signed his own death warrant.

As soon as night fell, the Velazquistas would begin loading the last of their stores of oil, water, cassava and fish on board the caravel *Potencia* which, with the collusion of its pilot and crew, they were going to steal. The crew Escudero had subverted for pitifully small sums, but the pilot, Diego Cermeno, had held out for a much larger amount, since his skills would be vital for getting the ship safely back to Cuba. Around 10 p.m., an hour before the *Potencia* was due to sail on the ebb tide, Alvarado was to stab Cortés to death in his pavilion – as though doing such a thing were a simple matter! – and then make his way down to the strand, where a longboat would be waiting to ferry him out to join the other conspirators.

So much for the plan. Instead, after parting company with Escudero, Alvarado went straight to Cortés and told him everything.

'Excellent, Pedro!' Cortés responded when he'd heard him out. 'Well done indeed. I knew I could count on you. Now we can take the whole nest of vipers in one fell swoop and rid ourselves of them for ever!'

'You may be surprised at how many they've managed to recruit,' Alvarado said. 'They're laying in stores for more than fifty.'

Cortés whistled. 'Fifty! That does surprise me. I thought I was loved by the men.'

He looked genuinely hurt, but then brightened. 'At least I'll know who my enemies are from now on,' he said, 'and take precautions against them.'

'You won't execute them all then?'

'Certainly not! We'll need every man we can muster if we're to defeat Moctezuma.'

Cortés led the arrest force personally. It was spearheaded by the squad of twenty-five trained killers under García Brabo, who'd done his dirty work for years, supported by another eighty of the best and most loyal soldiers to be found in Villa Rica. Amongst the captains and officers were Juan de Escalante, Alonso Davila, Gonzalo de Sandoval and Bernal Díaz.

The fact that the night was unusually dark and overcast made everything so much easier. The crew of the longboat waiting to pick up Alvarado after his supposed murder of Cortés were quickly overwhelmed; four other longboats drawn up on the shore were launched, and within minutes the *Potencia* had been boarded and the Velazquistas taken without a fight. Only Escudero put up any kind of resistance, but Alvarado had him at sword-point in a trice. 'You should have offered me fifty per cent,' he whispered in his ear as soldiers bound his hands and led him away.

A little later, after the rank and file conspirators had been sent back to shore under guard, Cortés and Alvarado made their way to the stateroom, where the ringleaders lay trussed and gagged on the floor. Cortés felt a mixture of emotions: triumph that the whole operation had gone off so smoothly and that he was now in a position to lance the Velazquista abcess once and for all, but sadness at the evidence now before his eyes of so much bad faith and treachery.

He walked from one man to the other, occasionally nudging them with the toe of his boot. Here was Velázquez de Léon and here Ordaz. Hardly surprising to have this latest confirmation of their eagerness to betray him; after all, they'd been Velazquistas from the start. Yet it hurt when he remembered their previous rebellion just a few weeks before and how he'd jailed them, then bribed them and finally freed them, in return for promises of loyalty. Ha! So much for loyalty.

Escudero was lying on his stomach. Cortés got the instep of his boot under the bastard and rolled him over onto his back, where he lay, glaring up furiously, mumbling and choking through his gag. He'd been jailed and bribed and freed and sworn loyalty too, but in his case Cortés had never expected the oath to be kept. 'Do you recall, Don Juan,' he now said, 'certain words we exchanged that night in February when the fleet sailed from Cuba?'

Escudero shook his head violently.

'Let me remind you.' Cortés rested his foot on Escudero's chest. 'If I recall correctly – and I believe I do – what you said to me was that given enough rope I'd be bound to hang myself . . . Does that ring a bell?'

Another violent shake of the head and more grunts from Escudero.

'Yet look at where we find ourselves now,' Cortés said. 'You have mutinied in time of war against the duly appointed captain-general, namely myself, of a lawfully constituted colony of Spain, namely Villa Rica de la Veracruz. Do you know, my dear chap, what the penalty for that offence is?'

Escudero was struggling mightily as the question was posed, shouting and barking through his gag, straining his wrists against the stout length of rope that bound him.

'The penalty,' continued Cortés, reaching to remove the gag, 'is death, and if my memory of the statutes does not betray me – and I don't think it does – the prescribed means is hanging.'

'You cannot hang me!' Escudero yelled, but there was real fear in his voice and his eyes were rolling in a most satisfactory manner. 'I do not accept your jurisdiction. I do not accept that Villa Rica is a legally constituted colony. I appeal to the authority of Governor Diego de Velázquez in this matter, for he is the king's representative in these New Lands and he alone has the royal warrant to plant colonies.'

'Ah yes,' said Cortés, 'but you see, most unfortunately for you, your patron the governor is in Cuba, sitting on his fat arse, while I am captain-general here, and I assure you that I do mean to hang you.' He stooped again, pulled up the gag, adjusted it tightly over Escudero's mouth and continued on his rounds.

Here was Alonso de Grado, who'd pretended friendship for so long but was always a traitor at heart. There was a spreading damp patch around his crotch. 'Tut tut, Alonso,' said Cortés, fixing his glance on the stain. 'You appear to have embarrassed yourself.' Next in line on the floor was Cristóbal de Olid: no dribbles of piss on him. Like Ordaz he was fearless in battle and a great swordsman – qualities that must surely save them both from the gallows, Cortés thought.

Onwards, and he came to Alonso Escobar and Bernardino de Coria. Like De Grado, they'd been his professed friends until very recently, but now their true allegiance was revealed. And who was this with one eye and lank black hair if not the verminous priest Pedro de Cuellar, who'd come to his pavilion back in May with Ordaz, Escudero and the other Velazquistas. At least he hadn't tried to hide his connection with them. But a priest, for Christ's sake! Taking part in a mutiny! What was the world coming to?

There were others here on the floor whom Cortés knew more or less well and was more or less surprised or disappointed to see. Perhaps most depressing of all was the pilot Diego Cermeno, a good man, highly skilled at his job, but drowning in debt, with an extravagant young wife to keep. Cortés had advanced him a thousand pesos after visiting him in his home in Santiago when he'd recruited him six months before. 'Why did you do it, Diego?' he now asked. He reached down and removed the gag. 'Could you not have stayed loyal to me? Did I not pay you well?'

'They promised me twenty thousand pesos, Caudillo,' Cermeno sobbed. 'Enough to clear all my debts and start again. Enough to change my life forever.'

'You would have made far more if you'd just been patient, Diego, but now there's nothing I can do for you . . .'

'What do you mean, Caudillo?' A look of terror crossed the pilot's face.

'Stealing a caravel is a capital offence, Diego. Didn't you know that?'

'I didn't know, Caudillo. I swear it. I didn't think. Oh God, my God, what have I done?'

'You've changed your life forever, Diego. I'm afraid you're going to hang.'

The trial of the conspirators took place in the meeting hall in the presence of all the colonists on the morning of Saturday 10 July, within a few hours of their arrest, and by the middle of the afternoon Cermeno and Escudero were dead. A little later, near sunset, Pepillo hurried past them, averting his eyes. It was horrible to behold them dangling from the ropes, their faces purple, their eyeballs and their tongues protruding, their privy members seemingly erect and their breeches fouled, for both had lost control of their bowels as they were hauled, kicking and choking, up the gallows post.

On his master's orders, Pepillo had drawn up the death warrants before the trial even began, and felt that Cortés was being less than honest about his feelings – at least where Escudero was concerned – when he gave a loud sigh, clearly audible at the back of the meeting hall, and said, 'Oh, how I wish I did not know how to write, so that I could not sign men to their deaths.'

'Bloody liar,' Escudero yelled; 'Mercy,' Cermeno wept, as Cortés signed the document with a slow, deliberate hand – some element of theatre here, Pepillo thought – before going on to pass judgement on the other conspirators.

Gonzalo de Umbria, the most senior of the defecting sailors, was to have all the toes of his left foot hacked off with an axe, while the rest of the caravel's ten-man crew would receive fifty lashes each, the sentences to be carried out immediately. With the other plotters, Cortés was surprisingly merciful. Pedro de Cuellar, the priest, was told he would have been hanged had he not been a clergyman. He gave his warrant to engage in no more political activity and was released. Escobar, De Grado and Bernardino de Coria were likewise released after humiliating themselves before the caudillo and begging

306

forgiveness. Diego de Ordaz had muttered as the trial began that he was sure Cortés would have him beheaded, but he too was freed, promising – not the first time he'd sworn such an oath! – to be the caudillo's loyal man from now on. Velázquez de Léon and Cristóbal de Olid received the same lenient treatment.

All in all, Pepillo reasoned, Cortés had handled the mutiny with great skill. He'd had no choice but to execute Cermeno; even in peace-time men were hanged for far lesser crimes than stealing a ship! A mortal example had also had to be made of the detestable Escudero, who'd anyway had this coming. Umbria might have expected to lose something more important than his toes. The sailors had got off lightly with fifty lashes. And the exceptional mercy shown to everyone else had established Cortés's reputation as a generous and forgiving leader who was nevertheless, as the corpses swinging from the gallows confirmed, capable of extreme, uncompromising firmness when necessary.

Carrying an urgent message from Cortés for Father Olmedo, the expedition's chaplain, Pepillo looked back at the hanged men, at the blood still darkening the sand from the whippings, and shuddered. It would be his own blood, soon, that would be spilled, since only three days remained until he must fight Santisteban. Since Monday Escalante had switched their practice sessions entirely to staves, but there was so much to learn! Deeply preoccupied with how little he still knew, he took a shortcut through an alleyway between two rows of newly built barracks as dusk settled over Villa Rica, and ran full tilt into Santisteban himself.

'Where you goin' in such a hurry?' the older boy smirked.

'I'm carrying a message from the Caudillo,' Pepillo said. 'Father Olmedo's waiting for it. Get out of my way.' He turned to run but found his exit from the alley blocked by Hemes and Julian.

'Not so fast, young'un,' said Santisteban, grabbing a handful of Pepillo's hair. 'We're going to teach you a lesson while you don't have captains and the like standing by to protect you.'

Pepillo flung a punch at Santisteban, but was held at arm's length and couldn't reach him. He did manage to land a blow on Julian, who was edging closer to wrap him in a bear hug, but then Hemes was on him as well and the three dog handlers piled in with fists and boots flailing.

They rushed the beating, no doubt afraid of being caught in the act. Pepillo's hard new muscles stood him in good stead and he was beginning to think he might escape with nothing more than a few bad bruises and some broken teeth, when Santisteban dropped to his knees beside him where he lay curled up on the floor of the alley, grabbed his right hand and bent back his index finger. 'Don't think I haven't noticed you practising swords and staves with your friend Escalante,' he said. 'No doubt you're hoping that'll give you the edge when it comes to our battle.' He bent Pepillo's finger back further; the pain was dreadful now. 'Not that it would, mind you,' Santisteban continued, 'but I thought I'd fuck you up anyway.' A sudden violent increase of the pressure, a twist outward and Pepillo's finger snapped like a twig, snatching a high-pitched animal screech from his throat.

Santisteban leaned closer: 'One word of this to anyone,' he hissed, 'and I'll poison your precious dog. Got that?'

Pepillo clenched his teeth, said nothing.

'*Got that?*' Santisteban repeated, applying another twist to the broken finger. Hemes and Julian giggled as Pepillo screamed again, tears of agony misting his eyes, and replied, 'Yes. I've got it. I won't talk.'

'Of course you won't,' said Santisteban, releasing him and standing over him. 'See you on Monday then. Staves at dawn, eh? I'm looking forward to it.'

Chapter Thirty

Saturday 10 July 1519 to Monday 12 July 1519

When Pepillo delivered the caudillo's message, Father Olmedo made a great fuss about his freshly battered and bruised appearance, the two teeth he'd lost from his lower jaw, his hand clutched against his chest with its limp, twisted finger, his pallor, and the fury in his eyes. 'What happened to you, lad?' the beefy friar asked. 'Did a house fall on you?'

'Something like that, Father,' Pepillo replied, forcing a smile.

'But seriously, you've been in a fight, haven't you?'

'No, Father, a fall. It was an accident. No one's fault but my own.'

Olmedo was plainly sceptical, but refrained from asking further questions. Instead he made him sit down and sip a beaker of harsh red wine, while he called in Doctor La Peña who checked Pepillo's mouth – 'both teeth came out clean; you're lucky' – and splinted and bound his finger.

The next morning, Sunday 11 July, the pain in Pepillo's hand was almost unbearable, and his leg had stiffened around a huge bruise on his thigh where Santisteban's knee had slammed repeatedly into him. Missing church, he limped out to the headland at dawn for his morning sparring session with Escalante, who exploded with rage when he saw him.

'Those dog handlers did this to you,' he said immediately. 'I'll have their guts.'

'No, Don Juan. No! It wasn't them. I had a fall.'

'Fall my arse. You've been punched and kicked – it's as plain as the nose on my face. And your hand! Bloody hell, let me take a look. How're you going to fight Santisteban with that?'

'I don't know, Don Juan, but I'll have to try. They'll call me coward if I withdraw.'

'Which is exactly why they did this to you!'

'They didn't, Don Juan! Please believe me. I fell.'

'What? Did they threaten your dog? That's it, isn't it?'

Escalante would not relent; eventually Pepillo admitted the truth, but only after swearing the angry captain to silence. 'You won't help me by getting involved,' he explained. 'I have to deal with this myself.'

Escalante pursed his lips. 'Very well then.' He examined Pepillo's hand. 'The good news is it was your index finger Santisteban broke. Your little finger plays the more important part in controlling your weapon, but the ignorant bastard wouldn't have known that. Here,' he passed Pepillo his stave. 'Let's see what can be done.'

Since leaving Teotihuacan, Tozi had walked north for twenty days, stopping only to beg shelter and food for the night. At first there had been many towns and villages, but the further north her feet carried her, the smaller and more widely separated the settlements became. On two occasions where the villagers were hostile, she used her powers of invisibility to steal maize flatbreads and meat, but otherwise she chose not to fade, preferring to take and deal with life as it came.

About six days ago she'd noticed the nature of the landscapes through which she was passing beginning to change, as she left behind the dense vegetation, well-watered trees and green fields of the fertile valley of Mexico, and entered increasingly sere and inhospitable terrain – first savannah and scrub, but later desolate flatlands, where only rough grasses and cacti grew. Now, as she picked her way along the floor of an ancient river channel in the blistering heat of midday, concerned that her water-skin was empty – indeed it had been empty since the night before – she heard a distant roaring and felt a shaking of the earth beneath her feet and, suddenly, ahead of her, like a dream come true that was intent on transforming itself into a nightmare, a wall of foaming water appeared, filling the dried-out channel to its rim. Tozi scrambled up the crumbling bank and over its top onto the higher land above, just as the rushing torrent came through and passed her by, a great fast-flowing river where there had been no river before – a terrifying river, churning with mud and carrying along tumbling, broken branches and even a whole tree, torn out of the ground by its roots, when there were no other trees to be seen for miles around.

Tozi looked up in astonishment at the clear blue sky and the sun burning in it like a furnace – not a cloud from horizon to horizon – and wondered where all this water had come from. Was it a sign that she was at last entering Aztlán, the home of the gods? Was this impossible river evidence of their handiwork? A much-needed gift sent especially for her? For even as she found herself seriously entertaining the thought, the flow of the river began to reduce, steadily falling as the sun tracked an hour overhead, until finally there was almost nothing left.

Seeing that it was safe to do so, yet wary lest another such outburst should manifest itself, Tozi hopped down into the now rapidly draining channel, drank until her stomach swelled, and filled up her empty water-skin in one of the last remaining pools, then continued on her way, following her feet north, ever north across the flatlands.

That evening, as the velvet darkness of the desert fell and the stars shone bright in the vault of the sky, she made camp near a huge saguaro cactus. She ate the last of her cold maize cakes, and took a sparing drink from her water-skin, for she had already used up half of it in her long, hot afternoon trek. If she failed to find water again tomorrow, she realised, she would be in serious trouble.

But she felt no fear, confident the gods would send another miracle.

When she awoke at dawn, however, she discovered that the gods had sent a serpent instead, a baby of the deadly tribe whose tails rattled. It was too young to have yet grown a rattle of its own but, like all of its kind, it had been armed with fangs and lethal venom from the moment of its birth, and as she stretched and yawned, her hand touched it and it bit her. In an instant, without thinking, she drew her knife and sliced off its head. She could already feel its poison coursing in her blood as she remembered that rattlesnakes were the creatures of Quetzalcoatl, especially loved and protected by him.

Had she just killed his messenger?

* * *

At dawn on Monday 12 July, Pepillo made his way out of the gates of Villa Rica holding his stave under his arm, his bruised leg – exercised and rubbed down with balm – no longer troubling him greatly. Escalante, who had rebound and fashioned a new splint for his broken finger, walked with him. They spoke in lowered tones as the captain gave final advice, reminding Pepillo that footwork, speed and deception were everything.

When they passed through the stand of trees that hid the headland from the town, they found Santisteban already waiting, swinging a thick pole as long as a pikestaff, an ugly grin on his face. Vendabal was there to support him, together with Hemes and Julian. Catching sight of Pepillo's stave, cut to the same length as the broadswords he and Escalante used in practice, they all sniggered, since Santisteban obviously had the far bigger weapon.

'*Hola*, Pepillo,' said Vendabal with a sneer, 'I always knew you'd have a tiny tool.' At this, Hemes, Julian and Santisteban made predictably lewd gestures.

Pepillo was framing a response about the tiny size of Santisteban's brain, but Escalante gave him a warning look and said quietly: 'Waste no energy on banter. Calm your mind. All that matters is the fight.' He stepped forward into the middle of the flat, grassy patch where they'd sparred so often before, and beckoned Santisteban and Pepillo forward to stand on either side of him. 'This is a grudge match, lads,' he said. 'The only rule is no edged weapons to be used. Other than that we'll let you go at each other, fair and square, to settle your differences. Pepillo's at a disadvantage, his right hand having suffered an injury, supposedly from a fall – ' a hard look at Santisteban – 'although I have my doubts.'

'Whatever do you mean by that, sir?' asked Santisteban, twirling his staff.

'You can take it to mean what you like, boy, but I'm warning you I want to see no one killed here. You may fight until one of you is knocked out or yields, but that's when it stops.'

As he spoke there was a sound of footsteps and everyone turned towards the trees, where Cortés, Alvarado, Bernal Díaz and Gonzalo de Sandoval had appeared. Malinal was with them, but hung back while the rest milled around the combatants.

'We heard rumours of a fight,' said the caudillo cheerfully.

Vendabal hurried to explain. 'It's your soft, spoilt page – sir, begging your pardon, sir – who has been causing trouble for our dogs. It's past time he was taught a lesson, sir, and Santisteban's the lad to do it.'

'Hmm . . . what's happened to your hand, Pepillo?'

After delivering his message to Olmedo, Pepillo had contrived to avoid his master. 'Hurt it in a fall, sir. Broke my finger.'

'And you think you'll be able to fight?'

'I shall have to, sir. This is a matter of honour . . .'

'Ah, honour . . . I see. Well in that case I'll not stand in your way.' He nudged Alvarado: 'What say you, Pedro? Shall we have a wager? I'll put a thousand pesos on my page to win.'

'I'll take that bet!' said Alvarado. 'Always happy to pocket your money, Hernán.'

Amongst the beggars of Tenochtitlan it was generally believed that one must immediately cut and suck a snake bite to get as much of the venom out as possible, but Huicton, who was learned in poisons, had once told Tozi this was an old wives' tale and that a hasty incision was more likely to make things worse than better. Still, to do nothing seemed wrong, so she took up her flint dagger, made a crisscross cut over the bite site, already swelling and hot, in the webbing between the thumb and forefinger of her right hand, sucked vigorously (her blood seemed strangely bitter and thin), spat, and sucked and spat again.

The sun was rising fast, and the only shade for miles on these inhospitable flatlands was cast by the tall saguaro cactus Tozi had slept beside, so she decided to stay where she was. There was very little she could now do, far away as she was from any healer, except use her own magic to cure herself. She recalled the warmth that had radiated from her hands when she had worked on the terrible wounds Guatemoc had suffered months before in battle with the Tlascalans; there was no doubt in her mind that his swift recovery was her doing. No reason, therefore, why she shouldn't be able to deal with a little snake bite – unless, as she feared, she had lost the favour of Quetzalcoatl by killing his messenger.

Pushing the thought aside, she worked fast to cut away the spines from the base of the giant cactus so she could lean comfortably against it if she needed to. Then she sat down in its shadow with her legs crossed and her back straight. She was aware of a great deal of pain from the wound, and her breathing seemed laboured, her heartbeat fast, but she ignored these symptoms, focused her mind inward, and began a slow, insistent chant.

Santisteban attacked at once, as Escalante had predicted he would, and Pepillo was ready for him. 'Use what you've learned about foot-work,' the captain had advised. 'Keep moving, make him strike at you again and again but make sure he misses. Soon enough you'll tire him out.'

Santisteban was two spans taller than Pepillo, heavier and more muscled in the body, and the weapon in his hands was long and thick, blunt at both ends, as much a bludgeon or a club as it was a staff. He charged with a yell, swung the pole high and brought it crashing down in a blow that would have broken Pepillo's head if it had connected, which it didn't. Pepillo was in a strong stance, left foot forward as he had been taught, right foot behind, his toes turned out, his centre towards Santisteban, and as the pole came whistling down he simply pivoted on the ball of his left foot, swinging his right foot around through ninety degrees, leaned his torso back and allowed the strike to pass him harmlessly by, the pole moving so fast, with so much force behind it, that its tip clunked jarringly into the ground.

There was a second, just a second, before Santisteban regained his balance, when his whole upper body was exposed. The opportunity was too good to miss and Pepillo swung his stave two-handed in a rapid curving slice that brought its edge – crack! – into percussive contact with Santisteban's long hooked nose, effortlessly breaking it, producing a spectacular flow of blood and a screech of pain and rage. Santisteban's eyes flooded with tears, which seemed to blur his vision and disorient him. Seizing the advantage, Pepillo followed through at once with a downward cut that struck Santisteban's right wrist with a satisfying crack of hard wood against bone. Pepillo then continued to pivot on the ball of his left foot, swinging his right foot back a further ninety degrees so he was now positioned beside his opponent and facing in the same direction. He did not want to grapple with him, too much danger of being overmatched, but again an opportunity presented itself and he took it, letting go his grip on the hilt of his stave with his left hand and bringing his left elbow sharply up to strike Santisteban in the jaw, sending him staggering. Finally, Pepillo took three sliding steps back, keeping good balance and contact with the ground, returned to a two-handed grip and raised the tip of his stave into the Plough Guard, the hilt held close to his centre, left leg leading, right leg back.

There came a burst of applause and, out of the corner of his eye, Pepillo saw that the source was Cortés. 'Bravo!' the caudillo exclaimed. 'Very nicely done. Your thousand pesos are in jeopardy, Alvarado, don't you think?'

The momentary distraction cost Pepillo the initiative. With a furious bellow Santisteban came charging in again.

Tozi had lost track of time and felt strangely separated from her own body, as if it and its sufferings belonged to someone else. Thus, although she was aware at some level of the immense pain in her grotesquely swollen right hand and arm, she was quite indifferent to it. And although she knew the sun was blazing down on her, drying her out, heating her up, indeed slowly killing her, she was oblivious to its effects. Her whole focus instead was upon the deep subterranean labyrinth through which she was wandering; it seemed as real to her, indeed more real by far, than any of those remote, detached, unimportant physical sensations that occasionally called for her attention.

It was a most strange and wondrous labyrinth, winding through solid rock, its walls cold and damp with condensation, glittering with veins of gold and quartz and infused with a soft, enigmatical luminescence that enabled her to see where she was going – which was . . . ? Which was . . . ? She paused for a moment, suddenly perplexed. Where, in fact, was she going? Why was she here? She knew it must have something to do with the serpent that had bitten her, but she could not say exactly what. And if she was not in her earthly body with its distant messages of pain and suffering, then what was this body she

315

inhabited now – this dream body, this vision body, so very like her form of flesh and blood, yet certainly not the same? Moreover, there was the problem of choosing her direction, because every few paces she had walked so far there had been side passages, forks, branches in this huge system of corridors, any one of which she could have taken and perhaps should have taken. What made her think that the passageway she found herself in now was the right one out of the hundreds, thousands of ways that opened up all around her?

She began to walk forward again, a feeling of uncertainty haunting her. Very soon she came to a crossing. A corridor branched to the left, another to the right. Another seemed to go straight ahead. She heard Huicton's voice: 'Your feet will know the way.' But did her feet really know the way, or was she impossibly, hopelessly lost? And was any of this real or was she just out of her mind with snake venom and sunstroke?

She chose the left-hand path, which rapidly became winding and sinuous with a steep decline. Again there were options – at the next junction she counted no less than fifteen different side passages, bewildering in the complexity of the choices they offered her. She chose one which continued to spiral downwards, ever more precipitously, the light from the walls growing dim, red, hellish, as though she were descending into Mictlan itself. The corridor, which offered no further side branches, progressively narrowed as she followed it. Soon she had to turn sideways in order to continue to pass, until finally she could force herself forward no further. She edged her way back in the direction she had come, but that way also the corridor now seemed narrower than before, and again she found she could not pass.

An overwhelming sensation of horror gripped her, and she screamed.

Santisteban swiped his staff viciously left to right as he charged in, aiming to deal a crushing mid-body blow. Pepillo was only just able to block it by hastily rotating his elbow up and dropping the tip of his stave down, thus adopting the guard called Hanging Point to protect his right side. Santisteban followed through with another tremendous swipe, this time from right to left, and again Pepillo blocked him with Hanging Point, then adopted a Long Point guard by rotating his elbow down. He immediately went onto the attack, sliding his left foot forward and executing a lunging thrust at the full extension of his arms that drove the tip of his stave into Santisteban's mouth, splitting his lips and smashing his upper front teeth.

Spitting blood, Santisteban staggered back, windmilling his staff wildly, and Pepillo followed with a series of rapid lunges that the older boy, panic now showing plainly on his face, only just managed to bat aside. Each time their staves connected, however, though Pepillo tried hard to disguise it, horrendous pain surged through his right hand.

This was where he was weak.

This was where he would truly be in danger.

In the two-handed grip he was used to after weeks of practice with Escalante, it was his left that was presently doing most of the work, while his right forefinger had been splinted and bound so that it stuck out rigidly, leaving only the other three fingers and the thumb of his right hand to grip the hilt. Up to now he had managed to override the pain, but the repeated clash and shock of the staves was taking its toll and he could already feel the force of his own counter-strikes weakening. Sensing this, Santisteban's crazed eyes suddenly seemed to light up and he rushed in on the attack again, sweeping his staff low at Pepillo's ankles, forcing him to jump back, and then throwing himself bodily at him, shoulder-charging him, grappling him, taking one hand off the hilt of his weapon and snaking it out to make a grab for Pepillo's finger.

Tozi calmed herself. This was a vision. It was not real. And she had the power of magic. These corridors had been made by her mind and could be reshaped by her mind. She began to chant – *Hmm a hmm hmm, hmm hmm, hmm a hmm hmm, hmm, hmm* – invoking the spell of invisibility, her voice growing deeper, hoarser, more intense, her dream body fading, losing substance, until she found that she was free, untrammelled by any physical constraint, and could move along the narrow corridor with ease. It seemed, moreover, that she was no longer walking but floating, drifting like smoke – indeed, she realised, she was being drawn through the labyrinth at greater and greater speed, its walls flashing by her on either side until suddenly, without warning, she was debouched into a vast underground cavern, illuminated by a soft but pervasive glow that seemed diffused everywhere. The domed ceiling overhead glittered with a thousand stalactites of pure, transparent crystal. From the floor, made of the same substance and towering above her, soared a forest of stalagmites. At the same moment, her state of being changed from chimerical, tenuous vapour to something more solid, and she was back in her dream body again.

'Welcome,' said a voice. It was a woman's voice – warm, kind and strangely familiar. 'You have travelled far, you are tired; you may take your rest here.'

'What is this place?' Tozi asked.

'Don't you know?' that beautiful voice replied, so poignant with memory it made Tozi's hair stand on end as she caught a flash of movement; some shape, some form, a hint of flowing red robes; someone, some being – *some god?* – slipping momentarily into view from behind one of the massive stalagmites, only to disappear behind another.

'I know nothing,' Tozi said. 'I was in the desert, I was bitten by a serpent. I killed the serpent and now I am here.'

'The serpent was sent to you by Quetzalcoatl to bring you to me,' the voice replied. 'Do not trouble yourself that you killed her. Our lord has taken her spirit back into himself now.'

'What is this place?' Tozi asked again.

'It is Aztlán,' the voice replied. 'Homeland of our people and of the gods. You are in the Caves of Chicomoztoc.'

As they grappled, and as his hand snaked out, Santisteban's pock-marked, sweating face was pressed against his own, and even as he felt the older boy's cruel grip take hold on his bandaged finger and begin to twist and tear, even as he screamed in renewed agony, Pepillo reacted instinctively. Yes, his finger was broken, but Santisteban's nose was broken too! Without hesitation he opened his jaws wide and bit down hard on that hooked, twisted blob of bloodied flesh and cartilage, sunk his remaining teeth into it and shook his head violently the way a terrier shakes a rat.

The reaction was instantaneous. Santisteban let go of the finger,

dropped his own staff, howled and tried to pull away, beating ineffectually at Pepillo's head with his fists, and in the process tearing his
ruined nose still further. Pepillo clung on, chewing, and only when
his mouth filled up with so much blood that it threatened to choke
him, did he at last unclench his jaws, spit out a lump of something
vile and slide back three steps, raising his stave into the Roof Guard
with his hands held at the level of his shoulder, his left foot and elbow
forward and the tip of the weapon angled up behind his head.

Santisteban was roaring and sobbing, both his hands clamped over
his ripped and bleeding face. Pepillo could easily have transitioned
from the Roof Guard into the Master Strike to the head that Escalante
had taught him, the strike called Zornhau – the Strike of Wrath – by
the German schools. It would have finished the fight there and then
but, not wishing to be accused of taking unfair advantage, Pepillo slid
back another step and nodded to Santisteban's staff where it lay fallen
on the ground. 'Pick it up,' he said. 'We're not done yet.'

Tozi hurried through the forest of stalagmites with an increasing sense
of urgency. She knew that kindly voice. She *knew* it! But why did it
touch her so deeply? And why did it have the power to reach into the
core of her being where so much loss, so much grief, lay stored?

Ahead of her she caught a glimpse of red robes again, a slim figure
with honey-coloured skin and long black hair moving rapidly, elusively
from one place of hiding to the next. Now there was a burst of laughter
echoing from the walls and ceiling of the great cavern, a rippling,
gentle laugh filled with love and joy. 'Follow me, Tozi,' the voice said.
'Follow me, my dear.'

Tozi followed, her blood pounding in her veins, her breath rasping
in her chest. The stalagmites were growing less numerous now and,
up ahead, a great tunnel opened, leading out of the cavern, a tunnel
filled with light that seemed to emanate from some distant source
beyond this netherworld.

It was strange indeed! Tozi was so short of breath she thought she
might actually die in this vision – and what would happen to her then,
if she did? Yet she could not give up and take her rest as the being
she was pursuing had offered, for she had to know – *she had to know!*

– who it was who spoke to her, and why she felt this haunting, anguished sense of remembrance.

The figure ahead became, briefly, clearly visible in the tunnel, lit by that radiance from beyond, but she was moving incredibly fast and now, with a whirl of her robes, she faded and vanished as though she, too, could work the spell of invisibility. Dogged and determined, Tozi continued to stumble forward – what else could she do? – but her breath came only in tortured gasps and her heart was beating with a deadly, irregular rapidity as she emerged at last into what seemed another world, with a blue sun in a burnished sky. A little way off was a vast lake, dark as midnight, with a rock rising out of it near the shore. Seated on the rock, dressed in red robes, was a woman with her back turned, her bare feet dangling in the water. The woman had long black hair, which she was combing, combing, and there was something so known, so familiar, so wistful in the motion of her hands that it clutched at Tozi's racing heart . . . and stopped it.

Her vision swam and she collapsed on her back on the roasting sand and the sun blazed down on her, a burnished sun in a blue sky. As her consciousness fled, a man's voice, filled with urgency and wonder, addressed her in a language that was Nahuatl yet not Nahuatl, and she felt a powerful blow strike her chest.

Santisteban didn't pick up his staff. Instead, with a sob of fury, he charged forward again, so fast yet so erratically, that Pepillo's strike to the head missed and glanced off his shoulder, failing to stop him. Santisteban barrelled into him with tremendous force, knocking the breath out of his body, and Pepillo had to take his left hand off his stave, continuing to hold it only in his injured right, in order to grapple with him. Even so, he managed to unleash a powerful downward slice that caught the older boy a hefty blow on the shin, and was about to hit him again, despite the shocking jolt of pain in his hand, when Santisteban writhed, reached behind, drew a wicked-looking dagger that he'd kept concealed down the back of his pants and stabbed Pepillo savagely in the ribs.

'Ahhh!' Pepillo yelled, jerked back with more strength and power than he knew he possessed, smashed his left fist into Santisteban's jaw and broke free of the grapple. As he did so, Santisteban wrenched the dagger from his side – another massive shock of pain – and rounded on him once more, lunging wildly.

Pepillo could feel his strength draining away even as he saw the shocked look on the faces of the stunned, immobile circle of spectators. Time, motion, the world itself seemed to slow down. Someone shouted, and Escalante, Cortés, Alvarado all began to move in to disarm Santisteban, but they seemed to be sleepwalking and had too much ground to cover, way too much; they'd never make it. With nobody to rely on for his own salvation but himself, Pepillo rapidly back-stepped twice, opening up a little distance from his attacker, and used it to rap Santisteban's right wrist hard with the edge of his stave, took a further step back as the bastard still came at him and struck him again, this time succeeding in knocking the blade from his hand. There was still strength in the unbroken fluid arc of the strike, and Pepillo followed it through, bringing up his stave and flowing immediately into a thrust, both hands gripping the hilt, arms extended, stepping powerfully forward with his left leg, the knee bent, right leg out almost straight behind, driving the tip of his weapon deep into Santisteban's throat with the combined colliding momentum of their weight.

With a strangled gasp, Santisteban dropped to his knees. Pepillo surged forward in the full grip of battle rage, his stave raised to dash his enemy's brains out, but the older boy cowered, holding his hands over his head, and croaked, 'Yield!' Pepillo stopped in his tracks, lowered his weapon and stepped away.

'By God! The boy's a warrior,' he heard Alvarado say, 'and a gentleman. Well worth my thousand pesos to see that fight!'

Cortés made some approving reply, but Pepillo didn't hear it clearly. His head was spinning, blood was pouring from the stab wound in his side and his legs quite suddenly buckled beneath him. He would have joined Santisteban on the ground, but Escalante caught him as he fell. 'You did well, lad,' the captain said. 'I'm proud of you.'

With Escudero and Cermeno's dangling corpses already showing the first signs of rot in the suffocating summer heat, with the remaining

Velazquistas thoroughly chastised and humbled, and with the letter he had circulated unanimously signed by all the colonists, Cortés had no concerns for the outcome of the public meeting that took place at noon on Monday 12 July, a few hours after the fight. Pepillo was in no shape to keep the minutes, but Diego de Godoy, the expedition's notary, volunteered for the role and lent a certain gravitas to the extremely brief and otherwise rather informal proceedings.

'Well, gentlemen,' Cortés said when everyone was settled, 'it's very hot, we all have things to do and we've all given our agreement in writing already, but I'll just ask one more time for the record,' a glance at Godoy who sat with his pen poised: 'Does anyone still object to the plan to win the king's blessing for our enterprise by giving him the treasures we've thus far accumulated? Raise your hands any who do.'

Not a single hand went up. Ordaz, Olid, De Grado and the other prominent Velazquistas, who were sitting bunched up together on the first pew, all shifted their buttocks uncomfortably.

'Very well,' Cortés continued, 'I'd now like a show of hands from all those in favour of the plan – again, for the record.'

This time every hand shot up, with the Velazquistas demonstrating particular eagerness to comply. Under his breath, Cortés chuckled. 'Good,' he said in ringing tones, 'so that's agreed then. Now to the details. I propose we delegate two loyal members of this company, Don Alonso Hernández Puertocarrero and Don Francisco de Montejo, to carry the treasure to Spain, since both are of the nobility, with better access than most to the court of King Carlos. By a show of hands, please, are there any objections?'

No hands went up.

'All in favour of the motion.'

Again every hand in the room was raised high.

Cortés turned once more to Godoy: 'Let the minutes show that by unanimous vote of the colony Don Alonso Hernández Puertocarrero and Don Francisco de Montejo will serve as our representatives to carry our gift to King Carlos. The vessel *Santa Luisa*, belonging to Don Alonso, will be the treasure ship.' A glance in the direction of Martin Lopez, the expedition's chief carpenter: 'Don Martin, how long do you think you'll need to complete the repairs on the *Santa Luisa*?'

'We're working night and day, Don Hernán. Like all the ships, she's in poor condition, though in better shape than some. I reckon we'll have her seaworthy within twenty days.'

'Faster, if you please, Don Martin. I'd like to see her ready to sail within two weeks – which will be, let me see, Monday 26 July. Do you think that's possible, Don Martin?'

'Perhaps, Caudillo, if we suspend repairs on all the other ships.'

'Very well then, make it so.'

In the midst of this short exchange with the carpenter, the germ of an idea had come to Cortés. It was a radical idea, potentially dangerous. But what was the expedition itself if not a radical and dangerous undertaking and, without great risk, was it not rightly said that there never could be great gain?

Since there was no further business to transact, he expressed the colony's gratitude to Puertocarrero and Montejo for agreeing to be the couriers of the treasure and declared the meeting closed.

It was mid-afternoon, the meeting had gone well, luncheon had been served afterwards – the Totonacs of Huiztlan were nothing if not generous in their provision of food to the colonists – and Cortés appeared to be in an excellent good humour. He and Malinal were alone in his pavilion and he had a certain light in his eyes that she knew very well. Before she gave him her body, however, she was determined to raise the matter of Pepillo and his dog. Cruelty had a place in time of war; she recognised that. But the caudillo's unkindness towards the boy disfigured his own character and served no useful purpose; the fight this morning offered a chance to change that.

'You happy with Pepillo?' she asked now.

Cortés grinned. 'Yes. Who would have guessed it? He has the makings of a first-class swordsman . . . And he earned me a thousand pesos!'

'But badly injured,' Malinal said, composing her face into an expression that she hoped combined concern, commiseration and winsomeness.

'Not so bad, all things considered. He was lucky the knife got stuck in his ribs and didn't push through to his vitals. He'll be right as rain in a week or two . . . Here . . .' The caudillo stepped close to Malinal, embraced and kissed her, but she pulled away.

'He was brave,' she continued.

'Who was brave?' Cortés sought another kiss and again she resisted.

'The boy, Pepillo. He was brave.'

'Yes!'

'And gentleman?'

'Yes . . .' A guarded look had appeared in the caudillo's eyes. 'What do you want from me, Malinal?'

'Want you to give Pepillo his dog back.'

'You know I can't do that, my dear.'

'You are caudillo! Can do what you like. You say "Vendabal give dog" and Vendabal give dog.'

'Exactly!' The curtains hanging across the open door of the pavilion were swept aside and Escalante strode in. 'Vendabal's not the captain-general of this expedition, Hernán, you are! And we're not talking about treasure, for God's sake, just a bloody dog.'

The caudillo's face had darkened. 'Were you eavesdropping, Juan?'

'I was coming to see you anyway and I couldn't help but overhear. I've got a soft spot for that boy and I want to see right done by him. Give him back his dog.'

Cortés glanced at Malinal, then back to Escalante again. 'I feel conspired against,' he said with a rueful smile. 'My lover on one side, my dear friend on the other. What am I to do?'

'Give Pepillo dog, then we shut up?' Malinal suggested. She was determined to have her way on this.

'Go on, Hernán. Just say yes,' urged Escalante. 'The boy did win you a thousand pesos, after all, and I'd say our army's gained another swordsman. Not a bad exchange for a dog, all things considered.'

Strangely, because this really was such a small matter, and one so easily resolved, Cortés seemed locked in some fierce internal struggle. What was it, Malinal wondered, that she didn't know? What was driving him? To be sure, he placed great weight on his frequent dreams of Saint Peter, and she chose to believe the dreams were true communications from the heavenly powers. Even so, why would the dead Christian holy man, who the caudillo said held the keys of heaven itself, disturb his mind with dreams about a dog? It made no sense!

Cortés had reached a resolution. 'Oh very well, the pair of you,' he grumbled. 'I'm persuaded. Send word to Vendabal he's to return the dog to Pepillo.'

'I'll tell him myself,' said Escalante, turning to go.

'I thought you wanted to see me about something,' Cortés reminded him.

'I did, I have, and I'm very happy at the result.'

With a wide grin, Escalante stooped out through the curtains, leaving Malinal alone with Cortés. She moved towards her master, sensual now, ready for anything.

Night had fallen when they were done. Cortés was a forceful man but he had rarely made love with such urgency or such passion. 'You see,' Malinal said as she dressed. 'It is nice to be nice.'

'Bah! Bugger nice. I just wanted to tup you. I knew you'd be more willing if I gave you your way.'

They paid a visit to Pepillo in the colony's two-roomed hospital. Melchior, newly restored to his young master, was lying at the foot of the bed and regarded them with a baleful eye. The dog was huge now, though still little more than a pup.

'Thank you for letting me have him back,' Pepillo said.

'It's nothing, lad,' Cortés said, as though it were all his doing. 'You earned it. Keep him lean, keep him savage. That's my advice to you. If it comes to a fight with the Mexica, he'll be needed. Everyone will be needed.'

'What about Santisteban? Is he all right?'

'He'll live . . . until we hang him tomorrow.'

'Hang him, sir? You mustn't do that.'

'Why ever not? Treacherous bastard pulled a knife on you. Broke the one rule of the duel. That's a capital offence. I thought you'd be happy to see him dead.'

'No I wouldn't, sir. Not at all.'

'So shall I have his hand cut off? What about that? Or maybe a good scourging? A hundred lashes should serve him out if he's to escape hanging. Since you're the injured party, you get to decide.'

'Pardon him, sir, is my request. I've suffered no serious injury and, as you say, we'll need every man if it comes to a fight with the Mexica.'

Pepillo sounded so tired, thought Malinal. *Gentle, sweet-natured boy. If there were more like him, this world would not be so dark.*

After the pair had gone, Pepillo received a visit from Escalante, who was carrying a cloth-wrapped bundle. 'Glad to see you've got your dog back,' he said.

'I still can't believe it.' Pepillo rested his hand on Melchior's head. 'The caudillo can be so kind.'

'He can – though sometimes he needs a little encouragement to bring out his better side. Like all of us, he has a devil whispering in one ear and an angel in the other.'

Escalante unwrapped the bundle as he spoke, and Pepillo recognised the beautiful broadsword he'd been allowed to use in their practice session. 'I've brought you a present,' the captain said. 'You fought like Amadis himself today, and a bold knight errant must have a sword of his own.'

'Oh, but sir, you can't give me that!'

'I keep telling you not to call me sir!' Escalante smiled. 'First names are good between friends. And I certainly *can* give you this sword – ' he passed it over – 'so here it is.'

'But Juan, it was for your son . . .'

'He's in a better place now. With him gone, I can think of no one more deserving of it than you. Indeed, Pepillo, if you will allow me to say so, you've become a son to me these past weeks, and since you're an orphan, I've taken steps with the notary to name you as my legal heir.'

Pepillo was so overwhelmed with emotion at Escalante's nobility and kindness that he began to cry.

'There, there, lad,' said the captain. 'Dry your eyes, for I wish you joy.'

When Tozi awoke, it was dark. Her chest and her right hand hurt mightily, and a small flickering fire built under a rocky overhang revealed a lurid scene. She sat up fast. Three wizened old men with something of the appearance of spider monkeys, naked but for loincloths, their faces and bodies painted with fantastic designs, were crouched around her chanting very softly, almost as though they did not want to be heard. She recognised some words in their chant but others were completely alien to her. 'Who are you?' she asked. She resisted the urge to fade, but couldn't quite hide the alarm in her voice.

'Ah,' one of them replied, speaking now definitely in Nahuatl. 'The sleeper awakes . . . You have fallen into good hands, my dear, don't you worry. If we'd been Chichemecs you'd be dead by now, and most likely eaten – certainly not cured of that very nasty snake bite. But luckily for you, we're not furious cannibals who dine on helpless maidens . . .'

Tozi gave him a suspicious glare: 'Who are you then?'

The elder who had addressed her puffed out his scrawny chest. 'We are medicine men of the Huichol nation,' he said. 'Good fortune put you in the path of the greatest healers on earth.'

Tozi gingerly touched her own chest. She felt battered, as though she had been punched repeatedly. 'You hit me,' she said accusingly.

The elder's deeply lined face took on a severe, scolding look. 'Well, what do you expect?' he said. 'Your heart had stopped. Would you have preferred we didn't restart it?'

'No! I'm grateful to you for that.' Tozi realised that her throat was parched. 'Do you have water?' she asked.

The elder reached into the shadows behind him, found a half-full skin and passed it to her. She drank greedily before a thought struck her and she paused. 'You have more?'

'We have more,' he said, 'you may finish that one if you wish.'

The other two watched her with glinting eyes, saying nothing as she upended the skin and finished it in five swallows. 'They don't speak?' she asked when she was done.

'They do.' A sour face from the elder. 'Usually too much, with boringly pointless excursions from the subject, long-winded soliloquies and tedious self-congratulation, so you may consider yourself doubly blessed, not only that we found you and saved your life, but also that only I amongst the three of us speak the barbaric pidgin of the Mexica, which abomination I was forced to learn as a child.'

'So you were chanting in Huichol, you and your friends?'

'Yes. The noble tongue.'

'It sounds a lot like Nahuatl . . .'

'Ugh! Yes, I have to agree. There are some family resemblances. But it is true, is it not, that within the same family one may sometimes find one brother who is intelligent, tall, comely and perfectly formed in features, limb and manners, and another who is small, retarded, ugly, misshapen and vulgar . . . This is the case with our beautiful Huichol and the hideous argot of the Mexica.' He paused, seeming to consider something: 'You are not, I suppose, Mexica yourself?'

'No,' said Tozi. 'I hate them. I was five years old when I first set eyes on Tenochtitlan. My mother always told me we came from Aztlán.'

The elder glanced quickly at his friends. They glanced back. The three of them then conversed in urgent whispered tones, of which Tozi understood perhaps one word in twenty, but those few words included 'witch', 'magic', 'Aztlán', 'Chicomoztoc', 'sacrifice', 'Chichemec', 'Moctezuma' and, most chillingly of all, 'Acopol'.

'What are you talking about?' she asked.

'You, my dear,' the elder replied. 'It seems it's not enough that we must save you from snake bite, sunstroke and dehydration . . . A witch of Aztlán is spoken of in our prophecies. It's said she will do battle for the light against the forces of darkness.' His eyes narrowed and a look of fierce concentration animated his lined, expressive face. 'Tell me . . . Is the name Acopol familiar to you?'

When she made no reply, he leaned closer, studying her. 'You've met him!' he said a moment later. 'I can see it in your eyes! You met Acopol in Tenochtitlan! Do I guess right? Is he the reason you're here now?' Urgency entered his tone: 'You must allow us to tutor you, my child!'

Tozi felt acutely uncomfortable and defensive at the mention of Acopol, but at the same time intrigued by the reference to prophecy. 'I don't need tutoring,' she said. 'I can take care of myself.'

'I'm sure you can! We saw how you summoned the spell of invisibility when you were sleepwalking in the desert. That's quite a formidable skill you have there. It's more than enough to protect you in the normal way of things. But Acopol is not a normal man. I'm afraid your magic tricks won't work with him.'

Tozi desperately wanted to change the subject. 'It doesn't make sense that you saw me walking in the desert,' she objected, her voice rising, a hint of anger in it. 'After the snake bit me, I sat under a saguaro cactus. I didn't go anywhere.'

'Well, so you may think, but you certainly weren't sitting when we found you. You were walking. You had been walking in the open desert for a very long while with your arm swollen and your heart beating too fast and your breathing very harsh and irregular. Sometimes you became invisible; perhaps this was how you avoided the Chichemec scouts.'

Other than in her visions, Tozi was sure she hadn't walked anywhere. Yet when she looked more carefully at her present surroundings, she realised she was in a very different place from the flatlands where she'd been bitten that morning. The flickering flames of the little fire under the overhang didn't reveal much, but there were bright stars overhead and – by the light of these – she saw they were camped in a narrow defile no more than a dozen paces wide, perhaps a side branch of a canyon, between high walls of sheer rock.

'What Chichemec scouts?' she asked suddenly.

'You mean you don't know the Chichemecs are on the war path?'

'I've seen no sign of Chichemecs or anyone else in these parts until I met you.'

'Then you're either exceptionally lucky, or protected by some god, because Acopol really stirred them up before he left for Tenochtitlan and they're swarming like hornets from a broken nest.'

'If they're swarming like hornets, what are you doing here, the three of you? Huichols are no friends of the Chichemecs, as I recall.'

'This is the season of the deer hunt,' the elder said, 'and we follow where the deer lead.'

'Deer?' Tozi laughed. 'In this desert? You must be joking.'

'Ah yes, but, you see, ours are a very special kind of deer . . .'

Chapter Thirty-One

Monday 26 July 1519 to Monday 16 August 1519

'Among other things that we are sending to Your Highness by way of these our representatives are our instructions that they plead with Your Majesty on no account to give any governorship in perpetuity, or judicial powers, to Don Diego de Velázquez. If any shall have been given him, then they should be revoked forthwith, because it is not for the benefit of the Royal Crown that the aforementioned Diego de Velázquez should have authority or favour in these New Lands of Your Majesty, which, as we have seen up to now and as we hope, are very rich. Should the afore-mentioned Diego de Velázquez be granted any powers, far from benefiting Your Majesty's service, we foresee that we vassals of Your Royal Highness, who have begun to settle and live in these lands, would be most ill treated by him. For we think that what we have now done in Your Majesty's service, that is to send You such gold and silver and jewellery as we have been able to obtain in these lands, would not have been his intention.'

It had proved difficult, but not impossible, to write with a broken index finger; though far from ideal, Pepillo had discovered he could grip the quill between his thumb and his second finger. For the past week, since his other injuries were healing well, he had been hard at work. The task was to create a final draft of the letter to the king that Cortés had been dictating virtually every day since the end of February, to do so in such a form that it would appear to come from the settlers of Villa Rica de la Veracruz rather than from the caudillo himself, and to ensure that it not only described all the events, negotiations, battles and travails they had passed through, but also that in every way possible – both subtle and direct – it served to blacken the name of Diego de Velázquez and put Cortés in the best possible light.

Now, on the morning of Monday 26 July, just in time to be carried aboard the *Santa Luisa* with all the treasure that Puertocarrero and Montejo had been charged with delivering to the king, the letter was complete. Pepillo read it aloud to Cortés with a sense of quiet satisfaction at a job well done.

'We, the inhabitants and citizens of this town and colony of Villa Rica de la Veracruz,' the letter concluded, 'do entreat Your Majesty to order and provide a decree and letters patent in favour of Don Hernándo Cortés, Captain and Chief Justice of Your Royal Highness, so that he may govern us until this land is conquered and pacified, and for as long as Your Majesty may wish, since he is a person well suited for such a position. The treasures which we send you herewith, over and above the one-fifth which belongs to Your Majesty, are offered in Your Service by Don Hernándo Cortés and the Council of Villa Rica de la Veracruz and are the following . . .'

The itemised list of the treasures annexed to the letter excluded certain items that had been given to Puertocarrero and Montejo, but still ran to many pages. 'Truly a king's ransom, sir,' Pepillo dared to comment as he finished the reading and passed the complete document to his master.

'Let's hope the king sees it that way!' Cortés replied, 'for if he does not, there's damn all I can do. The die is cast.'

The final touch was to have the letter signed on behalf of all the colonists by the *alguacil*, *regidores*, treasurer, *veedor* and other officials of the town, as well as ten of the common soldiers.

Three hours later, taking advantage of the afternoon ebb tide, the *Santa Luisa* sailed.

Cortés stood with Alvarado on the headland, watching the *Santa Luisa* as she left the bay under a cloud of sail, drawing a clear, straight wake behind her. It would be three hours at least before she disappeared from view over the western horizon, but there was no calling her back now and the die was indeed cast.

'Any chance they'll betray us, do you think?' Alvarado asked, giving voice to Cortés's own thoughts.

'In this life I've come to expect treachery,' he replied, 'but honestly

I don't think so. Puertocarrero will act as a check on Montejo and Montejo on Puertocarrero. Besides, both men are in my pocket – quite apart from the previous bribes they've had from me, the treasures they'll deliver to the king exclude ten per cent for each of them, skimmed off the top before the inventory was prepared.'

'Ha!' Alvarado exclaimed, 'ten per cent per man, eh? Escudero tried to convince me you were giving Puertocarrero a full thirty per cent just for himself . . .'

Cortés raised his eyebrow. 'That would have been excessive . . .'

'But of course he also wanted me to believe that the treasure would never reach the king – that Puertocarrero would take his thirty per cent and your father would hold the other seventy in safekeeping for you.'

'But naturally you didn't believe any of this?'

'If I had we wouldn't be standing here now, Hernán, and Escudero wouldn't have had his neck stretched. You're a snake and the very devil, but I know you're playing for higher stakes than treasures that can be packed in a single ship.'

'You are right, Pedro. I am playing for a world.'

'Then make sure my share will be a kingdom at the very least, old friend.'

That night Cortés dreamed of Saint Peter again.

It was a strange dream, for he met his patron on a ship, unlike any he had ever seen before, tall as a palace but forged from steel with huge guns, set in swivelling turrets, mounted fore and aft. Amidst thunder and flashes of fire, winged engines, also of steel and of wondrous design, soared into the sky at impossible speed from a great flat deck. Other devices, shaped like bodkin points but of vast size, roared up from the bowels of the ship and split the firmament, trailing lightning and clouds of smoke until they vanished over the horizon.

'What is this, Holy Father?' Cortés asked in amazement.

'This is the future, my son,' the saint replied. 'Come, let me show you a vision of the world I have brought you to these New Lands to create.'

Then suddenly they sat side by side in one of those winged engines, a battery of illuminated panels in front of them, tearing through the sky so fast Cortés was stunned and bewildered, gazing in astonishment at the earth below that seemed to curve beneath them as though it were a gigantic sphere. 'Now observe,' said the Holy Father, pointing to an enormous metropolis, its streets seething with throngs of gaily clad men, women and children – a populous city of glass and steel and towering minarets spanning both banks of a mighty river and rising up out of a limitless desert. 'It is a habitation of the Moors,' the saint explained, 'ancient enemies of Christendom; your people fought them for seven hundred years, now you will see them destroyed. Look! There!'

Cortés looked where the saint had indicated and saw a pair of fiery bodkins, each as long as a jousting ground, pass above them, arc down towards the city, then strike it. There were twin explosions of flame, brighter than the sun, and these rapidly merged into a single prodigious conflagration, dazzling to the eye, stupefying to the mind, and the very air trembled, seeming to burn and melt, and a gigantic cloud in the form of a great dark flower blossomed into the heavens, and a sound like the crack of doom struck Cortés's ears with the force of a blow to the head, leaving him dizzy.

The saint was grinning, laughing. 'Look,' he said, 'how the Lord has smitten his enemies,' and they flew closer towards the steaming shadow of the river, now empty in its channel, while all around it the city was no more, reduced to the twisted, molten remains of devastated buildings, tortured outcrops of fused metal and stone and glass rising from a field of glowing ash, strewn with blackened, contorted corpses. 'See! Some have lived,' the Holy Father said as they flew to the most distant outskirts of the devastated metropolis, where people ran screaming into the desert, their clothes smouldering on their backs, their hair in flames, their faces livid with burns. 'But they will not live for long,' the Saint added, 'for the explosions transmit a great and terrible poison that melts flesh from bones and eats a man out from within and that cannot be escaped.'

'Holy Father,' said Cortés as they soared back into the sky, 'give me weapons like these that I may better serve you.'

'Such weapons will not come to you,' the saint replied, 'but to your descendants, for out of your enterprise in the New Lands a mighty and ingenious nation will grow and that nation will master the world and lay waste to all the enemies of the Lord.'

Cortés felt a keen sense of disappointment, which the Holy Father seemed immediately to understand. 'Lament not, my son, for your part in this is the greatest and most noble. On account of your courage, on account of your cunning, on account of the strength of your hands, on account of your indomitable will, it is to you and you alone whom I offer the honour of creating this wondrous future and fulfilling the glory of the Lord. Nonetheless,' a sombre note of warning entered the saint's voice, 'your path will not be easy and you may yet fail. You have acted swiftly to destroy those who would have destroyed you, and I applaud you for that, but greater dangers still remain. Amongst your followers there are many whose hearts quail at the prospect of war with Moctezuma, who quiver with fear at the thought of his mighty armies, who secretly yearn for the safety of Cuba. You have taken these waverers by storm with your eloquence and your promises and they are ready to march into the interior with you, but at the slightest reverse – and you will face many – they will turn and run, knowing their ships await them ready to carry them across the sea.'

A mood of deep dismay threatened to overwhelm Cortés because he knew in his bones that the saint was right. His men had their qualities; for the present they would be loyal enough, but they were fair-weather friends and, when the going got difficult, there were many who would desert him if they could. 'What, then, am I to do, Father?' he asked.

'You already know the answer to that question, my son, for I have put the thought into your mind.' Around them, as the saint spoke, the scene had changed: day had become night, and the winged craft that carried them now circled over the bay of Villa Rica, where the Spanish fleet lay at anchor under the stars.

Cortés remembered. The idea had come to him when he had urged Martin Lopez, the expedition's carpenter, to complete the refit of the *Santa Luisa* by 26 July. Lopez had said the deadline could be met only if he and his team suspended their work on all the other ships. Cortés had agreed and the carpenter had been as good as his word.

Now, with the *Santa Luisa* on her way, the badly needed repairs to the rest of the fleet were scheduled to resume in the morning unless . . . unless . . .

'You mean the thought that I should sink our ships, Holy Father?'

Saint Peter beamed. 'Indeed so, my son! If there are no ships left to sail back to Cuba, your men will have no choice but to conquer or die.'

Something was bothering her caudillo, but Malinal could not persuade him to speak about it. He was restless, out of sorts, bad tempered. At night he tossed and turned, groaning frequently in his sleep and, three days after Puertocarrero had sailed, he arose from their bed in the darkest hour and did not return. When she found him in his pavilion the next morning, he was deep in conversation with the other captains, and with Martin Lopez, the carpenter.

Though he never showed it publicly, Pepillo knew that Cortés had been deeply shaken by the Velazquistas' plot and by the way that men like Ordaz, whose loyalty he believed he had bought, had been willing to betray him. What particularly seemed to haunt him was the thought that others might at any time choose to steal a ship, or several ships, and sail for Cuba to cause him further trouble there.

He resolved the problem in a most unexpected and characteristically daring way.

On 2 August, which was by chance Pepillo's fifteenth birthday, a week after Puertocarrero and Montejo had sailed, and following much behind-the-scenes manoeuvring with his captains, who agreed to allow Martin Lopez to drill holes in the bottoms of their already leaking and storm-battered ships, Cortés called the men together and announced an unfortunate discovery. With the exception of the *Gran Princesa de los Cielos*, the newly refitted caravel that Francisco de Saucedo had arrived in from Cuba on 5 July, the rest of the fleet, including his own *Santa Maria*, had been rendered unseaworthy as a result of a galloping infestation by a species of wood-beetle known as the *broma*.

It was a deception, of course – indeed the word *broma* in Castilian meant 'prank' or 'practical joke'. But since the ten 'infected' ships were by then half sunk, listing and foundering in the bay, the men were persuaded, and made no complaint when Cortés ordered the failing vessels to be sailed onto the sands and broken up, their timbers to be used to complete the construction of Villa Rica. By so doing, he pointed out, the conquistadors would be spared the expense and effort of maintaining the useless vessels and would benefit from the addition of their crews, numbering close to a hundred men in total, to the strength of the army. As well as their timbers, which were immediately made available for construction work, all the salvageable parts of the ships – sails, rigging, cannon, anchors, chains, cables and other tackle – were to be carted up to the headland and deployed to the advantage of Villa Rica, or stored for future use.

'The time has come,' Cortés said, 'to strike inland to Tenochtitlan and pay Moctezuma a visit.' Everyone knew that 'paying Moctezuma a visit' was a euphemism for seizing the Mexica capital by force, and there was a great cheer. 'Don't lament the loss of our fleet,' the caudillo continued. 'What use would the ships have been to us anyway? If we succeed in this great enterprise of conquest we shall not need them, and if we fail we shall be too far into the interior to reach the coast. Have confidence in yourselves. You have set your hands to the work; to look back is ruin! As for me, I remain in this land while there is one to keep me company. If there be any so craven as to shrink from the dangers, let them go home, in God's name. There is still one vessel left. Let them take that and return to Cuba. They can tell there how they deserted their comrades and patiently wait until we return loaded with the spoils of the Mexica!'

Pepillo remembered with a smile how the men had responded. Not one of them had voted to return to Cuba. 'To Mexico!' they all yelled, 'to Mexico!'

It was now 16 August, two weeks after those daring shouts rang out. Every preparation for a major expedition of conquest had been made, and all the men were gathered in Villa Rica's assembly ground. More than eighty of the original five hundred expeditionaries had died of wounds, bilious fever and the bloody flux since Potonchan, but the army's ranks had been replenished by the hundred sailors from the scuttled ships and the sixty soldiers of fortune brought by Saucedo. The total muster was therefore around five hundred and eighty. Of these, some two hundred and thirty, under the command of Juan de Escalante, would be staying behind to garrison Villa Rica. That number, however, included many who were still too sick or too badly injured to be much use in a fight. The other three hundred and fifty, all in good health and supported by a thousand Totonac warriors and as many bearers, were arrayed in marching order to begin the thrust into the interior. The Totonacs, and Cortés himself, were convinced Moctezuma's fierce enemies – the Tlascalans – would join them, so it was to Tlascala they would go first to win allies and increase their strength.

Wearing his new sword, its scabbard fixed to a strong leather belt around his waist, and with Melchior bounding by his side, Pepillo went to Escalante and embraced him. 'Thank you, Juan,' he said, 'for everything you have done for me. I'll never forget.'

'I'll not let you forget, lad!' the captain said gruffly. 'I plan to be seeing you again soon enough. In the meantime, keep up your practice with the broadsword! I'm sure Bernal Díaz will be willing to spar with you and, if you get the chance, see if you can talk Don Pedro de Alvarado into giving you some lessons. He's the finest swordsman in this or any army that I've ever known—'

'Not so fine as you, Juan,' Pepillo protested.

But Escalante would have none of it. 'No, no,' he said. 'Don Pedro's more than a match for me – more than a match for five men! But luckily enough I'll never have to fight him since we're friends.' He clapped Pepillo on the shoulder: 'Now, off you go, lad. It's time to march.'

'Will you be safe here, Juan?'

Escalante looked up to the strong stockade surrounding Villa Rica, with cannon mounted at strategic points along the battlements. 'I'll be safer than you will, Pepillo. But my God how I wish I could come with you. New Lands to conquer! Great adventures to be had! Instead I'm stuck here, nursemaiding the sick and injured!'

Cortés had walked over quietly to join them. 'It's so much more than that, Juan,' he interrupted. 'Villa Rica gives the whole expedition legitimacy. We need a strong rearward base that can maintain lines of supply for us and to retreat to if necessary, and I need a strong man to run it – a man I can trust completely.'

'And unfortunately you chose me,' said Escalante, making a long face.

'There's no one I trust more, Juan. But you won't be stuck here for long, I promise you. Once we get to Tenochtitlan, I'll relieve you here with another commander, and you can come upcountry and join us.'

The two captains said their farewells and Pepillo embraced Escalante again. It was painful, to know a father, mentor and guide for the first time in his life, only to be separated from him so soon. 'Off you go, lad,' Escalante repeated. 'It's time to march.' He turned to walk away, then looked back: 'Remember, Pepillo, if anything does happen to me, everything I have is yours. The papers are with Godoy.'

Pepillo nodded, his throat too constricted to speak. He beckoned Melchior to heel, and went to stand with Malinal, as Cortés climbed into Molinero's saddle, from where he gave a final short address to the men.

'Ours is a holy company,' he bellowed, 'and we must conquer this land or die. But be sure that our blessed saviour and Saint Peter himself will carry us victorious through every battle with our enemies. Indeed, this assurance must be our stay, for every other refuge is now cut off but that afforded by the Providence of God, and by your own stout hearts.'

That said, with Malinal and Pepillo walking at his stirrups, Cortés led his little army out past the gallows, where the mouldering skeletons of Escudero and Cermeno still hung, towards the distant mountains of Tlascala. Beyond those looming peaks, the golden prize of Tenochtitlan lay hidden like the Grail, promising either unimaginable wealth and power, or a terrible death, to those who dared seek it.

Part III

24 August 1519–02 November 1519

Chapter Thirty-Two

A fast, direct road, patrolled by Moctezuma's guards, ran from Huiztlan, close to the new Spanish settlement of Villa Rica de la Veracruz, and thence through the sacred city of Cholula all the way to Tenochtitlan. Had the Spaniards and their Totonac auxiliaries chosen to take this road, and to travel at the pace of a forced march, they could – assuming there were no ambushes to delay them – have reached the Mexica capital in four or five days, completely bypassing the free state of Tlascala. Moreover, Cortés had not forgotten the dream Saint Peter had sent him in the middle of the month of May, when they were still camped on the dunes at Cuetlaxtlan – the dream in which the Holy Father had quite specifically told him that he must go to Tenochtitlan 'by way of a city called Cholula, a vassal city to the Mexica. I am preparing a great victory for you there.' Cortés had every intention of obeying this command from on high. However, he was determined to visit Tlascala first, for there he hoped to recruit strong allies to stand by his side in whatever battles lay ahead. The route of march, proposed by Meco, whom the fat cacique had placed in overall charge of the Totonac warriors and bearers, avoided areas of heavy concentration of Mexica power, and led for the most part through uninhabited mountainous country. It had proved to be a long and circuitous journey that had exposed the troops to great discomfort, freezing fog, rain, hail, and a series of high-altitude passes. Finally, however, on the morning of Tuesday 24 August, after an arduous eight-day trek, they came down into a warm, pleasant valley, dominated by the town of Xocotlan, the last Mexica outpost before the Tlascalan border.

Because Xocotlan housed a large Mexica garrison, Meco's advice was to press on directly to the Tlascalan capital – called, simply, Tlascala: a journey of thirty-eight miles, less than two more days' hard march. But the men needed rest, so Cortés overruled him and instead had him select two emissaries, Mamexi and Teuch, both minor Totonac chiefs in their own right, who he sent ahead to Tlascala that same morning, bearing gifts, a message of friendship, and a specific request for safe passage.

Almost as fat as Tlacoch, Xocotlan's chief was a truculent, irritable man named Olintecle. Initially he was hostile, but within a few hours his frowns turned to smiles and he offered food and hospitality. Cortés's suspicions were aroused by the marked change of attitude, but Malinal remained unruffled. Mexica spies, who would be maintaining daily contact with Tenochtitlan by relay messengers, must have followed them from the coast, she said, and undoubtedly had a standing instruction to ensure the Spaniards were well treated. 'Moctezuma is coward. He frightened. He keep changing mind what to do. Now he think you gods, now he think you men. First he want keep you far away, then he think bring you Tenochtitlan, deal with you there. He coward. He feel safe in his city. Maybe once we inside he think he cut the . . .' – she searched for the word: 'Roads that are bridges?'

Cortés suggested 'causeways'.

'Yes,' Malinal said, 'causeways. He cut! He surround us! His armies very many; they trap us in narrow streets, no good place for our cavalry, and he destruct.'

'Destroy,' Cortés said.

'Yes. Destroy. That his plan. So we safe, I say, until Moctezuma get us where wants us.'

As was increasingly the case, Cortés found Malinal's arguments persuasive. She might be a woman, she might not speak perfect Castilian yet – although her grasp of the language was improving every day – but she was calculating and intelligent. If she was right, and he believed she was, then it was all the more urgent that the Spaniards recruit stronger, more steadfast allies than the Totonacs before they reached Tenochtitlan. Hence the importance of Tlascala, with its warlike reputation and its implacable enmity towards Moctezuma.

Here again, however, Malinal disagreed with Meco, who seemed certain the Tlascalans would be delighted to enter an alliance with Cortés against the Mexica. 'Tell you once, tell you again,' she told Cortés. 'Tlascalans mountain people. They stubborn, think for selves, fierce to protect Tlascalan land. If they decide you enemy – and maybe they *already* decided you enemy – they fight you and fight you hard.'

The Totonacs were a cowardly, devious people in Shikotenka's opinion, and he'd never trusted them. 'I propose we kill these two,' he said to the assembled senators, 'and if the white men cross our border, I propose we kill them as well.'

Tied hand and foot on the floor of the senate, Mamexi and Teuch, the two Totonac emissaries, shuffled uncomfortably. Town chiefs with a few grey hairs, they were vassals of fat Tlacoch of Cempoala, whose name they'd waved about like a charm. They'd clearly not expected to be taken prisoner and beaten bloody when they'd turned up in Tlascala late that afternoon after a hard trek of a day and a half from Xocotlan. Mamexi was so upset he was sobbing like a baby, with tears running down his face and snot dribbling from his nose.

'I propose a more temperate course,' said Shikotenka's wizened father, known to one and all – for the avoidance of confusion – as Shikotenka the Elder. 'The white men claim they want peace with us; in fact they claim they want to help us in our . . .' He paused and looked at the Totonacs: 'How did the leader of the white men put it?' he asked.

Mamexi, who had the big ears and narrow chin of a climbing rat, was too distressed to speak, but Teuch, stolid and practical, had a better grip on himself. 'The lord Cortés,' he stammered, 'bade us tell you he comes to help Tlascala in her heroic struggle against the tyrant Moctezuma.'

'There's nothing in that I find offensive,' said the elderly chief. 'I say we welcome this Cortés and learn more.'

'We don't need his help, father,' said Shikotenka, 'and besides, I don't believe his sweet words. My spies have watched the strangers since they first made camp on the sands near Cuetlaxtlan—'

'Where you rashly picked a fight with them,' interrupted Shikotenka the Elder, 'and your friend Alcolmiztli was killed. It's since then you've borne a grudge against these strangers. Try to set

343

your personal feelings aside, and choose only a policy in the best interests of Tlascala.'

'I am doing so, father, and I repeat that we have watched the white-skins closely since Cuetlaxtlan. Our spies followed them when they moved to Cempoala and Huitztlan, and now we see them in Xocotlan. They've been served by the Mexica and their slaves the Totonacs all the way, and they've received three top-rank embassies from Tenochtitlan, one of which included Prince Guatemoc. Now the white men gather their strength in Xocotlan, close to our border, where they're treated as honoured guests on the orders of Moctezuma himself. It makes no sense for them to be there, enjoying the tyrant's hospitality, unmolested by his garrison, if they've really come to aid our struggle against him. Surely the opposite is true? Surely they've come to aid Moctezuma against us?'

'The lord Cortés is very cunning, sire,' Teuch dared to interrupt, 'but we have learnt to trust him. He means to destroy Moctezuma.'

'Which he's going to do with things like this?' sneered Shikotenka, picking up the long, gleaming metal knife that the emissaries had brought as a present, together with a strange kind of bow with a string that was stretched so tight it couldn't be drawn.

'These and other things, lord. The things they call "guns", from which thunder and lightning blast forth to kill their enemies.'

'Some say these "guns" are fire-serpents,' offered venerable Maxixcatzin, who served as deputy to both Shikotenkas. 'I'm told they killed thousands of the Maya with them at Potonchan.'

'And we've seen they ride on the backs of deer and wear metal armour,' added Tree. Although he'd recovered from the wounds he'd received months before in the fight on the beach at Cuetlaxtlan, he bore, as a memento of that night, a hideous, jagged scar down the left side of his face. 'Some say they are *tueles*.' He stuck out a large bare foot and gave Mamexi a shove. 'What say you, Totonacs? Are these strangers *tueles*?'

Again it was Teuch who did the talking: 'Truly they are *tueles*, lord. They are the *tueles* who captured the great Moctezuma's tax gatherers and ordered that no one in the hills and cities of the Totonacs should pay tribute or send sacrifices to the Mexica again. They are the *tueles* who threw our *tueles* out of our temples and put their own in. They are the *tueles* who conquered the people of Potonchan and Cintla. They have great strength, these *tueles*. None may stand against them.'

Shikotenka had suddenly had enough of this womanish gabble. What his father said was true. He'd hated the white-skins with a passion since the one with golden hair had killed Alcolmiztli on the beach at Cuetlaxtlan and now, the more he heard about them, the less he liked them. They were not *tueles*! They were invaders, intruders, interlopers. They had no right to be here, riding in their metal armour on the backs of deer, deploying fearsome unknown weapons, double-dealing with the Mexica and bullying and commanding the other peoples of this land. He ran his thumb down the edge of the long metal knife – as long as a man's leg, sharp as obsidian, heavy and horribly strong. Residing within it was a cold, lurking power, like some deadly serpent; the power that had gutted and skewered his friend Alcolmiztli and drowned him in his own blood.

Out of nowhere, an awful premonition shook Shikotenka. These strangers were indeed here to destroy Moctezuma, as they had already boasted they would, but they would not be content with that. Unless they were stopped, and stopped now, they would sweep over the whole land and destroy everyone else as well. The Maya, the Totonacs, the Tlascalans, the Huexotzincos, the Texcocans, the Tacubans, the Otomies, even the Chichemecs in their remote deserts – all would fall, all would be made slaves, all would be humbled, never to rise again. As the stated target of the strangers' relentless advance, and as the greatest power in Mexico, it was Moctezuma – surely above all others? – who had the responsibility to confront them and drive them out; but instead of fighting them, the cowardly fool had befriended them, sent them rich gifts, sent his nephew Guatemoc as his ambassador to them, and obliged his vassals to provide them with warriors and bearers.

Shikotenka realised that at some point in the past few moments he'd made his decision, and now neither his father, nor his deputy Maxixcatzin, nor any of the other senators were going to talk him out of it. He got to his feet and prowled around the cowering emissaries. 'You came here with lies and falsehoods from that traitor Moctezuma,' he roared. 'And you tell us no one can stand against those you name *tueles*. But we Tlascalans will stand! We're going to kill your so-called *tueles* and eat their flesh. Then we'll see whether they're as strong as you say.'

Following his spectacular victory over the Mexica six months before – and it had been *his* victory, since he'd planned it, prepared it, carried out the decisive raid and bested, though unfortunately not killed, Guatemoc in a knife fight – Shikotenka's status had never been higher. He was a king and the son of a king, but while his ancient father still ruled supreme in civil matters, in matters of commerce and business, in matters of law, custom and religion, the fact was that he, Shikotenka the Younger, was the battle-king of the Tlascalans and his word carried the greatest weight when it came to war.

'The white-skins are not *tueles* but men,' he said, turning on the balls of his feet, looking round the benches and addressing every one of the thirty senators. 'I know because I have fought with them; so too has Tree, so too Chipahua, so too Ilhuicamina, and we all say they are men, and it is as men, not gods, that they are dangerous – a powerful military force supported by the vassals of our sworn enemy. I say we cannot and must not welcome them. I say the only honourable course of action open to us is to fight them to the death if they take even a single step onto our land.'

As Shikotenka had expected, Tree, Ilhuicamina and Chipahua immediately seconded him. All three of them had been injured fighting the white-skinned warrior on the beach at Cuetlaxtlan, and Tree and Ilhuicamina had only recently recovered their full faculties after resting long in the infirmary. They knew in the most direct and immediate way possible how dangerous the white-skins were, and their word carried weight with the senators who one by one cast their votes in support. Shikotenka's father was the last to agree to war in the event that the strangers crossed the Tlascalan border. 'My young son,' he said, deliberately echoing the words of his famous song, 'you leader of men. I will not stand in your way but I fear this is a decision you may come to regret. You are brash and full of confidence now, but tell me, if you lose on the battlefield, what then do you propose?'

'We are Tlascalans, fighting for our homeland. We will not lose.'

'But even so, if these white men defeat you, what will you do?'

'What would you wish me to do, father?'

'You must take it as a sign from the gods that the cause of the white men is just, and if they truly mean to march against Moctezuma, then you must march at their side.'

Shikotenka smiled. 'I accept, father . . . but we will not lose!'

'And in the meantime, what shall we do with these Totonacs?' The question came from Maxixcatzin, who was pointing his staff of office at the two bound emissaries on the floor.

'Hold them in the fattening pen while I ready the army,' Shikotenka replied. 'We'll sacrifice them and eat their flesh with chillies before we depart.'

A loud wail from Mamexi was cut short as Tree's foot slammed into his belly. 'Any more of that snivelling,' the big Tlascalan told him, 'and I'll sacrifice you now.'

'I hate it here!' said Pepillo.

It was Friday 27 August, their fourth day in Xocotlan, and he was exploring the town with Malinal, Melchior prowling by their side with his hackles raised. They were in a great square, which had a small pyramid topped by a temple on its north side, and three other temples at ground level on its east, west and south sides. In front of the pyramid steps, and in front of each of the temples, were huge piles of human skulls, so neatly arranged they could be counted. Pepillo was good with numbers and volumes and he reckoned that the four piles, added together, contained more than a hundred thousand skulls.

There were in addition other grisly collections of human remains – a heap of femurs and a macabre display of skulls and bones, some with flesh still attached, strung between wooden posts and guarded by three filthy priests whose long hair was matted with dried blood.

'Why do they do this?' Pepillo asked, feeling sick.

'It's the same throughout Mexico,' Malinal replied. 'Everywhere the same. Our gods are demons and they've got inside our minds and driven us mad, making us murder each other in their name. That's why Cortés has been sent to us, to stop all this.'

*   *   *

After the debacle of the summer solstice celebrations, Moctezuma had at once summoned Acopol from his work in Cholula and demanded an explanation from him, but the sorcerer had seemed unconcerned. 'Stay in your palace, Lord Speaker,' he'd said. 'You will be safe from the witch here. Venture no more beyond these walls until I discover her hiding place and kill her.' Acopol had then gone sniffing around the palace, indeed around the whole of the sacred precinct, even venturing up the great pyramid to the temple of Hummingbird, but had found no trace of her. Next he'd walked the streets of Tenochtitlan for three days, only to report at the end of his investigations that the witch was not in the city. 'It seems, sire,' he suggested, 'that after her attack on you at Teotihuacan, she did not return here.'

'Then where has she gone?' Moctezuma snapped.

Acopol shrugged: 'My powers are great, Lord Speaker, and they come from the god himself, but even I cannot search the whole world for this witch child. When she returns I will find her. Until then, I charge you to remain here, where my warding spells will protect you, while I complete the great task that the god has honoured me with in Cholula. What I have set in motion in that city will ensure the total destruction of the white-skins, but I rely entirely on you and your ministers to lure them there.'

'I have already invited them to come to Tenochtitlan,' Moctezuma said. 'I have offered them guides and the most direct road passes through Cholula, but we cannot *force* them to take it.'

The expression in Acopol's eyes had frozen Moctezuma to the bone. 'They *must* take it,' he'd said in the most sinister of tones, 'and they must come through Cholula, for if they fail to do so, then the wishes of the god cannot be fulfilled . . .'

And now, some sixty days later, the very problem Moctezuma had foreseen had come to pass. As he knew from the daily reports brought from his spies by teams of relay runners, the *tueles* had left a force to guard the town they had built for themselves on the coast, and had ventured into the interior, spurning all offers of guides and the fast, direct road that would have taken them through Cholula, and choosing instead to travel by a tortuous and difficult mountain route. In due course, this route had brought them to the Mexica stronghold

Xocotlan, ruled for Moctezuma by his vassal Olintecle, and there they had taken up residence, enjoying the lavish hospitality and gifts that he had ordered Olintecle to provide to them. From Xocotlan it was an easy march to Cholula, but alarming reports from the spies had indicated this was not what the *tueles* intended to do. Instead it seemed they planned to make a diversion into the lands of the hated Tlascalans.

The prospect of an alliance between the Tlascalans and the *tueles* froze Moctezuma's blood, so he had sent urgent word to Olintecle to dissuade them from this course of action, and now sat brooding in his palace, waiting to discover what the outcome would be.

Allowing a minimum of a day and a half journey time each way, and a day for deliberations, Mamexi and Teuch should have been back in Xocotlan by Saturday 28 August, but when they failed to appear, Cortés called his captains together and gave orders for the army to make ready to depart for Tlascala in two days' time on the morning of Monday 30 August. Getting wind of this, Olintecle came to him and urged him through Malinal not to go to Tlascala under any circumstances – for the Tlascalans were the enemies of Moctezuma. In his opinion they had already killed Mamexi and Teuch and now, forewarned, would certainly be preparing to attack Cortés. It would be much better, the chief suggested, for the Spaniards to avoid Tlascalan territory entirely and go by way of the city of Cholula, whose people were closely allied to the Mexica and would welcome them.

Speaking through Malinal, assisted in the translation by Pepillo, who improved and smoothed out her Castilian, Meco put the opposite point of view. 'Don't risk it,' he advised. 'The Cholulans are treacherous and Moctezuma has a large garrison in their town, much larger than here at Xocotlan, while the Tlascalans have always fought to keep their independence. They're frank and fearless and they're our friends. Mamexi and Teuch have simply lost their way and we'll see them soon enough. To change your plans now, Lord Cortés, will make you look weak. We must go through Tlascala.'

'What do you think?' Cortés asked Malinal later that night when they were alone.

'Same like I told you before. Tlascalans are – ' she sought for the word – 'unpredictable. Meco rely too much on Totonacs' friendship with them.'

'And Cholula?'

'It sound like twisted scheme of Moctezuma. Maybe some test. Cholula is sacred to god Quetzalcoatl, who he fears you are. Maybe he want see what happen when you go there. Maybe he hope his god Hummingbird send him sign so he know what to do next.'

Again Cortés was reminded of his dream of Saint Peter, in which the Holy Father had promised him a great victory at Cholula. It was intriguing to learn now from Malinal that this city was sacred to Quetzalcoatl. 'Could the Cholulans be potential allies for us?' he asked.

'I don't think so. They Moctezuma's – how you say? – lapdogs. Too afraid of him to be your allies, but the Tlascalans, maybe. Who knows? They crazy people. They might fight you or they might join you.'

'God, Saint Peter and my clever Malinal always guide me honestly,' said Cortés as he drew her close. He was more determined than ever to visit Cholula, but equally certain he was right to pay a visit to the Tlascalans first.

'Husband, show mercy,' said Xilonen. 'You have many faults but you are not a bully.'

They had made love in the garden on the palace roof and now lay side by side within their private bower, gazing up through the leaves at the vast star-strewn depths of the night sky. Xilonen crooked one long, naked leg, lightly sheened with sweat despite the chill in the air, and rested her knee on Shikotenka's scarred belly. 'I beg you, husband, let them go. The Totonacs may be weak but they have never been our enemies. You've already had their envoys in prison for three days, but to sacrifice them because you don't like the message they bring is unworthy of you. I would expect such an act of Moctezuma. Don't demean yourself by stooping to his level.'

Shikotenka sighed. He was always at his most susceptible to his wife's gentle persuasion when she had satisfied him so completely. 'Why shouldn't I sacrifice them?' he complained. 'They came here with treachery in mind—'

'What treachery?' She sounded scornful. 'They offered you an alliance, not poison.'

'The offer itself was the poison – to make us trust the very thing we should most suspect.'

'Pah!' Xilonen rolled fully on top of him. 'Too much suspicion!' He felt the pressure of her full breasts and her firm thighs. She supported herself on her hands and he saw the glint of her dark eyes as she gazed down at him. 'Let those poor men go,' she whispered. 'It's a small thing. Do it for me. The gods will bless you.'

'Now you're bringing the gods into it!'

'Whatever works. I want you to let them go.'

For the first time, Shikotenka found himself giving serious thought to the possibility. Nothing would be gained by sacrificing the emissaries, but perhaps some good might come from freeing them. 'Very well,' he said to Xilonen, 'if it pleases you I will release them. It seems I can refuse you nothing.'

'In that case, may I ask your attention for one more matter?'

'Wife,' Shikotenka said gruffly, 'do not try my patience.'

'It's a big thing,' she continued, 'but I feel strongly about it, so I am compelled to speak.'

'Speak then.'

'Do not rush into battle with the white men. Find some neutral ground and talk to them. Perhaps, after all, you should consider this alliance they propose.'

'Aiyee! Enough!' Shikotenka rolled Xilonen onto her back and spread her legs. 'Here's a big thing I feel strongly about,' he said, 'and it demands your immediate attention.'

There was a soft chill in the mountain air, the stars were bright, the sky the deepest midnight blue. On the roof of the guest quarters that Olintecle had provided, Malinal lay side by side with Hernán Cortés, the man she had set out to use as a weapon of vengeance against the Mexica, but had grown to love. He was, in every way that mattered, the most exceptional, extraordinary and contradictory man she had ever known: tender and imaginative in their sex play, ferocious in battle, clever and quick witted, a loyal friend and an indomitable enemy,

351

kind-hearted by nature, yet capable of great cruelty when it served his interests.

'What your plan,' she asked, 'when we get to Tenochtitlan?'

Malinal had described the Mexica capital to Cortés many times before: how it stood amidst the waters of a great lake, with its houses built on islands or on stilts; how every house had a flat roof which, with the erection of breastworks, could transform it into a fortress; and how the city could be approached only along the three causeways that connected it to the mainland, each causeway having multiple openings, allowing the water to flow from one part of the lake to another and spanned by wooden bridges which, if removed or raised, made entry – or escape! – impossible.

Nor was the problem simply one of Tenochtitlan's unique situation. Moctezuma had recently suffered a severe reverse in his war against the Tlascalans; nonetheless, Malinal estimated he could still command a standing army of at least a hundred and fifty thousand men and call in perhaps a hundred thousand more from his remote garrisons and vassal states, as well as Otomi and Chichemec mercenary forces, numbering in the many tens of thousands, that he was reported to have hired recently.

So Cortés knew all this when, lying there in the dark beside her, his hard naked body still alien to her in its bone-white beauty, he replied calmly, 'If we can continue to play the game well, as I believe we have done until now, we will enter Tenochtitlan as Moctezuma's guests, with smiling faces, exchanging gifts, knowing all the while he means to trap us and kill us there. But we will never let that happen. Once we are within his walls, I will make him my hostage and rule his city and his empire and all his armies through him, and take everything that belongs to him and make it mine.'

Malinal was momentarily stunned by the audacity and simplicity of the strategy, which Cortés had never hinted at before, and by the realisation that it might actually work. Because Moctezuma was a coward, because of his superstitious fear of the white men, but above all because he was an absolute dictator in whom all the power of the state was concentrated, it was just possible, if the caudillo could face him down with daring and succeed in taking him prisoner and terrifying him enough, that the whole Mexica empire might fall into line, without the need to storm its impregnable capital, or do battle with its myriad armies, or shed even a single drop of blood.

'It could work,' she breathed, thinking out loud.

'Of course it will work,' said Cortés. He sounded supremely confident.

But then he always did.

Telling Xilonen to keep the bed warm, Shikotenka went to Tree's home and found him, morose and belligerent, drinking pulque in the back yard. The big warrior had lived alone since the sudden death of his own wife a year previously. They'd not been blessed with children, and Tree refused even to have servants to tidy up after him. As a result his place was a mess, with a bad smell about it.

'Come on,' said Shikotenka. 'I need your help with something.'

'A fight?' said Tree hopefully.

'Not a fight. Not tonight anyway! I'm going to do something a bit odd and I want you to witness it.'

'Almost everything you do is odd, so why do you want a witness? Leave me alone.' Tree upended his cup and poured himself another hefty draft of the milky liquor.

'No, I really need your help,' Shikotenka insisted. 'I'm going to give those two Totonacs a chance to escape and their guards will feel better about the whole thing if you're there to witness it. Otherwise they might fear they'll be blamed.'

'I'm drinking, can't you see?'

'Yes, and too much these days. You'll lose your edge in battle if you go on this way.'

'Like you're losing your edge with all this mercy?'

'Xilonen persuaded me to let them go,' Shikotenka answered honestly.

'Right there,' growled Tree, 'I hear the sound of an edge being lost.' He paused: 'Are we still going to fight the white men, or did she talk you out of that as well?'

'If they cross the border,' said Shikotenka. 'We're going to fight them with everything we've got.' He grinned. 'So let's stay sharp, both of us.'

He walked with Tree to the fattening pens, where hundreds of prisoners were held in bamboo cages and fed on a special diet to make them plump for sacrifice. The two Totonac emissaries were kept in a cage of their own.

Shikotenka took the warders aside. 'Keep your voices down,' he warned. 'An hour after midnight, when the whole city's asleep, I want you to let the Totonacs escape.'

'Escape, lord? It's more than our lives are worth.'

'It will be more than your lives are worth,' Shikotenka whispered, 'if they're still here in the morning.'

'Yes, lord.'

'Take food in for them and tell them they must eat. Tell them they're to be sacrificed the day after tomorrow and we want them to be pleasing to the god. But when you go out, leave the gate of their cage open. Make it look accidental, but make sure they notice . . .'

'We'd prefer to discharge them into your custody, lord. Then you can set them free yourself.'

'They'd think I've gone soft and that won't help us. Just know you'll have done a great service to me personally if these men are long gone in the morning. I'll see you're well rewarded for it. Tree here will witness there's been no dereliction of duty on your part.'

'But lord—'

'No more questions. I'm counting on you. Get this done.'

'Get it done,' rumbled Tree, looming over the warders.

As they nodded their agreement, Tree strolled across the courtyard to the cage where the emissaries were held, snatched a flickering brand from a bracket and shoved it through the bamboo bars, revealing the terrified prisoners hunched in a corner. 'Snivelling Totonac bastards,' he observed.

The one called Mamexi gave a nervous squeak, while his companion Teuch got to his feet. 'What do you want with us?' he asked.

'Just checking your meat's still fresh,' said Tree with a horrible laugh. 'Day after tomorrow, the priests will take your hearts and me and the boys get to eat your thighs with chillies and beans before we march out to slaughter those *tueles* of yours.'

Mamexi was sobbing inconsolably now. 'We've done nothing wrong.'

Tree threw the brand down near the gate where it flared and flickered. 'See you for breakfast, day after tomorrow!'

'What was that all about?' Shikotenka asked a few moments later when they'd left the prison yard.

'You want those fools to escape?' said Tree, 'so I gave them a motive and some light to see by.'

Chapter Thirty-Three

Sunday 29 August 1519 to Monday 30 August 1519

The news from Xocotlan was as bad as it could possibly be. The *tueles* were preparing to march to Tlascala. Since they constantly demanded gold, Olintecle had tried to register the Great Speaker's disapproval by withholding further presents from them, but this had only caused them to advance their plans. They would depart at first light the next day.

In a fury, Moctezuma despatched a command to his vassal to give the *tueles* more gold. The messengers would carry the order from relay post to relay post, running without cease through the night. The entire team of runners, Moctezuma had made clear, would face execution if his instructions failed to reach Olintecle before the *tueles* marched.

When Olintecle walked his thighs slapped together – slap! slap! slap! slap!; this sound announced his arrival as he bustled into the square where the conquistadors were mustering on the morning of Monday 30 August. It was early, not long after dawn, the sky was clear but the air was still cold, and in patches here and there a light mist lay close to the ground. Olintecle came bearing gifts – a dozen necklaces, three pendants and some lifelike lizards, all of pure gold – which was surprising because over the previous days he had politely sidestepped Cortés's persistent requests for presents to send to King Carlos in Spain. But the motive for the chief's change of heart was transparent. 'You must not go to Tlascala, Lord Cortés,' he protested through Malinal, his face crumpling with insincere concern. 'Your emissaries' failure to return is a sure sign that danger awaits. Those evil savages have murdered them and they will murder you if you enter their lands.'

'The Lord is my shepherd,' said Cortés. 'I fear no evil.' He handed the gifts to Pepillo to pack away in Molinero's saddlebags.

Olintecle tried another argument: 'Besides, the Great Speaker himself commands it. He will be most offended if you fail to visit Cholula as he has ordered.'

'Compliments to the Great Speaker,' Cortés replied, 'but I take orders from no man except my king. My mind is made up.' He gave a wink to Pepillo who, as they'd prearranged when Olintecle had first appeared, loosed Melchior's leash. The huge hound bounded forward to sniff the chief's groin at which, breaking out in a sweat, he made his farewells and hurried away – slap! slap! slap! slap! When he was gone, Pepillo called Melchior back to his side.

All was now ready for the departure. Father Olmedo stood to the fore to lead the march out of Xocotlan. On such occasions the cheerful friar carried a standard embroidered with the cross of Christ. It hung limp, but now a soft morning breeze blew in from the west and the cloth rippled and flapped.

Perfect, thought Cortés. *A sign*. He swung himself into Molinero's saddle, stood in the stirrups and turned to review the disciplined ranks of adventurers. With the four additional mounts brought by Saucedo, and the six left behind with Escalante to defend Villa Rica, the spearhead of his force was his cavalry, numbering sixteen. They were followed by the foot soldiers grouped in seven companies of fifty, their shields, weapons and armour shining in the sun. Next came the dogs in five packs of ten – for half the animals had stayed at Villa Rica. Behind them, in their feathers and paints, were the thousand Totonac warriors provided by the fat cacique, and bringing up the rear were the *támanes*, also numbering a thousand, shouldering the baggage and hauling the artillery.

Signalling to Olmedo, who strode forward raising the billowing standard high, Cortés bellowed so that all could hear: 'Gentlemen, let us follow the banner, the sign of the Holy Cross, and by this we shall conquer.' There was a great cheer from the men followed by the steady tramp of marching feet and, with the whole population of Xocotlan now lined up to watch them go, the conquistadors wound their way through the narrow streets of the town heading west towards Tlascala.

*   *   *

An hour's march west of Xocotlan, Bernal Díaz stood at the head of the foremost squad of infantry, looking up at a pair of massive wooden gates set into a gigantic wall fifteen feet high, twenty feet thick and more than three miles in length. Crossing the whole breadth of the valley, the battlements of this impressive fortification, which marked the border with Tlascala, were patrolled by a thousand Mexica sentries in full war panoply. They willingly opened the gates, but as the Spaniards entered they found themselves confronted by a second parallel wall that overlapped the first for a distance of forty paces, somewhat in the manner of a ravelin. This device obliged them to make a right turn along a passageway ten paces wide, commanded by the battlements of both walls, from which the defenders would be able to rain down spears, arrows and stones on any attackers attempting to force the gates from the Tlascalan side.

'Thank God we don't have to fight our way through this lot,' observed Alonso de La Serna, looking up at the grinning, heavily armed sentries.

'We'd take losses,' Francisco Mibiercas conceded.

'More likely we'd be wiped out!' said Díaz, who was examining the immense blocks of stone, laid together without cement in the joints, from which the hulking fortification had been built. 'Has to mean the Mexica are pretty damn afraid of their neighbours.'

'Has to,' agreed La Serna, with a cheerful wave to the sentries. 'So let's hope all this talk about the friendly welcome we're supposed to get in Tlascala turns out to be true.'

Díaz hated confined spaces and was relieved to emerge from the shadow of the ravelin, but feelings of apprehension followed as he gazed into the wild, empty country that lay beyond. Already there was a marked change in the land from the pleasant meadows and fields around Xocotlan – the sky itself seemed less blue, the sun less bright. Though it had long-since healed, the arrow wound he had taken in his thigh at Potonchan now unexpectedly flared, piercing him with a sudden sharp stab of pain.

He shivered.

'Someone just walk on your grave?' asked Mibiercas.

Díaz forced a laugh. 'You'll not bury me yet,' he said.

A few moments later – the ravelin still lay no more than two hundred paces behind and scouts had not yet been sent out – Díaz heard faint shouts and cries carried on the breeze. He recognised he was in a dark mood, but something in the tone of these voices suggested terror. Mibiercas and La Serna were also listening, and the three friends exchanged concerned glances. Soon half the army was peering anxiously ahead; hands fell to sword hilts, spears and pikes were raised, musketeers fussed with their guns, archers cranked their crossbows.

They'd been hidden from view by the lie of the land, but now two Indians appeared at the top of a slope ahead and stumbled across the heath towards the conquistadors. So great was their haste, so frequently did they look over their shoulders, that they collided, tripping and falling twice before picking themselves up and darting forward again.

Cortés urged Molinero into a trot, and they soon reached the pair. They were battered and bloody, their clothing torn, their hair dishevelled. Still he recognised them. These were Mamexi and Teuch, the Totonac envoys he'd sent to the Tlascalans. *Well,* he thought, *that's one mystery solved, anyway!* He rode past them to the top of the slope as Alvarado, Davila, Olid and Sandoval joined him at a gallop. They all reigned in, looking for whatever horror the men were fleeing from and seeing nothing but miles of wild, empty terrain framed by high and jagged peaks.

The envoys were in such a state of terror – Mamexi tearful, Teuch frozen – that they could hardly speak. Little by little, however, through Malinal's gentle but insistent coaxing, and with help from Pepillo to put their words into flowing Castilian, the story came out.

The night before last they'd escaped from the fattening pen in the city of Tlascala, where they'd been held for three days awaiting sacrifice. They had run under cover of darkness, hidden themselves in a cave the following day, and run again all the previous night, convinced every moment they were followed and about to be recaptured, until finally they approached the wall, and safety, that morning. It seemed they'd only got away because the Tlascalans were so busy making preparations for war with the conquistadors that their jailers had become careless and left a gate open. 'Otherwise those devils would have killed us,' whimpered Mamexi, whose small, rat-like eyes seemed to contain inexhaustible reservoirs of tears. 'They wanted to rip our hearts from our chests. They wanted to eat our flesh with chillies and beans.'

'But didn't you explain we're on their side?' demanded Cortés, 'that we seek to be brothers to them – that we're as much against the Mexica as they are?'

'We explained,' wailed Mamexi. 'We explained a hundred times but they wouldn't believe us. They said you're in league with Moctezuma! They said they're going to eat you as well!'

'Not all felt that way,' interrupted Teuch, who was regaining his composure. 'There were different opinions. The elder Shikotenka wanted peace. It's his son, Shikotenka the Younger, who persuaded the Senate they should make war on you.'

'He's the battle-king of the Tlascalans,' volunteered Meco, who'd been standing nearby.

'The man you were so confident would want to be our ally?' sneered Cortés. 'So confident you had me turn down the hospitality of Cholula to come this way instead?'

'I don't understand what went wrong, lord,' said Meco. 'The Tlascalans are our friends. I was sure they'd welcome us.'

Mamexi cackled hysterically: 'Do you call this a welcome?' He showed his multiple cuts and bruises. 'They beat us like thieves. They humiliated us.' He turned to Cortés and glared at him through a flood of tears: 'Beware *tuele*,' he said, his voice cracking, 'they are animals, these Tlascalans. They're mobilising their whole army against you. They mean to fight you to the death.'

For an instant Cortés contemplated turning round and going by way of Cholula instead. It was what Saint Peter had wanted him to do, after all! But he put the thought out of his mind at once. Certainly he would go to Cholula, but he would do so in his own good time after he'd settled things with the Tlascalans. No matter the adversity, no matter the risk, the high-stakes game he was playing with Moctezuma meant it would be fatal to back down or show even the slightest irresolution or weakness now. 'Well, so be it,' he boomed cheerfully, 'if that's how things are, then forward, and may fortune be on our side.'

Sandoval, Alvarado and some of the other cavaliers had dismounted to listen to the envoys' story. 'Gentlemen,' Cortés said, 'to horse! Let's scout ahead and learn what awaits us here.'

The foot soldiers were following at a fast march and should now, Sandoval estimated, be about six miles west of the wall. It was already past noon. Eight of the horsemen – half the cavalry – had remained with the infantry, but the other eight, Sandoval amongst them, had been riding at a brisk trot for more than an hour – their mounts could keep this pace up all day if necessary – and were now some twelve miles west of the wall.

As always, Sandoval was immensely happy to be riding Llesenia, the chestnut mare the caudillo had allocated to him at Potonchan and allowed him to keep ever since. Ortiz, nicknamed 'the musician', who owned the animal, was less happy with the arrangement, but a bribe from Cortés had persuaded him to go along with it. The fact was that Ortiz was a poor rider, while Sandoval had been born to the saddle.

He looked around, taking in the feel and flavour of the country; it reminded him, in its harsh, untamed beauty, of the remote uplands of Cantabria. A fast-flowing river, its waters whipped into white foam, ran through a deep gorge a mile downslope, and in the distance jagged peaks and high forbidding cliffs clutched the sky.

It felt good, Sandoval thought, to ride free like this, scouting unknown terrain, with men he admired, men he knew would stand by him through thick and thin, on a quest of high adventure! Cortés was up ahead on Molinero, Alvarado beside him on Bucephalus, the two huge stallions neck-and-neck while their riders talked and joked. Fanned out behind them came Olid, Velázquez de Léon, Morla, Moran, Davila and Sandoval himself.

Suddenly Cortés was gesturing, pointing. A group of Indians, fifty warriors armed with spears, their heads plumed with feathers, stood silhouetted on a ridge a mile ahead. They were visible only for a moment and then vanished as suddenly as they had appeared.

Cortés and Alvarado spurred their horses and went after them, riding like demons, stretched out at full gallop, lances levelled. With a thunder of hooves, Sandoval and the rest of the troop followed.

* * *

Damn but these Indians could run! As Alvarado reached the ridge where the warriors had showed themselves, he saw them streaking away across the wild moorland, which sloped down into a long, gentle valley then up again towards a second higher ridge about a mile further west. They were still maintaining a good lead. He glanced at Cortés, who rode close beside him and yelled: 'Kill them or catch them?'

'Catch them,' Cortés replied, the wind snatching at his voice. 'We want peace with these fellows if we can have it.' Deliberately he put up his lance.

Well and good, Alvarado thought, putting up his own lance. *But what do we do with them when we've caught them?* He glanced back and saw that Sandoval, Davila and Olid were close, Morla, Moran and Velázquez de Léon a little further behind. All, following Cortés's example, had put up their lances.

The Indians were indeed incredibly fast on their feet, but the galloping horses were much faster and the gap between them began to close rapidly. Alvarado grinned, knowing the fear the big destriers provoked in primitive minds. None of the riders were fully armoured themselves – cuirasses seemed enough to enter what had, until they'd passed the wall, been thought of as friendly territory – but both he and Cortés had taken the precaution of having their mounts fully barded before leaving Xocotlan this morning; so too had Sandoval and Davila, and their shining armour, gleaming in the sun, made a magnificent and no doubt terrifying sight. Olid, Morla, Moran and Velázquez de Léon all rode unarmoured horses, but the savages would be so intimidated by the animals themselves it would make no difference.

Maintaining a surprisingly disciplined formation of ten ranks of five, the Indians were naked but for loincloths and sandals, their bodies painted a gruesome shade of red, bright green feathers fixed in their long black hair. All carried spears and all were armed with daggers hanging at their waists and their simple broadswords, made of wood with obsidian blades, slung in sheaths on their backs. Unlike other natives who Alvarado had run down on Bucephalus, they weren't peering anxiously over their shoulders, but seemed focused on their flight, arms and legs pumping, still covering a lot of ground very fast.

As the distance closed to a hundred paces, then fifty, Cortés signalled for the riders to split into two files – Sandoval, Davila and Velázquez de Léon following him to the left, Alvarado, Olid, Morla and Moran to the right. They galloped along the flanks of the Indian band, dropping their speed to a canter as they drew level. Now at last some of the warriors turned to look at them, but without panic, their fierce faces, daubed with stripes of black and red paint, showing no fear whatsoever. *Interesting*, thought Alvarado. *We might have a fight on our hands here.*

'Hey,' Cortés yelled, as if they could understand him. 'Stop! We just want to talk. We mean you no harm.' He switched his lance and Molinero's reins to his left hand and held up his right hand, palm outwards, in a sign of peace. But the Indians paid no attention, just kept on running, grim and silent.

Waste of time, thought Alvarado. With a nudge of his knee he swerved Bucephalus sharp left into the midst of the fleeing column, aiming to knock a few men down and make them listen to reason, but they were amazingly agile; the ranks simply melted away from the warhorse, and suddenly a big Indian, missing his front teeth, was attacking him with vicious, sweeping blows of his broadsword. Just as Alvarado realised that he recognised the man from the night fight on the beach back at Cuetlaxtlan, one of the cuts connected with the steel plates of the *crinet* protecting Bucephalus's neck, and he was obliged to swerve away as another slashing blow narrowly missed his own unarmoured thigh and crashed into the barding just in front of his saddle. 'What the hell?' he yelled as he spurred the animal clear.

Seeming to realise there was no point in continuing flight, the Indians stopped running and quickly formed up into a disciplined, defensive circle, bristling with spears. *Real soldiers!* Cortés thought. *Not like the Maya.* The ridge they'd been making for still lay half a mile upslope to the west but, though they'd been caught in the open, they seemed calm and unafraid. Hoping to take them alive, he again made signs of peace and waved his horsemen back until they formed a skirmish line fifty paces below the Tlascalans – he assumed they were Tlascalans – who brandished their weapons and shouted war cries.

'I think at least one of these fellows was amongst the band who tried to snatch Pepillo on the beach at Cuetlaxtlan,' said Alvarado. 'If it's them, then they know how to fight. Shall we have at them?'

'Not yet,' said Cortés but, as he spoke, out of the corner of his eye he saw Olid level his lance. 'No Cristóbal!' Cortés warned, but Olid wasn't listening. With a whoop he charged in towards the Indians, the hooves of his sorrel mare kicking up clods, and in the same instant a tall, massively built warrior, the braids of his long hair tangled and filthy and a great scar down the left side of his face, leapt out from the circle and ran to meet him, blocking his path with a ferocious aspect and a horrible yell, making the mare rear and whinny before he could thrust.

'That's another one of those bastards I fought on the beach,' Alvarado had time to say before something shocking and incredible happened, something completely unprecedented in all the battles the Spaniards had faced since their arrival in the New Lands. While Olid was still struggling to regain control, the huge Indian took an unexpectedly graceful step forward, shifted his weight to his right forefoot, pivoted half a turn, whirling his heavy wooden sword with its wicked obsidian blades, and struck the horse such a monstrous blow on its unarmoured neck that the animal was cleanly decapitated. Its head dropped with a heavy thud to the turf, its severed arteries jetted a tremendous gushing shower of blood, and its body toppled over so fast that Olid couldn't jump free and lay struggling vainly with his left leg trapped beneath its flank.

Sensing a disaster in the making, Cortés was already at full gallop before the mare went down. He mis-aimed his lance and settled for barging Molinero into the attacker, sending the man stumbling as he swung to kill Olid on the ground. A dozen Indians darted out towards them from the defensive circle, screaming hate, but the other riders thundered down on them, brushed aside their puny spears, killed five with lance thrusts, scattered the rest and charged on, lances levelled, into the main mass, thrusting and stabbing. In the pandemonium Cortés vaulted down from Molinero and, with a mighty effort, pulled Olid free, but immediately came under attack from three fierce-eyed, painted warriors who, far from running as he'd expected, were already back on the offensive. Drawing his sword, he ran the first of them through, disembowelling him, while Alvarado, who had lost his lance, rode Bucephalus between the other two and cleaved their skulls with his falchion. Davila charged in, reached for Olid and hauled him across his saddle. Snatching up Olid's lance – Alvarado would need a replacement – Cortés at once remounted and shouted an order to the rest of the troop to disengage.

The white men rode a distance of three hundred paces downslope to the east before wheeling their strange deer and forming a line again. 'Well,' growled Tree, 'at least they're mortal – the deer anyway.' He was examining the teeth of his bloodied *macuahuitl*, unbroken after scything through the animal's neck.

'Watch out for their armour though,' said Chipahua. He held up his own *macuahuitl*. It was badly damaged where he'd slashed it against the hard, shiny clothing of one of the deer. 'It's like the metal the white-skin we fought on the beach at Cuetlaxtlan was wearing.'

'I think the same man's amongst them today,' said Shikotenka. He pointed. 'There, with the golden hair, the one you just attacked. Don't you recognise him?'

'You're right,' said Chipahua. 'I didn't get a good enough look at him on the beach to be sure, but now you mention it – and the way he fights – yes, it's him.'

Shikotenka was remembering that night, how the white-skin had squared up to him at the end after Alcolmiztli was killed, the challenge he'd shouted in his strange language. He offered a silent prayer to the gods that the man would come under his knife today and surveyed the battlefield without emotion. Twelve of his men, mostly new recruits who'd joined the squad after the raid on Coaxoch's pavilion six months before, lay dead. Three others were too badly injured to put up a fight. He looked up again at the line of riders.

'I suppose we should count ourselves lucky these ones aren't carrying fire-serpents,' observed Ilhuicamina.

'If they have fire-serpents at all,' challenged Chipahua. 'I think it's a story the Chontal Maya made up to explain their defeat.'

Tree was standing nearby. 'Fire-serpents or not,' he said, 'it looks like they're getting ready to charge us again.'

Shikotenka narrowed his eyes. The one whose deer Tree had killed had been placed on the ground, where he sat nursing what was obviously an injured leg. The other seven had split into two units, one of four, one of three, and this second smaller unit now surged forward at a tremendous pace, the animals' hooves thundering upon the earth. They charged past the Tlascalans' right flank at a distance of a hundred paces and pulled up three hundred paces above them to their west.

'They'll come at us from both sides,' said Shikotenka. Normally he would have laughed at the suicidal notion of seven men doing battle with a force that was still thirty-five strong, but these strangers couldn't be judged by normal standards. He was quite sure they weren't gods, but he'd seen enough to know they were brilliant, disciplined, deadly warriors, utterly formidable on the backs of their rapid, heavy deer and armed with weapons of immense killing power. 'Throw your spears on my signal,' he said, speaking loudly enough for everyone to hear, 'then grab the bastards' lances as they come in. Grip them tight and don't let go no matter what they do. Try to pull them down where we can deal with them.'

There came a shout from the leader of the white men, and both groups charged at once, lances levelled, closing in on the Tlascalan circle with stupefying speed. Shikotenka wasn't afraid; he felt sure none of his squad was afraid. They had come here to confront a new challenge and learn how to deal with it.

He gave the signal, and thirty spears flew through the air, enveloping the riders in a storm of wood and flint. Most of the projectiles bounced harmlessly off their metal armour, but one drove home into the shoulder of an unprotected deer, causing it to swerve and run off madly at a tangent, while another took a man high up in the leg and stuck there, though he wrenched it free and did not break formation.

'Hold,' Shikotenka yelled, 'hold,' as his attention focused on a gleaming lance tip, aimed at his chest, being driven towards him with tremendous force by a big brute of a man whose frowning, black-bearded, green-eyed, white-skinned face glowered at him like some fiend out of Mictlan. There was no time to think, only to act. Shikotenka's body reflexes took over and he swivelled sideways, letting the thrust slip past him, pulled his dagger from its sheath with his right hand, grasped the shaft of the lance firmly in his left and continued to swivel, accelerated the turn, extended his left hand with a sudden jerk, sensed the resistance and heard the harsh cry of the man holding on at the other end, felt the hot breath of the deer on his head, swept the lance tip sharply down, and suddenly found himself exactly where he wanted to be. He stabbed rapidly right to left across his own body, buried his dagger to the hilt four times – *tac! tac! tac! tac!* – in the deer's neck, pulled the rider out of his seat and brought him crashing to the ground. With a snarl of pure joy, Shikotenka fell on the man and, seeing his upper body was heavily armoured, slashed open his right leg from knee to groin, opened the big artery there and released a rush of bright blood. Knowing he would be dead within minutes, Shikotenka leapt to his feet, saw with satisfaction that the deer too had collapsed, and was bleeding out, and stalked off in search of other prey.

When Cortés saw Pedro de Moran and his horse both brutally slaughtered by a lean, muscular savage, he immediately disengaged his remaining cavalry and withdrew them three hundred paces downslope to where they'd left Olid. The loss of not just one but two of their precious – and presently irreplaceable – mounts was a grievous and unexpected blow; he needed to preserve the remaining horses and their riders. Olid was on his feet now, so it seemed he had at least not suffered a broken leg, which might have put him out of action for several months. But Velázquez de Léon had a deep cut in his forearm and his unbarded horse had been speared through its shoulder, Morla had taken a spear in the muscle of his thigh, and his horse – also unbarded – had sword cuts to its rump and withers. Davila had been stabbed through his boot, and Moran was dead! Quite a tally for a skirmish with a band of primitives. Only Alvarado, Sandoval and Cortés himself were uninjured, but all three of their horses, though barded, had cuts about their lower legs and had only escaped hamstringing by a miracle.

The Indians had taken heavy losses, too, with a dozen men killed in the first clash, ten more in the second, and at least a further ten suffering lance and sword wounds that were more or less debilitating. The plain truth was, however, that as many as twenty-five were either completely uninjured or still sufficiently able-bodied to brandish their weapons, shout threats and begin a hostile advance on the Spaniards, rapidly closing the distance from three hundred to less than two hundred paces.

Cortés could not contemplate leaving the field, though the horses would see them clear in moments. To run, even from this little battle, even as a prelude to a larger attack with his whole force, would signal cowardice and bring disaster in its wake. The Mexica would hear that the feared cavalry of the Spaniards was far from invincible against a determined foe, while the formidable Tlascalans would gain heart and meet any further attempt to penetrate their territory with even higher morale and even more martial valour than they'd shown already. He made some quick calculations. Though it had felt like only moments, the pursuit and the two engagements here had consumed the best part of an hour, which meant the infantry, proceeding at the fast march he'd ordered, should now be only two miles behind them – a distance that a horse at full gallop could cover in less than five minutes. 'Davila!' he barked. 'Your horse is in the best shape. Ride like the wind back to the army, bring the rest of the cavalry up to reinforce us at once and order the infantry to come on at the double.'

Davila nodded, threw his lance to Morla, who'd lost his own in the last affray, wheeled his mount and was gone.

Cortés was calculating again. Five minutes there, a few minutes to make things clear and five minutes back with the other eight cavalry – it meant they should be reinforced within fifteen minutes. The foot soldiers would require a little longer to cover the two miles but, even so, if they hurried, they would be here in thirty to forty minutes. Meanwhile, with Moran and two mounts dead, and Davila temporarily out of the picture, Cortés had just five men on horseback and one – Olid – on the ground, to see off the howling mob of Indians who had now broken into a run and were closing rapidly.

'Gentlemen,' he said. 'Hold your lances short, aim them at the enemy's faces as we break through the ranks and give repeated thrusts. If your lance is seized, use all your strength and put spurs to your horse; then the leverage of the shaft beneath your arm and the headlong rush of the horse should let you tear your lance free or drag the Indian along.

Above all keep moving. Charge and withdraw, charge and withdraw. Don't let them swarm you . . .'

He was already at full gallop, Sandoval and Velázquez de Léon to his left, Alvarado and Morla to his right, when he saw a great mass of armed men, their heads dressed with wild plumes, pour over the top of the western ridge half a mile away and surge in ordered ranks down the slope towards them.

A man on horseback came galloping out of the west, the dazzle of the afternoon sun at first making him hard to recognise. 'It's Davila,' said Díaz, shading his eyes. 'He's whipping all colours of shit out of that horse. Looks like trouble to me.'

Moments later, the cavalryman reined in before the army. His mount was lathered. His own right foot had been pierced through his boot by some weapon and was dripping blood. 'All the horse!' he yelled. 'With me now! Cortés is in danger. Infantry follow our tracks as fast as you can. Two miles to the west.'

He was already wheeling his mount, the eight remaining riders mustering around him, when Ordaz, whom Cortés had entrusted with command of the infantry as he had done at Potonchan, shouted: 'What are we dealing with?'

'Scouts,' Davila replied. 'Maybe thirty of them still alive when I left the field. But they're not like any Indians we've ever fought. Killed two of our horses already. If there's a whole army like that, they won't be easy to beat.' He called for and was given a new lance and led the cavalry west at a gallop.

Assigning Mibiercas and La Serna as his deputies, Ordaz gave Díaz command of a vanguard of two hundred Spaniards, including thirty musketeers and thirty archers, supported by all the Totonac warriors. 'You'd better take Malinal with you as well,' Ordaz said, 'in case there's talking to do. And make haste – if the enemy have scouts out, their army won't be far behind. I'll follow with the rest of the foot and the dogs, but the artillery's going to slow us down.'

Díaz set off at once, urging his men forward at a pace faster than a forced march, almost a run. It was a risk, for he must not exhaust them to the point where they'd be unable to fight, but Ordaz was right

369

– scouts meant an army and there wasn't a moment to lose. Malinal, he was pleased to see, kept up without difficulty, her face serious and intent.

'Do you have a weapon?' Díaz asked as she strode along beside him.

She pointed at her mouth: 'Speech is my weapon,' she said.

He smiled, realising – as he had a hundred times before – how much he liked her. She was a great beauty, which some might say was enough in itself, but she was also tough and smart – the speed with which she was learning Castilian was remarkable – and, like a good soldier, she never complained. She was Cortés's woman, of course, and therefore beyond his reach, but that didn't stop Díaz admiring her from afar. He felt annoyed the caudillo had not thought to arm her.

'You should have something more than your tongue to defend yourself with,' he said, and on impulse he took his pack from his back as they marched, found the short stiletto he kept hidden there and passed it to her.

It was a fine weapon. She pulled its narrow blade from its sheath and examined it with a look of almost childlike wonder.

'For stabbing,' Díaz explained. He made a punching gesture with his fist. 'Thrust that into a man's gut and down he goes.'

'Thank you,' she said. She gripped the hilt and mimicked his punch. 'Down he goes!'

'That's right.' He fished in his pack again and found a leather thong. 'Attach the sheath to this, loop it round your neck and keep it out of sight until you need it.'

He looked away, surprised to find he was blushing as she followed his instructions. An awkward silence fell between them, and they hurried on, but moments later, carried on the light breeze, they heard distant shouts and then the unmistakable clash of battle. 'Stay behind the men,' Díaz warned. 'You're too valuable to lose to some skirmisher.'

Malinal grinned and made the punching gesture again. 'If skirmisher comes,' she said as she fell back, 'down he goes!'

Summoning La Serna and Mibiercas to join him, Díaz scrambled up a long gentle slope to the top of a ridge and saw a second, higher ridge about a mile ahead to the west. In the valley between the two, Cortés and all the cavalry were heavily engaged with a large force of Indians. So much for thirty scouts, then! This was an army, as Díaz had feared.

'How many do you reckon?' he asked.

'Three thousand?' guessed La Serna.

'More than that,' said Mibiercas. 'Four thousand, maybe five.'

Cortés's strategy was clear enough. The horsemen repeatedly charged the enemy, killing with their lances, withdrawing and charging again. Fourteen riders against so many seemed like lunatic odds, yet the truth was that everything about this campaign was a sort of romantic madness straight from the pages of *Amadis de Gaula*, where the few, if they had courage enough, could indeed sometimes prevail against the many. There was even, Díaz thought, a fairy-tale princess in the form of Malinal.

He waved his men forward, signalling that they should spread out along the ridge, the Spaniards in two squares of a hundred each, the thousand Totonacs behind. The odds were much better than at Potonchan but, unlike the Maya, this new enemy fought in disciplined companies, holding their lines, none of them showing the slightest inclination to panic, break and run.

Díaz called for his trumpeter. 'Sound the advance,' he said, 'and make it loud. I want the caudillo to know we're here.'

As the first notes rang out, he drew his sword. 'Santiago and at them!' he yelled and, with Mibiercas and La Serna running at his side, he led the way down the slope.

Shikotenka wasn't surprised to see more white men appear at the top of the ridge. He'd been expecting them and had mustered the biggest army Tlascala had ever seen to annihilate them.

But not today. Today was just a skirmish to test their strength, get a clear idea of their skills, their weapons and their fighting spirit, and lull them into a false sense of security. This was why he'd first confronted them with his fifty, luring them on, and why, even now, he'd allowed only five thousand to come against them. In the end he would leave them the field, and let them think themselves the victors, but tomorrow he would bring them to battle against a hundred thousand warriors.

A horn sounded up on the ridge and the ranks of the white men and their cowardly Totonac allies surged down towards him. At the same time the deer riders, realising they were reinforced, disengaged, drew back onto the lower slopes of the eastern side of the valley and waited for their troops to join them.

Shikotenka barked orders that were relayed along the Tlascalan fighting line. 'Hold! Hold here! Form up. Do not attack until you see the signal.' He and his men occupied the lower slopes of the western side of the valley and were separated from the deer riders by no more than a hundred paces. If the other white men had fire-serpents, he thought, they would surely use them now.

'Hold!' he yelled again. 'Whatever they put against us, hold! If any man goes in before the signal, he dies under my knife.'

Ilhuicamina and Chipahua passed the command along. Tree stood by Shikotenka's side, gripping his *macuahuitl* two-handed and glowering at the enemy.

'What in hell do they think they're doing?' asked Alvarado. He sat loosely in the saddle of Bucephalus, his bloodied lance resting on his shoulder.

A hundred paces away, across the bottom of the valley, if this hollow in the moor could be dignified with the term 'valley', the Tlascalans were simply standing their ground, five thousand of them in straight ranks of two hundred – rank after rank, massed all the way up the western side of the valley, almost as far as the ridge. Only moments before, the air had been filled with their wild whoops and war cries, but now they were utterly and completely – almost oppressively – silent.

'I'd say they're challenging us,' hazarded Cortés.

Alvarado scoffed: 'Challenging us to what?'

'To do our worst?'

'Why would they do that?'

'Find out what we're made of. Find out what we can do. It's a reasonable tactic, actually.'

'Well in that case,' said Alvarado, 'why don't we show them?'

'I want to try to parlay first.' Cortés turned to Díaz who was standing close. 'I hope Malinal's with you, not following on behind with Ordaz?'

'She's here.'

'Well, bring her forward. I've got a job for her.'

Moments later, Malinal was at Cortés's stirrup, looking up at him. Her face, Díaz saw, was radiant with some powerful emotion. Was it love? He felt a twinge of jealousy, but put it out of his mind.

Cortés nodded to her: 'Tell them we serve a great king who lives across the seas and we've come here in his name to seek their friendship. We seek their alliance in the war we will make against their enemy Moctezuma. Tell them we admire their long struggle against the tyrant and we've come to help them. Tell them our friendship will be greatly to their profit and that we will teach them and show them many wonderful things.'

While Malinal put this into Nahuatl, her voice ringing out across the valley, Cortés turned to Díaz. 'Are your musketeers and crossbowmen loaded and ready?'

'They are, Caudillo.'

'Pick the five best marksmen,' Cortés said, 'and have them take aim at whichever Indian replies to this. If it comes to a fight, they must make sure to kill him.'

'And the rest of the shooters?' Díaz asked as he strode towards the infantry, who were drawn up in two squares of a hundred men each.

'They should spread their fire widely. Do all the harm they can.'

Shikotenka had heard from Huicton of this Indian woman who spoke for the white men, but he didn't believe her honeyed words any more than he'd believed the Totonac emissaries. When she came to the end of her little speech, he was too angry to reply and turned to his standardbearer. 'Make the signal,' he said, and as the man raised the attack banner of wicker covered in iridescent quetzal plumes, he gave a great yell, drew his *macuahuitl* and charged the enemy line. Responding instantly, the five thousand battle-hardened Tlascalan warriors, who he'd picked to test the white men's strength that day, surged forward around him as one being, one blood, and he felt the air vibrate with the fury of their war cries and the ground tremble beneath his feet with the massed weight of their onslaught.

For a moment, as he closed the distance, there was surprise, even

373

shock, in the faces of the enemy. But only for a moment. Groups of them in each of the two defensive squares they'd formed were holding long objects to their shoulders, hollow metal tubes mounted on wood, and now smoke and flame belched forth from these, accompanied by a sound such as he had never heard before, an awful sound, a loud, popping, booming roar followed at once by an eerie, unsettling whirr as of a swarm of insects flying very fast. Something hot seared his ribs, something powerful that clutched at him and left the skin it had touched stinging as though he'd been whipped, sizzling as though he'd been branded, while men to his left, men to his right, men behind him were screaming, tumbling, skulls burst open, bodies broken, a mist of blood rising between them, and that hideous sound went on and on, echoing across the valley, reverberating off the ridges, swelling and multiplying as though it would never end.

'Fire-serpents,' he heard men whisper, 'weapons of the gods,' but even so they didn't break – they were Tlascalans! – and the first rank, with Shikotenka in its midst, flung itself against the two squares with a tremendous crash, as shields smashed against shields and swords against swords. The second rank followed and the third and the fourth, enveloping the enemy, surrounding them, battling to break through on all sides even as the deer riders reared and wheeled their animals, charging into the melee with war cries of their own, their vicious lances jabbing and thrusting, while the Totonac auxiliaries danced round the outside of the fray, spearing and cutting the throats of Tlascalans who already lay sprawled and gutted, piled up in groaning heaps.

Shikotenka hammered at the white men's shield wall, hacked at their snarling faces and armoured legs with his *macuahuitl* in his right hand and his dagger in his left, twisted, dodged and parried as the metal swords of their front rank darted out wickedly, and as huge spears held by men two or even three ranks back stabbed down at his neck and his head. The *macuahuitl* he'd taken from Guatemoc all those months before, and which he'd once thought so lethal, so perfect, seemed like a useless toy in his hands. Its obsidian blades shattered against the unyielding metal of the white men's bucklers, and once – only once – did he succeed in hooking his dagger past their defences and slashing open a bearded face.

Everywhere it was the same – brave Tlascalans uselessly assailing the bulwarks of the squares, which seemed as immovable and impenetrable as cliffs, and which yet bristled with fatal points and edges that cut men down like maize at harvest. Unlike Tree, Chipahua, Ilhuicamina, Shikotenka himself, and the rest of his squad, all of whom wore only sandals and loincloths for speed, many of the five thousand who'd come over the ridge to reinforce them carried wooden shields and wore wooden helmets and quilted cotton vests that could frustrate all but the hardest *macuahuitl* blows and stop flint-tipped arrows. Such devices had served Tlascalans well in battle for centuries but proved useless against the white men's metal blades, which cut through them as though they were paper, slicing to pieces the soft human flesh and bone within, while the Tlascalans' own weapons were miserably ineffective, with even their arrows and spears and fire-hardened *atlatl* darts bouncing off the helmets and armour of the foe.

Now, suddenly, men within the squares lifted their fire-serpents to their shoulders again, and some were holding those strange little bows like the one the Totonac emissaries had brought to Tlascala as a gift, and then the crashing, rolling thunder echoed out as it had before and a storm of death tore through the Tlascalan ranks.

Shikotenka could only watch as close friends from his own squad, who'd lived through the raid on Coaxoch's pavilion six months before, were now smashed down – Tlachinolli and Camaxtli, Milintica and Huitzlin, felled by the spears and the swords, the fire-serpents and arrows of the white men. With a great roar of fury, Tree was about to charge again, but Shikotenka held him back and ordered the standard-bearer, who'd stuck by him throughout, to signal the retreat.

Chapter Thirty-Four

Monday 30 August 1519 to Tuesday 7 September 1519

Discouraged by their losses, or perhaps by the timely appearance on the eastern ridge of Ordaz and the remainder of the conquistadors with the artillery and the baggage train, the Tlascalans abruptly disengaged, retreated up the side of the valley and streamed away westwards. Cortés watched them go, leaving the field in good order, and refrained from mounting a pursuit as he regrouped with Ordaz. The afternoon was already drawing on and the men and horses were tired after the sixteen-mile march from Xocotlan and the fight at the end of it.

A harder fight than he'd expected.

Taking a quick inventory, Cortés found that a dozen of the Totonac auxiliaries had died and thirty more had been injured in the hand-to-hand fighting. Things had gone better for the Spaniards within the protection of the squares. Happily there were no fatalities, but twenty-three had been injured, two seriously. Since the army had no oil to dress their wounds, he ordered the corpse of a stout Tlascalan butchered and his fat used instead.

Scouts reported no further hostile forces massing in the area so, after La Peña had finished doctoring the wounded, Cortés marched the army out of the valley in the tracks of the retreating Tlascalans and occupied a deserted village offering a good defensive position on an eminence overlooking a stream. The inhabitants had departed in haste, leaving behind more than a hundred small dogs bred for food, and these the Spaniards killed, cooked and ate, having first posted a strong guard.

They were not disturbed that night but, before the men lay down in their armour to sleep, there was much talk around the campfires of the military bearing and superb discipline of the Tlascalans, and Cortés sensed an undercurrent of fear. The Spaniards had driven off an army of five thousand, but what if ten or twenty times as many of these ferocious fighters were to be thrown against them?

Since the only answer to such concerns was action, Cortés had the troops under arms and on the march again before dawn the next morning, Tuesday 31 August. After less than a mile they came under attack, this time by a smaller force than the afternoon before – at most a thousand warriors, who burst out from behind a low hill and threw themselves furiously against the column, battered the shield walls for a few moments, fell back and then charged in again.

The assaults continued in this manner, never halting but greatly slowing the Spaniards' advance, goading and infuriating them with spears and arrows, assaulting their ears with the screech of conches and the beat of drums. After each onslaught, the enemy withdrew to cover in the broken rocky terrain and shadowed the column just out of musket range for a few hundred paces before charging in again. Finally there came a frenzied and sustained offensive. Upwards of fifty Tlascalans were killed and the rest of the force fled in apparent disarray into rough, broken country fractured by gullies and ravines.

'No pursuit!' Cortés yelled, 'keep formation!' But it was useless. With all the fighting and killing, after two hours of constant provocation, the men's blood was up, and hundreds of them raced after the bolting Indians into a narrow defile, only to come under immediate attack from a force so immense its numbers could not be estimated. The squares quickly reformed but the terrain made it impossible to deploy the cavalry or artillery to good advantage. Cortés again found himself with no choice but to keep moving, with his little army surrounded on every side, smashing its way through the swarming ranks of the enemy by force of arms and will, deafened by hideous whistles and war cries and the loud insistent beat of drums.

'I see nothing but death for us,' Meco muttered to Malinal. 'We'll not get through this pass alive.'

'Don't fear,' she answered. 'The caudillo will lead us to safety.'

In the thick of the fighting, Cortés yelled a warning that went unheard as three of his cavaliers, Miguel de Lares, Juan Sedeno and

Jerónimo Alanis, charged a great mass of the enemy across a patch of open ground, only to falter and fail as hundreds of warriors rounded on them, laying hands on their horses. Somehow, slashing wildly with their broadswords, trampling their attackers beneath the hooves of their destriers, Lares and Alanis broke free, but Sedeno was not so lucky. His mare was pulled down under him by sheer weight of numbers and hacked to pieces by the Indians. He himself, though armoured, received so many wounds he was already half dead and being dragged away for sacrifice when Bernal Díaz and Francisco Mibiercas, at the head of a flying squad of twenty infantry, hewed a murderous path through the press of Indians and snatched him from his captors.

'Fucking cavalry,' complained Mibiercas as they surrounded the fallen mare, cut its girths so as not to leave the saddle behind and fought their way back to the shelter of the squares.

'Fucking cavalry,' Díaz agreed as Sedeno died in his arms. Eight of his squad had been injured – and all for what? A saddle!

Refusing to show the alarm he felt at the loss of another horse, and at the greater loss of the semi-supernatural status his cavalry had been accustomed to enjoy amongst the Indians, Cortés stayed mostly at the head of the column, riding repeated charges with Alvarado and Sandoval to clear space for the infantry to march through, but from time to time fighting his way back along the line of march to re-form and encourage the troops. 'If we fail now,' he cried, 'the cross of Christ can never be planted in this land. Forward, comrades! When was it ever known that a Castilian turned his back on a foe?'

Such words were simple enough but, in the din of battle, confronted by the choices of annihilation or victory, they seemed to touch the hearts and spirits of the men, and in this manner, careless of the personal risks he ran, Cortés finally shepherded the army through the canyons and ravines and out onto open ground. There the enormous numbers of Indians they faced, filling the plain ahead of them and sending up a great din, finally became clear. This was a far greater force than they had confronted at Potonchan – seventy thousand men at least, perhaps even a hundred thousand. But they were so many, and so close packed, a chaotic throng of helmets, weapons, banners, and brightly coloured plumes, that their very mass and bulk would now work against them, while the cavalry were at last on ground where they could serve their purpose, and the artillery, which the Tlascalans had not faced to date, could be deployed to devastating effect.

Some of the cannon had been left at Villa Rica, but Cortés still had two lombards and ten falconets with the baggage train, and had kept them all fully loaded with grapeshot, and well protected by infantry, throughout the morning's march. Now, using the cavalry to disrupt the enemy formations and open a space for manoeuvres, he formed his men into a single large defensive square, ordered the artillery forward, recalled the horsemen out of the line of fire and let loose a devastating salvo.

The whistling grapeshot from the dozen guns was a fatal storm that tore through the massed enemy, killed hundreds at a single blow, littered the ground with bleeding and shattered bodies and opened up wide, undefended gaps in their ranks. Through these gaps Cortés sent his cavalry, lances thrusting, broadswords swinging, cutting down the dazed and disoriented Indians in an orgy of killing, while Mesa's gun crews worked feverishly to reload. Then a signal from the trumpeter called the horsemen back and the guns roared again.

It was not as it had been at Potonchan. There was dismay amongst the foe but no panic – not even when Vendabal let the dogs loose amongst them. But little by little the conquistadors won through and the Tlascalans began to move off the battlefield in as good order as any trained and disciplined army of Europe.

Other than securing a few prisoners, Cortés ordered no pursuit, for a whole day had passed and his troops were so tired they could barely stand. He watched the enemy go with mixed feelings of vindication and admiration. It had been a close thing, but God and Saint Peter had given him victory again, as he had known they would.

An hour's march brought the army to a suitable haven in which to pass the night – a low hill crowned by a small stone temple, surmounted by a tall tower that seemed almost purpose-built for a sniper's nest. The place was named Tzompachtepetl, or 'the hill of Tzompach', according to the prisoners, and it appeared to have been deserted in great haste only moments before the arrival of the Spaniards. The temple had a bubbling spring in its courtyard and was surrounded by well-made outbuildings, all easily defensible. Cortés had the whole complex fortified and lookouts posted before the sun had fallen below the horizon, then sent men out to loot the neighbouring village of the same name. This was also deserted, but caged fowl and small dogs were found in sufficient numbers to give the army a modest dinner.

Again the men slept in their armour, fearing an attack, but none came and, after taking his turn at watch, in the small hours of the morning Cortés lay down with Malinal in the single-roomed building off the courtyard he had requisitioned as his headquarters. He had remained outwardly cheerful and optimistic all day, knowing any sign of doubt or weakness on his part would rapidly infect the whole army, but he saw no need to hide his true feelings from this woman, who had done so much to help him understand the Indian mind, and asked her frankly: 'Can we win? I came here confident we'd find allies and instead we face a determined, resourceful, disciplined enemy. They seem to have no fear of us and don't give credence to this nonsense about us being gods that works so well with Moctezuma.'

'I warned you not easy,' Malinal replied. 'Tlascalans are warriors, fierce and free. You must defeat them before they join you.'

'I've defeated them twice!'

'You made bleed,' she demurred, 'but did not defeat.'

'At this rate I wonder if I ever will. Three of the horses and that fool Sedeno killed in two days. Upwards of sixty injured. We can't go on taking such punishment for ever.'

'So maybe send prisoners with a peace message for Shikotenka?' Malinal suggested. 'Might work! I think his biggest fear is you are secret friend of Moctezuma. You need to show him that not true.'

Cortés's eyes were growing heavy. 'Very well,' he nodded, 'we will try.' Sleep swarmed over him like a hostile army and then at once he stood before a giant wall, a hundred feet high, made entirely of mother of pearl, surrounding a great city of spires and towers built on the sides of a hill. Set into the wall, and reaching to its full height, loomed an immense double gateway with a wicket door, before which stood a familiar, glowing figure that was at once human and more than human.

Cortés fell to his knees. 'Your Holiness,' he said.

He felt Saint Peter's huge, calloused, soldier's hand rest in his hair, a burst of radiance filled his eyes and a jolt of some tremendous power, like lightning, suffused his body.

'Welcome, my son,' said the saint.

Cortés looked up as that massive hand was lifted from his head. 'Am I at heaven's gate, Your Holiness?' he asked.

'Do you doubt it?'

'It is just that you brought me here before, Holy Father, but the gate seemed different.'

'Heaven has many gates,' said the saint, 'and I hold the keys to them all. The day will come when I will admit your soul to take its rest here. But you have much work to do first.'

'All these months, Holiness, I have been vigilant for God. I have thrown down the idols of the heathen as you instructed . . .'

'You have, my son, and heaven is pleased with you. But the task I chose you for will not be complete until the tyrant Moctezuma is laid low and the cross of Christ planted firmly in the heart of Tenochtitlan.'

'I work towards that, Holiness. Day by day I work towards it.'

'And you are working towards it here, amongst the heathens of Tlascala? Amongst these devil worshippers?'

'I hoped to make allies of them, Father, and bring them to Christ. I offered them words of peace but they rejected me.'

'They are a stiff-necked people.'

'Their resistance is fierce, Holiness. It seems I will be forced to defeat them utterly before they accept my friendship.'

'Then defeat them.'

'Such a defeat of so stubborn a people may not be accomplished on the battlefield alone. I will have to spread terror amongst them, lay waste their villages and homes and farms with fire and sword, before they bow their stiff necks to me.'

'Do it,' the saint urged. 'Do it, my son! You have the blessing of the Lord.'

'Women will die, Holiness. Children will die. Is this not a sin?'

'When you do the work of God there is no sin in it. You must punish the wicked ways of the Tlascalans and lay my vengeance upon

381

them. Only then will they hear your words of peace. Only then will they accept your mercy. But when that is accomplished, my son, remember what I told you once before. Move on with your army to the city called Cholula where I have prepared a great and terrible victory for you.'

The big hand was back on Cortés's head and, as he looked up into the saint's eyes, black as midnight, he saw reflected in them the fires of burning villages.

He awoke in the dark, calm, resolved, determined, and lay still for a few moments, listening to Malinal's soft breathing beside him.

He needed her for now. She was a good woman. She had been baptised.

But she was and always would be an Indian.

He stood and strapped on his sword.

While his forces had been occupying the hill of Tzompach the evening before, Cortés had climbed the temple tower and looked west into the setting sun at the countryside that lay beyond. Unlike the wild moorland and broken ravines they'd passed through to get here, it seemed rich and well populated, with numerous farms, abundant plantations of maize and maguey, and many villages – small and large – perched on high points above wooded slopes and green valleys.

Now, before dawn on the morning of Wednesday 1 September, he announced his intention to mount a reconnaissance in force and quickly assembled two hundred infantry, ten musketeers, ten crossbowmen, and five hundred Totonac auxiliaries, all armed to the teeth. So rapid was the muster, they were already marching down from the hill of Tzompach when the sun rose.

'What's the plan?' Alvarado asked him, riding at his side.

'You'll like it, Pedro,' Cortés replied. 'We're going to do some harm.'

An hour later, climbing silently up a forested slope, they reached a cleared hilltop occupied by a large village of perhaps five hundred wattle-and-daub huts. The few men in sight were old or infirm, the young and able-bodied having no doubt been conscripted into Shikotenka's army, but there were a great many women and children crouched around the cooking fires preparing breakfast.

Cortés levelled his lance. 'Kill them all,' he roared, as he spurred Molinero to a gallop.

They sacked and burned four villages that morning. Sandoval witnessed all the atrocities – feet and hands amputated, women raped and murdered, old men castrated, the noses and ears of children cut off – and although he did not participate himself, never once drawing his sword or bloodying his lance, there was nothing he could do to prevent the carnage.

By noon, knowing that Shikotenka must have been alerted by the plumes of smoke, Cortés led a forced march back to the camp at the hill of Tzompach. 'This morning's work too strong for your stomach?' he asked Sandoval.

'I didn't join your expedition to kill women and children, sir,' Sandoval replied formally, unable to bring himself to use the first-name terms they'd fallen into months ago. 'God will not forgive us for this.'

'Nonsense, man!' Cortés snapped. 'We've served God this morning and we'll be rewarded for it at the gates of heaven. We've caused some suffering – yes, I admit that. But by so doing we'll shorten this war and save thousands of lives.'

'So you're saying, with Señor Machiavelli of Florence, that the end justifies the means?'

Cortés smiled. '"Every prince should desire to be accounted merciful",' he quoted, '"not cruel; but a new prince cannot escape a name for cruelty, for he who quells disorder by a few signal examples will, in the end, be more merciful."'

'I've read *The Prince*, sir, as you obviously have,' Sandoval replied, 'but I can't agree with that philosophy. Only bad things come from bad things, and what we did today, sir, with all due respect, was a bad thing.'

'And is it not a bad thing when we load the lombards and the falconets with grapeshot and mow down five hundred men with a salvo? Is it not a bad thing when we slip the leashes of the war dogs and encourage them to feast on our enemies? Correct me if I'm wrong, but were not you, yourself, the first of us to use the dogs in your battle with the Maya when you went to find Aguilar? I don't think you hesitated then, when it came to saving your own life and the lives of your men, and I don't see why I should hesitate now.'

'But it's different, sir—'

'Look, stop calling me "sir", will you? We've been Hernán and Gonzalo long enough and I'd like it to stay that way, even if we disagree over policy.'

'Very well . . . Hernán. But it's still different. To kill men in the heat of battle is one thing. But to kill innocent women and children, to mutilate them, to rape them, to burn their villages and the crops in their fields – how can that be right? What outcome can possibly justify such wickedness?'

'I've told you. Peace! Peace soon. Peace now! An end to this brutal war with a violent and stiff-necked foe and an alliance that will make us strong enough to overthrow Moctezuma himself without further bloodshed. That's the outcome I seek.'

In the early afternoon, back within the fortifications at the hill of Tzompach, Cortés asked Malinal to select two of the prisoners to be used as messengers and bring them to him under guard.

Now they squatted before him in their Indian manner, eyes watchful, distrusting him, expecting violence. They both claimed to be minor chiefs, Malinal said, and had been confirmed as such by the others, so they would serve his purpose well.

'I'm releasing you,' he told them, 'to be messengers of peace to the courageous and honourable Shikotenka. You're to inform him – as our Totonac emissaries who he treated so badly have already done – that we are here in Tlascala to seek his friendship and make an alliance with him against the Mexica. He should not be misled because we have received hospitality from vassals of Moctezuma, for this means nothing. If that great fool wishes to feed and shelter us on our way to destroy him, why should we not accept? But destroy him we will, with or without the help of Tlascala, therefore it is surely better for Shikotenka to help us, and reap the spoils of our victory against his hated enemy, than hinder us and gain nothing. You have seen now what we can do; you have seen our power on the battlefield and you must know we mean what we say. So know this! We will come to the city of Tlascala

384

as friends to make peace, or we will come as warriors to vanquish you, but in the end it will all be the same. We will march on and we will destroy Moctezuma.'

It seemed that Shikotenka's war camp could not be far off because, two hours after nightfall, the messengers were back with his answer and repeated it exactly as he had given it to them. 'Shikotenka says this: "Come, white men, to the city where my father is. Come by all means! We will make peace with you there by filling ourselves with your flesh and honouring our gods with your hearts and blood".'

Cortés exchanged a glance with Malinal and Pepillo, who were again working together to render the translation into perfect Castilian. 'That's it?' he asked. 'That's all he has to say to us?'

'Not only that. Shikotenka said he plans to pay us a visit here tomorrow to give us a longer answer in person, and we will see what it is.'

'High and mighty language,' mused Cortés. 'Sounds like a threat.'

'Undoubtedly it is a threat.'

Resisting an instinct to cut out the messengers' tongues and return them to Shikotenka choking on their own blood, Cortés flattered them with mild words and ordered Pepillo to go to the baggage and bring them some strings of beads, which they accepted with smiles. The presents were theirs to keep, he told them, but they were to stay in the camp, for he intended to use them as messengers again.

The next day, Thursday 2 September, arousing a chorus of furious barks and howls from the dogs, Shikotenka came to Tzompach with a hundred thousand warriors. Their faces were painted with red bixa dye, which gave them, Sandoval thought, the look of devils.

Cortés would have ordered the cannon fired on them as soon as they came within range, had it not been for the fact that they were preceded by a long column of *tamanes* bearing bundles and baskets of food. 'Let them come forward,' he said. 'We'll see what this is all about', and the *tamanes* were allowed to wind their way up the hill. It soon became apparent that what they carried were hundreds of cooked turkeys together with baskets stuffed full of maize cakes. 'You see,' Cortés said triumphantly to Sandoval, 'our action yesterday worked. They want peace.'

But while the feast was being handed over, the huge warrior who had decapitated Olid's horse three days previously began to address the Indian ranks in booming Nahuatl and, as Malinal and Pepillo gave the translation, it became clear that no peace was being offered. 'What foolish and contemptible men these are,' the warrior roared with a dismissive gesture at the Spaniards, 'who threaten us without knowing us, who dare to enter our country without our permission and against our will. Let us not attack them too soon. Let them rest and eat the food we've sent them, for they are famished. We don't want anyone ever to say we defeated them just because they were hungry and tired. Only when they've filled their bellies will we attack them, but then we will eat them and in that way they'll repay us for our turkeys and cakes.'

Sandoval turned to Cortés. 'So much for peace,' he said. 'Do you still believe good things come from bad things?'

Thus far, while allowing Pepillo to wear his sword, Cortés had ordered him to remain with the baggage train, well protected by a mass of infantry, though his index finger was fully healed now and he was eager to fight. Even so, he'd not been entirely insulated from the action, and had been given an oversized cuirass to strap on and an ancient helm to protect him against the enemy spears and arrows that came raining in. Shrieking warriors had broken through the shield wall twice, but on each occasion they'd been struck down in moments by the guard and trampled to bloody pulp underfoot. They had got nowhere near Pepillo.

Today it looked as though he might be given a more active role to play. As the conquistadors prepared for the massive attack of the Tlascalan force, Bernal Díaz came to Pepillo bearing armour. 'Try this for size, instead of what you're wearing,' he said gruffly.

The padded lining of the cuirass he held out was heavily stained with dried blood. 'It was Sedeno's,' Díaz explained. 'He was about your height and he's got no use for it now. Try this too,' he added, handing over Sedeno's helm.

Pepillo strapped the armour on and the helm; both fitted him well. 'Thank you, Bernal!'

'But stay well back if you can. You've no experience in the line of battle and these Tlascalans are the very devil.'

Pepillo resolved that under no circumstance would he stay back – after all, he'd had no orders from the caudillo to say that he should – but he decided to do what he could to keep Melchior safe. Holding the dog by his leash, he sought out Malinal and asked her to look after him. 'Better you put him inside,' she said, pointing to an empty hut with a proper door. 'Maybe the caudillo need me any time.'

Pepillo nodded and, with some misgivings, closed Melchior away, blocking the door with a stone. Objecting to being shut in, the big lurcher barked indignantly and battered the door with his huge paws, but Pepillo was satisfied he wouldn't be able to break out. He looked over to the other dogs, straining at their leashes; they were in five packs of ten, evenly distributed around the low rubble wall, bristling with cannon, which the conquistadors had built to protect the summit of the hill. Amongst the handlers was Santisteban, who had been watching him and now gave him an evil glare.

All around the hill, their ranks stretching back miles in every direc-tion, the Indians were making a furious din but had still not attacked. Cortés had been watching them closely, even as the conquistadors made a hasty breakfast of the unexpected bounty of food. 'I've had enough of this,' he said. Pepillo saw his master summon Francisco de Mesa, the grey-haired chief of artillery.

'You're loaded with grapeshot?' Cortés asked.

'Loaded and ready, Caudillo.'

'Then fire on the bastards, Mesa, and may God save their souls.'

The first salvo, from all guns, did tremendous damage, but not to the tens of thousands of Indians clustered closest to the base of the hill; the incline was steep and the barrels of the falconets and the lombards could not be depressed sufficiently to be brought to bear on them. Further back in the packed enemy ranks, however, ragged gaps now appeared, a great shrieking and wailing filled the air and the nearest warriors, ululating and blowing conches, charged up the hill into a withering volley of musket and crossbow fire. Men fell in droves, fouling the feet of those around them, but still the mass of Indians came on and, before the cannon could be reloaded, they'd reached the perimeter wall where the conquistadors met them with swords, pikes and spears.

Seeing a gap in the line of defence, Pepillo rushed forward, drawing his sword and plunged its point into the naked stomach of a painted, grimacing savage. He was startled by the wet suck of guts as he withdrew, seeing the blood gush forth, having no time to feel shock or revulsion that he'd just killed his first man, already raising his blade to parry a blow aimed at his head by another warrior, relieved that his attacker was immediately struck down by a Spanish pike.

From then on, as wave after wave of Indians surged up to batter at the defences and were again and again thrown back, Pepillo lost all track of time, and seemed rather to be embedded within an endless nightmare present, surrounded by a sea of heaving bodies, his ears assaulted by the roar of cannons and muskets firing into the attacking throng at point-blank range, the clash of blades, the screams of the enemy, the battle cries of the Spaniards and the stinking sweet stench of blood and shit and piss. Many times obsidian-edged swords and spear points struck harmlessly against his armour, and thrice his unprotected arms and legs took cuts and stabs that he barely noticed, so intense was the press all around him, so urgent the need to stab and thrust, parry and block. Then, just when the Indian throng pressed closest and threatened to overwhelm the perimeter, the dogs were unleashed and tore into the attackers, a host of vengeful demons ripping out throats and bellies, feeding on spilled bowels, here worrying a man's face, there tearing open a thigh in a spout of arterial blood. And amongst them – how could this be? – Pepillo caught a brief glimpse of Melchior, his brindled body unprotected by armour, running in the pack with Jairo, the mastiff that had become his friend during the weeks he spent with the hounds.

The onslaught of the dogs, coinciding with a powerful massed salvo of grapeshot from the cannon, broke the attack on the stronghold of Tzompach and the Indian horde turned and fled down the slope of the hill towards the plain below.

'Santiago and at them!' shouted Cortés, leaping into Molinero's saddle and jumping the huge horse clean over the perimeter wall, closely followed by Alvarado, Sandoval, Davila, Velázquez de Léon and the other cavaliers. 'Santiago and at them,' bellowed the men all around Pepillo, as he found himself amongst a mass of yelling, cheering foot soldiers running full tilt after the cavalry and the retreating Indians, who they pursued far out onto the flat land below until suddenly they rallied and turned upon the Spaniards with savage glee.

Even as Pepillo searched desperately for Melchior and could not find him anywhere in the bewildering, heaving melee, he noticed how the character of the fight had changed and wondered if the Indian retreat had perhaps been a ruse. The cannon up on Tzompach could no longer be used for fear of hitting the Spaniards below, who now found themselves surrounded by numberless Indians with no barricade except their shields to protect them. Amongst the enemies were hundreds of slingers, who sent stones whizzing through the air, thick as hail. Men in full armour, their heads protected by steel helms, were struck down by lucky shots. Then there were the bowmen whose arrows, double-barbed and hardened in the fire, darkened the sky as they came pouring in, and again men fell and the ground underfoot sprouted with spent shafts, thick as corn waiting to be threshed.

While the Spaniards were thus discomfited, raising their shields to deflect the constant volleys of slingshots and arrows, disciplined bands of warriors charged in on them, trying their luck with spears and wooden broadswords, often seeking to lay hands on the defenders rather than to kill them immediately, no doubt intending to drag them off for sacrifice. But that tactic was their undoing, opening them up to the furious thrusts of the defenders, whose blades of good Toledo steel cut through primitive shields of wicker and hide to kill and maim indiscriminately. Pepillo lost count of the number of men who came at him, tugging at his hair, his shoulder, his arm, with almost suicidal bravery, only to fall to his sword and be replaced by another. One sweating savage, his eyes rolling, the teeth in his gaping mouth filed to sharp points, did succeed in jerking him off balance and pulling him out of the line of defenders but, even as he stumbled, he lunged with the blade Escalante had given him, driving its point home through the Indian's exposed armpit and deep into his chest, causing him to emit a high-pitched screech of pain – *aieee!* – and let go his hold long enough for Pepillo to jerk his blade free and scurry back into the Spanish square.

Four defensive squares of different sizes had formed, an automatic tactic for the conquistadors, the moment the pursuit of the Indians fleeing out onto the plain had transformed into a massed counter-attack. Meanwhile the cavalry ranged free, the thirteen remaining riders sometimes drawing up in line abreast and charging the Tlascalans with shocking effect, the ground shaking beneath the steel-shod hooves of the heavy destriers, sometimes wheeling round to defend the infantry squares where they came under heaviest pressure. As to the hounds, Vendabal and his assistants had lost all control of them, but the dogs knew what to do and darted amongst the enemy, protected by their own plate and mail and doing terrible harm. From time to time, Pepillo caught a glimpse of his Melchior, unarmoured, covered in blood – although whether it was his own or from those he tore and rent with his teeth was impossible to say. In the heat of battle, Melchior was fearless, and seemed to have turned feral, working with Jairo to hunt down and kill the enemy.

For a moment, despite shouts of warning from Cortés and the other captains, one of the squares was disrupted by a ferocious Tlascalan onslaught, five hundred men at least who fell upon the defenders and broke their shield wall, driving a wedge into their midst. It seemed all was lost, but a cavalry charge spearheaded by Cortés and Sandoval, and incredible feats of swordplay, allowed the defenders to repel the screaming throng from their midst and re-form their ranks.

The sun had begun to fall into the western half of the sky, and Pepillo was weary to his bones, dust clogging his nostrils, blood clotting and drying on his clothes, all the men around him in an equally exhausted and dishevelled state, their water bottles empty, the energy and even their courage flagging, when a further change began to come over the battle. It was not so much a single dramatic incident as something slow and evolving – a gradual, phased withdrawal of the Indian horde. For the past hour – with great difficulty because their crews were under constant attack – six of the falconets had been brought down from the hill and deployed amongst the infantry, firing grapeshot out of the squares into the massed ranks of the enemy, killing so many that they could not be numbered and their bodies lay thick on the ground.

It seemed it was this, more than any other single factor, that had turned the tide, and the Tlascalan withdrawal, while never becoming a rout, grew increasingly rapid, so much so that Vendabal issued an order to call the dogs back. There were still sizeable bands of Indians retreating from the field, however, so groups of soldiers were assigned to protect the handlers as they pulled the dogs away from corpses they were feasting on. Pepillo had just spotted Melchior – Hemes and Julian had him and Jairo by their collars – when a disciplined group of the enemy, perhaps fifty in number, who'd seemed moments before to be in full flight, isolated Santisteban and Vendabal from the others and swarmed around them, seemingly intent on carrying them off.

It all happened very fast. The big dour conquistador Guillen de Laso, who'd several times taken Cortés's side in meetings to decide the future of Villa Rica, was placed to Pepillo's right. 'Santiago and at them,' he roared, raising his battle-axe above his head and charging towards the skirmish with the rest of those who'd defended the square, Pepillo amongst them, streaming out behind him. At the same moment Melchior and Jairo tore themselves away from Hemes and Julian and raced to join the fray, Jairo taking the ankle of one of the Indians between his huge jaws, bringing the man down and leaping forward to seize his throat, while Melchior vanished into the throng around Vendabal and Santisteban, snarling and biting. Seconds later, Guillen de Laso threw himself into the fight and struck a series of huge blows with his axe, splitting men's heads like cords of wood. Pepillo was right behind him, the tip of his sword licking out. Several times he felt the shock of blows against his cuirass, but the steel saved him and he cut his way through to where Vendabal and Santisteban stood back to back, defending themselves with knives, both bleeding from multiple wounds, as Indians tried to grapple them and drag them off for sacrifice. But Melchior was amongst them, his jaws dripping gore, his teeth tearing their unprotected thighs and buttocks, oblivious to the daggers and spears that cut down at him as Pepillo rushed to his aid, striking two men dead before Guillen de Laso's whirling axe drove the remnants of the band onto the swords of the other conquistadors.

Suddenly silence fell, and Pepillo dropped to his knees beside Melchior, urgently checking his bloodied hide for wounds. Miraculously there were only a few deep cuts; most of the blood, as he'd hoped, must have come from others. 'Good boy!' Pepillo said. 'Good boy!' The big lurcher, who had seemed such a fiend moments before, no less savage than any of the other war dogs, now wagged his long tail with evident joy at the praise and nuzzled Pepillo's face.

When he looked up he found Santisteban watching him. There was something unfathomable in his eyes. Was it sadness? Anger? Guilt? Jealousy? Pepillo was about to ask, but before he could do so the older boy turned abruptly and walked away.

All the horses and sixty-three Spaniards had been injured in the day's fighting, two of the foot soldiers so severely that they perished from their wounds. Cortés had their bodies buried in a deep hole with a mass of earth heaped over them to disguise the smell of rotting flesh.

That night he dreamed of Saint Peter again, and before dawn the following morning, Friday 3 September, he led a hundred infantry and five hundred Totonac auxiliaries out to lay waste the country, sacking and burning ten villages.

The largest of these, built at the top of a hill around a tall pyramid surmounted by a temple, had more than three thousand houses. There were no warriors but the priests and women put up a fierce resistance when they realised they were all to be killed. Cortés himself was attacked by a screaming mother who clawed his face as he picked up her infant by its feet to dash its brains out against a stone wall. After disembowelling her with his dagger, he finished off the child, just one of hundreds who died in the same fashion at the hands of his men, and ordered all the priests thrown down from the top of the pyramid.

It was harsh, bloody, thankless work, but it had to be done. He was only glad he had not brought Sandoval along this morning to judge him. The man was a fine soldier, but seemed unable to grasp the finer points of the war of conquest in which they were engaged.

Cortés arrived back at Tzompach in the early afternoon, just ahead of a large enemy force that was repelled without further Spanish losses after five hours of fighting. Finally, in the evening, he called Pepillo and dictated some passages of a new letter he was preparing for King Carlos. 'I burnt ten villages,' he reported of the day's activities, 'in one of which there were more than three thousand houses. The inhabitants resisted us strongly but, as we were carrying the flag of the Cross and were fighting for our Faith and in the service of your Sacred Majesty in this your Royal enterprise, God gave us such a victory that we killed many of them without ourselves suffering any harm.'

After dismissing Pepillo for the night, Cortés summoned the two Tlascalans he had selected as messengers. 'Inform Shikotenka,' he told them through Malinal, 'that it is still our wish to treat the Tlascalans as brothers and we would never have harmed them if they themselves had not given us constant cause to do so. Inform Shikotenka that if he does not want to join us as our ally in our war against Moctezuma, and enjoy great glory and rich spoils, then we will not compel him. But in that case he must stand aside and not disturb us as we visit his capital and pass through his country on our way to Tenochtitlan. Tell him he must accept these terms, and accept them now, or we will kill all his people, leaving not a man, woman or child alive in the whole land of Tlascala.'

The messengers did not return, but the following afternoon, Saturday 4 September, fifty Tlascalans wearing robes woven from black feathers, accompanied by five elderly women and a long train of bearers carrying baskets, appeared at the foot of the hill of Tzompach. Malinal called down to them and asked them their business and they replied that they had brought greetings and gifts from Shikotenka.

On Cortés's command, she told them to come up, and a few moments later they were admitted within the fortifications. 'Who are the ones in black feathers?' Cortés whispered.

'Supposed to be priests,' Malinal replied, 'but too clean to be priests. More like spies trying to find where we weak. See how they looking around!'

It was true, Cortés thought. Their eyes darted and wheeled everywhere and many carried battle scars – surely not usual for priests. The leader of the delegation had at some point in his life been hit across the width of his face with an edged weapon, probably one of the native broadswords. He had a huge puckered scar running from cheek to cheek and a hideous prosthetic nose made from a mosaic of the green stone so favoured in these parts. Now he approached with the rest of the delegation, the old women and the train of bearers behind him, as Spanish soldiers armed with pikes, swords and battle-axes clustered round them and musketeers looked down from the temple tower.

'Welcome,' Cortés said through Malinal, who had now been joined by Pepillo. Cortés liked the way the pair worked together on the inter-preting task, so as to give him translations in fluent Castilian. 'Do you have a message for me from Shikotenka?'

'Sir,' answered the man with the false nose, 'he sends these five slaves for you.' He gestured to the miserable, cowering old women. 'If you are fierce enough to eat flesh and blood, eat them and we shall bring you more. If you are a benevolent god,' he pointed to three of the baskets, 'here are incense and feathers for you. If you are men,' the rest of the baskets, numbering more than a hundred, were indi-cated, 'take these fowl and bread and cherries.'

'Tell him,' Cortés said wearily, 'he should release those poor crones and that we are here on behalf of Christ and the king of Spain to teach him and all the people of this land not to sacrifice humans or eat human flesh any more. Tell him also that we are men of flesh and blood, precisely like him. Tell him this is the truth and that I have always told the Tlascalans the truth. Tell him that I wish to be their friend and that they should not be stubborn fools for they will only suffer greatly by more fighting. Have they not seen how many of them have died and how few of us. Do they really wish to continue in this way?'

'I will pass your words to my king,' said the man with the false nose, who gave his name as Ilhuicamina. 'Now, please, since you are men, eat of our bread, eat of our turkeys.'

While the baskets were unpacked, the delegates in the black cloaks wandered freely round the compound, looking everywhere, and Cortés, who seemed to have contracted a fever in the night, felt his mood suddenly darken. Malinal was right about these men. They were spies – he was sure of it now. They had entered his camp under the guise of friendship and reconciliation, offering food, seeming to consider his proposals, and all for the purpose of treachery! With a surge of anger he ordered their arrest and placed them under strong guard, selecting one of the youngest, who gave his name as Yolotl, for interrogation. Despite loud protests from Ilhuicamina, this youth was taken aside into a small closed building, off the courtyard, where Cortés had him savaged by two ferocious mastiffs and interrogated through Malinal. Very quickly he admitted he was indeed a spy. He had come here with all the others to see and note the weak points in the defences through which the army of Tlascala might most easily attack and destroy the Spaniards.

More of the delegates, subjected to the same treatment, told the same story adding, furthermore, that Shikotenka was bringing ten thousand of his crack troops to attack the hill of Tzompach this very night.

It was enough for Cortés. Without further talk, ignoring their appeals, he had all fifty lined up in front of a chopping block, summoned Guillen de Laso and ordered him to strike off their hands with his battle-axe. Many fainted as the blade came down and their bleeding stumps were cauterised with a bar of red-hot iron.

Ilhuicamina was the last to be brought struggling and kicking to the block. 'Why are you doing this to us?' he asked Cortés through Malinal. 'You speak to us of friendship, you speak to us of truth, you condemn our sacrifices and yet you cut off the hands of brave soldiers and upright citizens?'

'I do it,' Cortés fumed, 'because it is unworthy of brave soldiers and upright citizens to dress in the robes of priests and stoop to the odious stratagem of spying.'

Ilhuicamina did not cry out, did not say another word, when the axe fell. 'Tell Shikotenka we are ready to receive him in battle at any hour,' Cortés shouted, spraying spittle. 'By day or night, whenever he wishes to come, he will see what manner of men we Spaniards are.'

As the delegates left the hill of Tzompach, reeling with the shock of their injuries, their bearers and even the five old women who were to have been sacrificed hurried after them.

The priests, wizards and soothsayers of Tlascala had worked their witchcraft, consulted their charms, cast their lots and, at the end of it, told Shikotenka what he already knew: the white strangers were men, not *tueles* as the Totonacs claimed; they ate turkeys, dogs, bread and fruit; they spurned the flesh, hearts and blood of warriors they killed, and if he continued to fight them he would in the end defeat them. The sorcerers did, however, add one useful and novel piece of information – the formidable powers and great courage of the white men deserted them after sunset and in the night they had no strength at all.

Many Tlascalans disliked fighting at night when ghosts and vampires walked abroad, but Shikotenka had never shared this superstition and, many times, though not yet against the white men, had led his warriors into battle during the hours of darkness. He therefore resolved to make a night attack on the hill of Tzompach. Even if the wizards were wrong – highly likely in his view, since they were rarely right about anything – things could hardly go worse than in the catastrophic battles he'd already fought against the white men in daylight. To be sure, they were not gods, but they seemed to lead charmed lives: their weapons, particularly the large fire-serpents, made them nigh on invincible, and their coordination and tactics were superb. Why, therefore, should he not try to take them at night? At least the sorcerers' mutterings would give his warriors heart, and perhaps the spies he'd sent in this afternoon with food and other distractions would gain useful intelligence on the state of the white men's defences. So he'd assembled ten thousand of his best warriors in a valley just out of sight of the hill of Tzompach, and now, as the day wore on, he waited for Ilhuicamina to return and join the battle lines.

He did not have to wait long.

After sending the spies back to their master in a condition that would make any reasonable man think twice, Cortés mustered his entire force in the courtyard on the hill of Tzompach. 'Feast on the enemy's food,' he told them, indicating the generous heaps of turkeys and maize cakes. 'You'll need all your strength, for I have sure intelligence we'll be attacked tonight.'

'I thought these savages never fight in the dark,' growled Guillen de Laso, who stood leaning on the long haft of his axe.

'Don't speak of us as savages,' Malinal spoke up sharply, 'when you're savages yourselves.' She pointed to the bloodstained chopping block. 'To take men's hands like that. It's not right.'

'Tell her to hold her tongue, Don Hernán,' complained the axeman. 'I'll take no lessons from a woman, least of all a woman of her colour and race.'

'Shame on you, De Laso.' Bernal Díaz strode furiously towards him. 'She has more manly valour than half of us soldiers. Though she hears every day how the Indians will kill us and eat our flesh with chillies, and though she's seen us surrounded in recent battles and knows we're all wounded and sick, yet she betrays no weakness.'

It was as though, Cortés realised, Pandora's box had been opened, as the argument between the two men spilled over into a general debate about the conditions that the Spaniards faced here at Tzompach. To his extreme annoyance, the endlessly vacillating Alonso de Grado, who he'd so recently pardoned for joining the Velazquista rebellion, seized this opportunity to press for an immediate retreat to Villa Rica, where they might sail the one remaining ship to Cuba to summon help. 'We're all weary and wounded,' he grumbled, 'some of us with two, even three, wounds; some who will die soon if not properly tended to. We're all ragged and sick from disease and chills and the cold of the mountains – yourself included, Hernán, if I'm not mistaken. It's going to be a tough business to march to Tenochtitlan and defeat the Mexica with their huge armies when we cannot even defeat the Tlascalans, who the Totonacs told us would be our friends! It's true God has given us victory in each battle, great and small, since we left Cuba, and by his mercy has continued to support us while we've been amongst these fierce Tlascalans, but we ought not to tempt him so often, or our fate might be worse than that of Pedro Carbonero.'

'This is unexpected from you, Alonso,' Cortés said, and his one-time friend, who had fair skin and thin blond hair, flushed with embarrassment and looked as though he wished he had not spoken. Still, the barb had sunk home, and a murmur of discontent swelled across the courtyard – for Pedro Carbonero, fighting to expel the Moors from Spain a century before, had unwisely led his men deep into enemy territory where they'd been surrounded and killed. Since then his name

397

had been synonymous with any military venture that overextended itself and ended in disaster.

Cortés was deeply hurt by the insinuation. He considered ordering De Grado flogged, or even hanged for incitement to mutiny in a time of war, but relented when he sensed the mood of the camp might not support it. 'Gentlemen,' he said, 'this is no time for such talk. We face imminent attack and we must prepare for it.'

Sandoval, Alvarado, Davila and Díaz had moved to stand at his side, De Grado mumbled an apology and Guillen de Laso laid down his axe. For the moment, as the men fell upon the food the Indians had brought, soon laughing again as they filled their bellies, the insurrection was over.

'Look what they've done to me,' Ilhuicamina said, hunched with pain as he showed his bloodied stumps. 'I won't even be able to wash my arse, let alone fight again. I might as well be dead.'

Speechless with rage, Shikotenka wanted to rush at once up the hill of Tzompach and butcher everyone there, but that was something easier thought about than done, and all around he sensed a loss of heart amongst his men. The harrowing battles they'd fought in the previous days, their friends and brothers killed, the villages and towns the white men had destroyed, the women and children they had so cruelly murdered, the strange and awesome weapons they deployed, the blast of death unleashed by their fire-serpents, and now this wicked harvest of hands – it all added up to something hitherto unknown, a dark and horrifying threat, the very shape of which defied comprehension.

'Not yet,' said Tree, as though reading Shikotenka's thoughts. 'Wait until dark, as we planned, when the white men are weak – then we'll have our revenge.'

'You don't really believe that, do you – that they'll be weak?'

'I believe it,' said Tree, his big scarred face showing no expression, 'and besides, the night attack will take them by surprise – the way we took Coaxoch.'

Ilhuicamina groaned. 'No it won't! Some of our men were mauled by their wolves and gave away the plan. It's not a surprise. Not any more. We have to call it off.'

'Call it off?' said Shikotenka. 'Never. We wait until midnight, when the moon will be high. Then we go in.'

It was another disaster.

At first, as Shikotenka's warriors surrounded the hill of Tzompach and advanced slowly and stealthily up its sides towards the fortified temple, all went well. The compound was plunged in the deepest hush and it really did seem possible that the white men and their beasts slumbered, bereft of their powers, while lady moon reigned in the heavens.

Then, off on the left flank, a sandal slipped on the gravel and there was a sliding, scraping fall followed by a burst of whispers and abrupt silence. Everyone stopped, ears straining for any hint of a challenge from above, but nothing came, nothing, and after a moment, cautious and careful, they began to climb again.

It must be true, Shikotenka was thinking, *they must lose their powers after dark* – for if it wasn't true, then surely their wolves, which the Tlascalans had already observed to possess the most acute senses, would have heard that clumsy fool and raised the alarm?

Except, of course, they had heard, because exactly at that moment there came an urgent, choking, coughing roar – the by now all-too-familiar sound the wolves made when the white men unleashed them – and suddenly the slopes were alive with the streaking figures of the powerful beasts, their armour glinting in the moonlight, their fangs like rows of arrowheads set in their great, gaping mouths, and a shadowy form leapt from above and bore Shikotenka down on his back in a cascade of furious snarls. Shikotenka heard screams of terror and agony all around as he instinctively defended his face and felt the snapping teeth of the monster sink into his forearm and shake him violently, rending his flesh, spraying hot drool. He stabbed the creature once, twice, thrice in the flanks, but each time the blow glanced off its shining metal armour, leaving it unharmed, until Tree's huge hands appeared out of the dark, prised open its jaws, snapped its neck with a single mighty twist and smashed its limp body into the ground.

Shikotenka was scrambling to his feet when he heard the deep reverberating battle cry of the white men and saw a line of them, silhouetted by the moon, as they exploded out of the temple courtyard on the backs of their gigantic and unearthly deer. They came thundering down the hill like some unstoppable avalanche, and crashed into the already devastated and reeling Tlascalans, hacking and slashing with their glinting swords and forcing them back into the ranks below in a stumbling, chaotic, disordered retreat. Behind the riders came the foot soldiers, killing machines clothed in metal, wielding swords, maces and axes, grimly clubbing and impaling and dismembering men, turning the retreat into a shambles and the shambles into a panic-stricken, terrorised rout.

Shikotenka could only run – as Chipahua was running, as even Tree was running, as all his ten thousand men were running – in a blundering, careening flight from the slopes and out onto the open, moonlit plain below, where the silver figures of the riders, fast as the wind, were already amongst the fugitives, cutting them down. Obedient to a trumpet call from the fortress, they called off the chase and returned to the hill for a brief moment, while the fire-serpents roared and flames belched forth and death whistled amongst the Tlascalans – taking some, leaving others – and then came thundering back, remorseless, unbelievably fast, easily overhauling the fleetest runners, giving no quarter, butchering them without mercy.

And Shikotenka ran as they all ran, weaving away from the shining riders, dodging and ducking their flashing swords, and the bile of dishonour rose in his throat and tears of shame leapt from his eyes.

Cortés could not rest. Fever burned his brow, chills shook his body, fury churned in his heart.

In the slaughter of the night attack, hacking heads and necks until his arm grew weary, trampling the foe until blood drenched Molinero to his fetlocks, he had many times sensed the presence of a ghostly rider at his side, a rider with dark eyes and glowing skin and soldier's hands – Saint Peter himself, emerging from the world of dreams into the world of flesh to urge him on.

'Your work this night is not done,' the rider whispered when Cortés at last called off the chase. 'I have given you victory; now I would eat the fatted calf.'

'The fatted calf, Holiness?'

'There are towns nearby you have not yet attacked.'

It was true. On the previous days of raiding and burning, Cortés had seen and chosen to bypass three towns, one of them very large, all within five miles of the hill of Tzompach.

'Those towns,' continued Saint Peter, 'and all who dwell in them, are the fatted calf you must kill and offer up to me.'

Sudden understanding flooded through Cortés, energising and exciting him. An offering . . . yes . . . It was appropriate.

He stood in Molinero's stirrups and looked around. Bright moonlight flooded the plain where mobs of Totonac auxiliaries moved amongst the heaped bodies of the Tlascalan dead, looting their feathers and weapons. Alvarado, Velázquez de Léon, Davila and three other cavalrymen sat their horses in a line nearby. Two hundred infantry were forming up in their companies, making ready to return to camp.

'Our night's work is not done,' Cortés bellowed. 'I need a hundred volunteers to help me teach these Tlascalans a lesson they'll never forget.'

Alvarado trotted over on Bucephalus. 'Count me in, Hernán.'

'Me too,' said Davila, as the other riders followed suit and foot soldiers clustered close, eyes aflame with the lust of killing.

Much later that same day, Sunday 5 September, Cortés led the men back to the hill of Tzompach. The fatted calf had been killed and offered up in the greatest massacre of civilians Spanish forces had yet conducted in the New Lands. It had, he supposed, been a massacre of the innocents, but he felt no shame or regret, knowing he had done the work of God, commanded by Saint Peter himself, and there was no sin in it. Besides, good results had immediately been seen, results he hoped would bear fruit very soon. As he stripped off his blood-drenched armour and clothing, and bathed in the clear icy water of the temple spring, he took it as confirmation of the rightness of his policies that his fever had abated and he felt well and strong again.

Bubbling with renewed energy, he selected two more prisoners, asked Malinal to give them a strong and passionate message of peace for Shikotenka, and sent them off with the hope that at last his stiff-necked enemy might see sense. Then he summoned Pepillo and dictated the next section of his letter to King Carlos, describing the cowardly night attack by the Tlascalans, the valiant Spanish counterattack that had driven the savages back with heavy losses and, finally, though he chose not to share every detail, the massacre.

'In the hours before dawn,' he intoned as Pepillo's quill dipped and scratched, dipped and scratched, 'I attacked two towns where I killed many people, but I decided not to burn their houses as the fires could have warned other towns nearby. At sunrise I came upon another large town, this time with more than twenty thousand houses. As I took the inhabitants by surprise, they fled their houses unarmed, and the women and children ran naked through the streets, and I began to cause them some harm. When they realised there was no use in resisting, some men of rank came to me to implore me by signs not to harm them any more because they wanted to be my friends and vassals of Your Highnesses. They recognised that they were responsible for not having wanted to serve me, but assured me that thenceforth I would see how they would fulfil my commands made in the name of Your Majesty, and they would be your very loyal vassals. More than four thousand of them then came peacefully and they took me to a fountain where they served me a good meal and told me that the name of the town was Teocacingo. Afterwards I made them understand that they should go to Shikotenka, the Tlascalan Captain, and tell him of my mercy and urge him to accept my offers of peace. To this they readily assented and thus I left them pacified and returned to our camp . . .'

Malinal sat silently in the room while Cortés completed his dictation, and when Pepillo was gone and they were alone she asked: 'What words "some harm" mean, Hernán? How many you kill?'

Knowing she was still angered by his harsh treatment of the Tlascalan spies (would she have been happier if he'd executed them as they deserved?), he was tempted for a moment to be no more frank with her about the numbers than he had been with the king, but in the end he told her the truth. 'We killed about three thousand of them,' he said casually, 'before I accepted their surrender.'

'And if they no surrender, how many you kill then?'

'Many got away, but we'd rounded up more than ten thousand. I would have killed them all.'

'So this is your mercy they to tell Shikotenka? Cortés could have killed ten thousand but only killed three thousand?'

He narrowed his eyes. 'Yes. Do you have a problem with that?'

She sighed: 'When I came find you,' she said, 'I looking for god of peace; instead I found god of war.'

'I am a man,' he replied, 'as you know better than anyone else. And in this land steeped in blood and violence, I cannot be other than a man of war.'

He drew her to him. She was disappointed with him, he knew, but she did not resist.

The next day, Monday 6 September, despite the great things accomplished for God and the king in the past twenty-four hours, Cortés was disgusted to learn that De Grado's faction was still agitating for an immediate return to Villa Rica and ultimately to Cuba. There were open murmurings amongst growing numbers of the men that their lot was no better, in fact worse, than that of pack horses, 'Because when a beast has finished its day's work,' grumbled Guillen de Laso, 'its saddle is taken off and it is given food and rest, but we carry our arms and wear our sandals both by night and by day.'

Others complained incessantly about the scuttling of the ships, for the word was now generally out that their sinking had not been due to worms and rot but to holes drilled in their hulls on Cortés's orders. To be sure one vessel was left at Villa Rica, but it was only a caravel that could barely carry sixty men to Cuba. 'Neither the Romans, nor Alexander, nor any other famous captain,' said De Grado, renewing his criticism of Cortés, 'dared destroy their ships and attack vast populations and huge armies with so small a force as you have done. It's as though you are preparing for your own death, Hernán, and that of all of us. I beg you, preserve us by leading us back to Villa Rica, where we are at least amongst allies and won't suffer these unending attacks.'

Others – small knots and coteries of men who had plainly lost their nerve – were less forthright than De Grado, but their whispered complaints were noted and reported to Cortés by Alvarado and other loyal friends, though he told them to take no action. Passing one of the huts in the early afternoon to inspect the guard, however, Cortés himself heard the mutter of a group of soldiers talking in lowered, conspiratorial voices, and when he paused to listen he clearly heard one of them say: 'If our captain wants to make a fool of himself by going where he can't return and getting himself killed, let him do it alone; we shall not follow him. If he wants to come with us, well and good, but if he doesn't, let's just abandon him.'

Mutinous, ungrateful bastards, Cortés thought.

He could feel it in the wind. If he failed to act soon, his ability to command the men would unravel, and all he had worked for, every gain he had won against overwhelming odds, would be lost forever.

Shikotenka sensed that all he had worked for – every gain he had won against overwhelming odds to secure the freedom and independence of Tlascala – was about to be lost forever. Despite the humiliations the white men had heaped on him time after time in every battle they had fought, he was convinced that if he did not falter, did not lose heart, did not give ground, he would ultimately defeat them. They, too, were growing weak and demoralised after days of continuous fighting but, unlike the Tlascalans, they had no reserves and few reinforcements to fall back on, except the men in the distant fort on the coast near Huitztlan, no lands teeming with crops and game to feed them, and no populace – with the exception of the Totonacs, who counted for little – to support them. With hindsight it had been a boastful, stupid mistake to give them food, but he would not repeat that error. All he had to do now was keep the pressure up a little longer, perhaps even just one more big push would do it, and he could wipe them from the face of the earth.

The problem was that the mood of the Senate, never wholly in favour of the war, had turned decisively against him, and now his own father stood up, his wizened face set in a deep frown, to make the case for peace. 'Friends and brothers,' he began, 'you have seen how often these *tueles* who are in our country expecting to be attacked have sent us messengers asking us to make peace and saying they have come to help us and adopt us as brothers. You well know that we have attacked them again and again with all our strength, both by day and night, and have failed to conquer them, and that during these attacks they have killed many of our people, our kinsmen, sons and captains, Now they are asking us for peace once more and the Totonacs who have come in their company say that they are the enemies of Moctezuma and his Mexica, and have commanded the towns of the Totonac hills and Cempoala itself to pay him no more tribute. You cannot forget that the Mexica make war on us every year, and you know that our country is so beleaguered that we dare not leave it to find salt, and therefore eat none. Nor can we look for cotton, and so we have little cotton cloth. If our people even go out to seek it, few return alive. Those treacherous Mexica and their allies kill them or make them slaves. Now all who have fought against the *tueles* – even you, my son,' he said, looking directly at Shikotenka, 'have spoken of their bravery and their great skill as soldiers. It therefore seems to me we should be friends with them, and whether they are men or *tueles*, we should make them welcome and join with them in their war against Moctezuma.'

Shikotenka stood up. 'Father,' he said, 'I hear your words, but these men you say we should befriend are the same men who cut off the hands of fifty of our bravest warriors—'

'And those warriors,' interrupted Maxixcatzin angrily, 'were dressed as priests on your orders and entered the white men's camp as spies. That was unwise of you. That was inviting retribution. That put them in harm's way. We ourselves do not hesitate to execute the spies of other nations when we find them amongst us . . .'

'These men you say we should befriend,' Shikotenka continued, 'went at dawn to the town of Teocacingo and killed three thousand woman and children. Three thousand!'

'They might have killed more,' said Maxixcatzin. 'The elders of Teocacingo themselves have come to us and said that when they begged mercy it was given to them and the killing stopped. They have offered themselves as vassals to the leader of the white men, who they believe wants peace. They urge us to do the same—'

'In other words,' spat Shikotenka, 'they advise us to surrender our dignity and our honour and live like dogs rather than see our houses destroyed and our women and children killed.'

'You are wrong!' exclaimed his father. 'Your pride prevents you from seeing the truth.'

Shikotenka bowed: 'Pray then tell me, honoured father, what is the truth?'

'The truth is that thousands of our women and children – in numbers far greater than the white men have killed – are seized every year by the armies of Moctezuma for sacrifice on the altar of Hummingbird. The truth is that we live lives of constant oppression and terror, and must fight for our liberty every day of the year, draining our wealth and our blood to keep Moctezuma at bay. The truth is that peace and a military alliance with the white men offers us the chance, for the first time in our history, to defeat the Mexica and be rid of them for ever – and that, my son, will not be to live like dogs but rather to be a free people, a truly free people, as we have never been before.'

The debate went on throughout the day and far into the night as Shikotenka fought to convince the older chiefs of the appalling dangers that would follow from making peace with the white men and marching at their side against Moctezuma. No matter how attractive the prospect of defeating the Mexica might be, he believed that in the end Tlascala would only substitute a greater for a lesser evil, and that miseries such as the land had never before known would descend upon it and all its people. Far from the dawn of a new age of light and liberty that his father and Maxixcatzin foresaw, Shikotenka knew in his heart and his bones that the peace they sought would mark the start of an epoch of darkness and slavery in which the Tzitzimime, the monsters of twilight, would fall from the sky, bringing ruin in their wake.

Detailing Totonac auxiliaries to stand guard, Cortés called a muster of all his troops at 8 a.m. on Tuesday 7 September. They met out in the open in the courtyard of the fortified temple on the hill of Tzompach under a bright morning sky. Cortés had slept well and felt rested and refreshed. He told the men to be at their ease and sit down: he had something to say to them and would like them to listen well.

'Gentlemen and friends,' he began, 'I chose you as my companions and you chose me as your captain, for the service of God and the increase of His Holy Faith, and also for the service of our king, and even for our own profit. I, as you have observed, have not failed or offended you; nor, indeed, have you done so to me, up to this point. Now, however, I sense a weakening among some of you, and little taste to finish this war we have on our hands, a war which – with the help of God – we have now concluded—'

At this De Grado, who was truly asking for a good flogging, had the temerity to interrupt, saying there was no evidence whatsoever the war was concluded. True Shikotenka had not launched any assault yesterday, after the failure of his night attack, but this was most likely because the formidable Tlascalan leader was collecting his forces for another immense battle. 'In my opinion,' De Grado concluded, 'we should not stay for that battle. Let us leave now, for Villa Rica, while our way is still uncontested. We can take shelter there amongst our allies the Totonacs, until we can all be brought safe back to Cuba.' There was a murmur of support. Even Ordaz and Velázquez de Léon, whose rebellious spirits Cortés thought he had quashed for ever with the hanging of Juan Escudero, seemed to be edging to De Grado's side, though they had not yet spoken out openly in his favour.

'You are misinformed, Alonso,' Cortés told De Grado. 'If Shikotenka and his captains haven't returned, I'd say it's because they're afraid to do so. We inflicted great losses on them in the last battles and they can't reassemble their followers after such massive defeats. I trust in God and our advocate Saint Peter that the war in this province is indeed over, but even if I'm wrong and we must fight the Tlascalans again, it would still be an error – a fatal error, I say – to retreat as you advise. Do you imagine if we turn back now we'll be allowed to disport ourselves in idleness and sloth amongst the Totonacs while we wait for sufficient ships to come out from Cuba to bring us all to safety? Far from it! I tell you, Alonso, if our allies who at present hold us to be gods and idols were to see us return to their lands too faint-hearted to visit Tenochtitlan, they would consider us cowards and weaklings and would rise up against us too. Since we told them to pay no more tribute to Moctezuma, they would expect him to send his Mexica armies not only to extort the tribute and make war on them, but also to compel them to attack us – which, in order to avoid destruction and out of their great fear of the Mexica, they would certainly do. So where you expect friends, I say we will find enemies. And what would the great Moctezuma say on hearing we had retreated? That our whole expedition was a childish joke? What would he think of our speeches and messages to him? So, gentlemen, if one course is bad, the other is worse, and I say it is better to press on to Tlaxcala and thence to Tenochtitlan, overcoming all obstacles with the help of Saint Peter who gives us the strength of many. It is clearly true that wars destroy men and horses, and that we only sometimes eat well – I don't deny it! We didn't come here to take our ease, however, but to fight when the opportunity offers. Therefore I pray you, gentlemen, kindly behave like gentlemen. From now on, keep the island of Cuba and what you've left there out of your thoughts and try to act, as you have done hitherto, like brave soldiers . . .'

Cortés paused to let what he had said sink in; in the silence Bernal Díaz – a good man, one of the best! – raised his voice. 'Captain, don't trouble yourself a moment longer with the idle chatter of doubters and fault-finders.' He glared pointedly at De Grado, who shuffled uncomfortably. 'Don't listen to their tales! I speak for the majority, brave and loyal soldiers all, and with God's help we're ready to act together to do what's right.'

'Thank you, Bernal,' said Cortés, meaning it, and a ragged cheer followed, quickly spreading through the crowd in the courtyard, gaining strength and volume. 'Thank you all.' He looked round and, as the cheering subsided, he drove home his advantage. 'From here to Tenochtitlan, where resides Moctezuma, of whose great riches and possessions you have heard tell, is less than a hundred miles – ' another cheer – 'and most of our journey thither is behind us, as you know. If we arrive there, as I trust in Our Lord God we shall, not only shall we win for our emperor and our king a country naturally rich, but a vast domain and infinite vassals, and for ourselves great wealth in gold, silver, precious stones, pearls and other jewels.'

Cortés paused again. The men were lapping it up now, daydreaming of treasure. 'All that aside,' he continued, 'we shall win the greatest honour and glory that were ever won up to this time, not only by our own nation but by any other. The greater the king we seek, the wider the land, the more numerous the enemy, so much the greater will be our glory – "the more the Moors, the greater the spoils", as the old saying has it. Besides, we are obliged to exalt and increase our Holy Catholic Faith, which we undertook to do like good Christians, uprooting idolatry, that great blasphemy to our God, and abolishing the abomination of human sacrifice and the eating of human flesh – ' a glance at Malinal – 'which is so contrary to nature and yet so common here.'

Once more Cortés's eyes ranged across the men. 'So then have no fear,' he concluded, 'and do not doubt our victory. You vanquished the Maya at Potonchan, and in these last days you vanquished a hundred thousand Tlascalans, who are reputed to be fire-eaters. With the help of God, and your own strength, you will also vanquish the remaining Tlascalans, who cannot be many, as well as the Mexica, who are no better than they, if you will be strong and follow me.'

As another cheer rang out, the dogs began to bark and howl; one or two of them at first, but soon the whole pack.

Up on the fortified walls of the compound, the Totonac auxiliaries were pointing out towards the plain, jabbering fearfully amongst themselves.

Then the Spaniards in the courtyard began to hear what the dogs had heard, carried far on the clear mountain air – the steady tramp, tramp, tramp of marching feet. As one man, they rushed to the barricades to see the whole vast army of Tlascala on the move towards them, bright with its plumes and banners, bold with its standards and weapons, not decimated in the fighting, but somehow reinforced to its original strength, a hundred thousand men painted for war, ready for battle and less than a mile away.

'Artillery!' Cortés shouted. 'Artillery!' But Mesa was already racing his gun crews into position, spinning the cranks under the huge barrels of the lombards.

De Grado sidled up to Cortés and shaded his eyes, looking out at the numberless ranks of approaching warriors. 'Vanquished these fire-eaters, have we?' he sneered.

Chapter Thirty-Five

Tuesday 7 September 1519

The guard's cruel eyes and harsh face brooked no compromise. 'You go this way,' he barked at the child as he wrestled her from her mother's arms. The mother resisted, tried to snatch her daughter back. 'And you go that way,' snarled the guard. He gave the woman a shove, sending her stumbling, and followed up with a kick to her buttocks that stretched her out face down on the ground.

They were at the edge of a crowd of at least two hundred women and girls amongst which many other guards, some of them women themselves, were also at work, separating children and young teenagers from their elders. Shielded by invisibility, harder to catch than the morning air, Tozi had been amongst them for an hour, watching and listening, trying to work out what it was all about. The crude categories of separation that were being applied were intended to put virgins on one side and sexually active women on the other. Further investigation of the members of both groups was then carried out, and finally those confirmed to be virgins – the great majority being children under twelve years of age – were led off across the plaza to the women's fattening pen. During the seven hellish months that Tozi had spent in the same pen, it had contained females of all ages and sexual status, but now it was filled exclusively with young, virgin girls.

Nor was it the only pen re-dedicated to this very specific purpose. Tozi had acquired a further alarming piece of information in the past hour: two of the four pens on the other side of the plaza, which had previously held only male prisoners, had been emptied of their former inmates and now also housed young girls. Adding all three together, she estimated close to six thousand virgins must presently be imprisoned, and awaiting sacrifice, around the plaza.

The child who had just been separated from her mother looked to be about eight years old. She had a sweet, innocent, serious face. 'No!' her mother screamed as they were forced further apart. 'No! She can't care for herself. She's simple. She needs me! For pity's sake let me stay with her.' But the guards were pitiless and the mother was beaten again and dragged away still crying out, 'No! No! Miahuatl. Oh Miahuatl.'

So . . . the girl's name was Miahuatl. Unseen, invulnerable, Tozi fell into step beside her as she was moved on with a dozen other children of about her age into the larger group, whose private parts were being exposed and inspected, like fruits at the market, by a coven of toothless crones.

How long had this been going on?

Perhaps as long, Tozi realised, as she had been away from Tenochtitlan – and she had been away for a very great while. Except for the past thirty-five days, she had not kept an exact count, but she knew it had to be close to a hundred and twenty days since Acopol had seen through her invisibility and driven her in terror from Moctezuma's palace, and close to one hundred and ten days since she had last attempted to penetrate the palace and been driven back by the sorcerer's warding spells. Afterwards she had succeeded in her magical attack on Moctezuma during the summer solstice festival at the pyramids of Teotihuacan – even that was now almost eighty days in the past – then continued the quest for Aztlán and the Caves of Chicomoztoc that Huicton had sent her on, telling her to seek out the visions that would prepare her to confront Acopol again.

Well, there had been no shortage of visions.

In the desert, twenty days' walk north of Teotihuacan, while mortally stricken by the snake bite, she had left her body and wandered in spirit through a mystic labyrinth, where she met a being dressed in red, a being in the form of a woman whose face she never saw but who told her she had found Aztlán and the Caves. All that had occurred in the realm of vision, while she drew close to death in the physical world, and she would certainly have died, and never returned, had she not been rescued in the desert by a group of Huichol medicine men, rightly known as *mara'kate* – shaman-priests – who restarted her heart, brought her spirit back into her body and took her under their care. With them she had travelled for eight further days through the hostile and dangerous Chichemec badlands on what they called their 'deer hunt', which was in reality an expedition to gather a year's supply of *hikuri*, the vision-inducing cactus that the Mexica knew as *peyotl* and that the Huichol symbolised as a deer.

'Why a deer?' Tozi had asked.

'Because,' the *mara'kate* replied, 'deer was the magical animal that gave *hikuri* to our first forefathers on their first hunt in the long ago.' And, even today, they explained, their strategy was to watch for the descent of the deer from the heavens and mark the point where it alighted on earth 'for there, and there only, we will find *hikuri*.'

All this had sounded like so much foolishness, and Tozi might have laughed at the three wizened elders, had it not been for the fact that they, like her, knew how to work the spell of invisibility. They had used it, effortlessly casting the net wide enough to hide her as well as themselves, when a large band of Chichemec nomads had passed near their camping place the morning after they'd brought her back to life. Subsequently, as they led her through the desert, stopping here and there to gather *hikuri* buttons, they'd been obliged to deploy the spell many more times, for the Chichemec were in a boiling turmoil, ranging far and wide on the war path, and frequently threatened to discover them.

However, it was not their command of powers similar to her own that had persuaded Tozi to stay with the Huichol, but their story of a prophecy that spoke of her and of Acopol. She also instinctively liked and trusted the three *mara'kate*, whose names were Irepani, meaning 'Founder', Taiyari meaning 'Our heart', and Nakawey, meaning 'Owner of the stars and water'. It was Nakawey who served as her interlocutor throughout the time she spent with them, for the others spoke no Nahuatl, but she noticed he consulted with them on almost every point before communicating with her, with the result that their conversations were often frustratingly long and convoluted.

The prophecy itself seemed simple enough: 'In the time of darkness will appear the harbinger of the light. She will fight against the evil

412

one for the future of the world. By these signs you shall recognise her. She will be an orphan born of Aztlán. She will be a witch and the daughter of a witch. She will be a protector of children. She will be offered as a sacrifice to he who stands at the left hand of the sun, but she will escape this doom.'

'Have you escaped sacrifice?' Nakawey had asked at this point. Tozi confessed that she had been consecrated as a victim of Hummingbird – whose name Huitzilopochtli meant 'Hummingbird at the left hand of the sun' – and that she had indeed escaped sacrifice.

Nakawey continued to recite the prophecy. 'She will be tested in battle', he said with a knowing nod, 'against one who shall be named Acopol, a man who is not a man, a sorcerer whose power comes directly from the evil one.'

'From Hummingbird?' Tozi asked.

'Yes, child. Acopol has sold his soul to Hummingbird in return for great power, and we have seen the result this past year amongst the Chichemecs, who he has driven to madness. At his urging they, who were once wild and free, now offer themselves as soldiers in Moctezuma's armies; at his urging they make war upon each other, tribe upon tribe; at his urging they eat the flesh of their own children; at his urging they have even ranged up into the sierras, seeking out the villages of the Huichol to take victims from us.'

Tozi did not tell the *mara'kate* that she, too, had received an increase of her powers from Hummingbird. It was none of their business, was it? And besides, she would only use what she'd been given for good purposes – to serve the god of peace Quetzalcoatl – and never, ever for evil. But the one question in her mind was whether her powers were sufficient for the burdens she'd been called upon to bear. 'I've been tested in battle against Acopol already,' she admitted, 'and I failed. He defeated me.'

'Which is why we must help you, Witch of Aztlán.'

So she had walked with them for the eight days that remained of their 'hunt' in the desert gathering *hikuri*, and then for three more days as they had climbed into the high sierras, finally coming to the village that the *mara'kate* called home. There, after a two-day fast, when she was allowed only water for sustenance, they placed Tozi in a darkened room and made her eat twenty of the small, green *hikuri* buttons.

The visions that had followed had been terrible and strange, of a world utterly unfamiliar to her, a world devastated by pestilence and famine and war, a world patrolled by huge devices made of metal that crawled across the ravaged face of the earth and screamed through the skies, a world in which there were no green places left, no fertile fields, no lakes or oceans teeming with fish – a world that seethed with death.

But while these visions were unfolding, Nakawey, Irepani and Taiyari sat with her chanting in their Huichol language, and their songs lifted her up out of that place and took to her a different world, a world filled with light and joy and peace where she witnessed the peoples of many different lands coming together in love, teaching one another, learning from one another, a world of abundance and beauty, teeming with vibrant and colourful life.

This was the first of her lessons and the *mara'kate* made no attempt to explain it to her, or any of the other wondrous mysteries she witnessed over the next seven days of continuous eating of *hikuri* and visionary ecstasy. Finally, at the end of it, they told her that her powers were stronger than their own, that they had been mistaken, suffering from the sin of pride, in imagining they could tutor her, and that the time had now come for her to return to Tenochtitlan and fulfil the prophecy.

'But how does the prophecy end?' she asked, feeling disappointed and in some way cheated. 'You told me I would be tested in battle against Acopol, but you didn't say what the outcome will be. If I confront him again, will I fail again or will I win?'

'We told you the whole prophecy,' said Nakawey, his voice flat, his eyes narrowed, his wrinkled features expressionless. 'It says no more about you.'

'The whole prophecy? But what about the world – the future of the world that I'm supposed to fight the evil one for? Will it be that place of darkness that I saw, or that place of light?'

'We told you the whole prophecy,' Nakawey repeated. He looked to his left at Irepani and to his right at Taiyari. Irepani merely shrugged, but Taiyari hunched forward and said something in Huichol. His voice had a singsong quality, as though he were reciting a verse.

'What did he say?' Tozi demanded.

'She will be an orphan born of Aztlán,' Nakawey translated. 'She will be a witch and the daughter of a witch. She will be a protector of children.'

The words from the first part of the prophecy! 'But that doesn't tell me what will happen and it doesn't tell me what to do,' Tozi protested.

Nakawey sighed. 'What Tayari means,' he said, is that 'you should go and protect children.'

Thirty-five days had passed since the *mara'kate* had dismissed her; thirty-five days of continuous walking, which took Tozi from the high sierras of the Huichols, through the burning deserts of the Chichemecs and finally back to Tenochtitlan. During the long and arduous journey there had been a great deal of time for her to reflect on the meaning of her adventures and her visions. In Teotihuacan she had found her courage again, and amongst the Huichols she had learned that the only person she could depend on was herself. She could not make a better world come into being or prevent a worse one from being born; no prophecy could tell her what the future held for her. She did not know if she would face triumph or defeat when she confronted Acopol again, but until that day there was one thing she could do, and that was protect the little children who suffered under the knife of Moctezuma.

It was this thought, more than any other, that had brought Tozi directly to the fattening pens when, this morning, covered with the dust of her thirty-five-day journey, she made her way into the heart of Tenochtitlan, and crossed invisibly through the gates of the sacred precinct into the shadow of the great pyramid, with the temple of Hummingbird, towering on its summit, looking down on all.

There were dreadful memories for her here, from the time at the beginning of the year when she and Malinal had narrowly escaped sacrifice at the hands of Moctezuma and been separated from her friend Coyotl, a little castrated boy, mistaken for a girl, who she'd taken under her wing in the women's fattening pen. Afterwards, convinced he could not be dead, and that he, too, had somehow cheated the knife as they had, Tozi had stolen invisibly into every one of the fattening pens in Tenochtitlan, hoping to find him. But that search had proved fruitless and at last she'd turned her back on those places of terror that awakened such painful memories for her.

Now she'd come back, determined to spirit away whatever children she found here – to protect them the way she'd failed to protect Coyotl – only to discover they numbered in the thousands and that three of the five huge prisons within the sacred precinct, once mostly populated by adults, seemed to have been given over entirely to the selection and preparation of children as sacrificial victims.

What could this great change signify? What force had set it in motion?

It was not long before Tozi had the answer.

'Reckon we'll hit the target,' she overheard one of the guards ask another, 'before the god's birthday?'

'The full ten thousand? Reckon so. Just had orders to begin moving the men out of the last two pens tomorrow to make room for more girls.'

'Beats me where they're all coming from . . .'

'From all over! Increased tribute payments where we can get them, raids where we can't – Zapotecs, Mixtecs, Totonacs, Mazatecs, Purupechas, Tlapanecs, Tarahumaras, some Maya, some Tlascalans – though they're hard bastards to catch these days – some Huichols, even some Popoloca and Yaqui, I'm told.'

The target, Tozi was thinking, *the full ten thousand, the god's birthday.* And suddenly, as though a lantern had been lit in a dark room, it all made sense to her. Moctezuma was going to sacrifice ten thousand virgin children to Hummingbird to mark the annual celebration of the war god's birth at the beginning of the month of *Panquetzaliztli.*

If it couldn't be stopped, this abomination would take place less than seventy days from today – and Tozi knew she was powerless to prevent it. Only Quetzalcoatl, the god of peace, could halt the bloodshed, but to do that he must reach Tenochtitlan in time.

When she'd left the city on her quest, the *tueles* had been far away on the coast, camped on the dunes near the town of Cuetlaxtlan.

Where were they now?

Chapter Thirty-Six

'No!' Malinal screamed, running along the top of the wall in front of the guns, her skirts flying, fear giving her strength. 'Don't fire! Name of God, don't fire!'

Mesa's face, smudged with black powder, was set in an expression of fury. 'Get out of the way, woman.' He was holding a lighted taper a finger's width from the touchhole of one of the two huge cannons.

Malinal stood square in front of the barrel: 'No! No fire!'

'What's going on here?' It was Cortés, angrier than Mesa, thrusting himself forward, reaching to drag her from the wall.

She struggled with him. '*No, Hernán!* They fly peace banner.'

'What? What's that you say?'

'Peace banner! Blue! Four arrows, white feathers, point down.'

'You can see arrows on a banner at this distance?' Though well within range of the lombards, the nearest Tlascalan units were still more than half a mile away.

'I see very good. I sure of it, Hernán. Peace banner. Must not fire!'

Some doubt showed in his face. 'You're sure?'

'Sure! Fire now and lose chance of peace forever.'

'It's a trick,' scoffed De Grado. 'Don't fall for it, Hernán. Fire the guns before they're all over us.'

She saw Cortés narrow his eyes, squinting into the distance. 'I see the blue,' he said, 'but not the arrows.'

'I see arrows,' said Díaz. 'Four of them, pointed down.'

Sandoval agreed: 'I see them too.'

'It means peace,' Malinal said again. 'You must give them chance, Hernán. Hear them! Hear what they say.'

He frowned: 'I don't like it! They don't need their whole army to make peace. Shikotenka and fifty men of rank would be quite sufficient.'

Malinal was almost crying with frustration. 'They are Tlascalans! Tlascalans different! Do things own way in own country!'

The banner was now close enough for everyone to see, but the men advancing beneath it came on at a fast march and were dressed for war.

Cortés called for his horse and lifted Malinal off the wall. 'Ride with me,' he said. 'We'll talk to them.' He turned to Mesa: 'Hold your fire.'

On an afterthought he sought out Pepillo. 'Follow behind us,' he said. 'Don Pedro will bring you on his horse.'

They galloped down from the hill of Tzompach, Malinal before, Cortés behind, and as he reined in a few hundred paces from the Tlascalan front line, the whole army of savages came to a halt.

'Tell Shikotenka to come forward,' Cortés said. 'Just him. No one else.' As he spoke, he could already hear Alvarado with the rest of the cavalry riding to join him. He waved his hand, signalling them to stay back.

Malinal called out a few words in Nahuatl. Although her voice was steady, clear, proud and unafraid, Cortés could feel her lithe body trembling.

For a moment there was no response, and then from under the huge, fluttering blue banner, which did indeed bear an emblem of four white-feathered arrows pointed down towards the ground, a warrior strode forward. Dressed in sandals, a loincloth and a fine purple cloak, he was of middling height, perhaps a little taller than Cortés, and powerfully built with lean, muscular legs, a narrow, athlete's waist and broad shoulders. His black hair was long, tied in braids, and he wore a scarlet headband into which was set a diadem of iridescent green and gold feathers. On his left forearm was a sturdy circular buckler of some dark wood painted with the white figure of a heron, its wings outstretched, perched on a rock. In his right hand he held a large native broadsword, its obsidian blades glinting black in the sun.

'Is he coming to make peace with me,' Cortés asked, 'or fight me?' But just at that moment, now less than fifty paces away, the advancing warrior paused, laid down his sword and shield, revealing bloody bandages covering a wound to his forearm, plucked a long flint dagger from his waistband and set it down also, then continued to stalk towards them. There was something of the panther about the way he walked – something dangerous, poised and confident.

'You think this is Shikotenka himself?' Cortés whispered in Malinal's ear.

'I sure of it.'

'Then we'll dismount.' He turned to where Pepillo sat with Alvarado and beckoned the boy forward. 'Get down off that horse and come with us, lad. Later I'll want you to write an account of what's said here, word for word. You can help Malinal put what this great chief has to say into good Castilian and, while you're at it, you can hold Molinero's reins and my sword.'

Vaulting from the horse, Cortés helped Malinal down, passed his sheathed sword to Pepillo, and stood waiting as the battle-king of the Tlascalans approached. His face was not handsome, but strong – a broad brow, a firm chin, high cheekbones, watchful oriental eyes, the nose somewhat flattened, full lips, a wide, sensual mouth. He was, Cortés thought, thirty or thirty-five years old – about his own age. And, like him, this was plainly a man of experience and calculation, a man who had lived in the world, a man who had killed and who had faced death, a man of decisive action. All this was written on his face and much else besides – pride, humour, sadness, even a certain wisdom. Without having exchanged a word, Cortés found he liked him and sensed he could do business with him.

The usual introductions began, Cortés affirming that he was a man, that he came from a land, Spain, that lay far away across the sea, that he served and worshipped the one true God, and that he was vassal to the greatest and most powerful king in all the world.

Shikotenka, for his part, stated that he was a king and the son of a king, but that both he and his father ruled at the will of the people and the Senate of Tlascala, and could be removed from office and replaced at any time if they did not serve well. In his capacity as battle-king, he said, he was solely responsible for the decision to make war on the Spaniards, whom he had considered to be enemies as they came to his land from Xocotlan, and with a force of Totonacs, who were the allies and vassals of that tyrant and bully, Moctezuma. Above all, he said, he was a man who loved his country and he had fought Cortés not out of malice or wickedness but because he wished to preserve the independence Tlascala had maintained throughout centuries of wars. 'Be not astonished,' he said, 'that we have never desired an emperor, have never obeyed anybody, and dearly love liberty, for we and our ancestors have endured great evils rather than accept the yoke of Moctezuma and the Mexica.'

'And now?' Cortés asked. 'What is to happen now between you and us?'

'You have not conquered us,' said Shikotenka, 'yet you have defeated us in many battles and have proved yourselves strong and invincible. Though we sent all our men to attack you and employed all our strength by night and day, we had no luck against you. Therefore our Senate has voted and the decision is made. We will have peace with you, we will become vassals to your king in his far-off land, and we promise to obey you and to serve you if you admit us to your alliance. In return we trust and require your assurance that you will respect our liberty and treat us and our women with dignity, and cease to destroy our houses and fields, and that if we are attacked you will come to our aid.'

'And your army?' Cortés said. 'Why is it here armed for war when you seek peace?'

Shikotenka seemed in the grip of some powerful emotion, and there were tears in his eyes – the tears of a brave soldier humbled. 'My army is here for you to command,' he said simply. He dropped to one knee and, behind him, in silence, a hundred thousand men followed suit.

To his surprise, Cortés found that he, too, had begun to weep. 'I'll not have you kneel to me,' he said, and he reached for Shikotenka's hand and raised him up.

Chapter Thirty-Seven

'Where are they?'

Tozi stood before him, dusty and sweat-stained, as though from a long journey, lean, sunburned and strong. Yes, definitely, a new strength about her! Huicton did not know yet what had befallen her after he'd last seen her at Teotihuacan on the day of the summer solstice, but whatever it was seemed to have filled her with fresh resolve, restored her self-confidence and revived her courage.

'Where are who, my dear?' he asked. Taking advantage of a lull in the flow of pedestrians passing him by, Tozi had materialised right in front of him as he sat on his begging mat on the south side of the city near the entrance to the Iztapalapa causeway. It was not his usual place, but he was here to observe the comings and goings of the spies who Moctezuma sent out daily to risk their lives in Tlascala following the progress of the Spaniards. The Great Speaker was in a state of abject terror about the white men he believed to be gods, and reports from Huicton's own network left little doubt why. Although massively outnumbered, Cortés's army had inflicted a series of bitter defeats on the Tlascalans, and in recent days had added to what must be a very painful experience for Shikotenka by massacring the populations of several towns and villages. Huicton had it on good authority that the Tlascalan Senate was about to order the battle-king to surrender – indeed, given the time it took for messages to go back and forth, he thought it likely that the surrender had already occurred. If and when that happened, Cortés would be able to add the Tlascalan forces to his own and march on Tenochtitlan at the head of a vast army.

Tozi stamped her foot: 'I mean the *tueles*, of course. Where are they?'

'They are in Tlascala, my fierce friend. Now come, embrace me, as friends should who have not seen one another in a very great while. After that you will first tell me what you've been up to all these many months—'

'No, Huicton. This is urgent!'

'Nothing is so urgent that it excuses bad manners. So you will tell this old man your story, Tozi, patiently, in as much detail as you can bear, and then I will tell you about your *tueles*.'

She made a face and stooped to hug him. *The child has become a woman*, he thought as he held her in his arms. While she'd been away, though it would have meant nothing to her, she had passed her fifteenth birthday. He patted the rug beside him, and with obvious impatience she sat, folding her legs under her. 'There you are,' he said. 'Very good. Now you may begin.'

By the time they rolled up the begging mat in the late afternoon, Huicton had a good understanding of Tozi's adventures and experiences, and she knew everything that he knew about the movements of the Spaniards up to their latest battles in Tlascala. Huicton had also confirmed the awful truth she'd learned at the fattening pens, although he himself had been aware for several months of the unfolding of Moctezuma's insane plan, namely that ten thousand virgin girls were to be sacrificed to Hummingbird in honour of the war god's birthday during the four days before the start of the month of *Panquetzaliztli*.

'What you can do,' he told Tozi, 'what we can both do, is continue to undermine Moctezuma and help the Spaniards defeat him. Ishtlil has asked me to follow their progress, for he seeks an alliance with them, and I've learnt that everywhere they go they make an end to human sacrifice. Our best hope to save those ten thousand young girls will be to bring the Spanish soldiers into Tenochtitlan.'

'They are not soldiers! They are *tueles*! They are Quetzalcoatl and his retinue.'

'They *are* soldiers and I've told you before that the name of their leader is Cortés, not Quetzalcoatl. I've told you before he's a human being, not a *tuele*. Even so, he detests human sacrifice just as Quetzalcoatl did, so maybe that god does work through him and his men. Such questions are of small importance, in my opinion, so long as they help us end the wicked reign of Moctezuma.'

'Whether they're soldiers or *tueles*, they should be here now to stop the sacrifices,' said Tozi. 'Why are they wasting time fighting a war in Tlascala?'

Huicton frowned: 'They went there in search of allies but that stubborn fool Shikotenka turned against them.'

'And he's slowed them down! They're needed here. Needed urgently. If they don't reach us before *Panquetzaliztli*, all those girls will die.'

'Then we must pray they reach us in time,' said Huicton. He was aware, even as he said the words, how calculating he was being – for he had a goal and a purpose that only Tozi could fulfil and this was the way he would lead her back to it.

'I want to do more than pray!'

Ah, he sighed inwardly. *That's my girl!* 'There is something you can do,' he now said, 'but it involves Acopol. Are you ready to face him again?'

'It's for that you sent me on my journey – to strengthen my powers so I could stand up to him.' She paused, seeming to collect her thoughts, then said: 'When I went away, Acopol was in Cholula. Is he still there?'

'He's still there and he's spent these months working a terrible and wicked necromancy, a patient, cunning magic intended to trap and destroy the Spaniards when they enter that city.'

'But will these Spaniards – I'm sorry, I can't call them that! These *tueles* – will they even go to Cholula?'

'Your friend Malinal has remained in contact with me through my messengers,' said Huicton. 'She says that Cortés will surely go to Cholula when he's dealt with the Tlascalans.'

'I remember you told me she'd become his lover.'

'She has.'

'Then she should know, I suppose.'

'I believe she does know and that we would be wise, if we can, to try to neutralise Acopol. But he's far beyond my reach, Tozi. Only you, with your powers, might be able to get to him. So I ask you again, do you think you are ready?'

'I don't know if I'm ready,' Tozi said. 'I honestly don't know. But I do know I'm supposed to protect children, and if that means doing battle with Acopol again, then I'm willing to try.'

'The last time we spoke of Acopol,' Huicton reminded her, 'you said his magic still guarded Moctezuma in his palace, even though Acopol himself was in Cholula.'

'That's right, I was hurt badly when I tried to enter. But at least I proved at Teotihuacan that Acopol's magic wouldn't protect Moctezuma outside the palace.'

'Indeed so,' Huicton chuckled, 'and the result is that the Great Speaker has confined himself to his palace like a frightened rat ever since! So it seems to me now that the first way to test your powers is to see what happens when you try to penetrate the palace again. If the warding spells that Acopol put in place still harm you, as they did before, then to go to Cholula and confront the man himself would surely be a hundred times more harmful.'

'But if I can get past the warding spells without being hurt?'

'Then that has to mean your powers have strengthened and, if that is so, then perhaps you could risk an encounter with Acopol.'

'And what would I do when I encounter him?' Tozi asked.

'Why, my dear,' Huicton said, 'you would do battle with him, of course, as you yourself have said. His powers come from the dark side of magic; your powers, I believe, come from the light. If you can overcome him, if you can foil his plans in Cholula, then you will render the greatest possible service to those ten thousand girls you seek to protect.'

Even as he said it, Huicton hated himself, realising he might be sending Tozi to her death. At some level he hoped she would fail the test of the warding spells, in which case there would be no need to go any further.

But if she did not fail . . . ?

Well, if she did not fail, then desperate times called for desperate measures, and he knew that he must urge her onward to Cholula.

Tozi did not fail.

Two nights later, after visiting poor little Miahuatl in the fattening pen again to strengthen her resolve, she crossed the great plaza and slipped invisibly into the palace.

The warding spells were there! She could see them, smell them, feel them in the velvet darkness. They had shape and form, like murderous spiders lurking in corners, like filthy cockroaches scuttling underfoot, like killers on the loose, but it was child's play for her to brush them aside – with a flick of her finger, with a wave of her hand; the gestures came naturally to her – and as she moved rapidly along the corridors and up the grand stairway that led to Moctezuma's sleeping quarters, no spirit knives and no spirit razors attacked her, her head did not burst, her brain did not bleed.

The heavily armed guards at the door saw nothing as she drifted past them and the door itself was no obstacle; it put up no more resistance to her invisible form than mist or a shower of rain.

Then she was within the vast high-ceilinged chamber, slipping silent as air across the polished floor, coming in a moment to the great bed where Moctezuma lay slumbering. She heard him mutter some indistinct phrase and started back in surprise. His eyes were wide open, moving rapidly from side to side, the whites gleaming in the light from the waning moon filtering through gaps in the window shutters. And not only his eyes! His lips and his tongue were moving also and words, whispers, groans ushered forth from his mouth. Yet he did not seem conscious, either of her presence or of anything else in this world.

What was this? Tozi looked around and found the answer. An open linen bag hung loose in Moctezuma's limp hand. She reached out, making herself more substantial for a moment, took it and peered inside, seeing a few fragments of mushroom, sensing a bitter, earthy smell. The Great Speaker had been eating *teonanácatl* again, the flesh of the gods, his preferred means of communion with Hummingbird.

The thought struck her: *Is he talking to his god now?* She replaced the bag, faded back into full invisibility again, studied him closely and that was when, in an almost blinding flash, the vision came to her. The same vision that he was seeing – she was sure of it!

A vision of Cholula.

Tozi had been to Quetzalcoatl's city only once in her whole life when, years before, as a child of six, her mother had taken her there.

425

Even so, she could not forget that immense pyramid, so huge people called it a man-made mountain, except now she observed it from above, looked down upon it as though flying like a bird and saw the sacred precinct that surrounded the pyramid, filled with fighting men. On one side were the *tueles*, those white-skinned soldiers Huicton called Spaniards, a tiny force, no more than a few hundred strong, and on the other, swarming all around them, filling the precinct from wall to wall, were countless thousands of Mexica warriors. As the fighting reached its climax, and the resistance of the *tueles* faltered and failed, she saw Moctezuma's jaguar knights and eagle knights seize them and take them prisoner, trussing some in hammocks so they could not move, holding others like slaves at the end of long poles, with collars fastened tight round their necks, and leading them off towards Tenochtitlan for sacrifice.

'Will it be so, lord?' she heard Moctezuma mumble in his trance.

'It will be so,' another voice answered, a voice Tozi had heard before, deep and filled with such power it made her hair stand on end.

There came a rumble of laughter that she knew Moctezuma did not hear, laughter that was intended only for her and, for a moment, just a fraction of an instant, Tozi saw Hummingbird again, looming over her like the shadow of death, and then he was gone.

Chapter Thirty-Eight

'The Tlascalans, the men of Shikotenka, were completely annihilated. The *tueles* destroyed them. They trampled upon them. They blasted them with fire-serpents. They shot them with metal bolts. They pierced them with spears. Not just a few, but great numbers they destroyed.'

It was following this crushing defeat on the battlefield, Moctezuma's spies explained, as well as massacres in many of their towns and villages, that the Tlascalans had surrendered to the *tueles* and made an alliance with them. Now the white-skins were free to come against Tenochtitlan, not only with their own small but mysteriously deadly army, but also with tens of thousands of Tlascalan auxiliaries to support them.

Moctezuma waited for the spies to complete their dismal and depressing report, then turned to Teudile, Cuitláhuac and Cacama, who he had summoned to join him in the audience chamber of his palace. 'What is your counsel?' he asked. He already had a plan but it amused him to toy with his three most senior advisers. 'Should we march out, do you think, and bring these *tueles* to battle?'

Teudile looked alarmed. 'The Tlascalan is a brave warrior,' he said, 'but he was helpless against them; they scorned him as a mere nothing. They destroyed him with a look, with a glance of their eyes. If we bring them to battle, will we fare any better?'

Teudile obviously did not think so.

Cuitláhuac made a strangled, furious sound. 'If Guatemoc was here with us,' he said, 'he would undoubtedly urge us to bring them to battle and to do so while they are still far from our city—'

'Well he's not here with us,' snapped Moctezuma.

'It's moot anyway, my lord,' soothed Cacama. 'The *tueles* are in

Tlascala, so they're already very close. I say let's make a virtue of necessity, allow them to come to Tenochtitlan as the legitimate embassy of a foreign king, and avoid battle with them if we can.'

Moctezuma smirked. Usually such news as the spies had brought would have plunged him into despair. But his spirits were soaring! The fattening pens were filling up with virgins to be sacrificed on Hummingbird's birthday, and the god himself had deigned to appear to him in the night, showing him again the vision of Cholula that he had shown him once before in which the *tueles* were vanquished by his brave jaguar and eagle warriors, captured by them for sacrifice, some trussed in hammocks so they could not move, others led away like slaves at the end of long poles, with collars fastened tight round their necks. To see that vision for the second time was to be reminded of the clear strategy it outlined – that the *tueles* must be lured to Cholula where they would be defeated if they could be taken by surprise in the sacred precinct that Acopol had wrested from the god of peace with his magic and re-dedicated to Hummingbird. Ah, what joy to see that victory again! It had given Moctezuma hope, so much hope, that the prophecy of Quetzalcoatl's return would indeed be reversed at Cholula, the ancient city of Quetzalcoatl himself! 'It is fortunate,' he said to his councillors with an indulgent chuckle, 'since all three of you have different points of view and never agree on anything, that I have consulted with the god—'

'With Hummingbird, lord?' gasped Teudile.

'Of course. Who else? I consulted with him in the night and he showed me again what we must do to be rid of the white-skins forever.'

Pepillo felt that he was living through a time of miracles and marvels straight out of the pages of *Amadis*. He had fought in a battle against worthy foes and bloodied his sword – and lived! – and his faithful hound Melchior had fought and lived too. There was no doubt now – for Malinal had witnessed it – that Santisteban was the one who had opened the door of the hut where Melchior was confined on the hill of Tzompach, and let the lurcher loose, unarmoured, to take his chances in the melee. So there was a strange, fated irony in the fact that Melchior and Pepillo had been in the forefront of the rescuers who had saved Santisteban's life and the life of his cruel, twisted master, Vendabal. Pepillo was under no illusions that this would turn either of them into friends; more likely it would only serve to increase their enmity. He would have to be more on his guard than ever, just as Amadis, surrounded by adversaries, had ever been obliged to be watchful. But like Amadis, too, he resolved he would not allow himself to be tainted by hate or envy. Love, truth, chivalry, and a kind heart; these were the qualities that would remain when all else was dust.

After the unexpected capitulation of Shikotenka and all Tlascalan forces on Tuesday 7 September, the Spaniards stayed in their camp at the hill of Tzompach for a further week, amply provided with food and other needed supplies from nearby towns and villages. Doctor La Peña had much work to do with the injured and the sick; almost all the horses required attention too, and all the weapons, particularly the guns, had to be cleaned and made good. Last but not least, Cortés wanted to be sure the peace was genuine and not some clever entrapment, so it was not until Wednesday 15 September that he put his soldiers on the march again. They proceeded at a leisurely pace, taking two days to cover the eighteen miles to Tlascala, and arrived in the capital around noon on Thursday 16 September.

Pepillo took delight in the noisy, festive exuberance of the occasion; the road into the city was lined on both sides for more than two miles by townsfolk who had come out to welcome them. They blew conches and trumpets, scattered bright flowers from baskets, shouted cheerfully and showed every appearance of joy, their faces wreathed with smiles, despite the cruel nature of the war so recently fought. Because their enemies the Mexica exercised a monopoly on cotton, Malinal explained, these Tlascalans were dressed in costumes of maguey fibre, rather rough but nonetheless magnificently embroidered and decorated. And, as well as ordinary citizens of all ages, there were also many priests, some wearing robes of black feathers, others white surplices with cowls resembling those of Mercedarian friars. Like all priests everywhere in the New Lands, they were filthy and a stink of rotting meat hung about them; their hair was so tangled and matted with blood it could not have been combed without first being cut, and their ears were torn by frequent acts of self-mutilation. Pepillo could also not help but notice their long twisted fingernails that gave them the appearance of wizards from some gruesome fairy tale. But they carried braziers filled with live coals and incense, from which they wafted clouds of sweet-smelling smoke, bowing their heads in humility to the Spanish soldiers as they passed.

Advancing ever deeper into the populous city, the thatched buildings of wattle and adobe became grander, many boasting flat roofs, crowded with spectators eager to catch a glimpse of the fabled strangers. Finally, on the approach to the centre, mighty stone temples appeared, painted in rich colours of red, blue and ivory, surrounding a giant pyramid on top of which stood a tower with a high conical roof, like a minaret, covered in gold leaf. The presence of gold caused much excitement amongst the Spaniards. Later that same day, as Cortés dictated further sections of his letter to King Carlos, he described Tlascala with its temples as larger, finer and more beautiful than Granada, which Spain had won back from the Moors less than thirty years before, and which Pepillo knew was renowned for its splendour and the glory of its religious buildings.

In the broad square in front of the great pyramid, with its lofty tower, framed in the distance by ranges of green mountains, Captain Shikotenka stood waiting, flanked by two old men of noble bearing – his own father, Shikotenka the Elder, and the revered chieftain Maxixcatzin. They moved forward to greet Cortés as he dismounted, each one of them gravely embracing him and telling him, 'You are our brother now.' Then they led him to his quarters, close to the pyramid, where a number of very pretty houses and palaces, sufficient to lodge the entire Spanish force, had been prepared and decked with flowers. A tremendous banquet was offered in the open square, where the conquistadors and their Totonac auxiliaries were sumptuously fed on turkeys, maize cakes and fruits. Even the war dogs and the horses, Pepillo noted with amusement, were offered their share of the bread and flesh.

The first friction between the Spaniards and their hosts came two days later, Saturday 18 September, when Cortés made a tour of the city. He was guided by Shikotenka, with Malinal, Father Olmedo, Alvarado,

Sandoval, Davila and a number of the other captains at their side, and Pepillo tagging along to take notes. While they were viewing the temples near the pyramid, Bernal Díaz came running up, a little out of breath, and informed Cortés of a discovery made by some of his men. Not far away in a walled compound, areas of which were visible from the street, it seemed a large number of captives were being held for human sacrifice. 'Is this true?' Cortés asked Shikotenka and, with some reluctance, the Tlascalan leader agreed that it was.

Cortés's face clouded over. 'Take me to see these captives,' he demanded.

'It is not permitted,' objected Shikotenka.

'You are a vassal now of the king of Spain,' Cortés insisted, 'and you have given me your surrender. Everything is permitted to me. I want to see these captives.'

Again reluctantly, after much argument and explanation, Shikotenka led the way into a dark warren of narrow streets lying to the south of the main square, and through the gates into a walled courtyard where hundreds of prisoners – men, women and children – hunched miserably in stout bamboo cages.

Pepillo felt shame at the massacres and atrocities he knew Cortés had committed during the war, but he was proud of what his master did next, for though it seemed to threaten the very fabric of the hard-won peace, the caudillo insisted that all the captives be freed at once and that Shikotenka should, on the spot, swear an oath in the name of his people that Tlascala would never again practise human sacrifice. Not only that, but Cortés seized the occasion to demand an immediate renunciation by the Tlascalans of all other aspects of their heathen religion, most notably their worship of idols, all of which must forthwith be smashed, followed by a full and complete conversion of the entire population to Christianity. If they failed to do so, they were bound to burn in hell, and Cortés did not see how he could maintain an alliance with such doomed sinners.

A huge argument ensued, Tlascalan warriors, gesticulating and shouting, began to crowd into the courtyard, many armed with native broadswords and spears; Alvarado and the other captains drew their own weapons. Díaz, who Cortés had sent off to bring reinforcements, returned – not a moment too soon in Pepillo's opinion – with two hundred Spaniards. At this point Shikotenka the Elder, Maxixcatzin and other Tlascalan chiefs also arrived and fell into urgent conference with the younger Shikotenka, while Pepillo overheard Father Olmedo urging Cortés: 'Wait, Hernán. This is not the way. I don't want you to make Christians by force. There's no use in overturning an altar if the idol remains in the heart. Give them time, lead them by example, and soon enough they'll feel the weight of our admonitions. Besides,' the friar added, raising a wry eyebrow, 'if you go on like this, the whole populace will rise in protest and then where will we be?'

After much more debate and rattling of swords, a compromise was reached that seemed to satisfy all parties. Shikotenka ordered the freeing of the captives, 'Even though,' he said, 'many of them are Mexica and we will see them again on the battlefield.' He also promised the matter of human sacrifices would be discussed at the next meeting of the Senate, the supreme ruling body to which even he and his father, as Tlascala's elected kings, must defer. Cortés, for his part, agreed not to interfere with any other aspects of Tlascalan religion, to throw down no idols and to leave the temples and the worshippers within them alone. He begged of Shikotenka, and was granted, one small temple that would be cleaned and whitewashed forthwith for use by the Spaniards as a church.

Pepillo was relieved that the day had ended well and the next morning, Sunday 19 September, the first mass was heard by Father Olmedo in the newly dedicated church in which Cortés had installed a large cross and a statue and several paintings of the Virgin Mary. It was noted by all that Maxixcatzin attended the service and afterwards asked, through Malinal, for an explanation of Christian beliefs, which Olmedo was pleased to provide.

By the following Sunday, 26 September, the Spaniards were granted the further right to hold open-air services in one of the town's many squares, where public masses were thereafter celebrated daily for the army in the presence of growing crowds of Tlascalans.

Tozi had been badly shaken when the war god had revealed himself to her as she'd spied on Moctezuma's vision but, seventeen days later, after many more secret visits to the palace, she knew that she could delay no longer and must proceed to Cholula at once. The final impetus had come that morning when she'd witnessed a meeting between Moctezuma and Teudile, at which the Speaker had sent his steward on his way to Tlascala at the head of a delegation bearing rich gifts and promises for the *tueles*.

The whole thing was a plot, a trick, a subterfuge! To persuade the *tueles* to travel to Cholula, Teudile was to tell them three things, all plausible, all seductive.

First – a sojourn in Cholula would allow trust to build between Moctezuma and the leader of the *tueles* who, as Huicton had said, had adopted the human name Cortés. Only once this trust was established would the *tueles* be allowed to proceed to Tenochtitlan.

Second – Cholula was the sacred city of Quetzalcoatl, whom Moctezuma believed Cortés to be. If Cortés were to refuse to visit Cholula, why then Moctezuma must needs doubt Cortés's identity as the avatar Quetzalcoatl. And if he was not the human manifestation of the Plumed Serpent, but a mere foreigner – and perhaps one with wicked intent – then why should Moctezuma allow him to move a step closer to Tenochtitlan?

Finally – if the *tueles* did go to Cholula, thus confirming the identification between Cortés and Quetzalcoatl and allowing trust to be built, then Moctezuma would willingly open the road to Tenochtitlan for them and, more than that, he would agree to become their vassal.

Tozi was convinced that such an offer, unheard of in the history of the Mexica, would surely lure the *tueles* into advancing their plan to visit Cholula, and if it did then truly, despite the terrible fear that held her back and had caused her to drag her feet shamefully, there was no time to lose. That fear, which she held deep in her heart and had hidden even from Huicton since she'd past his 'tests' with the warding spells, was simply and plainly that she was not yet ready – perhaps she would never be ready – to engage in magical combat with Acopol. Now, however, she resigned herself to her duty. The Huichol prophecy had named her as a protector of children, and the thousands in the fattening pens would be left defenceless if the tattooed sorcerer was not stopped.

She would stop him if she could, even if it meant she must lose her life. And because she believed that she *would* lose her life, and felt her doom swarming towards her like some unstoppable army, Tozi resolved to see Guatemoc one last time, despite the hatred she knew he harboured for the *tueles*, and to reveal herself to him before taking the road to Cholula.

That was why, as evening fell, after saying her farewells to Huicton without telling him what was in her mind, she gathered the clothes she would need, mingled with the crowds going back and forth across the Tacuba causeway, and made her way out to Cuitláhuac's Chapultepec estate, where Guatemoc remained a house prisoner. She would reveal herself to the prince, she decided, and she would make love to him if he would have her, because never before had she known a man in that way and it would be sad to depart this world for the next without having done so. Besides, if it were permissible for Malinal to become the lover of the *tuele* leader, then surely it was permissible for Tozi to surrender her virginity to the noblest warrior of the Mexica?

For many hours she waited invisibly within the mansion for Guatemoc to be alone and finally, after midnight, she followed him up to his chamber. There she waited again – for the handsome prince stood for a long while gazing up at the waxing moon riding high in the heavens – and finally, as he removed his clothing and stepped naked towards his bed, she materialised by his side. She had taken the precaution of wearing the finery and make-up of the goddess Temaz in which he had seen her before, but even so her sudden appearance startled him and he took a step back in surprise, then instantly dropped to one knee before her. 'My Lady,' he said, his head bowed. 'It has been many months since you graced me with your presence. I am honoured that you choose to visit me now.'

She reached out a hand and raised him, aware that she was trembling as he towered over her. 'Prince Guatemoc,' she said, 'in the next days I may die and, since I love you well, and may not see you again, it is right that I tell you the truth.'

'You cannot die!' he replied. 'You are a goddess.'

'I am no goddess, my prince! I am a simple girl blessed, or perchance cursed, with certain gifts. But know this, should you to attempt to detain me now, or in any way betray the trust I place in you, I shall vanish without a trace as suddenly as I appeared.'

The prince looked down at her, his eyes wide. 'I will not detain you, lady! I will not betray your trust! You have my word of honour on this for, whatever you are, or may be, I know with certainty you saved me from poisoning at the hands of Moctezuma and healed me from the grievous battle wounds I suffered. These great debts that I owe you would be ill repaid if I were to seek to do you harm now!'

'Would you still feel that way,' Tozi asked, her heart suddenly thudding, 'if I told you I am a witch.'

'A witch?'

'Yes, my prince, a witch. A witch who can render herself invisible. A witch with the gift of healing.' Tozi was preternaturally aware of the virility of the man who stood over her, of his handsome face, of his scarred and muscled body, of his big, heavy *tepulli* hanging between his legs, and of the power and charisma he radiated.

'A witch?' he repeated. 'Such a revelation would not change my feelings towards you at all, my lady, for I have long suspected it.' He grinned suddenly: 'Tell me, are you that witch who's been driving my wicked uncle mad?'

'I have done Moctezuma harm at every possible opportunity,' Tozi admitted.

Guatemoc's grin widened. 'It was you, then, who shamed him at Teotihuacan?'

'It was me,' Tozi allowed.

'Then I love you even more than I did before,' laughed Guatemoc, 'and my debt of gratitude to you is all the greater for every bit of distress you've caused that evil fool!' He reached out to her, wrapped his arms around her and held her close. She could feel his *tepulli* growing but then he stepped away, his features suddenly serious in the moonlight. 'I hope,' he said, 'that you've not come here to try to talk me into making war against the lord Hummingbird as you did once before, for if that's the case, my answer has not changed.'

'No,' Tozi said. 'I've not come here to ask you to make war. I've come here to ask you to make love to me.'

*   *   *

435

The sorcerer Acopol descended the long northern stairway of the great pyramid of Cholula with an easy, loping stride, the stride of a powerful animal, a predator, a killer.

Two nights had passed since Tozi had allowed Guatemoc to take her to his bed and her loins still ached at the memory. But, after leaving his quarters at Chapultepec before dawn the next morning, she'd rid herself of the finery of Temaz, put back on her beggars' rags and struck out at a fast pace on the road to Cholula.

She'd arrived here in the night and had already confirmed that extensive preparations were being made in the city for an expected visit by the white-skinned strangers who everyone thought must be *tueles*, perhaps even the companions of Quetzalcoatl himself, the god of peace to whom the great pyramid of Cholula had been dedicated in a former epoch of the earth. The preparations, however, were not friendly, as might be expected in Quetzalcoatl's own city, but hostile, with camouflaged pits dug in the streets to trap the strange deer on the backs of which the *tueles* were said to ride, and heaps of stones stockpiled on the flat rooftops to hurl down on them as they passed by.

Moreover, as Huicton had rightly informed her, an altar to Hummingbird had been raised on the towering summit of the pyramid, and there it had been her painful duty that morning to watch the tattooed sorcerer Acopol perform the loathsome ceremony of human sacrifice, taking the hearts of twenty young men and holding the dripping organs up to the rising sun. Such a thing had never happened in Cholula since time began, and Tozi understood in the depths of her being that what was being nourished by these acts was black magic of the worst kind – a shocking and corrupt inversion of everything Quetzalcoatl stood for, everything he represented, so that when the *tueles* came they could not draw on his power.

Reaching the bottom of the steps, Acopol turned right across the sacred plaza towards the palace of Tlaqui and Tlalchi, twin rulers of Cholula. The sorcerer's route, Tozi saw with alarm, would take him within a few paces of the corner where she sat on her begging mat beneath the overhanging roofs of two small temples.

He wore only a loincloth but, as she remembered so vividly from their last encounter, his entire body from his feet to his shaved head was covered in such a dense web of swirling interwoven tattoos that he seemed to be almost entirely black, black as a jaguar in the depths of the jungle – the creature she had seen him transform into that night in the courtyard of Moctezuma's palace. Behind him, in their filthy robes, followed the four priests of Hummingbird, who had assisted him with the morning's sacrifices, while the crowds of pilgrims paying their devotions in the sacred precinct shrank back.

Tozi, with her eyes to the ground, felt a prickle of fear run down her spine as Acopol approached, his bare, blood-smeared feet padding almost soundlessly across the flagstones. She had expected he would simply pass by and that she could observe him surreptitiously while she herself, just one more insignificant beggar amongst a hundred, would not be observed, or even noticed.

But that was not what happened.

Instead, with an awful inevitability, Acopol stopped directly in front of her, and loomed over her. She could feel his eyes boring into the top of her head.

'You, girl,' he said. 'What's your business here?' His voice was soft and mellow, rich and warm.

'I am Tozi,' she replied, 'a beggar seeking the charity of the god.'

'Look at me, Tozi.'

'It would be impertinent, sir, for me to gaze on a great one such as yourself.'

'But you are here to gaze on me, are you not?'

'No, great sir, I am here to beg.'

'I think not. You are here to observe. You are here to spy on me as you did once before.'

Tozi's eyes were still downcast, but she sensed the four priests manoeuvring into position around her. Her heart was beating fast, so loudly she knew the sorcerer must hear it, and though the morning was cool she felt a fat bead of sweat roll down her cheek. 'No, sir, I am here to beg, to beg only.'

'I said *look at me*, girl,' the voice was suddenly harsh. 'So you will *look!*'

Reluctant, but unable to resist, Tozi obeyed and saw the hidden nature of the man standing before her. He had the lean, rangy body of the race of nomads from which he sprang, the Chichimec people of the northern deserts, but his yellow eyes burned like molten gold out of a broad, flat, cruel face, writhing with intricate tattoos that twisted and intertwined, as though filled with a life of their own, revealing, in their dots and swirls and tendrils, a thousand transient, half-recognised shapes and forms.

The priests were moving again, moving in to seize her. Knowing she had gravely miscalculated, that visible or invisible she would always be a torch burning in the darkness to a man such as this, Tozi willed herself to fade as she had done a hundred times before, felt the hands that had reached out to grasp her close on the empty space where she had been, and heard the astonished, cheated shouts of her would-be captors.

She glanced back as she fled.

Behind her, undoubtedly *seeing* her, its golden eyes fixed on her with furious intent, loped a huge black jaguar. It was gaining on her, closing the distance between them too rapidly for her to escape. The creature opened its jaws and something, some shadow, some darkness, poured forth from its mouth, enveloping her in a mesh of fine black threads as sticky and entrapping as the web of a spider.

With a cry of terror, Tozi felt her strength drain from her and was dragged back against her will into full visibility. Dazed, confused, more afraid than she had ever been in a lifetime of fear, she found herself lying at the foot of the great pyramid of Cholula, with Acopol, once more in the body of a man, standing over her.

His face squirmed with triumph: 'You're mine now,' he said, as Hummingbird's foul priests swarmed round her, each one seizing an arm and a leg.

It was, Tozi realised with abject horror, the position of sacrifice.

On Wednesday 29 September, around mid-morning, Shikotenka visited Cortés in the palace he had been given for his headquarters. Their argument over religion had subsided. What had replaced it was a growing practical cooperation – Cortés did not imagine it was a friendship such as he was beginning to enjoy with Maxixcatzin – over the strategy that must soon be pursued against the Mexica. 'It's as I predicted,' Shikotenka now said. 'A delegation from Moctezuma has arrived under a banner of truce. They want to talk to you, Hernán. Do you want to talk to them?'

Cortés thought about it, his mind racing. He still didn't trust Shikotenka – perhaps he would never completely trust him; the man had too free and independent a spirit. And he wanted to be able to continue to play a devious game with the Mexica, assuring Moctezuma of his warmth and good feelings towards him, acting the part of an ambassador come to exchange gifts, and not suggesting for a moment he intended to conquer his kingdom and take the Great Speaker himself dead or alive. At the same time, Cortés had promised Shikotenka this was exactly what he was going to do, and that if the Tlascalans honoured their alliance with Spain, their reward would be the utter destruction of the hated Mexica and the death of Moctezuma. How much more difficult it would be to maintain such diametrically opposed positions with both parties in earshot of each other.

He smiled: 'Yes, Shikotenka, allow them to come. Let's see what Moctezuma has to say for himself now.'

'You're mine now.'

Hummingbird had used the same words all those months before when he had reprieved Tozi from sacrifice on top of the great pyramid of Tenochtitlan.

But today it was Acopol who claimed possession of her and, on his orders, the four strong young priests of Hummingbird were carrying her like a sack of maize into a corridor concealed behind a false wall beneath the eastern stairway of the great pyramid of Cholula.

Tozi struggled, but could not break free. She willed herself invisible but could not fade. She tried to send the fog but it would not come.

'Your powers have deserted you,' said Acopol, who was walking ahead holding a burning brand. 'I've put you under an enchantment.'

Tozi knew, without having to ask further, that what he said was true. Where magic had once been alive within her, she now felt only a numb, blank emptiness, so if she was going to escape it would have to be some other way. Craning her neck she saw the corridor she was being carried along was so narrow and cramped that the priests and the tattooed sorcerer had to stoop. The rough-hewn rock walls pressed in on them on both sides. 'Where are you taking me?' she asked, despising the edge of fear in her voice.

'The cave of the serpent,' said Acopol. 'The pyramid was built on top of it. In fact it's the reason the pyramid is here. It's the original sacred place of Quetzalcoatl. I had another girl set aside for this sacrifice, but when I saw you this morning and looked into your mind, I knew you'd be much more effective.'

Tozi struggled again but the priests held her firm; their stink filled her nostrils.

'We're not going to cut out your heart,' Acopol reassured her. 'Yours will be a sacrifice by slow starvation, a much worse death really.' He laughed – a horrible sound in this echoing place. 'As the vitality drains from your body, the power of Quetzalcoatl too will drain away.'

An immense stalagmite in the shape of a coiled boa constrictor gave the cave its name. A pile of quarried stone blocks stood at the end of the corridor, ready to wall in the victim. Acopol lit three other torches from his own to reveal a very large, high-ceilinged, irregular space, at least two hundred paces across, with several smaller lobes or alcoves branching off the main central chamber. 'Your tomb,' he said with a flourish, as the priests threw Tozi down at the base of the stalagmite. Then, while they tied her wrists and ankles and set to work building the wall with trowels and cement, he recited a lengthy rhythmic incantation in a language she did not recognise. Finally, without further explanation, he turned his back on her, walked off down the long corridor and was gone.

'Release me!' Tozi ordered the priests, putting all her will into a spell of commanding, but they ignored her and she understood again, with a tremendous, plummeting sense of despair, just how completely, and with what ease, Acopol had stolen her power. She was, truly, a witch no longer, and what was being done to her was going to be done and she could not prevent it. So while the priests cemented the final blocks in place and the light of their torches yet reached into the chamber, she looked round urgently for something, anything that could help her. At five different points on the cavern walls she saw glistening streaks of water that seemed to be seeping down from above and marked them in her memory. If she could slip her tethers she would, at least, not die of thirst. She also thought she felt a current of air blowing not only along the entrance corridor but also from the opposite direction, much deeper inside the cave. This too gave her a thread of hope, and when the last block was cemented into position and complete darkness fell, she refused to let panic take her but began work at once, twisting and turning to loosen her bonds.

'The lord Moctezuma sends his compliments,' said Teudile, giving his hollow-cheeked, insincere smile, 'and more medicine for your disease of the heart.' He indicated four large baskets that his bearers had placed on the floor of the audience chamber of Cortés's Tlascalan palace.

'My gratitude to the great Moctezuma,' Cortés replied as Alvarado leaned down to open the baskets, which were filled with small gold ingots in the shape of shrimps. 'This medicine will serve us well.'

Alvarado was already weighing the baskets on the expedition's scales. 'There's two thousand ounces here,' he declared after a moment, his eyes glittering with greed and calculation. The other Spanish captains, Davila, Velázquez de Léon, Ordaz, Olid and Sandoval, looked on with equally transparent interest. Only Pepillo, present as usual to help Malinal with the task not only of interpreting the words of the Mexica, but rendering them in flawless Castilian, seemed indifferent to the gold.

The Mexica delegation consisted of Teudile and three other lords, all splendidly dressed in sumptuous cotton robes that put to shame the rough, maguey-fibre smocks and tunics of the Tlascalans. Not that there were any Tlascalans here tonight, Malinal noted, since Cortés's powers of persuasion were such that Shikotenka had agreed to his request for privacy.

Teudile leaned forward, his voice lowered a notch. 'Tell the lord Cortés,' he said to Malinal, 'that his friend the lord Moctezuma rejoices in his splendid victory over our enemy Tlascala.'

I doubt it, thought Malinal, as she and Pepillo gave the translation. *I very much doubt it.* She felt quite sure the coward Moctezuma would have much preferred to hear the inconvenient Spaniards had been wiped out, thus saving him the trouble of wiping them out himself.

'My lord does wonder, though,' Teudile continued, 'why the lord Cortés chooses, now that he has defeated them, to stay with the enemies of the Mexica?'

'Because we are comfortable here,' Cortés replied, 'because our every need is met,' he waved a hand expressively around the large, well-furnished audience chamber. 'Because the people of Tlascala have made us welcome, and because they have agreed to become the vassals of my king, Don Carlos.'

Teudile lowered his voice further; it was almost a whisper now: 'The friendship they offer you is not sincere,' he hissed. 'Their promise to become vassals is empty. Everything they do is merely to dispel your suspicions so they can later betray you with impunity. Do not trust them, for they are traitors and they will surely kill you at the first opportunity and steal this present of gold we have brought you. The lord Moctezuma therefore requests that you leave this savage, dangerous place at once and proceed to our city of Cholula, where your safety will be guaranteed and he will show you the true meaning of welcome.'

'And this welcome of the great Moctezuma,' Cortés asked. 'What will it consist of?'

'My lord cannot negotiate with you while you are here in Tlascala,' whispered Teudile, 'but he gives his promise, if you show goodwill by making the short journey to Cholula, that he will heap upon you great presents of gold, a thousand times larger than this one – ' a nod at the gleaming baskets – 'and that he himself will become a vassal of your king.'

'A vassal, eh?' said Cortés, a sharp look – that Malinal recognised – crossing his face. 'And how much tribute in cloth, in gold, in silver, does the great Moctezuma propose to pay each year to my king?'

'All such details can be agreed once you are in Cholula,' Teudile insisted, 'and when they are agreed, and the tribute set, my lord Moctezuma will invite you to visit him in friendship in Tenochtitlan.'

Cortés turned to Malinal. 'I don't trust them,' he said in Spanish, at the same time giving Teudile a gleaming smile. 'Tell them we see no need to waste time in Cholula. Our preference is to march straight to Tenochtitlan and receive Moctezuma's pledge of vassalage there.'

Malinal knew very well that Cortés, on account of his dreams of

Saint Peter, was already firmly resolved to go to Cholula, but she put the bluff into the most scornful and ringing Nahuatl. As she did so, Teudile's face became stubborn: 'I regret that will not be possible,' he said.

'Why is it not possible?' Cortés asked. 'Why is the great Moctezuma so keen for us to go to Cholula?'

'There are two reasons,' Teudile replied. 'The first is that in Cholula, my lord Moctezuma hopes that he and the lord Cortés will learn to trust each other fully. He feels it is better for both of you that this trust is built before rather than after the lord Cortés comes to Tenochtitlan. Do you not agree?'

Though his mind had long been made up on the need to go to Cholula Cortés feigned an excellent impression of reflecting carefully on what he'd just been told. 'I can see the point of the argument,' he said finally. 'What is the second reason?'

'The second reason,' said Teudile, 'is that Cholula is sacred to the god Quetzalcoatl, whose manifestation on earth my lord Moctezuma believes the lord Cortés to be. It is right and proper, therefore, that the lord Cortés should visit this city before his arrival in Tenochtitlan. If he does not do so, if he is afraid to do so, it may cause my lord Moctezuma to entertain doubts about the identity – and the intentions – of the lord Cortés.'

'I am a man,' said Cortés sourly, 'as I have told you many times.'

'Nonetheless, this is what the lord Moctezuma requires – that you make a sojourn in Cholula before he permits you to enter Tenochtitlan.'

Cortés nodded and looked down at the gold. 'I'll think about it,' he said.

That night, Wednesday 29 September, while the Mexica delegation slept beneath the roof of Cortés's palace, under his protection, Saint Peter visited him in a dream.

'Moctezuma plans treachery,' the saint now revealed. 'He is gathering his forces. When you reach Cholula, he aims to bring a great army down on your head and destroy you utterly.'

'What then would you have me do, Holy Father?' Cortés asked, 'since you yourself have urged me more than once to go to Cholula?'

Saint Peter smiled, his eyes, black as coals, glittered with inner fire. 'Nothing has changed,' he said. 'I would have you go to Cholula and lay my vengeance upon that place. When you are within the city, when you judge the moment to be right, invite the lords, the heads of households, the soldiers, to gather in their thousands in the great plaza before the tall pyramid and there I want you to kill them all. Make a massacre for God in Cholula, my son. Repay Moctezuma in full measure for the treachery he plans there, and I will open the gates of Tenochtitlan wide for you.'

Teudile's delegation stayed until Sunday 3 October, and left with Cortés's promise that the Spanish would visit Cholula as they had requested.

'When?' Teudile asked.

'Very soon, when my men are fully rested and recovered from the injuries they received in our war against Tlascala. In no more than ten days from now, we will be there.'

'You must be mad,' Shikotenka told Cortés when he learned of this. 'Don't you know that everything the Mexica do is riddled with treachery and cunning, and in this manner they have subjected the whole land?' Speaking urgently through Malinal and Pepillo, he then informed Cortés of specific intelligence he had received in the past three days of a plan to trap the Spaniards once they were inside Cholula: 'Stones have been piled on the roofs of many houses ready to throw down on you; certain streets have been walled up to deny you free movement, and others have been mined with holes filled with sharpened stakes so your deer will fall and cripple themselves. The whole citizenry is being prepared and armed to rise against you and either kill you all or take you prisoner for sacrifice.'

None of this news seemed to come as any surprise to Cortés, and Pepillo saw from the look on his master's face that he had already made up his mind to go.

Later that same day, he explained his decision to his captains: 'Gentlemen, our goal is Tenochtitlan and the total subjection of the empire of the Mexica, so we cannot leave a city as hostile as Cholula between us and the sea. For this reason alone, even if there were no others, I would insist that we go there and either extract its surrender or destroy it. But even more important than this, in my view, is the matter of our honour. If Moctezuma sees us balk at Cholula and seek another way to reach him, he will know we are afraid, he will know we can be intimidated and this will strengthen his courage to resist us. It is still my hope, and my conviction, that we can conquer Tenochtitlan without having to fight but, if we are to do this, then we dare show no hesitation now.'

The next days were spent in planning and preparation. The Senate of Tlascala offered its whole army, close to a hundred thousand men, to defend against the expected treachery of Cholula, but Cortés declined, saying so many would amount to an open declaration of war on Moctezuma, and certainly cause him to close up and fortify Tenochtitlan instead of leaving the way open. Given the long history of enmity between the Mexica and the Tlascalans, it was better to proceed by stealth and misdirection, and for this reason, Cortés said, though he understood the risks were great, he would take no more than a thousand Tlascalans to Cholula and preferred that any fighting there should be done by the Spaniards alone.

On Monday 11 October, the Spanish captains gathered to make final plans before setting off for Cholula the next morning, a march of eighteen miles. Shikotenka, who would be leading the small Tlascalan force, was also present. 'Do you have some words for us?' Cortés asked him.

'Cholula is part of the Mexica empire,' he replied, 'and it's obvious the Mexica aim to deal with you there so they don't have to face you in Tenochtitlan. It will be a war to the death, so leave no one alive who you're able to kill; neither the young, lest they should bear arms again, nor the old, lest they should give good advice. The Mexica will show you no mercy and you must show none to them.'

There was a moment's silence, then Alvarado was on his feet clapping ostentatiously. 'Bravo!' he cheered. 'Bravo, Shikotenka! I knew it when we faced each other knife to knife on that beach at Cuetlaxtlan. You're a man after my own heart!'

445

Chapter Thirty-Nine

After they had crawled towards him across the smooth, polished flag-stones of his audience chamber, it pleased Moctezuma to keep Tlaqui and Tlalchi on their gnarled hands and knobbly knees while he conversed with them. As the secular ruler of Cholula, Tlaqui's impressive title was 'Lord of the Here and Now' and, as the spiritual ruler, Tlalchi was 'Lord of the World Below the Earth'. This morning, however, they looked more like the Lords of Grovel, or the Lords of Humiliation or, better still – Moctezuma suppressed a snigger at the thought – the Shit-Eating Lords, since he suspected they would gladly gobble up piles of their own filth, or any other noxious substance it might occur to him to nominate, if he would only grant the request they had come to him to lodge.

Both men were old, wizened, thin, grey-haired and cautious. Their mannerisms were curiously similar, in particular the odd way they held their hands before their mouths while speaking as though wishing to hide their teeth. They also frequently exchanged shifty eye move-ments – some sort of wordless consultation, doubtless built up over many years of collusion.

'If it would please Your Excellency,' Tlalchi was saying, his voice dry as an ancient corpse, 'we have certain doubts about the plan communicated to us by General Maza.'

'Doubts?' Moctezuma deliberately beetled his brows, giving the lords of Cholula a fierce, disapproving glare. 'Why should you have doubts? It is an excellent plan. I drew it up myself.'

In unison the pair wriggled uncomfortably.

'Meaning no disrespect to yourself, sire,' offered Tlaqui, 'but the plan as we understand it requires us to capture or kill the white-skinned

446

tueles in the streets of Cholula and we fear this will be difficult. We have heard reports of their fire-serpents and it is undoubtedly the case that great damage will be done if these powerful weapons are used within our sacred city.'

Streets of Cholula? Moctezuma thought. Maza, one of his most favoured generals, who he had appointed to oversee the Cholula operation because of his unquestioning loyalty, ferocity and cunning, had obviously been spreading misinformation – a clever way to keep the real plan concealed from prying eyes and ears. On a whim, he decided to play the old fools along for a few moments more. 'So what are you suggesting?' he barked. 'You want us to call off the attack because of possible damage to your precious city?'

'No, sire. No. No.' It was Tlaqui again, positively dribbling with anxiety. 'We are fully committed to the destruction of the *tueles*. We are loyal supporters of Your Excellency's plan. But in the narrow streets of Cholula there are so many obstacles, so many houses and temples for them to hide in, so many possible escape routes they may use to rally and regroup, that we fear things could go badly wrong.'

'And damage? You said you feared damage?'

'That too, sire, yes, but our greater concern is to bring overwhelming force to bear on the *tueles* and the very structure of the city will prevent that . . .'

'I don't see why,' said Moctezuma.

'The narrow streets, Excellency' – it was Tlalchi mumbling now, his hand back over his mouth. 'We understand General Maza is mustering six regiments to take the *tueles*, but it will not be possible to deploy all those men to good effect in our crowded city. Instead, Excellency, since the muster has already begun in the valley of Citlaltépec, four miles north of the city boundary, we suggest the general should lie in wait for the *tueles* there and ambush them when they march out of Cholula on their way to Tenochtitlan—'

'Fools!' fumed Moctezuma. 'The valley of Citlaltépec isn't even on the highway! That's why we chose it for the muster, so the regiments can assemble without attracting attention.'

'Of course, sire,' said Tlaqui with a sly smile, 'but our proposal is to block the highway – block it completely – and create a false road that will lead the *tueles* directly into the valley where the regiments will be waiting to annihilate them.'

'*No!*' shouted Moctezuma, suddenly bored with this charade. 'That is *not* how it will be done! The white-skins *must* be dealt with *inside* Cholula but *not* in those narrow streets you speak of. I cannot imagine where you got such a foolish idea! The white-skins are to be attacked and destroyed in the sacred precinct of the great pyramid of Quetzalcoatl *and nowhere else!* The god Hummingbird himself showed me this in a vision. Have you truly not, until now, understood the real reason for the ritual preparation of the pyramid by our excellent sorcerer Acopol?'

'We gave Acopol every cooperation, sire,' said Tlalchi, 'but we thought it better not to question.'

'Yet here you are,' Moctezuma pointed out, 'questioning me about narrow streets, and prattling like a pair of old women afraid of your own shadows when you should be preparing yourselves and your city. Don't you realise how soon the great moment will be upon you?'

A wordless look of concern passed between the two lords.

'I thought as much!' Moctezuma exclaimed. 'You haven't even taken the precaution of sending spies and runners of your own into Tlascala, have you?'

'No, sire. It is not safe there.'

'Not safe? *Not safe!* Bah! Spies are in the business of not being safe. Mine come and go and manage to survive and what they tell me is this. *The army of the white-skins marched out of Tlascala yesterday, supported by a thousand of Shikotenka's warriors!* They bivouacked in the open fields last night and they will certainly reach Cholula today. Most likely they are already there while you are here in Tenochtitlan, treasonously ill-informed and wasting my time with your petty concerns.'

Moctezuma stood, thrusting his stool back with such force that it crashed to the floor. He looked down at Tlaqui and Tlalchi, cowering beneath him. 'You will return to Cholula at once,' he said, 'and on the morning of the third day after today, when Maza has all his forces in place, you will spring the trap. Create some pretext, some subterfuge – I leave the details to you – but lure the white-skins to the sacred precinct, close and lock the gates, and have all your armed male citizens fall upon them there. I do not expect you to conquer and destroy them yourselves. That is not asked of you. Your task will merely be to begin the work and hold them within the walls of the precinct for the short time it takes – an hour at most – for Maza's regiments to reach you after the fighting begins. Do you think you can do that small thing for me without making a complete mess of it?'

The rulers of Cholula, it seemed, were absent from the city, and the lesser lords who had come out to greet Cortés had persuaded him to leave the small Tlascalan force camped in the surrounding fields. 'They're afraid of you,' Cortés told Shikotenka through Malinal. 'You should be flattered.'

'They should be afraid of *those*,' Shikotenka had said, pointing to the cannon that the foolish Cholulans had given entry to without a word of protest. The carriages were being pulled by Totonac bearers to whom, as Mexica vassals, the Cholulans had also granted access.

'Let us be thankful for small mercies,' Cortés replied with a wink. He paused thoughtfully, then added: 'Now hear me, Shikotenka: there are to be no rash actions, do you understand? I know how you feel about Cholula, but you must make no attack or do anything that could be interpreted as aggressive. Above all, although I know you're sorely tempted, don't bring in any more warriors from Tlascala. This is a delicate game I'm playing here with Moctezuma's fears and suspicions. You must leave me a free hand to play it as I think best.'

Five hours had passed since then, and the Spaniards had disappeared without a trace into the vast maw of Cholula, a city five times as large as Tlascala. 'I'm concerned for them,' Shikotenka admitted. 'I'm beginning to wonder if we'll ever see them again.'

'I don't understand you,' said Tree. 'Not so long ago you wanted to kill every one of them. Now you're worrying about them as if they're your children or something.'

'They're our allies,' Shikotenka replied gruffly. 'We have responsibilities for mutual protection under that alliance – responsibilities I take seriously.'

'It's more than that,' said Chipahua. 'The fact is, you like them. Why don't you just admit it?'

Shikotenka thought about this for a few moments. Finally he said: 'I like some of them. They're true warriors – courageous, skilful, loyal to one another, cruel to their enemies but willing to let bygones be bygones. Why should I not like them?'

'You could ask Ilhuicamina,' said Tree, 'if he hadn't died from his infected wounds. I'm sure he'd give you a thousand reasons why you should not like them.'

Shikotenka grimaced. They all missed Ilhuicamina. They were all still bitter about what Cortés had done to him. But war was war.

'What about Cortés?' Chipahua asked. 'Do you like him?'

'I do,' said Shikotenka. 'But I don't trust him. I'll never trust him. He would sell his own grandmother if the price was right.'

'Pity the poor Cholulans then,' laughed Chipahua, 'for allowing such a viper into their midst!'

Shikotenka lapsed into silence. Of course his friends were right. The Spaniards knew how to defend themselves. Even surrounded by enemies, in the midst of a hostile city, they would find a way to survive.

Yet still he felt restless, felt threat and danger in the air, felt the need to take action. As the sun set behind the great pyramid of Cholula, a pyramid so large it was known locally as *Tlachihualtepetl*, 'the artificial mountain', he called his men together and asked for a hundred volunteers.

Entombed in thick darkness in the ancient underground cavern beneath the great pyramid of Cholula, Tozi had long since lost any sense of whether it was day or night, and of how much time had passed since she was interred here. She had air to breathe, and after freeing herself from her bonds, she'd worked her way around the huge, irregular space, finding sufficient trickles of slime running down the rough rock walls to keep thirst at bay. Hunger was no great hardship, for she had been hungry many times before; eventually, as she'd expected, her contracting stomach ceased to trouble her with its sharp, demanding pangs.

What was strange was the way the darkness frequently yielded to light, and she saw extraordinary patterns, flows of dots merging together like waterfalls, scintillating zigzag lines, stars that burst and exploded, scattering flecks of fire, brilliantly coloured spirals that wheeled and spun, collections of dazzling triangles, circles and squares, and sometimes, thrusting forth through them, bizarre figures and forms she took to be spirits – a man with the head of a deer, a creature that was part fish, part alligator, a woman transformed into a puma, a giant serpent that wrapped itself around her and laid its great head upon her shoulder, gazing into her eyes with ineffable wisdom.

At some point a vortex of light opened up at her feet and she was drawn down into it in a rushing, whirling luminescent stream that carried her off helplessly, swirling and somersaulting through caverns and winding corridors until she was deposited gently on the shore of a vast midnight-dark lake in another world with a blue sun in a burnished sky. She had been here before! When the serpent had bitten her in the desert, just before the Huichol medicine men had found her and healed her, this was the place she'd been brought to in vision. And, just as before, she saw a woman dressed in red robes, with her back turned, sitting on a rock in the lake, her bare feet dangling in the water. The woman had long black hair which she was combing, combing, and Tozi was again overtaken by the poignant sense of familiarity that had tortured her in her vision of Aztlán and the Caves of Chicomoztoc, which had been left so hauntingly unexplained. She walked closer, stepped into the water which came only to her knees, and was wading out towards the rock when the woman looked round and she recognised her own long-lost mother.

Tozi was running now, splashing through the water, great sobs of joy wracking her whole body as she climbed up onto the rock and embraced her mother, who seemed absolutely present in that place – her scent, her warmth, the urgency of her embrace, everything about her, solid and tangible and real. 'Oh, mother,' Tozi heard herself saying, 'oh, how I've missed you', and her mother replied, 'I've missed you too, my darling,' and they held each other a moment longer until suddenly, cruelly, inexorably, the whole scene dissolved back into absolute darkness and Tozi knew the truth – that she lay entombed beneath the great pyramid of Cholula, bereft of her powers, cut off forever from all hope of life or rescue and unutterably alone.

It was the twins Momotztli and Nopaltzin, men of his old squad, men he'd trust with his life, who brought Shikotenka the news the following morning. They'd been amongst the hundred scouts he'd sent out in different directions around Cholula to see what they could learn. Well after midnight, they'd entered a steep-sided valley called Citlaltépec, about four miles north of the city, and started to work their way along the bank of a stream running through the valley floor, when they'd almost stumbled into a Mexica sentry post.

'There was no moon,' said Momotztli, 'otherwise we'd have seen the bastards sooner—'

'Or they might have seen us,' added his brother.

'But they didn't,' Momotztli continued.

'Which was just as well for them,' said Nopaltzin. 'I reckon we could have taken them any time.'

'But just as well for us we didn't have to,' said Momotztli. 'We were able to sneak up close, hunker down and listen to their gossip.'

Nopaltzin took up the story. 'Seems they're part of a big force that's mustering there. *Huge* force, in fact. Six regiments . . .'

'All in honour of our friends the Spaniards,' Momotztli added.

'So there's an attack planned,' Nopaltzin continued, 'two days from today in the morning. Seems the Cholulans are going to start it with a mass uprising inside the city to distract our friends' attention, then the regiments are going to pile in. They're going to try to take most of them alive . . .'

'They've been issued with special poles with leather collars on the end,' Momotztli elaborated. 'And hammocks! Lots of hammocks!' He laughed. 'The plan is to capture some of the Spaniards with the poles and tie the rest up in the hammocks and then carry them off to Tenochtitlan for sacrifice—'

'Except for twenty of them,' Nopaltzin remembered. 'They'll be handed over to the Cholulans to sacrifice here.'

Chipahua had been listening in: 'Hammocks!' he scoffed. 'Poles! Typical Mexica wet dream – nice warm fantasy followed by a nasty damp bed. You can tell they haven't faced the Spaniards in battle yet. If they had, they'd know six regiments are nowhere near enough.'

Shikotenka was sitting very still, thinking, calculating. Cortés had said he was to bring no more men to Cholula, and take no aggressive actions, but that was before either of them knew that close to fifty thousand Mexica warriors were mobilising for battle outside the city.

Chipahua nudged him: 'You're cooking something up, aren't you?' he said. 'You've got that look in your eye.'

Suddenly interested, Tree edged closer.

Pepillo brought his diary up to date on Friday 15 October, the second full day the Spaniards had spent in Cholula.

'We reached the city,' he wrote, 'on Wednesday 13 October, and entered it with all our cannon and cavalry, and our Totonac auxiliaries and bearers; however, the Tlascalans who had accompanied us were obliged to remain camped in the fields outside.

'The rulers of Cholula, Tlaqui and Tlalchi by name, were not present when we arrived. They were, we were told, in Tenochtitlan. They returned yesterday, Thursday 14 October, and installed themselves in their palace, but yet refused to see us. This the caudillo thought very rude, particularly so since they sent persons of no great importance to treat with us. He informed these minor lords through Malinal that an embassy such as ours, from such a great prince as Don Carlos, King of Spain, should not be received by men such as they, and that even their masters were hardly worthy to receive it. He gave orders that Tlaqui and Tlalchi should appear before him this morning, otherwise he would be forced to proceed against them as rebels who refused to subject themselves to the dominion of the king.

'This morning, however, Friday 15 October, even though we were quartered in two tall, spacious buildings overlooking the main plaza with its great pyramid, and adjacent to their palace, the rulers still did not appear. Instead they sent a message claiming they were both very sick. Adequate food supplies were provided to us yesterday and the day before, but none whatsoever were provided today. We all take this as an ominous sign, particularly since there is great unrest in the town, with large numbers of people, mainly women and children, leaving carrying their belongings. Malinal very bravely went out disguised as a local woman and found close to our lodgings some holes dug in the streets, covered over with wood and earth in such a way they could not be seen without careful examination. When she removed a little of the earth from above one of these holes she found it was full of sharp stakes to kill the horses when they charged, as our friends the Tlascalans had warned us. She saw that the roofs of many of the houses had breastworks of dried clay and were piled with stones, and this could be for no friendly purpose, since she also found barricades of stout timbers in another street.

'Worse, Malinal learned from gossip in the market that twenty young men are being sacrificed every morning to the Mexica god of war, Hummingbird, so that he will give the Cholulans victory in an attack they will soon launch against us. She also heard it said, she believes reliably, that many ropes and stout poles with leather collars attached had recently been prepared and stored in the armoury of the palace, ready to be used to hold us prisoner, as well as hammocks in which we are to be tied and carried off to Tenochtitlan for sacrifice.

'When the caudillo learned all this he showed no surprise, but became very grim and serious. "Since the Cholulans plan such treachery," he said, "we'd better make preparations to attack them first and teach them a lesson." He went at once with Malinal and twenty of our soldiers, all bearing arms, directly to the palace of Tlaqui and Tlalchi. I also followed, bringing Melchior on the caudillo's suggestion. There was an altercation with the guards at the gate of the palace, and Don Pedro Alvarado and several of our captains drew their swords, but Malinal calmed the situation and we were given entrance and led into the presence of the two peculiar old men who rule this city. They were very alarmed and so confused they could hardly speak. The presence of Melchior, who snarled at them and would, I think, have attacked them had he not been leashed, seemed to discomfit them particularly! They denied they had any intention of taking us prisoner, or that human sacrifices were being carried out, avowing that their god was Quetzalcoatl, a deity of peace, not the dread Hummingbird, but Malinal informed the caudillo quietly that they were lying. They said they would search for food for us but claimed their lord Moctezuma had sent them orders not to give us any and did not want us to advance any further.

'At this the caudillo announced they need not trouble themselves as we would depart Cholula tomorrow morning, Saturday 16 October, to proceed to Tenochtitlan to see Moctezuma himself and resolve all problems. He insisted that like other peoples we had encountered on our route of march, such as the Tlascalans and the Totonacs, they should provide us with a force of warriors from their city (he demanded no less than two thousand) and also bearers (again two thousand), for we should have need of them on the road. Finally he required that this escort of warriors and bearers should meet us in the plaza of the great pyramid in front of our lodgings tomorrow morning at one hour after dawn, and that all the lords of Cholula, including the two rulers, and all the heads of household of the population of the city should also assemble there. He wished, he said, to bid them a proper farewell and inform them of certain things that it would be greatly to their advantage to know.

'As Malinal translated these words, I noticed a very strange, sinister look, and hidden smiles, passing between Tlaqui and Tlalchi, who readily assented to everything the caudillo had asked. They then begged to be excused, saying they had many preparations to make for the morrow.

'It was late afternoon when we returned to our lodgings where the caudillo at once summoned all the principal captains, heads of companies and platoon sergeants to inform them of his plan for war.'

The gathering was held in the spacious, high-ceilinged audience chamber on the second floor of the grander of the two adjacent lodgings granted to the Spaniards. A balcony running the whole length of the room commanded a wide view over the city's main plaza, with many small, brightly coloured temples clustered at its edges, and the mountainous great pyramid of Cholula looming at its centre. The plaza itself, measuring a thousand paces on each side, was set within a high enclosure wall, decorated with richly painted reliefs of plumed serpents. These, Malinal said, were the emblems of the god of peace, Quetzalcoatl, to whom the pyramid had been dedicated in ancient times, and with whom Cortés, to his advantage, was frequently identified by the Indians.

Towering on the pyramid's summit was a tall temple, likewise dedicated to the peaceful Quetzalcoatl, yet at its east side squatted a fearsome and bestial idol of the war god Hummingbird – a recent addition according to Malinal – overlooking a hemisphere of stone, across which sacrificial victims would be stretched to have their hearts cut out. Standing beside that stone this evening, gazing intently down at the Spanish quarters, was the lone figure of a man, dressed only in a loincloth, his whole body covered in tattoos.

'Their high priest?' Cortés asked Malinal.

She shook her head: 'No! He *nagual* – very special sorcerer. Have great power.'

At this Cortés found he had involuntarily crossed himself. So too, he noticed, had Sandoval and Díaz, who stood nearby and had overheard. But Alvarado, who was with them, merely scoffed. 'Sorcerer my arse,' he said.

'I heard in town his name Acopol,' Malinal continued. 'Moctezuma gave him command of rituals at pyramid. He's the one makes the sacrifices there.'

'We'll put a stop to that,' said Cortés.

'Tomorrow?' Malinal asked. 'There will be ceremony at dawn, like today, like yesterday. Unless you stop it, twenty more young men die.'

She was looking Cortés directly in the eye and he shifted uncomfortably. Somehow the woman had the knack of making him feel guilty about almost everything he did. 'Unfortunately we have to allow the sacrifices to proceed tomorrow,' he said. 'To march up there and stop them would put the lords of this city on their guard, and that would be a mistake. I need that assembly of citizens they've promised in the morning.'

'Why do you need?'

'Because I have to take exemplary action here if we're going to avoid much worse trouble in the future.'

'Exemplary action? What that?'

'We have to make an example of them,' said Cortés. 'Not just of the sacrificers but of the whole city. They've defied us and they're planning to attack us and we need to teach them and others that that doesn't pay.'

'So you sacrifice them all then? Like you sacrificed people of Teocacingo?'

Cortés sighed: 'Sacrifice? Your Spanish is very good now, Malinal, but you have the wrong word. It's simply a matter of kill or be killed, attack or be attacked.'

Predictably not all the captains supported Cortés's plan. Some – De Grado again, always the most forward in urging retreat! – wanted to leave Cholula that very night and return to the safety of Tlascala. Others were also in favour of an immediate departure, but preferred to continue the advance, Ordaz in particular arguing for a new route to Tenochtitlan through the Republic of Huexotzinco which, like Tlascala, was in a state of open warfare with the Mexica, and might provide a source of additional allies against Moctezuma. The majority, however, were with Cortés in favouring a pre-emptive strike against the Cholulans. 'If we let this treachery pass unpunished,' Alvarado said, 'they'll never take us seriously again. I say let's fight them here. They'll feel the effect more in their homes than in the open fields.'

It was Cortés's way to allow his captains to speak, and sometimes to listen to them, but Saint Peter had convinced him that something momentous, something *exemplary*, must happen here. Had the welcome given to the Spaniards been different, had the city fallen at their feet in abject surrender, he might perhaps have spared it, despite the counsel of his dreams. But the evasiveness of its rulers, the preparations in the streets for war, the failure to deliver food supplies today, and the need to give Moctezuma an unambiguous demonstration of Spanish resolve, all made a massacre inevitable.

'Gentlemen,' Cortés said, holding up his hand to silence the series of noisy arguments that had broken out amongst the captains. 'Gentlemen! Hear me if you will.' He turned to De Grado and gave him a broad smile. 'Alonso, you are suggesting we run from a fight here in Cholula to seek the "safety" of Tlascala when not so long ago you were urging us to run from Tlascala to seek the "safety" of the Totonac Hills! I think it's obvious, if I'd listened to your counsel of despair then, that Tlascala would *not* be a place of safety for us today, filled with willing allies, but a place of danger filled with triumphant enemies. By the same logic, therefore, I shall not listen to your counsel of despair now! We must impose our will on Cholula as we did on Tlascala. Anything else would be pure folly.'

Cheers from Alvarado's faction filled the room, De Grado blushed and lowered his head, and Cortés turned to Ordaz: 'As for you, Diego, I could not be more in agreement. It has long been my strategy to win the allegiance of the Huexotzincos and form a grand alliance with them and the Tlascalans and others who oppose Moctezuma. To do this, however, there's no need for us to spend our time marching to Huexotzinco, for they already know how matters turned out between us and Tlascala and when they see us win a great victory against their bitter enemies here in Cholula, I assure you they'll come flocking to our standard.'

Ordaz nodded slowly. 'You're right, Hernán,' he said. 'I'm with you.'

Cortés looked round the room and asked: 'So are we agreed, gentlemen? Shall we teach these Cholulans a lesson in the morning?'

It was Bernal Díaz who stood up: 'Let's give them the beating they deserve,' he said, and it was plain he spoke for everyone. 'I say forward and good luck to us!'

After that it was just a matter of sorting out the details.

As though it was really the Spaniards' intention to leave in the morning, a great show was made of packing and tying the army's baggage which, as the evening progressed, was stacked up under guard out on the plaza ready to be transported by the bearers the Cholulans had promised to provide. Meanwhile Francisco de Mesa set his Taino slaves and Totonac bearers to work, hauling both lombards and six of the falconets up to the audience chamber, where they were loaded with grapeshot and placed on the balcony overlooking the plaza. At the same time, Cortés sent Bernal Díaz with Sandoval and García Brabo to reconnoitre the four main gateways in the enclosure wall surrounding the plaza, and to organise teams of soldiers to take possession of them in the morning.

When all preparations had been made to his satisfaction, Cortés retired to his private quarters with Malinal and took his pleasure on her, but he was too excited to sleep. Restless, he rose and dressed in the half-light before dawn, walked through the audience chamber to the balcony, leaned against the cold barrel of one of the lombards and observed, fascinated, the great crowds of Indians beginning to gather in the plaza as twenty captives were led up the steps of the great pyramid.

The savage blare of conches and the beat of drums welcomed the rebirth of the sun, its first rays glinted on the monstrous granite visage of Hummingbird, and the sacrifices began.

Moctezuma had spent the night wakeful within his chambers in the warded confines of his palace, and at each of the hours of darkness dedicated to the nine Lords of the Night, he had sacrificed a three-year-old girl to Hummingbird as a token of the birthday present he was preparing for the war god. He had left instructions that any messenger from Cholula should be brought directly to him, and now, as the sun rose and the hour of Huehueteotl, god of fire, ushered in the dawn, an exhausted runner was admitted to his presence.

'Sire,' the man said, throwing himself down on his face. 'I am to inform you that all has been done as you commanded. The lords Tlaqui and Tlalchi have devised a cunning plan. Even now, the white-skins will be gathering with all their belongings in the sacred plaza of Cholula, where they have been summoned to bid farewell to the lords and heads of household of our city, while a great escort of soldiers and bearers prepares to assist their march to Tenochtitlan. There will be some exchange of speeches, sire, to allay the suspicions of the white-skins, and when he divines the moment to be correct, the sorcerer Acopol will blow three blasts on the war trumpet. This will be the signal for the regiments of General Maza to move into the city and for our citizens and soldiers, bearing secret arms, to fall upon the white-skins—'

'I don't want them all killed!' said Moctezuma sharply. 'I must have captives brought here for sacrifice. I trust Tlaqui and Tlalchi understand this.'

'Orders have been given accordingly, sire. The lords and all the citizens of Cholula understand that every effort must be made to take the white-skins alive.'

'Very good,' said Moctezuma. Dismissing the runner, he summoned the priests of Hummingbird, who stood in attendance to bring him another child.

* * *

459

Malinal was with Cortés on the balcony where Mesa's gun crews stood poised by the cannon ready to fire. Behind them in the audience chamber was Pepillo, sitting by Melchior; the caudillo had permitted him to chain his dog for safekeeping in a corner. The rest of the war hounds were penned below in the courtyard, since there was no plan to deploy them in today's battle. Vendabal had offered them, but Cortés had replied 'only in extremis', which Malinal understood to mean only if the fighting went against the conquistadors. Otherwise, Cortés had said, the animals were better kept out of the way. In the enclosed space of the grand plaza there was a danger they would be killed by the Spanish guns and tangle the hooves of the cavalry.

Thirteen cavalry horses had survived the war with the Tlascalans; these were now lined up right beneath the balcony at the edge of the plaza. All were fully barded, twelve with their riders in armour already in the saddle, while the thirteenth, Molinero, was held steady by a groom awaiting Cortés's arrival. Lined up in front of the horses in five disciplined squares of fifty were two hundred and fifty foot soldiers, also heavily armoured. The remainder of the men, in four teams of twenty, had quietly taken up positions at the north, south, east and west sides of the plaza by the four massive gateways.

Separated from the main body of conquistadors by a strip of clear paving a few dozen paces wide, Tlaqui and Tlalchi were hunched in their ceremonial robes, surrounded by a hundred other lords of the city. Behind them, in sullen, threatening ranks, were the two thousand Cholulan soldiers Cortés had requested, here supposedly to provide the Spaniards with a safe escort to Tenochtitlan, and by their side a large group of two thousand 'bearers', themselves all obviously soldiers. Many of the latter were in pairs with hammocks suspended between them, in which they repeatedly invited the Spanish to lie down. 'Come, *tueles*,' they called out, elaborating their meaning with extravagant signs and gestures, 'take your rest, great lords. Let us carry you to Tenochtitlan to meet our god.' Their knowing grins and grimaces left Malinal in no doubt they were mightily pleased with themselves. Poor ones! They clearly believed they'd fooled Cortés and were going to have an easy time of it.

Behind them the whole plaza seethed with the men of Cholula

– ten thousand at least, Malinal thought. Making little effort to conceal the *macuahuitls*, clubs and knives they held, they filled every available space, lining the tops of the walls, occupying the roofs of the gate towers where piles of rock were clearly in evidence, lapping at the base of the great pyramid, clustering up its sloping sides and milling in their hundreds around the temple and idols on its summit platform. Equally ominous was the excited, buzzing murmur of the even larger crowd that had gathered beyond the walls: clearly the whole city had turned out to witness the humiliation and destruction of the Spaniards.

'It's time,' Cortés whispered, taking Malinal by the elbow and guiding her forward to the edge of the balcony. They stood side by side for a moment, looking over the multitude, before he began his address in his usual ringing tones, pausing at intervals to allow her to give her translation.

'Lords and citizens of Cholula,' he said – and at once all faces turned towards him and a pregnant silence descended. 'I know all of your evil plans. I know of the poles you have gathered with nooses you intend to slip round our necks, I know of the real purpose of those hammocks you invite us to lie down in. I know of the holes you have dug in your streets, the sharpened stakes you have planted, the barricades you have erected. I know you have sent your women and children from the city because you expect fighting and wish to keep them from harm. I know that in return for us coming to you like brothers, you hope to capture us and kill us and eat our flesh, here and in Tenochtitlan. I know of the vile sacrifices you have offered to your god of war in the vain hope he will give you victory – but he is wicked and false and has no power over us. All this treachery you have planned is about to recoil on you. Your city will be destroyed so that no trace of it will remain and all of you, every one of you, will die for your crimes.'

As Malinal put these last threatening words into Nahuatl, a great roar went up, weapons were brandished and there was a general surge of movement forward towards the Spanish squares. 'Now, Mesa!' said Cortés calmly, and at once all eight guns on the balcony belched flame and smoke and sent their whistling storm of death into the further reaches of the crowd, causing instant panic. At the same instant Malinal saw a flying squad of ten men led by García Brabo dash out from one of the squares below, cut down the guards around Tlaqui and Tlalchi, lift the astonished lords bodily from the ground and carry them back into the Spanish quarters. There came a pounding on the stairs and seconds later the two chiefs were thrown to the floor of the audience chamber and tied hand and foot.

'Stay here,' Cortés commanded Malinal. 'Keep an eye on them. I'm going down to get in the fight.'

As he hurried off she heard the rolling thunder of a concentrated volley of musket fire in the plaza and, rising above the din of battle, the familiar, hideous screech of a Mexica war trumpet sounding from the summit of the great pyramid.

Three distinct blasts were blown and Melchior, still chained in the corner of the audience chamber, howled mournfully as though in answer.

Díaz cursed, ducked under his raised shield and hurriedly ran out of range as a new shower of rocks pelted down from the roof of the gate tower. Ten or fifteen men were visible up there, but the musketeers had already fired a volley and had been forced to pull back to reload.

Because of the huge bulk of the great pyramid in the centre of the plaza, none of the four gateways were in the line of fire of the cannon on the balcony. Since the Spaniards' lodgings stood on the east side of the plaza, however, the slaughter unleashed was fully visible from the east gate, and much of the devastation could also be seen across the corners of the pyramid from the north and south gates. Only the west gate, on the opposite side of the monument, was completely out of sight, and Díaz had known, when he'd elected to secure this gate, that the mob was likely to be less demoralised and put up more of a fight here. Even so, the mere sound of the cannon salvo, and the wails and screams that rose up immediately afterwards, had worked their magic, scattering most of the defenders, and the first volley from his five musketeers had killed or chased off the rest. Once the men on the tower were dealt with, resistance here would be over and his squad could keep the gate closed and barred, as they'd been ordered, until the grim work of killing in the plaza was done.

The tower had an internal wooden stairway, also vulnerable to

462

attack from above, that zigzagged to the roof in three flights. On a signal from the captain of the musketeers, Díaz yelled to his men, shuffled into rank between Mibiercas and La Serna as they raised their shields, locked the edges together with the shields of the rest of the squad and darted forward in a mass under a solid armoured carapace. Glancing up as he charged, Díaz saw that all the defenders on top of the tower had crowded forward near the edge of the flat roof, the better to push down heaps of stones and, in the process – these men knew nothing of guns! – had made themselves easy targets. As the barrage of falling rocks beat down on the shield carapace, he heard the crash of the second musket volley and screams from above. He knew the shooters had found their marks when tumbling bodies joined the avalanche, hit the shields with tremendous force and fell limp and dead to the ground.

Then Díaz was inside the tower and taking the stairs three at a time, with Mibiercas ahead of him, La Serna behind and a dozen other men following. A few rocks came flying but they brushed them aside with their shields. Mibiercas gutted a screaming warrior who jabbed ineffectually at him with a spear on the second landing, and then, as they bounded up the final flight, they heard the tremendous percussion of the second cannon barrage, followed by some other, even louder and more ruinous sound, and burst out unopposed onto the roof to find the remaining defenders had cast aside their weapons and thrown themselves on their faces. The Spaniards fell upon them without mercy, quickly killing them all before they realised what had caused their abject surrender. Somehow Mesa had cranked up the elevation of one of the lombards sufficiently to fire a seventy-pound ball into the great temple perched on the flat top of the pyramid, and the projectile had clearly hit some crucial structural element, for it had brought half the edifice tumbling down amidst a thunder of collapsing masonry and a huge pall of dust that rapidly billowed out to fill the sky above the plaza like the smoke of hellfire.

Looking down from the roof of the tower, Díaz saw his five musketeers with their backs to the gate, swords drawn, stabbing and hacking at a screaming, hysterical throng desperate only to escape the plaza. But they would not be allowed to escape. Not one of them. Cortés's orders were quite specific on that point. 'With me, men,' Díaz yelled, as he led his squad down the stairs again at a run, soon reinforcing the musketeers at the gate and joining with them in the general slaughter. A troop of cavalry led by Cortés thundered round the south-west corner of the pyramid and charged the rear of the crowd with lances levelled. In the wake of the cavalry came a square of fifty infantry, their swords already steeped to the hilt in blood, driving further hordes of screaming refugees before them. Seeing the gates barred, some of those who fled climbed on one another's shoulders in desperate efforts to scale the walls, where they made easy targets for the teams of snipers who'd begun to work their way methodically around the plaza.

Díaz tasted the metallic tang of blood in his mouth as he killed and killed again, his face set, his sword arm already aching.

Deep beneath the great pyramid, Tozi heard the crash and roar of distant thunder and felt the cave floor shake. If these sounds were from the outside world, as they seemed to be, then they were the first to reach her since the start of her imprisonment here. 'No,' she said out loud, instinctively resisting the idea, her voice croaky and wavering, 'No. I don't think so.'

There had, after all, been many strange visions, many encounters here in the dark, and all of them, every one, had proved to be false – so there was no reason why this should be any different.

With a groan, she rolled onto her belly. She was so far gone in hunger and weakness now that she found it hard to stand. With great difficulty and low moans of pain, she got her hands and knees under her and began to crawl along her familiar track towards the wall. At last she found the trail of sour slime she was seeking and pressed her parched lips and tongue against it, lapping at the moisture.

Alvarado dismounted from Bucephalus, handed the reins to his groom and stalked off across the plaza on foot, swinging his falchion. He had enjoyed himself enormously, galloping around with the rest of the cavalry, running down the panicked and fleeing Cholulans, driving them up against the barred gates, killing thirty or more with his lance and watching many times that number trampled underfoot by their own compatriots in a dozen hysterical stampedes. What with the activities of the other cavaliers, the infantry running rampage with their swords and pikes, many volleys of musket fire, and the mass slaughter worked at the outset by the two salvos of grapeshot from the eight cannon on the balcony, the whole plaza was now so densely covered with fallen, broken, gutted Indians that he walked over nothing but bodies and heard nothing but the groans of the wounded and the dying.

Alvarado made for a knot of twenty or so dazed Indians milling near the steps that ascended the east face of the great pyramid. Some of them were still armed, but they were so shocked and disoriented they didn't look capable of using their primitive spears and native broadswords and, as they saw him approach with the huge falchion in his hand, they threw their weapons down. Fools and cowards! Better by far to fight, and sell their lives dearly, for not one of them would leave this place alive! Sprinting the last few paces, his mailed boots crunching over the skulls and throats of fallen men, Alvarado began coldly, systematically, precisely to cut the group of survivors down. None of them tried to come against him. They just stood there like dumb animals awaiting slaughter, as he chopped the heavy blade of the falchion into their unprotected heads and necks. Very few needed more than a single blow, but some he disdained to kill, hacking off their legs or arms instead and leaving them to die slowly of their injuries, screaming in agony. A few tried to run from him, fleeing up the steps of the pyramid; with a wild laugh, his armour dripping blood, Alvarado went after them.

The steps were hurdled with fallen masonry from the ruined temple on the summit. *Good shot there by Mesa!* Alvarado thought as he hacked another fugitive to death. With a despairing wail, the next man turned and tried to grapple with him, but Alvarado slashed the falchion across his belly, left him holding his guts and steadily, remorselessly, continued his climb. By the time he reached the top he'd killed all the men he was pursuing and he wasn't even breathing heavily. God, it felt good to be alive!

He looked around the summit platform. Several hundred Indians had been up here at the beginning of the morning, but most now lay crushed under gigantic blocks where Mesa's seventy-pound wrecking ball had torn the temple apart, and the rest, it seemed, had fled. However, the great structure was by no means completely flattened; large sections of it still stood and, where a dark corridor led into an intact wing, Alvarado saw a flicker of movement. He grinned and swung the falchion. Good! Still some murder to be done up here then.

The squads at the gates had done their work well: not one of the Indians who had come here, so puffed up with bravado and treachery that morning, had been allowed to escape. Blood flowed everywhere in rivers and pooled in lakes; thousands had died beneath the swords and spears of the conquistadors, and thousands more beneath the guns and in the resulting crush and panic. Sporadic bursts of musket fire could be heard as little groups of Indians who'd somehow survived until now were rounded up and finished off, and there were still pockets of resistance in some of the temples at the edges of the plaza but, rather than risk losing men storming these, Cortés had ordered great fires to be started. A dozen structures were already ablaze, sending up palls of acrid smoke; in some cases the defendants chose to remain inside and burn to death, while those who ran out screaming for mercy were butchered on the spot.

Cortés dismounted and handed Molinero's reins to Pepillo. Cortés had not allowed him to participate in the morning's action, but he'd come down from the audience chamber to meet the caudillo. Despite the courage and fighting spirit he'd shown at the hill of Tzompach, the boy was white faced now at the sight of so much death. 'You're a good lad,' Cortés said, tousling his hair with mailed fingers, 'but you need to cultivate a stronger stomach – you and Malinal both.'

'Malinal's stomach's strong enough,' the boy said with a surprising hint of defiance. 'The things she's seen, the things she's done. She's fearless, sir, but she has a kind heart. No one can blame her for a kind heart.'

Cortés nodded. No one could blame Malinal for her kind heart or deny her courage, he reflected, and Pepillo was right to remind him of this. 'Out of the mouths of babes and sucklings,' he said quietly, 'hast thou ordained strength because of thine enemies, that thou might still the enemy and the avenger.'

'What's that, sir?' asked Pepillo.

'Oh, nothing, lad, nothing. Take Molinero into the courtyard with the other horses, then go back to the audience chamber and guard Malinal well. She's a precious jewel to us.'

Pleased to see Pepillo was wearing the broadsword Escalante had given him, Cortés turned away from the boy and walked towards the steps of the great pyramid. All resistance there had ended when the temple had come crashing down; the summit platform, cleared of the foe, would provide an excellent vantage point to consider what should be done next. Pepillo's horror had touched him more deeply than he would have thought possible, and he realised he was beginning to reconsider his original plan to sack the entire city and kill every man, woman and child left within it. There was much to be said for mercy and perhaps, after all, the slaughter in the plaza would suffice to punish Cholula's treachery and send an unmistakable message to Moctezuma.

'Surely goodness and mercy,' Cortés recited as he climbed, 'shall follow me all the days of my life and I will dwell in the house of the Lord for ever.'

The audience chamber – with Tlaqui and Tlalchi still lying bound on the floor, Melchior still chained in the corner and straining furiously at his leash – had been deserted by the gun crews. 'Where's everyone gone?' Pepillo asked Malinal.

'Out into the plaza,' she answered, 'to join the killing and looting. It seems these are activities your people excel at; even the Mexica are not so thorough.' She walked to the balcony where the cannon stood silent and untended, and looked down on the heaps of bodies, the great pools and puddles of blood, the burning temples, and Spanish soldiers swarming everywhere, finishing off the wounded, going through clothing, helping themselves to the belongings of the dead. Pepillo joined her. 'It makes me ashamed,' he admitted.

'Me also,' Malinal agreed.

'The caudillo believes violence now will prevent more violence later,' said Pepillo.

'Then let's hope he's right. Tenochtitlan is a much larger city than Cholula. Twenty times larger, twenty times more people, twenty times better defended, but if we have to fight to seize it, I fear there will be a hundred times more deaths.'

Malinal's mind was in turmoil. Never until now had her determination to end Moctezuma's rule wavered, but looking down at the slaughter and devastation in the plaza, she wondered for the first time if she was doing the right thing. Still, despite it all, she knew she loved the great caudillo and continued to believe he was a good man sent to do the work of the god of peace.

Behind, in the audience chamber, Tlaqui groaned. 'Release us, kind lady,' he said. 'We are in pain.'

'Release us we beg you,' echoed Tlalchi, 'while none of the white demons are here. Let us flee this place. We know a way to escape.'

'We can't let them go,' said Pepillo.

Though he preferred to speak to her in Spanish, she'd seen the boy's grasp of Nahuatl improve enormously in recent months. 'They will be tortured,' she replied.

'Not if they tell the caudillo what he wants to know.'

'Even if they do, I still think he'll torture them. If they were just enemies, it wouldn't be so bad, but they lied to him, betrayed him. He never forgives betrayal.' She paused, tilted her head to one side. 'Did you hear that?' she asked.

Pepillo wrinkled his brow: 'What?'

'That. Listen.'

Then they both heard the sound – the stealthy tread of bare feet on the stairs, not coming up from the plaza or the courtyard, but descending from the floor above.

That floor gave access to the roof and there were no Spaniards there. 'Quick,' said Malinal, grabbing Pepillo's arm and running for the door. 'We have to get out of here.'

He shook her off and ran to unchain Melchior.

Alvarado was hunting a man, an elusive man, a cunning man, perhaps even a dangerous man, who ran and dodged and doubled back almost soundlessly through the labyrinth of chambers and passageways in the largely intact western wing of the gigantic ruined temple.

Even here, parts of the roof had collapsed, leaving some areas in complete darkness, while in others brilliant shafts of light pierced the gloom, revealing swirling clouds of suspended dust.

And much else.

In one long, narrow room, stinking of blood and incense, he found four hundred human heads threaded like abacus beads onto poles that penetrated them from ear to ear, and were fixed in orderly racks lining the walls. Pausing to examine the grisly trophies, Alvarado saw they had all been taken from young Indian men, some freshly butchered with the flesh and features still intact, some in such an advanced state of decomposition they must have been killed weeks before. Involuntarily his fingers tightened round the hilt of the falchion. He was not afraid. He was never afraid. But he had to admit to a certain sense of unease at the aura of evil filling this charnel house of the demon.

As he advanced towards the narrow doorway leading into the next room, a slither in the dust and a rapid, receding *pad, pad, pad* of bare feet told him his prey had been waiting silently there, no doubt hoping he'd give up the chase. *Hope on, dear boy*, Alvarado thought, increasing his speed, *but I will have your head and mount it on a spear if it takes me all day.* He was at a full run, pounding along a narrow corridor spanned by a low corbel vault, leaving the faint ghostly light of the chamber of skulls behind, plunging on into absolute darkness. He burst through into some larger chamber, almost blind now, and suddenly he heard a feral screech – something between a shriek and a roar that made the hair on his arms stand on end – as he was hit from behind by a snarling, powerful, muscled weight that felt like a man and yet not a man and exuded a rank animal stench and raked the steel of his cuirass with long, curved claws.

Instinct took over and Alvarado jabbed back viciously with his right elbow, caught his attacker full in the face, hearing some bone break, and simultaneously swivelled and lashed out with the falchion in a long curving sweep, shouting with battle joy 'Yes!' as the blade bit solidly into flesh and elicited a long, keening yowl of pain and fury. Something sharp – knife, claw, fang, he did not know – slashed along his left upper arm, cleaving the unprotected muscle (for he'd scorned wearing rerebraces today), but again his response was instant, a punching blow with the tip of the falchion that made another solid hit and drove the creature off.

Alvarado raced after it through the darkness, guided by sound alone, bleeding freely from his gashed arm and not caring, the need to kill so strong on him it ached like hunger.

Cortés reached the top of the eastern stairway. Ahead of him the granite idol of Hummingbird, squat and ugly, all tusks and fangs, had been thrown on its side, crushing three men, a great crack splitting its monstrous reptilian features. Beyond it the eastern wing of the temple brought down by Mesa's cannonball had been reduced to great chunks of rubble that lay scattered and piled everywhere, as though by an earthquake, upon more of the pulverised dead.

Cortés turned and looked down. An ocean of tumbled, bloody corpses stretched away from the base of the pyramid to the edge of the plaza, where the two tall lodging houses of the Spaniards were joined to the palace of Tlaqui and Tlalchi under a shared flat roof, the rear elevations of the three buildings towering above the massive enclosure wall surrounding the whole plaza. Cortés saw the cannon, the two great lombards, the six falconets, lined up on the balcony of the Spanish quarters, and tut-tutted that they appeared to have been left untended while their crews roamed amongst the dead, looting at will. Neither Malinal nor Pepillo were on the balcony, but he thought he saw movement inside the audience chamber, so that was where they must be – no doubt keeping guard on Tlaqui and Tlalchi, who he intended to put to torture very soon. Once their feet were basted with oil and held in a fire they would have much to tell him about Moctezuma's part in what had been planned here at Cholula.

Looking down again, Cortés saw Díaz and his friends Mibiercas and La Serna walking with Sandoval, picking their way amongst the heaped bodies in the plaza. They parted company at the foot of the stairway he had just climbed, Sandoval jogging up the steps towards him, Díaz and the others turning towards the Spanish quarters.

'Sandoval,' Cortés called down, 'how goes it?'

* * *

As Pepillo reached Melchior, ready to slip his chain, five heavily armed Cholulan Indians in loincloths and war-paint burst into the room. One seized Malinal in the doorway. Another threw himself across the floor at Pepillo, taking hold of him before he could free Melchior. Letting go of the dog's chain, Pepillo tried to draw his sword, but the Indian gave him a hard knock to the head that sent him sprawling, followed him, struck him again and ripped his sword away. Melchior barked and snarled, tugging frantically at the full extent of the chain, but could not break loose. Giving him a wide berth, the Indians dragged Malinal back into the middle of the room. One stifled her screams with a hand clamped over her mouth. Two others drew long flint knives and cut Tlaqui and Tlalchi free.

Pepillo lay limp, feigning unconsciousness, his Nahuatl quite good enough to understand from the rapid exchange of words what was happening. The intruders were part of the personal bodyguard of the Cholulan rulers. Left behind to protect the palace that morning, they'd seen Brabo's flying squad grab Tlaqui and Tlalchi from the plaza just as the fighting began, and had now crept across by way of the roof to rescue their masters.

The leader of the gang – a tall, sleekly muscled warrior whose name was Ecatepec – wanted to kill Pepillo and Malinal right away, but Tlaqui was against it: 'They're important to the white-skins,' he said, 'especially the woman. We can use them as hostages.'

'It won't work,' said Ecatepec. 'We have to get them up the stairs, across the roof, back into the palace, which the white-skins are busy looting, down the stairs and into the secret tunnel. Without them we might just make it, with them kicking up a fuss we're done for. Better to kill them and take our chances.'

Pepillo saw the elderly rulers exchange one of their secret looks and then Tlalchi said: 'Very well, kill them.'

Alvarado pursued his quarry into a vault that was dimly lit by a row of high, narrow windows. Unlike in the other chambers of the temple, there was no exit corridor here. This long narrow room, with a brazier of burning coals at one side and a stone idol of a huge plumed serpent twenty feet tall rearing up at the other, was a dead end.

The man, the creature – whatever it was – turned finally at bay. In this half-light, covered in blood from a broken nose, from the long cut the falchion had scored across the width of its chest and from a second deep wound in its shoulder, it did appear at first truly like a monster from another world. Though human enough, its arms, legs and body were densely inscribed with strange, hypnotic designs of black dots and spirals. These seemed to swirl and gyrate in constant motion, boiling in rich whorls and tendrils up its neck to cover its shaved skull, and giving its flat, broad face the aspect of some great, swart, yellow-eyed panther of the jungle.

Alvarado had paused in the middle of the room to study this apparition, recognising the so-called sorcerer he'd seen standing on the summit of the pyramid the evening before – the same ugly savage who'd also cut out the hearts of twenty young men at dawn that morning, and was no doubt responsible for every one of those skulls on the rack.

'They tell me,' Alvarado said conversationally as he stepped forward, light on his feet and swinging the falchion, 'that you're a sorcerer.' He moved the big blade faster, liking the sound as it sliced the air. 'But I don't believe in sorcery, so where does that leave you?'

The creature muttered some rhythmic incantation in its own brute language and executed a series of weird, hopping leaps in a big circle around him. As it did so, a beam of light from one of the windows caught its right hand, which seemed hooked and clawed. 'Ah,' said Alvarado, remembering the bleeding wound on his arm, 'that's what you cut me with.' He narrowed his eyes, wondering for a moment if this subhuman *thing* did actually have claws, then realised that it held some carved stone weapon in its fist with three scythe-like blades protruding from between its fingers.

It executed a second series of leaps, snarling and spitting, lashing out at him once, twice, three times with those scythes, but on the fourth attack Alvarado slid his right foot powerfully forward and put all his weight into a lunge, driving the tip of the falchion deep into the creature's tattooed belly, giving it a vicious twist and whipping it out again. It was followed by a great spurt of blood. 'There, my lovely,' he said, 'I expect that hurt you.'

472

Howling and screeching like a scalded cat, the creature made one more wild rush at him, which Alvarado easily sidestepped; as it went by he chopped the heavy blade of the falchion into the small of its back, cutting it down as one would cut down a tree, severing its spine and leaving it flopping convulsively on the floor, unable any longer to command its arms and legs.

Alvarado reached down, prised the peculiar weapon loose and threw it across the room, then dragged the screaming creature by its wrist across the floor, positioned its neck over the base of the idol of the plumed serpent, which made a convenient chopping block, and hacked off its head with a single blow.

'Sorcerer?' he said, looking down at his handiwork. 'That's what I think of bastard sorcerers.'

'Come walk with me,' Cortés invited Sandoval. 'Let's see if we've done enough here.' As he spoke, a great bellow of pain rose up from somewhere below.

Sandoval winced at the sound. 'So many wounded to finish off,' he commented. 'You're determined not to leave a single one of them alive?'

'I know it seems harsh,' Cortés replied, 'but yes. Those who came to the plaza to kill us this morning must all die. They knew what they were doing. They have to pay the price.'

'And the city? What are your intentions for it?'

'If we face no more resistance, I believe I'll spare the city. Once we've shown we can be firm, a reputation for mercy will not harm us. Cholula can thrive again; its people can return.'

While it was under way, in the thick of the killing, Sandoval had thought the massacre bad enough; but up here, from the top of the pyramid, the true extent of the slaughter was revealed to him and far exceeded his worst imaginings. He and Cortés had walked from the east to the south side of the summit platform, skirting the rubble and devastation of the ruined temple, and from this lofty vantage point it was obvious that every part of the plaza, from the base of the pyramid to the enclosure wall, was filled to overflowing with dead and dying Indians. Despite their hostile intent, the vast majority had perished without even defending themselves, and it was significant, Sandoval saw with feelings of revulsion, that their poor, broken bodies were most thickly clustered round the gates where they had sought and been denied escape.

The one consolation was Cortés's apparent decision to limit the destruction to the plaza and not continue it beyond the walls with a general sack of the city itself. Halfway along the west side of the summit platform, however, he suddenly stopped and pointed north. 'What's that?' he said.

Both men had been so focused on the scene directly below that they'd paid little attention to the surrounding countryside, but now, looking in the direction indicated by Cortés, Sandoval's hand fell automatically to the hilt of his sword.

The day's fighting and killing, which he'd believed to be over, had only just begun.

When Tlalchi said 'kill them', Pepillo's hand went to the sheath at his belt where he kept the wickedly sharp little dagger Cortés had given him months before at Potonchan. The movement went unnoticed by the Indians, one of whom, still talking in an urgent whisper to the others, was padding across the floor to where he lay. Pepillo got a glimpse of a huge club being raised, drew the dagger and stabbed it into the Indian's bare, dirty foot as he stepped in to straddle him, skewering the arch, finding a path through the bones and driving the point with a forceful thud deep into the wooden floor beneath.

The effect was extraordinary and instantaneous. The Indian let loose a great bellow of shock and pain, lost his balance as he attempted to free his foot and crashed down in a heap, narrowly missing Pepillo, who twisted sideways and leapt towards Malinal.

Things happened very fast after that.

In response to Tlalchi's order, Malinal's captor had clamped both hands round her neck and begun to throttle her, but when Pepillo's head smashed into his right side, he lost his grip and Malinal at once reached inside her tunic, pulled out a short stiletto and stabbed the man through the eye.

It all still would have ended badly, as the other Indians hefted their *macuahuitls*, if Bernal Díaz, Francisco Mibiercas and Alonso de la Serna had not at that moment charged into the room, blades flashing, and cut all three of them down. Tlalchi got in the way of Mibiercas's great and strong sword and was also killed, cut nearly in half at the waist, but Tlaqui, weeping and wringing his hands, was left unharmed, as was the Indian Pepillo had stabbed through the foot, who remained pinioned to the floor.

Seeing gentleness and concern on Díaz's face as he strode over to Malinal and enfolded her in his arms, Pepillo was struck by the realisation that this gruff, honest soldier loved her in a way that the caudillo never had or would.

Stretching away to the north of Cholula was a wide grassy plain, bounded at a distance of about four miles by a range of hills cut through with narrow valleys. The whole plain between the hills and the city was filled with the swarming regiments of an army at least a hundred thousand strong. 'We've fought as many before,' Cortés reassured Sandoval, 'and won. We can do it again.'

'We won't have to,' said a cheerful, confident voice.

The two men now stood on the north side of the great pyramid's summit platform, which commanded an unimpeded view over the plain. They turned in unison to see Alvarado strolling towards them out of the ruins of the temple, with his falchion resting jauntily on his shoulder. Impaled through the neck on the point of the weapon was a tattooed human head.

'What do you mean, Pedro?' asked Cortés, doing his best to ignore the glaring head with its baleful dead eyes.

'I mean we won't have to fight them. The Tlascalans are going to do that for us.'

'The Tlascalans?' said Sandoval. 'There's only a thousand of them. They can't fight an army this big.'

'Look again,' urged Alvarado. 'Our friends have been reinforced. I count close to fifty thousand of them out there now. Don't you recognise the banners?'

Cortés looked and suddenly understood. The massing regiments he'd estimated at a hundred thousand men were separated into two distinct blocks. The nearest, with their backs turned to the city, indeed held aloft the banners of Tlascala and were positioned to intercept the advance of the regiments further north.

'Let's ride, gentlemen,' he said, suddenly decisive. 'These forces look equally matched but the Mexica have never faced cavalry before. I warrant a charge or two will tip the balance.'

Chapter Forty

A glance was enough to reveal what had happened in the audience chamber – the corpses of the Cholulan warriors, Tlalchi dead, Tlaqui sobbing and wringing his hands, Díaz, Mibiercas and La Serna grimly cleaning their swords, Pepillo white-faced, Malinal shaken, her throat bruised, a blood-smeared stiletto still gripped tight in her fist, and that damned dog Melchior chained up in the corner where he'd clearly been no use to anyone. 'I'll hear more about this later,' Cortés said. He took Malinal by the arm. 'But now I need your services. There's speaking to be done. A matter of life and death.'

Minutes later they were mounted up, Malinal before him in the saddle, and riding at a gallop out of the north gate of the plaza. No sooner had the small troop of cavalry moved into position at the forefront of the Tlascalan ranks, however, than the Mexica regiments began to beat a hasty retreat. Seeing them on the verge of panic, Cortés was sorely tempted to pursue and destroy them, but he held back. His cannon and all his infantry remained in Cholula and, although the city seemed defeated, there might yet be hostile forces lurking within it. Besides, a pitched battle against the Mexica now would end the fiction of cordial relations he was attempting to maintain with Moctezuma, by means of which, and cunning diplomacy, he still hoped to see Tenochtitlan open its causeways and gates to him without a fight.

Cortés reined in Molinero beside Shikotenka. 'We'll let them go,' he said through Malinal.

'Let them go?' The Tlascalan leader's face darkened. 'Do that and you'll see them again on another battlefield.'

477

'I understand,' said Cortés, 'but my mind is made up. Let them go. Don't engage them.' He waited while Shikotenka barked orders to his captains, then added: 'Thank you, my friend. You saved the day for us here. I'll not forget it.'

'You told me to bring no more men.' There was a smile on Shikotenka's lips but not in his eyes as he gestured to the massed regiments of Tlascalans behind him.

'And you disobeyed me,' said Cortés. 'Thanks be to God!' He raised himself in his stirrups, looking south to the collapsed temple on the summit of Cholula's mountainous pyramid, and to the plumes of smoke billowing up from the fires in the plaza. 'I know the Mexica have deprived you of salt and cotton and other necessities for many years,' he said to Shikotenka, 'and I know they have used Cholula as a base to launch their attacks on Tlascala, but all that is ended now. We have conquered this city, and today and for the two days following, save only the temple precincts, I give it to you and your men to do with as you wish, take whatever revenge you choose, kill and rape as it pleases you and loot whichever commodities you require. That is my reward to you, Shikotenka, and to the warriors of Tlascala, for the great service you have done me here.'

The Tlascalans ran wild, but their sack of Cholula, though thorough and brutal, ceased at sunset on the third day, Monday 18 October, as Cortés had commanded. Nor at any point did the rampaging warriors seek to enter the great plaza with its palace and temples, which remained under Spanish control, yielding rich pickings in gold and jewels that were not shared with their Indian friends.

Under torture, Tlaqui protested repeatedly that the plan to trap the Spaniards in the plaza and kill or capture them for sacrifice had been entirely Moctezuma's idea, and Cortés put this accusation to a Mexica delegation, led once again by Teudile, which arrived in Cholula under a flag of truce on Wednesday 20 October. Teudile denied it, of course, so Cortés obliged him to witness a further more probing torture session, during which Tlaqui rather convincingly repeated the charges against Moctezuma as his fingernails were pulled out with pliers.

Working himself up into the appearance of a rage, though inwardly he was amused, Cortés told Teudile: 'I can scarcely believe that so great a lord as Moctezuma should send his messengers and such esteemed persons as yourself to me to convince me he is my friend while at the same time seeking to attack me by another's hand in so cowardly a way and hoping to evade responsibility if all did not come out as he intended! Well, Teudile, actions have consequences, as your lord will now learn to his cost. I have changed my plans. Before, it was my intention to visit Tenochtitlan to see Moctezuma and make myself a friend to him and speak with him in harmony and even ask his advice on all the things that must be done in this land, but now I will come to him at war, doing him all the harm I can as an enemy.'

Tlaqui chose this moment to convulse, foam at the mouth and noisily perish in the chair he was strapped to. Looking on aghast, Teudile himself seemed half dead with fear, his mouth gaping, his cadaverous features glistening with sweat as he insisted again that Moctezuma had never done anything to encourage the Cholulan rulers in their wicked plot against the Spaniards.

'How very odd,' Cortés objected, 'since I myself counted close to fifty thousand of Moctezuma's warriors outside Cholula, ready to make war on me. They ran away when we confronted them, but they were most assuredly there. I fail to understand how that could be, unless they were acting on Moctezuma's orders.'

Teudile's pallor worsened and, in a shaking voice, he begged Cortés not to cast aside his friendship for Moctezuma and not under any circumstances to make war on him until he was certain of the truth. 'Let me go to Tenochtitlan,' he said, 'and put these accusations to my master and return to you very soon with his answer.'

'How soon,' said Cortés with a ferocious glower, 'is very soon?'

'Not more than six days, great lord.'

'Very well,' Cortés replied. 'You have six days.'

Teudile and his fellow delegates departed in haste, but the following morning, Thursday 21 October, a new visitor was brought to Cortés by Shikotenka – the grave, stooped elder named Huicton, ambassador to the rebel Lord Ishtlil of Texcoco, who'd last visited him in early May in the camp on the dunes at Cuetlaxtlan.

'Welcome, Huicton,' Cortés said through Malinal and Pepillo. 'A pleasure to see you again. You'll know by now I took your advice and put Tlascala on my route of march.' A grin at Shikotenka: 'These fellows gave us a spot of bother, but we've since become firm friends. I hope very soon to make the acquaintance of your master Ishtlil and accept the offer of his allegiance that you brought me before. I recall he was badly wronged by Moctezuma. I hope to play some part in putting those wrongs to right.'

'Ah, good sir,' said the ambassador, 'there are so many wrongs to be righted in this unfortunate land.' Without ceremony, he then squatted on his haunches in the native manner. 'You'll forgive me if I rest my weary bones?'

'Of course,' said Cortés, sitting in his own comfortable folding chair and gesturing to Malinal to draw up the stool she habitually used.

Huicton smiled at Malinal. 'Greetings, my lady! So good to see you again. You're fast becoming the most famous woman in Mexico!'

'Famous and rightly so!' agreed Cortés. 'After God we owe our success in this land to Malinal!' He noticed she chose not to interpret this last remark.

'Indeed she is so famous,' continued Huicton, addressing Cortés again, 'that people are beginning to call you by her name. Those who don't think you are Quetzalcoatl, or some other deity, now often call you Malinche, which means "the master of Malinal". Did you know that?'

'Actually I didn't,' admitted Cortés. 'Malinal, Shikotenka, is this so?' They confirmed that it was.

'Hmm . . . Malinche,' Cortés mused, rolling the name around his tongue. 'The master of Malinal, eh? It has a certain ring . . . I think I like it. Now, to business. What can I do for you, Ambassador Huicton?'

'It is more a matter of what I can do for you,' said the old man. 'My master Ishtlil is ready to put twenty thousand of our rebel warriors of Texcoco at your disposal at any time you feel you need them. We know, of course, of the great support our friend and ally Shikotenka of Tlascala has given to you – ' a smile at Shikotenka – 'and we wish to do the same. My master also undertakes to bring the Huexotzincos and others who oppose Moctezuma to your cause.'

Cortés nodded approvingly: 'I welcome such support,' he said, 'and the time may come when I will rely upon it. But as Shikotenka and Malinal both know, I don't propose to take Moctezuma by storm, with a great army at my back, when guile and subterfuge might achieve the same objective without fighting . . . Shikotenka here has offered me fifty thousand warriors, but with all respect I've told him I will only take a thousand and keep the rest in reserve against emergency should it come. The same goes for your master's generous offer. To cement our friendship, let him supply a thousand warriors to me now. Should I find I need more, I'll ask for them.'

'You judge your enemy well. A large army will put him on his guard, but Moctezuma is more susceptible than most to guile and subterfuge, and you've already done much to weaken his will and confuse his wits and terrify his imagination.' Huicton leaned forward. 'In this work,' he said, and suddenly Cortés realised those opaque eyes were not as blind as he'd at first thought, 'you've had help – help no one else knows of. Help you did not ask for, but that has wonderfully served your purpose.'

For a moment Cortés was taken aback. Did this old man know about Saint Peter? But then Huicton seemed to change the subject: 'You love gold, do you not?'

'It has its place,' Cortés replied carefully.

'Suppose I were to tell you,' said Huicton, 'that a treasure more precious than gold lies within your grasp here in Cholula. All you need to retrieve it is a few strong men with hammers.'

'I'd be interested, of course,' said Cortés.

As Huicton stood up, his knee joints creaked and he paused to stretch his back. 'Come then, Malinche. Let me lead you to this treasure.'

The morning was bright and clear, the sky a rich, intense, cloudless blue. Yet as he climbed towards the summit of the great pyramid of Tenochtitlan, Moctezuma saw doom awaiting him: inexorable doom, inescapable doom, the doom of chaos, the doom of endings. So imminent was his sense of the disaster that pressed in on him that he had ceased to confine himself to his palace. With Acopol dead, the warding spells that had protected him there would no longer function anyway, so one place was no less dangerous to him than another.

Moctezuma could only guess at the precise intentions of the *tueles* until Teudile returned to court, but his spies had already informed him in the most graphic detail of the merciless sack of Cholula, the massacre of its people, the murder of Tlalchi, and the decapitation of Acopol, whose head, it seemed, had been impaled on a spear and left to rot at the foot of the steps of the pyramid of Quetzalcoatl.

How was it possible that the leader of the *tueles* could be the god of peace, returning to claim his kingdom, and yet have unleashed such horror and violence, such desecration and defilement, in the very heart of his own sacred city of Cholula?

The answer, Moctezuma knew all too well, must lie in Acopol's attempts to reverse the prophecy – the placing of Hummingbird's idol on the pyramid of Cholula and the human sacrifices performed there with the collusion of Tlaqui and Tlalchi. Such things were an abomination to Quetzalcoatl, and the spectacular vengeance he had inflicted on Cholula was the clearest possible sign of his wrath.

Of course Moctezuma would be next! It was he who had commissioned Acopol's dark rituals and set all this in motion, so it was he, ultimately, who must face the severest retribution for what had been done. Yet it seemed so unfair! So undeserved! For he had not acted alone, but on the express urging, advice and instruction of a higher power – no less than Hummingbird himself! – who had promised so much and delivered so little. As he reached the top of the great pyramid, all Tenochtitlan stretched out below him and the dark, blood-spattered doorway of the temple of Hummingbird looming ahead, Moctezuma felt such a wave of self-pity that tears sprang to his eyes and rolled down his cheeks.

His god had misled him. His god had lied to him! Suddenly angry, he strode through the door, passed the loaded skull racks in the antechamber, entered the inner sanctum and marched up to the hulking idol, squat and powerful, exuding menace, poised and motionless as a viper about to strike, flaunting its necklace of human hearts, hands and skulls. 'Lord Hummingbird,' shouted Moctezuma, 'Hummingbird at the Left Hand of the Sun, you have deceived me!'

The massive stone statue glared down at him out of the shadows, glittering with jade and jewels, its yawning mouth jagged with fangs and tusks, its eyes cold and appraising.

'You promised me victory in Cholula, lord,' Moctezuma complained. 'You showed me beautiful visions, you foretold that the white-skins would lose their power, you said I would be rid of them forever.' As he spoke his voice rose higher, and suddenly he was in the grip of a paroxysm of rage, wailing and screaming, gnashing his teeth, beating his fists against the carved feathers of the idol's granite chest. The fugue deepened, moving beyond his conscious control, so he had only the faintest idea of his own actions when he drew his knife from the sheath at his waist and used its serrated obsidian blade to slash his earlobes to shreds, spraying blood everywhere, and its point to stab repeatedly at his arms and shins. 'What shall I do?' he sobbed as he stabbed and sliced, stabbed and sliced. 'I am finished, lord. I am used up. I beg you, show me the way.'

But the idol remained silent, and later, when Moctezuma's cuts had begun to scab over and his blood had ceased to drip, he walked dejectedly from the temple, and down the steps of the pyramid, and made his way to his palace and his own private chambers, where he sat shivering and disconsolate on the floor, awaiting the return of Teudile and whatever tidings he would bring.

Ever alert to any talk of treasure, Alvarado had joined Cortés and Malinal and the two strong soldiers Huicton had suggested they bring, one equipped with a pick and the other with a sledgehammer.

Huicton walked with a pronounced stoop. Nonetheless, he was vigorous and surprisingly fast on his feet as he led the way from the palace Cortés had commandeered as his headquarters and out into the brilliant sunlight flooding the plaza. 'Where are we going, father?' asked Malinal, who was keeping pace with the strange old ambassador.

'Over there,' Huicton said bluntly, pointing to the eastern side of the pyramid of Quetzalcoatl and increasing his pace.

In the past five days, the plaza had been cleared of the thousands of corpses strewn across it on the morning of the massacre, but Alvarado had insisted that the head of the sorcerer Acopol, who he was very proud to have killed, should remain mounted on a spear that he'd set up at the foot of the eastern stairway. Catching sight of it as they drew closer, Huicton muttered something under his breath.

'What was that?' asked Malinal.

'Just expressing my surprise,' said Huicton. He gestured towards the head: 'I'd heard that one had perished, but I rather disbelieved the story – until now.'

Alvarado, whose enthusiasm, love of praise, general level of happiness and ability to kill without compunction frequently reminded Malinal of some great hound, came bounding forward. 'That's my head he's pointing at,' he observed.

'Yes,' said Malinal, 'it is.'

'Ask him – does he know anything about its owner? I've been trying to find out who the bugger was since I killed him, but everyone just mutters "sorcerer" and clams up.'

'This is Don Pedro Alvarado,' Malinal said to Huicton. 'He killed the man whose head this was and would like to learn more about him. Can you tell him anything?'

Huicton looked at Alvarado with interest, looked at the head, looked back at Alvarado. 'Sorcerer,' he said.

'See!' said Alvarado. 'See what I mean!'

Since the massacre, Malinal had stayed as far away from Alvarado's gruesome trophy as possible but now, as they approached it, she noticed that not only had the eyes not been plucked out by birds – a mystery in itself after five days – but also that they were wide open and seemed somehow still alive, filled with intelligence and malice.

Huicton was speaking again. At first Malinal thought he was simply elaborating on his answer to Alvarado's question: 'This is the head of a very bad man,' he said. 'A man called Acopol. According to information I received, he was responsible for the disappearance of your friend Tozi – but please, Malinal, don't translate that bit yet!'

Malinal suddenly felt faint and began to shake. 'What? What did you say?'

'Your friend Tozi – who is my friend also, as I told you when we last met. She's underneath the pyramid in a cave. She's been there for more than twenty days but she's tough and still alive, I hope. To get her out we have to find a secret entrance and then do some digging. I'm told these white men here will move heaven and earth for treasure, but I suspect they might do rather less for a missing girl.'

Alvarado was listening, looking puzzled: 'What's the old fool saying?' he asked.

'He's saying this head belonged to a very bad man called Acopol.'

Alvarado yawned: 'I know that already, dammit. But I want more. Can't he tell me more?'

Still trembling at the sudden and unexpected news of Tozi, who she'd had no word of since Huicton's last visit, Malinal's mind was full of unanswered questions. Why was Tozi here in Cholula? How was it that Acopol had buried her beneath the pyramid? And why, with her powers, had she not at once escaped? More important, was she still alive? Desperate to begin the search, but knowing Huicton had understood the Spaniards well, Malinal translated Alvarado's question.

'You can tell him,' answered Huicton, whose voice had a peculiar nasal thrum, like a swarm of summer bees, 'that he did a remarkable thing to defeat Acopol. Such a one is very hard to kill.'

'He put up a fight,' admitted Alvarado. 'Cut me here.' He pointed to a bloody bandage wrapped around his upper left arm. 'Not often a foe gets to cut me.'

'He was a *nagual*,' said Huicton. 'His power was to change his form, now a man, now a jaguar . . . Was this how he appeared to you when you fought?'

There was some confusion over the Nahuatl word for jaguar – *ocelotl* – which Huicton sought to clarify with the Mayan word *b'alam*, but neither had any meaning for the Spaniards. After some explication of the appearance and habitat of the animal, however, Alvarado gave a broad grin and said: 'Panther – that's what the bugger thought he was, leaping up and down, weapon like a claw. A big jungle panther.'

'*Thought* he was a panther?' Huicton queried the nuance. 'Or actually became one?'

'He was a mere savage,' said Alvarado without hesitation, 'pretending to be a panther. Silly bugger. Gave me a bit of a start, though, I have to admit, until I cornered him and cleaved his spine.'

Huicton glanced again at the ferocious head with its tattooed spots and whorls: 'Your magic was stronger than his.'

'I don't believe in magic,' said Alvarado. He dropped his hand to the hilt of his falchion. 'Just steel and the will to use it.'

'And no one uses it better than you.' Cortés stepped in and patted his friend on the shoulder: 'You did well to rid us of such a fiend, Pedro, but I for one have had enough of standing around in the hot sun admiring your handiwork.' He turned to Huicton: 'You said something about treasure, Ambassador?'

'Our magic,' said Tozi's mother, 'comes not from the gods, or from men, but from the source of all created things.'

'But the god Hummingbird changed my magic,' Tozi objected. 'And the man Acopol stole it from me.'

'They did not change it or steal it. To do so is beyond their powers. Gods and men may only divert the course of magic, as the course of a river may be diverted or the wind forced to flow around a barrier, but the magic is always there like the river or the wind.'

'So when Hummingbird made my magic stronger—'

'He only redirected it to flow more strongly through you, while Acopol deflected it to flow away from you. But the magic is still there, Tozi, and you can connect with it again.'

'Magic is a curse,' said Tozi. 'Because of your magic, the mob killed you and took you from me.'

'But magic is also a blessing,' her mother said, 'that has flowed through the women of our line in an unbroken stream, sometimes stronger, sometimes weaker, but always there, for ten thousand years. We pay a price for it, that's true. As I did. As you have. But our connection to it is a gift that cannot be denied, a gift from the source.'

'A gift for what purpose?'

'To work upon the world of created things and to magnify darkness or light, as we choose, to glorify good or evil, as we choose, to exalt love or hate, as we choose . . . The power is the gift but the choice is always ours.'

'I don't want to do such work any more,' Tozi said, surprised how certain she felt. 'I don't want to make such choices.' They were sitting side by side in the place where they often met, on the rock jutting up out of the waters of a lake under a blue sun in a burnished sky. Tozi wrapped her arms round her mother's warm body and rested her head on her shoulder: 'I'm so happy I've found you again. All I want is to stay here with you.'

'But you cannot stay, child.' Her mother's voice was gentle, overflowing with love, filled with sorrow. 'It's not your time. You are needed in the created world. You have to go back . . .' And already her appearance of substantial, corporeal reality was fading, and with it her scent, her warmth, her sheer, definite, unmistakable presence also evaporated like mist at dawn and, once again, as had happened so frequently before, this scene of reunion from which Tozi derived such comfort dissolved into darkness and she found herself back in her tomb beneath the pyramid waiting for death to claim her.

She lay still on the cold, comfortless rock floor and heard sounds – *crash! bang! crash!* – and imagined she saw flickers of yellow light, and laughed her mad, cackling, crazy woman's laugh, for she knew herself to be a princess in a palace of illusion where nothing was real.

Even so, the light drew her like a moth to a flame. With the last of her strength she clambered to her feet and stumbled towards it.

Pepillo had joined the growing crowd at the base of the pyramid, pushing through the soldiers to stand with Malinal as the stooped, grey-haired Texcocan ambassador explored the wall beneath the eastern stairway with the tips of his fingers, pressing and manipulating every crack and crevice. Then, just when it seemed there was nothing to be found here, and some of the spectators were beginning to drift away, Huicton gave a sudden grunt of satisfaction, there was a loud *click*, and a section of masonry wide enough for two men to pass side by side slid back to reveal a dark corridor beyond.

Alvarado laughed excitedly and plunged in, reappearing a moment later. 'Black as pitch in there,' he said. 'We'll need light.' Soon burning torches were brought and Huicton and Malinal led the way, with Alvarado and Cortés close behind and Pepillo, the soldiers with the pickaxe and sledgehammer, and the rest of the curious crowd following. After a dozen paces, however, Cortés turned round and bellowed: 'Out of here, the lot of you. Whatever we find, you'll know soon enough, but we need air and space to swing a pick.'

There was a rumble of complaint – rumours of a treasure trove had spread like wildfire – but eventually the corridor was cleared. Pepillo lingered close to Cortés, who gave him a cheerful nod. 'You can stay,' he said. He nodded towards Malinal: 'For goodness' sake try and cheer her up; she looks as if she's seen a phantom.'

Pepillo counted three hundred paces, perhaps a few more, before the corridor abruptly terminated in a wall of rough-hewn masonry blocks. Alvarado inspected it, dug the point of his dagger into the mortar between the joints and pronounced it freshly built. 'Come ahead, boys,' said Cortés, signalling the two labourers forward, and they set to work at once, rapidly smashing a hole in the wall with the sledgehammer and levering out the loosened blocks with the pick.

As the gap widened they all heard a cackle of high-pitched laughter.

Lurching towards them in the flickering glow of the torches, dressed only in a filthy, torn shift, her eyes wide and staring, was a skeletal, ghostly girl.

Chapter Forty-One

'I have spoken with the leader of the *tueles*, sire, the one all now call Malinche. I bring a message from him.' Teudile was caked with the dust of the journey, his clothing soaked with sweat, his face grey with exhaustion as he sat before Moctezuma in the House of the Eagle Knights.

Raising the index finger of his right hand, Moctezuma made the gesture of assent, the members of the Supreme Council leaned forward on their benches and Teudile began: 'The Lord Malinche holds you responsible, sire, for all operations that were to be taken against him and his forces in Cholula. He does not believe that Tlaqui and Tlalchi were acting alone, but rather at your instigation, and he cites as evidence for this the words of Tlaqui himself who he put to the most horrible torture before my eyes and who blamed you for everything—'

'The coward!' spat Moctezuma. 'The weakling!'

Teudile was trembling from head to toe. 'Tlaqui died under torture,' he shuddered. 'They tore his fingernails out one by one and to his last breath he refused to accept personal responsibility for the plot, saying you forced him to it.'

'Despicable traitor!' hissed Moctezuma. He could not believe the duplicity and faithlessness of his Cholulan vassal who had failed so miserably in his duty of silence and loyalty. His mind racing, he looked down at the perfectly manicured nails of his own fingers, stared at the pearly half-moons of the quicks.

'Sire . . . may I speak?' The interruption came from Apanec, Keeper of the House of Darkness.

'No you may not,' snarled Moctezuma. 'Be silent.' He continued to study his fingers. The thought that his own beautiful nails might one day be pulled out was almost too much to bear. At last he fixed his eyes on Teudile again. 'But surely,' he said 'the craven babble of Tlaqui is deniable? The word of a man under torture is meaningless; such a man will say anything to escape pain.'

'That is true, sire,' agreed Teudile. 'And I denied his accusations, declared your innocence in all these matters, promised Malinche that you bore nothing but goodwill for him and friendship in your heart. Regrettably, however, he himself saw the six regiments of your picked warriors under General Maza before they fled the field. He does not understand how such a force could have come against him without your express orders, and for this reason he says he no longer seeks your friendship. He says he will now advance on Tenochtitlan at war with you, seeking to do you all the harm he can.'

Moctezuma slumped on the plinth, careless of the judgemental stares of his counsellors. The fact was that Tlaqui had let him down; Maza, who he'd had skinned alive the moment he returned to Tenochtitlan, had let him down, and Hummingbird had also let him down. The great and perfect plan for the destruction of the *tueles* at Cholula, on which he'd placed all his hopes, had failed miserably, and now he alone must face the wrath of Malinche, who was no longer coming to him as the god of peace but as a warrior.

Malinche! Malinche! Moctezuma rolled the name and its meaning around in his mind. Ha! The Lord of that demon-woman Malinal – that harbinger of bad fortune, that omen of doom.

'*Advise me what to do!*' he roared at his counsellors, looking from one aghast face to the next. 'Is that not the purpose for which you are gathered here?'

As before there was a division of opinion.

Cuitláhuac, supported by many in the council, advocated war. 'We must mobilise all our forces and the forces of our allies before this Malinche leads every one of them into defection, and if he fulfils his threat to march on Tenochtitlan, as I fear he will, we must destroy him on the road. My son Guatemoc—'

'*You will not speak of that wretch here!*' bellowed Moctezuma.

'Very well, sire, then let me put it this way. I have consulted with military experts who know the craft of ambush and surprise, and they recommend a most suitable place between Cholula and Tenochtitlan where we may use our superior numbers and knowledge of the land to take the *tueles* at a disadvantage.'

'And where is this place?'

'Just below the high pass of Tlalmanalco, lord, now covered by snow and blasted by icy winds. Our forces are accustomed to such conditions, those of the *tueles* – we may presume – are not, since they have marched so recently from the hot lowlands of the coast. At the pass, where they will be cold, where they will be weak, the road divides, the left fork leading to Tenochtitlan by way of Tlalmanalco and Chalco, the right fork by way of Amecameca. If we block the road to Amecameca by felling many great pines and other stout trees across it, the *tueles* will naturally take the left fork. There, a little way down the mountain, we may make our preparations. Part of the hillside should be cut away, ditches and barricades prepared and a large force assembled, a force of at least one hundred thousand men, to fall upon the *tueles* like an avalanche and crush them utterly . . .'

But the opposite point of view was put by Cacama, Lord of Texcoco who remained in favour, as always, of inviting the *tueles* into Tenochtitlan. There was, he said, no guarantee that an ambush at Tlalmanalco would work. If the *tueles* were truly gods, with the powers of gods, as many suspected, they might not be adversely affected by the cold. Moreover, all previous attempts to take them by surprise, whether by the Mexica, or the Cholulans, or the Tlascalans, or even by the Chontal Maya, had failed dismally, and they had triumphed in every military engagement.

'No matter,' Cuitláhuac insisted. 'Should the ambush fail, it is still our duty to fight them whether they be gods or men. We must not hide. We must not flee. We must not be fainthearted. Rather we must shower them with stones and arrows and spears at every point of their march. In the event they reach Tenochtitlan, we must close and defend the causeways. Better we all die, *macuahuitls* in hand, than see our sacred city fall.'

Cacama disagreed. 'The Tlascalans thought that way,' he said, 'and look where it got them. If we try to prevent the *tueles*' entry into

Tenochtitlan, they will fight us in our subject towns – as even you yourself admit, Cuitláhuac – until we have no allies left. And all of this, in my opinion, is completely unnecessary! The *tueles* say they are the ambassadors of a powerful foreign king, and as such we should receive them courteously.'

After several hours of debate with no clear majority in favour of one view or the other, Moctezuma leapt to his feet and gave a great shout: 'ENOUGH! I have heard these arguments a hundred times and I am weary of them. You are a council of old women. I go to consult with the god.'

He summoned the High Priest Namacuix to follow him and strode from the assembly hall.

The moon was close to full that night and its baleful glare pierced the high, narrow windows of the temple of Hummingbird, adding a spectral glow to the flickering brands that lit the inner sanctum. 'The last time you came to me here,' said the god, 'you beat upon my breast with your fists like a spoiled child who has not been given his way.'

The great stone idol had quite suddenly come to life and was now filled with movement and a seething, restless energy. Moctezuma, who had consumed a dozen large *teonanácatl* mushrooms, dropped unsteadily to his knees. 'I am truly sorry, lord. I beg you to forgive me. I was bereft of my senses after the victory of Malinche in Cholula. I could not understand why you had permitted such a disaster.'

'It was not I who permitted it,' sneered Hummingbird, his eyes, blacker than obsidian, glittering in the moonlight. 'It was you. The sacrifices offered in Cholula were insufficient to reverse the prophecy. More blood should have been spilled. Precious blood – the blood of virgins, as you have given me tonight.'

'I left the matter in the hands of the sorcerer Acopol, lord.'

'You should not have done so. I required precious blood, female blood, the blood of virgins – and plenty of it. He gave me twenty males a day, males past the first flush of youth; captives of war. It was not enough.'

'My humblest apologies, lord. I hope tonight's sacrifice has proved more satisfying.'

Arranged around the floor of the Holy of Holies, propped up against the walls, their blood congealing in great pools, their hearts stuffed into the mouth of the idol until its fangs were clogged with matter and gore, were the butchered remains of the hundred virgin girls Namacuix had brought in fetters from the fattening pen to the pyramid. None of them, as Moctezuma had stipulated, was more than eight years old.

'More satisfying?' said Hummingbird. 'Without a doubt!' He extracted a great chunk of purple meat that had become lodged between his teeth, pushed it back into his maw and surveyed the bodies. 'I suppose these little ones are an advance on my birthday present?'

'They are, lord, but you will not go short on your birthday. I have promised you ten thousand and you shall have the exact count.'

'Very good,' said the god. 'I can hardly wait,' and with that – a miracle! – he transformed into a tiny hummingbird that hovered over one of the slaughtered children and dipped its long beak into her gaping chest cavity. A voice like a tinkling of bells filled Moctezuma's head: 'You have done well tonight, my son, and I am pleased. I sense you have a question for me.'

'I do, lord.'

'Then ask it.'

'What must I do about the *tueles*, lord? Guide me, I beg you. Show me the right path.'

'Be guided by your own heart, my son,' the god replied. 'I have placed wisdom there. Search within and you will find the path to glory.'

'I feel tricked by that cunning old fox,' said Cortés. 'He led us to expect a roomful of treasure and all we found was this wretched girl.'

'He said you find treasure more precious than gold,' replied Malinal. 'He spoke truth.'

'I've no doubt she's precious to you, my dear, after the ordeal you shared – but for the rest of us she has no value at all.'

Malinal was beginning to feel angry. Now she sat up in bed, moon-light pouring through the window of the large chamber they occupied in the palace that had once belonged to Tlaqui and Tlalchi, and looked down at her lover's stern, bearded face. 'Hernán. You said, after God, you owed success in this land to me. Was that joke? Or did you mean?'

Cortés appeared to think about it, which made Malinal, for a moment, even angrier. 'I meant every word,' he said eventually. 'We're winning here because I've been able to talk to people, threaten people, negotiate with people, and I couldn't have done any of that without you. We're winning because you've helped me understand the local customs, the local ways of thought, the local superstitions. I couldn't have done any of that without you either. Most important of all, we're winning because you've helped me get inside Moctezuma's head and defeat him on the battlefield of the mind and I certainly couldn't have done that without you.'

Malinal couldn't decide whether he was mocking her or serious. He sounded serious, but with Cortés you could never tell. Nonetheless, she decided to take his words at face value. 'In that case,' she said, 'my Tozi more precious than gold! Without her I not be alive today, and even if alive I not be here to help you. She saved my life in fattening pen of Tenochtitlan; you know already. But after – you don't know this, Hernán! – she make me come to Potonchan to search you out. She . . . how you say? Insist? She tell me it right. If she not do that, I never go to Potonchan! Never! I go somewhere else, safer for me, and you and I would not meet. I know you believe our Christian God put me in your path to win you victory – we talk about this many times! If he did, he used Tozi to do this. So in God's name, Hernán, I ask you recognise Tozi! Welcome her!'

Cortés grinned: 'Oh very well,' he said, 'besides, she's of an age to be a companion to Pepillo, and God knows he needs a companion other than that dog he's always clinging on to.' Another grin, lecherous this time: 'Now come here.' He reached out to fondle her naked breast. 'You're a goddess in this moonlight.'

On Tuesday 26 October, exactly six days after his departure, Teudile returned to Cholula with a train of *tamanes* carrying twenty gold plates that Alvarado valued at a thousand pesos each, an assortment of other fine gold ornaments worth a further ten thousand pesos, two hundred bundles of cotton garments including one thousand five hundred fine cloaks, and a hundred huge food baskets filled with cooked turkeys, quail, venison and maize cakes. As he had promised, the steward also brought a message from Moctezuma, a complicated one that Malinal and Pepillo worked on together to render into perfect Castilian.

'My lord commands me to convey to you his humble apologies for the treachery of his vassals in Cholula,' Teudile began gravely, 'and asks you to believe, in friendship, that he was not informed of it and played no part in it. It was an initiative entirely of those fools Tlaqui and Tlalchi, whom you have rightly put to death. As to the Mexica regiments you witnessed drawn up in battle formation outside Cholula to attack you, my lord again sends his apologies. He understands your suspicions but informs you these forces were not there with his knowledge or on his orders. Because of the need from time to time to suppress hostile elements in this region, we have been in the habit of maintaining garrisons at Izúcar and Acatzingo and at Cholula itself, and it was the commanders of these garrisons, acting misguidedly on the direct orders of Tlaqui and Tlalchi, who supplied the regiments that confronted you which, thanks be to the gods, you chased away. Those garrison commanders were arrested shortly afterwards on my lord's orders and suitably punished. He has pleasure – ' at this point Teudile summoned a bearer carrying a small basket which he opened with a flourish – 'to send you their hides.'

Cortés peered into the basket, wrinkling his nose with disgust at the bloody human skins, fresh and untanned, with glistening globs of yellow fat still attached, that lay folded within. 'Revolting!' he exclaimed, waving the bearer away.

'Such is our custom here,' said Teudile, 'for any who displease my lord, and those who wore these skins displeased the lord Moctezuma greatly in the inconvenience they caused you. In the same spirit, because he does not wish to cause you any further inconvenience or discomfort, my lord Moctezuma most humbly requests that you do not trouble yourself to make the arduous journey to Tenochtitlan, for the lands through which you must pass are very high, and cold, covered with snow at this time of year, and inhospitable. Moreover, as you may know, our city is located on an island in the midst of a lake, approached by long causeways, and all our food must be carried out to us on the backs of *tamanes*, or brought over the water by boat, so my lord fears he will not be able to feed you and all your men. He suggests you stay here in Cholula, or better still return with your company to the town you have built on our coast near Huitztlan, where the weather is warm and you may pass the winter in comfort. Only say what you need – food, cloth, gold and jewels, whatever you want, in whatever quantity you require – and my lord Moctezuma gives his solemn oath to send it to you, so long as you do not come to Tenochtitlan.'

'Please thank your master for his generous offer,' Cortés replied, 'and convey my regrets to him, but we will not turn back, neither will we remain here in Cholula, nor are we in the least daunted by any hardships we may face on our march to Tenochtitlan, even if we must go hungry when we get there. I have no choice in the matter as I am required by my own king, the most powerful monarch in the world, to give him a full account and description of your city and of the great Moctezuma. Since I must perforce do these things, the great Moctezuma must, on his part, accept the fact, and not make other plans – for if he does I will be compelled to cause him much harm and it would sadden me if any harm were to befall him.'

Teudile was tight-lipped. 'I will convey your words to my master,' he said. 'And may I tell him when you intend to proceed to Tenochtitlan?'

Cortés favoured him with a broad smile. 'We are making ready our departure now. Four or five more days at the most, and we will be on our way to you.'

'Very well,' said Teudile. 'I must return and report to my master at once. Perhaps he will wish to send you guides for your journey.'

Alvarado was still examining the gifts of gold, making no attempt to conceal his delight. 'A queer race,' he said to Cortés after the ambassador had taken his leave. 'On the one hand they show us their wealth – ' he lifted one of the heavy gold plates and bit its soft rim – 'and on the other they show us they don't have the courage to defend it.'

'Because they arrogant, strutting, loud-mouthed bullies,' contributed Malinal, whose own Castilian was improving so fast she soon would not need Pepillo's help to refine it. 'They used to pushing neighbours around. Only a few like Tlascalans stood up to them but you Spaniards are first people who bully them back. They don't like it! Don't know what to do about it! Have hearts of cowards.'

Thanks to Malinal's constant gentle tuition, Pepillo's ability to sustain a conversation in Nahuatl had advanced by leaps and bounds, so from the moment Tozi had been brought out from the cave under the pyramid, he'd been able to talk to her.

Not that she'd had much to say for the first few days, feeble and starved as she was, but whenever his duties allowed, Pepillo was in attendance on her, constantly urging food on her, nursing her back to health. Melchior, too, had taken a shine to her and vigilantly guarded her bed, where she lay as still as the dead, sleeping deeply and oblivious to the world. Little by little, however, as she gained strength, her skeletal form filling out, colour returning to her sallow features, she slept less and began to talk more. Often Malinal would be present, helping with the gaps in Pepillo's vocabulary, at first having to explain patiently to Tozi that he was not a god, that none of the Spaniards were gods, and that Cortés, their leader, who everyone now called Malinche, was most certainly not Quetzalcoatl as she seemed so much to want to believe.

During these days of slow recuperation, Malinal told Tozi the whole story of what had happened since she had first reached the Spaniards at Potonchan, and Tozi in her turn spoke of her own incredible adventures. Gradually Pepillo realised that this strange Indian waif, whose large earnest hazel eyes, high cheekbones and serious, pretty elfin face so entranced him, actually believed herself to be some sort of witch! Such an idea would have been very dangerous if Muñoz were still alive to do her mischief, but fortunately he was not, and Father Olmedo was too wise and generous-spirited a man ever to burn anyone at the stake. Even so, Pepillo cautioned Malinal and Tozi not to talk of such matters in the presence of Olmedo, or Cortés – or indeed any of the other expeditionaries.

'Why?' Tozi asked.

'Because Spaniards believe witches are in league with the devil, and fear them and kill them in cruel ways whenever they can.'

'The Mexica believe this too,' said Tozi. 'They killed my mother because she was a witch.'

'All the more reason to keep quiet about it then.' Out of long habit, Pepillo glanced uncomfortably over his shoulder, even though he knew the three of them were alone in the room.

But Tozi wasn't finished: 'The sorcerer Acopol took my powers away when he buried me under the pyramid,' she said sadly. 'I used to be able to make myself invisible and go wherever I pleased; I used to be able to send the fog, and put fear and terrible dreams into people's minds and know their thoughts, and command wild animals—'

'Shush!' Pepillo said. 'I told you not to talk of such things.'

'We're speaking in Nahuatl,' Malinal pointed out.

'Even so, it's dangerous. Better to say nothing.'

'Do you believe I'm a witch?' Tozi persisted. Her eyes, bright and intelligent, seemed to peer directly into Pepillo's soul.

'No, of course I don't!'

'Well you should,' she said, sticking out her lower lip in a certain stubborn way she had. 'Because I *am* a witch, even if I've lost my powers. My magic is still there and one day I'll find how to connect to it again.'

'It's true, Pepillo,' Malinal confided. 'Tozi did have these powers. She used them to save my life, not only once but twice.'

'Then if she's a witch she's a good witch,' whispered Pepillo. 'But even good witches get burnt.' He looked over his shoulder again. 'We have to stop talking about this. I'm sorry.'

A week after being rescued from the cave, Tozi was up and about, hobbling restlessly around her room, supporting herself between Pepillo and Malinal, and around noon on the eighth day, Friday 29 October, dressed in a fine new cotton blouse and skirt from the hoard Teudile had brought, she declared herself ready to go outside. She'd asked many questions about Acopol and his fate and now insisted she wanted to see his head.

Nearly two weeks had passed since it had been hacked from the sorcerer's shoulders. There had been calls for it to be removed from the prominent position it occupied in front of the pyramid, but Alvarado had resisted these and Cortés had supported him, saying the trophy sent an important message to the surviving Cholulans who were now returning in good numbers to reoccupy the town.

Approaching it, squinting in the harsh midday glare reflecting off the flagstones of the plaza, Tozi shook herself free of Malinal and Pepillo and walked independently for the first time, while Melchior danced and gambolled at her heels. She stopped about five paces from the head, still impaled on a Spanish spear as Alvarado had left it, and looked at it closely for several minutes with a firm, resolute stare. Then, keeping the same distance, she shuffled slowly round it until finally she stood in front of it again. The face was in such an advanced state of corruption, Pepillo saw, the teeth bared like fangs as the tattooed flesh melted away, that it did more and more resemble some monstrous jungle beast rather than a man.

Now Tozi moved closer, peering into the creature's rotting eyes, yet closer until she was only a hand's breadth away from it, and began to mumble rapidly, a spine-tingling, sibilant whisper that little by little became an incantation, more sung than spoken, rising in volume, growing coarse and somehow menacing. As the sound spread out across the plaza, Melchior suddenly whined and Pepillo looked nervously round, hoping no one would approach and witness this eerie, frankly witchy, scene. That was when Tozi's frail, skinny body seemed to shimmer, the way a heat haze shimmers in bright sunlight, shimmered a second time, and then, just for an instant vanished so completely that even her shadow disappeared. Pepillo stared in amazement, blinked his eyes twice and she was back, thin but solid, casting a shadow again. It had all happened so fast he at once began to convince himself he had imagined it.

Tozi's whispered chant stopped and she turned with a tired smile. 'I'm ready,' she said.

'Ready for what?' asked Malinal. If she too had witnessed the illusion, she gave no hint of it in her expression.

'To fight Moctezuma again,' Tozi said. 'We don't have long.' She linked arms with Malinal and Pepillo. 'Let's go inside,' she said, 'and I'll explain.'

Pepillo had always been good with numbers, so he did not find it difficult to reconcile the Mexica and Christian calendars for the weeks ahead. The Mexica year had three hundred and sixty-five days, as did the Christian year, but instead of being divided into twelve months, it was divided into eighteen months of twenty days each, plus one short month of five 'nameless' days, the *nemontemi*, which fell during January in the Christian calendar and were considered by the Mexica to be unlucky and potentially cataclysmic.

Today, Friday 29 October, was four days from the end of the Mexica twenty-day month of *Tepeilhuitl*, 'Feast of Mountains', that had begun on 11 October. The following month, *Quecholli*, 'Flamingo', would begin on 30 October and end on 19 November. Then came *Panquetzaliztli*, 'Raising of Flags', sacred to the war god Hummingbird, whose birthday was celebrated with human sacrifices on the first day of that month – corresponding with 20 November in the Christian calendar.

This year, Tozi said, Moctezuma was planning an unusually grotesque and wicked festival of sacrifices to honour the birthday of the war god; sacrifices on a far grander scale than any that had gone before, in which the hearts of ten thousand young girls, all maidens and most under twelve years of age, would be cut from their bodies on the summit of the great pyramid of Tenochtitlan. The murder of this huge number would take four days and nights to complete and would therefore begin on 16 November, in order to culminate with the offering of the last of the 'basket' of ten thousand victims at sunrise on 20 November, the birthday itself.

At first Pepillo found it impossible to comprehend that such a thing could happen, but Malinal and Tozi reminded him in alarming detail how they'd witnessed the sacrifice of two thousand women in February and had only by a miracle escaped the knife themselves. Long before they'd finished their account, he was persuaded that the almost unimaginable holocaust that Moctezuma was now preparing could and most certainly would take place between 16 and 20 November, unless Cortés and his conquistadors were able to reach Tenochtitlan in time to prevent it.

'This is the reason that Malinche was called to Mexico,' Tozi insisted, her eyes blazing. 'I care not whether he is Quetzalcoatl returning to claim his kingdom as I once believed, or just a man as you have told me, but the fact is he's here, with the power and the will to prevent this horrible and grievous wrong. It's our responsibility to ensure that he does . . .'

'It won't be so easy,' said Pepillo. 'My master Cortés – Malinche as you call him – can't be *made* to do anything. He long ago set his mind on reaching Tenochtitlan, but he'll take us there at the time he believes is best. He may wish to win more allies first, in which case he might halt our march in towns along the way – who knows for how long? Also, there's the matter of the Mexica. We'll make slow progress if they attack us – and they'd be fools not to, though I pray they don't.' He turned to Malinal: 'Remember how it was in Tlascala? We stayed two weeks on the hill of Tzompach without moving a mile.'

'The Tlascalans made us fight for our lives,' said Malinal, 'and they were led by a brave man. The Mexica are bullies led by a coward.'

'Even so, we're in their homeland.' Pepillo felt a responsibility not to give Tozi false hope. 'And they have hundreds of thousands of soldiers. God knows what sort of fight we'll face.'

The next day, Saturday 30 October, Huicton returned with a thousand warriors from the rebel faction of Texcoco, and left that same afternoon taking Tozi with him. Before her departure she sought out Pepillo and found him grooming Molinero, with Melchior looking on, in the makeshift stables in the courtyard of the palace. 'I have to go back to Tenochtitlan,' she explained. 'There's work for me there.'

'But how?' Pepillo was suddenly panic-stricken at the thought of losing this mysterious girl. 'You can't go. You can't even walk properly.'

'Huicton's *tamanes*,' she said. 'They've made a litter. They're going to carry me.' She rested a slim hand on Pepillo's arm and he felt himself blush to the roots of his hair. 'You've been very kind to me,' she said, 'but I have to go. Work on your master, make him come quickly to Tenochtitlan. I'll see you there . . .'

'But . . . But . . .' Pepillo was speechless. He wanted to run and find Malinal, hoping she might persuade Tozi to stay, but Tozi seemed to guess his thoughts. 'I've already told her,' she said. 'She knows better than to try to talk me out of anything. These are terrible times and we all have to do what we can.' She stooped and petted Melchior. 'This one has a noble heart,' she said. 'Something tells me he has a part to play in the events that are to come.'

Only after she was long gone did it occur to Pepillo that Tozi had done more than guess his thoughts.

She'd known exactly what he was thinking, not just about Malinal persuading her to stay, but *everything* that was in his mind.

He blushed again, though there was no one to see him.

On the morning of Sunday 1 November, a mass was held by Father Olmedo in the great plaza of Cholula. As the burly friar gave thanks to God for the many blessings He had bestowed on His servants in the conquest of these new lands, and requested His further help and support in the venture that lay ahead, Cortés knelt amongst the men and silently offered up his own prayer for victory to Saint Peter.

Soon after the mass, Meco, the commander of the loyal Totonacs who had accompanied the Spaniards all the way from the coast and fought bravely for them in the Tlascalan campaign, took Cortés and Malinal aside and informed them, with some trepidation, that he and his men would not complete the journey to Tenochtitlan. 'To go to that terrible city means certain death for us, lord, and for yourselves. We beg you to turn back.'

'We will not turn back,' Cortés replied. 'We will never turn back. But you have served us well, Meco. Go home now with honour and our blessings.' He rewarded him with many of the loads of rich cotton cloaks that Teudile had presented a few days earlier. Then, summoning Pepillo, he dictated a letter for Meco to carry to Juan de Escalante at Villa Rica, giving him news of everything that had happened since they'd parted company on 16 August, and informing him that the army was about to proceed to Tenochtitlan, there to take Moctezuma dead or alive. 'My dear friend,' Cortés concluded, 'fortify Villa Rica well, look after our settlers, keep a good watch and be alert by day and night. The Mexica are a cunning and vicious race and, as we march on them, it becomes more probable they will attempt some cowardly attack on you.' He sealed the letter and gave it to Meco to deliver. 'This is the first thing you must do,' he told the Totonac. 'Before even you go to your own family, you must place this letter in the hands of Captain Escalante.'

'As you command, Malinche, so it will be done,' replied Meco.

The following morning, Monday 2 November, no further word yet having been received from Moctezuma, Cortés summoned the troops to marching order and signalled the advance. Scouts had given the lie to Teudile's tales of a long and arduous journey. To be sure, a range of high mountains must be crossed, but Tenochtitlan and the looming, murderous power of the Mexica and their hellish gods now lay less than sixty miles to the west.

Time Frame, Principal Settings and Cast of Characters

Time Frame and Subject Matter

War God: Return of the Plumed Serpent unfolds in the seven-month period between 20 April 1519 and 2 November 1519. The book, which continues directly from the story told in Volume I (*War God: Nights of the Witch*), deals with the crucial second phase of the Spanish conquest of Mexico. After routing the Maya at the battle of Potonchan (described in the closing chapters of Volume I), the conquistador Hernán Cortés turns his attention to the much bigger prize of the Mexica (the Aztecs) and their golden city Tenochtitlan. But in order to win the Mexica gold, Cortés and his small force of just five hundred men will have to defeat the psychotic emperor Moctezuma and the armies of hundreds of thousands he commands. Cortés expects the warlike Tlascalans, hereditary enemies of the Aztecs, will join him, but instead finds himself locked in a life-or-death struggle with the Tlascalan battle king Shikotenka, who sees that the Spaniards will not stop with the destruction of Mexica power but will go on to annihilate all the ancient cultures of Mexico unless the invaders can be driven back into the sea.

Note on names

Some ancient Mexican names are extremely difficult for modern readers to pronounce and I have taken the liberty in a number of cases of simplifying them. To give just a few examples here, the town that I call Huitztlan is correctly written Quiahuitztlan, I have abbreviated the name of the Texcocan rebel leader Ixtlilxóchitl to the more manageable form of Ishtlil, I have abbreviated the name Temazcalteci, the Mexica goddess of medicine and healing, to Temaz, and the name Shikotenka is more correctly written Xicotencatl.

Principal Settings

(1) **Tenochtitlan**, capital city of the Mexica (Aztec) empire of ancient Mexico, 1325 to 1521. Built on an island in the middle of a huge salt lake (Lake Texcoco) in the Valley of Mexico. The Valley of Mexico is ringed by distant snow-capped mountains. At the heart of the valley is Lake Texcoco. At the heart of Lake Texcoco is the island on which Tenochtitlan stands, accessed via three huge causeways (varying in length between two and six miles), extending to the southern, western and northern shores of the lake. At the heart of Tenochtitlan, surrounded by a vast walled enclosure (the grand plaza, or sacred precinct), is the Great Pyramid, which is surmounted by the temple of **Huitzilopochtli** ('Hummingbird'), War God of the Mexica, to whom tens of thousands of human sacrifices are offered every year.

(2) **Tlascala**, an independent republic, with elected kings, at war with the Mexica. Both the republic as a whole, and its capital city, are known as Tlascala. Tlascalans captured in raids and battles are a prime source of sacrificial victims for the Mexica.

(3) **Cuetlaxtlan**, a coastal town on the Gulf of Mexico, ruled and colonised by the Mexica, but with a subject population of Totanacs, to whom the town originally belonged.

(4) **The Spanish military camp** on the dunes a few miles north of Cuetlaxtlan.

(5) **The military camp of Ishtlil**, leader of the rebel faction in the Mexica vassal state of Texcoco.

(6) **Huitztlan**, a Totonac town on the Gulf of Mexico that will offer friendship and allegiance to **Cortés**.

(7) **Villa Rica de la Veracruz**, the first Spanish town in Mexico, built close by **Huitztlan**.

(8) **Cempoala**, capital city of the Totonacs. The Totonacs will become the first allies of the Spaniards in Mexico.

(9) **Teotihuacan**, ancient sacred complex dominated by three pyramids, thirty-five miles north of Teotihuacan.

(10) **The Chichemec desert**, twenty days' walk north of **Teotihuacan**.

(11) **Xocotlan**, a Mexica garrison town on the border of **Tlascala**.

(12) **The Hill of Tzompach**, principal camp of the Spaniards during their war with the Tlascalans.

(13) **Cholula**, city sacred to **Quetzalcoatl** and dominated by a huge pyramid dedicated to Quetzalcoatl.

Point-of-View Characters

(1) **Tozi**. A witch. Age, fifteen. Tozi never knew her father. Her mother was a witch but was cornered and beaten to death by a mob when Tozi was seven, at which age Tozi's own training had just begun and her formidable supernatural powers were not fully developed. She survived as a beggar on the streets of **Tenochtitlan** for the next six years until captured and placed in the fattening pen at the age of fourteen to await sacrifice – a fate that she escaped as described in Volume I, *War God: Nights of the Witch*. Tozi's origins are mysterious. Her mother told her they came from Aztlán, the fabled homeland not only of the Mexica but also of the Tlascalans and other related 'Nahua' peoples who speak the language called Nahuatl. But Aztlán is a mythical and legendary place, the home of the gods, where masters of wisdom and workers of magic are believed to dwell; although the Mexica say their forefathers came from Aztlán, no one knows where it is any more, or how to find it.

(2) **Malinal**. A beautiful courtesan, and formerly a sex-slave of the Mexica, she was held in the fattening pen awaiting sacrifice with **Tozi**, and escaped with her (these events are described in Volume I). Age, twenty-one. Malinal is Maya in ethnic origin and is fluent both in Nahuatl, the language of the Mexica, and in the Mayan language. She hates **Moctezuma** and intends to use the conquistador **Hernán Cortés** as her instrument to destroy him.

(3) **Huicton**. A spy working to destroy **Moctezuma**. Huicton is in his sixties and passes unnoticed through the streets of **Tenochtitlan** disguised as an elderly blind beggar. However, he is not blind. He is the mentor and protector of **Tozi**.

(4) **Pepillo**. Spanish, approaching fifteen years of age. An orphan, he was given shelter, reared and taught numbers and letters by Dominican monks, who brought him from Spain to the New World, first to the island of Hispaniola and then to Cuba, where he worked as a junior bookkeeper and clerk in the Dominican monastery. He is the page of the conquistador, **Hernán Cortés**.

(5) **Moctezuma**. Emperor – his official title is Great Speaker – of the Mexica. Age, fifty-three. Moctezuma frequently enters a trance state induced by the use of hallucinogenic mushrooms in which he communicates directly with the War God – demon – **Huitzilopochtli** (Hummingbird). The demon, whose purpose is to maximise human misery and chaos on earth, urges Moctezuma on to ever more cruel and brutal mass sacrifices.

(6) **Shikotenka**. Battle king of **Tlascala**, sworn enemy of the Mexica. Age, thirty-three.

(7) **Guatemoc**. Prince of the Mexica. Age, twenty-seven. Nephew of **Moctezuma** (he is the son of Moctezuma's brother **Cuitláhuac**).

(8) **Pedro de Alvarado**. Age, thirty-three. Close friend and ally of **Hernando Cortés**. Alvarado is handsome, excessively cruel – a charming psychopath. He is also a brilliant swordsman and a notorious lover of gold.

(9) **Hernando (Hernán) Cortés**. Commander of the Spanish expedition to Mexico. Age, thirty-five. A brilliant military commander and political operator, he is clever, Machiavellian, manipulative, utterly ruthless, vengeful and daring, but with a paradoxical streak of messianic Christianity.

(10) **Bernal Díaz**. Age, twenty-seven. Down-to-earth, honest, experienced Spanish soldier on the expedition to Mexico. From farming stock, no pretensions to nobility, but literate and keeps a diary (even though he self-deprecatingly refers to himself as an 'illiterate idiot'). Admires **Cortés**, who has recognised his potential and promoted him to ensign rank.

(11) **Gonzalo de Sandoval**. Age, twenty-two. From *Hidalgo* (minor nobility) family, but fallen on hard times. New recruit to the expedition to Mexico. Promoted to ensign in same ceremony as **Díaz**. Unlike Díaz, Sandoval has a university education and military and cavalry training but no personal experience of war.

Supernatural Characters

Huitzilopochtli (referred to throughout the novel as Hummingbird), war god of the Mexica. The full translation of the name Huitzilopochtli is 'The Hummingbird at the Left Hand of the Sun'. Like all demons, through all the myths and legends of mankind, the purpose of this entity is to multiply human suffering and corrupt all that is good and pure and true in the human spirit. He appears to **Moctezuma** when the Mexica emperor is in trance states induced by his frequent consumption of hallucinogenic mushrooms. A tempter and a manipulator, Hummingbird deliberately stokes the flames of the conflict between the Mexica and the Spaniards, and ultimately backs the Spaniards because he knows they will make life in Mexico even worse than it has been under the Mexica. It is a historical fact that within fifty years of the Spanish conquest, the indigenous population of Mexico had been reduced through war, famine and introduced diseases from thirty million to just one million.

Saint Peter, patron saint of **Hernán Cortés**. As a child, Cortés suffered an episode of severe fever that brought him close to death. His nurse, María de Esteban, prayed to Saint Peter for his salvation and the young Cortés miraculously recovered. Ever afterwards, Cortés felt he enjoyed a special relationship with this saint and believed he was guided by him in all the great and terrible episodes of his adult life. Like **Moctezuma**, Cortés encounters Saint Peter in visionary states – in his case, dreams.

Quetzalcoatl, 'The Plumed Serpent', the god of peace of ancient Central America. Described as white-skinned and bearded, an age-old prophecy said he had been expelled from Mexico by the forces of evil at some time in remote prehistory, but that he would return in the year *1-Acatl* ('One-Reed'), in ships that 'moved by themselves without paddles' to overthrow a wicked king, abolish the bloody rituals of human sacrifice and restore justice. And as it happened, the year 1519 in our calendar, when **Cortés** landed in the Yucatán in sailing ships that 'moved by themselves without paddles', was indeed the year One-Reed in the Mexica calendar. Whether this was pure chance, or whether some inscrutable design might have been at work, **Malinal** would eventually teach Cortés how to exploit the myth of Quetzalcoatl. What followed was a ruthless and spectacularly successful campaign to dominate **Moctezuma** psychologically long before the Spaniards faced him in battle.

Whether in some mysterious sense real, as I rather suspect, or whether only imagined by Moctezuma and Cortés, Hummingbird (**Huitzilopochtli**) and **Saint Peter** played pivotal roles as agents of mischief in the events of the conquest, while the prophecy of the return of Quetzalcoatl was equally fundamental.

Secondary Spanish Characters who appear frequently in the story

Diego de Velázquez. Age, fifty-five. Governor of Cuba. Rival and enemy of **Hernán Cortés**.

The Velazquistas. The name **Cortés** gives to senior figures on the expedition to Mexico who remain loyal to his enemy and rival **Diego de Velázquez**, the governor of Cuba. Cortés must either bribe, manipulate, or force members of the Velázquez faction to change sides. They include Juan Escudero (ringleader of the Velazquistas), Juan Velázquez de Léon, cousin of Diego de Velázquez, Francisco de Montejo, Diego de Ordaz, Cristóbal de Olid and Alonso de Grado.

García Brabo. Age, forty. Tough sergeant who leads a squad of men dedicated to **Hernán Cortés**. He does Cortés's dirty work whenever required.

Significant allies of Cortés on the expedition. In addition to **Pedro de Alvarado**, Cortés can rely on Alonso Hernández Puertocarrero, Alonso Davila and his particular friend Juan de Escalante.

Alonso de la Serna and Francisco Mibiercas. Soldiers on the expedition. Friends of **Bernal Díaz**.

Dr La Peña. Doctor with the expedition to Mexico.

Father Bartolomé de Olmedo. Mercedarian Friar, a gentle good-hearted man who participates in the expedition to Mexico. Opposed to forced conversions.

Jerónimo de Aguilar. Spanish castaway in the Yucatán. Spent eight years as a slave amongst the Maya and became fluent in their language. Having been rescued by **Cortés**, Aguilar joins the expedition and becomes Cortés's first interpreter and, soon, **Malinal**'s rival for this role.

Francisco de Mesa. Cortés's chief of artillery.

Diego de Godoy. Notary of the expedition.

Telmo Vendabal. Keeper of the expedition's pack of one hundred ferocious war dogs.

Andrés Santisteban, Miguel Hemes and **Francisco Julian**, assistant dog handlers and tormenters of **Pepillo**.

Secondary Mexica, Tlascalan, Texcocan, Totonac, Cholulan and Huichol characters who appear frequently in or have prominence in the story

Namacuix. High priest of the Mexica.

Teudile. Steward to **Moctezuma** and a high-ranking lord of the Mexica empire.

Cuitláhuac. Age, forty-eight. Younger brother of **Moctezuma** and father of **Guatemoc**.

Acolmiztli, Chipahua, Tree, Ilhuicamina. Commanders in **Shikotenka**'s squad of Tlascalan warriors.

Shikotenka the Elder. Civil king of the Tlascalans (**Shikotenka**, his son, is the battle king).

Maxixcatzin. Deputy to both **Shikotenka** and **Shikotenka the Elder**.

Ishtlil, commander of the rebel faction in Texcoco.

Pichatzin, governor of **Cuetlaxtlan**.

Big Dart (Huciimuh), **Starving Coyote** (Nezahualcoyotl), **Fuzzy Face** (Ixtomi), **Man-Eater** (Tecuani), and **Mud Head** (Cuatalatl), particular friends and comrades in arms of **Guatemoc**.

Meco. A Totonac warrior whom **Cortés** saves from sacrifice.

Tlacoch, Paramount chief of the Totonacs.

Acopol, powerful **Chichemec** *nagual* (sorcerer, shape shifter), appointed by **Moctezuma** to conduct sacrificial rituals at **Cholula**.

Tlaqui and **Tlalchi**. Rulers of **Cholula**.

Nakawey, Irepani and **Taiyari**. Shaman priests of the Huichol who befriend **Tozi**.

War God and History

War God is a novel about an extraordinary moment in history but it is not a history book. Rather it is a work of fantasy and epic adventure in the tradition of *Amadis of Gaul*, the post-Arthurian tale of knight-errantry in which the conquistadors of the early sixteenth century saw their own deeds reflected as they pursued their very real and perilous quest in the strange and terrible lands of Mexico.[1] Wherever I felt it served the interests of my story, I have therefore not hesitated to diverge from a strict observance of historical facts.

For example, Malinal (who was also known as Malinali, Malintzin and La Malinche and whom the conquistadors called Doña Marina) was more likely a Nahua woman of the Mexican Gulf coast who had learned the Mayan language than a Mayan woman – as I have her – who had become fluent in Nahuatl. On the other hand, her biography as I relate it – daughter of a chief, disinherited and sold into slavery by her own mother after her father's death (because her mother favoured a son by her second marriage) – conforms to the facts as they have been passed down to us.

Other similar examples could be cited here (for instance Guatemoc was probably Moctezuma's cousin, not his nephew) but, by and large, while responding to the narrative needs of a fantasy adventure epic, I have worked hard to weave my tale around a solid armature of historical facts. This is not to say that the fantastic and the supernatural are not prominent themes in *War God* – because they are! – but there is nothing 'unhistorical' about this. Such concerns were of prime importance both to the superstitious Spanish and to the Mexica. Indeed Mexico-Tenochtitlan has, with good reason, been described by Nobel Prizewinner J. M. G. Le Clezio as 'the last magical civilization'.[2]

Take the case of Tozi the witch, one of my central characters. Some might think that an obsession with sorcery, animal familiars (even transformation into animal forms), the ability to make oneself invisible, the concoction of spells and herbal potions by women and the persecution of women for such practices were purely European concerns; but in these matters – as in so many others – the Spanish of the sixteenth century had much more in common with the Mexica than they realised. Witchcraft was widespread in Central America and endemic to the culture of the region.[3]

Then there is the matter of human sacrifice, a recurrent theme throughout *War God*. Do I make too much of this? Do I dwell on it at a length that is not justified by the facts? Honestly, no, I don't think I do. The facts, including the fattening of prisoners and their incarceration in special pens prior to sacrifice, are so abhorrent, so well evidenced and so overwhelming that the imagination is simply staggered by them. In saying this I recognise that the prim hand of political correctness has in recent years tried to sweep the extravagant butchery and horror of Mexica sacrificial rituals under the table of history by suggesting that Spanish eyewitnesses were exaggerating for propaganda or religious purposes. Yet this cannot be right. Let alone the mass of archaeological evidence and the surviving depictions of human sacrifice, skull racks, flaying and dismemberment of victims, cannibalism, etc, in Mexica sculpture and art, we have detailed accounts of these practices given to reliable chroniclers within a few years of the conquest by the Mexica themselves. Both Bernardo de Sahagún, in his *General History of the Things of New Spain*,[4] and Diego Durán in his *History of the Indies of New Spain*,[5] based their reports upon the testimony of native informants, and both give extensive descriptions of the grisly sacrificial rituals that had been integral to Mexica society since its inception, that had increased exponentially during the fifty years prior to the conquest, and that the conquistadors themselves witnessed after their arrival. The historian Hugh Thomas sums up the matter soberly in his superb study of the conquest.[6] 'In numbers,' he writes, 'in the elevated sense of ceremony which accompanied the theatrical shows involved, as in its significance in the official religion, human sacrifice in Mexico was unique.'[7]

Political correctness has also tried to airbrush out the Quetzalcoatl mythos of the white-skinned bearded god who was prophesied to return in the year One-Reed, and Cortés's manipulation of this myth, as largely a fabrication of the conquistadors – but this too cannot be correct. Again Sahagún's immense scholarship in his *General History* contains too much detail to be ignored.[8] But there are many other sources too numerous to mention here, and we should not forget the universal iconography of the 'Plumed Serpent' throughout Central America. Some of it – for example at La Venta on the Gulf of Mexico – is very ancient indeed (1500 BC or older) and is associated with reliefs of bearded individuals with plainly Caucasian rather than native American features.[9]

Other 'fantastical' aspects of my story, such as Moctezuma's visionary encounters under the influence of hallucinogenic mushrooms with the war god Huitzilopochtli (Hummingbird), and Cortés's conviction that he was guided by Saint Peter, are also thoroughly supported in numerous historical sources.

Last but not least, there is the matter of the incredible disparity of forces – the few hundred Spaniards against vast Mayan, Tlascalan and Mexica armies and the apparent miracle of the conquistadors' triumph. But, as I show in

War God, this 'miracle' was really science. The guns and cannon the Spaniards were able to deploy, their terrifying war dogs,[10] and the stunning impact of their cavalry gave them decisive advantages. No dogs larger than chihuahuas had previously been known in Central America, and whereas European infantry had accumulated thousands of years of experience (and had developed specialised tactics and weapons), to withstand charges of heavy horse, the armies of Mexico were completely unprepared for the seemingly demonic beasts and supernatural powers that Cortés unleashed on them.

But there was something else, ultimately more important than all of this, that brought the Spanish victory.

If Moctezuma had been a different sort of ruler, if he had possessed a shred of kindness or decency, if there had been any capacity in him to love, then he surely would not have preyed upon neighbouring peoples for human sacrifices to offer up to his war god, in which case he could have earned their devotion and respect rather than their universal loathing, and thus might have been in a position to lead a united opposition to the conquistadors and to crush them utterly within weeks of setting foot in his lands. But he was none of these things, and thus Cortés was almost immediately able to exploit the hatred that Moctezuma's behavior had provoked and find allies amongst those the Mexica had terrorised and exploited – allies who were crucial to the success of the conquest. Of particular note in this respect were the Tlascalans, who had suffered the depredations of the Mexica more profoundly than any others and who were led by Shikotenka, a general so courageous and so principled that he at first fought the Spanish tooth and nail, seeing the existential danger they posed to the entire culture of the region, despite the liberation from Moctezuma's tyranny that Cortés offered him. Only when Cortés had smashed Shikotenka in battle – as described in this volume – did the brave general finally bow to the demands of the Tlascalan Senate to make an alliance with the Spaniards, an alliance that soon put tens of thousands of auxiliaries under Cortés's command and set the conquistadors on the road to Tenochtitlan . . .

References

[1] See, for example, Hugh Thomas, *Conquest: Montezuma, Cortés and the Fall of Old Mexico*, Simon & Schuster Paperbacks, New York and London, 1993, pp. 61–62 and 702.

[2] J. M. G. Le Clezio, *The Mexican Dream: Or The Interrupted Thought of Amerindian Civilizations*, translated by Teresa Lavender Fagan, University of Chicago Press, Chicago and London, 2009, p. 41.

[3] See for example, Jan G. R. Elferink, Jose Antonio Flores and Charles D. Kaplan, *The Use of Plants and Other Natural Products for Malevolent Practices*

amongst the Aztecs and their Successors, Estudios de Cultura Nahuatl, vol. 24, 1994, Universidad Nacional Autónomo de México. See also Daniel G. Brinton, Nagualism: A Study in Native American Folklore and History, MacCalla and Co., Philadelphia, 1894. And see David Friedel, Linda Schele and Joy Parker, *Maya Cosmos: Three Thousand Years on the Shaman's Path*, William Morrow and Co., New York, 1995, pp. 52, 181, 190, 192–193, 211, 228. See also Le Clezio, *The Mexican Dream*, pp. 104–108.

[4] Fray Bernardo de Sahagún, *General History of the Things of New Spain* (Florentine Codex), translated from the Aztec into English by Arthur J. O. Anderson and Charles E. Dibble, School of American Research, University of Utah, Salt Lake City, 1975. See for example book 12, chapters 6, 8 and 9.

[5] Fray Diego Durán, *The History of the Indies of New Spain*, translated by Doris Heyden and Fernando Horcasitas, Orion Press, New York, 1964. See, for example, pp. 99–102 (from where the oration given to sacrificial victims in chapter 28 of *War God* is quoted), pp. 105–113, 120–122, 195–200 and many other similar passages.

[6] Thomas, *Conquest*, pp. 24–27.

[7] Ibid., p. 27.

[8] Sahagún, *General History*; see, for example, chapters 2, 3, 4 and 16.

[9] See, for example, Graham Hancock and Santha Faiia, *Heaven's Mirror: Quest for the Lost Civilisation*, Michael Joseph, London, 1998, pp. 38–42.

[10] An excellent source on the conquistadors' use of dogs trained for war is to be found in John Grier Varner and Jeannette Johnson Varner, *Dogs of the Conquest*, University of Oklahoma Press, Norman, 1983.

Acknowledgements

First and foremost I am grateful to my wife and partner Santha, my fiercest critic and constant companion who has read every word of this book and of the volumes that precede and follow it and who never lets me get away with any short cuts. My children Sean, Shanti, Ravi, Leila, Luke and Gabrielle, as well as my sons- and daughters-in-law Lydia, Simone, Jason and Ayako, have all also been helpful and inspiring presences, reading draft after draft and offering encouragement and advice.

My literary agent Sonia Land of Sheil Land Associates has, throughout, played a most important role in this book, giving me the benefit of her professional judgement and her kind and wise guidance at every stage of the process, and championing my new career as a novelist with tremendous verve and energy. I'm very grateful to you, Sonia, and can't thank you enough. Deep appreciation also to Gaia Banks and to all at Sheil Land, the best literary agency in Britain.

Mark Booth, my editor at Coronet (Hodder & Stoughton), was brilliant as ever, seeing what needed to be done at each stage of the writing process, and keeping me on the right course with amazing professionalism and insight.

Others who have read and been kind enough to comment on the manuscripts of the evolving *War God* series and who have given me much valuable advice, but who are of course not responsible in any way for the shortcomings of what I have written, include Chris and Cathy Foyle, Luis Eduardo Luna, Father Nicola Mapelli, Ileen Maisel, Jean-Paul Tarud-Kuborn, Ram Menen and Sa'ad Shah. I'm grateful to each and every one of these good and true friends of mine for their generosity with their time and their many constructive suggestions. Xavier Bartlett Carceller kindly provided translations of selected passages of the letters of Hernán Cortés. I found Adam Sharp's *The True Swordsman* particularly useful as background to my descriptions of sword training and combat.

My communities on my Facebook author page (http://www.facebook.com/Author.GrahamHancock) and on my Facebook personal page (http://www.facebook.com/GrahamHancockDotCom), and also my website community (www.grahamhancock.com) have been incredibly supportive of me through the several years of my life that *War God* has dominated my writing and my creativity.

Last but not least I want to put on record my appreciation for those Spaniards and Mexica of the sixteenth century who were caught up in the events of the conquest and wrote about it at first hand, leaving accounts luminous with the spirit and terror of the time that I have been able to draw on in creating this book – sometimes even putting the exact words of the individual concerned into the mouth of his or her character in my story. A number of modern scholars have also written important works on the events of the conquest, without which I would not have been able to develop a full appreciation of the period, and again I am grateful for the tremendous job they have done. Needless to say none of them is responsible in any way for the shortcomings of *War God*, but if the book has strengths it is in large part owed to them. Many more works of reference on which I have drawn could be cited here, but I list in particular the following texts to which I have most frequently had reference as primary and secondary sources for the first and second volumes of the *War God* trilogy:

Primary sources

Hernán Cortés, *Letters from Mexico*, translated and with a new Introduction by Anthony Pagden, Yale University Press, New Haven and London, 1986.

Bernal Díaz, *The Conquest of New Spain*, translated by J. M. Cohen, Penguin Classics, London, 1963.

The Bernal Díaz Chronicles, translated and edited by Bernard Idell, Doubleday, New York, 1956.

Fray Diego Durán, *The History of the Indies of New Spain*, translated by Doris Heyden and Fernando Horcasitas, Orion Press, New York, 1964.

Patricia Fuentes (translator), *The Conquistadors: First Person Accounts of the Conquest of Mexico*, Orion Press, New York, 1963.

Miguel León-Portilla (ed.), *Broken Spears: The Aztec Account of the Conquest of Mexico*, Beacon Press, Boston, 1990.

Francisco López de Gómara, *Cortés: The Life of the Conqueror by His Secretary*, translated by Lesley Byrd Simpson, University of California Press, Oakland, 1966.

Fray Bernardo de Sahagún, *General History of the Things of New Spain* (Florentine Codex), translated from the Aztec into English by Arthur J. O. Anderson and Charles E. Dibble, School of American Research, University of Utah, Salt Lake City, 1975.

Secondary sources

J. M. G. Le Clezio, *The Mexican Dream: Or The Interrupted Thought of Amerindian Civilizations*, translated by Teresa Lavender Fagan, University of Chicago Press, Chicago and London, 2009.

David Friedel, Linda Schele and Joy Parker, *Maya Cosmos: Three Thousand Years on the Shaman's Path*, William Morrow and Co., New York, 1995.

C. Harvey Gardner, *The Constant Companion: Gonzalo de Sandoval*, Southern Illinois University Press, Carbondale, 1961.

John Eoghan Kelly, *Pedro de Alvarado, Conquistador*, Kennikat Press, Port Washington, NY, and London, 1932.

William H. Prescott, *History of the Conquest of Mexico*, The Modern Library, New York.

Laurette Séjourné, *Burning Water: Thought and Religion in Ancient Mexico*, Shambhala, Berkeley, 1976.

Karen Sullivan, *The Inner Lives of Medieval Inquisitors*, University of Chicago Press, Chicago and London, 2011.

Hugh Thomas, *Conquest: Montezuma, Cortés and the Fall of Old Mexico*, Simon & Schuster Paperbacks, New York and London, 1993.

Hugh Thomas, *Who's Who of the Conquistadors*, Cassell & Co., London, 2000.

John Grier Varner and Jeannette Johnson Varner, *Dogs of the Conquest*, University of Oklahoma Press, Norman, 1983.

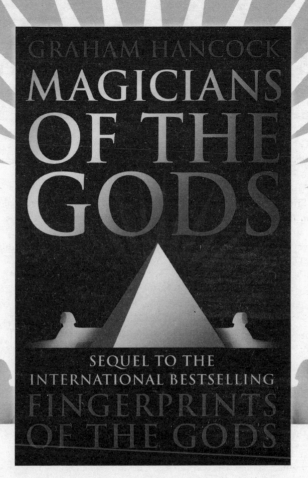

Graham Hancock's multi-million bestseller *Fingerprints of the Gods* remains an astonishing, deeply controversial, wide-ranging investigation of the mysteries of our past and the evidence for Earth's lost civilization. Twenty years on, Hancock returns with the sequel to his seminal work filled with completely new, scientific and archaeological evidence, which has only recently come to light…

OUT 10TH SEPTEMBER 2015

Do you wish this wasn't the end?

Join us at www.hodder.co.uk, or follow us on
Twitter @hodderbooks to be a part of our community
of people who love the very best in books and reading.

Whether you want to discover more about a book
or an author, watch trailers and interviews, have the
chance to win early limited editions, or simply browse
our expert readers' selection of the very best books,
we think you'll find what you're looking for.

And if you don't,
that's the place to tell us what's missing.

We love what we do, and we'd love you to be part of it.

www.hodder.co.uk

 @hodderbooks

HodderBooks

HodderBooks